PIMLICO

310

THE FORGOTTEN TRADE

Nigel Tattersfield was educated at Solihull
School, Warwickshire, and at Reading
University where he studied English and Art
History. After graduation he spent six years
travelling around the world before returning
to London and entering advertising as a
copywriter. He is now a freelance writer
and researcher, currently engaged on an
extensive study of the eighteenth-century
English wood engravers Thomas and John
Bewick. The first fruit of this research, a bio-
graphical dictionary of bookplates engraved
by Thomas Bewick, is being published this
summer.

THE FORGOTTEN TRADE

Comprising the Log of the *Daniel and Henry* of
1700 and Accounts of the Slave Trade from the
Minor Ports of England, 1698-1725

———

NIGEL TATTERSFIELD

With a Foreword by John Fowles

PIMLICO

Published by Pimlico 1998

2 4 6 8 10 9 7 5 3 1

Copyright © Nigel Howard Tattersfield 1991

Nigel Howard Tattersfield has asserted his right
under the Copyright, Designs and Patents Act 1988
to be identified as the author of this work

First published by Jonathan Cape 1991
Pimlico edition 1998

Pimlico
Random House, 20 Vauxhall Bridge Road,
London SW1V 2SA

Random House Australia (Pty) Limited
20 Alfred Street, Milsons Point, Sydney,
New South Wales 2061, Australia

Random House New Zealand Limited
18 Poland Road, Glenfield,
Auckland 10, New Zealand

Random House South Africa (Pty) Limited
Endulini, 5A Jubilee Road, Parktown 2193, South Africa

Random House UK Limited Reg. No. 954009

A CIP catalogue record for this book
is available from the British Library

ISBN 0-7126-7343-1

Papers used by Random House UK Limited are natural,
recyclable products made from wood grown in sustainable forests.
The manufacturing processes conform to the environmental
regulations of the country of origin

Printed and bound in Great Britain by
Creative Print and Design (Wales), Ebbw Vale

To my grandfather
George Frederic Howard (1891–1976)
artisan engineer with the Gold Coast Railways
1920–1941
and his tales of long ago

Contents

Foreword   xi

Preface   xiii

Spelling and Punctuation   xvii

A Note on Dates and Currency   xix

Part One
The Logbook of the *Daniel and Henry* of Exeter, 1700

1   An Introduction to the Slave Trade   3

2   Merchants versus Monopoly   9

3   Background to the Voyage   22

4   Slave Ship Cargoes   34

5   A Description of the *Daniel and Henry*   46

6   The Voyage Out   53

7   Africa and the Africans   69

8   Forts, Factors and Fraud   81

9   Along the Guinea Coast   93

10   The Financial Reckoning   123

11   The Middle Passage   141

12   Jamaica Bound   155

13   Counting the Cost   184

Part Two
Merchants, Mariners and Ports in the Provincial English Slave Trade of the Early Eighteenth Century

14   A Lawful Calling?   195

15 Berwick to Weymouth 202
16 Lyme Regis 227
17 Exeter, Topsham and Dartmouth 277
18 Plymouth, Barnstaple and Bideford 298
19 Falmouth to Lancaster 308
20 Whitehaven 326
21 The Re-export Trade in Slaves 350
   Epilogue 357

Appendix 1   Vessels Clearing Deal, Portsmouth, Southampton, Cowes and Weymouth for Africa, 1698–1720 359

Appendix 2   Vessels Clearing London, Bristol and Lyme Regis for the Burridge Family of Lyme, 1704–25 363

Appendix 3   Vessels Clearing Exeter, Topsham and Dartmouth for Africa, 1698–1725 369

Appendix 4   Vessels Clearing Plymouth for Africa, 1698–1719 Including the *Elizabeth Galley* of Bristol Freighted by Bideford Merchants to Africa in 1700 372

Appendix 5   Vessels Clearing Falmouth for Africa, 1698–1719 375

Appendix 6   Vessels Clearing Whitehaven for Africa, 1698–1725 377

Appendix 7   Minor Outport Involvement in the Re-export Trade in Slaves, 1698–1722 380

Appendix 8   Vessels Clearing Plymouth for the West Indies, 1697–1704 383

Appendix 9   Vessels Clearing Minehead and Bridgwater for the West Indies, 1697–1703 387

Glossary of Trade Terms 389
List of Abbreviations 395
Notes 397
Select Bibliography 445
Index 451

Illustrations

The *Daniel and Henry*; an impression by Geoff
    Hunt, RSMA   *frontispiece*

1 The Cargo of the *Daniel and Henry* from the Royal
    African Company records   37

2 European merchants dealing with the King of Sestos for
    slaves, c. 1690   76

3 View of the Cape Coast or Cabo Corso Castle   89

4 View of Cape St Appollonia   98

5 Africans ferrying slaves aboard ship   104–5

6 Chart of Port Royal harbour, Jamaica   178

7 Map of minor ports of England in 1700   194

8 Deal   204

9 Southampton   213

10 Lyme Regis   228

11 Dartmouth   287

12 Plymouth   300

13 Falmouth   310

14 Whitehaven   327

Sources and acknowledgements for illustrations. Illustration 1
from Royal African Company records PRO T.70/350. Crown-
copyright material in the Public Record Office is reproduced by
permission of the Controller of Her Majesty's Stationery Office.
Illustrations 2, 3, 4, 5, from Awnsham and John Churchill's
Collection of Voyages and Travels (1732) Vol. V. Illustration 6

Foreword

When I first read an early draft of Nigel Tattersfield's sharply revealing book, it was like some innocent stepping into a familiar next room, only to discover he had plunged straight out into empty space. What had caused this fall? My own almost whole swallowing of the illusion that in the seventeenth century and the first decades of the next all good, religious, political and ethical, had lain with Dissent, the complex aftermath of the Puritan movement. Had its Baptists, Independents, Quakers and the rest not heroically battled against the barbarous persecutions and the stifling authoritarian conformisms of the last Stuarts? Wasn't the bravest movement in Lyme's own history the withstanding of the Royalist siege in 1644? Where else did the obstinately free spirit of England, that quintessential 'againstness' or contra-suggestibility, spring from? Nigel's book, if not quite a step off a cliff edge, was certainly a very cold douche on all of that. My romantically canonised 'saints' of Dissent were only too like those gaudy plaster images that generations of militant Protestants once despised and hated the Catholics for worshipping.

It still puzzles me a little that my supposed pillars of Nonconformist virtue should have failed so miserably and universally to realise the monstrous cruelty and injustice, the total denial of all Christianity, that poisoned their involvement in the slave trade. They were not all greedy-blind merchants or naively simple mariners; indeed one of those last, Captain Thomas Coram of Lyme, was by means of the Foundling Hospital to provoke England in the 1730s and 1740s into a long-needed crisis of social conscience. Of course the other side – all the other sides, both internationally and in Britain – were quite as bad, often worse.

Yet that not one man of genuine conscience, one feeling pastor, one proleptic Niemöller, felt driven before 1750 to cry the truth! We are treating the blacks as mere livestock, as inhumanly as we do sheep or cattle, committing one of the most bestial crimes in all recorded history . . . but I must leave Nigel Tattersfield to discuss more coherently this appalling indifference, this near-total blindness, in our ancestors – even worse, in those on whom some light of humanity had supposedly begun to dawn.

I know that Nigel is proudest of the second part of the book, but it is surely the extraordinary log and account of the 1700 voyage of the *Daniel and Henry*, bringing the reality of the period so sharply to life, that will most attract the more general reader. I will say nothing of the assiduity of his research into slaving, especially his penetration of the murk surrounding many of the smaller provincial outports, not least here in Lyme Bay and the South-West. I had thought to have some closer knowledge of those last, but Nigel has given that most valuable help to all local historians – greatly cleansed, indeed almost revolutionised, their own stock views of the past. I pray people will read this richly detailed and absorbing book, with its vivid renaissance of a matter most of us English seem to have wished into oblivion. If this century has not burnt all meaning out of the concepts of guilt and conscience, *The Forgotten Trade* will at least cause some sober reflections. An abundance here to fascinate historians; but singularly little to make patriots purr.

John Fowles, 1990

Preface

Of all the differing categories of merchant shipping that plied the seas in the seventeenth and eighteenth centuries, perhaps none carries a more powerful stigma than the Guineaman, the African slave trade ship.

The appalling stench of the slave-holds, a miasma of death, madness, degradation and human suffering, is one which has carried down the ages and continues to taint much of capitalist society.

The trade made bedfellows of the strangest vessels. Anchored off trading stations along the West African coast were Bristol privateersmen and Quaker merchant vessels, ex-Navy ships of the line and north of England colliers. Each sought that most dreadful of all cargoes, human beings.

Detailed records of the early independent slave traders, those merchants and sea captains (not employed by the Royal African Company) who commenced, after 1698, to trade for human beings on payment of a 10 per cent tax on their outgoing cargoes, are few and far between. Yet it was these ten per centers (also known as separate traders) who contributed in no mean measure to the solid wealth of London and the major outports of Bristol and, later, Liverpool. Their vessels, however, remain shadowy ghost ships of infinitely tenuous substance.

Perhaps none are so veiled as the ships which set sail from England's small provincial outports; slumbering ports now little more than convenient harbours such as Lyme Regis and Topsham. Search in vain for their names in the standard histories of the slave trade. Only the crumbling pages of Port Books and Colonial Shipping Registers throw a faint and flickering light upon their passing. Not for these merchants and captains was there the luxury of large purpose-built slave ships, nor the financial benefit of being backed by major consortia of wealthy merchant venturers. And all too often surviving journals and log-books were expunged by later members of their families, ashamed of the powerful slave trade stigma and fearful of vilification.

Even as early as 1709, at the height of the argument whether the Royal African Company – henceforward called 'the Company' – should have its monopoly over African trade reinstated, their pamphleteer Charles Davenant had complained that the ten per centers

> have neither fixed place nor common trustees or servants . . . for keeping any general record of their proceedings, correspondencies, discoveries or observations . . .[1]

Thus the early eighteenth-century slave traders successfully covered, if not their tracks, then the details of those tracks. Such details were trade secrets, and the passage of time, involving as it has a U-turn in public attitude to the slave trade, has virtually extinguished both knowledge of the ventures and the bulk of the details themselves. Nearly three centuries on, first-hand material describing the activities of an early ten per center from a provincial port is of exceptional scarcity.

In this respect the *Journal* of 1700 which forms the heart of this book is unique among contemporary sources in its scope and detail. Even so, the original was lost from sight some seventy years ago, and this virtually complete version derives from a fair copy written out – with great prescience – in 1857.[2] It was originally the work of Walter Prideaux, supercargo of the ten per cent merchantman *Daniel and Henry* of Exeter, which sailed for the Guinea Coast from Dartmouth. As supercargo it was Walter Prideaux's duty to record the day-to-day business aspect of the voyage: goods loaded, goods exchanged, number of slaves taken aboard, their age, sex and condition, and general observations on trade practices on the Guinea Coast. As a tyro supercargo he relied heavily upon Gerard Malynes' great classic *Lex Mercatoria or the Ancient Law Merchant*.[3] Basically a trading handbook (if that can possibly describe such a massive folio volume) it contained chapters on factors and commissioners, freighting of ships, bills of lading, duties of the master to the merchants, and the duties and privileges of mariners. Unusually, the *Journal* also includes a virtually complete log-book, suggesting that Prideaux intended to pursue a career at sea.

No detailed account of this slave ship has ever been made, nor have any similar log-books or journals been the subject of publication. This may be partly explained by an unwritten rule which determined that the less said about the slave trade, the better. So research into the history of the *Daniel and Henry*, and into the broader context of the slave trade from the minor ports of England in the early eighteenth century, has resembled nothing so much as the piecing together of a vast antique jigsaw puzzle, from which, over the years, fragments have inevitably disappeared. Nevertheless, a substantially complete picture can be our reward. As with the best of jigsaw puzzles – those that make demands on our intelligence, interest and stamina – the way to start is by fitting together the background. Unfortunately the result, in this case, is not a pretty picture. For, unlike their partners in terror, the pirate ships, enshrined in folklore, fiction and on the silver screen, the slave ship lies beyond redemption as the maritime symbol of man's inhumanity to man.

Not being in any formal sense an historian, and feeling very much an interloper in that trade, I would never have written this account were it not for a host of individuals and organisations who contributed their help and advice with great generosity. (Nor would it have been possible without George Jeffery, on whose legendary book barrows in London's Farringdon Road the fair copy log-book of the *Daniel and Henry*, now in the possession of the writer, came to light.)

Once the book got under way, many people facilitated its course. Accordingly I am grateful to Professor James Rawley, Dr James Walvin, Dr Stephen Fisher, Dr Michael Harris, Dr Helen Forde, Dr Nicholas Rodger, Brian Dolley, Ted Cocksedge, Roy Prideaux, Brian Lake, Teresa Chris and my editor at Jonathan Cape, Tony Colwell.

One organisation above all dealt sympathetically with the interminable questions, demands and wanderings of a tyro historian; the Public Record Offices at Chancery Lane and Kew, the patience of whose staff was tried to the limit and not found wanting. They bore the brunt of my ignorance (and enthusiasm). I should also like to thank the staff of the British Library, their Department of Manuscripts, the Guildhall Library and the Archives of the Bank of England. The provincial record offices of Devon, Dorset, Cumbria and Somerset – at Exeter, Dorchester, Carlisle and Taunton respectively – made me most welcome, as did the splendid National Maritime Museum library at Greenwich and the tiny Whitehaven Museum in Cumbria.

Finally I am especially indebted to three people. The first is Olive

Tapp for typing what must have seemed endless drafts and revisions with great expertise, patience and good humour. The second is Captain A. J. B. Naish, RN (retired) who deserves much of the credit for illuminating the ways of ships and the sea. As an armchair sailor, steering a course by pen and ink, I have freely availed myself of his enormous fund of maritime knowledge. And thirdly John Fowles, whose most obvious contribution is the Foreword, but whose interest and support has gone well beyond the narrow confines of the chapter on Lyme Regis. His 'presence' has been a constant source of inspiration and encouragement and I am most thankful for it.

N.H.T.
Belsize Square, NW3
St Luke's Day, 1990

NOTE TO THE PIMLICO EDITION

Since the original edition of this book was published I have incorporated a small number of revisions and additions. I am particularly grateful to the anonymous reviewer for the University of Virginia who highlighted new research with especial relevance to the voyage of the *Daniel and Henry*, specifically the fatal effects caused by dehydration on the middle passage or transatlantic section of a slave-trade voyage.

N.H.T.
1 April 1998

Spelling and Punctuation

Had I kept strictly to the original spelling much of the *Journal* would have been puzzling and possibly misleading. In addition, because I have not had the advantage of transcribing the original, but a fair copy which itself contains occasional errors, I have opted for ease of comprehension rather than strict adherence to archaic forms.

Thus *Daniell and Henery* has become *Daniel and Henry*, 'ye' has become 'the', 'brickenteen' has become 'brigantine' and so on. Abbreviations were a notable feature of the *Journal*, since much of it was written as a log-book. These have generally been amplified. Personal and place names (especially those relating to Africa, and occasionally the names of English ships and their captains) were a recurring nightmare for Walter Prideaux. Where appropriate I have silently introduced more conventional equivalents in the belief that there is no point in prolonging his misunderstandings.

As a whole the *Journal*, rather like a series of jottings, lacked all punctuation. This has now been supplied. Extracts are symbolised thus

Long-forgotten trade goods, their weights and measures, played a central role in the slave trade and loom large in both parts of this book. To avoid endless footnotes these have been gathered together into a comprehensive glossary at the end. Maritime and navigational terms are both more widely understood and more easily accessible via modern dictionaries and so have not been the subject of such treatment.

Finally, as regards both spelling and punctuation, I have sought throughout to be as unobtrusive as possible. In the final analysis, however, there is only one criterion: does it make sense? I fervently hope it does and that what small liberties I may have taken to achieve this end may be forgiven by the purist.

A Note on Dates and Currency

Time marches on. But in the years covered by this book England marched to a different drum and slower beat than that heard upon the Continent.

For England, following the Julian calendar, lagged some eleven days behind its contemporaries on the Continent, whose days and months were calculated according to the Gregorian calendar. Nor were years free from enigma. The English year ran from 25 March (Lady Day) to the 24 March following.

In order to present a concerted and intelligible narrative of events, all days and months follow the English Julian calendar, which remained in use until 1752. All years, however, have been standardised to the modern style and the year taken to begin on 1 January. Thus, where an original document may be dated February 14 1699 (or $\frac{1699}{1700}$), this has been silently emended to 14 February 1700.

As with time, so with money. Britain resisted the continental system of currency until 1971 when decimalisation of sterling took place. In the belief that such action would not be appropriate, no attempt has been made in the following pages to convert financial data into the current system. All prices and costs are expressed in traditional pounds, shillings and pence.

Part One
The Log-Book
of the *Daniel and Henry*
of Exeter, 1700

CHAPTER ONE

An Introduction to the Slave Trade

I T IS tempting to view the involvement of ports such as Exeter and Dartmouth in the late seventeenth and early eighteenth century slave trade as transient provincial aberrations. But isolated as such ventures may have been, they nevertheless formed part and parcel of England's bid for supremacy in trade, on the high seas and ultimately in world affairs.

It has suited the English temperament (and civic pride) to see national involvement in the slave trade as predominantly abolitionist. Before it assumed an abolitionist character, however, it was fiercely generative, a stance it shared with every other major European power.

Slaves were pawns in the much wider game of the European commercial revolution. As national states emerged from the Middle Ages, national activities expanded and burgeoned. Trade blossomed, towns grew, commercial horizons broadened. And with the development of the middle classes there arrived a distinctive and positive viewpoint on competition and profit.

This was as much a factor in southern as in northern Europe. Exploration and exploitation often went hand in hand, for one thing very much led to the other. Inevitably attitudes of mind were reflected in the language, most notably in Portuguese where the verb for 'explore' and 'exploit' is one and the same. Perhaps Columbus encapsulated that when on his return from the first voyage he informed Ferdinand and Isabella he could supply as many slaves as they wanted from the newly discovered West Indies. On his second voyage he was as good as his word and packed 500 Indians aboard returning caravels. A reversal of the later Atlantic slave trade, when Africans were carried from east to west, this voyage saw the inauguration of the dismal tradition of slave mortality: about 200 of the Indians died on the way and were cast into the sea.

Though there has always been a tendency to see the slave trade as peripheral to the development of the West, it was in reality of central importance. The triangular nature of the points of contact – Europe, Africa, the Americas – defined an area of immense opportunity. It favoured the export of conventional European products in exchange for exotic luxuries. It created an insatiable demand for manufactured goods overseas which led inexorably to the introduction of power machinery at home to satisfy that demand. It stimulated shipbuilding and all associated trades and service industries such as insurance and banking. Slavery furnished the labour that had been one of the main deficiencies of colonies in the New World, and the proceeds from slavery reinforced the power and the wealth of African chieftains amongst their own people, and the pre-eminence of their tribes in the long series of coastal wars in which they took part. And finally, from the bricks of the slave-grown crops such as tobacco, sugar and cotton, empires were built. These raw materials were transformed by the mother country into manufactured articles which were then re-exported for even greater profit. Nor was that the only benefit to accrue, for each article sold in the colonies strengthened the mother country's economic and cultural penetration and reinforced the colony's economic dependence and thereby its value to the imperial power.

With the increase in trade, all services within its terms of reference underwent revolutionary change. Shipbuilding and banking were two of the areas most affected. The inexorable rise to dominance of European maritime technology was occasioned by innovations in rigging and hull construction, quadrants to determine latitude, growing expertise and accuracy in map and chart-making. A powerful combination of sophisticated navigational aids, sails and guns gave European ships superiority on the high seas and aided their pursuit of empire.

Banking thrived on finding answers to unfamiliar problems and matched the new spirit of shipbuilding with entrepreneurial enthusiasm. New commercial practices such as credit, bills of exchange, partnerships and joint stock enterprises were developed to mobilise the capital for long-haul, high-risk ventures. Those who could afford to fund these ventures – as the seventeenth century progressed the emphasis moved firmly from the Court to mercantile families – found themselves possessed of a powerful voice in determining the affairs of their nation in both public and foreign affairs.

Though Columbus had introduced the idea of a transatlantic slave trade, the enduring demand for slaves was to come from the European colonisers of the Americas, not from Europe itself. As gold and silver poured into Europe from Peru and Mexico the Amerindian miners died in such numbers that in 1510 King Ferdinand of Spain ordered 250 Negroes to be sent there. From that one decree grew the transatlantic slave trade of the sixteenth, seventeenth and eighteenth centuries.

Though hunger for precious metals provided the impetus for the first phase of the slave trade, sugar was never far behind. Virtually unknown to Europe before the Middle Ages, it began to be grown around the Mediterranean towards the mid-fourteenth century and then spread rapidly to islands off the African coast such as the Canaries and Madeiras, ultimately to São Tomé on the Equator. The first group of islands was held by Spain, the latter two by Portugal, and both colonial powers introduced African slaves from the adjacent mainland to work the plantations. It was Portugal, however, which opened up the concept of large-scale sugar plantation slavery in its possession of Brazil, and from there it spread across to the Caribbean during the seventeenth century.

Aided by its geographical location, Genoese knowledge and capital, Portugal monopolised the early Atlantic slave trade in particular and African trade in general. Its island of São Tomé was in essence a prototypical plantation and the lessons learned there during the sixteenth century with regard to slave labour, crop cultivation and refinement cleared the way for the full-scale exploitation of the jewel in Portugal's colonial crown, Brazil. Nor was demand limited solely to the sugar plantations. As this immense colony was developed gold, tobacco, cotton and coffee successively sharpened the demand for slaves from the seventeenth well into the nineteenth century. Not content with simply having castles like Elmina on the African coast, Portugal established formal colonies such as Angola and Mozambique well before other European powers arrived on the scene. But there were flaws in her alliance with Spain which exposed her to Dutch hostility. Holland's eighty years' war for independence eventually destroyed Portugal's monopoly of the Atlantic slave trade and even cost her the temporary loss of north-eastern Brazil (including the sugar capital of Pernambuco) and Angola, and the permanent loss of her one capital castle on the Guinea Coast, Elmina. An English sea captain and erstwhile slave trader, Nathaniel Uring, put it in a nutshell when he wrote in 1711, 'the Portuguese may be compared to Setting Dogs or Pointers who have taken great pains to spring the Game while others reap the benefit'.[1] Uring then goes on to refer modestly to the Dutch gaining the advantage, but in reality it was the English who overtook the Portuguese as masters of the slave trade.

Geographically close to Portugal and sharing a common heritage, Spain always remained in the wings of the slave trade rather than centre-stage. This can be accounted for by the fact that Spanish merchants had to trade under the most restricted commercial system in Europe, a system that was geared single-mindedly to the production of bullion rather than tropical produce. The mines were in existence long before the *conquistadores* arrived on the scene and so was the technology. Virtually no capital needed to be invested in the New World to exploit the bullion: no manufactured goods had to be exchanged for slaves so no commercial enterprises were formed to pursue overseas trade opportunities: as a result no adequate merchant fleet was ever developed. Unlike all the other colonial powers, Spain shipped no slaves of her own, relying instead on contracts with other merchant nations for her supply[2] – the basis of that infamous El Dorado of the slave trade the 'Asiento', which is simply the Spanish for 'contract'.

By the early seventeenth century it was the turn of the Dutch, and despite the close political links between Holland and England from the end of that century, both fought as bitter rivals in the trade and commercial arenas until the end of the nineteenth century. Holland stood at the crossroads of north-west Europe by the mid-sixteenth century, with a thriving merchant fleet and a substantial cloth industry. Dominated by Amsterdam, at that time and for virtually the rest of the century the financial heart of Europe, trade was Holland's life-blood. Its unrestricted flow was aided by particular skills in navigation, chart-making and weaponry. Though perhaps now best known for the covetous eyes she cast towards the East Indies, Holland fought long and hard for a share of the Americas. In 1630 she invaded Pernambuco, the sugar production centre of Brazil, and annexed it.

The colony's total dependence on imported African slave labour acted as a practical imperative for the Dutch to enter the slave trade and in 1637 they took a major step towards achieving this by capturing and retaining Elmina Castle on the Gold Coast from the Portuguese. Having lost Pernambuco to the Portuguese seventeen years later they exported their knowledge of sugar planting and refining to other foreign-held islands in the Caribbean such as

Barbados. One of the earliest histories of Barbados relates that 'Sir James Drax bought the model of a Sugar Mill and some Coppers from Holland'.[3]

The stimulation of the sugar trade was no act of altruism by the Dutch, for it also encouraged the consumption of slaves. Fortunately they were in a peculiarly advantageous position to supply them, having a large merchant marine, excellent contacts on the Guinea Coast and virtually no plantations of their own in the Caribbean or Americas to satisfy first. Though the Dutch West India Company, in league with the Dutch Navy, attempted to suppress all interloping voyages from Zealand, the profits for those merchants prepared to take the risks were irresistible. The presence of these Dutch interlopers on the Guinea coast made life difficult for the English ten per cent captains, whose freight had already been taxed by the Royal African Company:

> An Interloper fitted out from Zeeland, which with Cost of Cargo, Charges, and Outset from the River Mas may amount to £3000, is equal to a Ship of the same Bigness and Cargo fitted out from the River of Thames which will cost £4500 . . . the Dutch having no Dutys on Naval Manufactures can fit out their Ships one-third cheaper than we, and have East India and all Commoditys proper for Africa, except woollens, 30 per cent cheaper than we . . .[4]

The expansion of Dutch interests in the West Indies and America met with stiff opposition in the shape of English and French empire building, maritime, mercantile and colonial. The English interest in the slave trade was inextricably linked with a general interest in trading with Africa, but France was a late arrival. She made up for this with an abundance of zeal. After gaining a number of minor possessions in the Caribbean she invaded Jamaica in 1694 in an abortive attempt at annexation. Though beaten off she continued to be a thorn in the side of the English West Indies. In 1697 France was granted the cession of Santo Domingo by the Treaty of Ryswick and set up a powerful naval base at Petit Goâve, which constantly monitored English naval movements, and was in turn under continuous observation by the Royal Navy. Her entry to the slave trade on a grand scale came when she gained the Asiento with Spain in 1701 for an exclusive ten-year span. In the mean time her bid for colonial representation on mainland America had been successful, for in 1699 she gained the province of Louisiana.

Of all the countries in western Europe, only Italy was notable by its absence. As a group of princely states rather than a nation state, Italy could not draw upon national resources. Despite her reputation for navigation, Italy limited herself to trading largely within the Mediterranean. She had no Atlantic seaboard, and no colonies desperate for labour. Nor did she possess an African Company with strategic forts along the Guinea Coast, as did all the other European powers.

Nevertheless, English eyes were forever open to the danger of others meddling in their hard-won trade. In June 1699, Consul Boughton at Venice reported that the sloop *Seaflower*, freighted by Robert Davis, an English merchant resident in Venice, to Guinea and Honduras, had returned importing 30 tons of logwood.[5] Though imported into Italy, not England, Boughton believed he had the right to 5 per cent of the logwood's value. Caleb Phippard was the commander of the *Seaflower*, Thomas Crawford, a Scotsman, its supercargo. Though the Commissioners for Trade and the Plantations ruled Consul Boughton's attempt to impose English taxes in Venice out of order, he obviously believed he had stumbled upon an incipient threat to English trade on the Guinea coast. Later the same year Boughton reported

> there is at present a ship fitting out of this port called the *Golden Cross*, two Venetians that are brothers, are owners thereof, and one of them called Capt. Biazio Valentini is commander, and will be ready to sail hence in a few days for Guinea. The ship is burden about 250 tons, carries 40 men and 30 guns etc. An English engineer Mr Pearson . . . has been the Chief Director in fitting up the said Ship for the Voyage and Mr Crawford aforesaid is to be the Manager . . . both go on the Ship, having picked up an English mate and some seamen who have been in this State's service. A noble Venetian called Signor Morosini is an encourager and Protector of this design . . .[6]

Though a vessel cleared London early in 1702 for Venice with a cargo of beads for the African trade,[7] no more was heard of Venetian involvement. Despite all the European powers – with the exception of Italy – having excellent reason for seeking to dominate the trade to Africa, and pursuing that end with vigour, none surpassed the attempts of the English. The broad reasons behind this, its reflection in many areas of English trade, the dissatisfaction felt by merchants with the Royal African Company monopoly, and the attempts by the Company to control the trade are outlined in the following chapter.

CHAPTER TWO

Merchants versus Monopoly

WHEREAS every other European nation involved in the slave trade moved up or down in the table of ships sent or slaves exported as the seventeenth turned into the eighteenth century, England forged steadily ahead. Owing to a peculiar conjunction of advantages there was little to hold her back despite the prevalence of bitterly contested European wars in the opening years of the century. The legacy of the Commonwealth and of the Revolution of 1688 had bestowed a strong national government upon her which saw supporting commercial interests overseas as hand in glove with the political dream of empire.

Unlike Spain, England possessed a large merchant class whose voice was heard at the highest level of public affairs. Unlike both Spain and Portugal, England had industrial products to export: woollens from the south-west and east of the country, metal manufactures and weaponry from Birmingham, a variety of goods from manufacturing centres such as Newcastle upon Tyne, Manchester, Sheffield, Kidderminster and ultimately from the metropolis itself. Unlike any of the other European nations it shared no common border (except for Scotland) with a rival. Its command of the Channel, immediate access to the Atlantic and domination of the North and Irish Seas allowed it to monitor mercantile developments on the Continent, and – thanks to growing maritime superiority – to impose its will.

When the nature of England's overseas possessions is taken into account her involvement in the slave trade becomes a foregone conclusion. For neither the Portuguese nor the Dutch possessed any sugar-producing islands in the Caribbean nor tobacco plantations on the American mainland. France's ambitions for Martinique and Guadeloupe were frustrated by internal hostilities that rendered the islands ungovernable and unproductive for two decades. And Spanish eyes were dazzled by gold and silver alone, blinding them to sweeter riches.

As produce from the English plantations leaped spectacularly in value, the traffic in the means of production – slaves – responded in kind. With the harvests of sugar and tobacco stimulating shipbuilding both in the plantations and at home, the merchant tonnage increased from 90,000 to 261,222 between 1663 and 1701.[1] Furthermore the government acted to protect English mercantile interests by extending and reinforcing the Acts of Trade and Navigation, to the detriment of the Dutch.

Introduced in 1647 specifically to frustrate the merchant traders of any other European nation from making capital out of English plantations, the original Act entitled 'An Ordinance for encouragement of Adventurers to the several plantations of Virginia, Bermudas, Barbados and other places of America', stated that no plantation should suffer any goods or produce therefrom to be shipped to foreign ports except in English vessels. In 1650 all foreign ships had to be licensed for trade with the plantations. In 1651 Cromwell updated his 1647 Ordinance in order to tackle the problem of English ships manned by predominantly foreign crews. Described as an 'Act for Increase of Shipping and Encouragement of the Navigation of this Nation', no goods or commodities of Asia, Africa or America could be imported into England, Ireland or any English colony except in English-built ships owned by English subjects and of which the master and three-quarters of the crew were English in origin. In addition Cromwell loosed off a broadside against the Dutch carrying trade by further specifying that no goods from any country in Europe could be shipped into England except in English ships with English crews, though foreign ships were allowed to bring in goods solely from their country of origin.

As if that was not enough, more was to follow. Between 1660 and 1672 further legislation was enacted whereby all colonial produce had to be exported in English vessels, some sorts of produce could be exported only to England and her dependencies, colonies could not receive any goods whatever in foreign vessels and, finally, virtually no goods of whatever description could be imported except in English ships of predominantly (minimum 75 per cent) English manning. Such was the shaping of commercial policies to promote national interests. Such was the power of the English mercantile and naval marine – and the efficiency of the country's bureaucracy – that these policies could be enforced.

Sir John Hawkins of Plymouth is generally regarded as England's first slave trader, but after the débâcle of Hawkins' third voyage for slaves in 1567–9 there was little English enthusiasm for the trade. Gold had always been the motif of African trade before Hawkins and the desultory interest which remained towards Africa following his ventures concentrated once again on the precious metal, with ivory, redwood and pepper lagging some way behind. Even encouragement by the Crown in the form of privileges did little to help, though Richard Jobson's oft-quoted remark when offered slaves on the Gambia in 1621 that the English 'did not deal in such commodities, neither did we buy or sell one another, or any that had our own shapes' sounds too good to be true.[2] Less than ten years later Nicholas Crispe had already carried out at least one slaving venture to the Guinea Coast, and had been granted a vessel specifically furnished as a slave-trading ship by the Privy Council.[3] Admittedly his Company of Merchants Trading into Africa, whose patents were granted in 1631, had gold as their declared objective, but one suspects they would have had little compunction in loading slaves if they were offered. It should also be borne in mind that the Company was under unofficial orders to explore the sugar industry on the island of São Tomé, presumably with a view to gleaning enough information to assess the suitability of various islands in the Caribbean for future sugar production.

In place of the existing haphazard approach to African trading, Crispe brought a refreshingly businesslike approach. From the Dutch West India Company he poached Arendt de Groot, a man well versed in the Guinea Coast gold trade, and established a series of resident English merchants and lodges along the West African coast. Much of the building of these factories, including the fort at Cormantin, seems to have been financed by him personally. Gold was supplemented by São Tomé sugar in these early days, and of all produce redwood was the most profitable in the decade 1630–40. In 1651 his reconstituted Guinea Company brought slaving into the mainstream of its operations, though outside its declared charter of intentions. But given the sugar boom in Barbados, and the recent conquest of Jamaica, the slave trade could now hardly be described as of peripheral interest.

There was, however, an even more potent reason for the rise of interest in black labour: the decline in white indentured labour seeking a passage to the Caribbean. At one time the American colonies and Caribbean plantations had relied completely on white indentured servants to make up the deficiency in labour, but the early influx of white hopefuls was not sustained. During the mid-seventeenth century there was a marked reduction in the number of whites seeking indentured futures in the West Indies and a coinciden-tal change in attitude by the plantocracy. This was due to an aggravated disappointment which affected both sides. White servants, whose long-term aim was settlement, found that the most fertile and productive areas (most notably the Caribbean islands) had already been acquired by powerful mercantile interests, the very interests that had dominated their lives in Britain. Rumours had also reached England of cruelty to indentured servants and not all of these rumours were false. In Barbados abuse had reached such a stage that in 1649 a huge uprising was planned by the indentured white population; fuelled by the example of Cromwell and the Common-wealth, their object was nothing less than wholesale destruction of the plantocracy and control of the entire island.[4]

Even by 1685 friction between Barbadian planters and their servants – both black and white – had not ameliorated and a year later an uprising was rumoured of black slaves in collaboration with white servants. The plantocracy's fear of such a coalition was heightened by large numbers of Monmouth rebels who had been transported to the colony as felons. Nor did the white servants' quality of life invariably improve after their period of indenture had expired. As late as 1695, Governor Russell of Barbados wrote to the Lords of Trade and Plantations:

> there are hundreds of white servants in this island who have been out of their time for many years, and who have never a bit of fresh meat bestowed on them nor a dram of rum. They are domineered over and used like dogs . . .[5]

Such was the lot of the poor whites. The reasons behind the plantocracy's decision to dispense with indentured white servants as a labour force were largely economic. Wages had risen in England between 1640 and 1645,[6] and articles of indenture had increased both in complexity and in the safeguards they offered. This was due in part to potential servants' fear of exploitation and oppression. As the seventeenth century came to a close, it became plain that the West Indian islands were essentially throwbacks to a feudal past, albeit in a tropical climate. Dreams held by poor immigrant whites of fertile smallholdings when out of their indentures rapidly became disen-chantment on discovering that all the best land was already spoken for. Such indentured servants as did arrive during the late seventeenth and early eighteenth centuries were predominantly 'white-collar' workers fulfilling the functions of overseers or supervisors.

Black slaves brought with them no such complications, few expectations, and a better resistance to disease than their white counterparts. A planter owned them not for a limited span of four or five years, but for life. And therein lies the key to the rapid supersession of the white indentured system by black slavery. In 1695 a planter could, in Jamaica, purchase a slave for £20; a white indentured servant would cost at least £12 to £15 plus the cost of transportation. But whereas the white would work for perhaps four years, the black had a potential working life of twenty. Clearly the man:year ratio in terms of cost favoured investment in a black slave.[7]

Beyond bare economic considerations, slaves conferred certain pecuniary and non-pecuniary benefits on their owners. Apart from being capital assets, capable of acting as collateral for loans, and possessing a liquidation value, slaves served as soldiers and concubines. The more trusted often secured relatively light domestic duties inside the great plantation house. And for the planter himself they brought enhancement in social standing within a community rife with competition and paranoiacally conscious of status.

Not all slaves were appreciating assets. Despite having generally acquired useful skills and at least a fragmentary command of English, there came a time in their lives when they passed the point of no return in terms of the age:value relationship. To the white planter's mind a decent old age for a black slave was an unheard-of compassion. Everything was done to minimise the drain they would be on the profits of the estate; this despite the fact that, humanitarian principles apart, they had paid for themselves many times over during their working lives. Indeed it has been estimated that two-thirds of the value of a slave investment could be recovered in the first year of his or her labour on the plantation.[8] Rarely, if ever, do profit and humanity go hand in hand, and the plantations were no exception: old slaves were 'encouraged' to die.

Meanwhile, forty years after Richard Jobson's proud boast that Englishmen did not deal in commodities with their own shapes, it was left to the Company of Royal Adventurers into Africa to acknowledge that slave trading was of primary concern. Founded by James, brother of Charles II, in 1660 and justly described as an aristocratic treasure hunt rather than an organised business, it was reorganised in 1663 as the Company of Royal Adventurers of

England Trading into Africa. Its accounts reveal that cotton cloth, wax, hides, redwood, gum, pepper, ivory and especially gold were together much more important at that date than slaves. The 1665 estimate of its gross annual income in the African trade shows 25 per cent of their income derived from slaves (or as they termed them 'servants') sold in the plantations, and the remainder from gold, elephants' teeth (ivory), wax, hides, dyeing wood (redwood) and Guinea grain (mallaguetta pepper).[9] Their promising start was ruined by the Second Dutch War when de Ruyter destroyed their main base of operations at Goree Island on the Gambia. In 1672 the Company was wound up, and was superseded by the Royal African Company, henceforth usually called the Company since it is destined to play a major part in the following account of the slave trade.

The formation of this company marked the beginning of a new era.[10] It was not simply a monopoly but was also expected to play a key role as an instrument of imperial policy. Unfortunately the temper of the times did not look upon monopolies with favour and the Company attracted criticism from many quarters, most notably from the merchants whose financial and political muscle made them a force to be reckoned with. By the late 1690s opposition to the Company was almost solid.[11] If it wasn't merchants who felt the monopoly was against the free trade which they held most dear, then it was clothiers and suchlike who distrusted the Company's method of business. The policy which caused much of the latter opposition was the practice the Company had adopted of selling its Guinea redwood (used for dyeing cloth) by private contract to three or four dealers instead of by public auction in small lots. This attracted the fury of clothiers from Berkshire, Wiltshire, Somerset, Norwich, York, Gloucester and Devonshire before Parliament acceded to their request and ordered the Company to adopt sale by public auction.[12] Though most petitions from the provinces concerned the cloth trade in one way or another, the cutlers of Hallam in Yorkshire got their teeth into another angle altogether:

> since the Trade to Africa hath been ingrossed into the Hands of one Company, the Petitioners cannot be furnished with Ivory Teeth but from them; for which they pay double the Rates they were used to when the Trade was open and free; and the Dutch, who formerly bought great Quantities of Knives hafted in ivory have here of late by Reason of the Cheapness of Ivory among themselves, gotten the Trade from the Petitioners.[13]

Despite the Company's best efforts, the monopoly was never a viable proposition. Interlopers nibbled profitably at the edges of the trade until 1695 when the slave trade was opened up – but only east of the River Volta – to any trader willing to pay £1 per slave shipped.

In 1698 the merchants had their victory. With the 'Act to settle the Trade to Africa' (9. Will.3c.26) the African trade and the length of the Guinea Coast were thrown open to all on payment of a 10 per cent tax (based on the value of their Guinea-bound cargo) to the Collector of Customs at the port from whence they cleared. He then – in theory – remitted the proceeds to Africa House, headquarters of the Company. Merchants taking advantage of this enfranchisement of trade to Africa became known as 'ten per centers'. Later, as feeling grew increasingly strong that the 10 per cent tax was an unnecessary and burdensome restriction, they styled themselves 'separate traders'.

None of these merchants were totally reliant on Africa for their livelihood, despite the exaggerated petitions they presented to the Commons. If these were to be believed, the African trade involved a large proportion of the working population of England, not only from the large urban centres of London, Bristol, Liverpool and Exeter, but also towns such as Chester, Taunton, Totnes, Westbury (Wiltshire), Minehead and Bridgwater. Disregarding the more extravagant claims, these petitions displayed a change of tactic after 1710. Whereas they had originally stressed the risk of their petitioners' livelihood being cramped by a return to a monopoly, in the final thrust of their campaign the provinces highlighted a point of democracy, following the lead of the royal boroughs of Scotland.[14] The core of this issue was that all the subjects of Great Britain should have full freedom of trade: they were already excluded from Asia by the East India Company; to be likewise barred from Africa, and in consequence see the plantation and Guinea trade monopolised and established in London, would be intolerable.

Pressure on the Commissioners for Trade and the Plantations was unremitting from inside and outside Parliament and reinforced by large vested interests such as the plantation owners. In 1712 the 10 per cent tax was abolished and the trade thrown open to all. The way was now open for Britain to dominate the slave trade to an extent no other nation had achieved before or, thankfully, since.

Although generally perceived as a body riddled with inefficiency, desperately unprofitable to its shareholders and hopelessly incompetent in delivering quantities of slaves to the plantations, it is doubtful whether the Royal African Company was quite the lumbering and ineffectual organisation which the ten per cent traders and others opposed to its monopoly have portrayed in their propaganda. Its main limitation was its commitment to the African trade: unlike the ten per centers (or 'interlopers' as they were termed by the Company after 1712) it could not move on to a different trade when conditions became difficult, or a series of ventures failed to turn a profit. The Company was wedded to Africa for better or for worse. As the century turned it definitely became for the worse.

Yet the Company tried to regulate the trade, both from a business point of view and from a humanitarian standpoint. It did the first with remarkable efficiency given the difficulties of communication at the time. Before 1698 it had protected its monopoly with some degree of success. Its agents in virtually every port of any size on the British coast combined with its factors on the Guinea Coast and in the plantations to report the departures and arrivals of any vessels thought to be bound to or from Africa, or sought to impound them when they arrived with slaves.

After 1698 the Company, already embattled and having lost the first round of its fight to protect its monopoly, had to rely on the Collectors at the Customs House of the various ports to pass on the monies accruing from the 10 per cent tax. Goods arriving from Africa were also subject to the same tax, as were ships which cleared their cargoes from the West Indies or America to Africa and back. Commission on every clearance for Africa (and entrance from Africa) was payable to the Collector by the Company as an incentive.

A considerable flow of letters in and out of Africa House, the Company headquarters, kept the Company reasonably well informed of shipping movements between all points on the triangular passage by Company ships and ten per centers alike. Occasionally transgressors were seized. Early in 1699 Charles Chaplin, Agent at Jamaica, seized the *Africa*, captain James Tanner, who had declared for Ireland, taken goods aboard there without paying the 10 per cent tax, and then traded on the Guinea Coast.[15]

If the Company had any obvious weakness it was for employing people whose family connection and contacts were opposed to any monopoly whatever, thus weakening the resolve of the Company from within. Dalby Thomas, appointed Agent-General on the Guinea Coast from the ranks of the anti-Company pamphleteers, was one such example. No less astonishing was the selection of Giles Heysham, the brother of well-known interloper Robert Heysham, as factor at Barbados in 1693.[16] In 1695 Giles was replaced by another brother, William, whose securities were provided by the selfsame Robert! All three of them continued to trade on their own account to and from Africa. The Company excused itself on the grounds that it sought to advance its cause by appointing politically powerful figures in the plantocracy. Since these planters were usually involved in the slave trade, Company options were limited.

After the freeing of the trade in 1712, the Company found it harder and harder to protect its interests. Although the trade had been made free and the 10 per cent tax dispensed with, independent traders were not supposed to clear for Guinea, since the Company technically retained its monopoly in this region. The Company foresaw correctly that 'though none [of the interlopers] have entered their Ships and Goods directly for Africa, yet many of them will come upon the Coast to trade'.[17] As time passed it became clear that the interlopers were entering clandestinely at the Customs Houses for Madeira or the West Indies, then brazenly announcing they were sailing for Guinea.[18] The Company was powerless to respond and was forced to accommodate itself as best it could to the situation.

For all its sins, the Company treatment of slaves aboard its ships was better – or marginally less inhuman – than the treatment meted out aboard those of the independent traders. The question of over-crowding and mortality constantly exercised Company minds, leading them in 1705 to insist that charter-party ships carried 'one of Mr Wallcott's Engines to make Salt Walter fresh . . . to render the Voyage much the shorter and . . . lessen the Mortality of the Negroes'.[19] (The Company had been persuaded to invest extensive funds in Mr Wallcott's project – an unwise but not inconsiderate gesture.) At the same time Dalby Thomas at the Cape Coast Castle continuously warned against the mortality attendant on overcrowding.[20] Although not a part of the captain's orders prior to 1700, in that year a new paragraph appeared. One example is dated 16 April 1700 to Patrick Bourne of the *Gambia Galley*, a Company-owned ship: 'To prevent the mortality of the Negroes you must observe frequently to wash your Decks with Vinegar, and divert them as much as you can with some sorts of music and play.'[21]

When it came to governing conditions aboard charter-party or hired ships, the Company was on much less firm ground. In those cases the owner was contracted according to the capacity of his vessel. Obviously he would attempt to 'tight-pack' the slaves to maximise the capacity and hence his return. The practice of 'tight-packing' verged on the insane, but merchants dug their heels in whenever it was brought into question. One example can be deduced from the fragmentary Company records and graphically illustrates the problem. On 1 August 1704 the Secretary of the Company, John Pery, advised William Coward, a London merchant and important nonconformist, that ship surveyors for the Company had seen his ship the *Gold* (or *Gould*) *Frigate* and reported as follows:

Length for stowage of Negroes – 63 foot
Breadth between decks –   23 foot 10 ins
Depth in hold –   10 foot 6 ins
Height between decks –   4 foot 5 ins

Which last mentioned spoils all for she is far too low to carry 2 tier of negroes without stifling, & if but one she will take in but 400 negroes . . .[22]

This assessment met with a storm of protest from Coward – known for his 'fiery disposition' – who entertained high hopes of chartering his ship for 800 Negroes. On this occasion the Committee of Shipping stood its ground and Pery replied firmly:

Tis morally impossible that 2 tier of Negroes can be stowed between decks in 4 foot 5 inches. Were she four or five inches more they would venture, but as the case stands tis neither fit for you nor them to undertake it; the mortality must be so great that both must lose per the voyage . . .

Not all the blacks who embarked on Company ships were slaves. Though convention impels us to regard all the crew as white, black crew members were occasionally present, performing menial tasks on Company ships, though references to them are scanty at best. It is very likely that there were many more examples than the black woman hired aboard the Company ship *Royal Africa* in 1702 to dress provisions for the slave cargo on the middle passage.[23] Agents and factors on the Guinea Coast also had orders to lend castle *grommettoes* – free black servants – to assist any Company ship whose crew had been depleted by death or disease. As trade ran its course these blacks occasionally found themselves 'guests' at Africa House.[24]

Senior Company officials were well placed to bring blacks to England, despite the fact that the blacks' status as slaves once they had reached this country was in doubt. Not that the blacks would be aware of that. As a result there was a persistent trickle of slaves into

England. The Company requested the Cape Coast Castle to send it 'Ten good healthy and Young Negroes' in September 1698.[25] Sir Dalby Thomas sent a group of five or six to influential friends once he had established himself as Agent-General at the Cape Coast Castle in 1703. In 1704 the Committee of Shipping brought a further five on their own account by the Company ship *Postilion*, which had been trading on the Guinea Coast for ivory, gold and redwood. They arrived in Milford in January 1705 and came to London in March. One member of the committee[26] kept his black boy as a personal valet; the rest were put to work on the Company ship *Nicholson*, then loading freight for the Azores, and sailed with her when she cleared for Fyall. Though she returned directly to London, no more is heard of them. The year 1705 seemed to mark a height in the fashion for black servants; John Pery also imported a boy on board the *Boughton* from Guinea which was chased into Waterford by a privateer and delayed. He wrote to Captain Daniel Thomas (brother of Dalby) begging him to furnish his black with clothes suitable for the northern latitudes.[27]

Whatever cosy domestic arrangements these slave-owners envisaged, things did not always work out according to plan. By the same June 1705 when John Pery was being so solicitous, another member of the committee was impatient to be rid of what had come to be an encumbrance: 'Mr Joliffe desires his black boy ... to be disposed of ... values him at £20, hopes to make £30 of him in the West Indies' ...[28] ran the orders to the captain of the Company ship at Portsmouth to whom the unfortunate black was consigned. Occasionally black slaves in England were hired back to the Company; on 19 September 1721 a Mrs Anne Clarke 'was paid £20:14:0 for wages due to her black servant Taggee on the Company's ships *Union* and *Boughton*'.[29]

The arrival of black slaves in England was increased from 25 May 1721 when captains of Company ships were allowed the privilege of bringing one black into England for free;[30] previously they had been restricted to four Negroes in every hundred delivered alive in the West Indies as an incentive to minimise the mortality on the middle passage. This 4 per cent commission was paid in money in London, no captain being allowed to import slaves into England. Unfortunately no records survive of the consequences the 1721 privilege entailed: the numbers of blacks imported and their fate remains unknown.

During all this time the legal status of slaves in England was open to considerable doubt. Though their white masters would blandly assert that they were property – objects rather than people, owing to their being heathen – the widespread belief was that baptism would amount to manumission. Despite most English owners taking infinite pains to prevent their slaves being made Christians, a few slave-owners in provincial English towns did allow baptism to take place. Before becoming dewy-eyed about these exceptions to the general rule, it does seem as though these few slaves were at death's door and that by this stage their owners felt they had nothing to lose, and perhaps much to gain, in saving a heathen soul from the clutches of the devil.

Those masters (and mistresses) who held that slaves were tanta-mount to property received a sharp setback in 1706 when Lord Chief Justice Holt decided that trover – a common law action to recover the value of personal property wrongfully taken or detained – could not cover slaves, for in his judgement the common law did not distinguish black from white. There is nothing to suggest that this greatly dismayed slave-owners in England, nor that his famous pronouncements 'as soon as a Negro comes into England he becomes free' or 'one may be a villein in England but not a slave',[31] had Africans dancing in the streets. Nevertheless this grey area in the law did worry the West Indian lobby (largely made up of absentee plantation owners who brought their domestic slaves with them to England) and eventually in 1729 the Attorney-General and Solicitor-General ruled categorically and all too predictably that a slave in the West Indies was a slave in Britain. And that is how the position stood for nearly a century.

Finally, as a footnote to Company involvement in Africa, it should be stressed that this was far from passive: Birmingham and London gunsmiths profited by selling guns to the Company, which in turn profited by exporting war. Even after the height of its influence had passed the Company continued to export a colossal amount of weaponry: between August 1713 and May 1715 the numbers of guns contracted for by the Company amounted to 11,986. Fuzees made up the bulk (11,402) followed by Jamaica guns (150) and black muskets (434). Of this total 11,246 had been shipped by June 1715. With typical professional myopia the Company washed its hands of whatever use the Africans made of arsenals such as this. The scale of hypocrisy is truly confounding: though shipments of weapons such as these had been a regular feature of Company business, it could still write to its factor at Anamabo, Josiah Pearson, in June 1707:

You write you were in daily expectation of the Arcadians coming to fight the Cabestera people, which if they beat you expect a glorious trade for Slaves and Gold, but in your letter (dated August from Commenda) you tell us you are more engaged in War, having hired another Nation to help you.

We are sorry any part of our stock is spent in carrying on a War amongst the Natives.[32]

Perhaps the Company expected the Africans who bought the guns from them to beat them into ploughshares.

Though no longer a monopoly, the Company, its policies, operations, factors and forts, are destined to contribute greatly to the ensuing narrative. Fortunately many of its records have survived intact to the present day, and provide a wealth of relevant detail to flesh out the otherwise sparse accounts of the 10 per cent slave trade ships. For the moment, having briefly mapped out the beginning of the European and English trade in slaves from Africa and the important part played by the Company, we will now turn to the other end of the spectrum, from the general to the particular, and examine the genesis of a slave trade voyage from a small provincial port in England.

CHAPTER THREE

———

Background to the Voyage

THOUGH England's emergence as a slave-trading power was inextricably linked with the exploits of John Hawkins of Plymouth, Devon merchants in general were loath to follow his lead. For over a century they contented themselves with developing the cloth trade to France and the fisheries trade to Newfoundland. However, with the opening of the American colonies in the second quarter of the seventeenth century, closely followed by the settling of Barbados and Jamaica, they were quick to seize the new trade openings thus presented.

Such colonies might almost have been on the Moon, for they stood in dire need – water and light excepted – of everything essential to support human life (as the European understood it). Consequently huge shipments of building materials, household stores and provisions, leatherware and ironmongery sailed westwards. But of all goods in the long manifests of cargoes, wool stood supreme. And wool was closest to Devon's heart. Serge flowed from Exeter and Axminster, baize from Barnstaple. From neighbouring counties Taunton supplied plains, Dorchester broadcloth, and Sherborne silk.

In return Devon merchants imported animal hides and timber. As the early settlers gradually and laboriously cleared the land, cash crops such as sugar and tobacco emerged to dominate trade. Exeter found itself well placed to profit twice over from the two-way trade to the plantations, being both a great woollen manufacturing centre in its own right and conveniently close to Rotterdam, then the centre of the European tobacco trade. By 1700 Exeter was the second wealthiest provincial city after Bristol, and merchants like Daniel Ivy and Henry Arthur were amongst those who had prospered mightily on the city's transatlantic trade boom.

Employed in the tobacco trade with the American colonies by her owners Daniel Ivy and Henry Arthur, the *Daniel and Henry* was a familiar sight both in Dartmouth and at Exeter where Ivy and Arthur carried on a substantial business as tobacco merchants. A sizeable ship of 200 tons burden, armed with ten guns, she was usually manned by a crew of twenty while on her customary annual voyages to Virginia or Maryland.[1] When she berthed at Dartmouth on 5 December 1699[2] she had just completed a typical trading voyage under her master, Samuel Stafford, which had taken her first to Patuxent in Maryland (in company with the *John* of Topsham and *Hopewell* of Plymouth) then to Portsmouth,[3] where she discharged a proportion of her Maryland cargo of 475 hogsheads of tobacco, on to Rotterdam where the bulk was delivered, and finally back to Dartmouth. The voyage had taken approximately fifteen months, regarded as average for the time, which was one of peace.

Amongst the holland linen, iron pots, clover seed, copy paper, twine and other assorted Dutch produce with which the *Daniel and Henry* returned from Rotterdam, were three items which bore a direct relevance to her next voyage. They were a grain kettle, two dozen chains and nine printed maps valued at 42s. 6d. To the innocent eye such artefacts had nothing in the least remarkable about them; but to those in the know a more sinister application could be envisaged. Grain kettles, huge circular pots looking more like witches' cauldrons than the cosy domestic variety, were used to prepare the maize pottage ('broth' is too nutritious a word) which was supposed to nourish a human cargo. Chains were installed the length of the hold, providing a secure line to which slaves could be manacled. And the maps reflected the pre-eminence of the Dutch in map-making, especially of that area of the West African coast called Guinea. Despite their high price, they were an essential business investment and, since charts of unfamiliar waters were highly sensitive information, might well have been acquired clandestinely. Though Holland and England were united politically, in 1700 they remained the deadliest of competitors on the Guinea Coast.

Though the premier maritime county of all England, Devon had few sea captains with first-hand experience of African waters, and even fewer with prior experience of commanding a slave ship. One who had was Roger Mathew. As master of the *Exeter* in 1682[4], he had taken command of her at Fyall in the Azores and sailed for Guinea as an interloper. The following year he delivered 123 slaves in Barbados[5] as an unlicensed slave trader, finally entering Dartmouth from St Kitts with a cargo that included 2 tons of Guinea redwood.[6]

Though Roger Mathew does not appear to have been commissioned for another Guinea voyage until the *Daniel and Henry* of 1700, his son Robert had commanded several slave ships. Robert Mathew was a friend and business associate of Henry Burwell who acted as 'ship's husband' for Robert Mathew's vessel the *Sarah* (named after his wife Sarah Mathew), a London ship of 90 tons which plied in the plantation trade,[7] but which in November and December of 1698 was loaded with cargo for the Guinea Coast. The *Sarah* cleared London for Africa in January 1699.

As soon as the *Daniel and Henry* had arrived at Rotterdam, Roger Mathew had assumed command from Samuel Stafford. On berthing at Dartmouth, Mathew would have been impatient to refit the vessel. She had long been at sea and would need her hull thoroughly scraped, and a myriad repairs both major and minor to planking, blocks, rigging and sails before leaving for Guinea. The workmen did not have time on their side. The most propitious season for sailing to Guinea – traditionally October and November in order to clear Africa before the enervating wet heat of West Africa's midsummer – was well past. It was already mid-December. Most slave ship departures from England left between January and March, although some left at any time and simply made the best of the conditions they encountered. The vagaries of weather and seventeenth-century mercantile endeavour made any attempt at scheduling haphazard at best. Departure times were determined only when the vessel berthed from its previous voyage. Doubtless merchants then, as today, were inclined to impose unrealistic turnround times in a fruitless bid to improve profitability.

Working to a shoestring budget and an impossibly tight schedule, Roger Mathew was responsible for making sure the *Daniel and Henry* was in a sufficiently seaworthy condition to withstand eighteen long months away from her home port. Extra holds had to be constructed between existing decks, but skilfully, so that handling would be affected as little as possible. A substantial crew would have to be assembled, for the business of trading for, guarding and feeding slaves was highly labour-intensive. Preferably the crewmen would be experienced sailors to whom gales in the Bay of Biscay, tornadoes off the Guinea Coast, doldrums on the middle passage, and the heady perfume of tropical Caribbean zephyrs would be all part of their job. Many of the crew would be skilled tradesmen; carpenters, coopers, sailmakers and gunners. Skills such as these were in perennially short supply during the war-torn seventeenth and eighteenth centuries. Luckily for Roger Mathew, 1699 and 1700 were years of peace, so there were more of these skilled workers available than usual, having been discharged from the armed services and looking for employment. They were absolutely crucial to the success of the voyage; maintenance of the ship and defence of her cargo could not be left to chance or makeshift. And as if that wasn't enough, it was Christmas.

Whether or not the festive season had anything to do with it, the call for men to crew the *Daniel and Henry* failed to elicit an immediate response. Years of peace rather than war usually resulted in an explosion of trade from the outports, freed from the worries of embargoes, impressment and enemy privateers. The volume of vessels clearing Exeter, Topsham and Dartmouth at this time meant captains faced stiff competition when recruiting experienced mariners, though in England generally the end of the seventeenth century was marked by acute unemployment. More than one in five of the total working population of the country was receiving poor relief in 1700 and starvation was commonplace. At least aboard ship, though the food was not to everyone's taste, nobody starved to death. As for the threat of infectious diseases that a voyage to Africa and the Caribbean posed, England's great plague of a mere thirty-five years before showed that exotic destinations did not enjoy a monopoly on mortality.

It took Roger Mathew some weeks to find the numbers of crew he required, and empty crew places remained virtually up to the moment of sailing.[8] Eventually the full complement, more than double the normal number for a conventional oceangoing voyage, were taken aboard. This was the usual practice for slave trade ships. Merchants feared slave revolts aboard, against which they could not insure; the process of barter was labour-intensive; looking after and guarding the slave cargo took many man-hours; and finally the death rate among the crew was high. In all forty-four hands shipped out aboard the *Daniel and Henry*. Of this number ten were to die from disease and accident, five ran away, one was discharged, one left to marry and settle in Jamaica, three were impressed into the Royal Navy at Port Royal or Kingston, and twenty-four returned. There is little evidence on the *Daniel and Henry* of crewmen being forced off the ship: she was tied up in Jamaica for nearly six months so any disaffected or homesick crew would have had ample opportunity to be paid off and take ship either for the American colonies or for home.

In the normal course of events it made good economic sense to 'lose' crew once the middle passage had been completed since the cargo of sugar on the homeward voyage was much less labour-intensive than slaves (and ballast even less so). This left the unfortunate sailors to find employment on some other ship. It was not unknown for bad captains deliberately to harass their crew in West Indian ports with the intention of forcing them to jump ship.[9] Other captains would simply sail for home without warning. Equally it was an unparalleled opportunity to jettison crew who were too troublesome either from temperament or from their lame, debilitated or diseased physical condition. Sometimes they were dismissed straight into the ever-open arms of the press-gang. West Indian ports were amongst the happiest of hunting grounds for Navy pressmen, they being well aware that incoming Guinea slave ships were heavily crewed and that, once the slaves were discharged, many of the crew would be surplus to requirements. They were also aware that by this time every sailor on a Guineaman was an experienced mariner and, seasoned by heat and exposure to disease, would be less likely to succumb to the Caribbean fevers that decimated crews fresh from England. Disease posed such a grave threat to the ability of the Royal Navy to defend English interests in the West Indies that regulations introduced in 1696 allowed Navy ships ordered to the West Indian station to carry larger than usual crews to allow for the invariable fatalities.[10]

Manning levels of Guinea trade ships are notoriously difficult to assess. The decision to carry a crew of forty-four on the *Daniel and Henry* seems to have been on a 'better safe than sorry' basis. In the *Journal* entries dealing specifically with the bartering for slaves on the Guinea Coast, the *Daniel and Henry* found herself alongside vessels of much greater tonnage and capacity such as the *Encouragement* of 240 tons and a crew of twenty, and the *Prince of Orange* of 456 tons,[11] also with approximately twenty hands. Both these crews included a high proportion of seasoned West Indian hands, and both ships were Royal African Company vessels. The accepted average ratio of seamen to tons burden in 1691–6 was 1:5.2 tons; in 1698, by comparison a time of peace, the ratio had fallen to 1:6.5 tons.[12] At the latter rate a crew numbering no more than thirty-one could be expected aboard the *Daniel and Henry*. Although not exactly contemporary with the *Daniel and Henry*, the *Florida* of 350 tons which set sail in February 1714 from London for Old Calabar and thence to Antigua, carried only a twenty-strong crew.[13] Eight died on the middle passage. She loaded 360 slaves in total, of whom 120 died. The anonymous writer of the *Florida*'s journal records that most of the twelve remaining crew who arrived safely at Antigua – including himself – were peremptorily discharged there, the captain having to wait months for the next sugar harvest and obviously reluctant to have redundant seamen eating into his profits.

By the time Walter Prideaux joined the *Daniel and Henry* from his home at Ermington, 15 miles west of Dartmouth, she would have been a hive of activity as gangs of carpenters, riggers and sailmakers sought to make her shipshape. The hull would already have been thoroughly scraped clear of marine growth and sheathed with an extra carapace below the waterline more as a gesture of defiance than any infallible shield against the ravages of the teredo worm. This tropical waterborne mollusc could turn a fine vessel into a leaky sieve within an astonishingly short time and it was not until the introduction of copper sheathing later in the century that its appetite was blunted. Above the waterline the seams in the planking of both hull and deck would have been packed with oakum and tar, and finally sealed with pitch. Sailmakers would have been hard at work repairing the patchwork canvases that were the *Daniel and Henry*'s usual embellishments: her best sails would be stowed for emergencies. Carpenters would be fitting replacement timbers and spars, block-makers fitting new pulleys, glaziers replacing windows in the cabin, and ship's chandlers supplying lanterns, oars, ropes and hawsers.

Amongst this bedlam Walter Prideaux's task was to account for every item of trade goods to be stowed aboard. The cargo, a classic mix of manufactured goods that was to stand English slavers in such good stead on the Guinea Coast throughout the eighteenth century, came from two sources. Ivy and Arthur tapped their usual supply of local manufactures – such as serge goods – which they exported to Virginia and Maryland in the normal course of business. And the third partner in the consortium, James Gould of Dorchester, pro-vided most of the exotic luxury items such as alcoholic spirits, Indian cotton cloth, beads, gewgaws and coral; plus two sets of drums and trumpets (which are not mentioned by Prideaux in his exhaustive list). This was shipped coastwise from London (where the 10 per cent tax on it was duly paid) to Dartmouth at the end of November 1699.[14]

Although the first ten years of open trade to Africa (1698–1708) were marked by accusations from pro-Company sources that the ten per centers habitually perjured themselves at the Customs on the value of their cargoes,[15] this was not the case with the *Daniel and Henry*. However, few vessels from the minor outports ever gave completely satisfactory accounts of the value of their cargoes to Africa during this period.

For all three merchants, – Daniel Ivy, Henry Arthur, and James Gould – the venture was a complete break with their normal pattern of trading and can be described as a typically speculative, shot-in-the-dark adventure that characterised much early eighteenth-century slave trading. Luck would play an important role in its outcome, for the equation barter = slaves = sugar was not an easy one to achieve. Africa was a law unto itself and the cargo might prove not to the tastes of the Guinea Coast caboceers. Supplies of slaves ebbed and flowed in quality as well as quantity as war and peace alternated in the African interior. Disease and dehydration on the middle passage could wreak havoc with intended profits. And sugar too was an unreliable quotient. A poor harvest or hurricane could reduce the crop dramatically, resulting in plantation owners paying off the slave captains with postdated bills of exchange or credit. Even when the harvest had been a good one, the parsimony (or good business sense) of many planters led them to expect slaves on credit: in cases such as these there was no revenue with which the captain could buy sugar or molasses. It took little imagination to visualise the *Daniel and Henry*, set forth with such high hopes from Dartmouth, returning with nothing to show for her trip but ballast.

If, on the other hand, the voyage was a success, a repeat was on the cards. The Caribbean lay close to Ivy, Arthur and Gould's major areas of interest, the tobacco plantations of Maryland and Virginia. Even more to the point, there was profit to be made in freighting sugar, molasses and rum to the American colonies once the middle passage from Africa had been negotiated and the slaves delivered. If the voyage was a disaster then they would console themselves with the knowledge that they had at least attempted it, but found it wanting. Unlike the Royal African Company, but in common with all minor port slave traders, they had a solid, bread-and-butter trade to fall back on. They were also wealthy men.

The two Exeter merchants, Daniel Ivy and Henry Arthur, were respectable burghers of the city. Of the two, Ivy was the more eminent. Originally a clothier, he was a freeman of the city and lived in the parish of St Kerrian in some style: his assessment of 6d. in the 1699 poor rate was amongst the highest in that locality. The strength of his financial standing was such that in 1691 he had been proposed as security in a petition by a local resident – Christopher Bale – to be confirmed as Receiver of Taxes for Devon and Exeter;[16] and by 1701 Ivy was Deputy Lieutenant of Exeter.[17] A clue to his rise from clothier to gentleman is perhaps to be found in the linking of the Ivy family to the powerful Courtenays of Devon when one Benjamin Ivy married Frances Courtenay in the early 1690s.[18] Frances was far from the Courtenay centre of wealth, being the third daughter of a third son who had captained a man-of-war and died in battle against the Dutch.[19] Nevertheless, though immediate wealth may not have been generated by this link, access to finance would have been greatly eased. Henry Arthur was a much more retiring individual and his career can be much less clearly documented except that he had always been engaged in trade,[20] and was admitted as a freeman of Exeter in 1691.

Partner number three, and perhaps the prime mover in the venture, was James Gould. Members of a powerful merchant family of Dorchester, closely related to the Goulds of Upwey House and suspected of harbouring strong Dissenting beliefs, James Gould and his younger brother George traded the length of the Devon and Dorset coasts; their outward-bound cargoes for the plantations of the Caribbean and North America can be traced at Weymouth, Lyme Regis, Topsham, Exeter, Dartmouth and Plymouth. They prospered on the hugely profitable sugar and tobacco which made up the bulk of the return cargoes. Trade was not the only string to James Gould's bow. As a local magnate he was closely involved in local government, being successively alderman, mayor, commissioner for assessment, sheriff and justice of the peace. He successfully stood for Dorchester and was returned to Parliament four times between 1677 and 1690,[21] where he was believed to be a Whig collaborator but made little or no impact, being tied up by his local and business interests.

The partnership, little more than a marriage of convenience between Ivy, Arthur and Gould, did not endure beyond the voyage of the *Daniel and Henry*. All three partners were in their late sixties or seventies, their fortunes apparently well secured by many profitable years in the tobacco trade,[22] and this gamble was one they could easily afford. Moreover they had formed part of the opposition to the monopoly of the Royal African Company and were no less drawn to the magnet of profit than any other merchants. When the 1698 Act curtailed the monopoly and sent ripples of excitement up the inlets, estuaries and rivers to England's maritime centres, they had responded to the lure of the Guinea El Dorado. Though it would be human beings and not gold they would be trading for, the human beings were conveniently both black and heathen. In any case mankind, when spurred by strong economic interests, has never shrunk from oppression and murder.

What were the factors that had brought Walter Prideaux, bearing one of the most prestigious of West Country surnames, aboard the *Daniel and Henry* as supercargo? For this one must look back, as so often in the seventeenth and early eighteenth centuries, to Oliver Cromwell and the Civil War. Being firmly on the Royalist side in this conflict, Walter's grandfather, Arthur Prideaux, had thought it incumbent upon him to raise a troop of horse for Charles I, an expensive action which beggared him financially and lowered the standard of living for two generations of his descendants in the process. Nor was there to be any compensation come the Restoration; though the main branch of the Prideaux family rose inexorably to power and influence, largely due to their close connections with Sir William Morice, Secretary of State for Charles II, Arthur Prideaux remained in reduced circumstances at Ermington in Devon, a small village between Plymouth and Dartmouth.[23]

Here Walter Prideaux was born on 19 October 1676, his mother Mary dying in the process. Brief though her life was, it was to be her family and relations that were to shape his career. She was from Dartmouth, where her father Walter Jago – after whom this Prideaux was named – was a wealthy merchant: her mother's family, the Dottins, were equally wealthy merchants of the area. Thus Walter, through his maternal grandparents, had unrivalled access to the two most active and wealthy mercantile families in South Devon, which enabled him to break with the stultifying tradition of High Church adherence and minor landed gentry that had been the destiny of virtually every male Prideaux in his branch of the family. By the time Walter was twenty-one, Thomas Jago, his second cousin, was Controller of the Port of Dartmouth and remained so for many years. On the Dottin side, his uncle George Dottin (mentioned briefly in the *Journal*) was one of the most energetic and industrious of Dartmouth merchants. In the period 1695–1701 he imported timber from New England, tobacco from Virginia and sugar, molasses, melons and lignum vitae from Barbados and Antigua. In return he exported train oil, cottons, broadcloths and serges to the American plantations, cable yarn to Rotterdam, strong beer to Barbados. He was also part owner of the letter of marque ship the *Nicholas*, a Dartmouth vessel of some 300 tons burden.[24]

As with many West Country mercantile families, there was a strong link with the plantations. The Dottins were early settlers in Barbados: by 1631 a William Dottin was a member of the council, and seven years later he was recorded as owning more than 10 acres of land, a measure which defined him as a plantation owner. His son, another William, inherited the estate: by June 1680 he was registered as holding three manservants and sixty Negroes. The family – like many plantation owners – were actively engaged in the slave trade: their vessel the *Dottin Galley*, of 70 tons and 6 guns, made many 'double voyages' to the Guinea Coast with rum, returning with slaves, in the period 1698–1709. William Dottin the second died in Barbados in 1703: his coat of arms – two lions passant in pale – was exactly that of the Devonshire Dottins of Ley, Walter Prideaux's grandparents. Later Dottins who achieved eminence in Barbados included James, a popular member of the Barbados Council, who was returned as president in 1732 and successively 1735–9 and 1740. Unfortunately they also achieved notoriety and left Barbados under a cloud to settle in Oxfordshire about 1780.[25]

There were no clouds above Walter Prideaux's career when he stepped aboard the *Daniel and Henry*. Indeed the future must have seemed dazzlingly bright. He was only twenty-three and already entrusted with the business management of a sizeable capital-intensive venture. He would, of course, rely heavily upon his captain, Roger Mathew. But since he was also his uncle he could be sure of support from that quarter. The destination to which the *Daniel and Henry* was bound was a reputed goldmine. And the African trade appeared, if the pamphleteers could be believed, to offer limitless vistas of profit. It would only be natural to imagine this as being the first in an extensive series of long-haul voyages which would eventually culminate in Walter becoming an eminent Exeter merchant: moreover the *Pedigree of the Prideaux of Luson*, a remarkably thorough account of the branches of Walter's family, credits him with being a 'Captain and East India merchant'.

Unfortunately this is little more than fanciful embroidery. The family by then (1889) was staunchly Quaker, and this extravagance served to cover Walter's involvement in the slave trade and deflect embarrassing criticism. Though Walter had probably completed his apprenticeship in a merchant's office in the years prior to the voyage of the *Daniel and Henry*, his subsequent career at sea up to 1721, when he was aged forty-five, was uninspiring. Until that date he had made just five voyages; to Jersey with lime in 1701, Newfoundland in 1710, San Sebastian in 1713, the Cape Verde Islands, Barbados and South Carolina in 1717 and to Rotterdam in 1721.[26] Nor does his name occur in any of the East India Company registers for the first half of the eighteenth century. When Walter's brother Arthur died in 1728, his will described Walter as a maltster, a firmly land-based trade.[27]

If Walter's career at sea turned out to be somewhat deficient, no such allegation can be levelled at him as a father. On Boxing Day in 1705 he married the daughter of a local Dartmouth merchant, Dorothy Ball, and produced four daughters and nine sons over the ensuing twenty-one years. One daughter and five of the sons died in infancy. Though there is nothing to suggest that Walter Prideaux was a Quaker his two eldest sons to survive him into adulthood – George and William – both joined the Society of Friends.

At the time Walter set sail for the Guinea Coast there were no restrictions on Quaker involvement in the slave trade, and numerous examples of their presence can be cited. William Penn, founder of Pennsylvania and a devout Quaker, owned slaves in the 1690s. The *Daniel and Henry* was to fall in with a Quaker slave ship, the *Society*, on her traverse of the middle passage in October 1700. Quakers were curiously slow to act on the question of trading in and owning slaves, and it was not until 1757 that the influential London Yearly Meeting registered profound alarm.[28] A committee was delegated to investigate and by 1761 the Yearly Meeting announced that the trade was beyond the pale: any Quaker slave dealer or trader ran the risk of immediate and permanent disownment. Though Walter died in 1757 the new Quaker awareness of the horrors of slavery might well have caused tensions within the family during the last years of his life: in his eighty-two years public opinion on the slave trade had changed course almost a full 180 degrees, though the road to freedom for enslaved blacks was yet a great distance away.

Ahead of us at this juncture lies the voyage of the *Daniel and Henry*. It carried with it the hopes and aspirations not only of its crew but of its merchant backers too. What would Daniel Ivy and Henry Arthur have seen had they the gift of foresight? Their *Daniel and Henry* arriving back in Dartmouth groaning under a massive cargo of sugar and tobacco advantageously purchased from plantation owners prepared to pay large sums for prime Negro slaves? Or would they become just one of the statistics for Charles Davenant's epitaph on the ten per centers barely a decade later:

finding most of their ships returning with scarcely one half of their complement of slaves, others perishing in their voyages, by reason of delays upon the Coast, beside many other losses following thereupon, the far greatest Part of these Separate Traders to Africa have already given that Trade quite over.[29]

CHAPTER FOUR

Slave Ship Cargoes

Although usually presented as a requirement generated by the Africans themselves, the mix of cargo taken aboard ship favoured both African buyers and Europeans sellers, helping to keep the price of each product at a profitable level for everyone concerned. Too great an availability of one particular item could easily swamp demand, as John Barbot found to his cost in 1679:

> at my first voyage to Cape Corso I had a pretty brisk trade for slaves and gold: but at my return thither, three years after, I found a great alteration: the French brandy, whereof I had always had a good quantity aboard, being much less demanded, by reason a great quantity of spirits and rum had been bought on that coast by many English trading ships, then on the coast, which obliged all to sell cheap.[1]

As might be expected, it was the rule for English merchants to deal with a wide range of goods on most of their long-haul ventures. A comparison of cargo loaded on a ship bound in 1700 for the new American colonies of Virginia or New England with that of a ship bound for the coast of Africa reveals few significant differences. After all, beads, baubles and cloth were valuable barter with North American Indians too. It was also the case that the process from goods to slaves and thence to sugar was by no means as cut and dried as merchants would have liked, so half an eye had to be open to the probable sale of any residual goods in Barbados or Jamaica. For example, though a powerful currency on parts of the African coast, cowrie shells were of minimal value in the West Indies. A sensible trader would ensure the bulk of the Africa-bound cargo was made up of goods that would find a ready sale in the West Indies too. Since the West Indies were notoriously short of virtually all commodities, that was not a problem.

None the less, the mix of cargo seems to have been a European obsession. Those slave captains on 'double voyages' – dealing direct between the West Indies and the Guinea Coast – loaded cargoes that consisted almost entirely of rum, which was readily available, easily traded and relatively cheap. These 'double voyages' initially originated as a response to the risk interlopers ran when clearing from English ports in the period leading up to the 1698 Act.[2] Merchants found the cheap rum produced in Barbados and Jamaica was a highly acceptable spirit on the Guinea Coast: since it had not entered an English port it did not attract the duties that inflated the cost of West Indian rum to the English slave trade merchant. West Indian merchants could thus undercut English competition on the Coast and accept the poorer returns caused by flooding the market. As the Royal African Company was later to discover,[3] and occasionally adopt, 'double voyages' enabled merchants to operate an advantageous debt collection system: plantation owners paid off outstanding invoices for slaves with rum. During times of war (endemic in the period 1680–1725), the ferocious impressment of ships' crews in English waters by the Royal Navy also contributed to the development of the 'double voyage.' Though Royal Navy ships on the West India station would not hesitate to impress men when needed, the scale of impressment, though aggravating, was significantly less than in England.

Contrary to popular opinion, trading off the Guinea Coast was not characterised by scheming white slave captains exploiting innocent black caboceers. By 1700 the natives of the Gold Coast had long experience of European traders hawking their wares. The halcyon days of early Portuguese traders dreaming of – and sometimes realising – a mercantile El Dorado where base merchandise could be exchanged for nobler, now lay firmly in the dim and distant past. Writing a few years before 1700 the French trader John Barbot (who later operated from London) commented that

> the Blacks of the Gold Coast, having traded with the Europeans ever since the 14th century, are very well skilled in the nature of proper qualities of all European wares and merchandise vended there . . . they examine everything with as much prudence and ability as any European can do.

They needed to. Sharp practice went hand in hand with both ten per cent and Royal African Company trading. Usual tricks included the diluting of alcoholic spirits with water, finely ground charcoal added to gunpowder, tampering with weights for coral and gold, and short measures of cloth. The problem was exacerbated by the general deterioration of goods packed into leaky holds in the humid tropics: in conditions like these every little extra gained by subterfuge could help offset losses.

What use did Africans make of the manufactured items?

> the broad linen serves to adorn themselves, and their dead men's sepulchers within. The narrow cloth to press palm oil: in old sheets they wrap themselves at night from head to foot: copper basins to wash and shave . . . of perpetuannas they make girts [girdles] four fingers broad, to wear about their waist, and hang their sword, dagger, knife and purse of money or gold . . . of serges they make a kind of cloak to wrap around their shoulders and stomach . . . with tallow they anoint their bodies from head to toe and even use it to shave their beards instead of soap.[4]

The *Daniel and Henry* carried all these goods and more. The person responsible for assembling such a cargo – including items rarely found imported into any Devon port such as coral and different weights of Indian cotton cloth – seems to have been James Gould. Indeed the Company Duty Book[5] and the Dartmouth Port Book[6] both attribute the cargo to James Gould and Company, not Daniel Ivy and Company, but this is a matter of detail not substance. The Port Book also clearly states, in reference to the cargo, 'all which paid duty out of time being bought of shopkeepers'. This indicates that the goods were not imported by Ivy, Arthur or Gould, but bought from suppliers. Had they imported the foreign goods themselves and exported them within the time allowed, then the duty payable on them being initially landed could have been clawed back and the 10 per cent tax evaded on those goods. Though the Dartmouth Port Book fails to show whether the tax was paid, the Company records show the cargo was fully detailed and taxed on 13 November 1699. Introduced with the preamble, 'due to be loaded on the *Rose*, John Cooke for Dartmouth to be shipped in the *Daniel and Henry*',[7] the cargo was valued at £2,251 19s. 4d., tax amounting to £225 3s. 11d. The only items not covered by the invoice details of the present log-book are 250 bushel of beans, 2 trumpets and 2 hogsheads of tobacco. Goods not separately detailed, either to Company or Customs officials, included rapiers, hangers, Negro knives, fuzees, carbines and pistols that the log-book reveals the *Daniel and Henry* carried. These probably travelled under the heading of ironmongery.

Captain Roger Mathew carried a personal venture consisting of 1½cwt. ironmonger wares; 200 coarse serges; 2½cwt. wrought pewter; and 8cwt. 3qr. 21lb. of gunpowder.[8] This not inconsiderable personal cargo was valued at £193 10s. and the 10 per cent of £19 7s. was duly paid on 23 January 1700. Though neither William Mathew (the captain's son), nor his cousin Walter Prideaux had separate personal ventures, it can be assumed they held a certain percentage in Captain Mathew's cargo.

The Royal African Company record of the cargo
taken aboard the *Daniel and Henry* revealing
the bulk of the cargo derived from London,
not Exeter or Dartmouth suppliers

Thus far the process appears to have been relatively above board in an era regarded as the heyday of trickery. The only query raised by the Customs (and answered by the Board) concerned

> over 310 new ironbound Casks of several sizes ... if you are satisfied with the truth of the allegation that they are really water casks for the use of the Negroes on the voyage and not to be sold as merchandise you may suffer them to pass for that purpose. And likewise the hogshead of vinegar if it be only for washing the Decks and sprinkling the Ship as usual to prevent Distempers amongst the Company in Guinea.[9]

Since Thomas Jago, a kinsman of Walter Prideaux, was Controller of the port, no doubt the Collector was easily satisfied. Though the number of casks is excessive, none are recorded as being sold on the Guinea Coast, but, as we shall see later, they undoubtedly were. On the face of it the *Daniel and Henry* seemed an exemplary slave trade ship (if that is not a contradiction in terms): with a total of about 450 slaves envisaged as the complement from the Guinea Coast and 310 casks, each slave could count on about two-thirds of a cask of drinking water for the middle passage, an unheard-of luxury. Unfortunately it remained an unheard-of luxury, though the illicit disposal of the casks was eventually to cost the venture dear.[10]

The strange case of the water casks was not the only subterfuge practised by the 'owners and setters-forth' of this voyage. In a curious footnote to the *Invoice of the Cost and Charges of Sundry Goods and Merchandise* (see pp. 41–5), Walter Prideaux complained that the true costs of the merchandise had been increased by 50 per cent in the details which had been handed to him and his captain. Thus his total of £3053 19s. 1d. should in reality read £2,036.[11] This piece of short-sighted deception by the merchant backers of the venture hampered the initial trading attempts of the *Daniel and Henry* and doubtless caused the captain and his supercargo more than a few sleepless nights as they pondered how the competition consistently outspent them in trading for slaves. Though displaying a regrettable lack of faith towards their employees, the only explanation for this artificial boosting of the invoice prices is that the merchants hoped to ensure that the slaves taken aboard the *Daniel and Henry* were purchased at rock-bottom prices; captain and supercargo, labouring under the delusion of the high prices contained in the invoices, would have to work much harder to secure their bargains.

Turning to the *Daniel and Henry*'s actual log-book, this reveals she was carrying a substantial proportion of English cloth – £613 worth out of a cargo valued at £2,252: there is, however, little evidence of other English manufactured goods. The worth of goods that can definitely be assigned to foreign manufacture comes to £523: the balance is made up (leaving aside expenditure allocated to packing such as hogsheads, chests and casks) of gunpowder, weapons, alcohol, glasses, brass and pewter ware, basins and tallow. The majority of these were not of local manufacture, may possibly have been of national manufacture, but in all probability were foreign produce. Indeed, when the wider picture is examined and the cargoes of the Exeter and Dartmouth ships *Dragon*, *Dartmouth* and *Surprise* taken into account, the inescapable conclusion is that the slave trade of this period benefited import–export merchants far more than local manufacturers.

But the question of the origin of items carried as cargo by Guinea trade ships is a vexed one. Even those cloths such as tapseils, nicanees, brawls and annabasses, ascribed to India in the general catalogue of fabrics, are not so easily pigeon-holed by 1700. For Davenant, whose position as unofficial public relations man for the Royal African Company does not completely disqualify him from statements of veracity, records:

> the new manufactures of annabasses, nicanees, topsails and brawles, were introduced by the Company's particular direction and encouragement, for the trade to Africa . . . the new manufactures of boysadoes and striped carpets, which are made in and about Kidderminster . . . were introduced by . . . the Company.[12]

Regrettably Davenant does not specify the dates at which these new products were introduced, but it is unlikely to have been subsequent to 1698 when the Company was already in a somewhat beleaguered trading position. Despite the potentially enormous purchasing power of the Company, manufacturers who won contracts to supply it with their goods found it paid handsomely. Though the standard history of the Company states that it was able to gain advantage by large orders placed in advance,[13] the view of the anonymous author of an early eighteenth-century pamphlet is radically different:

> The difference of the prices of goods exported by the private traders and company, sworn to by the exporters, is at least 30%

cheaper than the Company; those buying generally for ready money and the Company buying at a long time . . . so that £5 of the private traders buys as much as £7 of the Companies.[14]

By this time the propaganda battle between the Company and the separate traders over the freeing of the trade to Africa was intense, and veracity sometimes suffered accordingly. It is highly instructive to compare the prices recorded in the Journal of the *Daniel and Henry* with those recorded for two Company ships of exactly the same date trading alongside her on the Guinea Coast. Data for the Company prices is extracted from records pertaining to the *Prince of Orange* and the *Encouragement*.[15] (In the case of the two Company ships, neither carried any finished serge goods – apart from 250 perpetuannas on the *Prince of Orange* – despite serge goods having such prominence in Company contracts.)[16] In Table 4.1 all Ivy, Arthur and Gould prices have been extracted from the *Journal* and reduced by one-third.

Table 4.1 Comparison of cargo costs in 1700

Goods	Royal African Company	Ivy Arthur and Gould
Salempores each	£1: 0:0	16: 8
Knives per dozen	2:5	1: 4
Rangoes per hundred	16:0	16: 0
Brawles each	6:3	4:0–6:0
Fuzees each[17]	12:0	17: 9
Blue paper Silesias each	7:0	6: 2
Iron bars each	3:6	3: 2
Hogshead of brandy	£14: 0:0	£12:16:0 (£15:0:5)[18]
Perpetuanas each	£1: 1:0	16: 0
Sheets per chest	£9:10:0	£9:7:8 (£9:13:11)[19]
Coral per ounce	4:1	3:10
Powder per ½ barrel	£1: 0:2	£1: 0: 6
Tallow per ½ firkin	9:6	5: 0
Basins per lb.	2d.	2d.

Ultimately the sole criterion of profit was not determined by the wholesale price paid for an article, but how advantageously it could be exchanged for a man, woman, boy or girl slave.

Invoice of the Cost & Charges of Sundry Goods & Merchandize Loaded on board the *Daniel & Henry*, Captain Roger Mathew's Command for Guinea, being for the Proper account & Risk of Messrs Daniel Ivey & Company of Exon, Merchants, which Goods for Sales Consigned to the Said Captain Roger Mathew the 10 Feb, 1700.[20]

AG No 1 To No 9 are nine chests of
            sheets, a quantity of 65 in
            each chest charged at 4s 4d
            per piece is £126:15: 0
            To 9 chests at 9s 4d per piece   4: 4: 0

    No 10 A chest qty 80 pieces of
            ticking, 9 yards in a piece @
            6s 8d per piece 26:13: 4
            Brawles 4 in a piece at 24s   24: 0: 0
            To a chest 16: 0

    No 11 A chest, qty 170 pieces of blue
            paper slessia @ 9s 4d per
            piece 79: 6: 8
            To the chest 6: 8

    No 12 A chest qty 48 white salem
            powers @ 25s 4d per piece   60:16: 0

    No 13 A chest qty 80 pieces of single
            brawles @ 9s per piece   36: 0: 0

    No 14 A chest qty 40 pieces Neh:
            wares @ 30s 8d per piece,
            20 yd 61: 6: 8   £420: 4: 4
            & 44 pieces nickanees 18s 8d
            per piece 15 yards   41: 1: 4
            To a chest 16: 0

    No 15 A chest qty 43 topsails, 28s per
            piece £60 4s 0d a chest 16s   61: 0: 0

    No 16 A chest qty 20 pieces of blue
            baffts 34s 8d per piece . . . 34:13: 4
            Ditto 114 Guinea stuffs, 7s 8d
            per piece 43:14: 0
            A chest 16: 0   £182: 0: 8

            Sum carried over £602: 5: 0

	Sum brought over		£602: 5: 0
No 17	A chest qty 20 pieces of single brawles 9s per piece . . .	9: 0: 0	
	Ditto 17 sheets 4s 4d per piece	3:13: 8	
	Ditto 16 pieces blue papard slessia @ 9s 4d per piece	7: 9: 4	
	To the chest	9: 4	
No 18	to 21 are 4 packetts containing 50 Darnicks in each at 7s 8d per piece	76:13: 4	
	To 32 ells Crocus for wrappers, 7d per ell . . .	18: 8	
No 22	to 25 are 4 hogsheads of brandy viz: No 11: a hhd English brandy qt 64 galls @ 6s per gall	19: 4: 0	
	No 12 to 14 is 3 hhds malt spirits qt 188¾ gallons @ 4s 3d per gallon	41: 6:10	
AG . . .	is 100 whole cases of spirits @ 14s 8d per piece	73: 6: 8	
Ditto	is 100 half cases ditto @ 8s per piece	40: 0: 0	
	To 4 iron bound hogsheads	3: 6: 8	£275: 8: 6
AG No 26	to 34 are 1 chest, 2 casks & 6 matts viz:		
No 26	A chest qty 6000 rangoes at 24s per hundred	72: 0: 0	
	ditto 350 lbs of four sorts of beads at 2s 6d per pound	43:15: 0	
	ditto 263 ounces of currell at 5s 8d per ounce	74:10: 4	
	ditto 6 guilt rapiers at 12s per piece	3:12: 0	
	ditto 8 hangers with belts at 7s 4d. per piece	2:18: 8	
	ditto 2 hangers, 17s 4d per piece	1:14: 8	
	ditto 10 gross of negro knives at 24s per gross	12: 0: 0	£210:10: 8
	Sum carried over		£1088: 4: 2

	Sum brought over		£1088: 4: 2
	ditto 20 dozen looking glasses at 6s per dozen	6: 0: 0	
No 16	A barrel qty 27000 gun flints at 10s 8d	14: 8: 0	
	6 matts qty 12 nests of trunks at 23s 4d per piece	14: 0: 0	£34: 8: 0
No 35	to 39 are 5 chests of arms qty viz:		
	100 of fine fuzees, 26s 8d per piece	133: 6: 8	
	100 of carbines, 13s 4d per piece	66:13: 4	
	1 pair of superfine pistols	2: 0: 0	
	1 fine guilt fuzee	2:13: 4	
	100 cases for the fuzees . . .	3: 6: 8	
	5 chests at 16s per piece . . .	4: 0: 0	
No 40	to 96 are 50 whole barrels of powder & 6 hhds qty 30 barrels in 403 rundletts of ditto at £3:4:0 per piece	256: 0: 0	
	To 800 bars of iron marked X at one end & A at the other, qty 10 tons 9 cwt 3 quarters 3lbs at £18 per ton is 18s per hundred	188:16: 0	
	To 420 small cases of lead net weight 40 cwt at 16s per cwt	32: 0: 0	
No 98	to 101 are 4 bales qty in each 25 pieces of hounscott seas at 55s per piece	275: 0: 0	
No 115	is a cask qty 354 Guinea brasspans qty in weight 4 cwt at £11 6s 8d. per cwt	45: 6: 8	
No 1 & 2	are 2 ends of perpetuanas qty each 18 W & 16 half, in all 52 pieces at 24s per piece	62: 8: 0	£1071:10: 8
	Sum carried over		£2194: 2:10

Sum brought over			£2194: 2:10

| No 3 to 10 | are 8 ends ditto qty each 17 W & 16 half, in all 200 pieces at 24s per piece . . . . . | 240: 0: 0 | |
| No 11 to 20 | are 10 ends qty each 18 W & 14 half, in all 250 pieces ditto at 24s per piece . . . | 300: 0: 0 | £540: 0: 0 |

| No AB&C | are 2 hhd knives, & 1 hhd sheaths qty 32½ gross of slope pointed knives at 45s 4d per gross . . . . . . | 73:13: 4 | |
| | To 3 hhd cask . . . . . | 18: 8 | |

No 1 to 8 are 8 casks of pewter qty viz:

No 1	50 large plain tankards at 3s 8d per piece	9: 3: 4	
	25 large at 4s 4d & 25 quarts engraved at 3s 9d per piece	10: 2: 1	
	50 quarts plain at 3s 2d per piece	7:18: 4	
	50 pound basins weighing 48lb at 5d per pound	3: 0: 0	£104:15: 9

No 2	50 large plain tankards, 3s 8d per piece	9: 3: 4	
	25 large engraved ditto, 4s 4d per piece	5: 8: 4	
	50 quart plain ditto, 3s 2d per piece	7:18: 4	
	25 quart engraved ditto, 3s 3d per piece	4:13: 9	
	50 pound basins weighing 47lb at 15d per pound	2:18: 9	£30: 2: 6

No 3 & 4	200 4lb basins weighing 760lb at 15d per pound	47:10: 0	
No 5 & 6	are 200 3lb ditto weighing 624lb at 15d per pound	39: 0: 0	
No 7 & 8	are 200 2lb ditto weighing 404lb at 15d per pound	25: 5: 0	£111:15: 0

Sum carried over			£2980:16: 1

Sum brought over £2980:16: 1

No 1 to 100 are 100 firkins of tallow
qty 25lbs each is 22cwt
@ £3 6s 6d per cwt . . . . __73: 3: 0__   £73: 3: 0

£3053:19: 1

Copied by Walter Prideaux at sea.

☞ *In the foregoing Invoice all goods are charged 50 per cent*
more than the true costs – as appeared by the ship's invoice
which we found upon the [Guinea] coast, which is what
hindered the Sale at first; other ships selling the same goods
at 25 per cent under our invoice & the Captains declared
they advanced 25 per cent more than really the goods cost
in England.[21]

CHAPTER FIVE

A Description of the *Daniel and Henry*

MERCHANTMEN of the eighteenth century were built for capacity, not speed. Broad of beam and apple-cheeked of bow, they were a far cry from the fleet-winged clippers of the nineteenth century. Yet, though perhaps hopelessly clumsy to our eyes, which view perfection in terms of streamlining, these merchantmen represented the latest technology of their day. Unlike all twentieth-century vehicles – with the possible exception of the bicycle – they were astonishingly efficient and self-contained. Fuelled by the winds which, though occasionally contrary, are virtually constant and absolutely costless, they were capable of carrying within their wooden walls all the skilled men, equipment and supplies to keep them voyaging for many months. These vessels, never eulogised like the Royal Navy's *Mary Rose* or *Victory*, carried England's hopes for dominating Atlantic maritime trade to fruition.

In the late seventeenth and early eighteenth centuries (and indeed for many years to come) very few ships were specifically constructed for the slave trade. The *Daniel and Henry* was no exception. In 1700, when she entered this trade for the first time, she was between ten and fifteen years old, having spent the bulk of her career up until then carrying cloth and tobacco.

She was a floating world of wood. Wood that had been chopped, cut, sawn, planed, chiselled, sanded, scrubbed, oiled and varnished. Wood that had been drilled, pegged, mortised, tenoned, dovetailed, jointed and mitred. Wood that was regarded as a noble material, and worked by men proud of their craft. Both senses of the word are implicit here. For craft, whether of skill or ship, derives from the old English for strength.

And strong she was. Since much of a merchant ship's voyage would have been spent trading in uncertain waters of river estuaries, and occasional visits to harbours where when the tide ebbed it left the ship 'taking the ground', often fully laden, strength was vital. She was also surprisingly complex. Timber was her very being, and as many as five different varieties – oak, elm, beech, pine, mahogany or teak – played specific roles as planking, baulks, knees, frames, keels, masts, spars and yards. The masts, spars and yards numbered twenty or more. Sails totalled between twenty-five and thirty with spares in addition. Each sail was rigged with sheets that differed in thickness and was controlled by a complicated system of wooden blocks.

Even when placid the sea is a hostile environment, and every ship, no matter how strong, as vulnerable as driftwood upon its expanse. For the sea is in constant motion, setting up continuous stresses and strains. On an eighteenth-century merchantman every inch of timber reacted. Every joint, peg, mortise and dovetail spoke out against such usage with agonised squeals, creaks and groans. Below the waterline, especially in tropical waters, the enemies of wood were incessantly active, though they deployed their weapons silently. Weed attached itself to the hull and flourished mightily, so that many a Guinea ship arriving in the Caribbean could boast a full-length underwater beard sprouting from its hull. Though not dangerous in itself, the weed hampered steering and acted as a brake upon the vessel. It also provided a home for molluscs, including the destructive teredo worm. For the time being the *Daniel and Henry*, in common with other merchant shipping, would have been fitted with a second skin of timber beneath her waterline. A primitive mixture of tar, oakum, horsehair and pitch formed the filling in this rather unappetising sandwich. Yet it manifestly failed to deter the teredo's activities, much as the tallow smeared over the hull failed to halt significantly the onward march of marine weed.

Every natural element contains seeds of destruction. The sea upon which the *Daniel and Henry* floated constantly eroded her efficiency and, indeed, could totally overwhelm her. The winds, upon which she relied for her motive power, could desert her, or suddenly rip through her rigging, shredding sails like tissue paper. The sun provided navigational data, heat and light, yet shone pitilessly down upon the hempen ropes and cables, sails and sheets, weakening them with invisible ultraviolet rays. The sea, far from absorbing these rays, mischievously reflected them back. Nor did wear and tear diminish at the going down of the sun. Cool sea breezes reversed the daytime expansion of exposed timbers, causing them to warp and spring. Oakum started from the joints between planking. Heavy tropical rains swept in off the sea, soaking the sails and leaking through the upper decks.

It fell to the crew of each ship to preserve the delicate balance between what man proposed and nature disposed. The key to this was maintenance and a crew, like the elements around them, was never still. When time allowed they scrubbed the decks, packed fresh oakum into the cracks between the boards, and channelled hot pine pitch and tar into the crevices to be soaked up. They oiled, painted and varnished. They tarred the running ropes and blocks; repaired the sails; replaced rotting ropes and cables (picking the vegetable fibres apart to form oakum), and even careened the hull. On long voyages extensive repairs were often required either because of storm damage or because of changes in the nature of the cargo, which is where the carpenters aboard truly came into their own. Slave trade ships especially underwent extensive internal restructuring, first to provide layers of platforms for the transport of hundreds of human beings, then to accommodate colossal hogsheads of tobacco or sugar.

If maintenance was the key to survival on the high seas, equipment was the key to maintenance. So fitting out a ship for a long-haul voyage involved several levels of artefacts of which rigging and sails formed only the first. Secondary equipment included a stove or furnace, long-boat and anchors, while the third level encompassed a myriad minor objects crucial to the good management of the vessel such as water casks, side scrapers, scrubbing brushes, mops and lanterns.[1]

Such expenditure is generally forgotten when the profitability of the slave trade is discussed but the financial minutiae were far from marginal when taken as an aggregate. Unfortunately nowhere in the material relating to the *Daniel and Henry* is there an account of how much the merchants Ivy, Arthur and Gould spent in fitting her out for the Guinea Coast and Jamaica. Such business secrets were rarely noised abroad but one yardstick does prevail. Though not exactly contemporary with the *Daniel and Henry* the cost of refitting the *John* from the smaller provincial port of Lyme Regis for a voyage to the Gambia and Maryland in 1717 amounted to only a few shillings short of £550. That sum included £55 worth of insurance, but otherwise the vast bulk of the total related to wood, nails, iron hearth, carpentry and so on. A full inventory of the costs is included in Chapter 16 on Lyme Regis. Direct comparisons between the *Daniel and Henry* and the *John* cannot be made, for apart from a chronological discrepancy of seventeen years, the *Daniel and Henry* was a larger vessel, being of 200 tons as against 65 tons and mounting ten guns as against the *John*'s two.

The twentieth-century slogan that time equals money would have cut less ice with the early eighteenth-century merchant. He was more concerned over the tonnage of goods that his vessel could carry than the speed she made through the water. Tonnage is a term which has caused some confusion down the years. It does not describe the weight of the vessel; this is known as displacement and varies with the amount of cargo or ballast being carried. It does describe the volume of the vessel available for stowing cargo or accommodating passengers – its burden – and is clarified when the full description, tons burden, is applied. Though the term is far from unscientific, being based on a formula derived from length, beam and moulded depth, the most that can be said is that it provides some indication of the relative cargo-carrying capacities of different ships since it is quite normal to find the same ship described as of 100, 150 or even 200 tons burden, depending on who is doing the describing.

A similar confusion exists over the type of ship. The high seas were awash with galleys, frigates, brigantines, hack-boats, barques, pinks and snows. To complicate matters, nowhere in his narrative of the *Daniel and Henry* does Walter Prideaux describe the ship itself. For that we are indebted to an expert third party who, as we shall eventually see, identified the *Daniel and Henry* as a haggboat.[2] This should not be confused with 'hackboat', a sailing lighter used for short-haul transportation of cargo or passengers in sheltered waters. It was in the hull that the distinguishing features of a haggboat were most clearly visible, her apple-cheeked bow differing from the cat, barque and pink by the addition of the timber beakhead which provided an extended platform for the spritsail. During very rough weather the spritsail was reefed lest it should be carried away by heavy seas, and only the foresail set.[3]

The *Daniel and Henry* was probably built in the period 1675–85 and certain aspects of her rigging reflect this. Until about 1680 both the mainsail and foresail were made in two parts. The upper two-thirds was secured to the yard and the lower third laced to the upper; this could be detached when high winds threatened. The upper section was called the course (from the French for body)[4] and the lower the bonnet (possibly because it laced together). After 1680 reef points were used to make the sail smaller and the separate course and bonnet arrangement fell into disuse. Since there is no mention of the course being reefed, the *Daniel and Henry* appears to have continued to employ the old-fashioned course and bonnet foresail. Her topsails, on the other hand, did have reef points[5] – a practice that was not at all common until the very end of the seventeenth century.

Since 1700 was a year – unusually – of peace, privateers would not pose a threat. Though some pirates chose the Guinea Coast for their operations, the Caribbean, the *Daniel and Henry's* ultimate destination, was another matter altogether. She would not be an easy vessel to take. Her armament consisted of ten guns and amongst her crew were two full-time gunners. In addition the crew were well armed for fear of a slave uprising. Pirates tended to prey on shipping which had, for one reason or another, departed from the usual sea lanes. Exact navigation could make the difference between success and disaster, even life and death, and a log-book recording all the alterations, major and minor, in the course of a ship would be a valuable document of reference should another such voyage be planned.

Inevitably, much of the following *Journal* or log-book is uncompromisingly navigational rather than anecdotal in content. As a science, navigation was still in its infancy, and some of the detail may be incomprehensible except to the maritime historian. Hopefully the narrative which intersperses the log-book is not too taxing in nature: detailed explanations of more recondite navigational techniques have been placed in the notes.

The log-book was so called because it was initially a record of the distance a ship had sailed. This was determined with a log-ship – a stationary wooden float – and a sandglass. The float was attached to a log-line which was paid out over the stern as the ship moved ahead. This line was marked with knots in lengths. The distance between each knot was fixed and had been worked out in the same proportion to a nautical mile as the number of seconds of the sandglass was to an hour. The sand took 30 seconds to run through the glass. Since a nautical mile equals 6,080 feet, the length of a knot on the line was 6,080 divided by $\frac{60 \times 60}{30}$, or virtually 51 feet. For a reasonably accurate reading the log needed to be hove every hour.

Usually, as in the case of the *Daniel and Henry*, the only record that remained of a voyage was the log-book. It is highly probable that Roger Mathew kept the official version. This had a certain legal status: for example any punishment – such as stoppage of a day's pay – given under the authority of the captain, had to be logged. However the working document from which most navigational decisions (such as the next course to steer) were made was not the log-book but the chart. This was drawn on Mercator's projection in which lines of longitude (vertical) cross lines of latitude (horizontal) at right angles. If it was required to sail from point A to point B it was only necessary to mark the points on the chart and join them up with a straight line. The direction of this line was then compared to the lines of the compass rose drawn on the chart and the compass bearing would be established.

At noon every day the position of the *Daniel and Henry* was marked on the chart, with due allowance made for leeway tides and ocean currents. In deciding the compass course to be steered, corrections would be made for variation (the difference between true north and the direction in which the compass pointed), and deviation (the error in the compass due to the close proximity of iron). Though the *Daniel and Henry* was carrying over 5½ tons of iron bars as freight, this was stowed too deeply in the hold to have exercised any influence.

Whenever possible the ship's latitude was determined at noon each day by measuring the maximum angle by which the sun rose above the horizon with a quadrant. Obviously the maximum angle was achieved at local noon, but it was not necessary (or feasible at that time) to have an accurate timepiece aboard. Instead it was simply a question of observing the sun's upward rise at short intervals of time, starting slightly before noon. The quadrant was adjusted each time the sun was found to be still continuing on its upward curve until it was observed that it had passed its zenith. The maximum angle obtained was noted and, subtracted from 90 degrees, formed the basis of the ship's calculated latitude.

Neither observing the sun (known as 'by observation') nor calculating course and speed (referred to as 'by log') was free from error, but a compromise between the two could prove sufficiently accurate for the purposes of the voyage. Due to weather conditions such as storm, fog, cloud or rough seas, a ship might have to forgo a reading by observation and rely totally on estimates by log. The latter method was not foolproof either; a strong following sea and damp in the sandglass could return data of doubtful value.

Longitude was much more of a problem. When out of sight of land (upon which features like the Lizard could be distinguished) there was no means of ascertaining a ship's longitudinal position except by log. As the errors inherent in this method added up like compound interest from one day to the next, the longer a vessel remained out of sight of identifiable land, the greater the uncertainty of her true longitudinal position. Here the lack of an accurate timepiece had profound consequences. For longitude in degrees was easily found by taking the difference in minutes between local shipboard noon and noon at Greenwich – or in the case of the *Daniel and Henry*, the Lizard – and dividing it by four. Accuracy was of the essence; a four-minute error in the timepiece would mean 60 miles error in longitude at the Equator. The lack of an accurate chronometer was not overcome until 1759, when John Harrison at last produced an instrument which could maintain sufficient precision at sea. Used in conjunction with mathematical tables this chronometer was largely responsible for Captain James Cook's notably exact marine surveys later in the eighteenth century.

Until then the only way of reaching an oceanic island was to sail to its known latitude, well to the east (or west) of its position, and then to sail along this line of latitude until the island was sighted. This was tantamount to searching for the proverbial needle in a haystack, and several attempts might have to be made. Many years later, Walter Prideaux was prevailed upon to command the *Mary and Anne* on a lengthy voyage to the Isle of May in the Cape Verde group, then Barbados and Carolina before returning to Dartmouth. On the last homeward stretch, driven by strong gales and great seas, with wintry sleet showers curtaining visibility he 'made the land which we took to be the Isle of Wight, but coming to the westward, found it Wexford in Ireland'.[6] It took six days to beat back around Cape Cornwall and finally anchor in the narrows at Dartmouth. If mistakes like this could happen in home waters the possibility of misjudgement was far greater in the unfamiliar seas of the Bight of Benin or Caribbean.

CHAPTER SIX

The Voyage Out

Ever since the *Daniel and Henry* had moored at Dartmouth at the end of 1699, she had been the subject of speculation, which had been fuelled by the major refitting that was taking place with platforms being constructed between the existing decks. There had been the arrival of the London coastal trader the *Rose* with bolts of cloth from the Far East, trinkets, beads, gewgaws and semiprecious stones. The *Daniel and Henry* was alive with men. If it wasn't carpenters and fitters, it was sailmakers and chandlers: the Customs were aboard too, with the landwaiters checking the goods being loaded. Finally there had been the attempt to recruit a crew. Experienced men were needed, for the *Daniel and Henry* was bound for the coast of Africa, then on to Jamaica. Level-headed men too, for Africa still raised nameless fears, and the time was not long past when the world was deemed to end at Cape Bojador. The *Daniel and Henry* was bound well south of this dreaded Cape. Despite the new rationalism of the age, the superstition persisted that, once the Cape was rounded, skin would blacken and the sea would boil. Then again, times were lean on land.

As the *Daniel and Henry* got under way on the high tide at Dartmouth, moving steadily out of the river-mouth past the castle on its western bank and across Start Bay in a blustery south-easterly, the crew were mustered on the main deck. Some of them would have been well known to the officers, for many were of local origin.[1] Francis Snelling came from Plympton St Mary, and had been at sea for virtually all his sixty-odd years. He was a 'professional' boatswain who had almost certainly served in the Royal Navy at some point in his career, and who had sought action in the early 1690s aboard the Devon letter of marque frigate, *Franke*.[2] John Rudd came from Yealmpton, near Ermington; Philip Foxworthy from Buckfastleigh, though his family had strong Dartmouth connections; John Godferry (aged fifteen) Nicholas March (nineteen), John Fort and his son Nicholas all came from Dartmouth. Though the elder Fort was to perish on this voyage, his son went on to spend his life at sea, eventually becoming tidesman for the Dartmouth Customs in 1719.[3] One of his superior officers in that future day was to be his present captain, Roger Mathew. Of the remainder Richard Basnio – apparently of Italian extraction – and John Shutter (of Dartmouth), both settled in Jamaica. Neither left any trace in the island's records: no marriage records, no baptisms, funerals, headstones or wills. And then there is the sole black crew member, George Yorke. There were many more blacks of both African and neo-Caribbean origin employed aboard English merchant shipping than have yet been granted recognition. Most obvious were those employed aboard Company ships, usually in rather lowly occupations. Crew lists of early eighteenth century merchantmen have long since disappeared yet occasional references do surface; the London privateers *Antelope* of 1702 and *Union Frigate* of 1709 both employed black cooks.[4]

The majority of black crewmen were slaves rented out as shipboard labour by their English masters. Though England prided herself on being the land of the free and slavery on English soil constituted, technically at least, a breach of the law, those who had the power to enforce such laws were too busy owning slaves themselves. George Yorke of the *Daniel and Henry*, from the fact that he possessed an English Christian surname rather than a demeaning sobriquet, and was 'left in Jamaica' along with Philip Foxworthy and Thomas Rogers (in other words, impressed) was a free man, not a slave.[5]

Fear of forced servitude in the Navy, rather than conditions aboard the *Daniel and Henry*, probably lay behind the desertions of Richard Hutchings, Robert Wisehard and Thomas Locke in Jamaica. They would have absconded to work on an inland plantation seeking perhaps a passage to the American colonies at a later date. With the lonely exception of William Hodge who ran away in São Tomé off the African coast, the rest of the losses were deaths, mostly caused by disease but one or two by misadventure.

All this, however, was in the future. As the *Daniel and Henry* tacked across Start Bay and cleared Start Point, pursuing a westerly course that would deliver her safely from the treacherous waters of Bigbury Bay, the first and second mates took turns to choose their watches from the assembled crew. These watches worked turn and turn about 'to watch, trim sails, pump and do all duties for four hours'. In harbours and road anchorages only a quarter watch was kept involving half the number of the crew.[6] When leaving harbour or in emergencies all hands were called on deck. Chapman's selection mustered on the larboard (or port) side of the deck, Branscomb's on the starboard side. Little is known of Roger Mathew's first and second officers, save that Branscomb was thirty-four years of age and came from Withycombe Raleigh near Exmouth. The remaining members of the ship's complement numbered Walter Prideaux, William Mathew (the master's son, whose role is unrecorded), the hapless doctor Edward Fenner and his assistant William Hunt.

By no means all English vessels intending for the slave trade carried a doctor, and even fewer a doctor's mate. In fact the law did not require a slave ship to employ a certified surgeon aboard until 1788. Obviously Fenner and Hunt were employed primarily out of economic rather than humanitarian motives, but their presence served to indicate Ivy, Arthur and Gould's commitment to the success of the voyage, and may well have allayed crew anxieties about the fever-ridden Guinea Coast.

The *Daniel and Henry*, fully laden, rode deep in the bitter grey-green waters of the Western Approaches. Beneath decks the crew were stowing their gear. Life 'tween decks was not an edifying spectacle at the best of times, and on a fully laden, overcrewed merchantman carrying extra anchors, timbers, spars and sheets it was proportionately closer to chaos. The crew berths on an early eighteenth-century merchant vessel would have made the equivalent on a late twentieth-century submarine look positively palatial. Quite simply it was packed, a mass of humanity in which each man was permitted approximately 14 inches breadth to sling his hammock. There was little light to relieve the deep and constant gloom (candles making little impression on the almost palpable blackness), and less heating. The risk of fire on a timber ship, caulked and coated with combustible oakum and tar pitch, carrying 80 barrels of gunpowder and hogsheads of highly inflammable alcoholic spirits, constantly occupied the minds of her officers. Nor was ventilation the strong point of vessels of that era; although some light and fresh air entered through the scuttles and hatches, these were firmly closed in bad weather. Within a very short space of time the crew's quarters would have built up a stifling fug. The lack of fresh air was exacerbated by the full cargo aboard the *Daniel and Henry*. She was riding so low in the water that her gunports would have shipped water when she heeled over: accordingly they would have been made watertight with pitch and oakum.

Into these cramped quarters, already alive with vermin, came the flower of England's merchant marine. They had but the haziest idea of whence they were bound, little idea of basic hygiene, only the most meagre bedding for their comfort, and few clothes, though no crew member of the *Daniel and Henry* was in such straitened circumstances as William Bembridge of the Company ship *Faucon-bergh* who in November 1699 was 'ketched stealing ships hammacks and making briches of the same'.[7] But the *Daniel and Henry* was a fine breeding ground for diseases. Some would have been unwittingly brought aboard at Dartmouth by already infected crew members: others, such as malaria and yellow fever, lay in wait on the coast of Guinea. Once disease had started to take its toll in one watch, who all worked, messed and slept in the closest imaginable proximity (outside of marriage) it ran rampant. And so it proved on the *Daniel and Henry*'s larboard watch.

Finally, as if to emphasise the exiguous nature of the crew's tenure on life, their captain, Roger Mathew, received the news shortly before sailing that his son Robert, master of the *Sarah* of London, had perished on his voyage to Guinea and Barbados.[8] The omens for the *Daniel and Henry* were far from auspicious.

 Watch Bill of the *Daniel and Henry*. viz:
Larboard

John Chapman, Chief Mate, died 27 September
Francis Snelling, Boatswain, died
John Meacome, died
Hales Martin, Gunner's mate
John Rudd, Cooper's mate, died 27 June
Richard Hutchings, sailor, ran away in Jamaica
William Hodge   ditto   ran away at São Tomé
Richard Johnson, sailmaker, died 29 July
James More, sailor, died 27 August of smallpox
John Worth ditto
Nicholas Picsson
Christopher Baale
Humphrey Handcock, died 21 September of smallpox
James Thomas
Stephen Monney
Peter Price
George Yorke, Negro, left in Jamaica
Nicholas Fort
George Hale, carpenter, died on passage home
Richard Basnio, cook, discharged at Jamaica and there paid his wages.

Starboard Watch
Bartholomew Branscomb, second mate
John Fort, gunner, died 7 August
Samuel Wood, carpenter's mate
John Shutter, boatswain's mate, married in Jamaica
John Tremlet, cooper
Robert Wisehard, sailor, ran away in Jamaica
Henry Gould
William Devis
Phil Foxworthy, left in Jamaica
Ralph Matham
Thomas Rogers, left in Jamaica
Thomas Thorne
John Godferry
Thomas Locke, ran away in Jamaica
Nicholas March
Robert Savage
Peter Johnson, drowned 27 May
Charles Pippenose
John Clapp, ran away

Captain Roger Mathew and his son William Mathew; Edward Fenner, doctor; and William Hunt, doctor's mate.

In all forty and four hands.

Journal or day reckoning of a voyage intended by God's assistance in the ship *Daniel and Henry* of Exeter, Capt. Roger Mathew commanding, from Dartmouth in England to Guinea in Africa, begun the 24th day of February $\frac{1699}{1700}$ whom God preserve & send us a prosperous voyage & safe return. Amen.

God be merciful unto us & bless us & show us the light of his countenance & be merciful unto us.

The watches organised, officers and crew settled into their quarters, and lookouts posted, Roger Mathew initially set a pronounced westerly course. Every Africa-bound ship feared being blown into the Bay of Biscay; once trapped in that embrace a vessel could take weeks to extricate herself against the prevailing westerly winds. Although the weather was difficult, within a week the *Daniel and Henry* would be running south-west before favourable winds and a strong Atlantic swell.

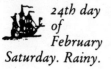

24th day of February
Saturday. Rainy.

This 24 hours have sailed SW by W 6° 15′ Westerly 30:5 leagues by the log and are in the latitude 49° 2′ with the wind from S to SE by E fresh gale: have seen several ships some to windward and some to leeward, we steering away SW by W with the wind at SSE.

25th day. Sunday. Thick weather with small rain.

This 24 hours have sailed W by S 1° 52′ Westerly 14:3 leagues and by the log are in the latitude 48° 55′ with the wind from SSE to W and W by N. Fresh gale, we now steering away SSW with the wind at W by N. See several ships; spoke with a pink bound for Madeira who stood away NW by N under a pair of riffle top sails,⁹ as they all did.

26th day. Monday. Hazy weather with small rain.

This 24 hours have sailed SSW 10° 30′ W 36:7 leagues with the wind from the W to WNW and are in the latitude 47° 55′ by the log, having not had an observation since came out. We now steer away SSW with the wind at NNW. At 2 o'clock this afternoon came on board of us Mr John Williams of Topsham, who came from Cadiz & bound home, by whom writ Uncle George Dottin I say by the *America Merchant*. A fresh gale at WNW.

27 day. Tuesday. Fair weather.

This 24 hours have sailed SW by S 4° 45′ Westerly 28:5 leagues by the log with the wind from W to WNW, under fore course & 3 topsails with a fresh gale. At noon this day we spoke with a pink of London bound for Madeira, commanded by Mr Benjamin Wollacott, burden about 80 tons, who steered away SSW and we steered away South with a fresh gale at noon, and brave weather in the latitude 47° 2′ by the log.

Four days out of Dartmouth, the *Daniel and Henry* was still plying in home waters. Walter Prideaux sends a letter to his maternal uncle George Dottin, then dominating overseas trade at Dartmouth, *via* the merchantman *America*. The *America* was smaller than the *Daniel and Henry* but similarly employed in the colonial trade, though 1700 saw her largely utilised in carrying cloth from Exeter to Cadiz, returning with large mixed cargoes.¹⁰ John Williams was her master, and among the Exeter merchants freighting her return cargo were Martha Brodridge and Arthur Jeffry, both of whom had substantial shares in the *Dragon* which had sailed for the Guinea Coast almost exactly a year before. Though the *America* sailed safely into port on 4 March, the *Dragon* – as we shall see later – was not to be so fortunate.

Accompanying the *Daniel and Henry* out into the Atlantic was an unnamed pink – a common type of merchantman of the day, characterised by an overhanging stern and popular in the timber trade. As with so many names in his journal, Prideaux fails to identify the master accurately. In this case it was actually Benjamin Wonnacott, who seven years later found himself commanding the company ship *Catherine* through the same waters, bound this time for the Guinea Coast and slaves.[11]

The term 'gale' denoted a good sailing breeze, such a good breeze in fact that the *Daniel and Henry* was deploying only a little more than half her total available sail area, her topgallant sails, main course and mizzen all being furled. Topgallant sails could only be set in a moderate wind, hence the expression 'topgallant gale' for such winds. All distances in longitude were taken from the Lizard as the ship had 'taken her departure' from there, usually the last identifiable point a navigator could sight and plot on his chart before heading out into the Atlantic.

28 day. *Wed.* *Fair* *weather*	This 24 hours have sailed S by W 10°:10' Westerly, 46 leagues by the log but at noon by observation were in the latitude 44:33 but by the log are in the lat. 44°:56'. We now steer away SSW with the wind at NNE having 84 leagues meridian distance or 6°:12' difference in longitude from the Lizard.
29 day. *Thursday. Fair* *weather*	This 24 hours moderate wind at NNE have sailed SSW 47:3 leagues being by the log in the lat. 42°:34' and meridian distance 102:7 leagues & difference longt. 7°24' from the Lizard, we now steering away SSW with the wind at NNE. Topgallant gale with a great sea from the northward.
March: 1 Day *Friday. Fair* *weather*	This 24 hours moderate wind at NNE have sailed SSW 56:7 leagues & are in the lat. 39°:58' by the log but at noon by an unvalued observation were in the lat. 40°:10'. We now steer away SSW with a great swell from the Northward & topgallant gale having

8°:43 diff:longt. from the Lizard and 124:4 leagues meridian distance I say this day at noon.

2 Day Saturday. This 24 hours have sailed SW by S 60 leagues and are
Fair weather in the lat 37:29 but at noon by observation are in the lat 37°:34′, have 11°:12′ differᵃ longᵗ from the Lizard. We now steer away SSW variable with a great sea from the northward and the wind at NNE fresh.

The wind continued to freshen. Running before it in a heavy sea, the *Daniel and Henry* was in danger of broaching to, swinging round broadside on to the wind and waves. To avoid this, sails were set on the foremast only which had the effect of pulling the ship along from the front. As the wind rose, Prideaux notes they 'handed' or furled the fore topsail and let her run before the wind under the fore course and bowsprit sail. In this situation foresail sheets were usually slackened off, which tended to lift the bow of the ship clear of the foaming seas which threatened to bury her fo'c'sle.

3 Day. Sunday Great sea from the north with strong showers of hail &c. Windy weather. This 24 hours with a strong wind NNE under the forecorse and foretopsails with a great sea and at ten at night handed the foretopsail & scudding away SW & SW by W under the fore and spritsail 59 leagues, my direct course being SW by S 7°:10′ have 13°:31′ diff longᵗ & being by dead reckoning in the lat 35°:50′ & have 9°:49′ meridian from the Lizard so that Madeira bears south 8°:22 E, 69 leagues.

4 Day Monday Fair weather. Little wind. This 24h have sailed south 40 leagues with the wind at NNE fresh gale having at noon by observᵃ 33°:26′ but by dead reckoning are in the lat. 33°:50′ & meridian distance 9°:49′ we now steer away S with the starboard tacks on board & little wind, Madeira bearing 48 leagues SE 7°:30′ E & Sanelo bears E by S 39 leagues with the wind at WNW. Small gale, smooth water.¹²

The *Daniel and Henry* was making good time towards the Guinea Coast. Some Africa-bound ships put in at Madeira or the Cape Verde islands for fresh water (and wine, which sold well to African chiefs) but Roger Mathew had no need of either. Less than two weeks after leaving Dartmouth, the African coastline was sighted. As the land

grew more and more distinct, soundings were regularly taken with
the lead, a practice that would continue the length of the coast. The
line attached to the lead was marked in fathoms: the lead itself had a
scooped base into which lard or tallow had been poured. As the lead
hit the sea-bed tiny particles of mud, sand or shell would become
embedded in the tallow, giving the navigator an idea of the ground
which lay beneath the vessel, its suitability for anchorage, and
perhaps a better indication of their position, for the composition of
the sea-bed was often marked on charts. Walter Prideaux's severe
headache would not trouble him again on the voyage.

 5 Day.
Tuesday.
Fair
weather.

This 24 hours have sailed S by E 34 leagues and are in
the lat 32°:9' but at noon by observᵃ were in the lat
31°:51' with the wind from the NW to NNW fresh
gale with the starboard tacks on board with the wind
at topgallant gale: being not all well myself having
my head in a raging pain.

6 Day.
Wednesday.

This 24 hours have sailed S by E 41 leagues and are in
the lat 30°:15' but at noon by observᵃ were in the lat
30°:8' with the wind from NNW to NNE, fresh gale
having 8°:48' meridian distance, we now steer S by E
& SSE.

7 Day. Thursday
We fell on the
coast of Barbary
being off Cape
Nom with fine
weather.

This 24 hours with small gale wind at NNW we have
sailed S 3°:00' Easterly 28 leagues & are in the lat 28°
51' but at noon by observᵃ were in the lat. 28°:32'. In
the morning saw the land bearing from SE to SSW.
Low land & level, much like the head of the Lizard
where it bears north from you about 4 leagues, have
stood in with it till noon we altered our course &
steered away WSW we then making it to be Cape de
Nom with very good land & fair weather.

8 Day Friday. At
noon were off
Cape Bojador in
the lat. 27°:9' &
long. 13°:26'
west.

We now steer away WSW, Cape de Sulis bearing
about SW by W 8 leagues of us. We passed by Ared
& Selva in the night at 10 o'clock & at 2, & in the
morning were off Bedelna when we steered away W
by S. At 10 o'clock the Point Curto being a low
point, bore SSW about 4 leagues. At noon by observᵃ
were in the lat. 27°:51', Bayadore then bearing SW by
S about 5 leagues. Having 18 fathom water being then
about 42 leagues off the land we still steer away WSW
and southerly.

9 Day. Saturday
Fair weather. A
strong gale.
Current sets to
the westward.

This 24 hours have (with a fresh gale) sailed SW by S 4°:15' W. 24 leagues and are at noon by observᵃ in the lat 26°:54' having very smooth water & topgallant gale at NE. We now steering away SW, not seeing any land since yesterday at 4 in the afternoon when Cape Bojador bore SE by E about 7 leagues having a current set to the westward, & 5° variation E wrought by the amplitude.[13]

The dreaded Cape Bojador, which earlier marked the edge of the earth beyond which mariners would plunge into oblivion, was rounded with little more than the odd case of sunstroke (which may account for Prideaux's headache) to mark its passing. Combined with the prevailing north-easterly trade winds the strong current helped the *Daniel and Henry* achieve daily distances of up to 43 leagues, nearly 130 miles. Later the vessel would encounter the favourable Guinea current, which would help sweep her round Cape Palmas and along the Gold Coast.

 *10 Day.*
Sunday
Fair
weather.

This 24 hours have sailed SW 10° Westerly 36 leagues and are in the lat. (at noon by observᵃ) of 25°:53' with the wind fron the NNW to NE. Topgallant gale & very smooth water with fair weather, we now steer away SSW with the wind at NE by E. Little wind.

11 Day.
Monday. Fair
weather.

This 24 hours with topgallant gale have sailed SSW 32 leagues & are in the lat. 24°:27' by dead reckoning & by observᵃ they both agreeing, having from the Lizard 248 leagues meridian distance. Fair weather & smooth water having 13°:24' diff. longᵗ from the Lizard.

12 Day. Tuesday
Fair weather

This 24 hours have sailed S 9° W 41 leagues & are in the lat. 22°:25' at noon by observᵃ. At 4 this morning fell in with land being Cape de Cintra. We then hauled off shore NW till 6 o'clock when we saw the land, being very low land, being set in by the current which set to the NNE & we steering S [blank]. At noon hove the lead & had 19 fathom water.

13 Day.
Wednesday. Fair
weather. Being
in [sight of?] the

This 24 hours have sailed SSW 8°:15' W 43 leagues & at noon by observᵃ were in the lat. 20°:34' with the wind from the NE to NNE, fresh gale. At 2 in the afternoon the land [bore ahead] of us as far [as we] *land being Cape St Ciprian. Currents.*

would well [see] being about 5 leagues, we then being offshore 2½ leagues. The land is very low & all along the shore sand heaps, & the shore but little else but sand. At sunset the land, I say the headland, bore S by E about 4 leagues, we then having 25 fathom water. Smooth water & a fresh gale at ENE, the current sets to the NNE very strong 4m in 4 hours or a watch by my nearest account.

14 Day. Thursday. Fair weather. A current.

This 24 hours with a moderate gale at NE by E have sailed S by W 2°:45′ to 42 leagues & are in the lat. 18°:32′ by observ^a in which find that the current has set to the northward this 24 hours about 9 leagues, the diff. between the log & observ^a. Have a fresh gale at North we steer away S with smooth water.[14]

15 Day. Friday. Fair weather with a strong current.

This 24 hours with the wind northerly fresh gale, have sailed S 39 leagues. By observations at noon find that the current hath set us to the North 5 leagues; and that by the observ^a have now 14°:6′ meridian distance from the Lizard or 14°:41′ diff long^t. beginning my long^t. from the Lizard also. We now steer away S with a fresh gale at N.

16 Day. Saturday. Fair weather. Strong current set to the northward.

This 24 hours with a fresh wind at North we have sailed S 37 leagues by observations which found this day at noon we have been set to the northward by the current 6 leagues having on the log 43 leagues, and our course hath been due South this whole 24 hours. We are now by observ^a in the lat. 14°:44′, Cape Verde lying in the lat. 14°:26′. We now steer away S with a fresh gale at N.

By now well clear of Cape Verde, the *Daniel and Henry* was sailing parallel to the Gambian coastline. Though Prideaux makes no mention of sighting other ships, many were in the vicinity. On 4 March 1700 the factors at the Royal African Company fort on the Gambia had written to London deploring the arrival of such ships as the *Daniel and Henry*:

The whole trade of the river is in the hands of the ten per cent ships, who are here at present, seven in number, some from Carolina and the rest from England, who daily increase the price of slaves in this river.[15]

Fair weather continued to render the passage an easy one. The deep seal lead was constantly hove as the dreaded St Pedro and St Anna shoals (*baixos*) were looming, especially dangerous as they rose very steeply from a sea-bed so deep that most soundings could not gauge it. On 18 and 23 March they lay directly under the ship as she picked her way cautiously across them. Since they were marked on the *Daniel and Henry*'s charts, the position of the ship could be accurately fixed by their presence, and a precise course set.

17 Day. Sunday. Fair weather with current set to the north.

This 24 hours with a moderate topgallant gale we have sailed S½ E 44 leagues & are in the lat 12°:34′ by the log; but this day at noon by observᵃ were in the lat. 12°:43′ with the wind at N fresh gale, we steering away SSE with smooth water & a current which sets to the N & 24 hours 3°:7′ by observᵃ. At eight o'clock last night hauled the lead & had 50 fathom of line out & no ground.

18 Day. Monday. Fair weather, no current but smooth water.

This 24 hours have sailed SSE½E 45 leagues & are in the lat 10°:46′ with the wind at N by W, fresh gale. Last night at 8 hove the lead & had 76 fathom of line out & no ground, but this morning were got atop the Baixos de St Pedro which lies in the lat 11°:15′, which lies SSE from Cape Verde. We now steer away SSE with the wind at N to N by W, fresh gale & smooth water.

19 Day. Tuesday. Fair weather.

This 24 hours have sailed SSE½E 33 leagues, & are in the lat. 9°:19′, have had fresh wind at NNW. We now steer away SE having this 24 hours made 15 leagues easting or meridian distance.

20 Day. Wednesday. Currents.

This 24 hours have sailed SE¼E 23 leagues, & are in the lat. 8°:38′ having made 18 leagues meridian distance this 24 hours and being with little wind. We now steer away SE with smooth water & fair weather. We at 2 o'clock got the boat out to try the current which we found set SW & NE 1 knot in ½ minute.

To be able to navigate more accurately Walter Prideaux needed to know the direction and speed of the ocean current. This he did by lowering a lead line from one of the ship's boats until the heavy lead rested on the bottom. The boat was then allowed to drift with the current, the lead weight remaining stationary. They found the boat moved a distance equal to one knot of the log-line (51 feet) in 30 seconds (the time it took for the sand to run through the log-line hour-glass). Thus he discovered that the current ran at one knot and by reference to the direction at which the lead line now lay, measured by a boat's compass, the set (i.e. direction) of the current was obtained. Its description as being both SW and NE – apparently contradictory – suggests the current was a tidal one which reversed its direction when the tide changed.

The fine weather continued to bless the voyage as the *Daniel and Henry* drifted south on favourable breezes, trailing the long-boat in its wake in case it became necessary to assess the current afresh. Taguarim, now in Sierra Leone and once the site of a long-forgotten Portuguese fort, lay off the port bow.

21 Day. *Thursday.*	This 24 hours have with the wind from NW by N, to SSE sailed E by S 9°:45′ southerly 15 leagues, and are in the lat. 8°:21′ having made 14:3 leagues meridian distance, being fair weather and the wind little. We steering away E by S with the small boat at the stern.
22 Day. Friday. *Fair weather.* *Current.*	This 24 hours have sailed ESE 8°:30′, southerly 17 leagues & are in the lat 7°:54′ when we saw the high land of Sherboro, I say the south side being Cape Tagrin; when hove the lead & had 20 fathom water, it then bearing E about 14 leagues. It's high land & full of hommets.[16] We now steer away SSE with the wind at NNW, the current setting ESE, 1½ knots in ½ minute.
23 Day. *Saturday.* *Current sets to the southward 1 knot in ½ minute.*	This 24 hours have sailed ESE½S 26 leagues, & are in the lat 7°:18′ by dead reckoning; having at 12 at night 13 fathom way, being on the middle part of the shoal called Boxo de St Anna. Having small breeze wind, we steering away E with smooth water. The sun having 3°:22′, northerly declination cannot observe.
24 Day. Sunday. *Fair weather with current setting south ½ knot in ½ minute.*	This 24 hours have sailed SSE 5°:20′ easterly 21:5 leagues & are in the lat. 6°:20′ by dead reckoning, having the wind from NW to NNW small gale, & at 2 in the afternoon we had 4 fathom water when we hauled off SSW; and from 2 till 8 we had from 5 to 7 fathom water; and at 10 hove the lead & had no

ground having 40 fathom of line out. We now steer away S & at noon steered E with a current setting south ½ knot in ½ minute; the wind is now at S by W, small breeze just under [?] gale. The sun having 5°:45′ northerly declination – could not observe yesterday. When shoal water we saw land bearing E, 10 leagues.

25 Day.
Monday.

This 24 hours have sailed E7:7 S, 8:3 leagues, & are in the lat 6°:17′ by dead reckoning, having very little wind; and at 10 last night we hove the lead & had 60 fathom of line & no ground. We then hauled up the courses being calmer, till this day 10 when had a little wind at NE being a current which sets to the S ½ knot & 2 fathom in ½ minute.

Little wind could be more damaging to sails than strong wind. The rolling of a ship in a calm caused 'slatting' of the sails, in which they flapped aimlessly about, rubbing against the masts and shrouds. The fore and main courses were particularly liable to wear and tear as their lower corners were not secured to yards (as were the lower corners of the topsails and topgallant sails), but held much less firmly by the tacks and sheets. To prevent wear the courses were hauled up to the yards by means of the clew and bunt lines and held steady there until the wind returned.

As it happened it was the quiet before the storm, the wind returning with a vengeance. Now all sails were furled except the foresail, which allowed the ship to run safely before the wind.

26 Day.
Tuesday.
Tornado.
Cape is very
high with a
saddle in the
middle & like an
isle.

This 24 hours have sailed SE by E 10°:30′ Easterly 7:7 leagues & are in the lat. 6°:8′ having at 4 in the morning a tornado with little wind but much rain, we then having the wind at E, steering west having all sails furled, but the forsail in the brails. And in the morning saw the land which is Cape Mount being 131 leagues meridian distance from Cape Verde, it bearing E about 10 leagues. And at 12 bore E by N, the wind at S by W, small gale, we steering away E.

27 Day.
Wednesday. Fair
weather with
smooth water.

This 24 hours have sailed ESE½S 19 leagues & are in lat 5°:44′. At 6 in the afternoon Cape Mount bore ENE 5 leagues, & at 10 it bore N by E 3 leagues. We then steer ESE. At 6 in the morning it bore NW by

Little or no
current.

N 4 leagues, when Cape Monserado bore ESE about 9 leagues offshore, it being all along sandy beach. We now steer SE.

Africa lay tantalisingly close but Walter Prideaux's first experience of dealing with Africans was to prove frustrating. The ship and her crew had made it safely to the West African coast only to find the natives seemed unwilling to trade. Without interpreters, and lacking knowledge of local customs regarding exchange and barter, little progress could be made with the canoes which came aboard. And the tropics presented new meteorological problems (as well as cultural and navigational phenomena). Sudden tornadoes could whip seas into mountains and tear unreefed sails into shreds before disappearing as suddenly as they had arisen.

The beginning of April marked the start of the tornado season, which generally lasted on the Gold Coast until June. Though three or four could strike in a day, their duration was generally short 'but accompanied with prodigious thunder, lightning and rain, and the violence of the wind so extraordinary that it has sometimes rolled up the lead the houses are cover'd with as close and as compactly as possible it could be done by the art of man'.[17]

28 Day.
Thursday.
Fair
weather. We had
a canoe on board
but no trade
with him.
Tornado at 4 in
the morning.

This 24 hours have sailed along the shore SE 22 leagues, Cape Monserado at 4 in the afternoon bearing N by E, and at 6 NW½N 1 league & 2 leagues, the southernmost headland then bearing SSE 4½ leagues, being about 3 miles offshore. All along the shore is a sandy beach with low land, & at 10 this forenoon were up with Barsaw when came off a canoe with 3 Negroes which place was [Rio] Corso, there being in the country over the shore a high land much in the form of a rainbow over the middle of the entrance, with several other hills to the westward. We now steer away ESE with the wind at N by W, small gale. Lat 4°:59'. This place is 12 leagues or thereabouts to the westward of Sisters.

29 Day. Friday.

This 24 hours we have sailed ESE 12 leagues we now being in the lat 4°:45'. The shore is all most rocky I say, the landing there being some high trees being higher than the others. We had a canoe come within pistol shot, but would not come on board; nor could we speak with them but went ashore again. There is

on the land, which is now ENE, a high land like a
hommett with a saddle in the middle, bearing as
above 3 leagues off, Sisters being about 4 leagues E
by N. We steering away SW with the wind at SE.

The days of plain sailing were now over, for the *Daniel and Henry*
(trailing her long-boat behind her in a bid to keep its seams from
opening in the heat) had arrived off the Grain Coast. Its name derived
not from wheat or barley but from the quantities of mallaguetta pepper
grains produced. Starting at Cape Mesurado the Grain Coast extended
coastwise to Cape Palmas; as well as acting as the border with the Ivory
Coast which followed, it also signalled the end of the 'windward' coast
which stretched northward to the Gambia. English Guinea-trade ships
traditionally bought pepper at Sisters (Rio dos Sestos) in order to spice
the 'slabber sauce' of salt, flour and palm oil which accompanied the
diet of rice, maize or horse beans traditionally fed to shipboard slaves.
The pepper was also believed to contain medicinal powers; it was
recommended – perversely one feels – for diarrhoea and dysentery.
The *Journal* now becomes far more detailed; not only was there much
more to record than the basic passage of the vessel, but there was no
printed account of the coast available as an *aide-mémoire*. If Prideaux
intended a life at sea, then the Guinea Coast would be a possible future
destination and his notes would be invaluable. For the moment,
however, we shall delay an examination of them and focus briefly on
Africa, the vast continent that loomed off the port bow of the *Daniel
and Henry* and on the Royal African Company, which carried the
major responsibility for the English attempt to exploit it.

CHAPTER SEVEN

Africa and the Africans

CONDITIONED as the modern European is to regarding the West
African Coast from the Gambia to Angola as erstwhile colonial
possessions, the reality that greeted the *Daniel and Henry* was very
different indeed. And though European nations had set up – through
the medium of African Companies with monopoly status – a network
of trading posts, forts and castles along the coast to funnel slaves to
their ships anchored offshore, this trade, though lucrative enough as
far as local chiefs were concerned, was small in comparison to more
conventional trading patterns. It was far from unimportant however,
for the large number of weapons exchanged by the slave ships for
their cargo helped reinforce local chiefs' dominion and assisted them,
by their firepower, to expand their territories. Gradually the importance of the slave trade was to assume such proportions that the whole
economic and political life of West Africa was dedicated to creating
a steady supply of slaves; at the time of the *Daniel and Henry*'s
arrival, such a state of affairs was, if not in its infancy, still far from
fully developed.

Given the myth of white ascendancy that was current in 1700 (and
has far from disappeared today) it must have come as a shock to the
crew of the *Daniel and Henry* to find that it was the white man who
courted the favour of Africans, and that even such an august body as
the Royal African Company had only the most tenuous of toeholds
on the Coast. The Europeans very much waited on the good humour
of the local caboceer and the determination of suitably assorted
goods for barter was again the African's prerogative. Many European
goods also met with stiff competition from locally produced articles.
Not only was the hinterland of Africa criss-crossed with a network
of well-established trade routes, but the goods that travelled these
routes were rarely inferior to anything the *Daniel and Henry* had to

offer. Though barely remarked upon by other contemporary writers, the ubiquitous Nathaniel Uring, who traded for slaves off the Guinea Coast in 1710 noted 'there is considerable Trade carried on, from one Nation to another, clear across that great Tract of Land, from the Gold Coast of Guinea to the Mediterranean Sea.'[1]

Indeed there was. The Akan, a large group of interrelated tribes of the area equivalent to central and southern Ghana and the eastern part of the Ivory Coast, roughly corresponding to that stretch of the coast from Cape Lahou to Accra, plus the Mande of the western Sudan, were pre-eminent amongst traders. By the early sixteenth century the Akan and the Mande traders held virtually all the mercantile cards, trading both with their northern Sudanic contacts and with the Europeans on their southern shores. Gold not slaves was the keynote of such trading.[2] For this precious metal the early Portuguese merchants exchanged brass bracelets, brass pans, red and blue cloth, linens and cloths striped with red, blue, green and white. The predominance of manufactured metalware and cloth was to prove of great benefit to the English when their time came to trade on the Guinea Coast. Even in the early sixteenth century a wide choice of goods was crucial to a successful transaction for gold. Accordingly the Portuguese presented for sale an extraordinary array of fabrics 'including panna . . . made from finely woven and combed cotton; pano branco or white sailcloth; calicoes; scarlet cloth from Portugal, Flanders, Venice, India; Bruges satins; muslin fustian . . . a weave manufactured from cotton and flax; and finally a group of eastern fabrics known as roupas pretas'.[3]

By 1700 local African weavers were successfully imitating European fabrics. A Frenchman, Father Loyer, who visited Asseney and Lahou in 1701 saw 'Turkish carpets' from the town of Begho to the north, 260 miles inland from the coast. At Asseney he was shown fine striped cloth from the same source.[4] In addition a substantial quantity of woven cloth was traded from the inland Sudanic markets of the Mande to the Ivory Coast where it was known as 'qua-qua cloth'.

Though the desire for gold was the driving force of early European (predominantly Portuguese) ambitions on the West African coast, it is doubtful whether they ever succeeded in gaining more than a minute percentage of the metal available for trade. Their dealings were restricted solely to the coastal fringe of the Akan regime, their cultural relevance was minimal and their economic influence slight. Nor were their goods for trade preferred above those of their

Sudanese competitors. The demand for cowrie shells, later to be a staple item in virtually every slave trade cargo, initially came from western Sudan where it was a regular currency. Imported by the Portuguese into West Africa, this enabled the Akan to increase their buying power with the Sudanese, leading to a reduction of Akan trade with the Portuguese. The spread of the cowrie currency into most of West Africa only serves to show how established and enduring the Sudanese connection proved to be.

The substitution of slaves for gold gradually occurred during the late sixteenth and seventeenth centuries. Two major factors contributed towards this change: on the African side, gold dust was now used throughout the Akan area as currency in imitation of the European practice, and the upsurge in home consumption meant that less was available to barter. In fact Africans often sought gold from slave trade ships in exchange for slaves; as we shall see, the *Daniel and Henry* exchanged gold for slaves in 1700. On the European side the opening of new plantations in the Americas and the discovery of gold in Portuguese-held Brazil had created an overwhelming need for labour (which would in turn generate wealth) in areas where indigenous labour was in very short supply. By the time the *Daniel and Henry* arrived the transformation in trade patterns was complete. Five years later the Dutch Agent-General at Elmina, William de la Palma, recorded that the Gold Coast had 'completely changed into a slave coast, for the natives no longer occupy themselves with the search for gold, but make war on each other in order to furnish slaves'.[5] This shift in emphasis can be seen as an intensification of an aspect of warfare long familiar to many Africans, which may have happened whether or not European vessels stood off the Coast.[6]

However the short and long-term consequences of this state of affairs were tragic. Whether or not authentic chattel slavery had existed in West Africa before the arrival of the European slave traders is still the subject of fierce debate, but it is quite clear that the transatlantic nature of the European trade took slavery into a new dimension. Neither can there be much room for doubt that the Atlantic slave trade stimulated the growth and development of whatever localised institution of slavery actually existed. By undermining values, political and social structures, and by creating social tensions and inter-group or inter-territorial misunderstandings, it deliberately encouraged frequent warfare.[7] Local chiefs, often working hand in glove with European factors at the castles and backed up with their weaponry, became robber barons. The object of their plunder and pillage was not property, but the actual people themselves. This was the one African commodity most in demand by the Europeans.

Nothing can be said in defence of the European role. Few gave it a second thought and it is rare to find such a clarity as that displayed by Alexander Falconbridge writing in the last quarter of the eighteenth century:

> I was once upon the coast of Angola . . . when there had not been a slave ship at the River Ambris for five years previous to our arrival, although a place to which many resort every year; and the failure of the trade for that period, as far as we could learn, had no other effect than to restore peace and confidence among the natives; which, upon the arrival of ships, is immediately destroyed by the inducement then held forth in the purchase of slaves.[8]

If the short-term effect of the slave trade was appalling in the misery, death and deprivation it engendered, the long-term effects on sub-Saharan Africa were catastrophic. It stunted the normal development of commodity trade between this region of Africa and the rest of the world. The forced imprisonment and transportation of upwards of 12 million Africans in the slave trade era resulted in a massive loss of labour, skill and knowledge. Africa was relegated to the periphery of the Atlantic area, which came to form the centre of the nineteenth- and twentieth-century world economic order. And the development of manufacturing was retarded. The ultimate result was vast underdevelopment – both economic and agricultural – in sub-Saharan Africa. This European legacy continues to trouble the African continent to the present day.

Nothing of this bothered the heads of the merchant backers, officers or crew of the *Daniel and Henry*. They were strictly businessmen attempting to manage profitable transactions in an unfamiliar environment. There is no reason to believe they would not have subscribed to contemporary attitudes towards slavery, which were predictably supportive of the trade. The generally accepted notion was that slavery was endemic to Africa, glossed over with the patina of a quasi-evangelistic idea that Europeans were not so much enslaving blacks as saving them from the clutches of the devil. Another fashionable sophistry, providing an indulgent release from any suggestion that slavery was unsupportable, was that Africa was so overcrowded the slave ships were actually doing the continent a favour by shipping the population off in chains to the plantations:

The Country is full of People, as may be supposed by every Man's being allowed as many Wives as he has the Ability to maintain; and if it were not for these Wars among themselves, and the Europeans carrying such great Numbers of Slaves from thence, it is highly probable that they would grow so numerous at last, that the Country would not contain them.[9]

Correlative to this idea, though rarely expressed by contemporary writers, was that the cost in home-grown manpower of annexing and maintaining Britain's colonial possessions in the Americas and West Indies would be prohibitive: England herself would be seriously weakened and at risk for any prolonged European conflict. By carrying Negroes to the plantations the problem of 'the exhausting of this Nation of its natural born subjects'[10] would be substantially alleviated.

Virtually all the slaves who were eventually crammed into the holds of the *Daniel and Henry* were from what is now known as Ghana. Whether this was achieved by accident or design is unclear, but slaves of Coromantine (Ghanaian) origin were most highly prized by the plantation owners of the Caribbean. Christopher Codrington of Antigua, one of the largest plantation owners in the West Indies and whose name has become synonymous with plantation slavery, remarked in 1701, 'they are not only the best and most faithful of our slaves, but are really all born heroes'.[11]

If the planters' bias in favour of Coromantine or Coromantee blacks puzzles us today, it was as much an enigma to slave trade captains. Although barely a day's sail from Accra, slaves from the Allampo region, which extended beyond the River Volta into what is now known as Nigeria, were regarded in an altogether unfavourable light by plantation owners. As a contemporary slave trade captain related:

They are esteemed the worst and most wishy-washy of any that are brought to the West Indies, and yield the least price; why I know not, for they seem as well limbed and lusty as any other negroes, and the only difference I perceived in them was that they are not as black as others, and all are circumcised.[12]

It is doubtful whether Roger Mathew, captain of the *Daniel and Henry*, could account for the prejudice of the planters, but it is quite possible that his sailing orders included specific areas where slaves were to be actively purchased. Given the intense competition along the Guinea Coast in 1700 (due to the 1698 Act which curtailed the Company's monopoly), it is extremely unlikely that Roger Mathew could have exercised any option in his choice of origin of slaves. However the voyage was blessed, if that is the right term, by an entirely fortuitous chain of events which led the *Daniel and Henry* to take more slaves of Coromantine origin aboard than could reasonably have been expected. Unbeknown to the captain, crew or freighters of the *Daniel and Henry* her passage off the Guinea Coast – and more specifically the Gold Coast – corresponded with one of the most powerful of the Akan tribes, the Ashanti, making a bid for power via a prolonged series of tribal hostilities. As was usually the case, substantial favours and tributes were exacted from the vanquished tribes. In 1700 the Ashanti imposed a ransom of 2,000 slaves upon the ruler of the conquered Dagamba people.[13] In all probability some of these found themselves within a very short time being haggled over by Roger Mathew and Walter Prideaux. It would be only a matter of hours before they were chained between the stifling decks of the *Daniel and Henry*.

Of all the men on the *Daniel and Henry* only her master, Roger Mathew, had any experience of trading on the African coast. If the Guinea Coast caboceers had been familiar with Europeans in 1600, by 1700 they harboured no doubts at all about their opposite numbers. Sophisticated, powerful and wealthy, the caboceers possessed a knowledge of the Europeans that was greater by far than the European's understanding of the African. This was the European's chief disadvantage in dealing with the caboceers, who had quickly learned that deviousness went hand in hand with European transactions. The Africans took their own, very sensible precautions. Thomas Phillips of the *Hannibal*, a newcomer to the African trade in 1694, was surprised to find that 'on the Gold Coast they know our Troy weights as well as ourselves and have weights of their own, which they compare ours with'.[14] Of course the Europeans took precautions too, for the Africans were not always the innocent party. Again Phillips reveals they carried 'touchstones to try the gold ... indeed we had need of all the caution imaginable to avoid being cheated by the negroes, which they often endeavour by mixing filings of brass with the gold dust, and filling the middle of their cast ingots with lead'.[15]

Naturally the caboceers kept an eager eye open for novices to the slave trade. When the monopoly held by the Company was dissolved, the influx of tyro ten per centers must have been a godsend. For here was an unparalleled opportunity to shift their 'refuse slaves', the halt, the lame, the sick and the old with whom more experienced slave trade captains would have no truck. However, a captain never had a completely free hand, for unless he agreed to take at least a percentage of the infirm he would receive no slaves at all. Phillips recorded the problem as he found it aboard the *Hannibal* at Whydah:

> When we were at the trunk [slave pen] the King's slaves, if he had any were the first offered to sale, which the cappashuas would be very urgent with us to buy, and would in a manner force us to it ere they would show us any other saying they were the Reys Cosa (i.e., belonging to the King), & we must not refuse them; though as I observed they were generally the worst slaves in the trunk, & we paid more for them than any others.[16]

That would have been far from the end of the story. In the packed holds of a slave ship, disease was transmitted with terrifying rapidity and the introduction of one diseased slave would severely affect the chances of survival of all the others. It is hardly surprising that the influx of the novice ten per cent ships triggered such appalling casualty rates on the 'middle passage'.

Trading for slaves involved a complex set of rules entirely of the Africans' making, and liable to change at any time. Unable to anchor close inshore due to a dearth of harbours and the presence of huge Atlantic rollers breaking on to the beaches, and unwilling to stand close inshore for security reasons, the slave ships were forced as many as three leagues offshore, and employed their long-boats for trading. More often than not these were unsuitable for driving through the crashing surf. Canoes had to be hired or purchased to deliver the goods for barter to the shore and return with slaves to the long-boat which stood in calm water beyond the breakers, or directly back to the ship. Such trading put a barely tolerable burden on the Europeans who – even if they escaped the ever-present diseases – burned in the sun, dehydrated in the heat and were soaked by frequent tropical downpours. They in turn lashed out at the only beings less fortunate than themselves, the slaves, the only innocents in the whole degrading transaction.

Local caboceers ruled these operations. A selection of goods for barter from the *Daniel and Henry* would be demanded, thoroughly inspected and responded to with signs of approval or disapproval. A liberal sprinkling of presents – *dashee* – to selected headmen would help the business along famously. The Royal African Company was

European merchants (C, D) dealing with the King of Sestos (A)
and his councillors (B) for slaves, c. 1690.

particularly careful in its choice of presents for it had more to lose
on the Guinea Coast than any ten per cent ship, and its Court of
Assistants particularly recommended lace fringed hats and *ketysols*
(parasols) which

> should be of Scarlet and Blue cloth, embroidered, well-lined and
> fringed, the sticks painted or stained with Birds and Beasts, on the
> Top carved or painted in its true colours; the small sticks within
> ... must be strong and well put together for playing up and
> down.[17]

For more ceremonial and official occasions, such as the arrival of
the new Company Agents to the Gambia in 1720, among the presents
judged as proper for presentation to the kings of the region was 'a
Clockwork Monkey that beats a Drum to be bought at Salmons Wax
Work for a small matter and is very diverting'.[18]

It would behove the surgeon of the *Daniel and Henry*, Edward
Fenner, to inspect the slaves presented in exchange for the goods as
carefully as the Africans checked over the goods themselves. His
mate, William Hunt, may have been the surgeon's assistant of that

name recorded at the Cape Coast Castle between 1696 and 1697, so he at least should have been of inestimable value. The caboceers were past masters in the art of dressing mutton up as lamb. Doubtful slaves for barter had their hair dyed if greying, and their bodies were shaved smooth and oiled to glisten with the appearance of health. Though age was fairly easy to estimate by an examination of their teeth, disease was far more difficult to spot, not least because the disease itself would probably be unfamiliar to an English doctor. Yaws was one such problem. Widespread amongst blacks and endemic to the Guinea Coast, it manifested itself in the presence of small strawberry-like swellings which were easily overlooked. Given the appalling mortality rate that was to be the fate of the *Daniel and Henry*'s cargo, it is doubtful whether the good Doctor Fenner or his worthy mate took as much trouble as the surgeons of the *Hannibal* did in examining prospective slaves: 'our surgeon is forced to examine the privities of both men and women with the nicest scrutiny, which is a great slavery, but what can't be omitted'.[19]

When both parties were satisfied with the bargaining, slaves were marked with the initial letters of the ship's name and consigned to minor caboceers until such time as the agreed goods were ferried ashore. These caboceers had differing responsibilities, and were often termed captains. Hence the captain of the trunk (variously known as 'slave pen' or 'barracoon'), the captain of the slaves (who secured the slaves at the waterside), and the captain of the sand (who looked after the merchandise offloaded by the canoes). A successful transaction involved much greasing of palms, especially as far as the captain of the sand was concerned, for pilfering of merchandise cost many a ten per cent ship dearly.

Alternatively, or as an extra precaution, a hostage or 'pawn' could be taken by either side as a means to guarantee the agreement. The form the hostage took was occasionally gold, more usually a human being. This was a far from perfect arrangement, as Nathaniel Uring discovered in 1710. He found himself stranded on the Guinea Coast, his captain having sailed after loading three slaves and a 'good quantity of corn' without paying. (Relations had been difficult between Uring and his captain prior to this event, so they must have been impossible afterwards.)

Ten per cent captains lived by their wits on the Guinea Coast, occasionally kidnapping (*panyaring*) local Africans in order to bring their slave cargoes up to strength. Royal African Company officials at the castles detested these interlopers (as they saw them) for their arrival signalled the beginning of the end of Company influence on the Coast. However, public detestation masked clandestine approval for no one was better placed to carry out private trade with the ten per centers than the Company men themselves. Most of them developed a very profitable sideline in trafficking for slaves (with Company and personal goods) which they then shipped aboard the separate traders. Occasional 'mishaps' such as fires and flood ensured that their books of accounts rarely made their way back to the counting house in London.

The fact that the separate traders were not tied to a specific trading location, as the Company ships were, was immensely to their captains' advantage. Without the sizeable overheads which bedevilled the Company's operations, they could offer considerably higher prices for slaves. If as a result of their generosity slave prices proved too high, the ten per centers simply weighed anchor and moved down the Coast in search of a more reasonably priced cargo. Company ships had little of this flexibility. Their cargo was determined in London and consigned to a particular castle, normally Cape Coast, for a particular quantity of slaves. For one reason or another this quantity of slaves might not be available on time, in which case the ship was directed to a Company out-station such as Whydah or Accra for its full complement. Though on the surface an ideal arrangement, it rarely proved so in practice. Relationships with the local caboceers were in a constant state of flux, complicated by the presence of other trading nations on the coast. As already noted, caboceers favoured ten per cent ships as offering better rates of exchange. The Company establishments were not cheap to run and employed substantial numbers of clerical staff, soldiers, servants and slaves who had to be paid, fed and housed; to say nothing of a large complement of sailors who manned the castle sloops used for riparian and coastal slave trading. Larger forts, such as the Cape Coast Castle, had huge slave dungeons capable of holding up to a thousand blacks in abject misery awaiting the arrival of the next Company ship.

Although the seaborne 'middle passage' is generally associated with mortality, slave deaths in the barracoons were far from infrequent, and have received little or no attention. Since these slaves had been paid for, their losses were a serious drain on Company profitability. By 1720 the problem of barracoon mortality was such that regulations were proposed 'for the preservation of the Shipping Slaves' at Cape Coast. They give some idea of how bad conditions were, and proposed:

(i) That a place be built for Sick Slaves to keep them separate from the others.

(ii) A platform to be made in the present Trunk or Dungeon for the Slaves to lay on in the Night to be raised 18 [inches] from the Ground; and the Sides of the Trunk to be lined with ½ inch Board to preserve them from the Dampness of the Walls.

(iii) The Trunk or Dungeon to be smoaked once a week at least, especially in the Sickly Seasons to refresh and sweeten it: to be cleaned every morning and sprinkled with Lime or Lemon juice (of which there is a sufficiency in the Garden) and strewed with green herbs.

(iv) To put Tubs in the Trunk for the Slaves to ease themselves in the Night.

(v) Troughs or Bowls and other Eatable necessarys to be provided for the Slaves and kept clean for their use.

(vi) The Slaves Provisions to be adapted suitable and agreeable to each Slave Eating in his Own Country.

(vii) To Wash and Rub them every day and Shave and Oil them once a Week.

(viii) To keep the Slaves Undermentioned always at the Cape Coast to attend the other Slaves only, who are to be taught English, viz:

Men	Women	Country
1	1	Gambia
1	1	Mallaguetta Coast
1	1	Gold Coast
1	1	Crupee

(ix) The Necessaries undermentioned proposed for the use of Shipping Slaves to Cape Coast for a year, viz:

Tobacco .... 6 cwt   Mallaguetta .... 1 cwt
Pipes .... 20 gross   Perpets, damaged 50
Rum .... 1 hhd   Rice, fish, salt &c.

(x) To provide Mills for grinding their Cankey or bread to be baked & not boiled, for which a Bakehouse must be built.[20]

Though the slaves for shipment were far and away the worst off, nobody living at the Cape Coast Castle could be called privileged. The same regulations plead for 'the better preservation of the White Men' at the Castle; they point up the necessity of a cookroom with an oven and a sickroom to replace the one over the smith's forge. A more unsuitable place for a sanatorium would be hard to imagine.

Despite the obvious common sense behind these suggestions it is doubtful whether more than a handful were ever effected. The finances of the Company, rarely satisfactory, were in a parlous state; and its future, never secure, was rapidly foreshortening. A new power had arrived on the Coast, from Gambia to Angola: the mulatto trader. Often claiming descent, like Zachariah Cumberpatch, from factors the Company had sent out to Africa the previous century, they combined the worst aspects of the African caboceer and English factor and owed allegiance to neither race, country nor class. In time, as the eighteenth century progressed, they became great powers along the coast, operating in tandem with the slave trade captains to oppress the Africans. In 1700 however, when the *Daniel and Henry* stood off Cape Mesurado, their time had not yet come, and the major power on the Coast resided firmly in the hands of local African chieftains.

Such power was coveted by most European nations trading to Africa. And of these nations none were more eager, or less veiled in their intentions than the Dutch and English. Accordingly, it is to the representative of the latter's interest, the Royal African Company, that we turn in the next chapter.

CHAPTER EIGHT

Forts, Factors and Fraud

P RIMARILY built to facilitate, defend and maintain Company
interests on the coast of West Africa against incursions by traders
of other European countries, the Company forts naturally became the
focus for all English ten per centers once the 1698 Act came into effect.
These vessels flocked to anchor beneath Company guns, as did ships
from friendly nations such as Portugal and Denmark. Stretching from
the River Senegal to Nigeria, the forts varied widely in type. A few
were properly constructed fortresses; most were little more than
thatched huts with rudimentary stockades hurriedly thrown up around
them. Strictly speaking, at the time the *Daniel and Henry* traded there,
only three castles were in existence. Elmina was the Dutch stronghold,
though built by the Portuguese. Christiansborg belonged to the Danes.
And the Cape Coast, or Cabo Corso, flew the English flag. The forts
really described the lesser, but still permanent, trading posts, while
temporary trade factories were more properly designated 'lodges',
though they occasionally retained the title of fort for official purposes.[1]
As the capability of the various European powers to defend their
Guinea interest waxed and waned, the establishments were captured,
purchased or usurped by whichever nation's Africa Company was in
the ascendant. Hence the Cape Coast castle was originally built by the
Spanish but was taken by the Danes in 1659, the Dutch in 1663, and
finally ceded to the English in 1664. Whatever nationality held the
forts, however, the tenure was a most insecure one. The forts were far
from being their own masters, and their presence was only counten-
anced by the favour (for which a substantial ground-rent was payable)
of the local African chiefs.

Each fort had a factor or agent. Cape Coast Castle, the Company
headquarters on the Guinea Coast, had three, plus a substantial retinue
of professional men such as surgeons, writers and accountants, and

tradesmen such as carpenters, armourers and bricklayers. The balance was made up by detachments of soldiers, gunners and sailors, all of whom were on the Company payroll and created huge overheads. There was also a substantial number of *grommettoes*; though the term has caused much confusion, the Company was clear about their status: they were 'free natives hired ... to do the work of the Garrison'.[2] Company forts also employed numbers of slaves on a permanent basis who often worked with both white men and *grommettoes* ashore and afloat in the sloops attached to the Company's forts. In 1700 the Company estimated it could muster 150 whites, 40 *grommettoes* and 50 Negroes (slaves) at the Cape Coast Castle. Its total workforce, the length of the Guinea Coast from Gambia to Nigeria, amounted to 606 whites, 176 *grommettoes* and 156 Negroes.[3] All Company waged-employees in Africa were also allowed a diet or contribution to living expenses: *grommettoes* were frequently paid in goods which they would then barter. Predictably the Company's profits, marginal at the best of times, were under constant threat from these overheads. The salary structure was a formal one (see Table 8.1), though small fluctuations did occur in individual cases:[4]

Table 8.1   Royal African Company salaries, employees on the Guinea Coast, 1700

	£ p.a.	£ diet p.a.
Chief merchant	300	100
Chief factor	100	50
Factor	40	50
Writer [clerk]	25	40
Surgeon-Chief	50–60	50
Surgeon's mate	30–40	50
Lieutenant	50	50
Sergeants	20–36	26
Soldiers	12	13
Gunners	18	13
Armourers	30	15
Carpenters	30	15
Sawyers	30	15
Coopers	30	15
Masons	30	15
Bricklayers	30	15
Blacksmiths	20–30	15
Bomboys[5]	17	17

At one extreme of the salary scale were the apprentices, paid nothing but clothing and diet. At the other was Sir Dalby Thomas, Agent-General of the Company from 1702, who was paid £1,000 per annum plus substantial living allowances and a commission of 2 per cent on all returns from the Gold Coast.[6] Salaries aboard the Company ships were roughly comparable with those of the rest of the merchant fleet, and far ahead of the Royal Navy, at least for the ordinary deck hand. Company sailors were paid approximately £21 per annum, third mates £30 p.a., second mates £36 p.a., first mates £40 p.a., and captains £60–80 p.a.

Since three years was the standard term of engagement on Company business, advances were payable in England to wives, relatives and nominees of both ship and shore-based employees. As far as ship-based employees were concerned, the Company probably followed the example of the East India Company in allowing crew to draw two months' wages in advance on joining the ship, and permitting a nominated party to draw one month's salary for every six months the ship was away. Two pay levels were in operation: a basic 'river wage' while the ship was in port, an enhanced, deep-sea wage which started as soon as the ship had cleared the port or estuary.

Wages were supplemented in a number of ways. The most popular were 'ventures', which took the form of personal trading in privately owned goods that were carried at company expense. Almost every member of the crew, whether shipped on Company or ten per center, took advantage of this. It was a practice that the Company had tried hard to stamp out aboard its own vessels. In 1675 it had forbidden all Company ships – whether owned or chartered – bound for the Gold Coast and Benin, to carry any goods on private account. From that date onwards the Company and its crews were at loggerheads until the Company was forced to capitulate and restore a private venturing allowance.[7] Predictably, this was comfortably exceeded by all concerned at every possible opportunity. Those at the top of the ladder of command were the best placed to profit from private ventures. Captains carried their own personal venture, often a substantial one worth as much as £200, to Africa for bartering. Those lower down the scale such as John Fort, gunner aboard the *Daniel and Henry*, had to content themselves with a few bolts of cloth. Like John Fort they formed small business partnerships in order to profit. Fort shared three pieces of serge with boatswain Francis Snelling, though neither lived to complete the journey nor to enjoy the reward on their outlay.

Occasionally Company ships and ten per centers held letters of marque from the Admiralty which gave them the right to capture vessels belonging to other nations. These letters were granted only in times of war and were intended to supplement the role of the Royal Navy. Letter of marque ships were essentially instruments of reprisal: their mandate did not extend beyond merchant ships or privateers of hostile nations. Merchantmen holding no such warrant had only the right to defend themselves if attacked; if they attacked a merchant-man, even of a country with which England was at war, they were guilty of piracy.

The terms 'letter of marque ship' and 'privateer' have been used interchangeably since the eighteenth century, but a privateer was originally a privately financed man-of-war which carried no cargo, and was fitted out specifically to cruise against the enemy once hostilities commenced. In theory the crews of letter of marque ships could earn themselves small fortunes: a third of the value of a captured foreign merchant vessel and cargo, once accepted as a genuine prize by the High Court of Admiralty, was payable to the ship's company.[8] (The remaining two-thirds went to a fund for the relief of the sick and wounded and the state.) In practice, the ship's crew rarely got their just deserts and were too poor and ill-educated to press their claims through the courts against the ship's officers who retained the bulk of the prize money. Quite what advantage a vulnerable, slow-moving, heavily laden Guineaman hoped to gain by carrying a letter of marque is a mystery. The letter itself was not freely issued, and the captain was obliged to present himself at the Admiralty with substantial bonds and financial assurances from approved backers. Guineamen rarely, if ever, took prizes; none of the vessels in these pages did so, and the function of the letters may simply have been to entice a crew aboard. The dangers of the Guinea Coast may have been rendered more palatable by the carrot of potential prize money.

Most Company wages were supplemented by the proceeds of fraud and deception. The opportunities were endless and the temp-tation extended from the time a vessel loaded its cargo at its point of departure to the time it berthed some eighteen months later from the West Indies. Opportunity sometimes got so much the better of discretion that the result was piracy. In an age prior to telegraph, telephone, telex and Interpol there was little a merchant could do to ensure his ship reached her intended destination. Even the Company was prey to such an occurrence and in 1721 their worst fears were realised. Their vessel the *Gambia Castle*, commanded by Charles Russell, went absent without leave. While Russell and the factors of the Company fort at the Gambia had been negotiating with the King of Barra for slaves, the ship's chief mate George Lowther and twenty-three sailors, aided and abetted by a contingent of Company soldiers (who were probably destined for the Gambia barracks), sailed out into the Atlantic. After fierce disagreements broke out between the sailors and soldiers, the ship was burned in Montego Bay the following year.[9] Those responsible were never caught and probably made their way into exile in the American colonies.

Fraud was not a practice peculiar to the ships. Those on dry land, especially in Company employ in Africa, rarely failed to take advantage of opportunities to line their own pockets.[10] It was not that they were poorly paid. Nicholas Buckeridge, Senior Agent at the Cape Coast Castle at the time the *Daniel and Henry* arrived, was paid a salary of £200,[11] of which £50 was payable in England to a named dependant at the start of the year. A farm labourer at the same time would be lucky to earn £20 a year. Employee mismanagement of business or misappropriation of funds and goods was an eighteenth-century commonplace. Company loyalty – of which so much is made today – is a recent phenomenon probably dating back no further than Victorian times in England. Until business ethics intervened, anything went. In the case of the slave trade, business and ethics could not have been further apart.

Despite the moral untenability of their position, it is not impossible to sympathise with the predicament in which Company factors found themselves. Isolated, far from home, stranded on the shores of an alien civilisation with no links with any known European model, faced with a climatic, political, social, philosophical and moral unknown, and braving the all-too-real daily possibility of inexplicable disease or political assassination, it is small wonder that Company employees went off the rails. Their chief business, when all was said and done, was to ensure their own personal survival. Blind to all this, the Company compounded the problem. No auditors were ever dispatched to Africa to check the books. No executives from the Court of Assistants or management cadre took it upon themselves to assess the local problems on site and create policies to deal with them. An enormous gulf opened between the Company factors in Africa and their nominal superiors in London. Not equipped by experience to respond quickly and effectively to their factors' demands and requests, the Company Assistants, made up for the most part from the gentry rather than the merchant class, seemed to thrive on confrontation rather than comprehension.

Though doubtless all factors hoped to profit greatly by their time in Guinea, they were hardly ne'er-do-wells interested in making a quick buck. Those who wished to join the Company in a senior position needed securities who would enter into bonds for their good behaviour. These were not insignificant by the standards of the day. Junior factors needed security for £400; merchants (factors and agents) for £900–£1,500, depending on the importance of the assignment and turnover of the fort; the Agent-General £2,000. All securities were closely scrutinised by the Court of Assistants and bad risks were subject to rejection.[12] During later years officers were allowed to post their own bonds but in 1700 this was not yet the case.

Despite all the care and attention, when transgressions came to light all this came to naught. Though the Company did commence a series of Chancery lawsuits against errant factors in the early eighteenth century, there is little evidence that it sought to claim the securities to offset its losses.

Life as a senior Company employee in Africa was never easy and was made a thousand times more difficult by the remote yet paternalistic Governors. They often required factors on the Guinea Coast to accomplish delicate political manoeuvrings that a senior diplomat in Europe would have approached with trepidation. Perhaps the Governors, in their ivory tower in Leadenhall Street, viewed Africans as naughty children who would respond favourably to the firm smack of government. Nothing could be further from the truth.

The case of Nicholas Buckeridge perfectly illustrates the failings of the Company from an individual viewpoint, and demonstrates the qualities of merchant, diplomat and military tactician that the Company expected of its senior factors. Chief Agent at the Cape Coast Castle in 1700 (in time we shall find the *Daniel and Henry* anchoring under its guns), Buckeridge had arrived as a raw recruit in 1686[13], posted to Sierra Leone. His immediate superior during those early days had been the redoubtable Thomas Corker (whose career is described in the chapter on Falmouth), and Buckeridge – if his later actions are anything to go by – proved an ideal pupil. Very little is heard of Buckeridge, however, until 1693 when he appeared at Winnebah, at that time little more than a trading lodge some distance to the east of the Cape Coast Castle. The authorities there considered Winnebah of some importance, but Buckeridge's title of factor was a resoundingly empty one. He lived on the beach in a little thatched hut with mud walls, spending his days constructing a fort which stood 'about a musket shot from the seaside' on a slight rise. Despite the intense heat and frequent bouts of disease, he had single-handedly constructed the walls to a height of 8 feet and dug a water tank within. All this had been achieved with neither labour nor materials – both of which he had been promised from the Cape Coast Castle. It was a slow and vexing business. He had to make the bricks himself, pounding oyster shells into powder to serve for lime to make mortar. The bricks themselves (as he was the first to admit) were 'sad, crumbling unserviceable trash'. A heavy day's rain could wash away the previous day's work, so he covered the tops of the walls with palm branches as a makeshift cover. As if these weren't problems enough, he was being harried and threatened by the Quamboers, an inland marauding tribe who occasionally sent out raiding parties to the coast. Phillips records that one night Buckeridge was so worried about the threat of all his goods being pillaged that he packed them up and stood by ready to come aboard the *Hannibal*. It was likely that the Quamboers had heard of the good trade in gold that Buckeridge was conducting and reasoned that without fort or retainers his position was extremely vulnerable.

But it was not quite all work and no play, for the queen of Winnebah, 'about fifty years old, as black as jet, but very corpulent', took him under her very considerable wing. She frequently stayed the night with him, which no doubt helped allay his feelings of vulnerability, politically at least;

> she was very free of her kisses to Mr Buckeridge, whom she seemed to much esteem; and truly he deserved it from all that knew him, being an extraordinary good humoured and ingenious gentleman, and understood this country and language very well.[14]

Nicholas Buckeridge was not quite as alone as some factors of the outlying stations, for his brother Thomas was also a factor on the Guinea Coast, albeit at its western extremity, Dixcove. There he was, like Nicholas, engaged in building a fort. When Phillips visited him he 'had a few small guns planted upon the rock under the fort open, which was all his defence then'.[15] Nor was the problem of isolation confined only to employees of the English Company: the factors of the French Company at Whydah in 1694 had not seen a French ship for three or four years. They were barely eking out a living in a poor mud hut and depended solely on the intermittent charity of a capricious local king.[16]

Conditions such as these must have bred enormous resentment against the Royal African Company in the minds of those it could least afford to alienate – its senior factors. Most adopted what might be regarded today as an alternative lifestyle, starting with a mulatto or African wife (or more correctly, a series of them). The term 'wife' is used in its loosest sense; mistress is more generally indicated. Phillips reports ironically, and perhaps with a sense of reserve, for despite being a sea captain he was never very far from his small Welsh home town of Brecon:

> this is a pleasant way of marrying, for they can turn them on and off and take others at pleasure; which makes them very careful to humour their husbands, in washing their linen, cleaning their chambers &c, &c. and the charge of keeping them is little or nothing.[17]

Despite the hardship and setbacks, Nicholas Buckeridge had decided to make his career on the Guinea Coast and made it known that he coveted the position of factor at the Cape Coast Castle. In 1694 he was requested to provide security for £1,600 as a step towards realising that ambition[18], becoming one of the three Agents at the Cape Coast Castle the following year.[19]

By 1700 Buckeridge was chief factor there and deeply involved in local politics. He kept open house at the Castle, encouraging local rulers and caboceers to visit with liberal – usually alcoholic – entertainment. The Castle's expenditure in brandy for October 1699 amounted to a staggering £48. In comparison the care lavished upon the slaves in the Castle's compound or barracoon was noticeable by its absence. Losses ran well into double figures: 20 men and 11 women died during January 1700, 13 men and 6 women the following March.[20] Though the Cape Coast Castle was the official residence of the Company's Agent-General on the Coast, the office had been discarded in 1687, so Buckeridge was answerable to nobody for his actions. With the curtailment of the Company monopoly in 1698 several appointees had been sent to the Cape Coast Castle, as the attentions of the ten per cent ships made it imperative for a senior Company official to govern the response of the factors to the new influx. Fortunately for Buckeridge none of the appointees survived the voyage out from England or the first few weeks on the Coast. Taking advantage of this hiatus in command, Buckeridge moved into the local political arena. His 'influence' was clearly felt in a local inter-tribal war of 1699. It was, of course, a clandestine involvement, but the Dutch Director-General at Elmina, van Sevenhuysen, was certain at whom to point the finger of guilt:

> The English premier agent Buckeridge, who by his murdering the King of Commany is the cause of the earlier mentioned war, went subsequently to Annamabo in order to move the Fantini to help him against the Commanys. But although this request was accompanied by a present of 300 bendas of gold, they refused.[21]

This was a classic instance of the pot calling the kettle black. In fact, though van Sevenhuysen was acting the innocent, he and his assistant, Wilhelm Bosman,[22] made Buckeridge look as though he was playing in a minor league. It was the Dutch who had kicked off the infamous 'Commenda Wars' which began in 1694 when they imported geologists to prospect for gold on a hill held sacred by the local Akan tribe, not far from Fort Uredenburg in Commenda.[23] The diminishing supply of gold was raising questions in the Dutch Exchequer. In response van Sevenhuysen shifted the blame to those traditional antagonists of the Dutch on the Guinea Coast, the English,[24] and blamed tribal wars deep in the interior of the country. In fact he and Bosman had instituted a system of terror and corruption such that the local tribes feared even to approach Elmina, let alone trade with the Castle.[25]

Nicholas Buckeridge was no better. The killing that Sevenhuysen referred to signalled the inglorious end of Buckeridge's career and blighted that of his colleagues, Freeman and Wallis. On 6 February 1700 the Company wrote to all three Agents, but upon Buckeridge in particular it vented its fury:

> You have not only broke your Trust by making private advantages upon our concerns and by assisting others in that trade contrary to our orders and your contracts with us, but you have, by suffering the King to be murdered in our Castle brought an odium upon all our managers and our whole affairs, increased the debt you pretended to lessen, and entailed a charge which to us has no prospect of an end, and by this means given all our competitors in the Trade an advantage over us, with all which we are daily upbraided.[26]

Generally, however, factors found it impossible to resist the temptation of a little local war, for the benefits were considerable. Advantageous links could be formed with important local chiefs, weapons could be sold for good prices, and an increased supply of slaves was almost guaranteed. Nor did the Company stand aside from meddling in local affairs if it believed its influence was under threat. In 1701 it wrote to the factors at the Cape Coast Castle:

> We are informed of a Negro Woman that has some influence in the Country, and employs it always against our Influence, one Taggeba; this you must inspect and prevent it in the best Methods you can and least Expense.[27]

What veiled menace underlies the last sentence. Such a covert state of affairs could not continue for ever. In 1702 the Company appointed a political heavyweight from within its own senior ranks – Dalby Thomas – to put its house in order on the Guinea Coast. Like many Company appointments, this was a curious choice. Before joining the Company (about 1697) he had been vociferous in his demands that it be stripped of its monopoly.[28] Two of his closest associates, John Gardiner and Sir Robert Davers, were extremely active ten per cent Guinea merchants. His brother Charles Thomas was a substantial Barbados merchant and plantation owner who also acted as Agent for the Company in Barbados where he 'confused all matters that were under his record'.[29]

Nevertheless Sir Dalby (as he became) applied himself to the task with commendable zeal. He fired off a broadside at the Company's Court of Assistants regarding the quality of the factors they had selected and grumbling that 'from weak and extravagant persons you cannot expect industry, diligence and judgement . . .'.[30] Some factors were singled out personally. Mr Searle, later a prominent London slave trader, 'is eminent in cheating the blacks by false weights that he has outdone all the rest on the Coast . . .';[31] Mr Peck was guilty of collusion with ten per centers. The Dutch interlopers were accounted a problem since the English ten per centers traded sheets and gunpowder for the slaves they held rather than buying from the Company. Little escaped his fulminations. The local chiefs and caboceers were blameworthy for drinking 'nothing but wine', and even the commanders of hired ships did not escape censure for they were learning the slave trade and gaining valuable contacts and experience at Company expense. It is for the ten per centers that he reserved his special contempt, though much of this would have been posture rather than practice. The scribe whose job it was to write the salient details of his correspondence reported:

> he says he treats them civilly, they eat and drink with him, laugh and are merry, he does them all reasonable civilities, gives them good words and breaks their voyages in every part as much as he can by directing our goods to be sold where they are as cheap or cheaper on shore than they do on board.

Sir Dalby had two great hopes. The first was to establish the Cape Coast Castle as a centre of excellence – 'a Nursery and Magazine' – from which his influence would spread in ever-widening circles to all the other Company establishments upon the Coast.[32] The second was to establish a direct colony on the Guinea Coast. This he initially conceived as a very limited scheme which could usefully employ Castle *grommettoes* and slaves awaiting shipment in 'planting corn, cotton, nay sugar canes' on Company territory.[33] Within a few years he was proposing a far more grandiose plan for a full-scale colony. The Company, which was having great difficulty in maintaining its existing facilities on the Guinea Coast let alone planning a full-scale colony, paid the scheme little more than lip service:

You have often expressed your Notion of the advantage if a Colony could be settled in the North Parts; if you could propose a proper Scheme and a fit place for the doing of it on the Gold Coast, I think people would more easily be induced to go over thither and . . . employ themselves in planting indigo, tobacco, cotton and country trade . . . [34]

With Sir Dalby's death in 1713 the scheme fell into abeyance. It was not until the nineteenth century was well into its stride that his vision became a reality. Only then was the oppressive weight of the British Empire brought to bear on virtually the whole length of the Guinea Coast, from Sierra Leone to Nigeria.

Such developments, inconceivable in 1700, were well in the future. Meanwhile the *Daniel and Henry* lay quietly off Cape Mesurado. Unbeknown to captain, crew and merchant backers, her presence signified a tiny nail in the coffin of millions of Africans.

CHAPTER NINE

Along the Guinea Coast

SINCE late 1699 the area around Cape Mesurado had been 'intolerably infested with pirates'[1] attracted by the rich cargoes carried by the Guinea-trade ships. Those aboard the *Daniel and Henry* would have been well aware of the target they presented, and in calmer waters closer inshore the gunports would have been opened as a measure of defence. They were approaching Sisters or Rio dos Sestos, which was marked by a saddle in the hills behind it, and the trading settlement boasted a fine natural harbour hidden by a narrow entrance. Since large vessels could ride safely there, it was a favourite port of call for interlopers and Company vessels and had been, until quite recently, a profitable place of trade for ivory. Excellent fresh water and fine timber could be supplied by local Africans in response to 'a bottle of brandy now and then to encourage them'.[2] Amongst the ships anchored at Sestos was the *Amity* commanded by Richard Smallwood of St John's parish, Wapping, London. She was the first ten per cent ship the *Daniel and Henry* had so far encountered. Owned and freighted by London ships' chandler John Smallwood and merchant Nathaniel Rouse, she had just arrived on the Coast. Described as a small plantation-built brigantine, she was one of the first ten per cent ships to trade in slaves after the 1698 Act, completing a 'double voyage' from Barbados and back during the first half of 1699. Like the *Daniel and Henry*, she was just beginning her trading pattern: both ships were to meet again further along the Coast and in Jamaica which was the *Amity*'s final destination.[3]

30 Day.
Saturday. This 24 hours have made no easting being near the same station, Sisters bearing ENE about 2 leagues, when you will see in over Sisters a high land like a sugar loaf, with a high land about E by N. When the

sugar loaf bears ENE, there's a ledge of rocks on the
east side which when you have them SE off, you may
anchor in 7 fathom water. The entrance is very
narrow, having on the west side about a mile from
the entrance three rocks, one of which is a white
rock. You will see the Parliament house standing on
the sand which is like a stick of wheat. Being in there
at the harbour's mouth on board the *Amity*, brigantine of London, Captain Richard Smallwood, of 70
tons, 8 guns, 22 men; have teeth very plenty and good
tin & from which Guinea ranters and cowries goes
off very well, but here nothing but teeth. Ships
commonly stop here to wood & water. The *Neptune*
of France, 7 months past, Capt. Jacob Nowell commanding, took a West India sloop who before took
from Little Sisters 7 negroes, they being both pirates,
the *Neptune* being a pink of 200 tons, 22 guns, 80
men, who has been out [of] France 2 years on that
account.

The curious 'Parliament house' noted by Prideaux as being like a
stick or 'stook' of wheat also caught John Barbot's attention, as well
as his eye for detail, on his voyage to the Coast twelve years before:

the council-house, the roof whereof, like that of the other houses,
is made of the same palm-tree sticks, adjusted close together,
covered over with large Banana and palm-tree leaves . . .[4]

31 Day.
Sunday.
Easter
day. Current sets
S & SSW.

This 24 hours have had little or no wind. Sisters
bearing at 4 o'clock NE, when stood on & off,[5] the
boat being on board a brigantine which lay at Sisters
for wood & water. At 5 the boat came on board,
when we tacked & stood on, but soon tack[ed] and
stood SW by S with the wind at SSE: and this
morning at 8 o'clock, Sisters bore NE by N about 4
leagues or little more when saw the brigantine coming
out, being bound on the Gold Coast. At 12 saw
another vessel bearing SSE 4 leagues, we being 3
leagues offshore. We now steering on ESE, little wind
being at SSE, smooth water.

April: 1st day.
Monday.

From yesterday 12 o'clock we have made but little
easting, being at noon about 5 leagues S by W½W
from Sisters, having but little wind, with the brigan-

tine about 2 leagues to the westward of us (a little wind at NNW), she being bound for the Gold Coast.

2 Day. Tuesday. From yesterday 12 to this day noon we have sailed along shore in sight of the land being now off Cape Formosa, there being three or 4 trees which are higher than the rest. A little to the eastward of the Cape is a long sand shore in which are some rocks. There you will see no high land from the water side, only a white rock in the middle of the bay which you will see very plain. 20 fathom water about 3 leagues off with good sandy ground; but if go nearer to the shore you'll have foul ground, but water enough.[6]

In comparison to her headlong dash from Dartmouth the *Daniel and Henry* was feeling her way along the African coast. The unfamiliarity of the waters could be measured by the lead and by such charts as they carried. But nothing could plumb the attitude of the African traders and provide them with an accurate reading. The stretch of coast around Setra Crou and Baddo was famed for the size and quality of its tusks, yet the *Daniel and Henry* failed to secure any, despite African canoes coming aboard. Perhaps Roger Mathew had forgotten that trading always opened with *dashee*, a present to the Africans. More likely it was a simple clash of cultures. Walter Prideaux would have been relieved to learn that Thomas Phillips, commander of the *Hannibal* off the same stretch of coast, had recorded only six years before:

came two canoes off near our ship with several teeth; but no persuasion we could use could prevail upon them to come aboard and trade with us, though we showed them diverse sort of commodities . . . all would not do, so that they returned ashore again.[7]

 *3 Day. Wednes-day.* From yesterday 12 to this day 12, we have sailed SE by E 10°:10′E alongshore. At 6 post meridian appeared Formosa, bearing N by W½W about 7 leagues. In the morning being off Settera Krou, came off 9 canoes with a great quantity of teeth (or mallafina); but meeting with some disheart they went all away verily without leaving [any]. As much as on this plain is well to be known, there being a ledge of rocks at the east side of the entrance which breaks

very much & all along the shore, rocky. At 12 we were off Badoe, where is a cliff which the sea breaks against more than anywhere else [you] shall see on the coast. This Badoe is in the lat. 4°:15′, the Cape being in the lat 4°:10′. We now steering away SE by E with the wind at SW, fresh gale; Cape Palmas bearing E, southerly of us about 9 leagues or thereabouts, being about 3 leagues offshore, 21 fathom water with good sandy ground.[8]

4 Day.
Thursday.

From yesterday 12 to this day noon. At 5 pm were off Grand Sester where a little to the westward is an island about a mile offshore, there being on the E side rocks & from the island to the river's mouth are foul ground & shoal, having 23 fathom water about 3½ leagues offshore; there being about 3 leagues to the eastward two round hills which you will see in over the land much in the form of a bowl's bottom with sand & rocks. From this place to the Cape, which is about 10 leagues, the Cape makes like an island with some trees which out seaward from it, showing as if it were not joined to the mainland, but it does when you are near to it. At 8 in the morning were due S from the Cape about 3 leagues, with a fair high land with no trees on it, there being no such place on the Coast having just to the eastward a plain, like a garden or cornfield, with some red clefts [i.e. cliffs] to the eastward. About a cable length distance[9] off the Cape is a shoal [which extends] a league offshore; we being about 3 leagues had 20 fathom with foul ground, rocks &c. At noon were off Ostend,[10] being about 5 leagues to the eastward [of] the Cape, being on both sides [of] the river sand with no rocks. Being about 2 leagues off have 14, 15, & 17 fathom water; we being about 3 leagues have 20 fathom, the ground rising gradually as you come near the shore. We had no trade at the Grain Coast, it beginning at Cape Monserado & ending at Cape Palmas. We now steer away E & E½N.

The Mallaguetta, Pepper or Grain Coast had now come to an end. It may well have been Roger Mathew's conscious decision not to trade there, for the coast had an unhealthy reputation:

the soil of the country, clammy, fat, all over woody, and watered by several rivers and brooks; which cause such a malignity in the air, that few Europeans can make any stay without danger of falling into malignant fevers, of which many have died.[11]

Things were not about to improve. The Ivory Coast was fast approaching, being deemed to commence at Growa. After the Grain Coast it was a little like jumping out of the frying-pan into the fire, for the natives of Drewin 'are the greatest savages of this Coast; and are said to eat human flesh. They take great pride in pointing their teeth as sharp as needles or awls, by filing them with proper files. I would not advise any person to set foot ashore here.'[12]

5 Day. *Friday.*	From yesterday noon to this day 12. At 2 in the afternoon were off Singi Robis, being about a league to the eastward of Ostend. At 12 at night were off Cavallie. At 6 in the morning were off Growa, and at about 12 – being noon – were a little to the westward of Tabbo, where you'll find double land with trees atop, some of the high land clifty & some sandy strand; you will also see some high land in the country, over the land by the shore, we being about 4 to 5 leagues off.
6 Day. Saturday.	From yesterday noon to this day 12. At 2 pm were off Buteroe which is to be known by 4 or 5 high hills with some naked places with little trees, which being off Berbay where is high land. At 12 at night were off Drewin being 4 leagues distant. Drewin is to be known by 2 white cliffs on the strand, not far from another by a little village. When you will see the high trees of Drewin [*there*] being 5, two to the westward & 3 to the eastward, the 2 to the westward are dead without leaves. At 2 were off Rio St Andrews when the briganteen stood into the bay, and soon came out again, we being about 6 leagues to the eastward of Drewin. At 8 in the morning were off the red cliffs & at 10 came off Rio de Frisco when came to an anchor to get some hatchets & mallagette from Capt Smallwood who lay at anchor in the road. We got two hatchets, but could get no mallagette. We could not trade for any teeth for when we were getting the boat out there were some Negroes on board, but leaped overboard & went off; but after came. We did not trade, they being very [surly?] not caring to speak.

The Prospect of Cape Sta Appollonia . Th.

a Village

Africans along this stretch of the Coast greatly distrusted all Europeans. They feared being kidnapped and sold into slavery, the fate of many of their countrymen during the past hundred years. Possibly as a consequence they had become expert swimmers. Thomas Phillips in the *Hannibal* gives an extensive account of meeting them and – like Prideaux – of his failure to do business despite his most earnest entreaties.[13]

7 Day.
Sunday. From yesterday noon to this day 12. At 5 we made sail from River Frisco and Cape Lahor. At 8 reckoned the value of Niggers received.[14] When we steered away E at 6 in the morning were off Cape Lahor, but no canoe came off. At 12 were off Caotre, it's a little place just standing in the scurts of a wood, with long palm trees off each side with several plain places & low land, not seeing any but [blank] by the seaside. You may anchor at either of these places in 12 or 14 fathom, but may go into 10 fathom, it being good sandy ground. The coast is all alongshore sand, with a great many trees on all the coast I say, from River Frisco to Caotre. We seeing at Caotre several canoes on shore and many negroes on the sand we had one canoe which came off to us from Caotre, but got nothing but a few limes, that canoe belonging to Jacque La Jacks.

8 Day. Monday. From yesterday noon to this day 12 we have sailed along shore from Cape Lahor being off Jacque La Jacks at 2 in the afternoon, & at noon were off Corby la Hore, being low land with some double land.

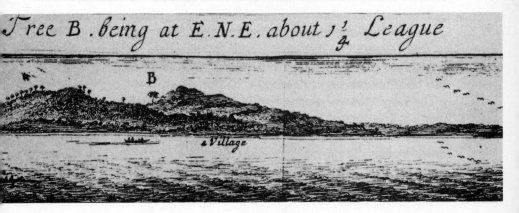

Tree B. being at E.N.E. about 1¼ League

B

a Village

9 Day. Tuesday. From yesterday noon to this day 12. At 6 were off Asseney & at 8 off Abeney when saw the high land of Cape St Appolonia making itself when you come from the Westward like two or three hills. In the morning were off Tres Points Castle when hauled in North & at noon anchored at said place in 15 fathom of oozey ground when I went on shore to the castle, Jan Devisser [commanding], a Brandenburgh. The fort stands atop of a hill having 48 guns & 70 white men. The lieutenant's name is Jan Mills. I came off again about 7pm in a canoe not being able to land with the boat, the sea breaking above twice the length of the ship offshore.

The purchase of 'a few limes' was probably not purely fortuitous for generations of seafarers had recognised the value of lemons against scurvy.[15] The importance of anti-scorbutic content in diet was not made manifest until 1753 when ex-Guinea Coast surgeon James Lind published his *Treatise on the Scurvy*, and an anti-scorbutic diet was not implemented on Royal Navy vessels until 1793.

Cape Three Points marked the end of the Ivory and beginning of the Gold Coast (now Ghana), and was dominated by the castle of the Brandenburg Company of Germany. Foreign vessels were encouraged to wood and water there for £10 a ship. Jan Visser had recently been promoted commander of the castle after a series of disastrous appointments, but his tenure proved to be a short one. Soon after the officers of the *Daniel and Henry* presented their compliments to him, several of his staff were apparently killed by local Africans. He too was then seized, taken inland and suffered a severe beating which broke virtually every bone in his body. Then he was returned to the coast, tied up, weighted with stones and tossed into the sea.[16] There is a strong suggestion that some of his staff collaborated in his demise.

The Cape was surrounded with good trading posts, all within an hour's sail of each other. Just to the westward was Axim and to the east the fort of Dicky's Cove or Dixcove. On 10 April, though not mentioned in the *Journal*, trading took place for gold,[17] and on the following day the *Daniel and Henry* took aboard her first slave. Business was about to begin in earnest.

10 Day. *Wednesday.*	This morning at six o'clock we weighed anchor & stood to the S, the wind at East, but some canoes coming on board we anchored again I say, at the Castle of Tres Points.
11 Day. *Thursday.*	This morning was brought on board a man slave which we bought for 3 Perpetuanna, 4 sheets & 2 knifes for a dark. At 2 in the afternoon we weighed anchor & got to the eastward of the Three Points and anchored again.
12 Day. Friday.	This morning we weighed anchor & came into Dickey's Cove, when came on board from the castle Wm. Coborn, an Englishman, who said we should never sell the goods being rated so dear. The castle at Dickey's Cove is commanded by Richard Crossman, being a Company's castle. We brought the castle north of us, in 11 fathom water a little offshore. To the eastward lies a ledge of rocks. Here is the best landing place of all of the coast to the eastward.

As this was the first English (Royal African Company) fort they had so far encountered, the officers and crew of the *Daniel and Henry* probably felt a sense of relief when they anchored under its guns.[18] William Colborn had been both surgeon and surveyor of the fort since 1698, and his remark about the value assigned to the cargo by Ivy, Arthur and Gould proved to be entirely correct. Colborn appears to have been factor in everything but name, but his tenure was not destined to be happy. In 1703 the fort was boarded up owing to a disagreement with the local African chief – Captain Dickey –

over the ground-rent. Colborn was kidnapped in retaliation for Company intransigence and Sir Dalby Thomas, Director-General of the Company, forced to ransom him for a considerable sum in 1704.[19] In reality Colborn had been pursuing a lucrative private trade with separate traders and interlopers of all nations. Either his dealings had led him to become embroiled in a local dispute or he had failed to provide 'Captain Dickey' with his percentage. In 1706 he embarked on leave for England, but his ship was taken by French privateers. Incarcerated in Dinant prison, he entreated the Company to secure his release. He was, however, low on their list of priorities and perished in Dinant in the early summer of 1707.

The *Daniel and Henry* lay at anchor off Dixcove for nearly a week loading Guinea corn (either maize or sorghum) via the long-boat. The cove itself, though an ideal landing place for such a boat, was too shallow to admit ships of any sizeable draught.[20] The trading post was surrounded by dense woodland from which good timber could be extracted for a price to repair vessels. The officers and men also took this opportunity to trade – officially and privately – for gold: they would have been less enthusiastic had they known that Dixcove was widely known as 'the fake Mint' of the Gold Coast because so much impure gold – and just plain brass shavings – were offered to European traders there. Apart from being a valuable commodity for export back to England, gold was often traded in part exchange for slaves further along the Guinea Coast. One Dixcove employee to fall victim to the gold-fakers (and who should have known better) was Richard Crossman: he spent a small fortune on 'gold' coins minted out of brass by a local chief ('Captain Noddy') whose skill surpassed all others, and returned home a ruined man in 1703.[21]

12 to 18. We have been at Dickey's Cove. The 18th, about 10 in the morning we weighed anchor. At 12 we were off Bottcave. At 2 were off Jararrary at which time we hauled into the bay till brought the breakers to the westward, WSW of us, when bore away. And at 4 came to anchor off Sekondi being a Dutch fort of about 8 guns where we lay; but the Dutch would not let any canoes come off to trade.

19 Day. Friday. This morning we weighed anchor when a canoe came on board & said the Dutch would not suffer any of the inhabitants to trade with us. At 10 came to anchor

off Sama, a little to the westward of River St Jan. At
12 weighed anchor again because no canoes came on
board to trade. At 1, being under sail, there came a
canoe on board and bought 4 sheets but gave us small
encouragement of a future trade. We are now in sight
of the flag at Commenda. A tornado just came home
from the sea with much thunder & lightning & rain.
When Commenda castle bore NE½E about 1½
leagues we came to anchor, being 6pm, at which time
came on board one Henry Clement, surgeon of
Commenda castle & gives us good encouragement.

Both the English and the Dutch had established forts at Sekondi,
but neither were successful despite the wealth of the local Africans.
In June 1698 the English fort was burned to the ground by tribesmen,
causing the death of several Company employees. The Dutch were
immediately suspected of engineering the tragedy. Relations between
the English and the Dutch had never been good. Phillips recorded
that 'the Dutch are very insolent upon this coast . . . endeavouring
by all methods to undermine and ruin our commerce there',[22] and
the situation had obviously not improved by the time the *Daniel and
Henry* appeared off the same stretch of coast six years later. In fact
the Dutch were attempting to run this coast as their own, being
possessed of the two forts – Sama and Uredenburgh – which flanked
the English settlement, Commenda. Sama was strategically located
upon a hill, but though the village was populous the inhabitants were
the poorest on the coast,[23] and understandably no canoes came out
to trade with Prideaux. Uredenburgh was a more serious proposition,
for it was a sizeable fort mounting twenty-four pieces of artillery.
Although at least one Dutch man-of-war patrolled the Guinea Coast
in 1700 (see the entry for 21 May on p. 111) there was no such
protection for English interests. The first vessel dispatched by the
Admiralty in response to Company and separate traders' petitions
was HMS *Milford*, which did not reach Cape Mesurado until 10
November 1700.[24]

Obviously there was little to be gained from the Dutch, so the
Daniel and Henry moved further eastward.

20 Day.   At this day till 10am were at anchor where we came
Saturday. to last night. At this time we weighed anchor and
came into Commenda road, saluted the fort – commanded by Mr Thomas Peck – and anchored in 7

> fathom of water, the fort bearing NNW. There is also
> a Dutch fort about a musket-shot to the eastward of
> the fort. We lay here expecting a fight between the
> Negroes, which they say will be in 3 or 4 days, being
> on the full of the moon.

Inter-tribal warfare usually produced an abundance of slaves, so Roger Mathew decided to anchor at Commenda for the duration of the expected hostilities. Though a newcomer to the Coast, Thomas Peck's attitude was typical of Company factors, blaming the ten per cent ships for interrupting trade and raising prices on the one hand, and actively encouraging them on the other. In 1702 Peck was found guilty of extensive private trading on his own account, the ten per cent ships being his main beneficiaries.[25]

In the event no inter-African conflict occurred. Local tribal wars were often 'manufactured' by chiefs favourable to the Dutch or English cause and caused untold damage and havoc. Neither the Dutch West India Company (whose fort at Commenda was Uredenburgh) nor the Royal African Company represented the interests of their parent countries, but were commercial undertakings. Whilst the two nations were governed in Europe by one and the same ruler – William III – in Africa they were at daggers drawn.

After sixteen fruitless days at Commenda it was obvious to Roger Mathew that no abundance of slaves was forthcoming. Along with Ralph Sadler of the Company ship *Encouragement*, also anchored at Commenda, Mathew decided to make for the Cape Coast Castle, headquarters of the Royal African Company. There he would expect to present his credentials and those of his senior officers to the Agents and assess the level of trade he could expect to achieve in the vicinity. As she anchored under the castle's guns the *Daniel and Henry* punctiliously saluted with five guns, but Mathew would have been dismayed to observe that the anchorage was crammed with shipping. Less than a month previously the Chief Factor at the Dutch headquarters at Elmina, well within sight of the Cape Coast Castle, had reported back to his superiors:

> the English say themselves that in a relatively short time not less
> than 80 recognition ships, from England as well as from Jamaica
> and Barbados have arrived here . . . interlopers and other foreign
> ships . . . have glutted the country and carried off the gold.[26]

The most Roger Mathew could hope to acquire was the mallaguetta pepper which had eluded him for so long.

This morning we made sail for Annamaboe. At 11 were off the Mine, being a Dutch fort about 3 leagues to the Eastward of Commenda.

At 2 were off Cape Corso castle and saluted it with 5 guns. At this time we sent the boat on board the

Africans ferrying slaves aboard European merchant ships anchored off the Guinea coast c. 1690. The Dutch castle of Elmina is to the west,

Prince of Orange, Company ship commanded by Josiah Daniell, to pay for a hogshead of Mallaguetta which he spared us, and whom we saluted with 3 guns.

Cape Corso Castle is commanded by Nicholas Buckeridge, Howsley Freeman, and Samuel Wallis who do all the Company's business.

Of the unholy triumvirate who governed the Company business on the Guinea Coast, Nicholas Buckeridge has been noticed elsewhere. Howsley Freeman was no angel either, being dismissed later the same year for 'arbitrary conduct'. More explicitly, his accounting procedures seemed too creative even for Company tastes and he was

and the Royal African Company headquarters of Cabo Corso or
Cape Coast Castle can be seen in the centre of the picture.

accustomed to harbour malefactors and help them escape from justice. (The Company believed he had caused them untold damage and following his death in 1705 prepared to revive the suit against his family for compensation, 'as an example to all such unfaithful servants'.) Wallis alone escaped censure.[27]

Of all the shipping that lay under the guns of Cape Coast Castle, none had achieved anything remotely resembling the career of the

Prince of Orange and her customary commander, Josiah Daniel of Rotherhithe in London. Part-owned by London merchant Dalby Thomas (shortly to become Agent-General at the Cape Coast Castle), she had been in turn a privateer (with Ralph Sadler as first mate), troop ship, fourth-rate Navy frigate on convoy duties to Maryland and Virginia, ship of the line under the overall command of Sir Cloudesly Shovell, and pirate hunter.[28] On being discharged from naval duties in 1697, she – and her incumbent captain – were contracted to the Royal African Company. This was her second consecutive voyage as a slave trade ship, though she was not due to load any slaves until she reached Whydah further along the coast. At the Cape Coast Castle she was delivering tallow, building materials, coal and timber. Although the area around the castle was – like Dixcove – heavily wooded, this wood was regarded as inferior to the oak of old England for building and ship repair, and oak imported instead.

Daniel's voyage was proceeding at a leisurely pace. Described as 'an easy, good-natured fellow',[29] he had sailed from the Thames a good two months before the *Daniel and Henry* slipped her moorings at Dartmouth. Company ships, despite the facilities of forts and factors that they enjoyed, were usually beaten hands down by the tight time schedule and fiercely entrepreneurial spirit of the ten per centers, but in this case the *Prince of Orange* was also engaged upon semi-official business. As well as his customary sailing orders Daniel had received instructions to investigate how trade at the Cape Coast could be improved:

> Having an extraordinary opinion of your good Judgement & fidelity, we do appoint that during your abode at Cabo Corso Castle you apply yourself to our Chiefs there and be of council with them. We have given them orders to admit you, & so often as you meet let all your resolutions be entered down in writing . . . we order that during your stay there the Dutch General of the Mine be sent to & that a Consultation may be appointed for the better Improvement of the Trade to the benefit of both Companies.[30]

By doing so, Daniel, never averse to a spot of meddling, was preparing the ground for the arrival of Dalby Thomas, whose job as Agent-General was to restore Company prestige on the Guinea Coast. As it turned out Daniel was not destined to see that development. He went on to Whydah with his command, loaded 600 slaves there, but perished on the middle passage to Barbados along with 254 of his cargo. The *Prince of Orange* sailed on into service as a troop carrier in the Navy at the start of the War of the Spanish Succession in 1702 (her experience in the slave trade making her an ideal candidate for such work), but three years later she returned to the slave trade. At Whydah in June 1705 she was hit by a tornado, driven ashore trailing her anchors and pounded to bits by huge breakers.

In 1700 all this was well in the future. In that year the *Prince of Orange* was shadowed along the Guinea Coast by the *Encouragement* of Barbados, another Company-hired ship. Her commander, Ralph Sadler, came from a prosperous Barbados family and his elder brother Thomas was to become Chief Justice of the island in the following year. His sister Mary had married Josiah Daniel, so Daniel and Sadler were brothers-in-law though their respective maritime careers had kept them apart for nearly ten years. Before embarking on the present voyage, Sadler and the *Encouragement* had been engaged in transporting nearly 200 white indentured servants from Scotland to Barbados. They formed part of a contingent of 2,000 disbanded soldiers shipped after the Treaty of Ryswick in response to continuous petitioning from the merchants of Barbados to the Council of Trade and Plantations for more white servants to help redress the huge racial imbalance that they feared would threaten the safety and stability of the island. One can but speculate whether Sadler appreciated the irony of his present voyage in which he eventually delivered 382 slaves out of the 450 he took aboard. Like Josiah Daniel, but for different reasons, he was never to go slave trading again. Instead he became enmeshed in the web of accusation and counter-accusation that typified the atmosphere of fraud, deceit and innuendo which permeated so much of the Company's affairs, it being alleged that he 'wronged the Company in the disposal of his cargo or in the running of negroes'.[31]

Aboard the *Encouragement*, and enjoying the voyage as a passenger, was Peter Duffield. Though later to be found guilty of collusion with ten per centers he was to survive this and many other serious allegations before dying at Whydah in 1710. For the moment he was the newcomer and had prepared himself for the rigours of life as a Company employee by shipping from London – along with a trunk and two boxes of clothing – a personal cargo of 2 cwt. of cheddar cheese, two cases of spirits, two firkins of butter and 200 empty bottles, the latter doubtless profitably filled at Madeira on the outward trip.[32]

In the time we lay at Commenda, being the 30 April the *Encouragement* came into Commenda road, Ralph Sadler in command, also a Company ship, which brought several things for Mr Thomas Peck from his father. On board we found Mr Peter Duffield who came to settle at Cape Coast, who now sends his respect to Mr Thomas Gibbs, having been out of England two months.

At 4 were off Morea being a small Dutch castle when came on board us [blank] mate of a brigantine, who this morning came from Alampo with 190 slaves; and sayeth that there are two ships at that place, one carrying 500 slaves and hath but 200 on board. However, we shall stop now at Annamaboe. The above brigantine is bound for Nevis with 130 slaves. At 5 we came to anchor in the road at Annamaboe at which time we saluted the castle commanded by Mr Curtis.[33]

Here we found 1 ship called the *New Adventure* of London, commanded by John Dunn of London, 1 brigantine commanded by James [*sic*] Smallwood, & a sloop commanded by John Davis of Barbados who is almost slaved, they being plentiful. Just to leeward of Annamaboe is Aggae where the Company have only a house, and a mile from that is Cormanlyn, a Dutch castle, where is a good place of trade for a small vessel.

The volume of shipping indicates the intense competition for slaves that faced the *Daniel and Henry*. The unnamed brigantine plying up the Coast from Alampo was the Company ship *Laurel* under Stephen Marsh, returning with surplus goods to the Cape Coast Castle. Shortly afterwards she cleared the African coast for Nevis with 132 slaves (64 men and 68 women) of which a scant 45 actually reached Nevis alive. They must have been in very poor condition for they found no buyers and were shipped on to Antigua. It had been, as the Company Court of Assistants drily reported, 'a very unfortunate voyage'.[34]

Trade at Anamabo for the *Daniel and Henry* was far from brisk, averaging little more than one slave a day. No gold was available and two of the slaves who were purchased had to be part-paid for in gold bought further back along the Coast. Perhaps most telling of all, Mathew and Prideaux found themselves competing against some of the sharpest slave trade captains in the business. Leaving aside the *Amity* under Richard Smallwood, John Dunn of the *New Adventure* and John Davis of the plantation-built sloop *Happy Return* were both Barbados traders, experienced and successful in dealing for slaves. On this occasion Dunn eventually reached Barbados on the return of his 'double voyage' on 17 October, discharging 103 slaves. John Davis, who, like Dunn, traded almost exclusively between the Caribbean and the Guinea Coast, had virtually completed his loading and was back in Barbados by the end of August with 99 slaves.[35]

Human nature being what it is, and Europeans believing implicitly in their superiority, it is doubtful whether these slave trade captains ever saw themselves as servants of the Coast's immensely wealthy Fanti chiefs. Exercising a stranglehold on all trade in the area, beholden to no one, the chiefs exemplified the fact – now usually forgotten – that the slave trade profited the two extremes of the labour–sugar equation. Black caboceers and white plantation owners, far more than any middleman, be he factor, merchant or slave captain, gained real wealth and power. Though Prideaux's account of Anamabo is lamentably terse, John Barbot had plenty to report a decade or so earlier.

> the great concourse of ships . . . very much obstructs the Company's trade with the Natives, whom the English factors dare not in the least contradict; but are rather obliged to bear with them, and sometimes so infested that they are close confined to the Castle without daring to stir abroad . . . the great wealth of the Fantineans makes them so proud and haughty that a European trading there must stand bare to them.[36]

Roger Mathew had traded for just nine slaves in his days at Anamabo and it was with a measure of relief that he heard of better trade to the east. Once again the *Daniel and Henry* weighed anchor.

May 15. Wednesday. Mr Mathews is dead & Mr Peter Duffield is now in his place at Tancomquerre, intending to live there.[37] This morning at 8 we set sail out of Anamabo road where left the above-named ships at anchor. We now design for Tancom:Querre, where at 5pm we anchored; where found at anchor Captain Dowrish in the *Arcana Gally*, who came from Alampo; his father died there. He hath about 150 slaves on board and is now going up to Anamabo. In the house at Tancom:Querre lives one Mr Mathew, where we corn'd, in 5 days taking in 200 chests at 2 ackeys per chest. Daggue is a little to leeward of Tancom:Querre, & a place of much corn.

Tancomquerry was very much an 'also-ran' in the Company's list of Guinea Coast establishments, being little more than a lodge thatched with palm leaves and subject to varying levels of trade. So far the *Daniel and Henry* had taken aboard thirty slaves in roughly as many days, so the decision to load 200 chests of maize (or perhaps sorghum, for the distinction was rarely made) must have been prompted by good news regarding the availability of slaves further along the coast. Here at least was an acquaintance, for William Dowrish came from a well-known Devon merchant family who traded extensively in cloth from Plymouth and Exeter to the plantations. Like the vessels anchored at Anamabo, the *Arcania Galley* was plantation built and owned. On behalf of her Barbados merchants, this frigate (of 120 tons and 8 guns) plied between Barbados and London with sugar, and regularly carried out 'double voyages' to the Guinea Coast with rum, returning to Barbados with slaves. The name of the vessel was no whim. *Akanni* referred to a consortium of African gold dealers and was first used by the early Portuguese and Dutch traders. The English seem to have employed the term after 1645 when they were overawed by the magnificent presence and fair dealing of over one hundred Akannis who arrived at Elmina to trade gold.[38] In the 1660s an *Arcaney Merchant* is recorded, and one suspects that the owners of Dowrish's command hoped their little flattery would not be lost on the all-powerful caboceers. The *Arcania Galley* landed 136 slaves in Barbados on 30 September 1700.[39]

One problem which faced every sea captain and supercargo trading off the Guinea Coast, whether for slaves or not, was the huge Atlantic breakers that rolled incessantly up the beaches. A ship's long-boat was far too wide and 'beamy' to guide safely through the mass of roaring water to shore, especially when heavily laden with goods for barter. It was equally difficult to launch the long-boat back from the shore, full of slaves. Though no lives aboard the *Daniel and Henry* had yet been lost (either from sickness or accident), it was obvious that canoes would have to be acquired if the *Daniel and Henry* was to stand a chance of trading competitively. Canoes were long narrow dug-outs and their descendants (including the canoe crews) still brave the rollers off the coast of Ghana to this day. They were measured on a scale from 2 to 12 hands. A seven-hand canoe, which Walter Prideaux had in mind, would be about 3 feet in width by 20 feet in length. Quite whom he envisaged manning this unfamiliar craft is a mystery. Usually a canoe crew would be hired at the beginning of the Guinea Coast and be paid off in goods when trading ceased. Nowhere in the accounts is there an allowance for a canoe crew, but the inference that the crew of the *Daniel and Henry* doubled up as canoe-men cannot really hold water.

Guiding a canoe through the breakers crashing on to the Gold Coat demanded a high level of technical expertise and extraordinary team-work. This was specialised seamanship of very high order:

> Those *blacks* manage [the canoes] ... with such extraordinary dexterity in the most dangerous places, that it is much to be admired; and if ever the canoe happens to be overset ... those people being used to such accidents, and excellent swimmers and divers, soon turn it up again, without any other damage than what the goods may receive by the sea-water.[40]

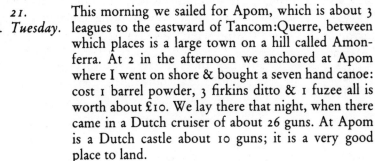

| 21. Tuesday. | This morning we sailed for Apom, which is about 3 leagues to the eastward of Tancom:Querre, between which places is a large town on a hill called Amon-ferra. At 2 in the afternoon we anchored at Apom where I went on shore & bought a seven hand canoe: cost 1 barrel powder, 3 firkins ditto & 1 fuzee all is worth about £10. We lay there that night, when there came in a Dutch cruiser of about 26 guns. At Apom is a Dutch castle about 10 guns; it is a very good place to land. |

22. Wednesday.   This morning we sailed from Apom, and at noon we anchored at Winnabey where is a castle of 16 guns, commanded by Samuel Salkeld. We intend to wood & water here.

27. [Monday].   The longboat went on shore for water and overset, Peter Johnson drowning & several other things being lost. We have had an indifferent good trade here, having taken a good quantity of gold & bought several slaves.[41]

The volume of work was growing all the time as more and more slaves were packed into the hold. Days were long. Trading started at daybreak and negotiations continued until sundown at six. Several trips to and from the canoes standing seaward of the breakers would have to be made in the long-boat, for the ship was usually anchored several leagues offshore as a security measure. After sunset the accounts would have to be rendered and stock levels assessed. The enslaved Africans in the steaming holds had to be fed, cleaned and exercised. Within a few days the *Daniel and Henry* had metamorphosed from an ordinary merchantman to a slave trade ship. Armed guards patrolled her day and night. Netting was strung out along her gunwales to prevent blacks leaping overboard to freedom. And worst of all was the incessant chanting of woe and despair which rose and fell, but was never hushed, issuing from the slave-hold. Officers and men, unaccustomed to the broiling heat and suffering from fever and dysentery, began to make mistakes. Peter Johnson, one of the youngest crew members, drowned when the long-boat was upended by a roller. Walter Prideaux neglects to record the day's business in anything but the sketchiest terms. The tropics were taking their toll.

June 7. This morning, endeavouring to weigh the small bower, the cable parted.[42]

8. This day the sea hath been so great we could not sweep for the anchor. In the afternoon came into the road the *Prince of Orange*, commanded by Jos. Daniel, at which we saluted him.

Sunday 9. This morning being smooth water we swept for the anchor, & got him up & sent the boat [i.e. the crew of the long-boat] on board Captain Daniell's to pay for a hogshead of Malaguetta. As soon as the boat came on board again we made sail for Accra. Between Winnabey and Accra is 12 leagues distance. All along the shore is low land, & within are very high hills. About 3 leagues to the westward of Accra is very low land with many trees and all sand on the shore with no rocks.

The doctor at Accra is called Thomas Wreight having an ill name. We anchored off Accra about 6pm & saluted the fort with five guns commanded by Gerrard Gore, having 26 guns in the Fort.[43] The English Castle is the westward, the Dutch the middle and the Danes the easternmost.[44] We anchored in 6 fathoms of water & good sand. You must mind at Winnabey, Accra & all along to the eastward to see your anchor every 24 hours.

The *Prince of Orange* appears to sail imperturbably onwards, yet Josiah Daniel had his share of problems. The news had just reached

him from London that his wife had died; he was also being charged
with carrying an excessive personal venture at Company expense.
Walter Prideaux's concern was for the anchor. Though not the largest
anchor carried by the *Daniel and Henry*, its loss would severely
hamper safe mooring. No one was to blame for the cables parting:
all the cables were hempen and became seriously weakened by warm
tropical seas, heavy rain and strong sunlight. At the end of the
seventeenth century the prevailing belief held that the West African
coast was easiest to navigate during June to August. This was a
serious error of judgement and one that James Barbot, supercargo on
the *Albion* off the Guinea Coast the previous year (1699), sought to
rectify. He advocated the carrying of a double quantity of anchors:
'for the sea is most days very high, and the wind at South south-west
very fresh, blowing on the land; accompanied with very heavy long
rains, which strain upon a ship continually, when at anchor . . .'

Even the weather could conspire to cause the maximum discomfort
for the ship's crews: 'during the five weeks past (May to June) we
have had continually a high sea, dismal dark, and very cold days and
nights, being as raw a cold as in the Channel of England in
September', added Barbot.[45]

Prideaux's interest in the anchors of the *Daniel and Henry* seems
close to an obsession, but it was far from unhealthy. Many a ship off
the Guinea Coast lost one anchor after the other, and failing to sweep
successfully for them, was reduced to making inferior substitutes
from iron bars. Sweeping for the anchor cable was a time-consuming
and wearisome task. Prideaux's remark about weighing the anchor
every 24 hours is echoed by Barbot the elder:

> before I leave Accra, I must warn sailors to weigh their anchors in
> the road every two or three days, because the ground being full of
> rock stones the buoy ropes and the cables are apt to be cut about
> eight or nine foot from the anchor. Thus we lost a sheet anchor in
> that road; and many other ships before and after me, have had the
> same fortune. The fresh SW gales, which generally blow from
> morning to night, except in the rainy season, from May to
> September, cause the sea to swell high, and the tide setting eastward
> very rapid with the wind, ships work very hard on the cables, and
> render it very tedious and troublesome to get up the anchor in the
> day-time; which is much easier done in the night, the weather
> being calmer.[46]

Apart from anchors the problem facing Mathew and Prideaux was the dearth of slaves on offer. Up until 12 June they had managed to secure a paltry 86 in all the long stretch of the Guinea Coast from Cape Mesurado to Accra. Their first slave had been bought at Dixcove on 11 April, so their average 'haul' was barely more than one a day. This was desperately slow going. Both knew that the secret of a successful Guinea voyage lay in embarking and discharging slaves as quickly as possible. The longer slaves lay in the oven-like hold off the Guinea Coast – some had now lain there for two and a half months – the fewer would be delivered in Jamaica.

There was no point in heading back the way they had come, so Mathew shaped a course for Poinyon (Poni), Prampram and Ningro which lay at the extreme eastern end of the Gold Coast.

12 [June]. This day at 10 we weighed anchor for Alampo and at about 4 in the afternoon we came to anchor in the road of Alim. Here we found an English ship of London commanded by Mich. Mack For, about 14 guns, 90 tons or thereabouts; and to the eastward of us there was a Danish ship carrying about 700 negroes, having about 500 now on board, slaves being very scarce and mighty dear. We anchored in ten fathoms of water; hard sand.

At Alim, a few miles east of Accra, the twin problems facing Roger Mathew – lack of slaves and intense competition from experienced slave trade captains – were not alleviated. Off this tiny settlement lay the *Wormley Berry* and a large merchant ship belonging to the Danish West African Company, whose final destination was probably the Virgin Islands and which had taken aboard most of her slaves at the Danish castle of Christiansborg near Accra.

The *Wormley Berry*, a London frigate, was commanded by a Scotsman, Michael Macpherson. Freighted by merchant John Peck (probably related to Thomas Peck, the factor at the Company fort of Commenda who had a reputation for collusion with ten per centers), the vessel was on a parallel course to that of the *Daniel and Henry* and reached Jamaica shortly before her. Macpherson was an old hand at the Guinea trade, having previously commanded the Quaker ship *Society* with which the *Daniel and Henry* would fall in later on the voyage.[47]

There was little to be gained at Alim so the *Daniel and Henry* slipped her moorings and moved further east.

All between Accra & Alempo is low land by the sea side, but high in the country, with sand all along and very few rocks. We anchored at James Town & lay there 9 days. Then we weighed anchor & came down to Poinyon & I was in the longboat trading at Pampran & at Ningroe & bought 102 slaves. We lay at Poinyon till the 15th day of August & came off with 452 slaves, mostly women & girls, men being very scarce.

At last the *Daniel and Henry* had encountered a regular supply of slaves, though predominantly female and expensive. To speed the buying process Mathew and Prideaux split the operation in half: Roger Mathew bartered and dealt from the ship, Prideaux from closer inshore in the long-boat. This two-pronged tactic produced the required result: a total of 366 slaves were embarked in eight weeks, of whom Prideaux was responsible for 102. For nearly one of every two Africans consigned to the hold it was tantamount to the death sentence.

During the months of June, July and August, the lottery of life and death picked its winners and losers from among the white crew too. Three died from disease during this period – John Rudd, Richard Johnson and John Fort. Others were infected and some perished later on the voyage. John Fort, gunner of the *Daniel and Henry*, died on 27 June at Alampo. He was not a wealthy man and his son Nicholas took custody of the few possessions for his mother:

Inventory of John Fort's goods, deceased (*viz*):

Goods of Adventure
3 Perpetts.
3 Pieces of Serge between the Bosun and him; 18½ yards, 15½ yards, 10½ yards.

Money for goods sold
38 Ackeys of False and bad gold.
18½ Ackeys of indifferent good ditto.
―――
56½
2 Ackeys Given the Caboceers for burying him on shore.

Wearing Apparell
1 Watch Coat, 1 ditto, new.

1 pair Serge Britches and Vest, new.
1 pair Serge Britches, half worn.
1 Striped flaning* Waistcoat.
2 blue Sheets, 1 White ditto.
2 pair blue Drawers, 1 flaning Sheet.
1 Serge Vest, half Worn.
1 Blue bunter sash.
1 Old Coat, 2 old Canvas Jackoats.
1 pair old Cloth Britches.
1 Rumal† Handkerchief.
2 Worstard and 3 pair Yarn Stockings.
2 Old Wigs, 1 Fur and 1 Muffle Cap.
1 breast Cloth, 4 Knives.
1 New Ticking Bed.
1 Feather Pillow and Pillowbie.‡
1 horn Tinderbox, 1 Inkhorn.
1 Comb Case, 2 Combs with a Request Trinket in the case.
1 small Lateen§ Grater.
1 Marking Iron,⁴⁸ 2 Gimlets.
1 Old quilt for a bed.
1 hatt for which I must pay 6 shillings.
1 pair New and repaired Old Shoes.
1 Shag waistcoat.
1 ditto pair of Drawers.
1 pair of Silver Buckles gave his Son.
All of which goods &c it was desired his Son Nicholas Fort should have
   for the Use of his Mother.

What his Son hath had before Delivered of the whole
1 Muffle Cape.
1 Knife and Sheath.
The wyre and lead which was between the Bosun and him, his Son hath
   also.

What He Took up in England
Twenty Shillings from John Cole of Totnes for which he was to pay 7d.
   per pound per month.

Money he Owes
To wire from the Bosun: 4 shillings.
For money Doctor Hunt oweth him: 5 shillings.

---

* Flannel
† Silk or cotton square, probably worn as a neckerchief.
‡ Pillowcase
§ Brass. The grater was for spice, possibly nutmeg or pepper.

Men who died at sea usually had their possessions auctioned before the mainmast; the revenue was then handed to the closest surviving relative ashore at the conclusion of the voyage.

The *Daniel and Henry* had now loaded 452 slaves. Since she was of approximately 200 tons burden, the overcrowding was severe even by contemporary standards. In addition forty of the original ship's Company were alive, if not well. At least six slaves were being carried as private ventures by the senior officers. So almost 500 souls packed the *Daniel and Henry* when she set sail from Alampo for the island of São Tomé, though some of the slaves taken aboard in April would already have perished.

Whilst the departure from Alampo was an unmitigated disaster for the slaves, who now recognised their hopes for freedom were fading by the minute, the white crew could allow themselves a sigh of relief. The hardest part of the trip was over, and their fate no longer lay in the hands of men but in the dispensation of the Almighty. They returned to the familiar tasks of manning the ship.

After the fever-ridden Guinea Coast the island of São Tomé, just over a week's sail away to the south-east, must have seemed like paradise or a latter-day Land of Cockayne. Unlike the flat coastline of Guinea, São Tomé was crowned by a lofty peak, heavily wooded at its base, and mantled with snow for most of the year. The vegetation was densely abundant and on its heavy, mist-laden equatorial breezes was wafted the sweet perfume of thousands of lemon trees growing wild in the valleys and hillsides. Fruit and vegetables grew to profusion on its well-watered rich volcanic soil. These were not exclusively African in origin: some had been brought from Brazil, others from Europe, and there were grapes, pineapples and sweet potato in abundance. Nor was meat a problem, for the island was liberally endowed with cattle, pigs and goats plus an assortment of fowl – turkey, goose, duck and partridge – that doubtless provided a feast for the eyes as much as it did for the stomach. Tropical birds such as scarlet-headed parrots fluttered amongst the lofty trees, and the waters around the *Daniel and Henry* swarmed with a vast array of edible fish.[49] The crew of the ship were far from unimpressed by São Tomé and one of them – William Hodge – saw no reason why he should give up this heaven on earth and jumped ship just before she sailed. Doubtless the dark beauty of the mulatto Portuguese *senhoritas* helped him to this decision, and it was not an irrevocable one. Many English slave ships were to call at São Tomé over the ensuing years with crews depleted by death and disease, and they would be happy to sign him on should he yearn once again for England.

Despite being only a relatively small island, São Tomé was easy to locate. The favourable Guinea current which had pushed the *Daniel and Henry* along the coast in an easterly direction swung south off Whydah and conveniently swept them to São Tomé. This was one reason the island attracted large numbers of slave trade vessels from the Gold Coast, Slave Coast (Nigeria), Old and New Calabar (Cameroons) and Angola. It functioned as a springboard for the middle passage to the West Indies, the English American colonies, the Spanish American colonies and Portugal's huge possession on the South American continent, Brazil. The traffic in this maritime 'bottleneck' in 1700 was intense. John Lorenz, Governor of São Tomé, informed the Danish Company in that year that the mortality on the vessels of the Dutch interlopers and English traders was particularly high. By the time they reached São Tomé some had little more than a third or a quarter of their original slave complement.[50]

 August 15. We sailed from Alampo for Sao Tome where we anchored to the northern part of the island there being a town in a bay to the north of us. Off the northern point is an island laying about a cable's length off the high land with a small neck which extends out to the Island. When at anchor, that island bore off us west, having 16 fathom of water & hard sand; the point to the south of us bears E½S, being a very good place to stop a tide, [i.e. while the tide is against you]. At the little town is very good watering & coconuts enough, and corn & wood, plantins & mananoes.

We came to Sao Tome on the 24th & found a Dutch Indian ship[51] which lost its passage laying at Sao Tome town where there is a castle. There is also to the N of Sao Tome town an island, about a mile offshore which is called Ann de Chares. The ruin which is at the town is called Ruin de Chares.

Prevented from anchoring straight away in São Tomé road by the volume of other shipping present, Walter Prideaux took the opportunity to see something of the island. It was one of the oldest colonial sugar plantations, for blacks had been shipped there by the Portuguese since the mid-sixteenth century. After the frenetic trading of the last eight weeks on the Guinea Coast, Prideaux obviously had time enough to write a long description:

There is also an island at the Southernmost part of Sao Tome called Isle of Roses; it lieth about a mile off the Southern point, there being 20 fathom of water between the shore & it. Between the town and this island are 9 small rocks or islands which they call the cabberrutoes. The island of Sao Tome is very good for provisions: I say water, wood, corn, plantains, coconuts, yams, ferrenoe[52] and other refreshments for your Negroes. About 2 miles to the south of Ile de Chares is a shoal which is from 5 to 2½ fathoms: we anchored on the southern shoal, the isle bearing NW & the castle S by W, and had 5 fathoms. It has very good sand, no rocks. You may sail between the Ile de Chares & the shore; but there's nothing got for you must haul to the eastward for the above shoal. The island is very bold all round.

The 27th we came to anchor in Sao Tome road in 3 fathom water having the castle SSE & the northern point NNW, the island being north about a league & a half off us. It's a very good road. You must keep the castle South shore till come in 3 fathom; when you come within the castle you must luff up & come to anchor. The watering is at the town. This day died James More of the smallpox, having been down 11 days.

Though justly famous for its good water, care had to be taken when filling the ship's casks. Night was the best time since the source was polluted during the day by men and beasts washing in it and 'throwing in all sorts of Filth'.[53]

Among the vessels riding at anchor in São Tomé was that apparent contradiction in terms, a Quaker slave ship. The *Society* was a square-sterned ship of 100 tons burden and 4 guns and had probably loaded some 250 slaves. Conditions aboard must have beggared belief. When Monk eventually made landfall at Barbados in November the total number of slaves delivered amounted to just twenty-two. John Grove, the receiving agent, 'would give no account of the sales, being a Quaker'.[54]

We found in the road the *Society* of London, Captain Edward Monk having been there a day and wants seven weeks from Old Calabar. Bound for Barbadoes, he has had 140 negroes die. He says that the *Elizabeth Galley* of Bristol, was lost at Calabar by letting fall the anchor on a shoal, & running atop of it – it went through the bilge & she sunk.

We have bought 10,000 ears of corn at 2½ dollars per [1,000?]; coconuts, a dollar per anker; yams, 2½ dollars, per anker; wood, 5 dollars per boat.[55]

Captain Monk seems to have been something of a Jonah, and brought nothing but bad tidings. His reference to the *Elizabeth Galley* was not gratuitous. She had been freighted by Daniel Ivy's son-in-law, the Bideford tobacco merchant John Parminter, and had cleared her home port of Bristol under William Levercombe in January. Captain Levercombe was no stranger to African waters. In 1698 he had commanded the Bristol ship *Beginning*, which made a successful slaving expedition in tandem with the *Betty Galley* of Exeter, and Daniel Ivy may well have recommended him to his son-in-law for the present voyage. Levercombe should have known better than to court disaster by anchoring in shallow water close to the notorious bar across the harbour mouth at Old Calabar – presumably while waiting for the tide to rise and carry her across – and then stoving in the vessel upon the anchor. The inrush of water would have been so sudden that the slaves packed below decks would have stood no chance of surviving. There but for the grace of God went the *Daniel and Henry*; Walter Prideaux's heartfelt prayers on making a safe landfall were not empty ritual.

Nevertheless, food for thought would not keep body and soul together, and his attention quickly turned to sustenance of a more practical value. Though provisions were abundant, victualling was not cheap at São Tomé. Few ships could afford to ignore the island's facilities, for slave ships consumed an astonishing quantity of food in the 8–10 weeks of the middle passage. More to the point, there was no equivalent source for provisioning between Africa and America. Slaves were generally messed twice a day. The first meal would be of large boiled horse beans with lard. The second of peas or maize with desiccated manioc, boiled with lard or suet or grease by turns.[56] Not surprisingly, the slaves loathed this food, especially the horse beans. Maize, manioc and yams, however, tended to rot and putrefy on a long sea voyage. Sometimes fish leavened the diet. In 1714 an anonymous writer recorded we caught sharks which were salted and preserved for the negroes. They eat this fish with much greediness. We brought horse beans and pease from England, but most of them were spoiled, the Negroes not caring for them.[57]

Shark meat was easy to come by; packs of sharks dogged the progress of every slave ship and fed upon the discarded bodies. Sometimes a dead Negro was dragged behind the vessel as bait.

As well as exorbitant food prices at São Tomé there were hidden service charges. In 1699 James Barbot, supercargo of the *Albion*, noted a payment of 41 ackeys (£9 16s. 8d.) to the Governor for anchorage; 10 ackeys (£2 8s. od.) to Raphael Lewis, principal contractor for provisions, and sundry other charges for porterage and carriage.[58] Care had to be taken not to offend the Governor or any of his officials. William Moses, captain of HMS *Milford*, assigned to protect English interests against pirates on the Guinea Coast in the latter half of 1700, crossed swords ill-advisedly with the Governor of the adjacent island of Principe. He had entered the harbour to replenish his water casks, but did so with such lack of courtesy that the Governor imagined Moses was a renegade slave trader seeking to raid the island's plantations. Despite Moses' commission and those of his officers, the whole command was incarcerated in the island's fortress and threatened with immediate deportation to Brazil.[59] No doubt Walter Prideaux and Roger Mathew's approach to the Governor of São Tomé had been far more conciliatory.

The first stage of the journey was now over. Walter Prideaux jotted down a few navigational remarks before he closed his account of the voyage from Dartmouth:

To the southern part of the Island of Sao Tome are three small islands which are called the Rowlers: you will not see these islands except if you go to the southward of the Island, where they lay all three almost north & south about ½ mile distant from each other & as much from the Island.

From Fernando Po to Prince, Sao Tome & Annabona the course is nearest NNE & SSW. Distance I say from Fernando Po to Annabona is 100 leagues, but the various setting of the current which no man can give account by reason that in sailing 5 or 10 leagues the current alters a point or two – sometimes more – but we generally observe that when the full and change[60] we have a windward current & a great sea all the coast over, I say from Cape Palmas to Alampo, having had experience of that myself in the aforementioned ship, the year afore.

Written by me
Walter Prideaux

Never again, should he live to be a hundred, would Prideaux experience such an intense six months. In comparison the impending voyage from São Tomé to Jamaica was a mere formality. Or was it? God would decide. In the mean time Prideaux took advantage of the cool Atlantic breezes to detail the trading that had ensued off the Guinea Coast. Though the *Daniel and Henry* was now a travesty of the spruce merchantman that had left Dartmouth only six months before, at least her accounts could be shipshape.

CHAPTER TEN

The Financial Reckoning

A LTHOUGH most of the commodities bought (slaves, pepper, redwood, ivory and gold) and services received on the West African coast could be set against goods (manufactured items carried as cargo), several currencies held sway on the Guinea Coast. These included reckoning in terms of bars of iron and strings of cowrie shells. Since neither of these methods would endear the factors of the various forts nor the captains of Company ships to their auditors in London, an anonymous currency, gold based, came into being.

This West African currency (which was also utilised by the Dutch and other European slave trading countries) was never coined or minted and when distributed then done so by weight and measure, closely reflecting its barter ancestry. It was predominantly for European traders an occasional currency of account. For European companies, however, like the Royal African Company, whose operations were on a much larger scale, and in whose factories manufactured goods could sit for a number of years, this intermediate currency of account was of vital importance.

Accordingly the sterling value of all Company goods from England (as well as the outgoings of the forts such as salaries, allowances and expenses for entertainment) was translated into this localised currency of marks, ounces, ackeys and tackeys.[1]

As an example, Company records reveal that Nicholas Buckeridge of the Cape Coast Castle was allowed an annual salary in 1700 of 4 marks 7 ounces 7 ackeys and 7 tackeys which, in addition to the £50 advance payable in England, made a total of £200.

Table 10.1 is relatively accurate for the period 1690–1710. Inflation grew slowly on the Guinea Coast: by 1730 an ounce of gold was worth £4, an increase of only 4 shillings in thirty years.

Table 10.1   Comparative currencies (1700)

Guinea Coast	Sterling
1 tackey	4¾d.
12 tackeys = 1 ackey	4s. 9d.
16 ackeys = 1 ounce	£3 16s. 0d.
8 ounces = 1 mark	£30 8s. 0d.

By the end of the seventeenth century, European weights were commonly used by the Akan, since they had been imported in large numbers for sale by European traders, and the currency achieved the following equivalents in gold:

$$1 \text{ ackey} = 1.9 \text{ grams}$$
$$1 \text{ ounce} = 31.1 \text{ grams}$$
$$1 \text{ mark} = 248.8 \text{ grams}$$

Unlike the Royal African Company, private traders such as the *Daniel and Henry*, whose operations were on a comparatively minute scale, made only marginal use of this monetary system. They could account for goods exchanged for slaves as transactions took place. But when trading for gold, the system came into its own as when, in an attempt to compensate for the poor slave trading opportunities experienced in the opening days of the *Daniel and Henry*'s sojourn on the Guinea Coast, Roger Mathew and Walter Prideaux turned to gold.

Ironically, most of their dealings for this precious metal took place at Dixcove – the 'fake Mint' of the Coast. They would not have expected to return to England with this gold, but purchased it with an eye to bartering it for slaves further along the Coast where they knew the caboceers valued gold above all other goods for exchange. The details of Walter Prideaux's log-book have thus far only hinted at this trade for gold (notably in John Fort's inventory) and the following account of goods exchanged for gold derives from the account book of John and Henry Burwell, probably ship's husbands to the *Daniel and Henry*.[2]

Account of Goods exchanged for Gold on the Coast of
Guinea, 1700

		Ackeys	Tackeys
10 April at Axim:	4 Looking glasses	1	
	3 bars of lead		3

11 April at Dixcove:	6 small knives	6
	1 dozen knives	1
12 ditto	17 looking glasses and 2	
	knives	5
	2 bars of lead	2
13 ditto	1 nest of trunks	8
	1 firkin of tallow	4
14 ditto	80 bars of iron & 1 sheet	128
	10 dozen knives	10
15 ditto	43 dozen knives	45
	3 sheets	3
	19 dozen knives	19
	5 firkins of tallow	20
	1 half case of spirits	2
	1 lead bar	1
17 Ditto	2 half cases spirits	4
	6 doz great knives	6
	2 firkins of tallow	8
	1 firkin of tallow & 1 small	
	glass	4
	4 sheets	4
(At Dixcove also gave 4 ackeys of gold for 2 chests of corn)		
9 May at Commenda:	1 looking glass	4
	2 whole & 1 half case spirits	10
	1 dozen great knives & 1	
	looking glass	1
	1 half case spirits	2
	2 whole cases spirits	8
	10 looking glasses	2
	2 firkins of powder	4

– END OF GOODS EXCHANGED FOR GOLD –

Trading for slaves took place from the ship and from the long-boat. Roger Mathew was in charge of the ship-based trade, Walter Prideaux of the long-boat trade. Roger Mathew originally indicated the proportion of gold included in his transactions with the cryptic term 'for parte', whereas Walter Prideaux openly stated when gold formed part of his bartering process.

In the following account from the log-book of the *Daniel and Henry* relevant data concerning the part-exchange of gold for slaves has been incorporated from Burwell's account book. This source has been identified with an asterisked bracket and refers only to the gold element involved in each of Captain Mathew's transactions.

ACCOUNT of what goods were put off for slaves on the coast of Guinea for account of Messrs Ivey, Arthur & Gould, merchants in Exon and London, on board their ship *Daniel and Henry* for their account and risk and bound for Jamaica.[3]

		Men	Women	Boys	Girls
1700					
April 11 To:	3 pieces perpetuannas, 4 sheets & 2 small knives	1			
Dicky Cove	(Gave 32 Ackeys of Gold, 28A of Gold & 32A of Gold for)* . . .	3			
18 To:	2 half barrels of powder & one small looking glass		1		
May 1 To:	2 whole cases of spirits (& paid 24A Gold)*	1			
Commenda 6 To:	48 dozen large knives, 39 sheets & 8 half cases of spirits		3		1
To:	64 sheets, 1 firkin of tallow, 2 perpetuannas (& 1A of Gold)* .		3	1	1
To:	33 sheets, 3 perpetuannas, 6 large knives (& 43A Gold)*	2			
Annamabo 9 To:	1 sea, 1 perpetuanna, 1 firkin of tallow, 4 × 3lb basins & 2 tankards	1			
10 To:	2 seas & 4 × 3lb basins	1			
11 To:	1 sea & 2 perpetuana	1			
12 To:	1 sea & 3 firkins of tallow		1		
13	(Gave 22 Ackeys of Gold for)*			1	
14 To:	2 firkins of tallow (& 16 Ackeys of gold)*		1		
To:	6 half cases of spirits, 6 perpetuannas & 6 looking glasses	2			
15 To:	2 firkins of tallow (& 38 Ackeys of gold)*		2		
Aponferra To:	7 darnicks				1
16 To:	3 firkins of tallow & 36 sheets .	1		1	
T:C:Querry					
17 To:	16 sheets, 4 seas, 1 half case of spirits, 2 tankards, 1 firkin of powder[4]	1	2		
	The sum carried to the other side is	14	13	3	3

	Men	Women	Boys	Girls
To the sum brought over	14	13	3	3
To: 1 half barrel of powder, 1 firkin of tallow (& 8 Ackeys of gold)*		1		
To: 5 whole cases of spirits, 3 half ditto (& 48 Ackeys of gold)*	1	1	1	
To: 24 sheets for		1		
18 To: 2 whole & 3 half cases of spirits (& 1 Ackey of Gold)*				1
20 To: 1 firkin of tallow, 2 whole barrels of powder, 4 firkins ditto [powder] & 6 sheets	2			
To: 2 sheets (& 24 Ackeys of Gold)*	1			
To: 1 fuzee, 6 large knives, 1 firkin of tallow, 1 whole case of spirits, (& 12 Ackeys of gold)*	1			
To: 1 barrel of powder & 6 dozen large knives	1			
To: 7 firkins of tallow & 1 darnick	1			
22 To: 1 nehallaware (& 1 Ackey of Gold)*		1		
Winnabey To: 1 barrel of powder (& 4 Ackeys of gold)*	1			
23 To: 32 sheets, 7 firkins of tallow & 28 dozen large knives	2	1		
24 To: 1 firkin of tallow, 1 barrel of powder & 1 × 3lb basins	1			
25 To: 1 darnick (& 32 Ackeys of gold)*	1		1	
26 To: 2 dozen large knives (& 17 Ackeys of gold)*			1	
To: 2 dozen ditto (& 24 Ackeys of gold)*		1		
To: 5 nehallawares & 3 dozen large knives		2		
(Gave 26 Ackeys for a young man)*			1	
To: 12 dozen small knives, 2 tankards, 2 dozen great knives & 2 firkins of tallow (and 25 Ackeys of gold)*	1			
The sum carried to the other side is	27	21	7	4

		Men	Women	Boys	Girls
	To the sum brought over	27	21	7	4
	To: 3 barrels of powder & 1 dozen great knives	3			
27	To: 2 darnicks, 2 firkins of tallow, 32 dozen great knives		2		
	To: 5 firkins of tallow, 2 × 3lb basins & 2 tankards		1		
28	To: 1 barrel of powder & 2 tankards for	1			
29	To: 2 firkins of tallow, 1 perpetuanna & 8 dozen great knives & 1 tankard		1		
	To: 13 dozen great knives & 4 firkins of tallow for		1		
	To: 1 barrel of powder for	1			
30	To: 1 barrel of powder & 2 dozen great knives for		1		
31	To: 2 barrels of powder for			2	
June 1	To: 1 barrel of powder & 1 firkin of tallow for	1			
	To: 18 iron bars & 1 dozen great knives for	1			
4	To: 26 dozen great knives & 1 barrel of powder for	1	1		
	To: 2 pieces of Nehallawares & 4 dozen great knives		1		
	To: 21 iron bars & 2 firkins of tallow for	1			1
6	To: 3 fuzees, 4 sheets, 1 perpetuana & 6 iron bars	1	1		
	To: 1 firkin of tallow, 15 sheets, 6 dozen small knives & 1 tankard		1		
Accra 10	To: 1 barrel of powder		1		
	To: 2 pieces of nehallawares & 8 looking glasses		1		
	To: 3 perpetuannas, 10 looking glasses & 3 × 1lb basins	1			
11	To: 2 fuzees, 1 × 3lb basin, 1 tankard & 8 looking glasses		1		
	The sum carried to the other side is	38	34	9	5

	Men	Women	Boys	Girls
To the sum brought over	38	34	9	5
Alampo 13 To: 4 tapseils, 1 blue sea, 9 × 2lb basins & 1 hanger	1	1		
To: 1 sea & 8 × 3lb basins, 1 tapseil & 6 darnicks		1		1
To: 2 perpetuannas & 16 sheets, 1 perpetuanna, 8 sheets, 1 tapseil & 9 darnicks		2		2
14 To: 2 tapseils & 12 sheets	1			
15 To: 24 × 1lb & 7 × 3lb basins & 1 nickanee		1		
To: 1 sea & 1 piece Nehallawares, 14 carpets, 8 tankards & 16 sheets	1	2		
To: 22 sheets, 11 darnicks or carpets for		1		1
16 To: 9 × 1lb, 1 × 3lb basins, 2 perpetuannas, 21 tankards & 1 tapseil	1	1		
To: 1 nehallaware, 2 × 3lb & 12 × 2lb basins & 3 perpetuanna		2		
17 To: 8 tankards, 3 iron bars, 2 perpetuannas, 8 sheets & 1 darnick	1			1
To: 11 darnicks, 2 tapseils, 2 tankards & 1 nickanee		1	1	
18 To: 4 pieces of nehallaware, 4 × 3lb basins, 11 sheets, 4 darnicks & 3 looking glasses		2		1
To: 2 seas, 2 tapseils & 7 sheets	1	1		
To: 1 half barrel of powder, 2 × 3lb basins & 3 looking glasses				1
19 To: 1 sea & 19 tankards & 1 case of spirits, 1 sea & 6 tankards		2		1
To: 12 looking glasses, 6 tankards, 4 darnicks, 8 × 3lb & 3 × 2lb basins, 1 case spirits		1		1
June 20 To: 6 carbines, 1 hanger, 28 sheets, 2 brass pans, 1 sea & 8 tankards	2	1		
The sum carried to the other side is	46	53	10	14

		Men	Women	Boys	Girls
	To the sum brought over	46	53	10	14
	To: 16 × 3lb basins, 8 tankards, 4 darnicks, 1 case of spirits & ½ barrel of powder		2		
	To: 3 salem powers, 11 × 3lb basins, 2 tapseils, 2 darnicks & 1 tankard .	1	1		
	To: 4 firkins of powder, 1 tankard, 1 sea & 9 × 3lb basins		1		1
	To: 9 × 2lb basins, 2 tankards, ½ barrel of powder, 2 half cases of spirits		1		
21	To: 4 perpetuannas, 12 × 2lb basins, 2 tankards & 1 half case of spirits .	1		1	
	To: 1 barrel of powder, 3 × 3lb basins, 1 tankard, 2 brass pans, 1 sea & 1 tapseil	1	1		
22	To: 1 sea, 8 tankards, 2 perpetuannas, 3 × 2lb basins, & 3 looking glasses		2		
	To: 12 iron bars, 7 × 3lb basins, 4 tapseils, 1 perpetuanna, 1 darnick, a brawle, 8 tankards .	2	1		
	To: 1 tapseil, 1 double brawle, 1 salem power & 5 tankards	1			
	To: 1 darnick, 3 firkins of powder, 10 × 3lb basins & 1 tankard . . .			1	1
23	To: 7 whole cases of spirits & 1 tankard for pte a man & 1 sea .	1			1
27	To: 6 perpetuannas, of the owner's servants for 2 women at 8A per piece		2		
	To: 1 barrel of powder, 1 sea, 9 × 2lb basins & 2 tankards		2		
	To: 1 sea, 1 whole case of spirits, 1 × 3lb basin & 2 tankards		1		
28	To: 2 brass pans, 3 × 2lb & 2 × 3lb basins, 60 rangoes & 1 tankard per pte		1		
	To: 1 sea, 17 × 3lb basins, 60 rangoes, 6 × 2lb basins & 2 tankards .		1		1
	The sum carried to the other side is	53	69	12	18

				Men	Women	Boys	Girls
		To the sum brought over		53	69	12	18
29	To:	2 seas, 2 darnicks, 15 × 2lb basins, 1 tankard, 30 rangoes			2		
	To:	16 darnicks, 1 × 3lb basin, 30 rangoes, 1 perpetuanna, & 1 case of spirits			1	1	
30	To:	3 tankards, 210 rangoes for pte	.	1	1		
	To:	5 firkins of powder				1	
July 1	To:	2 seas, 6 tankards & a nest of trunks – 8				1	2
	To:	24 brass pans, 6 carbines & 4 nickanees		1	2		
2	To:	1 perpetuanna, 13 brass pans, ½ barrel of powder & 60 rangoes .					2
	To:	1 sea, 32 tankards, 5 cases of spirits, 1 darnick & 3 firkins of powder			3		1
3	To:	3 perpetuannas, 1 darnick, 6 × 2lb basins & 8 tankards			1		1
5	To:	24 brass pans, 8 tankards, 1 sea, 4 × 4lb & 2 × 3lb basins . . .		1	1		
	To:	4 firkins of powder, 4 darnicks, 2 tankards & 3 × 2lb basins . . .			1		
	To:	2 perpetuannas 60 rangoes, & 4 darnicks		1			
	To:	4 darnicks, 2 tankards, 3 × 2lb basins, 2 brass pans & 60 rangoes					1
6	To:	3 perpetuannas, 8A per piece . . .			1		
9	To:	10 papar'd slesia, 18 brass pans, 2 ounces of currell, 2 darnicks, 30 rangoes & 2lb beads			2		
10	To:	1 sea, 3 tankards, 1 darnick, & 3lb of beads			1		
11	To:	2 seas, 1 tankard, 9 carbines, & 12 brass pans		1	2		
	To:	1 barrel of powder, 3 darnicks, 4lb beads & 3 perpetuannas		1	1		
12	To:	4 darnicks, 12 iron bars, 120 rangoes & 20 brass pans . . .		1	1		1
		The sum carried to the other side is		60	89	15	26

	Men	Women	Boys	Girls
To the sum brought over	60	89	15	26
To: 2 perpetuannas, 4 single brawles, 1 brass pan, 2 seas, 3 darnicks & 1 carbine		3		
July 14 To: 3 darnicks				1
15 To: 1 sea, 1 carbine, 1 darnick, 8 firkins of powder . . . . . . ′. . .		1	1	
To: 4 carbines, 1 carpet & 1 single brawle				1
16 To: 1 sea, 1 carbine, 2 papar'd slessia, 1 barrel of powder	1	1		
To: 27 brass pans, 1 ounce currell, 600 flints	1			
To: 60 rangoes, 1 single brawle, 1 papar'd slessia, & 12 iron bars .		1		1
17 To: 8 brass pans, 6 carbines, 26 × 4lb basins, 30 rangoes	1	3		
19 To: 26 × 4lb basins, 2 seas, 1 barrel of powder & 30 rangoes	1	3		
To: 21 × 4lb basins, 1lb beads, 25 brass pans	1	1		
To: 2 barrels of powder, 1 sea & 2 firkins of powder	1			2
20 To: 3 barrels of powder, 17 brass pans, 2 carbines, & 1 sea	1	4		
21 To: 1 sea, 3 iron bars, 30 rangoes, 2 fuzees & 3 barrels of powder .	1	4		
To: 5 × 4 basins 1lb beads, & a nest of trunks – 8		2		
22 To: 1 barrel of powder, 1 ounce currell, 60 rangoes, 2 × 4lb basins, 31 brass pans & 1lb beads	1	1		
24 To: 24 × 4lb basins, 12lb beads, 180 rangoes		2		
To: 1 sea, 3 Guinea stuffs, 4 brass pans & 12 fuzees	3	1		
To: 9 papar'd slessia, 3 Guinea stuffs, 2 seas, 14 brass pans & 2 × 4lb basins		1		2
The sum carried to the other side is	72	117	16	33

	Men	Women	Boys	Girls
To the sum brought over	72	117	16	33
25 To: 2 fuzees, 9 brass pans, 4 firkins of powder, 3 papar'd slessia . . .		2		
To: 2 barrels of powder, 3 fuzees, 2 salem powers, 1 brass pan, 1 piece of ticking & 21 single brawles	1	4		
27 To: 11 fuzees, 1 barrel of powder, 8 × 4lb basins, 4 papar'd slessia & 4lb beads	2	3		
To: 4 Guinea stuffs, 13 single brawles, 25lb beads		1	1	
28 To: 6 fuzees, 960 rangoes, 2 sea, 4 single brawles & 60 rangoes .		5		
To: 11 papar'd slessia, 60 rangoes & 4 perpetuannas		2		
29 To: 16 single brawles, 20 firkins of powder, 1 sea & 4 perpetuannas .	1	3		
To: 1 sea, 16 papar'd slessia & 25 ounces of currell	1	2	1	
30 To: 27 brass pans, 22 firkins of powder, 3 fuzees, 2 single brawles & 30 rangoes		4		
31 To: 4 seas, 22 papar'd slessia, 4 single brawles & 60 rangoes	1	4		
August 2 To: 28 Guinea stuffs	1	1		
To: 12 brass pans, 1 fuzee & 3 Guinea stuffs		1		
To: 1 sea, 12 firkins of powder, 1 Guinea stuff & 60 rangoes . . .		2		
To: 2 seas, 8 firkins of powder & 1 Guinea stuff	1	1		
3 To: 12 Guinea stuffs & 360 rangoes .		1		1
The sum carried to the other side	80	153	18	34

Here the existing details of goods exchanged from the ship come to a premature end. To this date, 3 August 1700, the *Daniel and Henry* had taken on board a total of 387 slaves: 102 of these had come from Walter Prideaux's endeavours in trading from the long-boat, and this account is detailed in the following pages.

ACCOUNT of goods put off for slaves in the ship *Daniel & Henry's* longboat by Walter Prideaux on the coast of Guinea for account of Messrs Daniel Ivy & Company. It is as follows:

	Men	Women	Boys	Girls
June 14 at Poinyon To: 1 Barrel gunpowder & 7 firkins ditto, 10 × 1lb basins, 4 tapseils	1	2		
To: 8 sheets, 1 tapseil, 1 sea & 16 × 3lb basins		2		
To: 9 × 2lb basins, 1 tapseil & 12 × 1lb basins		1		
17 To: 1 sea, 2 perpetuannas & 1 tankard		1		
To: 1 sea				1
18 To: 3 pairs double brawls & 1 tankard		1		
To: 1 sea & 8 × 3lb basins		1		
To: 9 firkins gunpowder, 3 tapseils & 1 salem powder	1	1		
To: 3 tapseils, 2 salem powders, 1 Nehallaware, 2 hangers, 1 sheet & 1 × 3lb basin	1	1		
To: 14 × 2lb basins, 3 × 3lb ditto				1
To: 1 hanger, 8 looking glasses, 1 tankard & 1 sea		1		
21 To: 3 blue baffts		1		
To: 3 tapseils & 1 blue bafft	1			
To: 3 × 4lb basins, 4 × 3lb & 3 × 2lb ditto & 2 Ackeyes money			1	
To: 6 × 4lb basins, 6 × 3lb, 6 × 2lb & 6 × 1lb basins		1		
To: 2 blue baffts, 1 whole & 1½ case of spirits		1		
22 To: 3 tapseils & 1 blue bafft	1			
To: 3 blue baffts		1		
To: 1 sea & 8 sheets		1		
To: 3 blue baffts		1		
To: 1 Nickanee & 5 blue baffts		2		
24 To: 3 tapseils & 8 tankards	1			
To: 3 double brawles & 1 sheet		1		
To: 2 Nehallawares & 5 sheets		1		

The sum carried to the other side is   6   21   1   2

	Men	Women	Boys	Girls
To the sum brought over	6	21	1	2

		Men	Women	Boys	Girls
	To: 1 sea, 22 small knives, 18 great ditto, 10 × 1lb basins & 2 Ackeyes in money .	1			
	To: 2 double brawles, 4 × 3lb basins & 4 tankards		1		
	To: 7 carbines & 1 cutlass	1			
	To: 1 × 1lb basin & 1 half case of spirits given away[5]		-----		
25	To: 3 whole & 2 half cases of spirits, 3 × 4lb & 2 × 3lb basins		1		
	To: 5 nickanees & 2A in money	1			
	To: 6 carbines for	1			
	To: 2 carbines, 2 × 2lb basins & 1 ackey in money				1
	To: 5 carbines & 1 × 3lb basin		1		
	To: 6 tankards & 24 sheets	1			
	To: 2 blue baffts, 2 Nehallaware, 3 sall. powders & 3 × 2lb basins		2		
	To: 5 looking glasses given away				
28	To: 2 double brawls 3 × 4lb & 4 × 3lb basins		1		
	To: 10 small brasspans, 7 × 3lb & 9 × 4lb basins		1		
	To: 10 × 3lb & 9 × 2lb basins				1
	To: 3 salem powders & 2 nickanees	1			
	To: 15oz currell & 1 carbine	1			
	To: 3 salem powders, 9 looking glasses & 6 × 2lb basins		1		
	To: 2 double brawls, 1 whole case of spirits, 2 carpets & 3 × 1lb basins		1		
30	To: 2 perpetuannas, 8 sheets, 6 tankards & 1A in money	1			
	To: 4 nickanees		1		
July 2	To: 2 seas	1			
	To: 1 sea & 1 Nehall ware		1		
	To: 1 sea, 1 whole case of spirits & 1 tankard		1		
	To: 1 sea, 6 × 2lb basins & 3 tankards & 2A in money		1		
	To: 8 carpets & 6 tankards		1		
The sum carried to the other side is	14	36	2	3

		Men	Women	Boys	Girls
	To the sum brought over	14	36	2	3
	To: 5 Salem powders	1			
	1 sea & 6 tankards		1		
	To: 7 × 3lb, 15 × 2lb, 7 × 1lb basins & 2 tankards		1		
	To: 2 double brawls, 1 salem powder & 1 tankard		1		
5	To: 1 sea & 8 tankards		1		
	To: 11 Darnicks or carpets		1		
	To: 11 ditto		1		
	To: 2 whole cases of spirits, 10 × 2lb basins & 4 darnicks		1		
9	To: 1 sea & 4 × 4lb basins & 1A in money		1		
	To: 3 double brawls, 5 × 4lb & 1 × 1lb basin	1			
	To: 2 seas	1			
	To: 1 sea & 4 carbines	1			
	To: 6 carbines		1		
	To: 18 brass pans & 3 carpets	1			
	To; 1 sea & 6A in money		1		
	To: 9 carpets & 3 × 4lb basins		1		
	To: 9 carbines, 6 tankards & 6A in money .	1			1
July 12	To: 2 seas	1			
	To: 8 carbines	1			
	To: 5 carbines, 1 carpet, & 1A in money .		1		
14	To: 1 sea, 2 carpets & 1 carbine		1		
	To: 1 barrel powder		1		
15	To: 2 salem powers, 3 carpets & 6 tankards .		1		
	To: 1 sea, 4 sheets & 2 carpets		1		
17	To: 3 salem powers, 3 × 4lb basins & 1 carpet		1		
	To: 1 sea, 1 carpet, 8 brass pans		1		
	Sold: 2 nest of trunks & 4 ankers[6] . . .				
18	To: 1 sea, 1 carpet, 3 × 4lb & 6 × 1lb basins .		1		
19	To: 1 Tapseil, 1 Neh'll ware & 14A in money	1			
	To: 1 barrel of powder		1		
	To: 2 seas & 1 × 1lb basin	1			
	To: 17 × 4lb basins, 2 × 1lb ditto		1		
20	To: a barrel of powder		1		
	The sum carried to the other side is	24	58	2	4

			Men	Women	Boys	Girls
	To the sum brought over		24	58	2	4
	To:	6 × 1lb, 3 × 4lb basins, 2 firkins powder & 2 small knives		I		
21	To:	1 sea				I
	To:	1 barrel of powder		I		
	To:	2 seas, 9 × 4lb, 3 × 1lb basins, 2 sheets & 1 tankard		2		
	To:	2 seas	I			
22	To:	1 sea, 3 × 4lb, 10 × 1lb basins		I		
	To:	4 salem powers		I		
	To:	1 sea, 6 × 4lb basins		I		
	To:	4 salem powers		I		
	To:	1 sea for				I
	To:	3 perpetuannas		I		
	To:	A man & a woman who we had from the king's son per acct	I	I		
			26	67	3	6

26 Men
67 Women
 3 Boys
 6 Girls
───
102

Purchased with the aforesaid goods &
put on board the ship *Daniel & Henry*
for the owners account and bound by
God's permission for Jamaica, which
God preserve.

1700 To: The King's son of Prampram

	Dr	Per Contra	Cr
July 2 To: 2 sheets for a canoe to send on board	2A	Pr: a woman slave which sent on board	24A
To: 2 whole & 1 half case of spirits . . .	10A	Pr: a man which I took from Coffee being the last canoe which came on board, otherwise should have lost[7]	32A
To: 5 carbines to himself	20A		
To: 1 fuzee	10A		
To: 1 carpet for bringing my canoe	2A		

To:	12 strings of rangoes	4A
To:	12 small knives . .	1A
To:	money a black owes us of the same town	4A
To:	brandy, beer & provisions which they took in the canoe	3A
		56A 56A

The unusual nature of this last account is highlighted by its being assigned to a separate page in the original log-book, and serves to illustrate the pitfalls that faced the unwary trader on the Guinea Coast. Customarily traders sought the protection of local chiefs to whom they made presents – the *dashee* or *bizzy*. They could then either offer goods on credit and take an agreed pawn or hostage to be redeemed when the slaves embarked, or wait for trade to arrive. (Goods on credit was a practice that extended right up to the slave source in the African hinterland, and across to the West Indies, where plantation owners' letters of credit were often an integral part of the slave-buying pattern.)[8]

Here at Prampram there seems to have been confusion over what goods constituted barter, and what was intended as a present. Reading between the lines it would seem as though the purchase of the woman slave was fairly straightforward but the King's son viewed the rest of the goods as his *dashee*, and that to balance the books and not having taken a pawn, a man was simply snatched from the last canoe that came aboard.

The prices in ackeys (56 = £13 6s.) are those current on the Guinea Coast: the actual cost of the goods was little more than £5 (the 50 per cent overvaluation allowed for).

Later, on the middle passage to Jamaica, Walter Prideaux summed up his trading experiences in a memorandum, estimated in the local currency of account. This was not solely for his own benefit, but also for that of his employers. The original *Journal* had commenced with a long list of 'goods sortable for the Coast of Guinea, I say the Gold Coast. Taken from Willm Hunt's original in which have found many Errors and himself very little acquainted with the Guinea Coast'.[9]

Curious though it may be to have a doctor's mate as an authority on Guinea Coast trade goods, the list was unremarkable, being in the main 'cutlesses, carbines, musketoons, small shells call'd cowries, perpetuannas and sayes, pentadoes, brandy and English spirritts, gunpowder, amber beads, ruff currell [rough coral], cristal beads and all other sorts [of] beads'. With the exception of cowries, all these items were aboard the *Daniel and Henry*, and all, with the exception of muskets, sold well. Prideaux, in the following testimonial, supplies his employers with a useful reference should they contemplate a further slave trade voyage.

The price of goods on the coast of Guinea

At sea, the *Daniel and Henry*, 10th October 1700.

		Ackeys	Tackeys
*	Brawles, 4 in a piece, Indian	8	
	Brawles, 2 in a piece, English	2	
*	Blue baffts	8	
*	Brandy per ankor	10	
	Beads per pound		7
*	4lb basins, 3 for	4	
*	3lb basins, per piece	1	
*	2lb basins, per piece		8
*	1lb basins, per piece		6
*	Currels per ounce, large	1	6
*	Carbines per piece	4	
*	Darnicks per piece	2	
	Gun flints per m[10]	3	
*	Fuzees per piece, 8A to 10A	10	
*	Looking glasses, 3 sorts:		
*	largest, 2 for	1	
*	second, 4 for	1	
*	smallest, 6 for	1	
*	Hangers, gilt per piece	2	
	Iron bars[11] per piece	1	6
*	Large knives per dozen	1	
*	Small knives per dozen		8
	Bars of lead per piece	1	
*	Nehallawares per piece	10	
*	Nickanees per piece	5	
*	Long cloths per piece	7	
*	Barrels of powder per barrel	24	
*	Anchors, 3 to a barrell, per piece	10	
	Brass pans, per piece	–	
*	Rangoes per string		4
*	Sheets, per piece	1	

	Ackeys	Tackeys
Blue papard Slessia per piece	2	
* Cases of spirits, per piece	4	
* ½ cases of spirits, per piece	2	
* Guinea stuff per piece	1	6
* Hounscott seas per piece	16	
* Perpetuannas, filletted,[12] per piece[13]	8	
* ½ piece ditto, filleted, per piece	4	
Ticking per piece	2	
* Tapseils per piece	8	
Nest of trunks, per nest	7	
* Tankards per piece	1	
* Firkins of tallow, per piece	4	
* Pentadoes per clout 2 for	4	
Firkins of powder, per piece	2	
Musketts per piece	8	
* Half barrels of powder per piece	12	
* Rum per anchor	10	

*The particulars aforegoing which are thus * marked, are most proper for
the Gold Coast; the others not much in request nor any profit to be had
by them. Thus by the experience of your servant,*
Walter Prideaux

CHAPTER ELEVEN

The Middle Passage

O F ALL THE elements that made up the capture, sale, transportation and forced labour of African slaves, perhaps none excites
our sympathy and outrage more than the horrors of the middle passage.
Accounts of the slave trade remain fixated by it – and justifiably so, for
there were no darker moments in history's most extensive forced
migration. The denomination 'middle passage' – that stretch of the
voyage from Africa to the West Indies or America – is an exclusively
European term, in the same way that 'triangular voyage' possesses a
similarly European connotation. For the small armada of plantation-
based slave trade vessels the middle passage was simply the return leg:
for those Company ships occasionally ordered to ply between the
West Indies and the Guinea Coast it formed the second stage of what
they called a 'double voyage'. These 'double voyages' with their
cargoes of rum were particularly valuable to the Company,[1] helping to
recover debts they were owed by plantation owners and delaying the
impressment of their sailors on the final leg back into English waters.
It is also a 'white' term: the middle passage for the blacks had started
with their capture – often some distance from the coast – continued
with their imprisonment in slave pens, barracoons or Company Castle
dungeons, and reached its nadir in their incarceration on board ship.
This incarceration was always of a lengthy duration: blacks did not
embark *en bloc* like passengers aboard an oceangoing liner, but were
taken aboard in dribs and drabs, one or two at a time over a period of
months. Therefore, though the actual transatlantic passage to Jamaica
might typically last ten to twelve weeks (shorter to Barbados, longer to
Carolina or Virginia), a slave who had been brought aboard and
shackled in the hold at an early stage in the venture might well have
been imprisoned for a total of seven or eight months by the time he or
she was delivered to the plantations.

A case in point can be provided by the *Daniel and Henry*. She is recorded as loading her first slave on 11 April 1700, but does not arrive in Jamaica until 17 November. Accounting for a few days in which entry port procedures had to be completed the earliest a slave could be expected to set foot on dry land would have been 21 November. Had the man loaded on 11 April still been alive, he would have spent thirty-two weeks chained in the hold. No wonder slave merchants in the plantations complained incessantly about the quality of the dazed men and women who stumbled uncomprehendingly on to the docksides, blinded by the unaccustomed sunlight, crippled by months of enforced inaction, and weakened by disease, poor diet and long-term dehydration. Food did not always improve in the West Indies: the islands, whose agricultural capacity had been engrossed by the sugar and tobacco industries, were in consequence chronically short of provisions. The vast number of vessels clearing from ports such as Plymouth and Minehead with pickled herrings, cheese and bread bore witness to the insufficiency of locally produced foodstuffs; in later years the Company unsuccessfully attempted to schedule their ships to arrive between December and June,[2] which was both the healthiest time of year to acclimatise and the period at which there were provisions in plenty.

For the black Africans the middle passage was the most intense expression, the epitome, of their new and unfamiliar slave status. Its effect was not experienced in purely physical terms: the depth of the psychological trauma cannot be minimised. From being men and women of honour and respect in their communities, they became debased creatures having no existence except as an expression of another's gain.[3] The state of being 'quintessentially a person without honour'[4] was simply too inhuman for many to bear. Believing that death would return them to their country, many stopped eating and starved themselves to death.[5] This was a common enough occurrence for slave trade captains to carry a 'speculum oris', an instrument of grisly appearance and application.[6] Shaped like a pair of scissors, the outsides of the blades were serrated: when closed the blades were forced between the teeth of any slave refusing to eat. Instead of holes for finger and thumb, this instrument was controlled by a hefty thumbscrew which was turned energetically to force the blades – and jaws – apart whilst food was forced down the throat.

Insanity, like death, provided an involuntary alternative for the hopelessly alienated and was a route that numberless African slaves took. It also became a survival technique that was consciously adopted once the plantation had been reached and slave status formalised. The helpless and apparently vacant 'quashee-slave' is a familiar figure in both plantation fiction and fact. Characterised by an evasion of all responsibility the stance marks, in effect, a form of passive resistance. On the other hand much insanity engendered by the middle passage was not assumed, but a real reflex to the deranging conditions that faced the freshly enslaved, torn apart as they were from husbands, wives, children, society and their futures.

Once aboard the slave ship they were in limbo, suspended between those who owned them and others who sought to purchase them. Yet they were looked after by a third party who had no financial stake in the voyage whatever and thus felt free to abuse them. Despite having worked alongside free blacks at some stage in their lives at sea, most crewmen on slave ships experienced no conflict in shipping human beings as commodities. If the crews thought about it at all – and there is no evidence that they did so – then their conclusions would have been that slavery was quite usual in Africa, and trading there for slaves was no different to attending the local cattle-market at home in England if you wanted to buy livestock.

Yet some must have been impressed by the Africans, black and heathen though they were. They had not spent their lives in grim, damp hovels with starvation just around the corner and a winter that never seemed to lift. Many of the male slaves were proud and powerful warriors, the women comely, their children enchanting. But gentler feelings had no part to play upon this brutal stage. Slave ships were there on business, and that business was domination and exploitation in its most absolute form. Consequently the white crew and their officers stamped on their own humanity as they whipped the slaves aboard and shackled them in the hold. The best looking of the women were set aside as ship's whores, but the term does not do justice to the hell and degradation to which they were forced to submit; quite simply, they were repeatedly raped. The children, distressed and traumatised beyond all comprehension, surrounded by the despair of their parents, survived the onslaught as best they could. But the damage to self-esteem, the abnegation of self-worth, abode with them for the rest of their lives and for succeeding generations who grew up knowing no other world than that of the plantation. Black society in the West is still coping with the white man's legacy of brutality to this very day.

The full extent of the misery engendered by the middle passage (let alone the slave trade in general) can never be measured. If it fell upon one group more than another then it fell hardest upon women. Many were pregnant when taken aboard and either miscarried or saw their babies taken from them and killed, for no slave merchant or plantation owner wanted the expense of a nursery full of children. Though men were highly sought after for their strength, plantation owners worked women to almost the same degree, not hesitating to employ them on hard manual labour. Women supplied by far the greatest bulk of the labour force on the plantations for the simple reason that they had been easier to capture in the first place and had a survival rate that was double the men's on the passage across the Atlantic.

Death stalked every slave ship in its headlong flight from Africa. Regardless of race, colour and creed it reaped its terrible harvest without interruption. Yet slave trade merchants aided and abetted the grim reaper in his daily task. Whether English, French, Dutch, Portuguese, Danish or Prussian in origin, the European traffic in slaves from Africa to the Americas and Caribbean is astonishingly similar in one respect: the almost universal disregard for slave survival. Despite representing a substantial capital investment and being the most highly perishable cargo imaginable, they were transported in obviously unsuitable conditions and subjected to unspeakable atrocities. In what other trade would sea captains have been allowed to get away with losses of up to 80 per cent? And with what other commodity would merchants have calmly written off such large potential profits? At no time during this epoch does it seem to have occurred to any of the undoubtedly astute businessmen engaged in the trade that to allow 20 per cent more room to the slaves in the hold (by carrying fewer of them) and thus enhancing their survival rate would actually reduce the number of crew (and wages) required for the venture in the first place. It would also significantly affect the capital outlay in terms of the cargo for barter (by an equivalent 20 per cent).

It was not until the end of the eighteenth century that slave ships (unlike troop ships which were allowed one man per ton across the Atlantic) were restricted by law to carrying a maximum of five slaves for every 3 tons burden, though the alarm bells had been sounded at least a century earlier. In 1681 the Company factors at the Cape Coast Castle had informed headquarters in London:

We find the covetousness of Commanders crowding in their slaves above the Proportion for the advantage of Freight is the only reason for the great Loss to the Company. If your Honours would be pleased to beat them down in their number though you gave them five shillings per head extraordinary your Honours would be considerable gainers at the year's end.[7]

However the Company remained resolutely convinced, like so many separate traders afterwards, that 'tight-packing'[8] the slave-hold was not the problem, but that the prime cause was the time spent off the Guinea Coast and on the middle passage. Today this seems almost wilful in its short-sightedness, but it should be remembered that understanding of the transmission of disease in the late seventeenth and early eighteenth centuries was extremely limited. Disease and death were still seen as acts of God, not consequences of man's actions or environment: as a science, aetiology was still less than a vague concept. The eventual conclusion though is inescapable. It suited the merchants all too well to maintain the status quo. Unrestricted by any statutory limits on loading, and unfettered by Christian charity – the slaves, after all, were heathen – merchants crammed their ships to bursting point. If the majority of the slaves survived, all well and good; if most died, then the value of those that remained was inflated.

The temptation is, because of the simple and incontrovertible fact that merchants and crews of slave ventures were white and that slaves were black, to view the degradation of and unconcern for the slaves as solely racially inspired. Though racial conditioning was indeed primarily responsible,[9] attitudes displayed towards slaves aboard ship and the conditions in which they existed also grew out of a general attitude towards the poor and dispossessed that was prevalent in England – and throughout Europe – at the close of the seventeenth century.

Without in any way attempting to gainsay or condone any part of the slave trade, it may be of value to bear in mind that poverty and intense hardship were the common lot of the average working man in the so-called civilisation which was England's pride. On land brutality and filth were an integral part of the everyday life of a labourer of the period, as cramped conditions were part and parcel of seafaring life, for the lower ranks at least. Whereas an African's experience of the dark, dank slave-hold and its close and insanitary nature would provoke both deep psychological trauma and severe physical stress, an English seaman's view would have been coloured by his own experience of the dirty, damp and smoky rookeries in which he and his family would huddle for most of the year, or the wretched dosshouses he would frequent in dockside slums. Add to that the real prospect of starvation in England, the prevalence of disease, lack of sanitation, high infant mortality rates, a barbaric penal code, and certain conclusions begin to be formed. The first is that the English working man was only nominally a 'free' man: the second is that some of the crew, despite the religious beliefs rigidly impressed upon them by their elders and 'betters', may have actually envied the Africans their comparatively easy existence, and looked back questioningly upon life in merry England.

Nevertheless, that should not distract us from the fact that whereas the number of options facing an English working man was deplorably limited, death was the only freedom for slaves packed on the *Daniel and Henry*. And die they did. Within thirty days of leaving São Tomé, Walter Prideaux records the number of slaves jettisoned by that date – 6 October 1700 – as 153. A recent study has asserted that 'the death rate per voyage among the crew was uniformly higher than the death rate among slaves in transit at the same period. The data are so consistent and regular in this respect that this can be taken as a normal circumstance of the eighteenth century slave trade'.[10]

Though undoubtedly possessing a general validity, this assertion is hardly borne out by the experience of the *Daniel and Henry*. In the end the number of slaves delivered and sold in Jamaica amounted to 246 out of a total of 452 loaded on the Guinea Coast. That is a loss of 45.5 per cent, whereas the crew loss on the same passage was a mere seven, or 15.9 per cent of the crew total. Even when calculated over the complete triangular passage, crew losses on the *Daniel and Henry* amounted to only 22.7 per cent. Perhaps it is less than a surprise to find racial and religious prejudices persisting even after death. Whereas dead slaves were simply thrown overboard or dragged behind the ship to attract sharks and provide shark meat for their helpless companions, dead crew members were slipped overboard or smuggled ashore if in coastal waters, as with John Fort of the *Daniel and Henry*. This was done secretly and at night to maintain the impression of white supremacy and conceal from the slaves the gradual decline in numbers of their white guards should an uprising be contemplated.

In any discussion involving mathematical computations in such circumstances, the residual sentiment is that they fail to take account of the scale of misery suffered by the slaves. They were heading for a lifetime of penal servitude: the crew, poor as they were, had at least undertaken the voyage as a calculated risk: a risk that was in all probability no greater than that of staying in England, and which on occasion could reward them handsomely.

Exactly why were so many slaves to perish on the *Daniel and Henry*? The overpowering reason appears to have been dehydration. For slaves shackled in the oven-like hold, water loss from sweating was exacerbated by further loss through vomiting due to sea-sickness, diarrohea and dysentery. Severe dehydration brought about a fatal affliction called 'fixed melancholy' in which slaves appeared to will themselves to die.[11] This was almost certainly the case aboard the *Daniel and Henry*, Prideaux remarking on the 5th November that the slaves were 'very bad ... the doctor not knowing what to do with them.' The '310 new ironbound Casks' loaded at Dartmouth as 'water casks for the use of the Negroes' were nowhere in evidence on arrival in Jamaica. Prideaux and Mathew had probably bartered them, counting on heavy rainfall during the middle passage to replenish whatever supplies they now carried.

Lesser factors also played their part. First, a Guinea trade ship carried the seeds of disease from three entirely remote environments – Europe, Africa and America – and the human beings consigned to its hold (and even the crew in their quarters) provided a fine breeding ground for diseases against which no resistance had been naturally developed.[12] Secondly, the *Daniel and Henry* was not a purpose-built slave ship but an ordinary merchant vessel whose two-month turn-round time in Dartmouth was far too short for any major restructuring to have taken place, apart from basic wooden stages being built between decks. Thirdly, by the end of her passage along the Guinea Coast she was significantly overloaded, even by the standards of the time. The usual ratio of slaves per ton of ship was 2:1, so with 452 slaves to 200 tons of ship the odds were already significantly stacked against a high slave survival rate. In tight-packing the vessel the merchants behind the *Daniel and Henry* characterised the independent traders: Barbot was under no illusion that: 'the great mortality which so often happens in slave ships proceeds as well from taking in too many as from want of knowing how to manage them aboard.'[13]

Fourthly, there is no way of knowing how healthy the slaves were when they were brought on board. Though the duty of the ship's doctor, Edward Fenner, and his mate, William Hunt, was to physically examine every slave for age, lameness, smallpox, ophthalmia, yaws,[14] venereal disease and 'bursten' (rupture or hernia), the year 1700 was one marked by intense competition for whatever slaves were available. In such times of scarcity, a blind eye was turned to suspected carriers of disease or those who were not too obviously infirm, eager as the captain would be to get fully slaved and clear the coast. In the insanitary cauldron that was the slave-hold, exacerbated by a poor diet, little fresh air and no physical exercise, disease raged unchecked amongst the physically debilitated and spiritually demoralised prisoners.

In comparison to the *Daniel and Henry* and others of her ilk, the professional slavers of the Royal African Company generally accomplished a far better – though still horrifying – slave survival rate. Records of the period 1680–8 indicate a mean loss in transit of 23.4 per cent, with a maximum annual rate of 29 per cent in 1682, and a minimum of 14.3 per cent in 1687.[15] Good reasons abound for the Company's ability to deliver the majority of its slaves alive. Their ships, if not purpose-built slavers, were extensively restructured for that purpose. Their captains and senior echelons often had first-hand experience of the West African coast. And the castle trade imposed its own discipline: trading for slaves would have been less frenetic and speculative, and Company factors had at least some control over the quality and health of the slaves offered to them. The forts themselves where the slaves were penned in barracoons or dungeons, awaiting the arrival of a suitable Company ship, also acted as 'buffer zones', allowing the slaves at least an interval of time in which to come to terms with the physical and psychological trauma of their condition, though many perished within the factory gates.

As far as the crew of the *Daniel and Henry* is concerned, their death rate may well have been abnormally low. Unlike slave ships from the maritime centres of London and Bristol (and later Liverpool), the *Daniel and Henry* drew the majority of her crew from the immediate locality. Of the more unusual surnames on the watches, Branscomb, Shutter, Tremlett, Snelling, Handcock, Foxworthy, Godferry, March, Rudd and Clapp were all from local parishes such as Withycombe Raleigh, Dartmouth, Plympton St Mary, Kentisbury and Buckfastleigh. The crew contained several family groupings: Nicholas and John Fort; Richard and Peter Johnson; Roger Mathew, his son William and nephew Walter Prideaux. Virtually every crew member would have known at least one other before signing on at Dartmouth; such solidarity of origin would be a reassuring source of support. As a crew of country rather than city upbringing they would have been healthier to begin with and none of them, coming from the premier maritime county of all England, could have been totally unprepared for the hazards of a life at sea. The voyage of the *Daniel and Henry* was no pleasure cruise, but it is with the slaves that one's sympathies lie.

Such sympathies are not solely a result of the awakening of the public conscience by the abolitionists at the end of the eighteenth century. Anxieties had been present, albeit muted, since the beginning of England's bid for a colonial empire and consequent domination of the slave trade. Nor did the voices of dissent emanate solely from recalcitrant members of the Society of Friends. The first historian of Barbados, Richard Ligon, wrote of the African slaves in 1656, six years after he had left the West Indies:

> I believe, and have strong motives to be of that persuasion, that there are as honest, faithful and conscionable people amongst them, as amongst those of Europe, or any other part of the world.[16]

Such scattered voices in the wilderness called not for immediate radical change but reflected a note of liberal concern. Later the middle passage provided a focus for that concern, best expressed by a long-suffering Guinea trade doctor called Thomas Aubrey. He wrote a lengthy, detailed tract on the humane treatment of blacks based on his experiences in the *Peterborough* off Calabar in 1717.[17] Though – like its author – now largely forgotten, it is a work of eminently good sense considering medicine at that time was at best a quasi-science[18] and complicated by European unfamiliarity with tropical disease environments. Aubrey pulled no punches in attaching both the ignorance of the average Guinea trade surgeon and the greed of the merchant venturers. His own profession was singled out for especial blame in the matter of slave mortality:

> Abundance of these poor Creatures are lost on board Ships to the great prejudice of the Owners and Scandal of the Surgeon, merely thro' the Surgeon's Ignorance because he knows not what they are afflicted with, but supposing it to be a Fever, bleeds and purges or vomits them, and so casts them into an incurable Diarrhoea, and in a very few Days they become a Feast for some hungry Shark; when, if he had spared himself the trouble of doing anything for them, but left all to Nature, they might have recovered, and become a Profit to the Merchant, and a Credit to him.[19]

Guinea trade surgeons were employed out of economic rather than humanitarian reasons, yet their presence – not required by law – betrays some attempt to diminish sickness and mortality and undoubtedly provided reassurance to crew members. Indeed Guinea trade vessels carrying doctors might well have found it easier to hire crews. Unfortunately these doctors had no control over either the merchants or their captains, who dictated the number of slaves to be loaded and had the final word on the quality and quantity of provisions or medicines taken aboard.[20] Aubrey knew that only money talked and advised every Guinea trade surgeon:

> tell the Commander . . . he must treat the slaves kindly . . . be sure to represent all these things to the Owners before you engage in their ship; for it's much better for them to bear a hundred Pounds charge more than ordinary, than to lose above half their Slaves, since the Death of a very few will be upwards of that money out of their way.[21]

As Aubrey saw it, everybody benefited from a more enlightened regime on board a slave ship: even the surgeon would get his reward, which would be an enhanced reputation and the right to a higher level of pay on the next voyage. In between discourses on the diagnosis and treatment of specific slave diseases, Aubrey reveals a fine knowledge and appreciation of the role diet plays in maintaining health. He recorded that the Africans' native diet consisted of meat, fish, oil and fruit and was far from confined to two meals a day. Even the 'middling sort of peoples' ate well, 'just as they have a fancy' for roast plantains, sweetcorn, yams, dates and coconuts. Small wonder that fluxes (dysentery) and diarrhoea were such common complaints in the slave-hold, once the slaves had been subjected to the disgusting mess of horse beans boiled in lard, with occasional lumps of salt beef, pork or shark thrown in for good measure, that was to be their only food for the duration of the voyage. Africans cared little for salt in their diet and Aubrey pleaded with slave ship cooks to soak salted meat in water before boiling. Water, however, was one of the many commodities that was traditionally in short supply aboard ship, especially one carrying a full complement of slaves and crew in tropical waters.

Amongst contemporary writers and commentators on the African, Aubrey is unusual if not unique in describing cleanliness as one of their many virtues, and pointing out that Africans habitually bathed in river or sea at least once a day. Heaven knows what his readers made of that. They would have been accustomed to bathing not more than once a week, relying on perfumes to disguise whatever malodorous effluvia they themselves gave off, and carrying a sponge liberally doused with attar of roses or an aromatic pomander to ward off the evil smells of others. Far from saving blacks from the clutches of the devil, Aubrey's contention was that the trade was forcibly transporting them from something like paradise: their trauma, he advised helplessly, can be ameliorated by 'drinking in moderation, smoking tobacco, a glass of brandy when you observe them melancholy'.[22]

Not all slaves were treated in the same way. Apart from black women who were singled out as ship's whores and received some scanty crumbs of comfort for the unmitigated degradation of their voyage, there were the 'privilege' slaves. They belonged not to the merchants behind the venture, but to certain officers who had received dispensation by the merchants to carry their own small ventures, and to transport one or two slaves free of charge. As may be imagined, the system was readily abused. Ships' officers generally exceeded their quotas and contributed greatly to the overcrowded conditions. 'Privilege' slaves were well fed, reducing the food available to the rest. They never died, at least on paper, for replacements were available below decks and silently substituted.[23] And their living conditions, though they were shackled, were immeasurably better than those of their fellow slaves. Some officers filled the long hours of the middle passage by teaching their 'privilege' slaves a skill – cooking, cooperage or carpentry. Far from being a primitive workshop therapy it was solely designed to increase their value when sold, for a slave with a 'European' skill could command a substantial premium on arrival in the plantations.

In the long stretch of the middle passage, punctuated by the deaths of blacks and whites alike, the attitude of the whites underwent a significant change. Though prepared to view Africans purely as commodities when trading and loading off the Guinea Coast, they could not fail to observe, in the impossibly close confines of an eighteenth-century merchantman, that they were more than just another inanimate cargo; they were human beings, as capable as the crew of joy, sadness, hope and despair. Far from land, voyaging on with no other sail in sight, constantly on the lookout against privateers and pirates, and at the mercy of the elements, a strange comradeship built up between crew and slaves. Though the crew initially brutally victimised the blacks, the only class with less status than themselves, it could not have been wholly lost on the lower ranks of the crew that their future was perhaps not so immeasurably better. The possibility of the crew themselves being impressed into the Royal Navy grew ever more real as they approached Caribbean waters. Royal Navy ships on the West India station suffered calamitous crew mortality and

Guinea-trade ships with their seasoned complement of experienced mariners were regularly raided – usually illegally – to make up Royal Navy deficiencies.[24] Captains of merchantmen so decimated were far from unhappy about the practice: sugar was a far less labour-intensive cargo than slaves and the less crew present on the homeward leg, the lower the wage bill would be for the whole voyage. So the apprehension with which the blacks regarded their arrival in the West Indies would have been mirrored by that of the white crew; some of the latter could well find themselves at sea for three more years and there was the finest of lines between impressment and imprisonment.

To those who would argue that whites would never have been treated so badly as blacks, the testimony of John Coad bears eloquent witness that this was not the case. Convicted by Judge Jeffreys as an adherent of Monmouth in 1685, Coad was dispatched to Jamaica to serve a sentence of ten years forced servitude in the plantations. The difference here of course is that Coad was a law-breaker (at least in the eyes of the Establishment) whilst the blacks were innocent of any such charge. Nevertheless the lack of humanity shown to both is the same; Coad was bleeding profusely from open wounds when he was shipped aboard:

> The master of the ship shut 99 of us under deck in a very small room where we could not lay ourselves down without lying on one another. The hatchway being guarded with a continual watch with blunderbusses and hangers, we were not suffered to go above deck for air or easement, but a vessel was set in the midst to receive the excrement, by which means the ship was soon infected with grievous and contagious diseases as the smallpox, fever, calenture, and the plague, with frightful blotches. Of each of these diseases several died, for we lost of our company 22 men . . . in the night fearful cries and groaning of sick and distracted persons . . . added much to our trouble. Some days we had not enough in five men's mess to suffice one man for one meal . . . our water was exceeding corrupt and stinking, and also very scarce to be had.[25]

Like hundreds of thousands of blacks before and after him, Coad – though white – was in such an appalling state on his arrival in Jamaica that he had to be specially fattened up before any merchant or plantation owner would even think about buying him (or rather a decade of his labour).

Occasionally Guinea-trade ships adopted this policy during the final fortnight at sea. Though correctly seen as good business practice to wash, shave and oil the bodies of slaves before arrival in port, it may well have represented a release of humanity, an attempt in some small way to make amends for the horrors inflicted. For the growing realisation that the slaves were human beings must also have brought the fear of divine retribution: no wonder Aubrey counselled his traders to be

> as careful of them as the white Men: for altho they are Heathens, yet they have a rational soul as well as us; and God knows whether it may not be more tolerable for them in the latter Day than for many who profess themselves Christians.[26]

Fear of retribution was never far from the slave trader's mind. Though a kind of suspension of disbelief could be achieved when faced with the 'savagery' of the Guinea Coast, the approach of the nominally Christian islands of the West Indies ushered in the need for atonement. For there the captains and crews would be liable again to the structures and strictures of the Church and state in which they had been born, raised, educated and perhaps oppressed. The slaves, traumatised, alienated, diseased and despairing in the holds could know nothing of this, and perversely frustrated any chances of crew absolution by continuing to die. The fury of the captains knew no bounds, backed as it was by the knowledge that they were also losing – along with a safe berth in the hereafter – valuable revenue in the here and now. Understandably, no slave trade captain wrote easily of these matters for fear it would prejudice his career: nevertheless Aubrey captures the spirit of white disenchantment with the middle passage when his captains ask angrily – much as Roger Mathew of the *Daniel and Henry* was doubtless to do –

> What a Devil makes these plaguey Toads die so fast? To which I answer: 'Tis Inhumanity, Barbarity, and the greatest of Cruelty of their Commander & his Crew, together with either Ignorance of the Surgeon, or downright cowardice, in not daring to advise his Commander better.[27]

Tension was further heightened by the white perception that black slaves were conspiring to die simply to frustrate the economic success of the voyage. Thomas Phillips in the *Hannibal* of 1693–4 showed much of his own state of mind when he wrote of his slaves:

> What the smallpox spared, the flux swept off to our great regret . . . after all our pains and care to give them their messes in due order and season, keeping their lodgings as clean and sweet as possible, and

enduring so much misery and stench so long among a parcel of creatures nastier than swine; and after all my expectations to be defeated by their mortality.[28]

The transfer of guilt from oppressor to victim, so familiar to those who have studied the psychological aspects of political repression and torture, is here made manifest: the captain is making the slaves responsible for their condition. Phillips himself did not escape scot-free from his slave venture. As a result of his voyage he contracted a prolonged illness marked by convulsions and shattering pains in his head: on his return to London he found he was almost totally deaf and, though still a young man, retired back to Wales.

As for the crew of the *Daniel and Henry* and its hapless ship's doctor, nothing is ever heard again of their involvement in the Guinea trade. Given the appalling results of the middle passage on which they are about to set out, that is no bad thing. Much less articulate than Thomas Phillips, the thin fabric of Walter Prideaux's narrative painfully fails to hide the magnitude of suffering which haunted the *Daniel and Henry*. If one could reverse history and interview Walter Prideaux or Roger Mathew for their own view of the slave trade their opinions would almost certainly concur with that of John Barbot, for they must have shared the ideology that was so prevalent at the time:

the fate of such as are bought, and transported from the coast to America, or other parts of the world by Europeans, is less deplorable than that of those who end their days in their native country; for aboard ships all possible care is taken to preserve and subsist them for the interest of the owners, and when sold in America, the same motive ought to prevail with their masters to use them well, that they may live the longer and so do them more service. Not to mention the inestimable advantage they may reap, of becoming Christians, and saving their souls.[29]

CHAPTER TWELVE

Jamaica Bound

Journal or day reckoning of a voyage intended by God's assistance in the ship *Daniel and Henry* of Exeter, Capt. Roger Mathew commanding, from St Thome to the Isle Jamaica. Begun the 6th day of September, being Friday, in the year 1700.

God send us safe to desired port. Amen.

WITH HER complement of slaves packed below decks, her crew settled back into their quarters (minus William Hodge who could not resist the considerable temptations on offer at São Tomé), and every spare inch of hold and cabin space crammed with provisions and water barrels for the imminent Atlantic passage, the *Daniel and Henry* rode dangerously low in the water. In the light equatorial westerly breeze her salt-soaked, sun-scorched canvas, patched and repatched by the ingenuity of her patient sailmakers, fitfully slatted about. Stained, patched and drab, her sails must have looked incapable of sustaining a trip across the Channel, let alone the Atlantic. Beneath the waterline the *Daniel and Henry* sprouted a flourishing beard of marine weed that, despite the best efforts of the crew to give the hull a limited careen and tallowing, would slow her down across the Atlantic.

What a sight she must have presented. Every scrap of paint and decorative gold leaf had shrivelled and flaked in the African sun. There was not a pristine white sail to be seen. Hardly a plank above water that had not warped in the heat of the day and cool of the night and been hastily recaulked. Barely a square foot of deck that was not crammed with roped-down chests and securely lashed hogsheads. And not a man on watch who was unarmed, for this was a prison ship. Though a few black children played in the fo'c'sle, every single one of the adults was chained below decks lest the presence of land prove too inviting: and every hatchway and grating boasted an armed sentry.

These gratings and hatches exhaled an effluvium which – no matter how fiercely the wind blew – seemed to imbue the very timbers of the ship and cling to its sails. It was accompanied by a rhythmic litany of despair that clutched at the heart. Perhaps even at the heart of Walter Prideaux, a capable and conscientious young man, carefully writing up this, his own log-book, in the vellum-bound ledger stamped with his coat of arms and the legend *Walter Prideaux – His Booke – Anno Dommini 1688*, given to him on his twelfth birthday as a commonplace book.

In the suffocating hold of the *Daniel and Henry* languished nigh on 450 souls. The ship rode deeply, so deeply that none of her scuttles could be opened for fear they shipped water. Though they had provided some measure of ventilation while she stood off the Guinea Coast, even this small relief was now stopped. Extending over her gunwales she wore the costume of the slave ship, gigantic net flounces supported by spars, hastily rigged to catch slaves who attempted to fling themselves over the side. It would remain in place until Jamaica was safely reached. And at her stern flew the proud symbol of England's maritime supremacy, the Red Ensign, a simple red flag bearing the cross of St George in the canton.

Doubtless the crew's loyalty to the flag remained unshaken, though their faith lay entirely with the Almighty. Accordingly, as in the first stage, Walter Prideaux opens his account with the ritual entreaty of God's blessing upon the voyage. This was no empty supplication, for nowhere was man more at the mercy of the elements than at sea. And, beneath the everyday navigational conventions of the log-book, there arises a suggestion that Walter Prideaux is far from easy about being employed upon a slave trade ship. As we shall see, little is communicated directly, but gradually the full horror of what he is engaged upon begins to sink home. In comparison with the voyage from Dartmouth to São Tomé, he grows more and more fearful; five prayers are invoked on this passage, though it is without incident (perhaps thus showing the power of prayer).

Changes occur in the recording of the voyage too. In the first part of the log only the overall distance and direction made good, between noon of one day and noon the next, were recorded. (Although there must have been several changes of course and speed during most days, these would have been only roughly noted.) In this section particulars of the individual short distances sailed are recorded in the left-hand margin in minutes (or nautical miles, identical in terms of latitude), and figures in the right-hand columns showed the distances made good from São Tomé. The latter are now gathered into parentheses at the end of each day. For convenience of plotting the course of the *Daniel and Henry* on the chart (which was the real physical manifestation of the voyage), the record of distances sailed is kept as so many leagues east and west but from 16 September the easting column is dispensed with as the ship now follows an exclusively westing course. Changes in a northerly or southerly direction are recorded under latitude, the readings being taken at noon as usual.

Account of ship's way from St. Thome to the Isle Jamaica. The former being in the northern latitude 10°:10′, the latter in the latitude 17°:50′. The distance between them is 81°:40′ I say meridian all the course is nearest W by N¼N. We set sail from St. Thome Road the 6 day of September, being Friday, in the year 1700. God send us safe to desired port. Amen.

Saturday 7. *Fair weather.*	This day at noon, the island bore NW of us about 14 leagues, with the wind at SW fresh gale: the current setting to windward strong. Being now in the south latitude 00°:14′, having made 8 leagues easting by course since we made sail. We now steer away west. (Latitude by LOG 00°:14′S; leagues Easting 2:7)
8 Day Sunday. *Fair weather.*	This 24 hours we have sailed W by S 17 leagues, with the wind from the SSW to S, topgallant gale. We have made 17 leagues westing & 3 leagues southing and this morning saw Sao Thome about 14 leagues ENE of us. We now steer away W by S, the wind at S by W fresh gale, & the current setting to the southward strong. (Latitude by LOG 00°:23′S; leagues Westing 14)
9 Day Monday. *Fair weather.* *Fresh wind.*	This 24 hours have sailed W¾N 25 leagues and have gone to the westward 24 leagues and 3 leagues to the north since yesterday 12 o'clock; the current is setting strong to the south west, the wind at S & SSW fresh gale. We now steer away west northerly, the current under the lee bow makes good a west course according to the best of my judgement. The sun has now 1°:7′N declination. (Latitude by LOG 00°:14′S; leagues Westing 24)

10 Day Tuesday. Fresh wind & a strong current sets to the SW. Great swell from the WSW. This 24 hours have sailed W by N 23 leagues & have gone to the northward 1 league & to westward 22 leagues with the wind from SSW to SW fresh gale, the topgallant sails handed. The current still sets strong SW with a great swell from the WSW. We now steer away WNW, the sun having 43'N declination, we being now in 2'S latitude & have made 60 leagues westing from Sao Tome. It is now so cold here as many times I have found it in England at this time of the year. (Latitude by LOG 00°:2'S; leagues Westing 22)

Compared to the stifling heat of the Guinea Coast and the sheltered anchorage of São Tomé in the Bight of Biafra, the open Atlantic breezes seemed bitterly cold. Walter Prideaux was by no means unique in finding open equatorial waters called for heavy jackets and mufflers. At the same place, though the previous year, James Barbot, supercargo of the *Albion* noted with surprise:

> we find the weather commonly so cold . . . though so near the line and at the time of the equinox, that it may well be said to be as raw and pinching as on the coast of Brittany: especially in the night, every man aboard, though never so hardy, is glad to put on more clothes[1] . . .

Curiously Barbot made this observation at exactly the same time of year as Walter Prideaux, for Prideaux now goes on to record that the sun has – on 11 September – 20 minutes northerly declination (meaning it was one third of a degree north of the equator), and on 13 September it has 27 minutes southerly declination. Therefore the sun crossed the Equator on 12 September, the autumnal equinox, when the *Daniel and Henry* finds herself virtually becalmed. In 1700 England still used the Julian calendar, at that time eleven days behind the more correct Gregorian calendar. A comparison of Walter Prideaux's figures with those given in a modern nautical almanac indicates that he had an accurate table of his own which showed how the sun's declination varied with the date throughout the year.

11 Day Wednesday. Little wind & a current sets to This 24 hours have sailed WNW 14 m & at night we tacked & stood to the South & have made southing 11 leagues & 2', & are now in the S latitude 36', the sun having 20' North declination. The current sets to the southward, the wind has been from SW to SW by

the southward & *a swell from SW.*	S. Little wind and a swell from the South West. We now steer away S by E half East with a little wind.[2] (Latitude by LOG 00°:36′S)

12 Day
Thursday.
S by E: 5m.
SSE:48m. SE by
S:11m. Showery
– little wind.

This 24 hours have sailed (with the wind from SW by S to SW) SE by S½E 64m & have gone to the southward 16½ leagues, & to the eastward 13⅔ leagues, and are in the South latitude 1°:25′ having gone to the westward since we came from Sao Tome 46⅓ leagues. We now have little or no current but a great swell from the southward & little wind. God send us a good passage. (Latitude by LOG 01°:25′S; leagues 13⅔ Easting, 46⅓ Westing)

13 Day Friday.
SSE:20m
S by E: 9m
SE by S:10m
SE:12m
W by N:10m
Showery with a
great swell & a
fresh wind.

This 24 hours have sailed SE by S 6°:30′ easterly with the wind from the SSW to the SWbyW, moderate. Have gone to the southward 10⅔ leagues & to the eastward 9 leagues. Could not observe the sun having but 27′S declination. We still have a great sea from the southward with showers. At 6am we saw a ship which bore SSW 3 leagues: at 8am she bore SW by W½W 5 leagues, she standing to the westward & we to the southward, at which time we tacked & in a shower lost sight of him. We now steer WNW with the wind at SSW, fresh gale which pray God continues. (Latitude by LOG 01°:57′S; leagues 9 Easting, 37⅓ Westing)

14 Day.
Saturday.
WNW: *3m*
S by E: *19m*
SSE   *18m*
S: *6m*
SE by S: *30m*
Fresh wind &
showery.

This 24 hours have sailed SE by S 25 leagues & have gone to the southward 21 leagues and are in the southern latitude 3°:00′. We have gone to the eastward 14 leagues having a great sea from the south west. This 24 hours have had the wind SW to the WSW, fresh gale: at 11pm rift [reefed] the fore top sail, being full of showers. We now steer away SSE with a fresh gale at SW & variable. (Latitude by LOG 3°:00′S; leagues 14 Easting, 23⅓ Westing)

15 Day. Sunday.
SSE: *21m*
SE by S: *6m*
W by N: *15m*
WNW: *38m*
Showery. Saw a

This 24 hours have sailed WNW 9°:10′W & have gone to the westward 9⅔ leagues & to the northward 2⅓ leagues with the wind from SW by S to SW by W, fresh gale & showers but little or no current. This day at 6am we saw a ship which bore S by W about 6 leagues: we suppose it to be the *Society*, Captain

ship.	

Edward Monk who sailed from Sao Tome 4 days before us, bound for Barbados. We steer away NW by W. (Latitude by LOG 2°:53'S; leagues 33 Westing)

16 Day.	
Monday.	
NW by W:	5m
S:	20m
SSE:	6m
S by E:	28m

This 24 hours have sailed SE 20 leagues & have gone to the southward 14 leagues & to the East 14 leagues, the current setting strong to leeward. At 4pm we tacked at which time Captain Monk bore down on us. At 8am he came on board us & says he makes but 1°:5' South of the equinoctial & that he saw Sao Tome Thursday last. (Latitude by LOG 3°:35'S; leagues 14 Easting 19 Westing)

17 Day.	
Tuesday.	
S by E:	5m
SSE:	18m
SE by S:	16m
W by S:	10m
W by N:	4m
W :	6m
No current.	

This 24 hours have sailed upon sea courses which wrought by a travers is S by W 10 leagues & 7 tenns [tenths?]. Have gone to the southward 10 leagues & to the westward 2 leagues, with the wind from S by W to SW, fresh gales & rain. We are still in the company of Captain Monk who sails much worse than we. We now steer away W & W by S with smooth sea & showery. Mr Chapman is sick & afraid of the smallpox. (Latitude 4°:5'S; leagues 21 Westing)

The *Society* had cleared São Tomé some days before the *Daniel and Henry* but had been hampered in her progress not by Captain Monk's poor sailing or management, but by her appalling condition.[3] This was also reflected in the fact that only twenty-two slaves survived her middle passage to Barbados, and that once the *Society* had arrived there she was condemned as unseaworthy and immediately broken up.[4] Monk continued to be employed in the slave trade, commanding the *Bridgewater*, a Company ship, to the Gambia in 1708. On that occasion the voyage was cut short by the intervention of the French, who captured her while trading up the River Gambia in February 1709, taking possession of 213 slaves and 2½ tons of ivory.[5]

The health of John Chapman, chief mate, was giving grave cause for concern. His importance to the success of the voyage can be judged by the constant monitoring of his state. In comparison Humphrey Handcock, a common sailor, simply merits a passing reference that he died of smallpox, which had made its appearance three days out of São Tomé.

18 Day.	
Wednes-	
day.	
W:	*15m*
W by S:	*25m*
W by N:	*17m*
Lat.3°53′S	

This 24 hours have sailed WNW 9°:55′ Westerly 18:5 leagues with the wind from S by W to SSW and have gone to the southward 4 leagues & to the westward 18 leagues, being still in the company of Captain Monk. We now steer away westward. We cannot have an observation of the sun having but 2°:25′ S declination & we in the latitude as in the margent; but little or no current with showery weather & the wind, variable with every shower, sometimes a point & a half. Mr Chapman still sick. (Latitude by LOG 3°:53′S; leagues 39 Westing)

19 Day.	
Thursday.	
W:	*46m*
W by N:	*11m*
W½S:	*7m*
Showery	

This 24 hours have sailed W by N½N 21 leagues, & are gone to the Northward 2 leagues, & to the westward 20 leagues, with the wind from the SSW to SW by S, moderate gale being still in sight of Captain Monk. We now steer away W by S with a fresh gale at S by W, showery. No observation of the sun, having but 2°:48′S declination & we in the south latitude 3°:47′. Mr Chapman still sick. (Latitude by LOG 3°:47′S; leagues 59 Westing)

20 Day. Friday.	
W by S:	*53m*
W½N:	*6m*
W:	*6m*
W by N:	*3m*
Showery.	

This 24 hours have sailed WNW 22:7 leagues, & are gone to the northward 8.7 leagues & to the westward 21 leagues, and are in the latitude 3°:21′:′S; & have had the wind from S by W to SSW½W with showers. This day could not see Captain Monk but at topmast head, bearing ESE about 12 leagues. We now steer away west, with the wind at SSW moderate, smooth water and little current. (Latitude by LOG 3°:21′S: leagues 80 Westing)

21 Day.	
Saturday.	
W by S:	*27m*
W:	*32m*
W½S:	*23m*
Showery weather	
with a strong	
leeward current.	

This 24 hours, with a fresh gale, have sailed by the log westward 4°:53′ Southerly; but allowing the ship 27°:23′ leeway[6] shall have made good a WNW course 27:3 leagues & have gone to the westward 25 leagues & to the northward 10.5 leagues & are now in the latitude 2°:50′ south. The Captain had an observation & found the ship in the south latitude 2°:54′. We now steer away west with the wind at SSW, little, with showers. (Latitude by LOG 2°:50′S; leagues 105 Westing)

At 9pm, Humphrey Handcock departed this life having been sick in the smallpox, which struck in again after having been out three days. Have not seen Captain Monk this 24 hours.

22 Day Sunday.
W: *10m*
W by S: *18m*
WSW: *35m*
SW by W: *9m*
W by N: *4m*
Showery

This 24 hours have sailed W by S½S by the log but with allowance for ship's leeway she has made good a W by N course 25 leagues & has gone to the westward 24:5 leagues, & to the northward 5 leagues, now being in the S latitude 2°:35′ with the wind from SW by S to S by E, fresh gale & showery. We now steer away SW by W with a fresh gale at S by E & a strong leeward current. (Latitude by LOG 2°:35′S; leagues 129 Westing)

23 Day.
Monday.
SW by W: *24m*
W by ½S: *23m*
WSW: *45m*
             ―――
             92m
Strong current.

This 24 hours have sailed by the log WSW 4°:10′ South; but with allowance for a strong leeward [i.e. northerly] current we have made good but a W by N 31 leagues & have gone to the westward 30 leagues & to the northward 6 leagues. The wind from S to S by E, fresh gale, & strong current setting NNE to the nearest of my judgment. We now steer away WSW. (Latitude by LOG 2°:17′S; leagues 159 Westing)

24 Day.
Tuesday.
SW by W: *7m*
WSW: *86m*
             ―――
             93m
Strong current and showery.

This 24 hours have sailed WSW 45′W by the log, but by the current & leeway we have made good but W by N distance 31 leagues, with the wind at South & S by E; fresh gales & smooth water. At noon by observation we were in the South latitude 1°:5′; we have gone to the northward this 24 hours 6 leagues; and to the westward 30 leagues. We have been set by the current 54m to the northward since we came from Sao Tome, having made 9°:27′ diff. longitude from the meridian of Sao Tome to the westward.[7] (Latitude by LOG 1°:59′S, by OBS 1°:5′S; leagues 189 Westing)

25 Day.
Wednesday.
W by S: *23m*
WSW: *47m*
Showers with strong current.

This 24 hours have sailed W by S 6°:25′ southerly by the log, but with allowance for leeway have made good a W by N course 23 leagues; & have gone to the northward 4 leagues & to the westward 22 leagues, & are now in the latitude 1°:47′ by dead reckoning. But at noon by observation were in 0°:00′S latitude, with the wind from S to SSE & moderate. We steer away W by S. (Leagues by LOG 1°:47′S, by OBS 0°:00′; leagues 211 Westing)

26 Day.	
Thursday	
W by S:	*36m*
WSW:	*29m*
	65m
Fair weather.	

This 24 hours have sailed WSW 3°:00′ westerly by the log, but allowing leeway & current she has made good but a W by N distance of 21 leagues, she having gone to the northward 6 leagues & to the westward 20 leagues with the wind from S by E to S by W. Little wind. Have differ^d my longitude 11:33′ to the westward. Smooth water. We now steer away WSW with the wind at S. (Latitude by LOG 1°:29′; leagues 231 Westing)

27 Day. Friday.	
W by S:	*66m*
W½S:	*8m*
W:	*7m*
	81m
Fair weather.	

This 24 hours have sailed W by S 25′ westerly by the log; but leeway & currents allowed, she has made good a W by N distance 27 leagues, & has gone to the northward 5 leagues & to the westward 26 leagues with the wind from S to SSW moderate, & a current set to the northward.

Last night at about 9 o'clock Mr John Chapman departed this life, he being before very bad in a cold.

We now steer away WSW with a moderate gale wind. (Latitude by LOG 1°:14′S; leagues 257 Westing)

The loss of John Chapman, chief mate, was a severe blow to the good management of the voyage. His health had given cause for concern since the time they left São Tomé and had steadily worsened. Though he feared he had contracted smallpox – like Humphrey Handcock who had shared his watch – his dying 'in a cold' after a two-week incubation period suggests a primary attack of malaria. From his inventory, detailed on pp. 164–5, he was obviously a professional seafarer and a man of some substance, able to afford a sizeable private venture (which he did not declare to the Customs at Dartmouth and so did not pay the requisite 10 per cent tax).

Possibly because of the intense competition for gold, slaves and ivory, much of this venture had failed to sell. However, Chapman was evidently a cautious trader and eschewed gold and all that glittered for the solid virtues of ivory which he branded with his initials. Though men slaves were extremely scarce on the Guinea Coast, Chapman had managed to procure one for himself, along with a girl, both marked for life with the same brand. Ship slaves, bought for the ship's merchant backers, were branded instead with the initial letters D and H.

Though there is nothing remarkable about his wardrobe, despite its displaying – with its lace neckcloth, silver-buckled shoes and

ivory-headed cane – a certain sartorial elegance, his collection of
books and instruments shows a thoroughly professional approach to
his work. Walter Prideaux's later comment on the *Daniel and
Henry's* relatively slow passage – 'much may be attributed to bad
steering' – will serve to emphasise their previous reliance on Chapman's knowledge and skill.

Amongst his possessions were a forestaff, used to take the altitude
of heavenly bodies; a quadrant; a nocturnall which ascertained the
hours by observation at night; and a Gunter scale, a flat marked rule
for mechanically solving navigational or surveying problems. This
hardware was complemented by a well-thumbed working library
including James Atkinson's *Epitome of the Art of Navigation*, John
Seller's *Practical Navigation or an Introduction to the Art* (probably
the second edition of 1673), Richard Norwood's *Seaman's Practice:
containing a fundamental Problem in Navigation . . . namely touching the Compass of the Earth and Sea . . . also an exact Method of
Keeping a Reckoning at Sea* and a Waggoner, a corruption of Lucas
Jancz Waghenaer, author of *The Mariner's Mirror*, the earliest sea atlas
or compendium of charts, first printed in England in 1588. Armed with
these in one hand and an assortment of Bibles, prayer books and
devotional literature in the other (like nonconformist divine John
Foxe's *Door of Heaven opened and shut*), mariners such as Chapman
extended and maintained Britain's maritime supremacy throughout
the eighteenth century.

 Inventory of Mr John Chapman's goods, deceased.
At Sea 9 October 1700.

13 Single Brawles
56 coarse callakew sheets
 2 Nickanees
 1 piece Pentadoes
   Pte a piece Blue Lyning
11 Sheets
 6 small Elephant Teeth marked J:C:A
 2 small   ditto   m'ked J:C:P
 8 small   ditto   m'ked J:C
 3 small   ditto   J:C
 1 man Slave }
 1 girl ditto } m'rked J:C
 6 Bars lead
Some Brass wyre

Clothes (viz):
4 Old Coats, 3 old Jackcoats
1 Waistcoat, 1 pair britches
2 Flanning Sherts, 1 pair flanning Drawers
1 old Broad Cloth coat & Jackcoat
2 old Hats, 4 pair old Stockings
6 old White Shurts
1 old Check Shurt & 1 pair Drawers
1 Lace Neckcloth: 10 old Muzling ditto
1 Rumall & 1 White Handkerchiefe
1 Bed, 1 Rugg, 1 blanket, 1 Pillow
2 pair old broad Cloth Britches
1 pair Serge   ditto
1 White Fustian Waistcoat
1 Serge Coat and Waistcoat
1 old Cloth Jackcoat
3 New hats, 1 pair old Gloves
2 pair old Shoes, 1 pair Silver Buckles
2 Nickers, 3 pair Sheets
1 hat brush, 1 Cane with Ivory head boss
1 Knife and fork, 1 pen Knife

Books and Instruments (viz):
1 Forestaff with 4 vanes
1 Quadrant with 4 vanes
1 Nocturnall, 1 Gunter scale
1 Plain & 1 Gunner scale
1 old Epitome, 1 old Callinder
1 Practical Navigation
1 Seaman's Practice
2 old Journal Books
1 pair Dividers, 1 pair Compasses
1 Bible, 1 Whole Duty of Man
1 Common Prayer, 1 quarto Waggoner.
1 book called Heaven Opened
1 paper Pocket Book
1 old atlass, all torn
1 old papered book
These Things are putt into two Chests which are marked J:C: and this
Inventory is attested by us
                    Francis Snelling
                    Walter Prideaux

Painful as the death of Chapman undoubtedly was, it did not compare with the sufferings of the slaves. By this time the movement of the ship would have rubbed their bodies raw in places, for there was no bedding to ease their discomfort.

Dehydration and disease continued to ravage their numbers. Dysentery, smallpox, ophthalmia, measles and yaws, not to mention malaria, yellow fever and typhoid, spread like wildfire in the cramped and fetid conditions. And the sun continued to shine with not a drop of rain in sight.

28 Day.
Saturday.
W by S: 10m
WSW: 77m
            ―――
            87m
Fair weather.

This 24 hours have sailed W by S 9°:5' southerly, but at noon by observation have made good a WSW distance of 29 leagues, & have gone to the westward 26 leagues & to the southward 11 leagues; with the wind from S by W to SE by S, & moderate gale. This day at 9am we set the fore & fore topmast studding sail.[8] Judge have a current which sets to the southward.

We have now 142 slaves dead & many queasy. (Latitude by LOG 1°:47'S, by OBS 1°:47'S; leagues 283 Westing)

29 Day. Sunday.
WSW: 74m
W by S: 16m
            ―――
            90m
Fair weather.

This 24 hours have sailed WSW 20' westerly by the log, but by observation are gone to the southward but 15 miles, so have made good a west 10°:00 southerly course & have been kept to the northward by a current and great sea a distance of 30 leagues; & have gone to the westward 29 leagues, with the wind from SSE to S by E, fresh gale. We now steer away WSW with the wind at SSE. (Latitude by LOG 2°:02'S, by OBS 2°:02'S; leagues 312 Westing)

30 Day.
Monday.
WSW: 87m
Fair weather.

This 24 hours have sailed WSW by the log but allowing 4° declination westerly & 18°:30' set to the northward by the current, have made good at way allowing her 26 leagues for westing, with the wind from SSE to SE by S, fresh gale. We now steer away WSW with the wind at SSE. (Latitude by LOG 2°:2'S; leagues 338 Westing)

1 Day. October.
Tuesday.
WSW: 10m
W by S: 57m
            ―――
            67m
Fair weather &
smooth water.

This 24 hours have sailed WSW 9°:5' westerly by the log, but at noon by observation were in the latitude 2°:6' having gone to the southward 4 miles since yesterday noon: so that from the 29th at noon to this day 12 o'clock have made but 4 miles southing by observations, so must allow her to have made good a west ¼ south course distance of 20 leagues with the wind from SSE to SE by S & moderate. Smooth water & sometimes almost calm & then showery with a little wind. We now steer away W by S, & differ^d. my longitude 17°:54' I say to the westward. (Latitude by LOG 2°:6'S, by OBS 2°:6'S; leagues 358 Westing)

2 Day.
Wednesday.
W by S: 51m
Fair weather
with a great sea
from the
southward & a
current from the
same.

This 24 hours have sailed W by S 17 leagues by the log, but by observation have made but good a W by N course having gone to the northward 3 leagues since yesterday noon, & to the westward 16 leagues; with the wind from SE by E to S by W. Small gale, with a great sea from the southward: I cannot get the longboat out to try the current but suppose it sets to the northward. There is now little wind, we steering away W by S with fair weather, having made 18°:45 diff. longitude I say westward. (Latitude by LOG 1°:57'S, by OBS 1°:57'S; leagues 375 Westing)

3 Day.
Thursday.
W by S: 50m
Fair weather.

This 24 hours have sailed W by South by the log, but by observation have made good a W½S distance 16:7 leagues with the wind from S to SSE, small gale. Have gone to the westward 15 leagues & southing 1:6 leagues with a little swell from the southward. We now steer away W by S with the wind SSE; have diff. my longitude 19°:36 to the west. (Latitude by LOG 2°:1'S, by OBS 2°:1'S; leagues 392 Westing)

4 Day. Friday.
W by S: 81m
Fair weather &
smooth water.

This 24 hours have sailed W by S by the log, with the wind at SSE fresh gale but at noon by observation were in the southern latitude 2°:12', so we made good but a W8°S course, & distance of 27 leagues, westing 26:7 leagues & 2:7 leagues southing. We have had smooth water and little current. Now we steer away W by S½S with the wind at SSE fresh gale, the studding sails set. (Latitude by LOG 2°:12'S, by OBS 2°:12'S; leagues 419 Westing)

5 Day. Saturday.
W by S: 105m
Fair weather &
smooth water.

This 24 hours with the wind at SSE fresh gale – the studding sails set – have sailed W by S 1°:45' southerly, a distance of 35 leagues by observation this day at noon & find we are in the southern latitude 2°:35' having differed in longitude 22°:39' to the westward southing 7:9 leagues, westing 34 leagues. We now steer away W by S, have smooth water & a fresh gale at SSE. Small sails still out. (Latitude by LOG 2°:35′S, by OBS 2°:35′S; leagues 453 Westing)

6 Day. Sunday.
W by S: 103m
Fair weather.

This 24 hours have sailed W by S by the log but at noon by observation have made good but a W1°:00′ southerly course; a distance of 34 leagues with the wind at SSE & S by E, fresh gale & the small sails set; have made 33:9 leagues westing & southing 6 tens with smooth water & fresh gale. We now steer away W by S.

We have now thrown overboard 153 slaves. (Latitude by LOG 2°:37′S, by OBS 2°:37′S; leagues 487 Westing)

7 Day. Monday.
W by S: 109m
Fair weather, a
short sea.
Diff. long^t.
26°: 9′

This 24 hours have sailed W by S by the log & have altered my latitude 00°:21′, but at noon by observation were in the latitude 2°:39′; so have made good but a W1°:00 southerly course, distance 36.3 leagues; westing 36 leagues, southing two miles since yesterday noon, with the wind from SSE to SE, fresh gale. We have had a short sort of a sea. Now steering away W by S with the wind at SE & moderate. (Latitude by LOG 2°:58′S, by OBS 2°:39′S, leagues 523 Westing)

8 Day. Tuesday.
W by S: 82m
Fair weather &
smooth water.
Distance
meridian 27:27.

This 24 hours have sailed W by S by the log & have altered in southing 16′, but by observation at noon have gone to the southward 17′: so my course is W by S, S 30′ southerly, distance 26:7 leagues, with the wind from SSE to ESE, moderate gale & smooth water. We now steer away west with the wind at SE by E. The currents are setting to the southward as appears by observation at noon, and much may be attributed to bad steerage. My diff. long. is 27°:27′. (Latitude by LOG 3°:14′S, by OBS 2°:56′S; leagues 549 Westing)

9 Day.
Wednesday.
W½S: 52m.
Little wind &
smooth.

This 24 hours have sailed W½S by the log, but at noon by observation have made good but a W 5° southerly course 17 leagues, southing 4m & westing 16:7 leagues with the wind from ESE to SSE. Little wind, the currents setting to the northwest which causes the difference between the log & observations. (Latitude by LOG 3°:19′S, by OBS 3°00′S; leagues 565 Westing)

10 Day.
Thursday.
West: 92m
Fair weather &
smooth water.

This 24 hours have sailed west by the log but by observation have gone to the northward 4m, so my course is West ¼ northerly distance 30:7 leagues, westing 91:9 & northing 4:5, with the wind from ESE to SSE fresh gale & smooth water. Diff. longitude 29°:45'. St Pauls[9] lying in the longitude 351°:30' & Acroll lies in the longitude 350°:20', my departure in the longitude 26°:00'.[10] (Latitude by LOG 3°:19'S by OBS 2°:55'S; leagues 595 Westing)

11 Day. Friday.
West: 91m
Smooth water.

This 24 hours have sailed W¼N by the log but at noon by observation have made good but a W 9° North course distance 31 leagues, westing 30 leagues, northing 4:9 leagues with the wind from SSE to ESE fresh gale. Meridian distance 31°:18' & we are in the longitude 354°:42'. We now steer away west, the wind at ESE. (Latitude by LOG 3°:15'S; by OBS 2°:41'; leagues 626 Westing)

12 Day.
Saturday.
W½N: 105m
Fair weather & a
fresh gale. A
great sea from
the SE.

This 24 hours have sailed W½North by the log but at noon by observation have made good a West 4° 00' southerly distance 36 leagues Westing 35:9 leagues southing 2 leagues with the wind from SSE to ESE fresh gale, the studding sails set. Diff. longitude 33°:6' are now in the longitude 352°:54', Acroll's in the longitude 350:20 & St Paul's in the longitude 351°:30'. We steer away west with the wind at ESE fresh gale. (Latitude by LOG 3°:6'S, by OBS 2°:47'S; leagues 663 Westing)

13 Day. Sunday.
West: 110m
W by N: 8m
———
118m

St Pauls
Long:351°:39'
Diff. 35
Sao Tome:
26°:30'
Fresh gale.

This 24 hours have sailed by the margent but at noon by observation found the ship has made a West½Northerly course distance 39 leagues; westing 38 leagues, northing 3:8 leagues with the wind from SSE to ESE fresh gale with a swell which comes out of the SE. We are now in the longitude 351° being 30 to the westward of St Pauls, having had a fresh gale wind with a great swell. My course by the log with a 4°:30' easterly variation is W3° northerly at 7pm.

Phil Foxworthy said he wished that King James & his followers had pissed but one clout. Witness Hales, master gunner, intimating before that he was forced to fly out of England for some crime which he did not declare. He very often speaks of being in the

South Sea & in New England & at Bermuda. (Latitude by LOG 2°:59'S, by OBS 2°:36'S, leagues 700 Westing)

It has proved impossible to find a reference for the remark uttered by Phillip Foxworthy, but the latter's evident distaste for James II and his followers[11] – who included Clarendon and Lord Chief Justice Jeffreys – plus his admitted forced exile from England, may point to an involvement with Monmouth's rebellion at Lyme Regis in 1685 and his defeat at Sedgemoor.

Next day a Portuguese merchantman is sighted bound to the north-east. In 1700 the south Atlantic was criss-crossed by Portuguese slave trade ships. Some slaved in Angola and carried their consignment to Rio de Janeiro, Pernambuco or Bahia in Brazil, returning to Lisbon with colonial merchandise such as sugar or gold. Others slaved on the same stretch of Coast as the English were wont to favour, capitalising on the strong political links between the two countries by frequently anchoring off Company forts and enjoying their protection. After a chequered last half of the seventeenth century in which north-east Brazil became Dutch territory, the colony was again under entirely Portuguese administration, and enjoying an unprecedented boom. Sugar played only a supporting role here; most slaves were channelled through Rio to the great central plateau of Minas Gerais and its mines. Now a state of Brazil, it was once described as having a heart of gold and a breast of iron: black slave labour was responsible for working both metals free from the earth's tenacious grip.

Far from every slave ship flying Portuguese colours was bound for Brazil however. The officially constituted Company of Cacheu, whose headquarters on the upper Guinea Coast was at Cacheu and Bissau, just south of the Gambia, had gained possession of the Spanish Asiento in 1696 for a period of five years. This exclusive contract gave the Company of Cacheu the monopoly of transporting slaves to any Spanish possession in the New World, so the vessel sighted here could have been homeward bound from Buenos Aires.

At this point, thirty-eight days out of São Tomé and with a little over half the middle passage covered, the *Daniel and Henry* alters course to the north-west. Both the wind and the north equatorial current help her achieve respectable distances every day, despite 'bad steerage' caused by marine growth on her hull and rudder. The 'thick horizon' obscures the rising and setting sun and prevents Walter

Prideaux from ascertaining the variation between magnetic and true north.

14 Day.
Monday.
W by N: 18m
WNW: 78m
—————
96m
Fair weather & a fresh gale with a swell from the SE. Variation 4°:30′ Easterly.
A thick horizon.

This 24 hours have sailed W by N 9°:45′ northerly by the log, but at noon by observation have made good a WNW 4°:30′ northerly course distance 32 leagues with the wind at SE by E & SE, fresh gale with a great swell which comes out of the SE. At 6am we saw a ship which stood away NE by E: we supposed she was bound for the coast of Guinea, a Portuguese. Acrolle is in the North lat. 10°:10′ & long. 350°:20′ & St Pauls in the N latitude 1°:25′ & longitude 351°:30′ we being now in the longitude 349°:36′ having made 36°:24′ Diff. longitude from Sao Tome. We now steer away NW & wind at SE fresh gale. We cannot judge of any current, only bad steerage which makes the difference between the log and observation, however we suppose the 4°:30′ variation easterly, cannot get an amplitude. (Latitude by LOG 2°:26′, by OBS 1°:54′S; leagues 728 Westing)

15 Day.
Tuesday.
NW: 99m
Fresh gale & a great swell from the SE.

This 24 hours have sailed NW by the log but at noon by observation have made good a W by N 10°:17′ westerly course distance 33 leagues, with the wind at SE; westing 22:9 leagues, northing 23:7 leagues. We are now in the Southerly latitude 00°:47′ & longitude 348°:27′. We steer away NW with the wind at SE fresh gale & a great swell from ditto. (Latitude by LOG 1°:16′S, by OBS 0°:47′S; leagues 751 Westing)

16 Day.
Wednesday.
NW: 112m
*Diff. long*ᵗ
38°:57′

This 24 hours have sailed NW by the log with the wind at SE, but at noon by observation found she hath made good a NW4°:00 Westerly distance 37 leagues; westing 27:9 leagues, northing 24 leagues, & are in the northern latitude 00°:25′ by observation: but by dead reckoning are in the latitude 00°:2′ North. We now steer away NW, the wind SE, fresh gale. (Latitude by LOG 0°:2′S, by OBS 0°:25′S; leagues 779 Westing)

17 Day.
Thursday.
NW: 118m
Fair weather fresh gale.

This 24 hours have sailed NW by the log, but at noon by observation were in the northern latitude 1°:44′ so have made good a NW2°:00′ westerly distance 39 leagues; westing 28 leagues, northing 26:6 leagues with the wind from SE to SSE, fresh gale with a great swell from the SE. We now steer away NW being in the longitude 345°:39′ having differed my longitude 40°:21′ from Sao Tome. (Latitude by LOG 1°:12′S, by OBS 1°:44′S; leagues 807 Westing)

18 Day. Friday.
NW: *124m*
Fair weather.

This 24 hours have sailed NW by the log, but at noon by observation were in the northerly latitude 3°:19′, so my course has been NW7°:00′ northerly, a distance of 41 leagues; westing 25 leagues, northing 32 leagues, with the wind at SSE fresh gale. We now steer away NW: are now in the longitude 344°:24′ & my diff. of longitude 41°:36′. (Latitude by LOG 2°:39′S, by OBS 3°:19′S; leagues 832 Westing)

19 Day.
Saturday.
NW: *107m*
Showery
weather.

This 24 hours have sailed NW by the log but by observation were in the northerly latitude 4°:14′, so my course has been NW by W 1°:45′ westerly, distance 35 leagues; westing 29 leagues, northing 18 leagues, with the wind at SSE in the longitude 342°:57′, difference of longitude 43°:3′ from Sao Tome. The wind SE by E & showery. (Latitude by LOG 3°:53′S, by OBS 4°:14′S; leagues 861 Westing)

20 Day. Sunday.
NW: *139m*
Showery
Great swell.

This 24 hours have sailed NW by the log, but at noon by observation were in the northern latitude 5°:30′, which is a NW by W distance 46 leagues, with the wind at SSE fresh gale with a great swell which came after us. Westing 38 leagues, northing 25 leagues. We now steer NW, the wind at SSE, fresh gale & showery. (Latitude by LOG 5°:29′S, by OBS 5°:30′S; leagues 899 Westing)

At this point the fair copy manuscript of the *Daniel and Henry*'s voyage comes to an abrupt and premature end. The story is taken up by edited extracts which first appeared in the *Mariner's Mirror* for 1920, and for which meteorological and navigational details were not included.

By now it was obvious to Walter Prideaux that his worst fears concerning the death rate of the slaves were being all too clearly realised. Conditions in the hold were beyond belief; one slave was now expiring every twelve hours. Little wonder Prideaux's narrative introduces a breath of superstition reflecting his fear he is aboard a ship of doom. His anxiety is manifest in the repeated description of a

flaming sword, suggesting divine retribution is imminent. The garbled
reference to Elam, which gains nothing in the transcription, seems to
be taken from Jeremiah chapter 49, verse 37; 'I will cause Elam to be
dismayed before their enemies . . . and I will bring evil upon them, even
my fierce anger, saith the Lord; and I will send the sword after them,
till I have consumed them.'[12]

As the *Daniel and Henry* is swept onwards by the Caribbean
current towards its nemesis, the slaves continue inexorably to perish.
So serious is the situation on board that even the sighting of Barbados
gives Prideaux no cause for joy. He is all too aware that the *Daniel
and Henry* is a ship of death, and all too conscious of his own fragile
mortality. Lucifer himself seems to sail with them, spreading disease,
twisting the currents and frustrating their best intentions of delivering
a choice cargo of slaves. Or is this the work of the Lord?

	22 Oct. Tuesday	Last night at 9 o'clock was seen a flaming sword in the Elam. Saw a star shoot which continued like a flaming sword for 3 minutes.
	23 Oct. Wednesday	We have had died 173 slaves which taken out of the 452, remained on board 279 for owners' account.
	25 Oct. Friday	The current is as uncertain as can be in these parts. We cannot hoist our boat out so cannot try which way it sets, only by estimation.
	27 Oct. Sunday	A current which sets to the Westward and a great swell which comes out of the Eastward. God send us good landfall.
	29 Oct. Tuesday	Sometimes our topgallant sails out in having much in the showers. The wind at an East and a great sea.
	4 Nov. Monday	At a ¼ after 4pm we saw Barbados and at 10am we saw St Vincent.
	5 Nov. Tuesday	We have now at this day noon 183 slaves dead and many more very bad. I wish may escape with 200 dead, the doctor not knowing what to do with them.
	9 Nov. Saturday	We have trimmed our longboat and are doing the same to the yawl. Have 206 slaves dead and many more still sick.

12 Nov. Tuesday From the topmast head I saw a barkalong going to the Eastwards.

Sighting another vessel was the signal for the *Daniel and Henry* to be placed on immediate alert. No vessel could be trusted, for they carried no names or ports of origin and frequently flew misleading flags. For aught the crew of the *Daniel and Henry* knew, the fragile peace brought about by the Treaty of Ryswick might well be ancient history. England could now be at war with one or other of her rival European powers, all of whom had colonial possessions and naval bases in the Caribbean. Added to which the area was infested with pirates who found the Guinea trade ships, slow of sail and weary of crew, easy prey.[13]

13 Nov. Wednes-day.
Moderate &
Fair.
Wind ESE.

Off Hispaniola we saw a ship who fired a gun; presently weighed and stood to windward, but the wind favouring [us] he hauled off SW.

14 Nov.
Thursday.
Moderate and
Fair. Breeze.

At 6pm the ship we saw yesterday came in upon us when we made our ship ready supposing her a pirate but at 12.30 at night she altered her course and hauled in for the land. In the morning she was within a mile of the shore when Cape Tiburon bore WNW½W, distance 7 to 8 leagues. We steered away with the wind at ESE fresh gale. God send us a good sight of Jamaica.

16 Nov.
Saturday.
Winds E by
North and NE.
Fresh gales.

In sight of Jamaica. The morning saw the *Margrett*, a man of war and a small sloop with him turning to the Eastward who we saluted with 5 guns.

Almost home if not dry, the sighting of HMS *Margate*, a sixth-rate ship of the line, was most welcome.[14] Under Captain Rupert Billingsly she had been sent to the Caribbean to deter the French at Petit Guavos – now Haiti – from launching an invasion of Jamaica. Two other ships of the line, the *Fowey* and *Scarborough*, were also on the West India station as reinforcements,[15] Admiral Benbow and his fleet having been recalled some months before.

The arrival of the *Daniel and Henry* did not go unnoticed. William Law, first lieutenant of the *Margate*, noted in his log-book for Sunday 17 November (the discrepancy in day is due to ships in coastal waters – or waters of pilotage – logging their entries from midnight to midnight as on land, rather than midday to midday as on the *Daniel and Henry*):[16]

> At 8 this morning spoke with a Merchant man from Guinea: she gave us 5 guns, we returned 3.[17]

Later the same day Joseph Lyne, master of HMS *Fowey* then lying closer inshore, observed: 'This evening a Haggboat of London, Captain Mathews, came in from Guinea'.[18]

Though the presence of the Royal Navy was comforting to Roger Mathew, it was less reassuring for his crew; for them it meant nothing but impressment, and several took the opportunity to run away the moment the *Daniel and Henry* anchored at Port Royal.

The indiscriminate firing of guns as salutes caused rumblings deep within the Admiralty, culminating in First Lord of the Admiralty Pembroke's *Regulations about Salutes* of 3 March 1702:

> Whereas heretofore considerable Quantities of his Majesty's Powder has been unnecessarily expended by frequent Salutes with Guns and by his Majesty's Ships returning Salutes to those employed in the Merchant's Service, which ought to be prevented as much as possible in the future . . . [19]

The regulations went on to forbid Navy vessels to respond to merchant ships with more than a one-gun salute, and not even that if the merchant ship failed to fire more than three.

Not all of the Navy's business was at the exclusive behest of King and country for there has been little or no acknowledgement of its role as a slave trader. Captains of ships on the West India station were particularly keen on this activity and HMS *Fowey* was no exception. On 1 February 1701, Joseph Lyne noted he supervised the loading of 150 slaves and provisions at Port Royal quay. Their destination was Bastimentos in Panama. Not all were sold there, however, for on 21 February he records 45 of them being sold at Orange Key.[20] Within a few years the Navy was involved in the slave trade on a transatlantic scale. Their large stores of guns, powder and shot, and their privilege of not clearing Customs at their port of departure, gave them an enormous advantage. When Navy ships were eventually sent to cruise off the Guinea Coast, as HMS *Oxford* and *Hastings* did in 1704, the Company complained that their captains 'had Gold and Teeth to our great Mortification, and carried Slaves to Virginia on their own Account'.[21]

More than a century later the Navy was regularly to employ black ratings on its ships, either those bought from slave traders or manumitted slaves who were unemployed. But as the *Daniel and Henry* made her way into harbour in 1700 the Navy's interest concerned only the free men aboard her.

 17 Nov.
Sunday.
Wind
NE by E and
ENE. Fresh gales
with a Great
Sea.

At 4am were off Yellow Point, being a low point full of trees about 3 leagues to the westward of Point Morant when we brought our ship to until 6am when we made sail for Port Royal harbour hauling in with Plum Point. At this time we saluted the *Soldados Prize* which lay there, the Commodore bound home. At noon we came to an anchor in Port Royal harbour – after saluting the fort with 9 guns – in 9 fathom of water, soft ground, where we found Captain Mackfor.

HMS *Soldados Prize* passed her, outward bound under Captain Peter Pickard for Portsmouth. She had been dispatched to the West Indies in June 1698 and recalled on 1 August 1699.[22] Her delayed sailing had been partly caused by the poor communications of the day, partly because HMS *Germoon* had overturned in Port Royal harbour and her men had to be accommodated aboard. She was a fifth-rate ship of the line carrying 46 guns and ended her life in 1712 being sunk as a foundation for part of Plymouth harbour. As for 'Captain Mackfor', coming from the other extreme of Britain to Scotland, Walter Prideaux could never manage much more than a stab at Macpherson's name. They had last met at Alim on 12 June when the *Wormley Berry* was trading for slaves.

Nine months had now passed since the *Daniel and Henry* left Dartmouth. But if Captain Roger Mathew thought that his troubles were over now safe landfall had been made at Jamaica, his optimism was to prove short-lived. For the moment though, Walter Prideaux was happy to to record his own final comments for posterity and offer heartfelt thanks to the Almighty for his safe deliverance:

You must be sure when you come in from the East to keep the shore close on board, by reason of several reefs which lie about 2 miles offshore. You will have, in going along the shore, 11 to 15 fathom of water with sandy ground I say after you come off Plum Point; which Point lies on the low land being to the eastward of Kingston. From 8pm to 4am we went along shore and our foresail, fresh gale at ENE, a strong windward current. You must bring the Castle about SSE or [   ] as the draught [of] water the ship shall draw [is] commonly more SE and NW; have your best anchor for the SE sea breeze.

For which above Preservation, God alone be Blessed and Praised, now and for ever more.

Amen.

We sold 246 slaves and six died in port.[23]

Slaves did not cease dying when the ships in which they were imprisoned arrived at their destination, and the middle passage continued to take its toll for many months afterwards. As evidence witness the report of the Jamaica Assembly, which reckoned that in the period 1655–1787, of the 676,276 slaves declared to the Customs House as arriving, the number that had died in the harbour totalled 31,181.[24]

Thus far the voyage of the *Daniel and Henry* was not a great success. Of the 452 slaves taken aboard in Guinea, 206 had died. It was perhaps as a relieved rather than a happy man that Captain Mathew went ashore in the afternoon of 18 November. His first duty was to report to the Colonial Naval Officer, a customs officer whose responsibilities included ascertaining whether the masters, owners, crew, vessel and cargo of any incoming traffic were legally qualified to trade with the colonies under England's draconian Navigation Laws. There he learned that the *John and Thomas* had arrived at virtually the same time and that the *Mayflower*, a Jamaican-owned vessel on a double voyage to Guinea and back, was due at any moment. The presence of three Guinea trade ships in port within a few days of each other could not fail to depress prices for slaves.

The Colonial Naval Officer would have taken careful note of all crew aboard the *Daniel and Henry* and passed the lists on to the officers of the Royal Navy ships then at anchor at Port Royal, the *Margate* and *Fowey*. Though fears of a French invasion of Jamaica had now subsided, seasoned hands were in constant demand on the men-of-war, most of whose crews had been assembled in England and were dropping like flies from the heat and disease of the tropics. Though they wouldn't bother Roger Mathew or his senior officers, the press-gang would shortly come calling. When they did, they took Phillip Foxworthy, his mess-mate Thomas Rogers, and the black, George Yorke.

Recently Benbow's penchant for wholesale press-ganging had aroused the ire both of the local authorities and of merchant shipowners trading to the West Indies. The Admiralty had taken note of

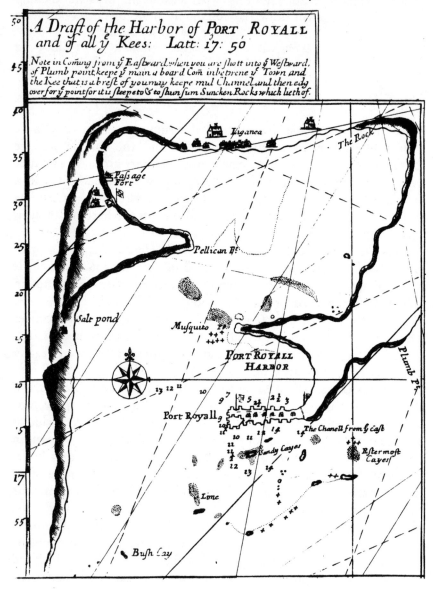

Chart of Port Royal harbour, Jamaica

this and the current regime was far more circumspect in its dealings. Roger Mathew would not have been unhappy at the loss of three of his crew. Their going reduced the wage bill aboard the *Daniel and Henry* but there were still men enough to overhaul the ship comfortably.

Next day Roger Mathew declared his cargo of slaves to Samuel Catchpole, Collector of Customs at Port Royal, producing at the same time his account books and certificates from London and Dartmouth as evidence that the 10 per cent premium on his original cargo had been paid to the Company. During the following days the slaves aboard the *Daniel and Henry* were given a final feed and oiling for slave merchants were already coming aboard to assess them. With the *Wormley Berry* recently arrived, the *John and Thomas* newly anchored, and the eagerly awaited *Mayflower* even now entering harbour, it was a buyer's market.

The buyers were not impressed with what they found aboard the *Daniel and Henry*. Nothing could hide the poor physical condition of many of Captain Mathew's cargo of slaves, and the high predominance of women served to depress the average price that the merchants were prepared to bid. A significant proportion went for little more than their initial cost and the cost of their keep on the middle passage. They were bought by the island's refuse slave specialists, who gambled on buying blacks at the very end of their physical tether, fattening them up, and selling them when (and if) they made a successful return to health.

So crowded was Port Royal harbour with English shipping that there was not enough sugar to freight more than a fraction of the vessels anchored there. Nor was there any sign of more becoming available before the next harvest in late May. Perhaps worst of all, Samuel Catchpole entertained severe misgivings about the disposal of certain items of cargo aboard the *Daniel and Henry* on the coast of Guinea. As if to underline that, four of his men arrived early one morning aboard her, marched down the deck, and nailed a writ to the masthead. If she left Jamaica now she would forfeit her bonds and face seizure at any English or colonial port she attempted to enter. Now the *Daniel and Henry* could be tied up in Jamaica until kingdom come, for both sides would need to appoint attorneys and the judiciary in the island moved at a snail's pace. The only bright spot was that juries in the West Indies, drawn from the colonies' merchants and plantation owners, notoriously failed to convict merchant ship captains for trading misdemeanours. Despite his confidence Catchpole was on a losing wicket.

To this day the nature of the offence committed by the master or freighters of the *Daniel and Henry* can only be guessed at. It will be remembered that her departure from Dartmouth had caused comment at the Customs House, particularly regarding the load of 310 new ironbound casks of various sizes, free of the 10 per cent duty on the understanding that they were 'for the use of Negroes on the voyage'. It must be assumed that the Excise Board informed the Company of the presence of these casks, and in turn the Company wrote to Catchpole setting out their misgivings. Catchpole's searchers, finding few if any of the casks still aboard the *Daniel and Henry* on her arrival, deduced they had been sold or bartered *en route* and so 10 per cent of their value (about £20) should have been paid to the Company. Perhaps even more incriminating was the enthusiasm shown by Walter Prideaux over the saleability of these 'anchors [casks] 3 to a barrell' in his list of 'goods most proper for the Gold Coast' which he had itemised while on the middle passage, and which may have been part of the documentation seized by Catchpole.

Whatever the reason, it cost the *Daniel and Henry* an enforced seven-month sojourn in Jamaica and substantial legal costs. Samuel Catchpole got nothing from this exercise except a legal bill for £6 15s. from his attorneys; in 1713 he was still attempting – unsuccessfully – to earn reimbursement for his pains from the Company. Less than grateful for his assiduity, and not having gained in the slightest by his prosecution of the *Daniel and Henry*, the Company maintained that as Catchpole was paid a handsome commission (5 per cent) to look after their interests, his expenses would have to come out of this.[25]

The irony for merchants Ivy, Arthur and Gould is that had the casks been put to their proper purpose, rather than being sold on the Guinea Coast, they would have profited by far more than their value as barter. Over 300 extra casks of drinking water may well have made all the difference to the mortality rate of the slaves, who would have sold better on arrival in Jamaica. Furthermore, no legal proceedings would have delayed the *Daniel and Henry*'s homeward passage. Like so much of the voyage the sale of the casks was a calculated risk. Captain Mathew gambled on spreading the sails in heavy rain to top up the existing casks but, as the *Journal* shows, rainful was scanty at best.

After nearly ten months on active service and approximately 7,000 miles of voyaging, most of it in tropical waters, there was much work to be done on the *Daniel and Henry*. Once the crew had recovered from their euphoria at having made landfall safely in Jamaica – a celebration which took them ashore for days and nights at a time, and might eventually have led John Shutter the boatswain's mate down the aisle – they were rounded up and put to work overhauling the ship. With the writ firmly nailed to the masthead, for once time was on their side.

Since the intention was to load hogsheads of sugar, the timber stages where the slaves had been shackled between decks were dismantled and stored. The *Daniel and Henry*, relieved of her cargo, rode high in the sheltered waters of Port Royal, allowing her scuttles and gunports to be knocked out and the hold given a thorough airing and scrubbing down. In addition pitch was burnt in the hold, rather in the manner of incense, in a vague attempt to fumigate and disinfect the area. All the decks and side walls were swabbed down with vinegar.

Generally, no matter what the vessel, the routine of an overhaul followed a set pattern. Sails were unbent and the rigging dismantled. Provisions were taken ashore along with gunpowder and the carpenter's and boatswain's stores. Even the guns themselves were occasionally taken ashore, but in this case they were probably left aboard as weights for when the time came to heel the *Daniel and Henry* over and careen the hull. As the gunner's stores, the cables, and any remaining unsold Guinea cargo was shifted ashore, caulkers came aboard to begin the process of packing the fissured seams of the planking with oakum.

For those crew detailed to clear the orlop and bilges the experience was a hard one. The deeper they descended into the bowels of the ship, the worse the stench became, proceeding from the accumulated sewage of the middle passage. As they moved through the Stygian gloom, clearing the accumulation of ship's stores, canvas, tarpaulin and rope, rats the size of small cats swarmed over the inner walls, scrambling desperately to find an exit. Every length of rope, every stowed sail, when disturbed released an explosion of cockroaches and mice. Only when sails were brought into broad daylight could the cost of the year-long verminous attack be counted.[26] While aloft new rigging and shrouds were fitted to the mainmast and worn ones to the foremast, below the unsavoury task of pumping the bilges clear of filth was taxing the crew. Whatever ballast remained was removed. The whole ship was then rerigged and the careening began in earnest, the guns being run to one side of the vessel so that she heeled over exposing her hull. Floating wooden platforms manoeuvred alongside and the graving and scraping commenced. Long trailing marine weed and thickly encrusted molluscs were patiently and painfully cleared, revealing the outer skin of the double hull riddled with the holes of the teredo worm. This skin was then stripped off, 'spoilers' driven into any holes which had penetrated through to the main hull, a 'sandwich filling' of oakum and tar slapped liberally upon the exposed hull before a renewed outer skin of planking was hammered tightly down. Finally a generous layer of lard or tallow was smeared thickly over the hull before the vessel was heeled over again for the same exhausting procedure to begin on the other side.

During this time the sailmakers had been far from idle, spreading the sails, drying them, patching and sewing. Ships' sails, far from being billowing acres of snowy pristine canvas, most closely resembled a tatterdemalion's stained patchwork quilt. Every member of the crew had a part to play. Some, like John Tremlett the cooper, who was responsible for constructing the colossal hogsheads in which the return cargo of sugar would be transported, were doing the work of two; his mate, John Rudd, had perished off the Guinea Coast.

Unfortunately most of Tremlett's work was to little avail for cargoes of sugar were few and far between. The fragile peace brought about by the Treaty of Ryswick some three and a half years earlier was holding and merchant shipping besieged Jamaica from a multitude of English ports in addition to the colony's own fleet of sugar trade ships. Accordingly the competition for sugar was extreme, and favoured those captains and supercargoes with ready money or gold. It is highly probable that Roger Mathew and Walter Prideaux had little of either. The bulk of the revenue from the sale of the slaves would have been on a credit basis, spread over one or two years. And the *Daniel and Henry* had been forced to meet unforeseen extra-curricular expenses at Port Royal. By the beginning of June, Roger Mathew's patience was exhausted. The case brought against the vessel by Samuel Catchpole had collapsed, only a mere 5 tons of muscovado sugar was stowed in the hold, and there were thirty head of merchant sail anchored in Port Royal harbour.[27] He decided to cut his losses and make a run for England.[28]

Dartmouth was reached on 23 July 1701,[29] with the loss of only one of the crew, carpenter George Hale, on the homeward passage. Though there would have been rejoicing at the safe return of most of those who had set sail seventeen long months before, it was doubtless tempered by the poor dividends returned by the venture. The general gloom was not improved by the fact that Daniel Ivy, despite his recent election as Deputy Lieutenant of Devon, had fast declined in health. He had died on 6 June 1701,[30] without ever seeing the *Daniel and*

Henry arrive safely home.

The shadowy Henry Arthur came to an altogether different end. As a result of some extensive borrowing – possibly to finance the Guinea venture aboard the *Daniel and Henry* – he and Daniel Ivy had run up a substantial debt of £600 with a William Hollwell, 'a doctor of physick' in Exeter. On Ivy's death, Arthur became liable for the whole sum, which he was unable to pay. Obviously both Ivy and Arthur, contrary to their image, were operating on the slenderest of economic tightropes and had been badly hit by the loss of John Parminter's *Elizabeth Galley* and by the poor returns registered by the *Daniel and Henry*.

Since no repayment was forthcoming from Henry Arthur, Hollwell issued a writ for the recovery of the outstanding £600. The writ was lodged with the Sheriff of the County, who immediately seized the *Charles*, a flyboat belonging to Arthur, and sold it in open market to Exeter merchant Roger Prowse for £300 (who promptly resold it for £30 profit). Shortly afterwards Henry Arthur went bankrupt and absconded abroad to escape his creditors. He died some time before 1705, never returning to England.[31]

As for James Gould, he had his fingers in so many profitable pies that he could afford to have them burned in one or two. He continued trading but never again to Africa. Likewise Roger Mathew, master of the *Daniel and Henry*, pursued his established career at sea as a merchant sea captain, but never again to Africa. He was to retire from the sea in 1720 on his appointment as tide surveyor and coast waiter to the Dartmouth Customs.[32] And as for Walter Prideaux, who had joined the voyage so optimistically, we have already seen that his career at sea was to prove lack-lustre at best.

Thus all those associated with the *Daniel and Henry* had nothing further to do with the slave trade, in fact gave 'that trade quite over', as Davenant was to record in 1709. Unfortunately whatever views Walter Prideaux expressed on his involvement in the slave trade have not been handed down to posterity. But perhaps a clue may be derived from his descendants, several of whom were baptised Walter, who became leading lights of the Society of Friends in Devon right into the twentieth century.

CHAPTER THIRTEEN

Counting the Cost

DESPITE – or possibly because of – the lack of any hard financial evidence, merchants engaged in the slave trade have traditionally been regarded as wealthy men whose involvement in the trade made them wealthier still. Certainly most began by having access to capital in the first place, an advantage denied to the poor, who were automatically excluded from any mercantile operation whatever, be it for slaves or a more conventional cargo. The first half of the eighteenth century was marked by a concerted bid by England to place herself at the forefront of colonial development: trade played a major part in this and the years of peace between intermittent bouts of hostilities were periods of intense trading activity in which many fortunes were made. Few were made in the slave trade however, and the 'reckless ascription of high profits'[1] (though undoubtedly disguising the stench of an unpalatable trade with the perfume of profit) is hardly borne out by a close examination of the relevant data. Too often the profits made in the slave trade have been calculated simply on the basis of prices paid in Africa for slaves set against prices secured in the plantations. The *Journal* of the voyage of the *Daniel and Henry*, although incomplete with regard to the final leg, affords a good opportunity to redress the balance.[2]

A clear warning as to the profitability of the slave trade was signalled by the continuous flounderings of the Royal African Company. Though heavily financed and more competently run than most organisations of its day, the Company generally made substantial losses, despite the strength of its monopoly. The separate traders who dominated the trade after 1698 did not necessarily fare any better. Their losses cannot be as clearly seen as those of the Company, for they were not publicly accountable and rarely engaged solely in the African trade; their account books were closely guarded at the time and are virtually impossible to discover now. Nevertheless, all the available evidence points to the difficulty rather than the facility of making a fortune from the slave trade. This is partly coloured by established traders seeking to discourage others from jumping on their bandwagon by publishing despondent accounts of their losses. One such example was John Barbot, whose record of trade off the Guinea and Calabar coasts is one long tale of gloom and doom.[3] Though interlopers in the trade prior to 1698, the passing of the Act enabled Barbot and a consortium of London merchants to set out the frigate *Albion* (24 guns and 60 men) for New Calabar with a cargo valued at £2,600. James Barbot was appointed supercargo and the *Albion* eventually sailed in 1699, taking 583 slaves aboard in just two months.

At this point what can only be described as professional pessimism settles as Barbot reports:

> all the ships that loaded slaves with the *Albion* frigate at Calabar lost some half, and others two thirds of them, before they reached Barbados: and such as were then alive died there, as soon as landed, or else turned to a very bad market: which rendered the so hopeful voyage of the *Albion* abortive, and above sixty per cent of the capital was lost, chiefly occasioned by the want of proper food and water to subsist them, as well as the ill management of the principals aboard . . .

Contemporary documents point to another end to the story. Under the very able command of Stephen Dupont the *Albion* entered Barbados on 22 November 1699 and cleared for London on 18 April 1700.[4] Amongst the cargo of cotton, ginger and molasses on the return leg of the voyage were 341 hogsheads of muscovado sugar. Since a hogshead was generally reckoned as 12 cwt., and one pound of muscovado was worth approximately 6d. on the London wholesale market, the muscovado alone was worth over £12,000 sterling: this undoubtedly made the 'abortive' losses on the middle passage easier to bear.

It is precisely the triangular nature of the trade which makes it so difficult to assess profits: indifferent trade on the outward leg to Africa and heavy losses on the middle passage could be redeemed by a highly profitable cargo of sugar for the final leg back to England. Because England and the rest of Europe (with the possible exception of Portugal) imported very few slaves for its own use – instead controlling the shipping and creating economic policies which governed both plantations and trade – the tendency has always been to view the slave trade as peripheral and as an adjunct to the sugar or tobacco trade.[5]

To vex the question even further, colonial currency did not exchange at par with sterling and was frequently discounted by as much as 30 per cent. This makes fixing the prices paid for slaves in the West Indies with any accuracy extremely difficult. Prices in Jamaica in 1700, the year of the *Daniel and Henry*'s arrival, vary considerably depending on the authority quoted, though by all accounts demand was extremely high. The Company reported an average £23 15s. per head;[6] another authority states the average was about £25;[7] a different reading of the Royal African Company's accounts produces figures of £30 14s. for each man, £28 10s. 6d. for each woman;[8] and finally Sir William Beeston, Governor of Jamaica, complained to the Committee of Trade on 5 January 1700 that the ten per centers were charging '£34 a head for slaves on harsh credit terms'.[9] As if that were not enough to obscure any clarity, local conditions also had their part to play. Competition for slaves on the Guinea Coast in 1700 was so intense that captains would consider taking delivery of all except the aged, infirm, disabled or obviously diseased. Poor delivery figures and high mortalities recorded by almost all the vessels with which the *Daniel and Henry* consorted off the Coast bear silent witness to that. Also the *Daniel and Henry* was not loaded with 'prime' slaves but mainly with women, whose value in the plantations was slightly less. To complicate matters further, three vessels arrived in Jamaica within a few days of each other: the *John and Thomas* on 18 November with 130 slaves, the *Daniel and Henry* on the following day with 246, and the *Mayflower* (owned and freighted by Jamaican merchants) on the 21st, with 73.[10] Such a cluster of Guinea trade ships could only spell disaster for prices, so the average prices previously referred to must be treated with care.

When discussing profits accruing from the slave trade, writers generally take little account of the host of expenses that accompanied any trading venture. Insurance is a case in point, varying widely with times of war and peace. Generally premiums varied accordingly from about 8 guineas per £100 in peacetime to double that in times of war. The London slave merchant Humphrey Morice records a payment of 8 guineas per cent on a cargo worth £2,190 in 1728:[11] this would have excepted losses by natural death of slaves and insurrections.[12] He also records a payment for porterage, lighterage, cartage and searchers' fees (at the Customs) of £43: the total of such charges over a seventeen-month voyage such as that undertaken by the *Daniel and Henry* would not have been small. Similarly the cost of converting a vessel of her size to engage in the trade was not cheap: costs for the *Daniel and Henry* can only be approximate, based on the charge of £812 recorded by the *Davers Galley* during conversion in 1709.[13]

Nor was it cheap to trade off the Guinea Coast: the local caboceers all exacted their dues. A constant thorn in the side of the slave traders was the *dashee*, or present, which opened all business negotiations. This was customary the length and breadth of the Coast and though not mentioned by many contemporary accounts, the practice clearly exasperated John Barbot:

> seeming at first of no great value . . . in process of time and having forty or fifty blacks or more everyday to give it to, it at last amounts to five per cent out of the cargo of the ship . . . [14]

Having paid off its interpreters and canoemen, the *Daniel and Henry* sailed to São Tomé to provision the major leg of the middle passage, and thus incurred additional heavy expenses. The final blow to any hopes of high profit margins on this voyage was delivered during the middle passage with the death of 206 slaves: mortality was always much higher amongst male slaves in transit than female,[15] and since their initial cost had been proportionately higher, their loss represented a substantial diminution in potential profits.

The *Journal* for the *Daniel and Henry* records a total of 452 slaves bought, but the breakdown of figures by age and sex is available only up to 387. At that stage the cargo consisted of 106 men, 220 women, 21 boys and 40 girls. Assuming that the pattern of trading remained similar for the further 70 slaves, the final consignment would consist of 122 men, 258 women, 23 boys and 49 girls. Of this number, a total of 246 were delivered to Jamaica, but these are not described in terms of age or sex. Assuming twice as many men as women died on the middle passage, the final delivery figures would have been in the region of 35 men, 180 women, 10 boys and 21 girls.

If fate had not dealt kindly with the *Daniel and Henry* up to now, the *coup de grâce* was not long in coming. As we have seen, instead of executing the quick turnaround in Jamaica that he had counted upon, Roger Mathew found himself bogged down in litigation. Though the action was brought by Samuel Catchpole, Collector of Customs at Jamaica, it was not a Customs-related matter but appears to have been generated by the Royal African Company. It was nothing to do with James Gould, who had clearly detailed his venture in London and paid £71 17s. 5d. tax in respect of 10 per cent of its value.[16] Nor was it Roger Mathew's private venture, worth £193 10s., on which he had similarly paid 10 per cent tax of £19 7s. to the Dartmouth Customs.[17] Ivy and Arthur's two-thirds of the venture had also paid the required 10 per cent, despite no entry having been made at Dartmouth. That leaves only the question of the vast number of casks (shipped free of the 10 per cent duty) which had caught the eye of the Customs searchers in Dartmouth, and which had been illicitly sold on the Guinea Coast. Though Catchpole did not win his case, the *Daniel and Henry* was tied up in Jamaica until early June: all she had to show for her time there was 104cwt. of muscovado sugar which George Dottin, Walter Prideaux's uncle, cleared through Dartmouth Customs for James Gould on 23 July 1701.[18] At London wholesale rates that was worth a mere £292 and only a proportion of that would have been profit. As for bills of exchange or promissory notes brought back from Jamaica, these would have been heavily discounted by London bankers.

On her arrival back in Dartmouth, the biggest bill the merchant backers of the *Daniel and Henry* had to meet was that of the seamen's wages. This, the largest single expense with the exception of the cargo, is also the most complex to assess. Wage levels varied by both occupation and location, 'river' wages being paid in port, 'deep-water' wages while at sea. It is presumed that river wages were payable while the vessel was anchored off the Guinea Coast. The task of assessing wages is not made easier by the disappearance of a quarter of the original crew by death, discharge, impressment or desertion, or by the lack of comparable data on pay. Seamen, unlike their labouring equivalent on land, have their board and lodging found for them, though not of course that of their families. Nor is seafaring on a long voyage a seasonal job. Wage scales in southern England for the year 1700 for building craftsmen reveal they were paid an average of 1s. 8d. and labourers 1s. 2d. per day;[19] building was an intensely seasonal occupation and the wages reflect this.

Finally there is the question of fraud. Merchant backers of slave trade ventures had little option – short of accompanying the vessel about its business – but to entrust all to the captain and supercargo. Little could be done to check up on exactly how many slaves had been loaded on the Guinea Coast, or the cargo that had been exchanged for them. The islands off the West Indies offered ample opportunity for a boatload of slaves to be smuggled ashore under cover of darkness and then marked dead on the slave muster. 'Prime' slaves were sometimes hidden in the ship whilst the bulk of the cargo was disposed of, then word put about that a few 'choice' slaves were available at premium prices. Though the Controller of the port of arrival was theoretically expected to note down an accurate account of the number of slaves delivered to the plantations, this was probably done by taking the captain's word rather than by an actual head count. In the case of the *Daniel and Henry* Walter Prideaux records that 246 slaves were sold, and six died in port. The Controller of Customs, in his account lodged with the Company, states that 250 were delivered.[20] His was a global figure that did not differentiate between slaves carried as personal ventures and those who formed the bulk of the numbers. As all Guinea-trade vessels arrived with dying slaves aboard, an accurate figure is impossible. The balance sheet of slaves sold (Table 13.1) is computed on the basis that 240 were actually the subjects of deals that were honoured. Payment on slaves who died shortly after being sold was usually refunded. Nor can the balance sheet take account of the profits on the return cargo of sugar from Jamaica since no details have emerged of its cost, nor whether it was funded by the sale of slaves. Lastly the importation of gold cannot be assessed. We know that the *Daniel and Henry* traded for gold during her first days on the Guinea Coast, but what proportion of it was fake, and how much was subsequently part-exchanged for slaves is not possible to ascertain. Gold, unlike pepper and ivory, did not attract a 10 per cent tax when landed in England, so no record remains of it being landed at Dartmouth. Equally no record of ivory being imported survives, though the crew of the ship had a quantity of tusks aboard. The turning of blind eyes towards certain aspects of the *Daniel and Henry* cargo – both inbound and outbound – may have contributed to the summary dismissal of Walter Prideaux's kinsman Thomas Jago as Controller of the port of Dartmouth in 1702. It was little more than a rap across the knuckles; shortly afterwards he was reinstated and served without further ado until 1713.[21]

Table 13.1   A speculative balance sheet

Outgoings	£
Actual cost of cargo	2,036
Insurance of cargo at 10 per cent	204
Insurance of ship (valuing vessel at £1,000)	100
Ten per cent taxes paid on the declared value of the cargo	225
Port charges at Dartmouth	20
Cartage, porterage, lighterage and searchers' fees	40
Re-equipping the *Daniel and Henry* for the Guinea trade	500
Provisioning of ship	150
Extra equipment (sets of sails, spare anchors etc.)	100
Charts	2
Presents to Guinea Coast caboceers	102
Purchase of a canoe	10
Hire of canoemen	10
Purchases of pepper etc.	5
Provisioning and harbour dues at São Tomé	25
Port charges at Jamaica	25
Customs charges (searchers' fees etc.) at Jamaica	10
Legal expenses	10
Provisioning of ship	50
Repairing ship – raw materials	20
Convoy charges when clearing Jamaica[22]	11
Wages[23]	1,145
Incentives to Captain Mathew[24]	207
Incentives to Doctor Fenner	12
Commission (5 per cent) to auctioneers on hammer price	273
Total expenditure (excluding cost of return cargo of sugar)	£5,292

Incomings

Slaves:
A total of 246 were sold but not all slaves aboard the
Daniel and Henry belonged to Messrs Ivy, Arthur and
Gould. At least 6 would have been the personal allowance
of Captain Mathew, Edward Fenner and John Chapman,
chief mate. The *Journal* records Chapman had purchased a
man and a girl slave while the ship stood off the Guinea
Coast. Captain Mathew would probably have carried 2
men on his account and Doctor Fenner 1 man and 1
woman. As has been noted, slaves which were personal

ventures never died – at least on paper – so these 6 slaves must be subtracted from the total belonging to the merchant backers of the *Daniel and Henry*; the incentives to Captain Mathew and Doctor Fenner have been adjusted accordingly.

The revenue from the slaves belonging to Messrs Ivy, Arthur and Gould has been conducted in the following manner:

31	men slaves @ £25 colonial currency/£17 10s. stg.	£542 10s.
179	women slaves @ £23 colonial currency/£16 2s. stg.	£2,881 18s.
10	boy slaves @ £20 colonial currency/£14 0s. stg.	£140 0s.
20	girl slaves @ £18 colonial currency/£12 12s. stg.	£252 0s.

Total revenue from sale accruing to Messrs Ivy Arthur & Gould in sterling (excluding any profit on the return cargo of sugar)   £3,816 8s.

Whatever the uncertainties about specific finances, the main revelation of the speculative balance sheet is clear. The voyage of the *Daniel and Henry* neither made rich men out of its participants, nor tempted any of them to re-enter the trade in slaves in the future.

Though the voyage of the *Daniel and Henry* is unique in that the greater part of the log-book has survived (although in fair-copy form), she was far from the only ship of her time to be freighted by a merchant consortium which originated outside the recognised centres of the slave trade – London, Bristol and Liverpool. As the following chapters show, voracious though the merchants of the 'big three' ports were, those of some minor outports were no less enthusiastic, though their contribution to England's involvement has largely been overlooked.

Part Two
Merchants, Mariners and Ports in the Provincial English Slave Trade of the Early Eighteenth Century

Principal Towns and Minor Ports of England in 1700

Glasgow
Edinburgh
Berwick upon Tweed

NORTH-HUMBERLAND
Newcastle upon Tyne

Belfast

Carlisle
CUMBERLAND
DURHAM

WHITEHAVEN
WEST-MORLAND

Ulverston

YORKSHIRE

LANCASTER
Leeds
Hull

Isle of Man

LANCA-SHIRE

Dublin

Liverpool
Manchester
Sheffield

CHESHIRE
Chester
LINCOLN-SHIRE

FLINT
DENBIGH

CAERNARVON
MERIO-NETH

Nottingham

Kings Lynn
Norwich
NORFOLK

To Cork
and
Kinsale
100 miles

Birmingham

Cambridge
SUFFOLK
Ipswich

CARDIGAN

PEM-BROKE

Gloucester
Colchester

ESSEX

Milford
Haven
GLAMORGAN

Swansea
Cardiff
Bristol

London
Southend

Gravesend
DEAL

SOMERSET
KENT

Barnstaple
Bridgwater
HAMP-SHIRE
Dover

BIDEFORD
Tiverton
Taunton
SUSSEX

DEVON
Axminster
DORSET
Southampton

Dorchester
Portsmouth
Brighton
Hastings

TOPSHAM
POOLE

PLYMOUTH
EXETER
LYME REGIS
WEYMOUTH
Isle of Wight

DARTMOUTH

Land's
End
CORNWALL
FALMOUTH
Start Point

Isles of Scilly
Lizard Point

N

| 0 | 25 | 50 | 100 | 150 Miles |
| 0 | 40 | 80 | 160 | 240 Kilometres |

CHAPTER FOURTEEN

A Lawful Calling?

I T IS sometimes difficult to remember, given the enormous amount of attention accorded to London, Bristol and Liverpool in the slave trade, that the English trade in slaves actually started from the minor outports. Plymouth, having caught the limelight with Hawkins' expeditions of 1562, '64 and '67, has been otherwise ignored by all histories of the slave trade. Yet the prospects of trading for slaves on the African coast clearly excited a great many provincial merchants. They were driven by exactly the same motives which prompted Hawkins and his backers, namely that 'Negroes were very good marchandise in Hispaniola . . . and might easily be had upon the Coast of Guinea'.¹ The city and merchants of Exeter, for example, were granted a charter to trade with Africa in 1588: the prime aim was gold, but slaves were never far from mind in any European's assessment of potential profits to be gained on an African venture.

The early predominance of the minor outports of south-west England – especially Devon – was no accident. Their geographical locations alone would have made them prime candidates, situated as they are on the Western Approaches to the Channel with direct access to the Atlantic. They are provided, by man or nature, with deep, sheltered harbours rather than windswept shallow estuaries. And they were populated with seafarers, to such an extent that hundreds of West Country sailors were transported to Rochester to man Queen Elizabeth's contingent of four vessels which were due to join Hawkins' nine-strong fleet from Plymouth in 1567.²

As the years progressed, trade with Africa fell into the doldrums. It was not until the middle of the seventeenth century that serious interest in it was reawakened by various African companies, and eventually put on a firm business footing by the Royal African Company. As a company with close political and financial links with

City merchants and policy-makers in Parliament, its headquarters were in London. So from the middle of the seventeenth century to the abolition of the slave trade in the nineteenth century, London dominated the stage. There were, however, powerful interests which lay outside the capital, in rich provincial cities like Bristol and Exeter, which campaigned against Company monopoly in the seventeenth century. Many of these cities were self-sufficient, providing from their own immediate hinterlands a range of manufactured goods for export. Though largely based on wool, 'the Staple Commodity of England, and the Fountain from whence all our Power and Riches took their Source',[3] woollen-based produce was supplemented with leather goods, glassware and quantities of provisions. In addition substantial cargoes of other fabrics, iron, earthenware and pewter were imported from abroad. All these formed the backbone of a growing trade from the outports to the new colonies in America and the Caribbean. The self-sufficiency of these ports even extended to processing the raw materials that arrived back from these colonies for home consumption, or re-exporting them to Ireland, the Channel Islands, France or Holland. By controlling this inward-bound trade the outports could maximise their profits.

Trade with the new American colonies was a vital prerequisite for any merchant considering venturing into the slave trade. He gained both experience of procuring and handling large mixed cargoes, and linked up to a network of potential slave purchasers on the other side of the Atlantic from whom he was currently buying or freighting cargoes of sugar, tobacco or cotton. They may well have suggested to him the profits that could be made by spending a few months trading on the Guinea Coast for, with the exception of specialities such as cowries, a cargo for Africa was very similar in its constituent parts to that of its West India or America-bound equivalent.

Behind these long-haul trading voyages were men of substance, often heading highly capitalised operations and throwing their weight behind every effort for less restrictive trade. Their entrepreneurial spirit is best exemplified by organisations such as the Plymouth Company and the Merchant Adventurers of Bristol, both vitally important in encouraging trade beyond England's immediate horizons. Merchants who responded to this challenge and developed a varied import–export trade were at a huge advantage when they turned to survey the possibilities of an African venture.

All this was as nothing if the outport did not possess significant maritime expertise which went well beyond a pool of experienced mariners. A seventeenth- or eighteenth-century trading vessel was constructed from the skills of dozens of professional craftsmen: to keep such a ship in a condition for extensive trading voyages to the coast of Africa, the Caribbean and back required the skills of dozens more. They included carpenters, sailmakers, ropemakers, blockmakers, riggers, caulkers, anchorsmiths, and chandlers: all needed to be available on a year-round basis.

Virtually all these conditions had to be fulfilled before a port could even consider, let alone mount, a long-haul trading voyage. Few of the minor outports found themselves possessed of such advantages. But, while the majority followed very conventional paths straitened by tradition, convenience and geographical outlook, a few minor outports had merchants prepared to break the mould.

Yet the African ten per cent merchant was rarely wedded solely to the Guinea trade but, like Daniel Ivy of Exeter, was engaged primarily in trading in a conventional commodity such as tobacco. Whereas it is relatively easy to assess the geographical and local economic factors that facilitated the entry of a minor port into the African trade, the origins from which these provincial slave trade merchants sprang is more complex. Basically, three distinct socioeconomic backgrounds can be identified. First there were the younger sons of the landed gentry who found a place in the merchant community by apprenticeship or marriage or occasionally both. Walter Prideaux of the *Daniel and Henry* is an example drawn from this tier. Secondly there were the sons of merchants who simply followed their fathers into trade. In third place, numerically very far behind, came those from more heterogeneous backgrounds who by luck, judgement or opportunity had completely outdistanced their origins.[4] These tiers were, of course, not mutually exclusive. Their overlapping often gave rise to vastly extended networks, hardly guessed at on the surface, but which could occasionally involve merchant, slave ship captain and plantation owner in a singular gavotte of mutual profit.

Like Daniel Ivy of Exeter, who rose to become Deputy Lieutenant of Devon in 1701, the slave trade merchants of the provincial ports were not irresponsible delinquents but God-fearing pillars of society. Up and down the country, in the great ports of London and Bristol (and later Liverpool) and among the small ports which peppered the English coastline, these prosperous and worthy men sought profit by buying and selling other human beings. To be sure, these human beings were black, heathen and regarded as little better than livestock, but from what moral or religious high ground did these merchants set sail, so confidently to enslave their fellow men? In other words, how did religion sanction the slave trade?

The answer can be found, not in Anglicanism, the established church of the nation, but in Dissent, in Nonconformity. The roots of Dissent lay well back in the sixteenth century, in the teachings of Calvin. This was the seed from which the great trunk of puritanism grew. Below ground the roots spread vigorously, penetrating the foundations of religious thought. Above ground, puritanism revolutionised accepted notions of government and determined political aspirations, business relations, family life and personal codes of behaviour.[5] During the early seventeenth century many of these changes were embodied by the Anglican church but as the century progressed the overwhelming desire for religious (and political) liberty of conscience went well beyond Anglicanism's limited response. Soon a number of branches could be observed growing strongly from the puritan trunk. Presbyterianism was one, though it was less than revolutionary in its adherence to a strict system of church organisation supported by a limited monarchy.[6] Congregationalism was another which, unlike Presbyterianism, insisted on the right of every church to organise itself and on the freedom of all churches from state interference. This branch bore fruit in the guise of a tradition of civil and religious liberty which we still enjoy today. Among the other branches was that of Quakerism. All these offshoots possessed characteristics in common, chief among these being a devotional regard for the activities of commerce and industry. This was hardly surprising since these were areas in which Dissenters, being neither of the landowning minority nor of the peasant majority, could flourish mightily.

Of course, Dissent and its disciples prospered mightily under the Commonwealth, but these intoxicating years evaporated quickly in the cold light of the Restoration in 1660. With it the old economic policies of Charles I's government, favouring an artificial and state-promoted capitalism based on the grant of privilege and concessions to Company promoters ensconced well within the oligarchy, reared their ugly monopolistic heads once again. Political dissent quickly became part and parcel of religious dissent as merchants fought hard to retain their independence. The governments of Charles II and James II tried, against all the odds, to turn back the clock. But Parliament now contained members who had invested heavily in colonial ventures and had their own ideas on commercial policy. Moreover they would not be dictated to by Church or state on matters in which they knew best. Their central demand was that 'business affairs should be left to be settled by business men, unhampered by the intrusions of an antiquated morality or by misconceived arguments of public policy'.[7]

Little appealed to Dissenting merchants as much as profit, and though they dressed the term up as economic expediency, it soon became sanctified as the first fruit of a religion called business. Profit did not arise without strings attached. Business itself had to be conscientiously discharged, prices kept within reasonable bounds, dealings characterised by honesty and diligence, debts settled with care and rapidity, and bankruptcy avoided at all costs. In short, an Englishman's word was to be his bond. Work was to be considered a duty to society, and an obligation to God. And lastly charity, the greatest obligation placed upon a Dissenter of means, had a major part to play in helping the less fortunate to stand on their own feet; bequests to the poor and the payment of apprenticeship fees figured largely in Dissenters' charitable activities.

Such revolutionary activities which – except perhaps the last – we consider commonplace today, put the wind up the Restoration establishment in no uncertain manner. It responded by ostracising Dissenters, paying mobs to destroy meeting-houses, hounding conventicles and preachers, and legislating to deny Dissenters the right to direct participation in public affairs (though not to Parliament), and even entry into the universities of Oxford and Cambridge (a rule not repealed until well into the nineteenth century).

Dissenters of intelligence and ambition, sensing that the *cordon sanitaire* thrown around them and all of their contagion could well become a rein of power, made a virtue of necessity. They threw themselves wholeheartedly into commerce and finance (areas unknown to the medieval backwaters which England was pleased to call universities), and did so without scruple seeing that religion itself had blessed their choice and charity provided an extra benison. The outcome of this was a powerful affinity between religious radicalism and business acumen that was to carry Dissent and great Dissenting families – like the Cadburys and Frys – effortlessly through into the mid-twentieth century, leaving Oxford and Cambridge floundering in their wake. In the wider arena of political freedom and social progress in England, Dissent has played a key role. In the words of one authority, democracy owes more to nonconformity than to any other single movement. The virtues of enterprise, diligence, and thrift are the indispensable foundation of any complex and vigorous civilisation. It was Puritanism which, by investing them with the supernatural sanction, turned them from an unsocial eccentricity into a habit and a religion.[8]

So overwhelming was the bullish mood of Dissenters and their casuists, and so persuasive (and pervasive) the idea that all commerce could and should be carried on for the greater glory of God, that few of their number cared to examine the darker aspects of trade. For the bottom line of trade is profit, and profit – more often than not – involves exploitation. Most exploitative of all commodities were sugar, tobacco and cotton, where no amount of charity could sweeten the basic wrong of using people as chattels. And what of the trade in slaves, already well established by the 1660s; how did that work for the common good?

If Dissenters felt themselves on the horns of a dilemma here, it lost them no sleep. Their religion sanctioned trade, this specific trade involved releasing blacks from their pagan backgrounds and exposing them to the superior benefits of the Christian world, so their consciences could have a clear run up until that point. When the slaves were sold it was the responsibility of the plantation bosses to inculcate them with Christianity. Traders were simply middlemen. In addition Dissenters held an additional card up their sleeves. For them the commonly held nineteenth- and twentieth-century doctrine that religion and economic interests form two separate and coordinated empires[9] was still in its infancy, but beginning to make itself felt.

Accordingly where fulmination and denunciation of the trade might have been expected, there was a vacuum. In all the great swath of sermons, tracts and books published during the heat of the commercial revolution launched by Dissenters between 1660 and 1700, none grappled with the potential embarrassment afforded by the slave trade. True, they did attempt to remind the plantocracy that their slaves were 'of as a good a kind as you . . . reasonable Creatures as well as you; and born to as much natural liberty',[10] but their main point was that slaves should be offered the salvation of a Christian baptism rather than immediate and unconditional manumission.

Having escaped the opprobrium of their ideological peers, who exhorted them 'whatever thy Hand findeth to do, do it with all thy might',[11] whilst reminding them to avoid oppression and cherish good works, Dissenters felt no qualms about the slave trade. Merchants of all Protestant denominations – Anglicans, Presbyterians, Independents, Congregationalists, Methodists, Baptists and Quakers – played their part. It was not to last for ever. In the mid-eighteenth century an obscure American settler of English background, French descent and Quaker persuasion called Anthony Benezet reached back over half a century to the Dissenting tracts of Richard Steele. There he found the dictum that, the dust of years newly polished off, reflected the very core of his opposition to the slave trade and illuminated the way towards abolition of both the trade and the institution of slavery. The text of this rule was simplicity itself: 'To do unto all Men as we would they should do unto us'.[12]

Nothing could be clearer, or more directly to the point. Yet the merchants of early eighteenth-century England, fired by free trade zeal, had ignored it, and no group had more flagrantly dismissed it than the slave traders.

CHAPTER FIFTEEN

Berwick to Weymouth

TAKING the coast in a clockwise manner, from Berwick upon Tweed in the north-east, round to Carlisle in the north-west, a glance at early eighteenth-century maritime trade from the minor outports initially displays little variation from that imposed by location. The further north-east the less the variation, so Berwick's overseas trade linked virtually exclusively with Scotland. Newcastle upon Tyne relied almost solely upon the export of coal to the continental ports of Europe, though an occasional plantation-bound ship did make a showing – the *Happy Return* left Stockton for Barbados in 1698, as did the *Reserve* in 1699 and 1700.[1]

Otherwise it was an unrelieved humdrum of coal, pewter and lead to Stockholm, Hamburg, Rotterdam or Gothenburg. Further south, Hull loaded the *Concord* with a massive mixed cargo for Barbados in 1699 and repeated the exercise to Jamaica in 1701.[2] A few other departures for the West Indies were swamped by the trade with Rotterdam. There is nothing to report from Boston, tightly locked into trade with Scandinavia, nor from King's Lynn, equally tied to a marriage of convenience with Norway, though Rotterdam figured as an occasional suitor. Yarmouth bravely attempted to break with a diet of herrings and cloth to the Continent and Scandinavia by loading its own *Bourdeaux Merchant* for Jamaica with bricks, pitch, beer, cheese, iron goods and leather in 1700.[3] This appears to have been a somewhat indigestible diversion, for no other departures for the Caribbean were recorded up to 1704. Ipswich concentrated on cereal and cloth to the yawning maw of Rotterdam; a pattern closely followed by the neighbouring port of Colchester.

The influence of London sapped all independent commercial flair from the ports of the Medway, Thames and Kent; later we shall find that Bristol blighted the trading aspirations of Bristol Channel ports to a similar degree. One exception to the absolute rule of London, however, was Deal.

Sitting in a now forgotten corner of England, but once frequently in the glare of history, Deal seems an unlikely contender against London's might. Yet in bygone days, when there were no satellite communications, long-range weather forecasts or electronic navigation aids and when sail ruled supreme, Deal, perched on the smooth rump of Kent with not even a harbour, inlet or pier to its name, had a major part to play in maritime affairs.[4]

A map will not reveal the reason why, but a sea chart will. There, four miles offshore from Deal, lurk the Goodwin Sands. This infamous procession of sandbanks, over ten miles long and four miles broad, was notorious for its capacity to enfold and devour unwary or unlucky ships, clutching them to a sandy bosom from which there was no escape. For on a rising tide the Goodwins become quicksand; and on an ebb tide, when they peep above the surface, the sands drain and compact, becoming hard as sandstone and easily capable of breaking the back of any storm-stressed vessel thrown upon them.

Despite their unforgiving nature, the Goodwins have saved more ships than they have savaged. For their presence has blessed Deal with a deep-water anchorage capable of holding several hundred ships. With the Deal shore providing shelter from the predominant westerlies and the Goodwins acting as a massive submarine breakwater against fierce easterly seas, the anchorage – known simply as the Downs – developed as a natural haven and rendezvous for both Royal and Merchant navies. It became customary for most London merchant shipping, which was inevitably delayed in the straits of Dover by contrary winds, to take its passage as starting from the Downs.

Wars meant prosperity for Deal. Small fortunes could be made provisioning the men-of-war and troop transports packed with soldiery that lay at anchor awaiting orders during England's frequent European conflicts. Peace meant adversity, or so the local saying went, but there was a pretty penny to be made then too.

Few London ships (or those from other east coast ports) attempted to navigate the Goodwins without a Deal pilot, and rarely anchored for less than a few days – and often for several weeks – in the Downs awaiting favourable winds. Inward-bound merchantmen offered even greater prizes, for smuggling was well established by the seventeenth century. Deal longshoremen ferried pilots and provisions to weary merchantmen bound up the coast to London and beyond, providing as they did so a ready outlet for luxury goods such as silks, lace, tea, tobacco, brandy and rum.

Over and above the Goodwins, shore batteries at Deal and Walmer acted as a powerful deterrent against marauding privateers in wartime, and the virtually continuous presence of naval men-of-war was a reassuring sight to merchantmen awaiting a convenient wind or convoy. But the Downs proved a mixed blessing for ships' companies. Though in theory the Navy had no right to impress there (this being the prerogative of the Warden of the Cinque Ports) in practice it frequently usurped the privilege.

So Deal stood in an enviable position at the very neck of a funnel. Through it poured almost all the shipping of London (and the east coast ports) to and from France, Spain, Portugal, the Mediterranean, West and East Indies, America and Africa. It became a convenient place for a London merchant, company or trading house to keep an agent, for last-minute instructions or delayed cargo could easily be dispatched by road and reach Deal within two or three days. In the early eighteenth century the Royal African, South Sea and East India companies all maintained representatives there.

As England's colonial ambitions in the seventeenth and eighteenth centuries were expressed alternately by force of arms and trade wars, Deal accommodated itself profitably to each phase. The town had its own merchants of course, prominent amongst whom were the Bowles, a Kentish family who had forged strong links with the Crispes of London during the early seventeenth century. In turn

they were deeply involved in the African trade through the activities of Nicholas Crispe, who had not only created the Company of Merchants Trading into Africa of 1631, but also largely financed the Guinea Company two decades later. As we have already seen, this was the direct ancestor of the Royal African Company, boasting an extensive string of trading posts along the Guinea Coast, resident factors, and a field of operations which emphatically included trading for slaves.

As a result of the family's connections with the Crispes, one of the Bowles was employed in the Guinea Company, coming to an untimely but spectacular end on the Guinea Coast in 1652:

> Mr Bowles, one of your factors going up with a cargo to Baracunda, was killed by an explosion of a powder chest on which he was sitting smoking a negro's pipe of tobacco under the impression it was a gold chest.

Perhaps as a result, this was the last time any member of the family made a personal appearance on the Guinea Coast, though it failed to dampen their collective ardour for the trade to Africa. In this they were well represented by brothers Tobias, Valentine and George Bowles. Of the three, Tobias was the most prominent, becoming a successful London merchant with a head office in Mincing Lane and property in both London and Deal. He traded predominantly for sugar and tobacco with Maryland, where an uncle, Colonel Seymour, had been Governor during the time of Queen Anne. In the late seventeenth century, probably during Seymour's tenure of the governorship, Tobias Bowles sent his son James out to Maryland. Initially he was employed as his father's factor but was soon appointed Royal African Company agent, attending to the importing of slaves and the exporting of colonial produce from the Patuxent district, an activity which made him a very wealthy man.

Doubtless using political preferment and the good offices of their relations the Crispes (who were now the Collectors for the Customs at London) various branches of the family secured rewarding sine-cures with eighteenth-century trading companies and, in Valentine Bowles' case, with the Royal Navy and subsequently the Royal African Company. A second lieutenant in 1693, by 1695 he had been appointed to his first command, the fireship *Machine*, and a year or two later he was promoted captain of the 32-gun man-of-war *Sheerness*. He was not a success with his brother officers, who observed he was rarely aboard when the *Sheerness* was in port or lay in the Downs, and was constantly drunk and 'seldom ever capable of knowing what he said or did'. Valentine Bowles was rarely parted from his bottle and cared not a whit who knew it, celebrating his drinking parties 'in wasting the King's Powder by firing it away in drinking healths when he has had Company on board him. Particularly at one time he fired after that manner 192 guns, at another time 202.'

Such a man needed no second bidding to make sail from Portsmouth for the West India station via Madeira, with four other ships of the line to convoy the outgoing trade, in 1697. Nor was he harbouring any illusions that the voyage was for the sake of King and country; Valentine Bowles was very much in business for himself. Accordingly, on arriving at Madeira after an eventful trip in which a contingent of French men-of-war was with some difficulty beaten off, he purchased ten pipes of wine. A pipe was no small measure, amounting to 105 gallons, so ten pipes added up to over 1,000 gallons of wine. To accommodate such indulgence the store rooms aboard the *Sheerness* were turned into a *bodega* and the rations of bread and beer decanted to a storage area between decks which could not be secured, and from which the sailors could, despite precautions, help themselves. Though this carelessness made Bowles popular with the ordinary seamen, the price was high. On arrival at Tobago, he saw the profits to be made in running timber for buildings to the expanding population of Barbados, and for a month 'used the Ship's Company like so many Slaves by imploying them in Cutting down the aforesaid Timbers every day, wet and dry, squaring the same, & drawing it to the Waters Side'. It meant a £60 profit to Valentine Bowles; for the sailors it meant blood, sweat and tears. One sailor, John Wilkison, refused to cut timber at Tobago and was 'whipped at the jeers,[5] giving him above a hund[d] lashes'.

For Bowles the voyage was turning into a global shopping trip. Next he turned his attention to a French merchantman in Barbados waters, from whom he bought 22 half-hogsheads of brandy, a hogshead of claret and bolts of linen cloth. These too he sold in Barbados, though his fury at the wine being discovered by the Customs (after a tip-off) led him to challenge the seaman he suspected of being the informer to a duel. The latter prudently refused and received a beating for his pains.

The catalogue of abuse, waste and alcoholism was such that the court martial held following the return of the *Sheerness* in 1698 swiftly upheld the complaints of her master, purser, gunner, carpenter and boatswain (all of whose careers had been compromised by Bowles' behaviour). Valentine Bowles was drummed out of the Royal Navy in ignominy, forfeiting a year's pay for his irregularities. However, it was difficult to keep a bad man down in such times. A year later, again due to his family's connections, he was appointed Royal African Company Agent at Deal (shortly before his nephew James was appointed at Patuxent river, Maryland), a far from onerous position and one which undoubtedly offered much scope for his talents. His generation of the family was not long lived and he died (possibly of cirrhosis of the liver) in 1711. As an act of remorse, or as a good Nonconformist, he remembered his obligations to charity and left a meeting-house to the Dissenting community of Lower Deal.

Amongst others of the Bowles family engaged in the slave trade of the time were Tobias and Valentine's first cousins, Thomas and William, who both held senior positions in the South Sea Company. Thomas was this Company's Agent in Madeira in 1715, well before the disastrous 'bubble', and during the Company's salad days immediately after it had gained the much-prized Asiento. At this period it was shipping nearly 5,000 slaves a year from Africa to the Spanish colonies at Buenos Aires, Caracas, Cartagena, Havana, Panama, Portobello and Vera Cruz. So impressed was Thomas' elder brother William with the performance of the Company (or because he considered it to be money well spent politically) that he purchased £1,100 of its original stock (as did Thomas) and later contracted for a £3,000 loan on the strength of it. When the 'bubble' burst in 1720, William not only survived it but superseded it, becoming a director of the reconstituted Company from 1724 to 1739, MP for Bridport in 1727 and for Bewdley in 1741.

With his own very successful trading houses in London and Deal, to say nothing of the information to be gained from family contacts, Tobias Bowles had no need of a company. He flourished mightily in the early eighteenth century, becoming mayor of Deal in 1700 and 1712–14. His prosperity took on a physical shape and he was satirised as 'that lump of magistracy' in contemporary squibs. Despite his generous appearance he had a reputation for tight-fistedness. When it was proposed to build a much-needed chapel at Lower Deal at a cost of £1,300 he 'was loath to spend so much on Heaven/But gave his vote to have it done for seven'. Neither did his charity begin at home. His niece Thomazine, daughter of his brother Phineas, found no other way to settle in Virginia but as an indentured servant, only being released from her servitude by a bequest of £60 in Tobias' will.

With his third brother, George, Tobias dispatched a number of vessels to the coast of Africa in the opening decades of the eighteenth century, although today only the faintest hints remain of their passing. In 1704, for example, they imported a cargo of ivory worth £430 (the equivalent to seven years' wages for a merchant sea captain of the time), consigned to them in Deal aboard a man-of-war from Guinea.[6] Precious commodities such as ivory and gold were often shipped aboard Navy vessels if the occasion arose, rather than subjecting them to the potential danger of the second and third Atlantic legs of the usual slave trade triangular voyage.

Nothing further is then heard of the Bowles involvement in the Guinea trade until 1715, when Tobias sent one of his Deal-registered ships, a snow (a small twin-masted brigantine-like vessel) to trade on the Gambia.[7] For one reason or another the captain became embroiled in a local dispute and the ship was captured by Africans loyal to the King of Barra; having been greatly weakened by disease the crew could offer only a token resistance and were easily overrun. Their ship was run ashore and wrecked, leaving the crew to make the best of their way to the Company factory. No slaves, gold, ivory or redwood had been loaded, and the attack came out of the blue. Though Bowles might not have intended the vessel for slaves, the King and his caboceers were generally all too ready to sell their fellow Africans into the slave trade, as Company records make plain. Unfortunately no records – where they exist – show the actual extent of Tobias Bowles' involvement in the slave trade. With his interests in sugar, his successful business career and excellent family connections, a much more substantial appearance in the slave trade drama should be his – and indeed Deal's – rather than a shadowy role somewhere offstage.

Though it is tempting to regard the Bowles family as the beginning and the end of the town's involvement in the slave trade, this wasn't absolutely so. Men of Deal, adept at handling long-boats between shore and ship, were particularly welcome aboard vessels bound for the Guinea Coast, where all trade was by the long-boat or native canoe. Occasionally such vessels took their loading aboard in the Downs, rather than at London, especially if they were on their maiden voyages in ballast or only lightly freighted from their previous voyage. The transhipment of trade goods must have been an arduous business, especially in the depths of winter and in the teeth of bitter easterly winds. It was the course followed when loading the sloop *Samuel* of London chartered by Deal wine merchant Henry Alexander Primrose for Guinea in December 1719. However, this too was essentially a Bowles venture, for Primrose was Tobias Bowles' son-in-law. Much of the *Samuel*'s cargo had been brought by land carriage from London, for Deal neither imported nor manufactured trade goods in the quantities demanded for such highly capitalised overseas ventures. Commanded by Joshua Anley, the *Samuel* sailed early in the new year, eventually delivering 98 slaves to Barbados slave merchant William Allen in June 1720.[8]

Apart from herrings from its fishing fleet, and beer made from the hops for which Kent was – and is – justly famed, Deal could contribute little in the way of cargo from its own resources. Accordingly vessels bound for far-flung destinations such as Buenos Aires, Madras or Barbados tended merely to 'top up' in the Downs. Hence in December 1722 merchant Daniel Mann of Deal sent two barrels – one of white, the other of 'shotten' or spawned red herrings – aboard the Company ship *Whydah*. They would have been intended to supplement the diet of beans fed to the slaves in the middle passage. Similarly in 1726 Thomas Baker furnished a ton of strong beer, probably intended for consumption by her crew, to the *Guinea Packet*, also outward bound for Africa.[9]

How many Deal men shipped out for Africa during the early eighteenth century is a matter of speculation. Certainly William Boys, son of a Deal woollen draper, did so. Though his strongly Presbyterian parents had intended him for the Nonconformist ministry, they had been discouraged by the difficulties this presented and instead apprenticed him to a merchant sea captain. By October 1726, aged twenty-six, he found himself stepping aboard the *Luxborough Galley* of London, which was anchored in the Downs, as first mate. A fine new ship of 340 tons and 26 guns, she had been fitted out for the Asiento slave trade by the South Sea Company. William Boys probably found himself aboard her thanks to the good offices of William Bowles, by that time one of the company's directors. If such was the case he would have cause to regret it, but there was little to cloud his optimism as he, accompanied by his sea chest and a private venture consisting of some 30 yards of finely woven India damask, was welcomed aboard the *Luxborough* by her captain, William Kellaway.[10]

Bound for Cabenda, well south of the Equator in the area now known as the Congo, the *Luxborough* aimed to load a complement of 600 slaves. For this she carried a sizeable crew, more than forty in all, notable for its multi-racial complexion. Amongst the ship's boys were Caesar (an Indian), Hammose, Merry Pintle, Sharper and Coffee (all Negroes) and Jemmy (a mulatto). The crew also numbered a celebrity in the shape of highlander Evander MackEvoy (or McIvor), who still bore the scars of his fight to the death with Edward Teach, also known as Blackbeard the Pirate.

Fortunately McIvor's prowess with the claymore was not required on the voyage, which progressed peacefully. The required number of slaves was taken aboard at Cabenda, though disease carried off one out of every three Africans during the middle passage. William Boys' only comment was that the ship's company 'endured a great deal from the many disgustful circumstances' of the slaves' plight.[11]

Otherwise it was proving to be a model maiden voyage. Loaded with sugar and rum in Jamaica, the *Luxborough* ran before favourable winds for England. Lunchtime on 25 June 1727 was a cause for celebration, being William Boys' twenty-seventh birthday. Wine flowed in the officers' quarters, and rum on the lower deck. The boatswain and carpenter, having consumed their rations, called for another bottle to be drawn off. Over a thousand gallons of rum were stored in hogsheads in the ship's lazaretto, a storage hold situated aft, which also held the water casks. Two of the ship's boys, the blacks Hammose and Merry Pintle, were detailed to attend to this task. With lighted candles – for the lazaretto was in pitch darkness – the two boys descended into the depths of the ship, only to find their bare feet splashing through a liquid which covered the deck of the storage hold. In a bid to ascertain whether this was rum or water, they bent their candles close to the liquid. Unhappily it was rum, and in an instant the hold was aflame.

Frantic attempts to douse the fire proved fruitless. Beneath the lazaretto lay the powder room and fear of a catastrophic explosion froze many of the crew. William Boys kept his head while all about were losing theirs, and got the yawl lowered alongside. Here at least was a boat he could trust, clinker-built in Deal by Stephen Bradley not two years before, sixteen feet long, five broad and just over two feet deep. She was sharp-prowed for easy rowing, but hardly ideal for the purpose to which she was about to be put. With twenty-two others Boys abandoned ship and crammed aboard the yawl, constructing makeshift rigging with oars for masts and frocks (sailors' smocks) for sails as the *Luxborough* went up in flames.

On all the broad expanse of ocean there was not another ship to be seen. Initially kind, the weather changed on the fifth day. A gale struck the tiny craft, putting all in the utmost jeopardy. The two black boys who had inadvertently started the fire had managed to scramble aboard the yawl and it was proposed to throw them overboard to lighten the boat, a move which Boys piously records he 'opposed strongly'. This situation resolved itself when one of the boys died the same day, as well as another member of the crew.

Devoid of compass, water or provisions the shrinking number of survivors found themselves in the direst straits. Thirst became intolerable: 'we all of us drank our own urine, but the quantity we evacuated was very inconsiderable'. Moisture was gained by wringing the makeshift sail, and 'everyone his neighbour's cloaths when wet with fog or rain'. The torments of thirst were thus a little assuaged, but hunger was not so easily satisfied:

> it was at this time we found ourselves impelled to adopt the horrible expedient of eating part of the bodies of our dead companions, and drinking their blood . . . with great reluctance we brought ourselves to try different parts of the bodies of six, but could relish only the hearts, of which we ate three. We drank the blood of four. By cutting the throat a little while after death, we collected more than a pint from each body . . . found ourselves refreshed and invigorated by this nourishment, however unnatural.[12]

Surrounded by the siren songs of imaginary church bells, cocks crowing and friendly merchantmen hailing them from alongside, the yawl drifted steadily northwards. The 7th of July marked their day of deliverance, when the survivors, now only six in number, were picked up by a fishing vessel and landed at Old St Lawrence harbour in Newfoundland.

With the exception of Captain Kellaway, who died the next day, none of the other survivors appeared to suffer any long-term damage from their experience, two of them living into their eighties. William Boys, though 'much afflicted with hemorrhoidal complaints' as a result of the diet – or rather, lack of it – aboard the yawl, was sent back to the West Indies as a manager by the South Sea Company. Later he made his career in the Navy, becoming Lieutenant-Governor of Greenwich Hospital in 1761. He died in 1774.

Unlike Deal, Dover, though only a few miles down the coast, channelled its energies solely to Dieppe, Calais and Boulogne. Nor is there anything to report from the great sweep around the English coast to Chichester. At Portsmouth, however, everything changed. Here the domestic toing and froing across the North Sea or English Channel underwent a metamorphosis, as befitted a port with a deep and extensive involvement with the Royal Navy. Though essentially a garrison town from the sixteenth to the nineteenth centuries, Portsmouth had a strong contingent of merchant traders. Their main interests lay in the wine trade, but the discovery of New England had opened fresh fields of commerce. Tobacco was the key to this, and in 1625 the merchants petitioned Parliament to grant them a monopoly of the tobacco trade,[13] with the intention that all ships bound for New England should be obliged to set forth from Portsmouth, and all inward-bound tobacco should be unloaded there. The petition was not successful.

During the first decade of the eighteenth century Portsmouth experienced an upsurge in trade with the West Indies. This reached its peak in the war years between 1705 to 1711, when merchants sought the protection of the Royal Navy at Portsmouth in order to set forth their ventures in comparative safety. During these years clusters of vessels cleared, usually in April and May, travelling in convoy. In 1708 the merchantmen *Lascelles*, *London*, *Newport*, *James*, *Satisfaction* and *Guilford*, all of London, departed simultaneously for various destinations in the Caribbean. This pattern was repeated until 1712 when, after a brief involvement with East India Company ships, Portsmouth bowed out of long-haul departures. After the Treaty of Utrecht in 1713 it finally settled down to a prosaic pattern of trade with Gibraltar, Lisbon, Dieppe and the Channel Islands.

Between 1699 and 1713, when records temporarily cease, a total of eight ships cleared Portsmouth waters for Africa. The majority of these lie outside our interest for they were owned or chartered by the Royal African Company whose preferred policy (as a quasi-government arm of foreign trade) was to ship from outports used by the Royal Navy, when London or Gravesend were not suitable. By far the vast bulk of the cargo was carried direct to Portsmouth by land carriage from the capital, having been entered with the Customs at London, so these voyages reflect little of local investment. That started in a small way in March 1699, when the *Ekins Frigate* of London, Francis Stretell commanding, touched at Portsmouth at the beginning of her long haul south to Guinea.[14] She was due to pick up thirteen soldiers and artificers for the Cape Coast Castle, but also took the opportunity to load three casks of shoes, an unusual cargo

for the Guinea Coast. Since these were shipped under Stretell's name and did not attract the 10 per cent tax, this particular cargo was probably bound for the West Indies. Just under a year after clearing Portsmouth, the *Ekins* arrived in Jamaica, delivering 359 Negroes from the total of 600 she had been chartered to take aboard.

Eighteen months later a local merchant, William Pafford, headed a consortium which set forth the *Mary Anne* of Warsash, a small village at the confluence of Southampton Water and the river Hamble, under Captain Israel Brown. The venture lay well outside Pafford's usual trading interests, and his involvement can only be seen as a response to the 1698 Act freeing the trade to Africa. A substantial and varied cargo was loaded aboard the *Mary Anne*, which bore witness to meticulous planning. Though much of the hardware and ironmongery was second-hand, the declared total value of the cargo – £283 – is astonishingly small, and one must suspect collusion between the freighters of the *Mary Anne* and the Collector at the port of Cowes. But the amount raised no eyebrows with the Company's accountants and the *Mary Anne* sailed on her way.

All might have been well with the voyage had the owners and freighters, William Pafford and Peter Hawkesworth, been luckier with their choice of captain. Though a local man from Titchfield in Hampshire and doubtless known to them previously, Israel Brown had an idiosyncratic approach to trading on the Guinea Coast which was destined to cost them dearly. His approach to navigation may have been equally odd; departing from Portsmouth on 24 August 1700, it was the middle of November before the *Mary Anne* arrived on the northern Guinea Coast, having touched at Tenerife and the island of Santiago in the Cape Verdes. According to Israel Brown, his duties were solely to navigate the vessel, all care of the trade being committed to John May (or Mayle), the supercargo.

Though slow, the voyage was proceeding normally. At Cape Mesurado just south of Sierra Leone, the *Mary Anne* took in wood and water, falling in with a Jamaican sloop similarly engaged, the *Endeavour* under John Walker. Both ships now sailed in tandem along the coast, trading as they went. Admittedly there was a little trouble at Boutrou, just west of Dixcove, when Africans stole a consignment of brass pans, pewter pots and beads that had been landed ashore in exchange for slaves. In retaliation the *Mary Anne*'s supercargo carried off one or two native canoes and turned them into firewood.

William Harris, first mate of the *Mary Anne*, took a less sanguine view of the proceedings. According to him the trouble had started at Cape Mesurado where Brown, far from taking a back seat in the trading, went ashore and stole seven men and a woman from the African caboceers. Within a day or two he turned on a Royal African Company factor, Alexander Richardson – who had presumably boarded the *Mary Anne* to remonstrate with her captain – and clapped him in irons. After three days Richardson was released – or ransomed – on payment of gold, ivory and rice by the master of the Company sloop in which he had sailed out to confront Israel Brown. Quite what the latter hoped to gain by such a hot-headed action is hard to imagine, but he had not finished yet. Further down the coast he committed more outrages, imprisoning the African traders who came aboard, with the intention of carrying them to the West Indies as slaves. Brown's creeping megalomania finally erupted in late November off the Ivory Coast, as William Harris was later to relate:

> There came on board to trade with us several persons some of which were seised by ye sd Israel and by his comand, put in Irons, and severall leaping overboard intending to Escape were Shott dead in ye water by ye sd Israel and his orders . . . this Examinant, denying to Joyne with the sd Israel in so bloody and Inhuman acts, was confined in the hoult [hold] of ye sd Ship in Irons.

Nor did it end there, for Brown developed a nice little line in treachery, ransoming kidnapped Africans to their fellow countrymen for gold and ivory and subsequently taking those who brought the ransom as prisoners too.

Such a train of events could not be expected to last for ever. On 22 December, at one o'clock in the morning, the *Mary Anne* and the *Endeavour* were joined by the *Betty Galley* of London, Edward Briscoe commanding for prominent London slave trade merchants Houlditch and Brook. According to Brown, Briscoe asked him to spare a hogshead of beer, which Brown agreed to supply once he had anchored at Dixcove. A few days later the *Betty Galley* followed the *Mary Anne* and *Endeavour* in anchoring off Dixcove (despite its inviting name the cove was suitable only for long-boats, ships having to anchor offshore). Briscoe immediately issued an invitation to captains Brown and Walker to dine with him. No sooner had they accepted (which they did with some alacrity) and boarded the *Betty Galley* with high hopes of a roistering feast – for it was now Christmas Eve – than Briscoe had them clapped in irons, threatening to bring them to justice at the Cape Coast Castle. He then signalled for the rest of their respective ships' companies who, reckoning they were on to a good thing and unaware of the fate visited upon their captains, lost no time in hastening aboard the *Betty Galley* to join in the seasonal good cheer, only to suffer a similar indignity. In such a manner did the crew of the *Mary Anne*, with the exception of William Harris and John May, both of whom had incurred Brown's severe displeasure, spend Christmas Day 1700.

The following day Briscoe (and his ship's surgeon) boarded the *Mary Anne* with the keys to her sea chests which he had taken from Brown's pockets and with information which Brown later alleged had been extorted from him by intimidation. He also carried a letter from Brown to William Harris, authorising the latter to release sixteen of the men slaves aboard the *Mary Anne*, plus a barrel of pitch, a flitch of bacon, a box containing 14 oz. and 7 ackeys of gold (worth £54 16s. 1d.) and £10 in Spanish dollars. This having been done to Briscoe's satisfaction, Brown was immediately released. Extraordinarily, instead of complaining to the Royal African Company factor at Dixcove, making a deposition of the events before the authorities at the Cape Coast Castle, barely two days' sail away, or mounting a reprisal against the *Betty Galley*, Brown swallowed his anger and sailed meekly away.

What had given Briscoe the right to take the law into his own hands? Nearly three centuries after the event, the suspicion must be that African caboceers had approached a Company trading post demanding restitution for their losses and a factor – possibly Alexander Richardson – had authorised Briscoe (though not a Company captain) to act on its behalf. Certainly no case was filed by Brown against Briscoe in the High Court of Admiralty, so he probably decided the summary justice meted out to him was not unwarranted and, indeed, that he had got off lightly.

In comparison with her lackadaisical progress to the Guinea Coast, the *Mary Anne* made a speedy crossing of the Atlantic, despite spending some days provisioning at São Tomé. But all was far from settled between captain, supercargo and first mate. On calling at the first land to be sighted, which turned out to be Nevis – a relatively small island with a poor reputation for buying slaves – John May the supercargo caused all the slaves to be put ashore. This despite orders from Pafford and Hawkesworth that their destination was to be Jamaica, a further two weeks' sail away. Furthermore, having sold all the slaves John May refused point blank to set foot upon the *Mary Anne*, preferring to make his own way back to Portsmouth.

Since John May had been entrusted with the business aspect of the voyage, he presumably received all the proceeds from the sale of the slaves. His refusal to ship aboard the *Mary Anne* meant that there was no revenue in her sea chests to pay for the cargo of sugar which she was scheduled to load at Jamaica. Israel Brown spent the next few weeks irresolutely plying between St Kitts for provisions and Nevis for the supercargo (who however remained adamant), before cutting his losses and making for England.

When a voyage started off on the wrong foot, it often had a habit of continuing so. Though backed by favourable winds for most of the journey, Israel Brown's hopes of an easy landfall on the English coast were frustrated. At the last moment contrary winds forced the *Mary Anne* into Castlehaven, Ireland, on 9 June 1701. By this time the crew were close to mutiny and marched to the mayor of Castlehaven demanding the arrest of their captain for not paying their wages. Faced with such a concerted action, Brown paid them all off except for his first mate. That was the last straw for William Harris, who made a deposition recording all that had gone before to Simon Dring, mayor of Cork.

By November 1701 the *Mary Anne*, presumably seized on orders from Pafford and Hawkesworth, was still lying at Castlehaven. Witnesses stated she was in desperate straits:

> She is in a perishing Condition, Lying on hard Strand, her decks leaky & noe Cables and ancors to hold her, in so much that she broke loose on Monday night last & was in danger of being lost . . .

Castlehaven proved to be the *Mary Anne*'s last resting place, but Israel Brown was not allowed to disappear so quietly. In the spring of 1703 he was arrested on a warrant from the High Court of Admiralty on a charge of piracy, which, if proven, carried a mandatory death penalty. It must be assumed that Pafford and Hawkesworth instituted proceedings against him, for no record of the part they played survives. Brown was committed to the Marshalsea prison in Southwark, a stone's throw from the shipping which packed the river Thames, and from which the aspiring bulk of the new St Paul's Cathedral could just be glimpsed, though still almost a decade from completion. From time to time Brown was released from the Marshalsea to face examinations before the Admiralty Court, eventually being granted bail of £100 (nearly two years' wages for a provincial sea captain) and discharged on recognizance of his sureties.

At every examination Brown predictably paraded a complete innocence of all charges, seeking instead to discredit his erstwhile first mate Harris and his employers Pafford and Hawkesworth. His initial allegation, that in 1699 Pafford and Hawkesworth had smuggled two packs of wool to Bordeaux and not their declared destination of San Sebastian in Spain, was small beer and par for the course. But he subsequently accused Harris, Pafford and Hawkesworth of dishonestly handling cutlasses, scimitars, pistols, guns and gunpowder from the Royal Navy base at Portsmouth, and of having illegally appropriated provisions, barrels, rigging and running tackle from HMS *Norfolk* (all the foregoing being loaded aboard the *Mary Anne* for her Guinea voyage), a much more serious charge. It will be remembered that the *Mary Anne*'s cargo for Guinea was astonishingly cheap, so did Israel Brown have a point?

If he did, he could not make it stick. Later in the eighteenth century William Pafford became a constable of Portsmouth corporation, which suggests the affair of the *Mary Anne* did him little harm, except financially. All those connected with the ship appear to have completely relinquished the slave trade. As with so many merchants of England's minor ports, once was more than enough. Except, that is, for Israel Brown. Having escaped hanging for piracy and reached some sort of settlement with Pafford and Hawkesworth, he returned to sea. In 1718 he returned to the Guinea Coast as master of the London vessel *Wright Galley*, and delivered 327 slaves to Barbados in March the following year.[15]

While Israel Brown was alternately languishing in the Marshalsea and appearing before Justice George Bramston at the High Court of

Admiralty, the first London independent slave trader was preparing to open his account from the Solent. John Cross had been heavily engaged in the trade ever since 1698 when he freighted the *Donegal* to Guinea. In the intervening years he had set forth the *Annapolis* (1700), captained the *Cape Mount* for Guinea on behalf of John Taylor and Company (also 1700), freighted the *Recovery* (1702), and captained the *Mary* for John Maccarell and Company. These ventures all cleared from the River Thames, Cross being a mariner of St Botolph's parish, Aldgate. The opening of hostilities against the French late in 1702 found him on the Guinea Coast trading for slaves in the *Mary*. On his return to London in the summer of 1703 he was granted letters of marque for his *Austria Galley* and proceeded to Portsmouth to fit her out. Though his own cargo was purchased from local sources, that of Elwick and Stevens (associates of his on the *Recovery* of 1702) and William Browne was dispatched from London by land carriage. No evidence survives of the success or failure of this voyage, but the presence of the Bristol ships *Molly* and *Broomfield* in the slave trade in 1741 and 1747 respectively, both freighted by John Cross and Company, suggests success. [16]

Whereas the documentation of so many Guinea trade ships presents little more than a faint outline, the next vessel is surrounded by a wealth of detail that providentially provides a beginning, a middle and an end. It also forms an exemplary account of the pitfalls involved in hiring a ship. In the case of the *Barbados Merchantman* of 1706, the disasters befell not a mercantile consortium, but the Royal African Company. Curiously the vessel in question was far from an unknown quantity. The Company had previously chartered her for a successful voyage to the Guinea Coast for slaves in 1704.[17] By this time the Company, which had preferred chartering vessels to owning them – thus avoiding the problem of procuring a return cargo from the West Indies to London – was moving towards a policy of purchasing its ships.[18] As and when the need arose, this fleet was supplemented by charter-party vessels. Since merchant owners could make substantial profits at very little risk to themselves by hiring out vessels to the Company, there was no shortage of offers. So when Joseph Bingham of Plymouth once again offered his ship *Barbados Merchantman* to the Company, he was met by a polite refusal and the assurance that the Company had sufficient tonnage at its disposal to meet current needs.[19] Even as this assurance was given, a train of disasters was already in motion. First the *Resolution* under Patrick Galloway, a hired ship which had sailed for Guinea from the

Downs at the end of December 1705, was chased and caught by a Navy man-of-war off Spithead and diverted to Portsmouth. Here the Admiralty was acting under orders from the Company, which had received irrefutable evidence that the *Resolution* had broken her charter-party agreement by being severely undermanned and appallingly ill equipped. Understandably, the Company was reluctant to consign a cargo valued at £2,775 to a ship of fools, and the contract was declared null and void. All the Company's cargo was speedily removed from the *Resolution* at Portsmouth and stored in a sealed warehouse.[20]

To make matters worse, the Company ship *Maurice and George*, *en route* for Cape Coast Castle and Whydah from London, and designed for 600 slaves, ran into a severe winter storm off Spithead. While making for shelter at Portsmouth she foundered; luckily her cargo (valued at £3,672) was recovered virtually intact as soon as the weather eased. This double blow to Company fortunes now rendered it imperative that a ship be hired. Bingham's offer of the *Barbados Merchantman* was now accepted.

After the aggravation caused by the *Resolution* the Company was in no mood to be crossed a second time, and Bingham received strict instructions as to what was expected from his side of the bargain. On 20 June 1706 he was informed he must carry eight men and 15 tuns of casked water to every 100 Negroes.[21] The ship was to be sheathed and provided with a Negro furnace, shackles and a mill for grinding corn. In July the Company contracted to slave her with 350 Negroes for certain (or 50 more if space could be found); if this number was not fulfilled they would pay compensation – dead freight – to the amount of £6 6s. 8d. per head. Ninety days was allotted to her on the Coast for unloading the cargo (valued at £6,620 including slave provisioning), and the Company would pay £11 per head freight for all Negroes delivered alive at Jamaica. Of every 104 slaves delivered, the Captain would have the right to the proceeds of 4 slaves as an incentive; as a gratuity the ship's doctor would be entitled to 12d. a head for every Negro delivered alive. In addition to the requirements laid down in their previous letter, the Company stipulated that Bingham should furnish the *Barbados Merchantman* with deal platforms, shackles, bolts, firewood and a separate cabin big enough to stow about a ton of horse beans. Each man of the ship's company was to be issued with swords and enough muskets and ammunition to quell any slave revolt on board. A surgeon's chest for the Negroes was the one concession made to humanity, though it was little more than a concession motivated by profit. Once landfall had been made in Jamaica, delivery of the Negroes ashore had to be completed within fourteen days. The *Barbados Merchantman* would then be discharged from Company service, though the Company reserved the option of freighting it back to England with 100 hogsheads of sugar.

Merchants of the time always had an inflated idea of the capacity of their vessels and none more so than those engaged in the slave trade. Though Bingham agreed to the conditions imposed by the contract without demur, he stuck to his intention to 'tight-pack' the vessel with slaves. After a further exchange of letters the Company agreed the *Barbados Merchantman*, of approximately 300 tons burden, could take in 450 Negroes 'and no more, by reason she is a crank ship'. To accompany this concession they stipulated that the 'mates and surgeons must be such as have used the Guinea trade'.[22] Far from satisfied with such barriers to greater profitability, Bingham ordered his captain John Russell to take out a letter of marque giving the *Barbados Merchantman* the right to attack the merchant shipping of France and Spain, with whom England was at war. Though the Company had previously entertained its own or hired vessels taking out such letters (the *Prince of Orange* and *Guinea Frigate* of 1689, the *Sally Rose* and *Hannibal* of 1696, the *Fauconberg* of 1697 and the *Royal Africa* of 1702 and 1704),[23] the conclusion had been reached that these licences to attack foreign merchant shipping only served to put its own cargo in danger. It also probably increased the insurance costs in a dramatic fashion. Accordingly the Company refused to have anything further to do with the *Barbados Merchantman* until John Russell withdrew his letter of marque. It was now the end of October and Company patience with Bingham was wearing decidedly thin.

Faced with such an ultimatum, Bingham had no option but to comply. It may well have been simply a lever to enable him to win a further concession on the number of slaves, for on 17 December he was reluctantly allowed a further fifty. Shortly afterwards the *Barbados Merchantman* cleared Portsmouth, put in briefly at Plymouth and sailed from there on 16 January 1707.

Since the cargo shipped by the Company had already been detailed in London and all taxes and duties paid, only merchant David Faulkener's contribution appears at Portsmouth. As on the *Barbados Merchantman*'s previous voyage of 1705,[24] Bingham had managed to wrangle permission to carry a limited cargo of his own for a strict personal allowance of fifty slaves, and the assumption must be that the cargo loaded by David Faulkener was actually on Bingham's behalf. Since the rest of the *Barbados Merchantman*'s cargo had already paid all relevant duties and taxes when aboard the ill-fated *Resolution* and *Maurice and George*, the Collector for Cowes was doubtless persuaded that Bingham's cargo of luxury items could be conveniently overlooked as far as the 10 per cent tax was concerned. That this cargo was intended for Africa there can be no doubt. Though tea was a commodity of unproven value on the Guinea Coast, the fine linen – including malmul, a species of sheer, silk-like muslin from the Far East – and the predominance of kittisoles, could have only one destination. These parasols were especially prized by African chiefs, who used them as traditional badges of majesty.

As it happened, the best-laid plans of both the Company and Joseph Bingham proved to no avail. On 4 April 1707 the ship fell victim to a French privateer of 30 guns after rounding Cape Palmas and making a desperate run for the Cape Coast Castle. This revealed Russell's application for a letter of marque as not only an irony but, more seriously, as an imposture since the vessel could not even defend herself, let alone capture enemy shipping. When the crew were eventually released, the first mate complained to Sir Dalby Thomas that the ship

> was a heavy sailor, ill-fitted in every respect and that the Captain made no manner of a provision to fight for they were to seek for shot, the guns being of so different a nature.

Following weeks of negotiation the vessel and its cargo were repurchased for the Company by Captain Willis, factor at Whydah. It is doubtful whether the luxury cargo loaded by David Faulkener was included in the deal.[25]

Redeeming the *Barbados Merchantman* proved a mistake. Her crew had reached the limits of their patience and were so disorderly that Sir Dalby Thomas could not trust them even to bring a letter back to London. More seriously, the first mate's criticisms of the vessel's handling proved only too accurate: her end was nigh. Condemned as 'not fit to keep above water' she was broken up in January 1708 and her timbers used to repair Cape Coast Castle.

The departure of the *Barbados Merchantman* from Portsmouth was followed by a succession of London ten per cent ships touching at the port to load limited cargoes before clearing English waters for the African coast. First was the *Adventure* in 1706 bound for Guinea and Virginia on behalf of Huguenot slave trader Anthony Tourney,

Thomas Colthurst, James Wayte, Abraham Houlditch and other London merchants. She took iron aboard plus chests containing a variety of beads. These had been supplied by Huguenot exiles Daniel Jamineau and his brother Claude, who had an unofficial monopoly of the supply of beads in London during the period 1698-1725. All the ten per cent merchants and the Company itself were forced to purchase beads – of crystal, amber and jet, with names like bugles, rangoes, olivets and gooseberries – from this single source. In the case of the *Adventure* they had been consigned to Portsmouth by land carriage from the capital. The *Adventure*'s commander was Daniel Lewis, who had experienced as much as anyone the varied fortunes that were a sea captain's lot. Five years earlier, in December 1701, while trading at Drewin to the south of Cape Palmas in the *Dolphin*, Lewis and his crew had been overwhelmed by a hostile band of coastal Africans. His vessel was totally wrecked, and he and his shipmates force-marched to the interior where they languished until a ransom was arranged.[26] The voyage of the *Adventure* from Portsmouth was considerably less traumatic, and she eventually delivered 92 slaves to Maryland in August 1707.

Second in the procession of London ships was the *Prince of Mindelheim*. She was owned by Houlditch and Brook and freighted almost entirely by them. Though Brook remains a shadowy figure, Abraham Houlditch was one of the few Company employees on the Guinea Coast in the late seventeenth century who turned his experience to good account as a ten per cent merchant. Her captain was John Gordon, who had declared letters of marque for the *Prince* early in 1707.[27] On that occasion her destination had been Africa and no further. She successfully traded for 47 tons of redwood, but her cargo of ivory was badly damaged by a fire in her holds. Following her refitting in London, her cargo for the present venture was loaded in March 1708; her only reason for putting into Portsmouth was to take ten chests of old sheets aboard. She cleared for the Gambia towards the end of August 1708 only to run into trouble with the French at their forts. Though still carrying letters of marque, John Gordon was unable to fend off the attention of pirates, and her cargo of 240 slaves was captured and transhipped. The *Prince* was retaken, but not the slaves. Early in 1709 Gordon was reported at Anamabo, 'making but little trade'. On 13 March 1709 he anchored in the Thames, discharging 27 cwt. of ivory and 6 tons of redwood on Houlditch and Company's account.[28] Houlditch had a fleet of ships engaged in trading with Africa, and it is likely that the *Prince of*

Mindelheim – having lost her slaves – was instructed to engage in bilateral trading and make directly back to London.

The final ship to touch at Portsmouth for the London separate traders was the *Three Crowns* under Digby Keeble.[29] She loaded four bales of perpetuannas for merchant Joseph Martyn. Other merchants concerned in the voyage were Edward Searle, Isaac Milner and Robert Atkins. She was designed for 205 slaves to be loaded on the Guinea Coast and delivered to the island of Nevis.[30] In the event she delivered 200, a survival rate little short of miraculous. The suspicion must remain that the figures were cooked in order to impress the Commissioners for Trade and Plantations (who were deciding whether to revive the Company monopoly of African trade or throw the trade open to all) with the efficiency of the separate traders. Both Milner and Martyn were heavily engaged with giving evidence before the Commissioners for Trade and Plantations during the latter's interminable deliberations.

As if to reinforce the surprisingly marginal involvement of Portsmouth with the slave trade, the final vessel, a French-built galley of 80 tons, 6 guns and 10 men called the *Isle of Wight* seems to have cleared from London. Under her captain John Mellish (who later commanded the slave trade ship *Betty* of London), the *Isle of Wight* discharged 123 slaves in Barbados on 13 July 1714.[31]

During the third decade of the eighteenth century, the Royal African Company, now rapidly entering the twilight years of its trading career, made extensive use of Portsmouth's boat-building and servicing facilities. Among their Guinea-bound vessels which called at Portsmouth were the slave ships *Sarah* for Virginia, *Martha*, *Royal African*, *Cape Coast*, *Wydah*, *Gambia Castle*, *Greyhound* and *King Solomon* for Jamaica, and the *Margaret* for Antigua.[32] The balance was made up of Company sloops, constructed in local shipyards. These were designed for the use of the Company forts whose names they bore and included the *Accra*, *James Island*, *Gambia* and *Congo*. Although not strictly slave ships in the sense that they never delivered slaves to the plantations and were assigned to Africa only on a local basis, they nevertheless created a significant 'feeder' trade, carrying slaves along the Guinea Coast to the Company barracoons. Later on in the eighteenth century Portsmouth entered the mainstream of the slave trade and sent forth two such ventures a year between 1758 and 1774,[33] when the American War of Independence intervened.

Despite the local presence of John Barbot, Southampton merchants evinced little interest in the trade to Africa beyond the sailing of the

Mary Anne of Warsash. Though John Barbot had been deeply involved in the Guinea trade at the turn of the century, all of his slave trade ventures departed from London and it was there that he and his nephew James continued to work for Huguenot slave traders and bead merchants Daniel and Claude Jamineau.[34] In general Southampton remained an onlooker as Portsmouth took the lion's share of long-haul ventures during this period. One vessel which did clear Southampton for Africa was the Dutch merchantman, *Dunker-vell*. Under Stephen Steydervil, she sailed for the Dutch settlement at Cape of Good Hope with 1½ tons of strong English beer in August 1699.[35] Her ultimate destination was almost certainly the Dutch East Indies.

Of the ports to the west of the Isle of Wight, Poole made the most promising showing. It shared with Weymouth a high level of activity orientated towards the plantations and Newfoundland fisheries which flourished despite local navigational hazards, for Poole was a less than ideal departure point for heavily laden merchantmen. Though possessing a capacious harbour at high tide, its waterways were comparatively narrow and its deep-water anchorage limited. Entrance to the harbour was difficult, and further obstructed by a shifting bar which in 1698 had little more than 16 feet of water on it even at high-water spring tide. Weymouth faced similar problems with occasionally only 3 feet of water on the bar, and a harbour that was liable to be choked by sand. Both ports suffered a catastrophic reduction in overseas trade following the outbreak of the War of the Spanish Succession and did not immediately recover their substantial trade to the plantations once it was over.

There is no evidence of early eighteenth-century involvement in the slave trade, yet Poole merchants in the second and third decades of the eighteenth century came tantalisingly close to entering it. They were already accustomed to trade with the Cape Verde islands for salt from the Isle of May, which neatly complemented their New-foundland fishery trade. In February 1716 Sir William Lewen, a prominent Poole merchant much concerned with the Newfoundland fisheries, dispatched the *William* of London under Robert Christian to Barbados via the Cape Verdes. Two years later Joseph Jones of Poole set forth the *William and John* upon the same voyage; the 1½ tons of hay in her hold pointed towards a cargo of *assenigoes* (small asses) rather than slaves.[36] In fact this triangular trade between Poole, the Cape Verdes and the colonies of Barbados, South Carolina and Newfoundland continued well into the eighteenth century, eventually overlapping with Poole's actual entry into the Guinea trade in 1751.

The two Poole merchants who spearheaded the port's involvement with the slave trade in the mid-eighteenth century were William Barfoot and William Jolliffe. As we shall see in Chapter 21, Barfoot was already involved in a peripheral leg of the slave trade – the re-export trade from Barbados to the American plantations – in 1722. Thirty-four years later he sent out a procession of three ships in two years to Bence Island in Sierra Leone. They were laden with building materials for Richard Oswald who owned and ran the island as a slave trading post, and one of Barfoot's vessels continued to Charleston with slaves.

William Jolliffe, son of the celebrated privateersman Captain Peter Jolliffe, had captained his own ship the *Jolliffe's Adventure* to Carolina as early as 1721 (when he was just twenty-three), and traded continuously with the colony henceforward.[37] He eventually sent nine ventures to Sierra Leone between 1751 and 1760 which traded with Richard Oswald[38] for slaves before sailing on to deliver them in Charleston.[39]

Despite problems with a sandbar that was progressively choking the harbour entrance, Weymouth was a popular port in the early eighteenth century with the colonial merchants of Dorset. Both James Gould of Dorchester (one of the backers behind the *Daniel and Henry*) and John Burridge of Lyme Regis frequently set forth voyages from there, though not to Africa. Prominent amongst the merchants of Weymouth itself were the Randall family. Strong supporters of trade to the American colonies, they were equally strongly in favour of the pleasures and profits of smuggling tea and rum. Perhaps inspired by, and almost certainly related to, Richard Randall of Topsham, who entered the re-export trade in slaves from Barbados to Charleston at about the same time, Weymouth merchant Thomas Randall essayed the Guinea trade in the spring of 1717. For this he chartered a London ship, the *Flying Brigantine*, whose captain and part-owner was Stephen Patrick, an ex-Company commander, who had delivered a consignment of slaves to Barbados in 1709 and was familiar with African and Caribbean waters.[40] The brigantine was not a large ship, being of barely 50 tons burden, and Randall had her loaded with a considerable quantity of alcoholic spirits and 6 tons of iron. Her ostensible destination was Madeira, but the presence of substantial amounts of beans aboard her betrayed her true intent. Later the same year, presumably having delivered the bulk of his slave cargo elsewhere – possibly Barbados – captain Patrick discharged seventeen slaves in Charleston, South Carolina. It seems the voyage did not match Weymouth's expectations, for the *Flying Brigantine* did not persist in the slave trade and the Randalls returned to colonial produce and smuggling.[41]

For both the Royal Navy and the merchant marine, the long stretch of coast from Portland Bill to the border with Devon was regarded with apprehension and fear. Shelter on this picturesque, cliff-girt shore was at a premium, and to be caught in its wide embrace by a gale from the westward invited destruction. Nevertheless at the very apex of Lyme Bay – the name of this benign, fickle and dissembling stretch of water – lay one of the most unlikely slave trade ports of all. It is there we turn our attention in the following chapter.

CHAPTER SIXTEEN

Lyme Regis

To the westward-bound traveller on foot, having forsaken the main highway for the clifftop path from Charmouth, there can be few more appealing sights at the end of a long summer's day than the town of Lyme Regis. The footpath, after winding along bosky cliffs, debouches on to a grassy knoll, part of the ridge of hills which form a semicircle at the back of the town before descending, by fits and starts, towards the sea.

From this knoll, high above Lyme, the eye is inevitably drawn through the tumble of pastel and whitewashed Georgian and Regency cottages, along the broad seafront promenade, to the massive yet curiously delicate bulk of the Cobb. Shaped by succeeding generations of builders from the thirteenth century into the form of a sickle, the handle of which juts out into Lyme Bay and the point of which barely grazes the tiny naze from whence it springs, this ponderous hybrid – part breakwater, part pier – is the town's very *raison d'être*. Without it Lyme would have been swept long ago from the annals of maritime history, for – when aroused – the fury of the prevailing westerlies brook few obstructions on this stretch of coast. Not even the Cobb itself, which has been endlessly overwhelmed and patiently rebuilt time without number, has been spared the indignity of an occasional collapse. That is, until the early nineteenth century, when the Royal Engineers rethought its foundations and cased it in local Portland stone.

If the Cobb is Lyme's chief ornament (the term not detracting in the least from its practical value), it is also its folk memory, an enduring symbol of its past. The shape of a sickle is the same as that of a question mark and Lyme has found itself more than once at the crossroads of history. This was especially so during the seventeenth century when Lyme, like Taunton to the north, proved itself firmly in the Parliamentary camp. Locals of Lyme firmly rebuffed Prince Maurice's summons to surrender, marvelling that he 'should expect to have whole towns given him in England, whereas they knew not so much as a thatched cottage that he was owner of here'.[1]

Obviously the Royalists had a problem on their hands with Lyme, and under the inspired generalship of Robert Blake the town remained adamant against every attempt of the Royalist army under Prince Maurice to subjugate them. They commemorated this resistance until well after the Restoration with 'shouting, feasting and the like'.[2]

Celebrations were again the order of the day when the Duke of Monmouth landed on the beach beside the Cobb one fateful day in June 1685, for the town's radical character, which sprang from its violent distaste for Catholicism evident even in the time of Mary Tudor who dubbed it a 'heretic town', had not been tempered by the passing years. It was to be almost extinguished by the all too predictable defeat of Monmouth at Sedgemoor and then by the wave of blood-letting ordered by James II through his ambitious lieutenant Judge Jeffreys. Of the poor unfortunates who featured on Jeffreys' list of proven and suspected rebels, 99 were of Lyme origin, 105 from nearby Colyton, 104 from Axminster and 48 from Thorncombe. By far the greatest number came, of course, from Taunton.[3] Even after the removal of James II and the firm entrenchment of the

Lyme Regis from the West, 1723, showing (B) Portland, and (C) the Cobb

Protestant Church of England, Lyme remained fervently anti-Catholic. Evidence of this persisted well into the nineteenth century every 5 November, when the image burnt on the town's bonfires was not Guy Fawkes but the Pope, his supposed master.

So the idyllic scene which confronts our casual observer upon his lookout above Lyme, the westering sun causing him to shade his eyes the more clearly to distinguish the fishing and pleasure boats pottering into the lee of the Cobb, the whole town seemingly embraced by the dense woods of the Ware Commons, was not always of such profound calm. For Lyme, now the epitome of the Regency watering-place and imbued with strong literary associations, was founded on the cut and thrust of trade.

Indeed it was to merchants that the town owed its existence from medieval times until well into the eighteenth century; the seaside mania – heavily promoted by fashionable doctors who regarded sea-water as a universal panacea[4] – did not affect Lyme until the 1760s. Even then it never reached the outrageous heights of Weymouth or Brighton, and was popular with impecunious families rather than dedicated followers of foppery. Lyme's position as a mercantile centre was highly anomalous, for it produced little of any commercial value within its precincts beyond small-scale cloth finishing and some lace and clothmaking. Across its surrounding hills, however, lay some of the richest woollen centres of Dorset, Somerset and Devon, and wool was England's greatest medieval currency, a commodity valued highly throughout Europe and the Mediterranean. Through Lyme (as through Topsham and Dartmouth) flowed the great river of woollen cloth on its way to the sea, and Lyme merchants grew wealthy on its passing. More often than not the river was in flood as Bristol merchants in the war-torn years between 1670 and 1713 sought to find a safe passage for their exports away from the privateer-infested Bristol Channel.

Though Lyme's natural trading partners were the cross-Channel ports of Morlaix and Rotterdam, its own merchants had not been backward in evincing a yearning for the fabled riches of Africa. In this they were perhaps spurred on by knowledge of the wealth accumulated by the Hawkins family of Plymouth, barely a day or two's sail to the west, or the substantial fortune amassed by the freebooting activities of local celebrity – and sometime mayor of Lyme – Admiral Sir George Somers.

Accordingly a group of merchant venturers, seeking a profitable diversion from their highly lucrative cross-Channel transactions, banded together as the Brotherhood of St Thomas Beckett to freight the barque *Cherubim* to Senegal and the Gambia in 1591. Meeting with a good response the experiment was repeated a number of times until by the early seventeenth century a lucrative trade in ivory and gold was being pursued off the northern Guinea Coast. Perhaps inspired by Lyme's example, the merchants of inland Taunton requested, and were granted, a charter from Elizabeth I in 1592 to trade to Guinea.[5] But England's scramble for empire lay in the direction of America, and when Sir George Somers of Lyme was appointed Admiral of the new colony of Virginia by the London company of that name in 1609, the trade with Africa fell off, though that other staple of Lyme long-haul trade, the Newfoundland fisheries, remained unaffected. Sir George's most pressing task was that of recruiting men and women for the fledgling colony, and many came forward from Lyme and its neighbourhood.[6]

Within a very short time Virginia replaced Africa as the new mecca for Lyme's long-haul merchant traders, for the new settlers and their followers needed every conceivable product from food to building materials to nurse along their young community. As the colony progressed and plantations became established, tobacco gradually replaced its early exports of timber and animal skins. The Virginia tobacco at first supplemented and then replaced the leaf imported from Morlaix which at that time held the French tobacco monopoly. So Lyme became one of a number of West Country ports with a thriving import trade in Virginia tobacco most of which, since it lacked the facilities to process the crop, was carried to Bristol or London, or re-exported to Rotterdam.

Breaking the lands of the new colony, planting and harvesting tobacco, soon proved beyond the physical capability of Virginia's colonisers, who envisaged tobacco plantations on a grand scale. The Amerindian tribes, initially friendly, eventually withdrew their support as the scale of European operations took on a more aggressive and intimidating dimension. In any case it would have required a major transformation in the Amerindian way of life and society to persuade them to work the land for profit let alone serve the white man in a menial capacity. So the colonisers looked elsewhere to make up the deficiency in labour, and once again Lyme merchants were encouraged to look towards Africa. Not for gold and ivory, but for men.

It would be a mistake to imagine that trade from Lyme swung wildly from cloth to gold and ivory, to tobacco and finally sugar. As in medieval times, so in the seventeeenth and eighteenth centuries, cloth formed the bulk of all exports and imports. Characteristically serges were exported to Morlaix, and lockrams – a coarse linen used both for clothing and domestic hangings and drapery – brought back from France. All Lyme merchants were cloth merchants though tobacco, wine, sugar and other luxury items inevitably formed part of their imported cargoes.

Whatever the trade, the Cobb played a central role. All ships anchored in its lee, and it was there that goods were loaded or unloaded. However it was not connected to the land until 1756, so a system of Cobb porters, strictly licensed by the mayor and borough, were responsible for carrying goods to and from the Cobb, via the Customs House at the Cobb Gate, half a mile distant at the bottom of Broad Street. This carriage of goods across the intervening half-mile was achieved by pack-horse at low tide, small boat at high. The horses were perfectly accustomed to shift for themselves, as appears from this eyewitness account of 1675:

> The Vessels of Burthen are loaden and unloaden by Horses, turning and returning upon the Sand between the Cob and the Town. And they have no Drivers, but are charged with Bales (for Instance) at the Warehouse, and away they trot to the Ship's Side, and stand fair, sometimes above the Belly in Water, for the Tackle to discharge them; and then they gallop back to the Warehouse for more. And so they perform the Tide's Work, and know by the Flood when their Labour is at an End.[7]

This picturesque scene held no charms for William Culliford, the scourge of smugglers and 'runners', when he arrived in Lyme in 1682. His tour of inspection of behalf of the Commissioners for Customs and Excise, jointly carried out with Gregory Alford – who was possessed both of the patronage of the Customs at Lyme and of fiercely Conformist views – revealed serious flaws in the system. Prominent among them was the habit the Customs officers had developed (with the connivance of the merchants) of examining incoming goods aboard ship at the Cobb. In the event of the goods carrying a false description or exceeding the stated quantity, they could not be forfeited as they had not been 'laid on land'. Fine French linens, then a prohibited import, were the main offenders. With the connivance of friendly tidesmen and other officials who turned a blind eye for a small consideration, the offending goods were quietly run ashore under cover of darkness.[8]

Smuggling remained the exception rather than the rule, and most incoming goods reached the Customs inspection at the Cobb Gate without incident. Having cleared Customs they were then either consigned to merchants' warehouses or transferred to pack-horses for the long climb up from the town centre in Coombe Street.

These pack-horses were vital beasts of burden, for until 1759 Lyme was hampered by a singular lack of roads passable by wheeled transport. Over the centuries a constant stream of pack-horses, loaded down with seams or dowsers (boxes and baskets slung either side of the horse) had made their way to and fro along the route known as the Via Regia, the King's Way, along Coombe Street to the little River Lym then along its banks to Uplyme Mill and across the hills to join the main Dorchester to Exeter highway. The route has long fallen into disuse.

From Dorchester, Exeter and Axminster came broadcloth and serge, from Sherborne woollens and silks; baize from Barnstaple and plains from Taunton. These were the very stuff of trade. Only from the mid-eighteenth century onwards, when the great medieval currency of wool was debased first by the metalware of Birmingham and Sheffield and then by the mass-produced cottons of Manchester, did trade at Lyme commence its terminal decline.

For all its status as England's staple commodity, wool and those associated with it – including dyers, spinners, weavers, tuckers, packers and merchants – had a radical thread running its length and breadth. That thread was religious, and ultimately political dissent. In Lyme such Dissent was the rule not the exception. Despite all the efforts of powerful Secretaries of State such as Sir Leoline Jenkins and his band of informers, Dissenting conventicles, their pastors and congregations, flourished. Dissenting doctrines permeated the very heart of Lyme mercantile life from before the Civil War until the mid-eighteenth century.

Prominent among this community of Dissenting merchants was Robert Burridge. Originally from the parish of St James in Taunton where the family were in business as clothiers (merchants dealing in cloth) Robert was dispatched to Lyme in order to process his family's shipments for export. Close to Taunton in both the political and religious sense, Lyme proved very much to Robert's taste and he prospered in the bustling seaport. As time went by he increasingly became engaged in business on his own account and was eventually granted the freedom of the town in 1647. Within a few years he married Elizabeth Cogan, daughter of a Bristol merchant of Lyme origin, Cogans having been at Lyme since Elizabethan times. Three of their children survived infancy. The first, Mary, married a Bristol merchant called Henry Gibbs and settled in that city; the second and third were sons John and Robert II, born in 1651 and 1653 respectively.

Following the Civil War, the era of the Commonwealth was sympathetic to Lyme and Robert Burridge flourished, exporting Dorset dozens, medley kersies, Taunton cottons and Bridgewaters to France, in exchange for lockram and canvas. But the promise of the interregnum was not to be fulfilled and when the political pendulum swung back in 1662 Robert Burridge was removed from the corporation of Lyme by the Commissioners of Corporations for refusing to take the oath of allegiance to the Crown.[9] Curiously for one who had made no secret of his Dissenting sympathies, his eldest son John had no trouble entering Wadham College, Oxford. Matriculating in March 1668, he eventually followed his younger brother into his father's business in Lyme.

Prominent as Robert Burridge was, the pride of place in Lyme's merchant community in the mid-seventeenth century was held by the four Tucker brothers, Walter and John of Lyme, Samuel of Rotterdam and William of St Michael's parish, Barbados.[10] As factors, agents and shippers they were strategically placed to handle the family's interests in Holland, Virginia and the West Indies. Walter and John dominated the trade to Virginia and Barbados from Lyme in the two decades 1650–1670, a trade in which Robert Burridge was an occasional partner.

Though occasional, Robert was far from uninterested. He communicated his enthusiasm for the plantation trade to his sons who, by 1678, were rapidly eclipsing the Tuckers and their descendants as the leading merchants, especially to the colonies. In that year, of the five clearances from Lyme for the plantations, one was freighted by Solomon Andrew & Co., one by John Anning (of and for Boston, New England), one by Walter Tucker (the *Concord* for Barbados) and two for Virginia (the *Charity* of Lyme and the *Endeavour* of Ramsgate) on behalf of John Burridge & Co.[11]

Such had been their rise to fortune that they now attracted the unwelcome attention of the authorities. In September of the same year a commission of inquiry into Customs frauds was set up, for an addiction to smuggling was viewed as part and parcel of an adherence to conventicles by those whose business it was to root out Dissent in the mercantile community. Leading lights on the commission were prominent churchmen, Thomas Strangways and John Pole (MP for Lyme in 1685 and 1689, though foisted upon the town on both occasions), who were not known for their expertise on import/export procedures but who could be relied upon to come down hard upon Dissenters. If this commission was intended to drive John and Robert Burridge off the corporation of Lyme and out of public life, then it failed miserably on both counts.[12]

Instead they dug their heels in deeper. The senior echelons of the Tucker family were now dead, except for Walter Tucker (died 1682), and with Robert Burridge II safely married to Walter Tucker's daughter Mary (who brought with her a considerable dowry and, within three years, an inheritance),[13] John now had a free hand to expand his horizons. Though the most eligible bachelor in Lyme he was destined never to marry, instead channelling his energies into commerce and politics. Usually in partnership with his brother and one or another of the local families of Tuckers, Courtenays, Gundrys or Cogans taking smaller shares of the ventures, John Burridge concentrated, like his father before him, on exporting cloth in return for linen and wine. Increasingly however, the colonial trade attracted his attention.

In the first four years of the 1680s the Burridges – and John in particular – completely engrossed Lyme's plantation trade, a hold which the family never relinquished until they faded out of Lyme commercial life in the mid-eighteenth century. As a measure of this, in 1684 John Burridge & Co. dispatched all four west-bound long-haul voyages from Lyme, to Barbados via Madeira, to Newfoundland, to Virginia, and direct to Barbados.[14] During these years the brothers were subject to a constant sniping by their Tory adversaries. In 1683 Bernard Granville (MP for Saltash in 1681 and Plymouth in 1685 and a fervent Royalist), shrugged off a petition for restitution of linen belonging to the Burridges and Tuckers which he had unlawfully seized in Plymouth, claiming their Dissenting beliefs made them reasonable targets:

> The loss of their goods on the condemning them according to law could be no hindrance to their trade or any prejudice to the customs, the inhabitants of Lyme being sufficiently known to his Majesty to be of dangerous and rebellious principles, the pretending owners being the most remarkable Dissenters thereof.[15]

Though the Tories seemed to be having everything very much their own way, even to the extent of having Robert Burridge removed as Lyme's mayor in 1684, their days were numbered. The following year the Duke of Monmouth landed at Lyme and started a chain of reactions that no one could have foreseen. For the moment the emotion his landing provoked most strongly amongst the merchant community of the town was curiosity. Even before he landed, merchants and former mayors Solomon Andrew and Andrew Tucker, accompanied by the more stout-hearted (or less circumspect) of Lyme's inhabitants, had rowed out to meet his little fleet of two ships and a frigate.[16] This could have been none other than a spur of the moment decision, and it is unlikely they fully appreciated the enormity of Monmouth's action. They were rewarded for their pains by imprisonment aboard the flagship of the fleet – the hired frigate *Helderenburgh* – which eventually set them ashore at St Ives in Cornwall after a nail-biting interval of two weeks.

The Burridges, with James Tucker, John Cogan, Thomas Pitts and others, had their spy-glasses trained beyond this fleet. Perched on the Church Cliffs, far more extensive than now and which formed a seventeenth-century marine promenade, they anxiously awaited sight of their inward-bound vessels from Morlaix, loaded with linen and wine, and wondered how to contact the captains and order them to lay off the coast while the situation resolved itself. Lyme was now thronged with Monmouth adherents and the normal pattern of trade totally disrupted.[17]

Though a ghastly period for Monmouth sympathisers, the aftermath of the rebellion, which was cowed at Sedgemoor and finally crushed by Lord Chief Justice Jeffreys, eventually brought considerable benefits for the Burridges, despite the slackening of long-haul trade from the port. James II, a fanatical Catholic, dreamed of Catholicising the country and envisaged a motley union of Nonconformists, turncoat Tories and renascent Catholics turning that dream into a reality. Accordingly an appeal was made to Nonconformists by his publication of a Declaration of Indulgence intended to secure liberty of conscience for all.[18] Lyme Dissenters were among the first to benefit from this measure, being granted royal letters of protection in January 1687,[19] Robert Burridge resuming his interrupted term as mayor in 1689.[20]

Despite these little local difficulties, the Burridges had caught the affairs of state on a rising tide. To be sure, there were some minor drawbacks. Lyme's Customs men decided (or were instructed) to suspend all connivance with John Burridge over the matter of smuggling West Indian sugar. Brown muscovado sugar attracted a much lower rate of duty than refined white sugar when landed from the Caribbean, and Customs officals found it paid them handsomely in backhanders to affect colour-blindness. At any rate, in 1687 John Burridge had imported some 9 tons of brown sugar which upon closer examination turned out to be 'fit for common use'[21] and he was heavily penalised for his false declaration. In the long-running game of cat and mouse all merchants played with the Customs and Excise, sugar provided a favourite scenario, not least because the Customs weighers used large scoops to draw and examine sugar; these were deployed three times on each hogshead under examination to the great mortification of the merchant (who did not get his scooped sugar back) and the great profit of the Customs men.[22]

All this was but a minor irritation to the Burridges for John was now on course to realise his dream of representing Lyme in Parliament. In 1688 the King's electoral agents approved him as court candidate, and he eventually scraped home by a single vote. He took his seat in January 1689, just in time to vote to expel James II.

John Burridge proved far more energetic as a merchant than as an MP and when he did sit on committees in the Convention Parliament of 1689 they were predominantly concerned with mercantile matters.[23] His presence in the capital and his awareness of Lyme's vulnerability in times of war contributed to his setting up a London commercial base. When the war against France commenced under William of Orange in September 1689, the wisdom of his actions became obvious. Overseas trade at Lyme went into a steep decline. Even six years later, when the war was a fact of life and some accommodation to its exigencies had become possible, the level of overseas trade from Lyme remained pitiful. In the first six months of 1695, for example, only three ships left the port for overseas destinations, and they were merely bound to the Channel Islands for Bridport merchant Nathaniel Gundry.[24] No overseas goods were imported. Apart from a few fishing vessels and coastal traders the Cobb was deserted, and the effect upon the townspeople little short of catastrophic. John Burridge was now settled firmly in London. Described as a merchant of that place as early as 1691, he had set forth the privateer *Elizabeth and Katherine* of that year in an attempt to repair some of the damage French privateers had inflicted upon his merchant ventures.[25]

None the less, though he was to remain both living in London and as MP for Lyme (in 1690, 1701, 1702, 1705 and 1708) he did not abandon the town to its fate. His brother Robert Burridge continued to live in Lyme, presumably acting as his agent and factor and kept busy by occasional Burridge ventures which originated at Lyme. In the second half of 1695, a year notable for the paucity of overseas traffic, two of John Burridge's vessels, the *Unity* and *Friendship*, anchored from Virginia and Barbados respectively, the only two ships to arrive in that year. Having discharged their respective cargoes of tobacco and sugar, they returned whence they came with fresh cargoes of woollen goods for John Burridge & Co.; Daniel Gundry also freighted a small proportion of the *Unity*'s cargo to Virginia. Both ships returned safely the following year but it was to be nearly a decade before the port grew prosperous once again. It is no exaggeration to claim that if any port in England owed its continued existence to one family, then it was Lyme to the Burridges as the seventeenth century turned into the eighteenth.

It should not be thought that the Burridges were exclusively devoted to the ports of London and Lyme when it came to shipping their ventures, but doubtless these ports remained the twin pivots of their mercantile endeavours. Perhaps as a result of John's base in London and Robert's in Lyme, the Burridges were remarkable for trading from ports the length and breadth of the West Country. Few merchants of any importance tied themselves to one outlet for their exports, yet the Burridges' indiscriminate use of so many bears witness to the volume of trade passing through their hands. In the period between 1697 and 1701, for example, the Burridges conducted more business to the colonies (and fisheries) from Poole and Weymouth than they did from Lyme.

Though there must have been solid reasons of economy behind these intermittent appearances at other ports, it did allow the brothers unparalleled opportunities to glean intelligence which, combined with John Burridge's access to political decision-making, provided an exceptional vantage point from which to anticipate charges of direction in trade and foreign policy. Good first-hand information was, in an age bereft of a reliable mass media, worth its weight in gold. Indeed the Burridges paid for it in gold; many years later John Burridge recorded in his accounts that he had paid 1s. 6d. for intelligence and contracted with a certain John King for supplying the same, on payment of 2 guineas every Lady Day.[26]

Up to now the emphasis has been firmly placed on the elder Burridge brother, whose career in the latter quarter of the seventeenth century was not without note. Robert Burridge II, the younger brother, appears to have remained in Lyme, again serving as

mayor in 1696 and 1699. The office was an influential one, the mayor
being the returning officer for parliamentary elections, and so it
suited John Burridge very well to have his brother running the arm
of local government. Not as financially secure as his elder brother,
and without his connections, Robert Burridge II remained in a
smaller way of trade. Much of his time would have been taken up
with his family. Five sons and two daughters were born to his wife
Mary between 1681 and 1698. Though the Burridges were generally
radical in politics, religion and trade, they were distinctly conserva-

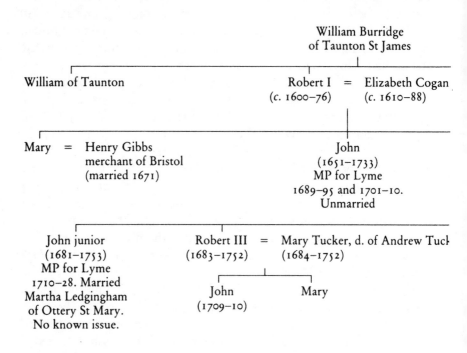

tive in naming their children, providing a tiresome rod for the local
historian's back. Regardless of future confusion, Robert and Mary
Burridge baptised their first two sons John and Robert, so an outline
family tree may help us to see the various Burridges as they really
were.

Robert II's eldest son John, named after his uncle, was usually
called John Burridge junior and often, but not always, signed himself
so. For various reasons that will shortly become evident it is virtually
impossible to differentiate clearly between uncle and nephew; a
similar situation occurs between Robert II and III, as it did between

I and II. The family was close knit and habitually supported each other's ventures by taking shares in freight and owning proportions of each other's ships.

Unlike his namesake, John Burridge junior, born in 1681, did not attend university. The Act of Toleration passed by the Convention parliament in which his uncle sat, though freeing Dissenters from forfeits for failing to go to church and suspending many other penalties imposed by the Clarendon Code, stopped short at allowing Dissenters into universities or civil and military public office. Both

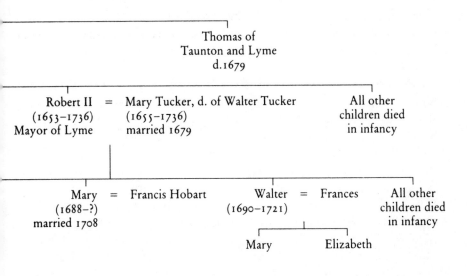

John junior and Robert III probably attended the school at Lyme run by John Kerridge II, before leaving at the age of fifteen to be apprenticed to merchants. In the case of John junior, it seems that he joined Benjamin Way's house in London rather than that of his uncle John, though it was to the latter that his brother, Robert III, was apprenticed.[27]

Whether in Lyme or London, the apprenticeship covered much the same ground, lasting roughly four years. During that time apprentice merchants gained a groundwork in mercantile practice that could be found in no university of the time. This 'hands-on' training covered negotiating ventures, organising and accounting for cargoes, arranging insurance, balancing books, clearing bills of exchange, and securing protection from impressment for ships' crews and release from embargoes in times of war. In addition they often accompanied ventures as supercargoes – much in the manner of Walter Prideaux of the *Daniel and Henry* – literally learning the ropes.

The Way family came from Bridport, eight miles up the coast from Lyme, where they had been settled since the time of Edward III.[28] Like Robert Burridge I, they were merchants in the cloth trade, shipping serge from Lyme and Bridport and importing lockram and canvas.[29] Thomas Way was the head of the family but died young (in 1649) leaving three sons and one daughter, Elizabeth. She married twice, first to a merchant of Lyme called Lee, by whom she had a son, Thomas Lee; and then to John Kerridge II, schoolmaster at Lyme and later pastor at Colyton, just across the county line in Devon.

Of Thomas Way's three sons it is Benjamin and his descendants who will interest us most. Born in 1629 at Bridport, from 1662 Benjamin lived in Dorchester as an independent pastor.[30] This brought him not only into conflict with the authorities, but – more fruitfully – into contact with Martha White, daughter of John White the puritan patriarch of Dorchester (later hailed as the founding father of Massachusetts) and sister of the Dissenting minister, John White II. They married and had five children, of whom Joseph and especially Benjamin are central to this narrative. In 1672 the Revd Benjamin Way established a Congregational meeting place in Dorchester and he remained there until he went to Bristol in 1676 following the death of his first wife Martha and his second marriage of 1675. With his constitution seriously weakened by endless persecution and several spells in damp and filthy gaols, he died at the relatively early age of fifty-one. In his will he left most of his property to his two eldest sons Joseph and Benjamin II, including the lease on a property in Back Street, Dorchester 'behind Mr James Gould's house'; the same James Gould who, two decades later, was to join in venturing the *Daniel and Henry* to Africa. Both eldest sons were already serving their apprenticeships and the Revd Benjamin left strict instructions for

my two younger sons Richard and John Way to be imployed when they are grown up . . . in some honest calling; according to the approbation and good liking of Jeremy Holwey ... of Bristol, merchant; Thomas Scrope of the same city, merchant; and Ichabod Chauncy of the same city, ... Dr in physick.[31]

Obviously the Revd Benjamin had all his sons earmarked for mercantile rather than pastoral careers. Perhaps less obviously two of the three guardians named here were also resolved Dissenters. Thomas Scrope was one of the sons of Adrian Scrope, Governor of Bristol in 1650, a devout Parliamentarian who was executed as a regicide come the Restoration. Thomas himself was to be implicated in the Rye House Plot in three years' time but survived to become alderman of Bristol in 1688. His son, John Scrope, was destined to cast a long shadow over Lyme for much of the eighteenth century. Ichabod Chauncy, described by a contemporary as a 'veritable bell-wether of the fanatics', was indicted at Bristol along with the young Joseph Way and both were sent to Newgate with a fine of 5 marks in 1684, presumably for their Dissenting activities during the Tory crackdown of that era. Unfortunately neither of the Revd Benjamin's younger sons survived into adulthood so their guardian's approval was never put to the test.

While the eldest son, Joseph, remained in Bristol once he was out of his apprenticeship, Benjamin went to London. (Both brothers operated in much the same way as the Burridges did, though in their case Bristol replaced Lyme as a pivot of business.) Benjamin Way was then about twenty-five and destined to become one of the foremost merchants of the metropolis. His trading ventures proved so successful that within a very short time he had moved to Walthamstow in Essex, now a rather ordinary east London suburb bisected by several major arterial roads, but then a leafy and salubriously select village bordering Epping Forest. It was greatly favoured by merchants and shipowners for the convenient access it afforded to their shipping anchored in the Thames between Wapping and Woolwich.

There he met Elizabeth, daughter of the late Henry Coward of Petworth, Sussex, and Port Royal, Jamaica, who was staying with her uncle William Coward at his splendid house. As luck would have it William Coward was not only an influential Congregationalist[32] but an important merchant and ship-owner whose vessels *Walthamstowe Galley*, *Somerset Frigate* and *Gold* (or *Gould*) *Frigate* (amongst others) were a familiar sight in Caribbean waters and off the Guinea Coast. Even more conveniently, Elizabeth Coward accepted Benjamin Way's proposal of matrimony and the couple were married about the year 1696. So Benjamin Way was being drawn irresistibly towards the West Indian trade, not only through his wife's interests – she may have inherited property in Jamaica from her father – but also through her uncle. William Coward's interests in shipping were substantial and he possessed, via his plantations in Jamaica, a vested interest in the Guinea trade; moreover he was happy – once the Royal African Company had lost its monopoly in 1698 – to hire out his vessels to them on contract.[33]

In all of this there is little to suggest that John Burridge junior was apprenticed to Benjamin Way rather than to his uncle John Burridge. Records of apprentices were not required to be registered until 1710, so there is nothing forthcoming from that quarter. It is little more than a theory which, as this narrative progresses, becomes increasingly credible. After all Elizabeth Kerridge, wife of John Kerridge the schoolmaster at Lyme, was Benjamin Way's aunt; the Kerridges and Burridges had been firm friends over several generations and Robert Burridge II might well have considered his eldest son would be better off with a merchant in his early thirties than an uncle in his late forties, who in any case was much taken up by parliamentary affairs.

As owners and freighters of sugar and tobacco trade ships from London, Lyme, Exeter and elsewhere, the Burridges were well aware of the demand for labour, which was ever the cry of the plantations. Though they never mounted voyages carrying indentured white servants alone, their ships would as a matter of course often carry several passengers who had usually sold four years of their labour to a colonial plantation owner in exchange for their passage to the New World. Such servants came not only from Lyme itself (ever since Sir George Somers and the Virginia Company the town had a reputation for supplying colonial labour) but from the surrounding countryside too. In fact the Virginia Company had been the originating body behind the concept of white indentured labour and by 1620 its main characteristic – that a plantation owner would pay a lump sum to an importer for the services of an immigrant – was well established. This lump sum vastly exceeded the cost of transporting an immigrant so white indentured labour (the indentures being assignable from one master to another without let or hindrance) became a commodity to be bought and sold. Since the cost of transportation was about £3 and the selling price of the servant between £6 and £30 (often taken in tobacco) depending upon age, sex and qualifications, indentured servants were greatly sought after. Emigration agents, known as 'spirits' or 'crimps', regularly plied their persuasive trade in tinsel dreams in markets, pubs and fairs in villages and towns the length and breadth of the West Country, and England in general. Such agents were paid by ships' captains and merchants at a fixed rate per head of all souls thus conscripted.[34]

After 1682 the law demanded that emigrating indentured servants be brought before magistrates at the ports of departure to ensure legal registration of their contracts, and that the servants were not being kidnapped. By this time Lyme inhabitants seemed loath to seek their fortunes in the West via this particular channel. Between September 1683 and December 1689, of the 28 indentured servants (21 men, 7 women) who passed through Lyme, only one came from there. The majority hailed from Taunton and its environs, some from other parts of Somerset and from Devon and one each from as far away as Hampshire (Eversleigh) and Berkshire (Hamstead Marshall). All but two were illiterate.[35]

Despite the number of Burridge ventures heading for Virginia and Maryland, few indentured servants were at first consigned to them, whereas some sea captains such as John Bull seem to have virtually monopolised the trade. Nevertheless, by the end of the seventeenth century, Burridge-owned ships like the *Unity* at Virginia in 1700[36] were carrying substantial numbers to the American plantations, but not to the West Indies, for black slaves had long been preferred to white indentured labour on those islands. Though the step from transporting white indentured servants to trading in black slaves was not an inevitable one, the Burridges' involvement in the former was perhaps a signpost towards the latter. In this transition they were not alone. Two London merchants, Peter Paggen and Micajah Perry, both made small fortunes for themselves transporting indentured white servants before turning to the black slave trade in the last years of the seventeenth century.

If the impression has been given that the Burridges were gradually leaving Lyme to its own devices, the truth was otherwise. In 1698 a new Customs House was erected at Lyme for £60 and mortgaged to Robert Burridge II for £150 payable at 6 per cent per annum.[37] As the peace brought about by the Treaty of Ryswick appeared to be holding there was an upsurge in overseas trade from the port, led in the main by the Burridges. Perhaps as a gesture of faith in the town he represented, and certainly because of his Dissenting sympathies, John Burridge senior purchased the old vicarage in Church Street from the heirs of Ames Short,[38] courageous Dissenting vicar of Lyme.

The see-saw of trade at Lyme came down with a predictably negative bump at the start of the War of the Spanish Succession in 1702. Shipping fled to safer ports where armed Navy convoys afforded some measure of protection. This time the Burridges stayed steadfastly on, though one suspects the majority of their long-haul ventures cleared from London. Nevertheless no other trading family of Lyme could even approach the contribution they continued to make to the town. In the dark days of 1703, for example, of a total of £1 2s. 7½d. received for Cobb dues by the town's corporation, the Burridges accounted for 14s. 9d. In the Christmas quarter alone for that year they imported 137,299 lb. of tobacco into Lyme from Virginia.[39]

During this period nothing could have been easier for them than to have dominated overseas trade to the exclusion of all other merchants. Instead they encouraged the participation of others by dividing ventures not into eighth or sixteenth parts, but into twenty-fourths and thirty-seconds. In the *Friendship* bound for Jamaica in 1704, John took $\frac{1}{24}$ part of the cargo, and Robert II $\frac{17}{24}$; in the *John* of the same year, John took a $\frac{10}{32}$ part and Robert II $\frac{5}{32}$.[40]

Nor did they forget their charitable obligations. The early puritan proclamation that God was a poor man's God was, by the end of the seventeenth century, buttressed by the more pointed belief that the devil finds work for idle hands to do. Of all evils, Dissenters abhorred idleness the most[41] and perceived charity as a tool capable of defeating that threat. The Burridges and their circle of like-minded merchants such as the Cogans, Courtenays, Tuckers and Fowlers, regularly contributed to a Lyme charity for the binding out of poor children. These children, occasionally orphans, sometimes fatherless – every seaport lost a substantial proportion of its adult male population through disasters at sea – and always without guardians or parents who could afford apprenticeship fees, were thus safely found a productive place in society.

Dissenting merchants were among the first to recognise the contribution circumstances, not natural proclivity, could make to anti-social behaviour. Without such charities poor children would gravitate to the criminal and marginal fringes of society, becoming vagabonds, beggars, thieves and prostitutes, in turn posing a threat to the merchants themselves. Thus the £3 10s. which John Burridge donated to the Lyme Charity in 1703, to be administered by Samuel Courtenay,[42] was not activated by entirely disinterested motives, though his concerns were genuine enough. The Burridges

made many such donations regularly in their lifetimes and as
bequests at their deaths. Their charity was still being administered
well into the twentieth century though by this time charity had
become a doubtful word, redolent of deterrence as much as of
relief. By this time too, merchants had undergone a profound
transformation in relation to religion. From being essentially spirit-
ual beings who devoted a reasonable amount of time to business in
order to survive, they had become businessmen who – aware of
their mortality – kept half an eye open towards their religious
obligations.[43] In the Burridges can be seen the rolling crest of this
profound sea change.

The final decades of the seventeenth century had also marked a
change in trade patterns. Lyme was no longer locked into a rather
humdrum European relationship but had expanded its horizons to
the west, to the blossoming colonies of America and the West Indies.
Their transformation was apparent, to a greater or lesser degree,
across the whole country. Merchants were gaining confidence and
chafing at the restrictive practices engaged in by monopolies such as
the Royal African Company. Though doubtless aware of the vital
role played by black labour in the development of the plantations
Lyme, unlike Exeter, Totnes and other neighbouring towns, played
no part in the general outcry against the Company monopoly of
transporting slaves from Africa to the colonies. Lyme's Brotherhood
of St Thomas Beckett was a forgotten episode in its long seafaring
history and commerce with Africa was a marginal issue. The war with
France, only ended by the 1697 Treaty of Ryswick, had made all trade a
desperately fraught business, let alone a voyage to the unfamiliar
waters of the West African coast.

Nor was there a manufacturing imperative to open new trade
routes to Africa. Essentially the difference between the merchants of
Bristol, Exeter and Totnes, who formed such a powerful phalanx for
change and eventually succeeded in clipping the Royal African
Company's wings in 1698, and the merchants of Lyme, was that the
latter town manufactured little of consequence. Instead Lyme acted
mainly as a funnel for the goods of its neighbours, even from as far
away as Bristol.

Yet it is inconceivable that the Guinea Coast did not figure in
conversations between Lyme merchants and sea captains in the last
two decades of the seventeenth century, and some Lyme mariners
undoubtedly shipped out on slave trading voyages during this time.
The numerous Bragge family of Lyme, merchants and mariners of

the middle sort, had three sons at sea in July 1682; two in the Caribbean and one on the 'Cost of Ginni'.[44]

All this paled into insignificance when compared to the homecoming of Richard Hallett. The Halletts were a Lyme merchant family who had made good – very good – in Barbados by a judicious mix of limited capital, native wit and advantageous marriages. In 1691 Richard Hallett, who managed the Lyme end of their enterprise, purchased Stedcombe House, just across the county border at Axmouth. He had little time to enjoy it since he died just four years later, and the property (and the bulk of his fortune) passed to his nephew and namesake in Barbados, Richard Hallett II, who was then under twenty-one years of age. The senior Robert and John Burridge, 'worthy friends', were instructed to act as his agents, collecting rents and looking after his lands until his arrival in England.

The Halletts of Barbados owned many slaves, both domestic and plantation workers. When Richard Hallett II eventually arrived in Lyme following the death of his father in 1699, he brought not only his newly wedded wife Meliora (daughter of John Hothersell, one of Barbados' richest plantation owners), but also a retinue of black servants. Presumably they all stayed at the house in Lyme he had inherited, for Stedcombe was being rebuilt and would have taken some time to be completed. The house, a charming and idiosyncratic overgrown doll's house of mellowed brick and white-painted quoins, topped by an unusual belvedere, stands to this day, now restored to all its former glory.[45] As well as Stedcombe, Richard Hallett also set about building a political career for himself, standing as a candidate for Lyme in the parliamentary election of 1701, but with little success.[46] Afterwards he settled down to live, very comfortably, as a gentleman of independent means, occasionally supplementing his considerable private income from his estates in Barbados by trading in sugar and rum.

Quite how many black slaves inhabited the servants' quarters at Stedcombe is impossible to estimate. Meliora had been brought up surrounded by black maidservants at her father's plantation great house in Barbados and undoubtedly brought one or two of them back to England. Her husband, Richard, definitely possessed a black manservant called Ando. Early in December 1702 he was accused of being riotously assembled in Broad Street in company with other inhabitants of Lyme, including Elizabeth Swain, a woman of the most doubtful reputation. All faced charges of unlawful assembly and the use of violence to rescue one Thomas Templeman from the custody of the Fowler family. The Templemans were close friends of the Halletts but the affair is an obscure one. A jury was empanelled at the Guildhall within the month and returned a verdict of unlawful assembly but no riot and the case – and Ando – dropped from sight. Neither he, nor any of his black companions, if they existed, were ever recorded on the very thorough Lyme census of inhabitants. However the fact that Ando was involved in such a disorder indicates that he was allowed at least a measure of his own social life.[47]

In general the Halletts of Barbados seem to have displayed a liberal approach to their domestic slaves. The father of Richard Hallett II, John Hallett, in his will of 1699, the year of his death, ordered 'my boy Virgil to have his freedom . . . and if he please to live in my family where he shall be maintained'. Richard's elder brother, also called John, who continued to live in Barbados, made similar provisions in his will of 1716 leaving to 'my negro woman Jane and my molatto boy called Johannes and my molatto girl called Nancy a piece of land called Cameroons and £10 a year each, and also to the said Jane a little negro boy by name Quashey'.[48]

Unlike the Tuckers and the Halletts, the marriages of the male Burridges in the seventeenth century had been blessed with few boys who survived into adulthood. Probably for that reason alone, no close members of the Burridge family established themselves in the plantations to handle the western end of their colonial trade. And though the Burridges owned a plantation-built vessel christened the *Africa*, which they employed chiefly in the tobacco trade between London or Lyme and Rappahannock in Virginia, there is no evidence that she ever plied in the Guinea trade. She was frequently captained, however, by Francis Read, who had few scruples about commanding slave ships when he wasn't working for the Burridges.[49]

There is evidence that it was Lyme's links with London that proved crucial in smoothing the port's entry into the slave trade. Amongst local merchant families who had settled in London were the Alfords of Winsham, some eight miles north of Lyme, whose scion Joseph Alford figured frequently as an export–import merchant at Lyme between 1657 and 1661. By 1698 his sons Joseph and Daniel were fully established in London and between November of that year and September 1702 they invested a total of £2,647 (exclusive of the 10 per cent tax) in part-freighting ten separate voyages for slaves,[50] the first of which was the *Sarah* captained by Robert Mathew, son of Roger Mathew, captain of the *Daniel and Henry*.

Next to evince an interest was Benjamin Way who, primed by his involvement in the West India trade through his father-in-law, could now see the appeal of slave trading. In September 1700 he was the major shareholder in venturing the *Cecilia* from London to the Guinea Coast. Shortly afterwards his brother Joseph of Bristol also ventured into the trade becoming, like his younger brother in London, one of that city's foremost slave trade merchants.[51]

In turn they were closely followed by Major William Cogan of Barbados, who was born and bred in Lyme where his father and grandfather before him had been cloth merchants, and indeed closely related to the Burridges by marriage. An earlier ancestor, John Cogan, had been one of the principals named in the 1592 charter granted to Taunton merchants to trade to Guinea. Now, a little over a century later, William Cogan was employed by the Royal African Company as Writer, a position which brought him into contact with the island's slave merchants and, in a private capacity, enabled him to join their ranks. Lacking English-style produce for barter in Guinea, Cogan made good the deficiencies by shipping colossal quantities of local rum in exchange for slaves. His first venture to clear was the *Guinea Hen* of May 1702. She was followed by a lull of five years during which Cogan may well have chosen to invest in the ventures of others. He reopened his own account by freighting a series of six ships on 'double' voyages between May 1707 and August 1709. Their total cargo of rum amounted to 25,766 gallons with a value of £1,909, exclusive of the 10 per cent tax.[52] Clearly, even if the two John Burridges had not been working in London, enough of their relatives, friends and contacts were already successful traders to the Guinea Coast should the time ever come for them to enter the trade in human beings.

The time came in 1703. Summer of that year found Benjamin Way at his busiest. Apart from his normal course of business he was also organising two Guinea-trade ventures. One involved his ship the *Way Galley* due to depart from London at the end of the year.[53] The other concerned the vessel *Union Galley*, which did not belong to him but to slave trader William Franklin of Bristol,[54] and was presently refitting at that port. In July 1703 Benjamin Way sent a cargo of tallow, old sheets, tapseils, niconees, perpetuannas, says, short cloth and iron by land carriage to his brother Joseph in Bristol.[55] This was destined for the *Union* though it was by no means the entire loading, for the bulk of the cargo was the responsibility of John Burridge junior. He was currently ordering that from London and Exeter using the good offices of Joseph Paice (his uncle's agent and fellow MP for Lyme from February 1701 to July 1702),[56] Roger Prowse, an Exeter merchant (who again acted for John Burridge junior in 1714), and David Arbuthnot. Something of a Burridge camp-follower, he had worked for the senior John Burridge nearly a quarter of a century earlier in Lyme, and had recently been engaged in the tobacco trade at Weymouth with James Gould of Dorchester,[57] backer of the *Daniel and Henry*. On the voyage of the *Union Galley* Arbuthnot acted as accountant, as appears in the following memorandum of John Burridge junior.[58]

Voyage for Guinea in the *Union Galley*

December [1703]	Joseph Paice for Cost of Iron & Hemp	£227:15:2
January [1704]	Cost of 6 chests of sheets & other linens	84:18:6
	Joseph Greenaway for 165½ bushels of Beans	25:19:9
	Roger Prowse for 500 single Ranters	240: 3:4
February	Cash paid for 2 indentures & 2 certificates from the Customs House to certify their being bound	0: 6:0
March	Cash advanced to Cross £2:9:6½, to Symms £2:9:10½, the two Apprentices	4:19:5
	Cash gave the Mate, 4 men & 2 servants their travelling Expenses to Bristol	1:17:6
	Cash paid for an Indenture, Certificate for Limbrey, another servant, his Expenses to Bristol	0: 9:0
	Cash paid Stoward for carriage of the seamens clothes	1: 1:6
	Cash for Symms, Express from Bristol, one of the boyes that was left behind .	0: 3:6
	Cash for a Protection for the Ship & 3 for the Servants to keep them from being impressed	0:14:0
	Cash for Diet of the Servants before they went for Bristol, & Symms since his return	1: 5:0
	The Balance I carry to the Debit of Mr David Arbuthnot who is the Accomptant	589:12:8

Owing to the lack of any surviving documentation[59] and the fact that the *Union Galley* made a subsequent voyage to Guinea in 1706 (for William Franklin), it must be assumed that this, the first overt Guinea-trade venture mounted by John Burridge junior, was successful. This was probably due more to Benjamin Way's watchful eye and careful tutelage than any other factor. Though the precise business relationship between the two of them is impossible to pin down, where Benjamin Way led, John Burridge junior followed.

In May 1705 the senior Burridge brothers dispatched their vessel *Friendship* to Jamaica under John Butcher (a favourite master in their sugar trade), with Benjamin Way taking a quarter of the venture. She returned a year later with sugar and once again departed for Jamaica with foodstuffs and dry goods. Aboard her at this juncture were three passengers, a woman and two Negroes, whose passage cost 5 guineas. Presumably the woman was white and had embarked for Jamaica as an indentured servant. The blacks are much more of a conundrum and it can only be surmised that they had been brought back to Bristol, possibly with others, by the *Union Galley* on her return the previous year. It is worth bearing in mind that the early 1700s were marked by a fashion for black servants (slaves) in England, no colonial merchant deeming himself complete without one following respectfully in his footsteps. The fact that these two were bound for Jamaica suggests they had outlived their novelty value and were being packed off to the plantations. After a year in England, possessing a few words of English and having picked up one or two European skills, they could command a premium in the colonies for their erstwhile masters. On her return the *Friendship* 'and her appurtenances' were sold for £116 and work started on a pink of the same name at Isaac Bellerby's stocks in Minehead.[60]

The desultory level of overseas trade at Lyme, a consequence of the War of the Spanish Succession which had commenced in 1702, was transformed in 1706 for no other reason, it appears, than that the Burridges wanted it so. Even smugglers had deserted the coast of Lyme Bay, so intimidating were the French privateers. A measure of French success can be gauged from the Treasury's resolve that

> the salary of Mr John Gould, the riding officer for inspecting the coast of Dorset and part of the coast of Devon (being £60 p.a. on the establishment of Lyme Regis port) to be sunk as useless in times of war.[61]

None the less in the opening months of 1706 (and perhaps

encouraged by the lack of a riding officer), the senior Burridge brothers started shipping large mixed cargoes to Jamaica and Virginia.[62] No less than five heavily laden vessels cleared the port on their behalf for the plantations. Some of these may have been escorted for the first few days of their voyage by the *London Galley*, commissioned as a privateer at the beginning of the year, and in which Benjamin Way and John Burridge junior owned the principal interest in both ship and cargo.[63] Their offices were situated in Coleman Street, then, as today, a busy commercial thoroughfare a stone's throw from the Bank of England and the Royal Exchange, and a short stroll from Africa House in Leadenhall Street.

Privateering was little more than a sideline for the *London*. She was bound for the Guinea Coast with a cargo valued at £1,265, the first of two slave ventures in which Benjamin Way (and by default, John Burridge junior) were involved during that year. (The second, which cleared London in May 1706, was the *Dorset Brigantine* of Bristol, owned by Joseph Way, but again freighted to Guinea by Benjamin with a cargo valued at £684.)[64] It was by no means rare for a slave trade ship – or rather her captain – to take out letters of marque entitling her to capture merchant shipping of nations with which England was at war. Many Guinea trade merchants seem to have approved of the practice though the returns were invariably negligible.

As it turned out, the returns from the *London Galley*'s voyage were negative. After a highly successful summer trading off the Guinea Coast she arrived in Jamaica at the end of 1706, discharged her slaves, and loaded sugar, logwood, indigo, cocoa and other commodities. This was effected at some speed since a convoy of merchant shipping was shortly to leave for England under the protection of HMS *Northumberland* and the opportunity of an armed escort was too good to miss. Working against the clock the *London Galley* only just made the deadline for the convoy. Seven of her crew had been impressed by Sir John Jennings' squadron, she was riding deeply, sailing slowly, and her replacement crew 'hired at very extravagant wages – £10, 12, 14 and 15 a month', assisted by a few French prisoners of war, were unfamiliar with the ship. It was nothing less than a recipe for disaster, and disaster accordingly struck. In a desperate attempt to keep up with the convoy her master Abraham Battell crowded on more sail, sprung her foremast in the partners, and brought down his mainmast.[65] Now comprehensively disabled, the *London* was left far behind by the convoy who, ignoring her distress signals, sailed onwards. Ship and cargo were lost, the total amounting to many thousands of pounds. Despite prolonged complaints directed to Prince George of Denmark, the Lord High Admiral, and to the House of Lords, the Navy predictably refuted the charge of negligence and left the merchants without a penny compensation.

Such a loss made little appreciable impact on either Benjamin Way or John Burridge junior. If anything, the year 1707 marked a turning point in the careers of both. For some years Benjamin Way had been consigned sugar from the Bybrook plantation in Jamaica owned by William and John Helyar of East Coker, Somerset, and had acted as their London agent. It was not a satisfactory relationship and Way frequently found himself out of pocket on their behalf:

> Not having an Opportunity to sell goods or none would buy Sugar at present, the two Mr Helyars will be considerable in my debt. I have already Disbursed a great deal from my Purse and am dun'd for £133 cost of mules bought last year, so that when I send home my Account passed by the Attorneys I hope Mr Helyars will allow the produce of the Sugars Shipt home to be paid to me: I allow you 25 per cent for the difference of moneys . . . [66]

Shortly afterwards Benjamin Way purchased John Helyar's half-share in the estate. For him it represented an acquisition sweeter by far than any sugar. The Helyars' father, Colonel William Helyar, had been a particularly fervid Royalist who, after the restoration, was notorious for the enthusiasm with which he harried Somerset Dissenters and hunted down their conventicles.[67] This was the revenge that Benjamin Way had worked all his life to achieve.

For John Burridge junior the year 1707 denoted his first appearance on the stage of public affairs, albeit closely shadowed by Benjamin Way. Initially he joined a concerted effort by a group of English merchants – including Benjamin Way – which opposed the granting of passes to four Spanish vessels intended for Honduras with wool. The grounds of their opposition rested on the belief that this would create a precedent eventually damaging the woollen trade from Jamaica to Spanish America. Subsequently he became an expert representative of the 'Separate Traders to Africa', a pressure group set up by slave trade merchants to oppose the attempts by the Royal African Company to regain its monopoly on the Guinea Coast.[68]

At first sight he would appear to have been completely out of his depth. All the other merchants, including Benjamin Way, Peter

Paggen, Isaac Milner, Richard Harris, Humphrey Morice, Abraham Houlditch, James Wayte and Joseph Martin, were slave trade heavyweights. No Burridge was even listed in the comprehensive official account of ten per cent merchants trading with Africa between 1702 and 1707,[69] so John junior must have been nominated by Way. Financed by some of the richest merchants in the land, the separate traders continuously lobbied Parliament and the Commissioners for Trade and Plantations from 1708 to 1712 as the debate raged over the Company's future.

Far from taking a back seat, John Burridge made an important contribution from the start, perhaps seeking to emulate his uncle (again elected to represent Lyme in 1708) and sensing that here was as good a way as any to win friends and make contacts within the powerful Whig mercantile elite. During 1708 he helped draft the influential open letter to the Commissioners for Trade, one of the most significant documents to emerge in the wrangle over the African trade. Appearing in 1707, the letter adduced evidence which clearly showed the huge disparity between the Company's delivery rate of slaves and the separate traders' rate.[70] The signatories formed a rollcall of the most prominent slave traders, amongst them John Burridge junior, a minor player in a very senior league indeed.

Included in the signatories was – of course – Benjamin Way. Whatever dreams he had envisaged of a hermetically sealed triangle of profit between London, Guinea and Jamaica were destined to come to naught. Dogged by ill-health he sought relief at the fashionable waters of Bath, but died there in May 1707.[71] Signing the letter of the separate traders had been one of his last actions. Now John Burridge junior stepped into his shoes for Benjamin Way, only forty-four years old at his death, had no sons older than seven to succeed him in the business. For John Burridge junior the years of waiting in the wings were over. The time had come for him to start trading to Africa on his own account.

By now Burridge had the contacts and knew the business, but how did he finance his initial solo venture? Undoubtedly he raised some capital from within the Burridge family, but the bulk probably came from his wife, Martha Ledgingham. We have already seen how Benjamin Way, the son of a poor Dissenting pastor, prospered by his marriage into the slave-owning Coward family. John Burridge junior profited by a similar manoeuvre. At some point during this time he had married the daughter, and only child, of Warwick Ledgingham of Ottery St Mary, a thriving woollen town which lay on the old road between Lyme and Exeter. About 1670 Ledgingham had paid a substantial capital sum for the manorial rights over the town, doubtless hoping to raise rents wherever possible and substitute leases at rack rent for customary holdings. His extortionate demands – including excessive distraints – led to proceedings being taken out against him in the Crown Office for oppressing his neighbours, and he was found guilty on three counts.[72] For better or for worse, Martha was his sole heir. Since he died before 1695, she was now in full possession of a substantial amount of Ottery land, building and perquisites, a pretty plum to fall into the persuasive arms of John Burridge junior.

He too, was not without resources. It was agreed upon his marriage that his uncle's manor of Thornfalcon would eventually be settled upon him. And he had shares in many potentially profitable ventures inside and outside the Guinea trade, including a one-sixteenth share in the *Emelia Galley*, a slave trade venture of Humphrey Morice's. By this time Morice, an energetic London merchant of West Country origins (and a distant cousin of Walter Prideaux, supercargo of the *Daniel and Henry*) was just getting into his stride as a slave trade merchant. Later he was to dominate the slave trade from London, using the Company forts as his own and taking Catherine Paggen, the daughter of slave trader Peter Paggen, as his second wife. Morice is perhaps best remembered as the Governor of the Bank of England who used his position there to run up the most colossal debts. They eventually totalled over £200,000 of which £29,000 was owed directly to the Bank.[73] As we shall see, some of Morice's attitude to finance rubbed off on John Burridge junior, and Morice may well have provided a model for the role that the latter sought to play.

All this lay well in the future, for both John Burridge and Morice were still, in 1709, relatively young men. Burridge withdrew his £200 share in the *Emelia Galley* and invested it in chartering the London frigate *Martha*. She had not been christened after Martha Ledgingham, but it was a pleasant coincidence and one that augured well for the success of the voyage. A sizeable vessel of 230 tons burden, the *Martha* had previously been employed by Huguenot slave traders (and purveyors of beads) Daniel and Claude Jamineau.[74] For insurance Burridge turned, not to Joseph Paice as one would expect, but to Humphrey Morice, who charged him the enhanced wartime rate of 12 guineas per cent, and which added a further £103 to the cost of the voyage.

The choice of captain was an important consideration, and here John Burridge junior turned homewards, picking William Courtenay, eldest son of Samuel Courtenay, mayor of Lyme in 1702 and a solid supporter of Burridge endeavours. Although only twenty-two years of age (John Burridge junior was only twenty-eight), William Courtenay had recently distinguished himself as first lieutenant of the enormously successful privateer *Severn Galley*. She was a 'professional' privateer of 160 tons burden, 24 guns and a hand-picked crew numbering a hundred. Though a Bristol ship, she operated from Poole and ranged the length of the Channel, Western Approaches and Atlantic trade routes with dramatic results. Amongst her owners was the Dissenting merchant and Bristol grandee Abraham Elton, a friend and associate of Joseph Way. The Courtenays had long been close to the Burridges at Lyme and the two families were linked through the Tucker sisters Elizabeth (William Courtenay's aunt) and Mary (John Burridge junior's mother). So it was hardly coincidence that the command of the *Martha* fell to William Courtenay.[75]

The *Martha* cleared the Customs House, London on 20 August 1709 for 200 slaves, her cargo being detailed and attested by Walter Burridge, John Burridge junior's youngest brother.[76] Two weeks later was under sail down the Thames for Gravesend and the Channel. For William Courtenay the voyage could be described as beginner's luck; his command ran into no unforeseen difficulties and trading along the Guinea Coast was completed without difficulty. He made good time to Jamaica, arriving there on 25 March the following year and delivering 160 slaves.[77] William Courtenay was also fortunate in expediting a quick turnround: a valuable cargo of sugar, indigo, cotton, logwood and lime juice was rapidly taken aboard during the latter half of April and early May and discharged in Bristol along with ivory from the Guinea Coast, on the *Martha*'s arrival on 26 June 1710. All in all it was a most encouraging start for John Burridge junior and William Courtenay.

Perhaps sensing he was on a winning streak and buoyed up by news of trading in Guinea sent back by William Courtenay, Burridge had already launched his second venture for slaves in February 1710. This involved the Burridge family's own tobacco trade ship the *John and Robert* and probably indicates that, though John Burridge junior was apparently acting alone in his attempt to break into the African trade, endeavours were firmly endorsed (and the ventures partly financed) by his father and uncle. The *John and Robert* was captained not by a tyro in the slave trade, but by Robert Collins, who had experience of African waters as commander of the Company ship *James* in 1702.[78] Once again Walter Burridge handled all the paperwork and cleared the cargo through the Customs House in London.

The voyage was an uneventful one. Designed to take 130 slaves[79] the *John and Robert* left no trail of misdemeanours or misadventures, in fact left no trail at all. Her final destination was almost certainly Virginia and it was probably from this vessel that John Burridge imported 4 cwt. of ivory early in 1711 at the port of London.[80] In the spring of that year the Burridges again dispatched the *John and Robert* for the Guinea Coast, this time from Plymouth, the voyage being separately noticed in Chapter 18.

Everything was coming up roses. His ventures were successful, the operational network laid down by Benjamin Way functioned well, and sugar continued to arrive in satisfactory quantities from the Bybrook plantation.[81] On the public front the campaign of the separate traders was making huge inroads into the credibility of the Royal African Company. A veritable tornado of petitions from cities and towns the length and breadth of Britain whipped up commercial sensibilities and Whig sympathies against any resumption of the Company's monopoly. In Lyme, John and Robert Burridge II were busy collecting signatures for their own petition, attesting

> that the Trade of this Port and your Petitioners Livelihoods very much depends on the Western Navigation and the Plantations whose Productions are Chiefly Raised by Negroes brought from Africa. That by Encouragement of the Late Act of Parliament [1698] . . . Divers of the Merchants and Inhabitants of this town became Adventurers therein.[82]

Thanks to John Burridge junior this petition was unusual in actually recording the truth. Again on the public front his dream of following in his uncle's footsteps as MP for Lyme was realised. The senior John stepped down in 1710 and John junior succeeded him in the Commons in the same year, remaining there until 1728, a tenure which, as we shall see, proved to be not entirely without incident.

So it was with high hopes that John Burridge junior awaited news of the *Martha*'s second voyage which had begun in September 1710. Since she had been berthed at Bristol on her return from her first trip, Burridge had used Joseph Way as his agent both to assemble and load her cargo, and clear her through Customs. The summer and early autumn of 1710 had been a busy one for Joseph Way. In addition to the *Martha* two of his own ventures, the *Expedition Brigantine* under Thomas Costin and the *Way Galley* under John Scott, were also being loaded simultaneously for Africa. Hoping to discourage attacks by privateers, the *Martha*, *Expedition* and *Way Galley* joined company with the *Anne* of Bristol, a brigantine commanded by Samuel King for merchant Richard Henvile, and the sloop *Mary* under Isaac Roberts for tobacco merchant George Mason, both also bound for the Guinea Coast for slaves.[83]

Alas, the little convoy attracted rather than repelled boarders. French privateers swooped down on them as they approached the African coast in late December, harrying them remorselessly and eventually cutting out the *Way Galley* and *Martha*. All William Courtenay's experience on the *Severn Galley* proved to no avail in this confrontation, for the *Martha* was a heavy merchantman laden with goods, skimpily armed and with an apprehensive crew of thirty-odd souls rather than a hundred hand-picked fighting men. Both ships were described as 'lost' by Company factors on the Guinea Coast.[84] There is no indication of the crews, ships or cargo being offered for ransom or simply released on some deserted stretch of the Coast as was frequently the practice. Nothing more is heard of William Courtenay until his father was granted the administration of his estate in 1714,[85] perhaps indicating his incarceration and death in a French gaol prior to the cessation of hostilities in 1713.

The loss of the *Martha* and her captain was a severe financial and personal blow to John Burridge junior and it was to be another eighteen months before his interest in the slave trade was reawakened. By this time the Royal African Company was at a crucial point in its long battle to regain the monopoly to Africa. Amongst its rules was one stating that the 10 per cent tax on an African-bound cargo could not be refunded if the cargo was lost *en route* before trading commenced. However as a conciliatory gesture to the uncertainties of overseas mercantile trade, another of the same value could be dispatched subsequently to Africa without incurring the 10 per cent penalty. Fearing that this concession might be lost in the unlikely event of the monopoly's reintroduction, John Burridge junior hastily assembled a Guinea-trade cargo which he swore amounted to exactly the same value as the *Martha*'s and shipped it aboard the *Mary and Elizabeth* at anchor in the Thames. Huguenot slave trader, Anthony Tourney (or Tournai), whom Humphrey Morice described as an ironmonger, supplied him with wrought or worked iron, and James Wayte, also prominent in the London slave trade, joined him with a separate cargo on his own account. Clearing London in March 1712, the *Mary and Elizabeth* shaped a course for the Gambia where she loaded about 200 slaves. On landing at the Potomac naval district of Virginia her master, Nathaniel Davis, reported 113 slaves still alive and 22 dead (not deceased on the middle passage but dead on arrival).[86] They sold for between £20 and £28 sterling a head. The *Mary and Elizabeth* returned to Lyme on 1 June 1713 with 10 cwt. of ivory for John Burridge junior and a massive 50 tons of tobacco for the mercantile triumvirate of John (senior), Robert Burridge II and Nathaniel Gundry of Bridport. (This was far from the first time the Gundrys had found it convenient to be linked with the Burridges in the tobacco trade from Lyme. In 1706, for instance, John Gundry had shared in venturing the Burridge's tobacco trade vessel *Africa* to Virginia, sending brother Daniel Gundry along as supercargo.)[87] Whilst the Gundry's were never overtly engaged in the slave trade, the Burridges' habit of splitting ventures into small fractions suggests that a number of local Lyme and Bridport merchants could be relied upon to speculate with ¹⁄₂₄ or ¹⁄₃₂ of the cost. Unremarkable as the arrival of the *Mary and Elizabeth* was in Lyme, it heralded a new departure in Burridge trade to Africa. From this date none of their ventures to the Guinea Coast cleared from London for Africa but all departed – with the exception of the *Surprise Galley* of Exeter – from Lyme.

To what can this shift be attributed? Amongst the agglomeration of possibilities the date is of major significance. The year 1713 marked the end of the War of the Spanish Succession, and a measure of normality returned to British trade with the signing of the Treaty of Utrecht. This promised vast benefits for merchants. The territories of Hudson's Bay, Nova Scotia, Newfoundland and the island of St Christopher in the Caribbean became indisputably British, and Britain's power in the western Mediterranean was confirmed by the retention of both Minorca and Gibraltar. In a concession ultimately shown to result in more harm than good, Britain was also granted the Asiento or monopoly contract to supply slaves from Africa to Spanish territories in South America. The trading company to which this contract was awarded was the ill-fated South Sea Company.

Enthusiasm for these new vistas of endless profit swept through the mercantile community. The good times were about to roll. In Parliament, the Commons voted to end the Royal African Company's monopoly for good, and African merchants were finally freed from the irksome 10 per cent tax. John Burridge junior and his committee of separate traders to Africa had won the day. Peace also removed the necessity of being in London to negotiate convoys, freedom for crews from impressments and ships from embargoes. Little by little, trade started to move back to the minor outports.

Transferring the Burridges' African trade to Lyme meant that John Burridge junior's key role in organising the ventures came to an end. Since he now had many irons in the fire, he was probably far from reluctant to hand over the responsibility to his father and uncle John, though he still kept a close interest and shipped substantial proportions of the ventures. His uncle had now moved back to Lyme permanently. (For him the year 1713 was momentous but far from pleasant: in October his house was completely gutted by fire and the contents destroyed.)[88] For other reasons too the move to centralise operations from Lyme made good economic sense. The Burridges were the most considerable traders of the port, both dominating the corporation and having the Customs in their pocket. They had also contributed greatly to the upkeep of the Cobb, had petitioned Parliament for funds for its maintenance, and generally served Lyme interests well. Though cargoes for African ventures might prove something of a problem in Lyme, this was more than offset by major savings in port fees, refitting costs, victualling charges, crew wages and the cost of locally produced serge goods for barter.

So in 1713 John and Robert Burridge II set forth the *John Frigate* (owned by John Burridge uncle and nephew) on a voyage of truly epic proportions. Tracing her convoluted passage also illustrates that the triangular pattern conventionally attributed to the slave trade had validity only as a general theme. Particular and individual variations constantly recur. Though a small vessel of little more than 65 tons burden,[89] and lightly armed with but two pieces of cannon, the *John* (built in Chester River, Maryland in 1697) was a firm favourite of the family and continuously plied between Virginia and Lyme in the tobacco trade. In recent years she had been commanded by Samuel Courtenay, younger brother of William of the ill-fated *Martha*, and like him an experienced master mariner.

Towards the end of 1713 the *John* was loaded with a substantial cargo of beer, dry goods and provisions for Barbados and Virginia. She was bound first for Cork where provisions were cheap and where a group of indentured white servants awaited their passage to the plantations. In March 1714 the *John* arrived without incident at Barbados, discharged her cargo and cleared for Virginia with a new lading of sugar and molasses. Although it was almost certainly

Samuel Courtenay's intention to load tobacco at Rapahannock (for Lyme), he was informed on his arrival that the course of the voyage had been altered. Owing to the nature of voyage that the Burridges now envisaged, or perhaps due to the death of some of the crew, three of the indentured Irish servants were hired as crewmen. The *John*'s course through the summer months of 1714 is speculative but included New England, for in November of that year the *John* sailed back into Barbados, registering her last port of call as Boston. During the intervening period an agent of the Burridges in Barbados had been engaged in purchasing barrel-loads of rum, for the *John* was now destined upon a 'double voyage' to Guinea and back for slaves. The identity of the agent who had so assiduously procured the 5,000 gallons of rum now being loaded aboard the *John* is unknown, but ex-Lyme resident and Burridge relative Major William Cogan – with whom the Burridges had had conventional business dealings since 1706 at least – undoubtedly had a hand in the proceedings.[90]

He also had a finger or two in the pie of profit, though this turned out to be less fruitful than expected. Having cleared Barbados with a target of 200 slaves the *John* limped back with 91, of whom 82 were sold to William Cogan for £1,719.[91] Here fresh instructions awaited Courtenay from Lyme ordering him to pay the men's wages from Guinea and refit the vessel for Sanlasey (St Lucia). Since the *John* had now been continuously at sea for nearly two years, much of it in tropical waters, the state of her lower hull and rigging must have given cause for concern. The cost of wages and the refit came to £469. For the next few months the *John* seems to have engaged in desultory inter-island trading in the Caribbean before returning once again to Barbados to have her hull resheathed and to be refitted for Saltatudos (Turks and Caicos Islands) where she traded for indigo, ginger and fustick. She returned to Barbados yet again in May 1716 and cleared the following July for Lyme Regis.

Though this should have been a straightforward enough trip it was tarred with the same brush of complexity as the rest of the voyage. In October, when the *John* should have been securely moored along-side the Cobb, she was anchored in Tralee Bay. As most of the crew had died on the preceding voyages, she was short-handed, carrying only a mate and five crew in addition to Courtenay. Three of these were the indentured Irish servants. When discharged from the *John* they each received £6 wages for the period 26 September 1715 to the day they arrived back in Lyme – a total of fourteen months. By virtue of foul weather or crew exhaustion it took the *John* another two months to clear Irish waters and reach Lyme Regis. This she eventually did on 6 December 1716, after three years wandering the trade routes of the North Atlantic and Caribbean. It took nearly two weeks to unload her cargo of muscovado, ginger, cotton, fustick and indigo. (During her three-year sojourn the Burridges had dispatched the *Surprise Galley* to the Guinea Coast from Exeter, and got her back with two years to spare.)

Samuel Courtenay was paid £4 a month for the voyage of the *John*. Such financial minutiae are generally forgotten when the profitability of the slave trade is discussed, as are the costs of setting a ship up for a long-haul voyage. No matter what the destination these costs were considerable, for an eighteenth-century merchantman was a complex and vulnerable vehicle.

Yet, contrary to the conventional view, the cost of building a ship from new was not necessarily prohibitive. As we have seen, in 1706 the Burridges ordered the construction of a replacement for their ageing vessel, *Friendship*. How much – if any – of the old *Friendship* went into the new is debatable, but the fact that captain John Butcher was taken off his seagoing duties for the Burridges and employed in overseeing the ripping up of the old *Friendship* suggests that its key timbers – probably the 'knees' and frames – were incorporated into the new vessel. Tried and tested timbers were well worth preserving. However that may be, the new *Friendship* came off the stocks at £854 16s.5d., proving in due course a valuable addition to the family's fleet; she was still engaged in the African trade in 1731 under Robert Read who had captained her earlier namesake to Virginia in the opening years of the century.

Ideally a merchantman such as the *John* would be completely refitted once every year. On her arrival from Tralee Bay, work started upon her even while her cargo was being discharged. For her next voyage she was intended for the Cape Verde Islands and Maryland, and the costs involved in setting her up for that were substantial, as the following extract from John Burridge junior's account book shows.

Sundry disbursements on the Ship *John* in refitting her from the 4 Jany 1717 to the 30 April 1717; viz:

For 3 barrels of Pitch 7 cwt:1:7 at 11s per
    cwt £4: 0: 5
12 deals at 20^d £1: 0: 0

Sundry disbursements on the Ship *John (cont.)*

6½ Dozen of Oakum with a bag . .	£0: 9: 6
18 dozen of nails delivered the Carpenter with a bag	£0: 5: 6
10 pieces of small canvas at 22s per piece	£11: 0: 0
11 pieces of the best sailcloth, 421 yards at 14d	£24:11: 1
8 pieces of seconds sailcloth, 300 yards at 12d abating on the whole 10s8d is but	£14: 9:10

£55:16: 4

For 26 cwt:0:11 of beef at 22s per cwt, less 4s	£28:10: 0
9cwt ditto	£9: 0: 0
1637 of pork at sundry prices	£17:13: 0
43 cwt:1:24 of biscuit flour	£26:11: 6
For tusk used in graving* the ship	£0: 6: 0
The Carpenter's bill for graving the ship	£7: 0: 0
Compasses, glasses & bringing empty pipes from Topsham	£2: 7: 0

£91: 7: 6

For a Register of Plantation certificate	£0:12: 0
47½ bushels of Peas	£5:10: 2
4 bushels of Grits, 20s. Mats under the beans 6s 6d	£1: 6: 6
½ cwt Cheese, Butter, Vinegar, Pots, Spice for suet	£2:12: 2
Making 2 pair of indentures for servants	£0: 7: 0
2 barrels of Tar at 29s	£2:18: 0
Paid John King's bill for making and mending of sails	£8:14: 0
Lent the Seamen in advance of wages .	£10:17: 0
Lent ditto on Bottom ree†	£10:10: 0
Geo. Mathews a servant	£1: 0: 0
Filling the Water Cask, 16s 6d. Making an Hearth, 10s 10d	£1: 7: 4
A copper kettle & pewter	£4: 2: 0
Cartridge paper, 3s 8d., Bills of loading, 8d	£0: 4: 4

* Scraping the hull clear of marine growth.
† Money lent on the security of the ship.

Sundry disbursements on the Ship *John* (*cont.*)

Sam Courtenay Junior for disbursements in refitting yᵉ Ship .	£10: 9: 5	
		£60: 9:11
For 15 hhds of Beer for Ship's use	£9: 0: 0	
16 seams of wood at 18d	£1: 4: 0	
2 bags, one for pease & the other for bread	£0: 2: 6	
The Doctor Fox with medicines . . .	£10: 9: 6	
Lights outward 7s 6d. 4 empty bottles 8d.	£0: 8: 2	
Barrel of 4d nails & one of 6d nails for Maryland	£5: 5: 1	
Nails for a store	£3:13: 1	
12 doz of strong Beer & cider with Bottles at 4s	£2: 8: 0	
2 doz of Red Wine with Bottles at 18s .	£1:16: 0	
Nath. Grundy note for empty cask, an anchor, Paint etc.	£11:13: 2	
42 cwt:2:20 Cordage at 31s. Dipsey‡ line at 8d. 28lb	£67: 0: 0	
Geo. Kearly bill for Candles, Tallow &c.	£7: 2: 4	
14 bushels of Bay Salt at 6s	£4: 4: 0	
18 ditto of White	£4: 5: 6	
A new ensign, making it & Bunt carried with them	£3: 5: 6	
For Glass & Glazing cabin windows . . .	£0:18: 0	
Portridge down & weighing the biscuit	£1: 7: 2	
Getting the ship to sail & Hawsers .	£1:14: 0	
Swetland's bill for timber, oars & work done by carpenters	£5: 5: 6	
Jnᵒ Kerridge & Co for work aboard the ship	£0:11: 0	
For diet of 2 servants taken this voyage	£2: 5: 6	
2 Sheepskins, Spirits & Tobacco, gave Harry & a Messenger	£0:10: 8	
For Looking after the Ship in Cobb 12 weeks at 4s	£2: 8: 0	
		£146:16: 8
To Jos: Paice & Son for £1000 insured to Gambia & Maryland with charges		£55: 5: 0

‡ i.e. deep sea line.

Sundry disbursements on the Ship *John* (*cont.*)

For Cookney the blockmaker's note, lead,
    oakum &c £5:18: 6
Use of my warehouses & cellars for
    salting of meat . . . .
Making sails & for Beans £1:10:0, 6
    napkins 4s 6d £1:14: 6
For a foreyard topmast & Mizzen
    mast £2:15: 0
Twine used about the sails & for a
    store £1:13: 6
Timber, treenails§ &c £1: 3: 3
1 cwt Sheathing Nails £1:13:6,
    Landing sails 8d £1:14: 2
Robert Salter's note for Ballast, carry-
    ing down provisions, water & c.   £4: 2: 6
                                        £19: 1: 5

Andrew Drake's note for work at the
    Cobb, painting the ship; Sheathing
    nails 1 cwt:0:15, Nails for the Store,
    Lanthorns, Deals used aboard &
    carried with them. Chairs &c. . . .   £19:11: 4
Geo. Pike the Smith for an Iron
    Hearth, Hoops, work etc. £26: 0: 0
Carriage by horse to & from Cob, .   £1: 5: 8
Mr Bunson for refitting the Arms,
    Handscrews, Stilliards &c £9:10: 0
Postage of Letters paid here during the
    acc° £3:12:10
½ per cent commission for paying the
    bills from Ireland & Mr Paice's
    postage above £1: 0: 6
                                          £61: 0: 4

To Cash lent Thomas Bevis on bottom .   £1: 0: 0
paid for 2 seams more of tusk to
    grave £0: 2: 0
                                          1: 2: 0

May: to sundries for the Cooper's bill,
    Hoops & nails £39: 9: 0
    to fees of entering & clearing the Ship
    & Landwaiter 0: 6: 0
June 1: To sundries, for further postage since
    the 25 March £0:10: 3

§ Hardwood pins for fastening timbers together.

> For commission and trouble in selling
> the cargo from Barbados, buying &
> shipping the cargo for Gambia,
> refitting the Ship & keeping the
> accounts £18: 0: 0   £18:10: 3
>
> £549: 4: 5

Such an account not only displays the 'hidden' costs of setting forth a ship on a slave voyage, but also the depth of marine expertise of which a relatively small outport such as Lyme Regis could boast. All the minor and major demands that keeping a vessel afloat entailed could be satisfied very close to home: carpenters, glaziers, provisioners, timber merchants like Joseph Swetland, sailmakers such as John King, smiths such as George Pike for the iron hearth, anchors and hoops, blockmakers like Cookney, watchmaker and locksmith Henry Bunston for metal artefacts, ropemakers like Nathaniel Gundry, tallow chandlers like George Kearley and a number of labour contracts placed with John Kerridge (the mariner not the schoolmaster of Lyme), Andrew Drake, carpenter and timber merchant (who was continuously in trouble with the Court Leet for blocking his street with lengths of timber), Robert Salter and others.

These were men of substance in Lyme, serving their turn on the Court Leet or, like Henry Bunston, serving terms as mayor. Not George Pike though. Perhaps as one would expect of an eighteenth-century blacksmith, he was something of a rough diamond who was readily to admit in a year's time that the newly delivered son of his servant Anne Dean was his. The following year 1710 found him under arrest during September and October for allegedly assaulting John Bowdidge, a local justice. Not content to let matters rest there he

> further misbehaved himself in the public market place . . . using braving and provoking Speeches there in breach of his Majesty's peace and to the disquieting and terrifying of his Majesty's subjects.

Nathaniel Gundry, mayor at the time, put him into custody to cool his heels or perhaps repent at leisure for his intoxicated state.[92]

Whilst the *John* was refitting at Lyme Regis her cargo was brought to the Cobb for loading. Much of the cargo for John Burridge's account was not recorded in the Port Book and so is not summarised in Appendix 2, on Lyme's involvement in the African trade. Some items – such as the Dutch landscape paintings – were obviously destined for the colonial market at Maryland rather than the Gambia.

And it is unusual, if not unique, to find bully beef amongst the provisions taken aboard for the slaves. For a fuller picture of the cargo carried by the *John* on her second voyage to Africa from Lyme Regis the following list should be read in conjunction with Appendix 2. Lyme merchant John Pitts accounted for one-third of the cargo, John Burridge for the balance:

1717. Voyage in the *John* frigate for Gambia & Maryland
for her owners.

Jan 26	To Jos: Paice & Son for cost of Goods bought in London as by their invoice & consigned Mr Sam: Courtnay Junr for sales		£283: 1:10
Feb	To Sundrys for 265 bushels of beans for the Negroes at 2s .		£26:10: 0
	To Cash for 9 cwt:1:14 of bull beef for ditto		£5: 8: 0
	To ditto for 2 dozen of felts [hats] for men, edged		£2: 5: 0
	To Sundrys for 2 pieces of Plains, 93 yds at 17½d	£6:15: 7	
	12 pieces of perpets with all Charges	£5: 5: 3	
	6 pieces of Barnstaple bays, 245 yds at 9d	£9: 3: 9	
	Carriage from Exon, 2s 9d; Mr Prowse, commission,[93] 7s 2d .	£0: 9:11	£21:14: 6
	To Sundrys a Cask of Sugar, 6 cwt at 32s	£9:12: 0	
	5 cwt of White Biscuit at 17s .	£4: 5: 0	
	6 Dutch Landskipps	£2: 0: 0	
	6 Musketts, Bayonets & Cartouch Boxes at 21s	£6: 6: 0	
	2 pair of Pistols with Swords, Belts & Cartouches	£3:18: 0	
	1 cwt of Cut Tobacco without the drawback at 5d[94]	£2: 1: 8	
	2 large Cases for Landskipps & Muskets &c	£0:10: 3	
	14 gross of Tobacco pipes at 11d	£0:12:10	
	for freight of the goods from London	£2: 5: 6	£32: 1: 3

1717. Voyage in the *John* frigate (*cont.*)

To Cash for custom of Goods outwards	£0: 9: 6		
110½ French crowns at 4s 6d .	£24:17: 3	£25: 6: 9	
To Sundrys for 2 hhds, 30 butts & pipes, some wine & some oil casks at sundry prices; for water besides what is on the ship's account		£10:11: 6	
March To Cash gave Landwaiters for weighing the iron at the Cob & victualling bill 10s, porterage of part of the cargo landed at the Cob 5s	£0:15: 0		
For charge of 5 debentures paid here	£1: 1: 6	£1:16: 6	
May For Roddon Samways[95] for fees of entries, Cob duties, searcher's fees, stamps &c. .		£0:14: 3½	
		£409: 9: 7½	

During March 1717 the *John* departed from Lyme Bay for the Gambia, though her 'official' goal was the Cape Verde Islands. This destination was characterised during the seventeenth and early eighteenth centuries by a certain breadth: the islands off Cape Verde, the Bissagos or Bijuagos Isles, and indeed the adjacent mainland, were no strangers to the slave trade. Known now as Guinea-Bissau, but then loosely referred to as Cacheu and notable as the headquarters of the Portuguese slave trade, the region shipped off 13–15,000 Negroes annually. While anchored off the African coast, Portuguese slave trade captains frequently exchanged their slaves for European goods, especially woollens and linen, brass and pewter, instead of carrying them directly to the New World. There now remains no trace of the *John*'s trading along the Guinea Coast, though it can be assumed that she aimed to slave a total of 200 blacks, as she had attempted when sailing from Barbados. Nor is there any record of her arrival in Barbados which, though not on her schedule, was where Captain Samuel Courtenay sold William Cogan four and one half masts of amber for £65 3s. which had failed to sell on the Guinea Coast.[96] The numbers of slaves delivered to Barbados is not recorded, but the *John* loaded 22 Negroes there for shipment to Maryland at £7 per head as part of a pattern of re-exportation of slaves from the West Indies to the American mainland: the existence of this largely ignored pattern and the involvement of Lyme and other provincial ports will be outlined in Chapter 21.

Early in 1718 the *John* was laden with £1,200 worth of tobacco in Maryland and cleared for England. On her arrival at Lyme in June 1718 the bulk of her crew were paid off, the wages bill being made up as follows:

To Sundrys for Wages to Guinea, Maryland thence to this
Place, viz:

Sam: Courtenay Junr at £5 per month, 15¼ months	£76: 5: 0
William Palmer, mate at £3	£45:15: 0
Nathaniel Pearce, doctor at £3	£45:15: 0
James Sadler, second mate at 35s	£26:13: 9
John Houston, carpenter at 45s	£34: 6: 3
Geo Jackson, Thomas Beves & Thomas Tucker each 28s.	£64: 2: 6
Charles Rowland £3:17:0, Thomas Cole £4:4:0. Walter Draker £3:10:0. These 3 died in the voyage	£11:11: 0
John Baker, cooper at 25s	£19: 1: 3
	£323: 9: 9

Not accounted for in this bill are two indentured servants and Harry, a Negro belonging to John Pitts, a merchant of Lyme Regis who held substantial shares in John Burridge's African ventures. Quite when Harry arrived in Lyme Regis is open to question, but in all probability he was part of the complement of slaves that the *John* had traded for on her first voyage to the Guinea Coast (from Barbados) in 1715. A persistent trickle of black slaves entered England at this period and were frequently hired out to shipowners as casual labour by their merchant owners. Thus early in 1717 John Burridge records an expenditure of 10s. 8d. on sheepskins, spirits and tobacco for Harry and a messenger, which suggests he was employed as night-watchman on the *John* while the vessel was undergoing refitting during the winter of that year. Harry's wages reverted directly to John Pitts; after his stint as night-watchman Harry accompanied the *John* to the Gambia, Maryland and back to Lyme Regis. He was classed along with the two indentured servants in the Burridge accounts for the subsequent voyage to Barbados and Virginia which record an expenditure of £4 1s. 6d. for 'Diet of the Negro and Servants'; in 1717 John Pitts was paid £6 5s. for '2½ years salary for his Negro Harry at 50s per annum'.

On her arrival from Maryland the *John* cleared directly for Rotterdam with the bulk of the Burridges' cargo of tobacco. She returned after a few months with tiles, Rhenish wine, gunpowder and pipestaves. Following a further refit she sailed for Barbados and Virginia in April 1719 with a large mixed cargo which included the tiles and wine from Rotterdam. Though on the face of it a conventional voyage to the West Indian and American plantations, there are certain quirks which give it a flavour all its own. The pattern of trade was normal enough – building materials and provisions sold well if not spectacularly in Barbados – and sugar, molasses and rum could then be purchased and profitably exchanged against tobacco in Virginia. Before the *John* departed from Lyme Regis, however, the Burridges had decided to ring the changes and freight slaves from Barbados to Rappahannock, Virginia to pay for tobacco. In this they were preceded by Nathaniel Gundry, now well established as a tobacco merchant in his own right, who had recently freighted the *Martha* under John Wallis to Barbados and thence to Potomac with fifteen slaves.[97] But this hardly marked a completely new departure for either the Burridges or their ship: in 1703 Robert Read in the *John* had taken nine slaves from Barbados to South Potomac.[98] Accordingly the *John* was now loaded with 134 bushels of beans (which could always be sold in Barbados or Virginia for the plantation slaves if there was any shortage of available blacks to ship into Virginia). In addition she carried '19 suits, 5 waistcoats, 4 petticoats for Negroes', which had been made up at a cost of £2 10s. (the materials cost an extra £1 13s. 6d.).

In Barbados a proportion of the *John*'s cargo was exchanged with William Cogan for slaves, rum, molasses and lime juice. Of the slaves, twenty-five were procured for Samuel Courtenay at £18 a head on the elder John Burridge's account. The voyage was the latter Burridge's responsibility, though his brother Robert owned three of the complement of slaves. A further twenty-one slaves were freighted on behalf of other merchants to Virginia at £3 10s. a head, and Samuel Courtenay took advantage of the situation to ship a private allowance of two more, making a grand total of forty-eight in all. As a gesture to profit first and humanity second it was thought worthwhile to hire a surgeon and accordingly £2 10s. was laid out for his passage to Virginia.

As the *John* shaped a course to the north-west the warm waters of the Caribbean were left behind and the climate became noticeably sharper. This is where the clothes for the slaves came into their own (and also generated a useful profit as the Burridges charged £6 5s. 2d. for them) for the *John* was heading into the Virginian winter. This in itself was unusual, for Maryland and Virginia – unlike the Caribbean – had peak and off-peak seasons. The winter, lasting roughly from November to April when slaves could only work in the fields spasmodically because of the weather and had difficulty in adjusting to the change in climate, was quite definitely off-peak. Planters feared that slaves acquired then would become an economic burden. At least so the traditional argument runs. On the other hand the planters would have sold most of their yearly crop of tobacco by this time so perhaps they were flush with cash. In any case the *John* had no trouble disposing of her cargo of slaves. All arrived alive at Rappahannock, though one of Robert Burridge's died a few days later.

Judging the venture a success the elder John Burridge dispatched the *John* in November 1720 on another voyage along the same lines, though this time via Cork. Amongst her cargo were 30 bushels of beans and a set of clothes costing £4 16s. 3d. On this occasion ten slaves were purchased in Barbados and sold at Rappahannock; three men and two women for £120 in bills, one man and a girl for £45 'current money of the country' and three of unspecified gender for tobacco valued at £69 12s. 11d. At this time the value of slaves – and incidentally of white indentured servants – was commonly expressed in pounds of tobacco. Back in London, Joseph Paice, the Burridges' faithful broker, discharged the bills for the slaves at ½ per cent commission, earning 10 shillings in the process.

The voyage of the *John* marks the end of John and Robert Burridge's involvement in the slave trade; the *John* herself was lost at sea in 1725,[99] though Samuel Courtenay survived, eventually dying in 1732. From 1718 onwards all the Burridge ventures to Africa passed into the hands of Robert Burridge III. He mounted five conventional voyages to the Guinea Coast between 1718 and 1725, captained first by James Wyatt junior of Wootton Fitzpaine, and latterly by Arthur Raymond.

Not on the face of it trading for slaves, the vessels carried exactly the same cargoes for barter as the earlier Burridge ventures had done. The likelihood is that these five voyages made a proportion of their profits from the short-term or 'coasting' slave trade, profits that were quick and comparatively free of overheads. Since the lengthy and deadly middle passage was not involved no surgeon needed to be carried; extra provisions for the blacks could be purchased on the

Guinea Coast or eked out of the ship's store: extra crew would not be needed for guard, feeding and cleaning duties; and since only a handful of blacks would be carried at any one time profitable cargo space was not compromised. There is now little evidence of this coastal trade in blacks, for historians like their facts cut and dried; so the slave trade is one thing and the trade for gold, ivory and redwood quite another. In reality they overlapped in much the same manner as sugar, tobacco, rum and slaves did on the other side of the Atlantic, where scores of vessels bound for the Caribbean found a handsome profit in running slaves on to the American mainland.[100]

As if to demonstrate the fact that there were no hard and fast rules in the slave trade the fifth of Robert Burridge's African ventures provides a case in point. By this time Arthur Raymond had replaced James Wyatt junior as Robert Burridge's 'African' captain. He was a useful man to have on the Burridge side, an energetic first-generation merchant and sea captain whose son was to become Surveyor of Customs at Lyme, but whose descendants were to manage the town as a corrupt pocket borough for the Fane (Earl of Westmorland's) interest from the middle of the eighteenth century. Though they deserve no monument whatever for they represented all that was undemocratic in late eighteenth-century Lyme, Raymond House in Broad Street and Raymond's Hill near Axminster bear witness to their passing.

The fifth of Robert Burridge's African ventures set sail in the dying days of 1725. A massive cargo had been assembled aboard the *Friendship*. Along with all the standard Guinea-trade goods there was a writing desk, 10 gallons of gin, drums, trumpets and bells, a hundredweight of Cheshire cheese, nearly 1,500 clay pipes (probably from Poole, which had an extensive clay pipe industry), painted sticks (probably toys featuring small wooden monkeys which could be worked up and down the shafts), and two dozen bottles of Staughton's Elixir.

Having called at Madeira to fill nearly 300 empty bottles with duty-free wine, the *Friendship* arrived off Sierra Leone about March 1726 and set about trading along the Guinea Coast for redwood and ivory. Late in May she fell in with the *Resolution* of London under John Carruthers who was trading for slaves, gold, ivory and camwood. Whilst at Bence Island off Sierra Leone the *Resolution*, having completed her trading but still awaiting her final consignment of slaves, ran upon a rock and was badly holed. Luckily for Carruthers and the slaves aboard, the *Resolution* was slow to sink and he had time to land all sixty of them plus the cargo of camwood and ivory. The rescue completed, he sent his crew back again – presumably the *Resolution* had settled in comparatively shallow water – to strip her of her rigging, which he sold for £220. Sails and ropes rotted quickly in the heat and humidity of the Guinea Coast and were always in demand.

At this juncture Carruthers received his final contingent of 70 slaves, making 130 in all. That was all well and good and there had been no loss of life; but Carruthers was stuck up a rather unpromising creek without a paddle. He had two options: either sell all his slaves and Guinea produce to another slave trade ship (which would undoubtedly capitalise happily on his forced sale), or charter a vessel in the vicinity.

The *Friendship* was the obvious choice. Though a small vessel of 90 tons burden, Raymond was not trading in slaves. The ivory and redwood already aboard her – and by this time her trading cycle was virtually complete – would hardly have filled her hold and could, in an emergency, be lashed to the deck. There was no time to lose. By 8 June, barely five days after the *Resolution* sank, Carruthers had concluded a deal with Raymond. For £500 of Barbados money together with the *Resolution*'s sheet cable and yawl, Raymond agreed to transport all Carruthers' cargo (and as many of the crew as wished to leave Sierra Leone, though he specifically excluded paying them wages) to Barbados. Mercifully the passage to Barbados was quick and extraordinarily healthy. The *Friendship* arrived there on 26 August 1726, delivered 119 slaves on Carruthers' behalf, and the deal was successfully concluded.[101]

The year 1726 marked the re-emergence in Lyme of John Burridge junior after an absence of some nine years. He had continued as the town's MP during this time but his commercial career had over-shadowed any concern he may have felt for his constituency. To say his mercantile efforts had run into problems would be an understatement. In 1717 his estates had been seized by the Crown on behalf of the Commissioners for Customs, whom he owed £2,600 for wine duties. As if that was not enough to persuade him to put his house in order, he became embroiled in an attempt to defraud the Commissioners for Taxes out of £1,800, which resulted in his losing virtually everything except his seat in Parliament.[102] Nevertheless the promise of easy money continued to grip John Burridge junior's mind, and an answer was soon at hand in the shape of the South Sea Company's extravagant visions of infinite profit. By the time that bubble burst he owed the Company nearly £11,000.[103] Once again elected as MP for Lyme in the election of 1722, he also took office as mayor in 1726.[104] Since the mayor was also the returning officer in the event of an election, John Burridge could not technically be elected as MP in 1727. He ran for Lyme regardless, causing a 'great outrage', was initially re-elected but lost his seat within six months to his opponent.[105] The following year he was again in trouble with the Customs, this time for smuggling.[106]

From being the great white hope of the Burridges of Lyme, John Burridge junior had become the black sheep of the family. While they continued to trade steadily from Lyme, making a solid but unspectacular contribution to the well-being of the town through their mercantile presence and charitable interests, he sought charity for his own sake. In August 1730 he importuned Robert Walpole for assistance from the secret service funds:

> Having really spent a fortune for his Majesty and the succession of his family . . . I beg you will represent my conduct and attendance in Parliament for near twenty years – my uncle and I having served in Parliament ever since the Revolution and I believe as much from such a principle as ever . . . I have for near twenty years received but £2,150 – and nothing this five or six years past . . . I trust . . . [the King] will be induced to serve me in this difficulty and necessity.[107]

Not to put too fine a point on it, the King didn't. Any hopes John Burridge junior may have entertained of inheriting under his uncle's will were shattered three years later. The senior John Burridge, who died in his eighty-second year, left the bulk of his property to his brother Robert II and nephew Robert III, but as for the estate at Thornfalcon (in which John Burridge junior had an interest for life) this he ordered sold to cover his debts.[108] Accordingly Robert Burridge III raised a mortgage of £1,500 on the estate, an indication of the difficulties in which John Burridge senior had found himself at his death.[109] His nephew John junior inherited next to nothing under the will; neither, in contrast to the will of Robert Burridge I, did the poor of the parish of Lyme, who benefited to the sorry tune of just £10.

Despite his humiliating reverse in the parliamentary elections of 1727, John Burridge was back in 1734 as a candidate for Lyme. He was heavily defeated by John Scrope, son of the Bristol Dissenting merchant Thomas Scrope who had – many years before – been a good friend of Benjamin Way's father.

Though fiercely Dissenting in his youth, John Scrope proved to be less than a good friend to Lyme, and his election was incalculably detrimental to the town. Not only was Scrope absolutely corrupt, he corrupted absolutely. Lyme, a stout-hearted independent town which had – though vastly outnumbered – held firm against the Royalist forces under Prince Maurice during the Civil War, was stealthily undermined by the dry rot of political and economic malfeasance introduced by Scrope. Though possessing neither property nor business in the neighbourhood, he obtained control of the borough by Customs House and other patronage.[110]

Scrope's influence was terminal. He strengthened his stifling grip on the town by reducing the number of freemen and introducing more non-residents favourable to his cause into the corporation, amongst whom were the Fanes, his wife's side of the family, Customs officials from Bristol. They were to bribe and extort freemen's votes until 1832 to ensure their family's hold over the town. Whereas a century and a half earlier the inspired puritanism of vicar John Geare had tolerated a measure of Dissent and encouraged the settlement of substantial merchant families, the Fanes, who by a genealogical fluke became the Earls of Westmorland, achieved quite the reverse. At their feet, fair and square, can be laid much of the blame for extinguishing the last vestiges of Lyme's commercial fire. They turned Lyme from a radical centre of revolution into a tame pocket borough.

Unabashed at having been rejected by Walpole for charity in 1730, John Burridge junior fashioned another ornate but equally hopeless petition some sixteen years later. This was addressed to his 'Most Generous & Bountiful Prince & Sovereign' George II,[111] following the defeat of the Jacobite Rebellion of 1745. At the heart of its baroque gibberish was a plea for £1,000, but it was a plea the sovereign saw fit to reject. Estranged from his family,[112] isolated from the mercantile mainstream in which he had played such a significant part, John Burridge junior faded into obscurity and died in 1753.

After a century of dominating trade from Lyme the Burridges, lacking a male heir to pick up the reins of family business, were also caught by a fundamental change in the tide of trade. After centuries of profitable wool trading the small ports of the west of England with their rich, wool-producing hinterlands now faced a bleak future. As ports like Lyme and Topsham sank into relative oblivion, the

major outports of Bristol and Liverpool, nourished by the emerging
metallic giants of Birmingham and Sheffield and by the cheap cotton
goods of Manchester, made colossal strides forward to dominate
Britain's overseas trade. Consequently the interests of the last Lyme
Burridge – Robert III – who had mounted ventures to Africa three
decades earlier, turned gradually landward, to brewing, though he
was dealing in tobacco and freighting ventures to Virginia as late as
1740.

Nevertheless he still stood for the Dissenting articles of diligence
and honesty which his elder brother had long since abandoned and
which John Scrope was so flagrantly to flout. Though a man of
considerable substance, having inherited much of his uncle John
Burridge's property, and owning houses in Broad Street and Combe
Street as well as the Hogchester Farm, Charmouth tenements and
various warehouses and cellars in Lyme, Robert Burridge III couched
his will in the exhortatory language of a century earlier with frugality
and probity the constant refrain.[113] The will reflected the man
himself. Unlike some in Lyme, he remained true to his Dissenting
forebears. Much of what he stood for can be found in Samuel
Wright's *Great Concern of Human Life*, a work he greatly admired
and held up for others to follow. In both style and subject matter it
harks back to the great Dissenting casuists of the previous century.
But passages of it must have struck Robert Burridge uncomfortably
close to home, especially regarding his errant brother John:

> We must deny also the Lust of Riches . . . a vehement and most
> grievous Lust in many, Spending themselves in vain and sinful
> Contrivances to gain a great deal of Wealth . . . it is a sufficient
> Gratification to some sordid Minds only to look upon their Heaps,
> or their Papers and Securities, and to think they can call so much
> their own.[114]

After the excesses of John Burridge junior, Robert's will, with its
accent on sobriety, diligence, honesty and fair dealing, is rather
refreshing. Nor was charity, 'the great Promoter, and Guide, and
Cherisher of all good Actions' forsaken. Robert Burridge had, in his
hands, a sum of £33 10s. and paid interest on this at 5 per cent to the
poor of Lyme. The original sum had previously been laid out for
charitable purposes by his mother and uncle in London insurance
shares but these had performed badly. In his will Robert Burridge
made the balance up to £100 and directed this sum to be invested in
blue-chip insurance companies. The dividends or interest thus accru-

ing were directed to be distributed amongst the poor of Lyme,

> with special regard to the Aged, infirm and such Poor as generally receive the Lords Supper in the Publick Church and Presbyterian and Anabaptist way, and some part of it for the teaching two poor Children to read Annually and some part of it in Books.

As Lyme slid imperceptibly into decline, the poor of the town increased. Robert Burridge's charity was still doing good work in the early nineteenth century though as the role of private charities was superseded by state education and welfare developments, it too was largely but not completely overtaken by events. Before the abolition of school pence, fees for the elementary education of six children had been effected. Afterwards, and indeed right into the present century, the dividends on its £227 worth of consols were being distributed in the form of shawls and blankets to sixteen poor people of the parish.[115] Perhaps even more remarkably, and exactly following the letter and spirit of Robert Burridge's will, the Burridge charity was until very recently funding a few prize books distributed every summer at Lyme's junior school.[116] In general however, over the ensuing years time, the all-consuming tide, has virtually erased the name Burridge as if it had been carelessly inscribed on the sands of Lyme. Even by the end of the eighteenth century long-haul overseas voyages had become little more than faded memories in the minds of a few aged mariners who gathered on the Cobb as if to summon up the ghosts of Virginia-trade frigates, sugar trade brigantines, and long-forgotten Guineamen.

Time had moved on and the overseas traders and sea captains had been replaced by a lesser breed of men, coastal traders, who swarmed around the Cobb from Newcastle and Hull. The Cobb itself, finally benefiting from substantial government grants, was solider than ever. But the town, bereft of overseas trade, lacking export goods and politically corrupt, became enfeebled. Turning in upon itself it began a second career as a fashionable seaside resort, its elegant and thronged Assembly Rooms effortlessly usurping the Cobb as the centre of attraction. With the coming of the railway in the opening years of the twentieth century the Cobb finally became redundant. Today the Assembly Rooms, like its summer butterflies, have long since gone. It is the Cobb which endures, its steadfast, monolithic bulk patiently celebrating Lyme's vibrant past, despite an uncomprehending and largely careless present.

CHAPTER SEVENTEEN

Exeter, Topsham and Dartmouth

Though Lyme Bay is the largest bite from the underside of England's outstretched south-western ham it is Devon and not Dorset which benefits from its lee shores. From Seaton to Start Point it is studded with numerous estuaries, inlets and bays affording shelter. In the case of Topsham, Torbay, Brixham and Dartmouth that shelter has the advantage of a secure anchorage. But the roll-call of Devon ports does not confine itself solely to Lyme Bay, for west of Start Point lies Plymouth. Nor does it restrict itself to a single coastline, for Devon possesses a northern seaboard too, stretching along the topside of England's outstretched leg and embracing the ports of Clovelly, Bideford, Barnstaple and Ilfracombe.

Ever since England spread its wings as a trading nation, a host of routes radiated from these maritime centres. Those from the north Devon ports carried on a profitable trade with southern Ireland and then became heavily involved in the Newfoundland fisheries. Meanwhile the south Devon ports prospered mightily on the export of woollen goods to Holland and France. By the middle of the seventeenth century England's acquisition of colonies in America and the West Indies had vastly widened the horizons that beckoned Devon merchants towards profit. Infant colonies demand much of their mother country and Devon responded by shipping vast quantities of woollen goods from the county's well-endowed cloth centres of Barnstaple, Crediton, Ashburton, Totnes and Exeter. Foodstuffs too were in demand, and the herring fleets of the north Devon coast pursued a profitable trade in salted herrings to the new colonies. In return the colonies sent back timber and animal skins and, as they became more established, sugar and tobacco. Soon transatlantic voyages were to become as regular a feature of Devon merchantmen as the humble Channel or Irish Sea crossings.

Without doubt Devon was England's premier maritime county, and its merchants entertained visions of trading ventures that to their conservative North Sea-facing East Anglian cousins (who also dealt predominantly in wool) probably appeared little short of madness. But for Devon merchants, strategically situated on the Western Approaches and with the Atlantic on their very doorstep, it was the West that summoned. Typical of this early entrepreneurial spirit was the Hawkins family of Plymouth who traded for ivory and gold to Guinea and Brazil in the early sixteenth century: most famous of the younger generation of Hawkins was John, whose swashbuckling reputation has largely obscured his brilliance as a merchant venturer. With his brother William he was ideally situated in a loose network of family, friends and business contacts to glean the gossip of foreign parts and catch the drift of international trade. More importantly he had a sound marine education, and first-hand experience of Guinea Coast trading.

Significantly, both English and Devon slave trading commenced with this same man. Albeit backed by substantial quantities of London and court capital, Hawkins' ventures were also underwritten by local backers and indigenous maritime expertise. In financial terms, his three expeditions to Africa between 1562 and 1567 were outstandingly successful. On his first voyage he sold 300 Negroes in Hispaniola: on the second he delivered 400 slaves from Sierra Leone to the Spanish main. The third voyage was intended to cap these achievements; together John and William Hawkins pledged £2,000 towards the risks – and in anticipation of the rewards – of this third slaving expedition. They also contributed no less than three ships to the six-strong fleet which left Plymouth in 1567.

Lest anyone should harbour any doubts as to the commodity Hawkins expected to trade for, his newly granted crest – a Negro bound by a cord – fluttered on a pennant aboard his flagship the *Jesus of Lubeck*. As luck would have it, and luck played an important role in all trading ventures of those times, a string of misadventures and unforeseen delays resulted in his arrival at San Juan de Ulua in the Gulf of Mexico at the same time as the heavily escorted Spanish silver fleet. Naturally his presence was seen as a threat: despite his best efforts and those of his mariners, Hawkins' tiny fleet was routed. Though many perished, he escaped with his life. So did his young kinsman, Francis Drake. Both lived to fight the Spaniard another day.[1]

Hardly a disaster in the financial sense – Hawkins returned early in 1569 with 25,000 gold pesos in all, which took four heavily laden pack-horses to transport from Plymouth to London – it was still a bitter personal defeat. Not a man known for his loquacity, he characterised the experience as a 'sorrowful voyage'. Perhaps as a sign of contrition or penitence, and certainly as a reflection of this expedition, he supplemented his crest with the traditional staves and scallop shell of the pilgrim. Whether from choice or compunction Hawkins never went slave trading again, preferring to channel his energy and seamanship into harrying his great rivals on the high seas, the Spaniards.

Without Hawkins' leadership and lacking a strong mercantile and court involvement, interest in the slave trade remained at a low ebb for the next hundred years in England in general and Devon in particular. Nevertheless there were one or two false dawns. Exeter merchants had followed the exploits of their Plymouth brethren with interest. In 1588 a licence was issued to eight merchants of Exeter, Colyton, Barnstaple and London for ten years' exclusive trading rights to the area between Senegal and the Gambia.[2] Though the results of this monopoly are unknown, they were probably limited to the acquisition of gold and ivory. The labour-starved plantations in the Caribbean and North America had yet to exert their baleful grip on the Africa trade.

The demands of the plantations did not make themselves heard until the middle of the seventeenth century, and interest in the slave trade revived with the formation of the Company of Royal Adventurers into Africa in 1660. With the opening up of the American colonies in the second quarter of the seventeenth century, quickly followed by the exploiting of the Caribbean, a flood of fresh trade opportunities surged up the quiet Devon backwaters. Vast quantities of woollen goods, household stores and provisions, building materials and leatherware, were required. In return the colonies offered tobacco and later sugar. Plymouth benefited hugely from this upsurge in transatlantic trade,[3] as did Exeter, Dartmouth, Bideford and Barnstaple.

By 1700, Exeter was second only to Bristol as the richest provincial city, and its pre-eminence was based solidly on the great medieval currency of wool. For centuries it had flowed into the pockets of its merchants, into the coffers of the Cathedral, and into the private banks, estates and businesses of its inhabitants. As Celia Fiennes remarked, visiting the city in 1698, 'It turns the most money in a week of anything in England, one week with another there is £10,000 paid in ready money, sometimes £11,500.'[4]

Clearly wool was very big business indeed. It was central to both the provincial and national economy, for England had little else to export. And for a period of about a quarter of a century, between 1695 and 1720, Devonshire serge was the most important expression of the nation's woollen industry in terms of exports.[5] Wool dominated all discussions of trade throughout the seventeenth and early eighteenth centuries. In 1680 an influential pamphlet on the 'Public Utility and Advantages' of the Royal African Company's monopoly presented its case largely in terms of wool:

> The Exportation of our Native Woollen and other Manufactures in great Abundance, most of which were imported formerly out of Holland – have of late Years (by the present Company's Direction) been Manufactured at home: and for the greatest expence thereof, have given express Orders to their Factors at Guiney to undersel all other Nations; whereby the Wool of this Nation is much more consumed and spent than formerly; and many Thousands of the poor People imployed.[6]

Barely a decade later another writer claimed that the Company actually introduced the making of boysadoes and annabasses (formerly from Holland)[7] as well as carpets, tapseils and niconees (formerly from India). But the Company apologists were on a losing wicket. Exeter wool barons did not take kindly to monopolies which restricted their freedom to trade and the African monopoly was vehemently denounced. Merchants throughout England bombarded Parliament with petitions demanding free trade to Africa and at the heart of the movement was the West Country. To the substantial weight of the Bristol Merchant Venturers was added the powerful and energetic presence of the Exeter merchants who petitioned for free trade to Africa in 1690 and 1691. Nor was protest the privilege of the cities alone; towns such as Kingsbridge and Modbury also chimed in.[8] The sum total was a solid national opposition to the very concept of monopoly, and this deeply influenced the colonies. Angered by the shortfall in deliveries of slaves, they clamoured equally for free trade. The Jamaican lobby, intensified by the French invasion of 1694 which carried off 1,300 slaves,[9] led the colonial pressure.

It would be naive to assume that Exeter merchants waited until 1698 to get the green light from Parliament before proceeding to Africa. Clandestine voyages using false destinations were a feature of the pre-1698 trade to Africa but are notoriously difficult to trace. By correlating records, however,[10] we can identify at least one: the *Speedwell* of Dartmouth of 1682. Freighted by Exeter merchant William Ivy,[11] she cleared the Customs for the Cape Verde islands and Barbados under Philip Varloe. In reality she was headed deep into the southern Atlantic and round the Cape of Good Hope. Eventually she took her cargo of slaves aboard in Madagascar[12] – a far cry from Cape Verde – in exchange for Barnstaple says, Exeter serges, Devon broadcloth, Norwich stuffs, beaver-fur hats, haberdashery, brassware, wrought iron and gunpowder. Cargoes such as this were commonplace for the Cape Verde Islands, and were usually exchanged for wine, salt, and small asses (assinegoes) which were popular in Barbados as pack animals, so the *Speedwell*'s declared initial destination would have attracted little comment. On 2 April 1683 she entered Barbados, delivering 170 slaves and 4 cwt. of ivory.[13]

Unfortunately, the clandestine trade remains true to its name and is impossible to assess. When the Act of 1698 allowed merchants to trade openly to Africa on payment of 10 per cent tax on the value of their cargo to the Company, Exeter merchants in a burst of enthusiasm declared they had profited greatly by the opening of the trade, which had given them a new market for coarse serges. Ashburton announced new levels of manufacture which employed most of the town. Even allowing generous room for doubt, these statements are patently untrue. In all probability they were little more than political post-rationalisations. The Company had habitually purchased serges of Devon manufacture for its African cargoes, buying either through its agent in Exeter or through a London intermediary.[14] As had been the case prior to 1698, in overall terms Rotterdam bought by far the largest quantities of serge; the plantations of Antigua, Barbados and Jamaica trailed well behind in comparison, as did North America. Serge needed a populous market that used wool for personal insulation against the cold: neither Africa (which produced excellent cloth of its own), nor the Caribbean possessed such conditions. Yet most slave trade ships did include serge amongst their goods for barter – often under the term perpetuannas (which reflected how long-wearing it was) or ranters – and the Company continued to purchase local Devon serge for its ventures.

Enthusiastic though the Exeter merchants had been to remove the Company monopoly of Africa trade, they were more circumspect about taking up the trade themselves. Perhaps they preferred to supply less faint-hearted London and Bristol entrepreneurs with serge or continue shipping it to Rotterdam where a proportion formed part of the Dutch West India Company's cargoes to the Guinea Coast. Thus there was no great rush for Africa, and when they did start trading it was the tobacco merchants who were to dominate the scene. Though leaving neither from Exeter nor Dartmouth waters, the first Devon ten per cent ship was the *Betty Galley* of Exeter freighted by John and Charles Ellard. A plantation-built vessel of 80 tons and 4 guns, she cleared Bristol under Charles Ellard in January 1698 bound for Cape Verde[15] in tandem with the *Beginning* of Bristol under William Levercombe. A tyro in the slave trade, Ellard completed a successful though slow first half of the voyage, delivering 97 Negroes and 400 tusks of ivory to Barbados on 15 November following. His turnround time at Barbados was exemplary. He cleared for Plymouth at the end of January 1699 with sugar, ginger and molasses and much of the cargo – including ivory and pepper – was landed there in June.[16] Exeter was finally reached in the first days of July, when Francis Lidstone took delivery of ginger and muscovado sugar, and Roger Prowse of tobacco.[17] Despite all the appearance of a successful venture, neither the Ellards nor the *Betty* went back into the slave trade. The former carried on much as they had done before, in the conventional way of trade; the *Betty*, come the War of the Spanish Succession, was transformed into a privateer.[18]

If the *Betty*'s career on the Guinea Coast was straightforward, that of the *Dragon* of Topsham, four miles downriver from Exeter, was anything but. Though Topsham now is an idyllic beauty spot with narrow streets lined by whitewashed Dutch-style houses, for over two centuries it was the channel through which the bulk of the vast Exeter trade in woollens flowed into the world. This status had been thrust upon it in an artificial, but spectacularly successful manner. In medieval times the Exe had been closed by the Courtenays, the Earls of Devon, who constructed weirs across the river to prevent vessels reaching Exeter.[19] By this simple but despotic measure, merchants were forced to discharge their inward-bound cargoes at Topsham (and load their outward-bound cargoes too). All the best legal efforts of the burgesses of Exeter failed to remove the weirs and Topsham, not surprisingly, became a flourishing port. It was still prospering when the *Dragon* cleared for Africa.

Little of this prosperity was destined to rub off on the *Dragon*. Owned and freighted by Joseph Anthony, William Pounick (or Penneck), Arthur Jeffry, Martha Broderick (or Brodridge) and

Christopher Butcher – all of Exeter – and Robert Corker of Falmouth, she cleared Topsham for Africa under Christopher Butcher on 15 February 1699,[20] sailing on 4 March of that year. Though Arthur Jeffry was named as the titular head of the consortium and may indeed have owned the greatest proportion of the venture, Robert Corker, whose brother Thomas was the erratic Company Agent on the Gambia at the time, was its guiding light.[21] Perhaps as a result, the cargo was particularly light on West Country serges and perpetuannas, and heavily reliant on import–export goods such as wrought iron and brass.

Unfortunately the success or failure of the voyage hinged upon Christopher Butcher's performance as captain and supercargo. In the heat and disease of the Guinea Coast, Butcher proved unequal to the task, succumbing to sickness and dying in the middle of June. The care of the voyage passed into the less capable hands of his first mate, the hapless Henry Taylor, a Jonah of the first water.

Until then the voyage had gone well, helped by a rapid 21-day passage to the Gambia. Once there Agent Corker had proved a handful, failing to provide constructive advice and disappearing for weeks on end to attend to the myriad irons he kept in his fire. To Butcher's credit he had little patience with Corker's cavalier attitude and threatened to up anchor for the Sherbro river in Sierra Leone. This would have been much against Corker's interests and he came to heel, providing a caboceer from his substantial extended Gambian family, a Captain Amber, to supply Butcher with slaves for two months. During this time 57 slaves, 10 kentels (cwt.) of ivory and 14 kentels of beeswax were loaded aboard the *Dragon*. This would hardly have caused the ship to ride deeply in the water, but perhaps the backers of the *Dragon* had severely underestimated the cost of slaves (the *Dragon*'s cargo cost no more than £400), or overestimated the influence of Agent Corker. Of course as Royal African Company employee he had no business dealing with a ten per cent ship in the first place, nor freighting it with twenty-nine of his own slaves in the second.[22]

By now Taylor had assumed command, and disaster accordingly struck. The *Dragon*'s departure from the Guinea Coast was delayed by a lack of provisions for the slaves and 'contrary winds', and during this time the crew of the ship were faced with that nightmare of the Guinea trade, a full-scale slave uprising. This cost the lives of two crewmen and seven slaves. When the crew opened fire many of the slaves who were milling around on deck still shackled to one another leaped overboard and five were drowned, their irons taking them swiftly to the sea-bed.

Late in September the *Dragon* reached Barbados and landed between 37 and 42 slaves (the accounts are contradictory) the majority of whom had been carried on freight by Agent Corker at £3 10s. a head. The total delivered for the backers of the voyage amounted to only 14, of which one died during the sale. They were consigned to merchant Joseph Hole, as were the ivory, beeswax and all the exported goods which had failed to sell on the Guinea Coast.

But Taylor's tribulations were only just beginning. He now had only two crewmen in good health, and by the beginning of October he claimed that all the crew had died. He too was desperately ill, lying at death's door for eight months, lacking even the energy to reply to the increasingly frantic letters from Arthur Jeffry and Company. They had heard from Joseph Hole that the *Dragon* had somehow (possibly in the confusion occasioned by the slave revolt) mislaid her plantation register, and had been quite properly seized by the Customs pending the production of another. With some urgency they had written to Taylor on 25 December 1699 displaying an attitude predictably devoid of any hint of Christmas cheer but informing him a new register had been sent,

> though we do admire w^t is become of the former. We are also very uneasy for want of a Letter from you to give us Some Light what was done on the Coast of Guinny & in the whole Course of the Voyage . . . the cargo we sent out from hence cost us above £500 first penny & to hear of but 17 Slaves for our Account aboard which could not cost above £100 is astonishing.

Eventually rising from his sickbed in June 1700, Taylor penned an extravagantly illiterate and hopelessly incoherent letter which could have done little to allay their misgivings. In it he recorded his hopes of sailing for Plymouth within a few days, but it proved to be April the following year before the *Dragon* was released from seizure by the Admiralty Court at Barbados. Even then she was cleared not for Plymouth, but for Trinidad and Tobago for timber and firewood on behalf of Joseph Hole, who was attempting to recoup some of the losses he had suffered in contesting the seizure of the *Dragon*, preventing her from being condemned, and having her resheathed and refitted on her release. Meanwhile Hole had taken the bulk of the *Dragon*'s export cargo which had failed to sell at the Gambia in 1699 (the rest had been damaged by being stored too long in his damp warehouse) and reshipped it to Africa in a valiant attempt to earn some revenue for the Exeter backers.

In June 1702 during the third of Taylor's series of voyages to Trinidad and Tobago, (Hole was determined to extract his money's worth from the *Dragon*), Taylor and his command were captured by a French pirate. The long-suffering *Dragon* was sailed off to breathe fire amongst the shipping lanes as a French pirate vessel, and Taylor was left to cool his heels in a Spanish prison at Comina near Caracas. Released on Christmas Day 1702 he made his way back to Barbados by shipping aboard various vessels via the Virgin Islands and St Kitts.

By now he had been away from his home, wife and family for nigh on four years, but it was with some degree of trepidation that he stepped aboard the *Phoenix* of Barbados as master commissioned to take her to London. It was not so much his reputation as a Jonah that caused his apprehension, rather the all too real possibility of a warrant for his arrest pending his arrival in England, and the threat of legal proceedings against him. Before leaving Barbados he extracted a promise from Joseph Hole that the latter would send him complete details of the Admiralty Court's seizure of the *Dragon*, Hole assuring him that the *Dragon*'s owners had been fully advised of the same as well as being remitted a full balance of accounts of monies spent upon the ship.

Taylor's joy at reaching London safely at the end of October 1703 was tempered by his arrest within a fortnight on an action instigated by William Penneck for the recovery of his share of cargo and vessel. The allegation contained in the warrant for his arrest complained bitterly and belatedly that Taylor had not acted according either to his duties or orders and

> hath applyed the said Ship and her Cargo and loading and the proceed thereof to his owne use or wasted and destroyed or wilfully cast the same away & hath not given the Owners any Acct. thereof.

Initially unable to find any surety to stand bail for him, Taylor was thrown into prison; John Baker, the London merchant to whom the cargo aboard the *Phoenix* had been consigned, eventually came to his rescue and he was released pending proceedings.

No such rescue was afforded for two of the *Dragon*'s unfortunate backers. Arthur Jeffry, whose business had been much concerned with Jamaica and Barbados during the closing years of the seventeenth century, had meanwhile been experiencing severe financial difficulties. His once-prosperous trading house had finally gone bankrupt during 1703, forcing him to flee abroad to avoid his creditors.[23] Nor had William Penneck himself escaped having his fingers badly burned by the *Dragon*; on 11 December 1703 he appeared personally before the High Court of Admiralty in London to testify 'that by reason of his great losses at sea and otherwise he is reduced to great necessity and is not worthe Five Pounds, his Debts pay'd . . .'

Christmas that year must have been a misery for most of those enmeshed in the affair. Though Taylor had been released from prison, neither he nor his wife had been paid any of his wages accruing from the *Dragon*'s initial voyage, so he in turn sued Penneck for two years' wages at £6 per month, a total of £144.

The case was still rumbling through the Admiralty Courts in spring of the following year but without being clearly resolved. Perhaps the parties simply dropped their respective suits. Certainly they suspended for all time any further thoughts of trading to Africa. Henry Taylor never again shipped out for the coast of Guinea, nor – with the exception of Robert Corker who had mounted a single venture to Guinea from Falmouth in early 1701 at the instigation of his brother Thomas – did any of the *Dragon*'s backers tempt fate a second time. Only Robert Corker successfully surmounted his losses on the *Dragon*, becoming the leading Cornish merchant of his day and, as we shall see, dominating trade from the ports of Falmouth, Penrhyn and Truro.

The fate of the *Dragon*'s backers curiously foreshadowed that which befell those of the *Daniel and Henry* whose voyage forms the heart of this book and whose career has already been examined in some detail. Both the *Dragon* and the *Daniel and Henry* had the advantage of peacetime voyages (though it seemed to bring neither of them any reward), but the outbreak of war in 1702 naturally forced any West Country merchant planning a slave venture to reconsider its chances of success. The Channel ports and their approaches lay under virtual siege during the first few years and long-haul trade suffered accordingly. It was not until 1709 that John Harris and Company of Exeter felt sufficiently emboldened to mount a voyage to Guinea. As with the *Daniel and Henry* of 1700, Dartmouth was chosen as the point of departure in preference to Exeter. John Harris appointed Silvanus Evans to assemble and supervise the loading of the cargo. Evans might well have had a share in the venture for he and Harris had formed partnerships before;

later Evans was to captain the privateer *Sorlings*, a large ship of 400 tons, 30 guns and 100 men, which he owned in conjunction with Harris.[24] To enhance the voyage's prospects Harris hired an experienced London and Bristol Guinea-trade captain called John Blake, to take the *Dartmouth Galley* to Africa and the West Indies. Her cargo was valued at £1,151 14s.7d and her intention was to trade for 300 slaves; in September she cleared the Customs House at Dartmouth, paying the statutory 10 per cent tax.[25]

Despite all precautions and the high hopes of the owners, the voyage of the *Dartmouth* was a disaster. Though Blake negotiated the passage to Africa with ease, he was captured by French privateers operating off the Guinea Coast in January 1710. Factors at the Cape

Coast Castle reported this loss to London in February,[26] and the news would have reached Exeter some time in the spring of that year. This was not, however, the end of the *Dartmouth*. With her crew in shackles, the privateersmen sailed her in company with the *Joseph and Thomas* with which she had been travelling, along the coast to Whydah. There they approached William Hicks, factor for the Company at the fort, with an offer to sell him both the *Dartmouth* and her cargo. After consultation with Sir Dalby Thomas, his superior at the Cape Coast Castle, Hicks was instructed to refuse any deal with the French and it was left to the Dutch to pick up the bulk of the cargo at rock-bottom prices. (A suggestion remains that Hicks, unable to resist the temptation, bought some of the cargo for his own ends.) Eventually the *Dartmouth* and her crew made their way back to England. On 27 March 1711 her owners, merchants James Doliffe of London, James Evans of Dartmouth and captain

Robert Holdsworth (also of Dartmouth), were granted letters of marque for the *Dartmouth*, described as 160 tons burden.[27] Victualled for sixteen months and armed to the teeth, the *Dartmouth* set out with the *Holdsworth*, also of Dartmouth and captained by Arthur Holdsworth (whose letters of marque bore the same date), to avenge the losses sustained on the Guinea Coast.[28] Though doubtless the original cargo had been insured, the costs of setting up a vessel for Africa were substantial and were not covered. Neither were the crew's wages, nor the cost of provisions. Probably most bitter of all, the 10 per cent tax payable to the Company was not recoverable either. Should John Harris and Company care to mount another venture to Africa of the same value then the tax would be waived. Harris, once bitten, was twice shy; he never attempted trade with Africa again.

The period since 1706 had been marked by the Royal African Company on one hand, and the ten per centers on the other, drawing up their respective battle-lines over the future of the trade to Africa. Naturally the Company wished for a return to pre-1698 days and a total monopoly. Equally understandably the mercantile community did not, and repudiated even the irksome 10 per cent tax on their Africa-bound cargoes. If the Company had been in the habit of buying much of its woollen goods from local Devon manufacturers, it showed remarkable reluctance to pressure them into petitioning Parliament for the return of the monopoly. In fact the Company appears to have been purchasing very little in the way of serges from the Exeter region at that time. Only Mathew Barrett was a regular supplier, and it was he who had approached the company at the end of 1706.[29] Winning an initial order for 350 double pieces of perpetuannas in February 1707, he quickly secured a subsequent contract for 200 double pieces per week for three months. At the rate of 14s. a piece this contract was worth £1,680 and ensured valuable continuity of work. Curiously, in an area of England known for the abundance and excellence of its serge, Barrett found great difficulty in maintaining the quality of his product. His ploy of introducing substandard cloth into the bales received short shrift from Company quality controllers:

> one bale is of a very inferior sort and none of them weigh as they ought, so unless the Comp[a.] can be assured of a good commodity They will not be encouraged to proceed with you for they are much importuned daily to alter their Method and buy their goods in town.

Fearing the loss of business, Barrett fired off a string of apologies, blandishments and assurances, apparently to little avail.

> The Comp^a are not well pleased that you should write to them so often that the goods you buy for them are better than the goods bought by the 10 per cent men. You are in the wrong to suppose the Comp^a will be bought by letters. They are judges of matters of fact and know the 10 per Ct. men have better goods than some of those they have had from you.

The belief that the ten per centers acquired better-quality goods was a constant irritation to the Company and never failed to be employed as a weapon to keep their suppliers up to the mark. Whether it had any basis in reality is difficult to judge but the volume demanded by the Company for their orders would certainly have facilitated attempts to slip in the odd bolt of substandard cloth. And whereas the ten per cent men paid ready money, the Company often demanded extended terms of credit. None the less as the lobbying on the trade to Africa reached new heights, no side could afford to alienate its supporters. A merchant such as Barrett in a city such as Exeter could provide much-needed support in the battle with the ten per centers, and the Company eventually regarded it as politically expedient to overlook his shortcomings. In March 1708, however, they turned the screws by making it quite plain that if he valued his contract with them he would have to secure a goodly number of illustrious signatures to a Company petition aimed at reinstating Company monopoly. No doubt Barrett realised he was backing a loser. He made a half-hearted attempt to glean a few signatures, which the Company regarded with ill-concealed disdain. A further pathetically small supplement was returned to Africa House the following June, and business predictably ceased between the two parties. Thereafter all woollen trade between the Company and Exeter merchants appears to have been conducted through London intermediaries, with the sole exception of Joseph Veale. In 1720 he supplied the now declining Company with over £8,250 worth of woollen ranters between August of that year and the following February.[30]

Devon was a lost cause as far as Company attempts to retain its monopoly were concerned: it bombarded Parliament with more petitions than any other shire to free the trade to Africa. From March 1708 to May 1714, Exeter, Dartmouth, Plymouth, Ashburton and Totnes burgesses, town councils and merchants lodged a total of ten petitions against the Company.[31] Only one petition (that of the Weavers, Tuckers and Dyers of Exeter) supported the Company's endeavour. Yet despite the clamour for free trade to Africa, the merchants of Exeter, Dartmouth, Topsham and Plymouth hardly fell over each other in the rush for the Guinea Coast once the Company monopoly was dismissed by Parliament.

Why then had the monopoly attracted so much vituperation and attention between 1690 and 1712? First it was a monopoly, and a royal one at that, which the merchants, predominantly Whigs, found extremely irksome. Secondly, unlike the monopoly operated by the East India Company, it incorporated no democratic mechanism by which a merchant could join and trade under its aegis. And last but by no means least, Africa was not the real focus of the merchants' concern. Their interest lay primarily in the West Indies and American plantations. But as trading partners these colonies were still fledgelings, possessing no population of any size and producing commodities which, though profitable, were fitful and unreliable in quantity. Only by large-scale immigration of labour could these colonies be placed on a firm footing; only then would England have a numerous and highly receptive audience for its manufactured goods, and only then would the vastly increased production of sugar and tobacco enable viable – indeed colossally profitable – return cargoes to be virtually guaranteed. And that is where Africa came in, not as a trading partner but as the sole supplier of manpower, the vital factor in turning these colonies into centres of profit. The Company's monopoly was perceived as hampering, not facilitating, the speed of this development.

With the monopoly out of the way, peace in Europe, and without even a 10 per cent tax to rail against, the merchants of the Devon ports still fought shy of venturing to Africa. A curious stab at the Guinea trade was attempted, however, by the captain of the *Anna* of Topsham,[32] Thomas Wills. Having loaded a small cargo of cotton cloth, perpetuannas, serge and barley in November 1713 with Oporto as his ostensible destination, Wills made landfall at the Gambia early in January 1714. Faulty navigation seems not to have been to blame. If anything, he had failed to secure an expected return cargo at Oporto and been persuaded by a Portuguese merchant that rich pickings could be his on the Guinea Coast. The holds of the *Anna* were now packed with foreign produce and his crew supplemented by a detachment of Portuguese sailors under a captain of their own. In reply to close questioning by the Company factors on the Gambia,

Wills maintained he was destined for Brazil and requested their assistance in trading for slaves. Still smarting from the loss of their monopoly, they resolutely opposed any such dealings.[33] Like many another Guinea-trade ship the *Anna* sailed haphazardly into oblivion. Her master, who appears to have been captain in name only, may have survived. In 1722, on successfully taking the pirate Bartholomew Roberts and his ships *Fortune* and *Ranger* off the Guinea Coast, the Royal Navy found Thomas Wills aboard the *Fortune*. He was not there of his own volition, having shipped out of Bideford aboard the *Richard* as boatswain, bound for the Caribbean, and subsequently having had the misfortune of being taken by Roberts. He must have presented a strange contrast to the pirates, since 'he was never heard to swear, never given to Drink, and called Presbyterian for his sobriety . . . and appeared Sorry when ever they saw Sails or had a Prospect of getting Prizes or doing Mischief'.[34]

Shortly after the *Anna*'s departure from Topsham, John Burridge junior of Lyme Regis mounted another of his African ventures in February 1714, this time from Exeter. Chartering an Exeter brigantine called the *Surprise Galley*, he instructed Joseph Tibby, a Southampton sea captain, to take her to the Guinea Coast.[35] Exeter merchant and long-time associate Roger Prowse handled the cargo for Burridge. Notable for its pronounced Guinea flavour, the cargo included vast numbers of beads and semiprecious stones including olivet, a mock pearl specifically made for the African trade and particularly acceptable at Senegal, and 6 cwt. of mock coral necklaces. Other items included lace-fringed hats and buccaneering guns. The hats, like the heavily adorned parasols used as badges of rank amongst African chieftains, were much in demand by caboceers, and especially prized when adorned with a fanciful blue feather.[36] Despite their name, the guns did not derive from swashbuckling buccaneers, but were long muskets originally used to hunt wild cattle. John Burridge's ventures were generally successful, and though nothing is recorded of the *Surprise* following her departure from the Guinea Coast, it is highly probable she delivered her complement of slaves to Jamaica. She would then have loaded a cargo of sugar, molasses and rum, some of which – the rum especially – would have been traded in Virginia for tobacco, before she returned to London in the late spring of 1715.[37]

Despite the example set by John Burridge of Lyme, Exeter merchants continued to fight shy of direct involvement in African trade, and it was left to George Barons, an Exeter merchant resident in Holland, to carry the flag to Africa. The son of an Exeter distiller, he was born in Crediton and later apprenticed to Exeter merchant Malachy Pyne. Making his way to Amsterdam in the early 1690s and subsequently to Rotterdam, Barons built a reputation as a successful import–export merchant. Since his extensive business dealings kept him active between Exeter and Rotterdam on a virtually continuous basis, he appointed his brother Samuel to look after his wide-ranging interests, from the Newfoundland fisheries to the Virginia tobacco trade, on the English side of the Channel. Both brothers' preferred aim of trading activity centred around South Carolina and it was there that Samuel, by now resident in London, transported indentured servants aboard his merchantman *Neptune* in 1717.[38]

George Barons had initially ventured into the African trade from Plymouth, but Dartmouth was the starting point – albeit a nominal one – for his two ventures of 1714 and 1715. Both involved the same ship – the *Sylvia Galley* of 40 tons and 4 guns[39] – and the same master, John Vennard junior. The Vennards were a seafaring family from Topsham whose knowledge of American and Caribbean waters had first been acquired by John junior's grandfather James Vennard, master of the *George* in the 1670s on her regular runs to Barbados for sugar and Virginia for tobacco.[40] His son, John senior, an ex-Navy captain, also plied regularly in plantation waters, as master of the *Anne* of Exeter, freighted by Daniel Ivy and Henry Arthur to Virginia in 1698, and of the *Orange Branch* of Topsham to Carolina in 1701 and several times subsequently. He too was destined to enter the slave trade on George Barons' behalf, but from Plymouth, not Exeter or Dartmouth.

Both the *Sylvia*'s voyages to Guinea commanded by John Vennard junior proceeded along identical paths. On her first she cleared the Dartmouth Customs House in September 1714 for Terceras in the Azores,[41] having loaded little more than a couple of hundredweight of pewter goods. On leaving Dartmouth the *Sylvia* made, not southwest for the Azores, but eastwards for Rotterdam. There she loaded a cargo of Dutch slave trade goods such as old sheets and weapons and linens, beads and cotton cloth from the Dutch possessions in the East Indies. October saw Vennard trading off the Gambia in the company of two other English 'interlopers', both of whom had also taken their cargo aboard in Holland.[42] Being a small ship, the *Sylvia* was quickly slaved and had probably cleared the African coast by Christmas. Nothing can be traced of her progress from that time, but from the evidence of her cargo, discharged on her return to

Dartmouth in August the following year, it included Jamaica and South Carolina.[43] Within the month the bulk of her cargo of rice, logwood, ivory and beaver fur was exported aboard the same ship to Barons in Rotterdam.

Here the process repeated itself, though with some delay, for it was not until well into 1716 that the *Sylvia* found herself on the Gambia. All did not go quite according to plan. When almost fully slaved, Vennard found himself faced with quelling a slave revolt that threatened to jeopardise the entire venture, and which was suppressed only with the help of the Company factors at the Gambia and their soldiery. From that time on the factors displayed a marked change of heart towards Vennard (presumably he had rewarded them well for their assistance) recommending him as 'the only Civilised Commander that hath been here'.[44]

Whether as a result of the uprising, a poor middle passage, or because the majority had previously been delivered to another Caribbean island, Vennard landed only nine slaves to merchant Benjamin Hole (resident in Barbados though of Devon origin, and owner of the slave ship *Trial*) in July 1716.[45] Now homeward bound to Dartmouth, the *Sylvia* was loaded with over 40 tons of fustic and quantities of ivory. As before, this was immediately exported to Barons in Rotterdam as soon as the *Sylvia* returned to England.[46] During this time both Vennard father and son were working for Barons; while John junior was at the Gambia, John senior was master of the *Clarinda* plying between Exeter, Rotterdam and Antigua,[47] a pattern of trade that was adopted by the *Sylvia* after her second slaving voyage. By 1719 Barons had lost interest in the slave trade (probably because of the losses caused by the slave revolt, an eventuality which was specifically excluded in the conditions of insurance), and his subsequent ventures, mostly between the plantations, Exeter and Rotterdam, were all of a conventional nature.

On the other hand brother Samuel did maintain a dilatory interest in the slave trade. Eschewing the advantages of West Country seaports, he set forth the *Ludlow Galley* under Arthur Lone from London in September 1716. She delivered an unknown number of slaves at Charleston early in 1717, but there the venture ran into trouble with the crew. They complained of being forced to take their wages in current Carolina money, not sterling. The currencies – nominally the same – did not exchange at anything like par, and Samuel Barons was accused of 'Imposing a notorious Fraud' before the court which had been hastily assembled to hear the case.

Witnesses for Samuel Barons instead maintained that he was 'a considerable Trader and a man of Great Reputation upon the Exchange of London and was never known to be guilty of any Fraud in any Contract or dealing'. Whatever the result of the case, Samuel Barons subsequently concentrated his mercantile skill on other areas of colonial trade. It seems, though, that he was loath to relinquish the slave trade absolutely; in 1734 he (and Nathaniel Paice, originally of Lyme Regis), both signed the petition of London merchants against the Act of that year which applied a duty of £10 per head on all slaves imported into South Carolina.[48]

So direct Exeter and Dartmouth interest in the slave trade fell into desuetude. The covetous eyes with which the merchants of Exeter had regarded the trade to Africa in the last decade of the seventeenth century were not, in the event, matched by their stomach for it. They were happier sitting on the sidelines as suppliers or contented themselves with investing in other ventures from London or Bristol. Amongst those who did so was Henry Burwell of Exeter (already noted in connection with the *Daniel and Henry*), whose interests in London encompassed ships' factoring, insurance and procurement of cargo. Between 1696 and 1700 Henry Burwell handled, in the course of his business, a number of Guinea ventures from London including the *Fly*, the *Wydah* (in which he owned a two-eighth part of the venture and which his purser accompanied as supercargo), Robert Matthew's command the *Sarah* (in which he owned 3/32 of both ship and cargo), the *Wydah*'s second voyage, and the *Two Brothers* in which he had a one-sixteenth part of the cargo.[49]

To what can be ascribed the lack of activity in Exeter towards the trade to Africa? First, the merchants believed they were sitting pretty: wool had formed England's staple export since time immemorial and they could see no sign of change in their fortunes. Whether the Royal African Company wrested the trade back from the separate traders or not, Devon serge would still form an important element in African cargoes, though the total amount was insignificant beside the colossal quantities shipped to Rotterdam. Secondly, the importation of many Guinea-trade goods such as Indian cottons and beads of all types was largely restricted to the entrepôt ports of London, Bristol and later, Liverpool. Exeter merchants planning a Guinea-trade venture had to bear the cost of shipping the bulk of their intended cargo coastways from London, as did the backers of the *Daniel and Henry*. Little of the cargo aboard a Guinea-trade ship, with the exception of woollen goods, was of indigenous manufacture. Even the lead and iron bars were from the Baltic; old sheets generally from Rotterdam; sletia linens from Germany; brawls, niconees, nehalla-wares and so on from the Far East. Very few of these items were easily available in Exeter. Thirdly, the hinterland of Exeter did not possess a large and varied manufacturing capacity, such as was available to London or Bristol merchants who had industry – if not exactly on their doorstep – at least within easy carriage distance and on good connecting roads. Exeter's natural hinterland was small, rural and of limited economic importance.[50] It was unable to provide the wide range of goods increasingly demanded by the American and West Indian colonies, and crucially incapable of processing the raw materials deriving from the plantations, be they tobacco, sugar or cotton. Finally the port was not without its difficulties of access and egress. The bar at Exmouth was a geographical inconvenience; but the fact that Exeter was not accessible by larger vessels, which had to tranship goods to and from lighters for the canal trip to the legal quay at Exeter, involved merchants in extra financial expenses which they resented. Within a quarter of a century of Celia Fiennes' laudatory description of Exeter trade, the city's overseas interests were perceptibly – and irretrievably – declining.

Before forsaking Lyme Bay and proceeding around the coast to Plymouth, mention may be made of a long-forgotten incident involving Topsham which functions as a sad postscript to its role in the slave trade nearly a quarter of a century after the *Dragon* had started it. The last few days of April 1722 had been marked by capricious spring weather: strong westerly winds battered the coast and high seas made shipping scurry for safe ports. Beating down the Channel and across Lyme Bay came the Company ship *Northampton*, 110 tons, commander John Sharrow.[51] He was due to call at Falmouth to embark a group of Cornish miners under a Captain Paul, continue with them to the Guinea Coast and then make for Delagoa Bay beyond the Cape of Good Hope. Since Madagascar and Delagoa fell within the boundaries of the East India Company's monopoly, the ship had been licensed by them to land at Delagoa but not permitted to trade. Privately the Royal African Company had issued Sharrow with an *aide-mémoire* entitled *Directions for the Bay of Delagoa and the Rivers therein, with some Memorandums concerning the Trade of that Place*. The detailed navigational directions and minute accounts of the 'goods which go off best' reveal that the *Northampton* was certainly intended to trade there and indeed carried a cargo valued at £1,015 to enable her so to do:

Sharrow's orders included the exhortation 'the Manner of Trading is always at the Muzzels of your Muskets'.[52]

It was rare for the paths of the two great trading Companies of England to cross in such a manner. Ostensibly the reason for the *Northampton* landing at Delagoa Bay was to return 'two persons commonly called the Two Black Indian Princes' to their homes. They had been in England for about a year, fêted by the Royal African Company, presented at Court, and generally seeing the sights of London. This was by no means unusual: the Company had a policy of entertaining – and even educating – children of selected African potentates in order to forge closer and more profitable links between them.

As the *Northampton* bucketed her way into the Atlantic approaches the weather, already bad, took a turn for the worse. Sharrow correctly chose to run for the mouth of the Exe rather than risk making for Falmouth, which would expose the ship to much greater danger. Unfortunately, while going over the notorious bar at Exmouth the *Northampton* grounded heavily and damaged her hull.[53] Prince James, one of the Africans, became greatly alarmed, fearing perhaps that he would never see his native land again. So concerned was Sharrow at his disturbed state that he immediately wrote in some trepidation to London: the Company merely advised him to 'use all the fair means you can to reduce him to quietness and ease, having at the same time a regard to yourselves & the safety & success of your voyage'.[54]

Whatever disguised threat the last phrase entailed is open to question. On the 4 May, Prince James apparently hanged himself and was buried ashore. The Company remained unperturbed:

> the violent death of Prince James . . . was what might have been expected from his late behaviour . . . it is certainly very happy that Prince John (to whom pay my humble services) keeps his Temper, it makes Amends for the Loss of the other who was a Wretch whose being was not to be regarded nor his Death lamented.

This shabby episode sums up the division between the concerned public stance of the Company towards blacks and the private reality that all were expendable. As a footnote, the *Northampton* cleared Topsham after repairs and eventually delivered Prince John to Delagoa. If her outward voyage had been marked by tragedy, her return voyage was close to farce. The Company factors at Cabenda reported in May of the following year that the *Northampton* had arrived and been dispatched on her final leg to London with Guinea redwood and ivory; but the crew were so mutinous that a parcel of gold, part of the proceeds deriving from the sale of blacks to Brazil-bound Portuguese slave ships, was withheld from consignment, the factors fearing the Company would see neither ship nor crew again if the gold were entrusted to them.[55]

CHAPTER EIGHTEEN

Plymouth, Barnstaple and Bideford

By 1700 Plymouth was a substantial town and a far cry from the motley collection of fishing villages that had once been scattered along the shores of Plymouth Sound, Cattewater and Hamoaze, a transformation that paralleled England's own development as a maritime power with colonial aspirations. Owing to its strategic location and deep-water anchorages, the port had become a naval station in the sixteenth century, the springboard from which England's largely successful campaigns against the Spanish armadas were launched. This new status was encouraged by the representatives of two Plymouth merchant families – Sir Francis Drake and Sir John Hawkins – being respectively Treasurer and Comptroller of the Royal Navy at that time.[1]

With England's growing maritime ascendancy, the threat from Spain receded, and so did the fortunes of the town. That state of affairs was not destined to last for long. France rose to take the place of Spain as England's enemy and the demand for a western naval base was renewed. This time the base was seen as a permanent necessity and by 1696 the great naval dockyard had come into existence, an existence nourished by the frequent war footing upon which England found herself during the eighteenth century.

Thus by 1698 the town of Plymouth (though three miles distant from the dockyard and not connected by road until 1775), already displayed a pronounced naval flavour. The interests and manufactures of the town were inextricably bound up with supplying and servicing the wide range of needs generated by Navy vessels both at primary and ancillary levels. The merchant marine happily took advantage of these services, especially in times of war when the presence of the Navy and the possibility of joining a protected convoy made Plymouth an expedient alternative to beating down the

Channel fully laden from London and risking privateer attack. In addition the area had a large pool of experienced seamen and artisan-mariners such as sailmakers, coopers and carpenters, all of whom were vitally important for long-haul ventures to the Guinea Coast and the Caribbean. Though the threat of the press-gang taking a significant number of a merchantman's crew remained stronger in Plymouth than anywhere else (except perhaps Portsmouth), merchants regarded this as a minor disadvantage compared to the benefits of security, servicing, a quick turnaround time and immediate access to the Atlantic. However the lack of a strong manufacturing base in Plymouth[2] meant that much of the goods exported to Africa and the Caribbean,[3] with the exception of woollen produce and herrings, had to be shipped coastways from London – itself a hazardous undertaking in times of war – or carted by land carriage. This option was not satisfactory as the highways deteriorated markedly the further west they went from London, and were virtually impassable during the winter months. Both methods of supply, sea and land, involved merchants in unwanted extra expenditure. During this period, as soon as the depredations of war diminished, the Guinea-trade merchants reverted to their favourite ports of Bristol and London, and their affair with Plymouth ceased. This break with Plymouth was made easier by the fact that the town had no facilities and little local interest in processing or purchasing imported goods such as tobacco and sugar from the plantations; being predominantly a town of poor artisans and labourers, it is doubtful whether any but a minute proportion of the inhabitants could afford such luxuries.

Until the start of the War of the Spanish Succession in 1702 there was little direct trading between Plymouth and Africa, though a substantial quantity of shipping cleared for the Caribbean (see Appendix 8). With the sole exception of the *Rochester* of London, bound for Guinea in 1701 under Captain John Dennis, which called to pick up tobacco for merchant Edward Nicholson, no vessel cleared for Africa until 1703.[4] In October of that year the *Michael Galley* of London,[5] John Prior commanding, loaded a substantial Guinea-trade cargo for Mordecai Living. Apart from 475 yards of red plains and long cloths, and 40 pieces of Guinea stuffs, none of the items were of local Devon origin. Nor was Mordecai Living, a London-based slave trade captain and merchant who had previously been engaged on 'double' voyages between Barbados and Guinea for slaves.[6] The *Michael* was followed in July 1705 by the *William* of

London, a brigantine.[7] Her captain was John Collingwood and she was freighted by Joseph Martin, or rather by his company. At that time Consul in Moscow, later he was MP for Hastings and a director of the South Sea Company, though not associated with its collapse. The *William*'s cargo is notable for the considerable quantities of local serge, Barnstaple says and woollen goods it contained. Martin's company was simply using Plymouth for the sake of convenience, for despite sailing annually to the Guinea Coast – until 1709 when both ship and captain were taken by a French privateer[8] – the *William* never again cleared from there. Surviving the loss of his command in 1709, Collingwood remained in the slave trade as a merchant and agent. Many years later, in 1716, as supercargo of the *Anne and Priscilla* of London, he was lucky to escape with his life when the slaves she had taken aboard fought their way to freedom by slaughtering virtually all her crew.[9]

Similarly, the next departure from Plymouth for Africa had little connection with the port, but the cargo loaded was unusually interesting. She was the latest addition to the Royal African Company's fleet, a newly built galley of 240 tons burden, 16 guns and 40 men, called the *Pindar Galley* after a Governor of the Company. She had left the Downs on her maiden voyage late in September 1706 with a huge cargo valued in excess of £5,500,[10] of which perpetuannas, Guinea stuffs and fustians accounted for almost one-fifth. Her passage down the Channel had been delayed by a mandatory convoy system, so it was not until late December 1706 that she arrived in Plymouth. Awaiting her captain, John Taylor, was a solitary apothecary's chest weighing three-quarters of a hundredweight,[11] consigned to Sir Dalby Thomas, Agent-General at the Cape Coast Castle. Two years previously Sir Dalby had earnestly entreated the Company to supply him with both seeds and drugs.[12] His intention was to plant the seeds in Africa and monitor their progress as part of his growing belief that England should directly colonise the West African coast and develop plantations there. To this end he sought plants not only from England but from the Caribbean, and amongst his papers can be found recipes for growing and manufacturing indigo. With the drugs, Sir Dalby proposed to alter the balance of influence, if not of power, on the Coast. Perceiving the considerable political advantage to be gained from reducing the caboceers' dependence upon their influential witch doctors (who relied primarily upon fetishes to effect their cures) and encouraging them to use white man's medicine (which he hoped would be more efficacious), Sir Dalby had taken steps to order the apothecary's chest which was now loaded on to the *Pindar* at Plymouth. As a matter of record and to satisfy the more hypochondriacal reader, the medicine chest prescribed by Mr Carless, surgeon, and conveyed aboard by John Addis, Company Agent at Plymouth,[13] consisted of the following:[14]

Bass Sulphur iii vel iv	Camphor made up well in a	iv
Elix: propriet lls	large quantity of linseed	
Sp. Cornu Cero iv		
Sal.Arn iv		
Sal:vol:ol ivi	Radix Liquour llvi	
Sp.Nitr.Dulc iv	Hypococvan[15] iv	
Salis cond vi	Ther.Andr. llii vel iii	
Laud liquid vi	Cassia fistularis llii	
Laud opiat.iii	Dates best & largest llx	
Gum alves sunot vi	Merc.Dulcis vi vel viii	
Mirrh vi		

Though some of these herbal preparations were remedies in themselves, they basically provided the ingredients for pills, plasters, ointments and draughts for a variety of afflictions. Sulphur was used as an ointment for scabies, burned to disinfect rooms, and taken internally as a laxative. The elixir would have been prescribed during the convalescent stage of fever, which had supposedly been cured by liquid laudanum, theriaca and dates. Spirits of cornu cervi, otherwise known as hartshorn, were particularly efficacious in treating rheu-

matism and rheumatic fevers; sweet spirits of nitre functioned as a
diuretic; laudanum for dysentery; myrrh as an antiseptic and expec-
torant; cassia as a purgative; camphor as a liniment; and the mercury
dulcis was often taken for intestinal worms.[16]

Unfortunately none of these remedies could cure the *Pindar*'s
teething troubles; despite being newly built, she was further delayed
at Plymouth by repairs and replacement of defective components;
her 'masts, bolts and pritts &c were not sound and good'.[17] Eventually the *Pindar* sailed for the Cape Coast Castle and thence to
Jamaica, where she landed 285 slaves almost exactly a year after
clearing Plymouth.[18]

So far there had not been a single departure for Africa on behalf of
local Plymouth or even Devon merchants, and the clearing of the
Joseph Galley of Bristol, in November 1708, was no different.[19]
Captained by Robert Mullington, whose previous command had
been the *Indigo Merchant* to the Guinea Coast in 1706,[20] the *Joseph*
was owned by Bristol merchants and privateersmen Jacob Elton,
Thomas Smith and Joseph Gotley. Not surprisingly the *Joseph* had
been granted letters of marque for this voyage,[21] and Mullington
himself had experience of privateering as commander of the *Deny
Galley* of London against the Dutch in June 1696.[22] The merchants
freighting the *Joseph* to the Guinea Coast were Houlditch and Brook,
who operated as ten per cent traders from both Bristol and London.
Though little is known of Brook, Abraham Houlditch was a leading
slave trade merchant who had been Agent-General at the Cape Coast
Castle at the time of the Company's foundation in 1672, and ever
since leaving its service had fought – successfully – against its
monopoly. While most of the *Joseph*'s cargo loaded at Plymouth was
brought by land carriage from London, much was of recognisably
local origin including bays and long cloths plus nearly 2,500 pieces
of English fustians. Usually thought of as cotton and often lumped
together with annabasses in the long catalogue of cloths, there is
good reason to believe that these English fustians were actually made
of wool in the same way that 'Manchester cottons' of the same period
were. Mullington made a successful voyage in the *Joseph*, delivering
280 slaves to Jamaica and loading 100 tons of fustick and 6 bags of
cotton for the return trip to Bristol in January 1710.[23]

Given the wealth of maritime expertise available at Plymouth it is
surprising that the number of clearances for Africa were so episodic,
and that no local or metropolitan slave trade merchant employed its
facilities on a more consistent basis. But for Devon slave traders the

county was already too well endowed with ports to make Plymouth anything other than a second or third choice for departing to Africa. None the less it was from Plymouth that the Exeter merchant, George Barons,[24] long resident in Amsterdam and trading largely from Rotterdam, chose to send his first venture to the Guinea Coast late in 1710. Retaining John Vennard senior from Topsham as captain, he freighted the *Sylvia Galley* to Guinea with a paltry £235 worth of cargo.[25] The cargo had been assembled and loaded by agent Philip Pentyre, the son of a Plymouth sailmaker,[26] who had risen to become the port's principal merchant in the early eighteenth century, and it can only be assumed that the bulk of the *Sylvia*'s cargo subsequently awaited her in Rotterdam. As demonstrated in Chapter 17, Barons was to employ the *Sylvia* again in the same capacity (the vessel presumably belonged to him), following the same Guinea route via Rotterdam, under not Vennard senior but Vennard junior. George Barons was nothing if not consistent.

It could only be a matter of time before the ubiquitous Burridge family (who had extensive dealings with George Barons in the tobacco trade) put in an appearance at Plymouth. Earlier they had used the port to trade in more conventional cargoes but in April 1711 Robert Burridge and Company freighted the family's vessel *John and Robert* to the Gambia.[27] Under her captain, Robert Collins, she had just completed a successful voyage to Africa, the plantations and back for John Burridge,[28] and she was probably ordered to Plymouth to refit. Once again Philip Pentyre was responsible for the cargo, notable for its complete lack of woollen goods. How successful this venture proved to be is impossible to ascertain, for the vessel does not appear on any surviving Caribbean shipping registers, and the records for Virginia – where she probably loaded tobacco for London[29] – are fragmentary at best. Nor does any trace of the *John and Robert*'s voyage appear in Company documents. Nevertheless this trip was doubtless a profitable one – Burridge ventures tended to be successful – and seven years later the same vessel carried out a conventional African trading voyage for Robert Burridge junior of Lyme Regis (see Appendix 2). During the period 1698–1725, this vessel was the last to leave for the African coast from Plymouth.[30]

However the paucity of African-bound departures from Plymouth did not restrain extravagant displays of enthusiasm by the burgesses and merchants of the town for the trade. Even as the *John and Robert* cleared for the Guinea Coast, the House of Commons was being presented with Plymouth's principal merchants' petition that the trade be made free and open to all. As with all petitions of this type, it seems to have been formulated with a blithe disregard for the truth:

> since the laying open of the Trade to Africa, divers Ships have been fitted out from this Port to that Coast, to the great Benefit of this Corporation, and Parts adjacent, employed in the Woollen Manufacture . . . [31]

In reality, as shown in Appendix 4, only five vessels cleared Plymouth with cargoes taken aboard there, and of these only two carried substantial quantities of locally produced cloth.

Though the merchants of Devon's south coast had joined vociferously in the late seventeenth and early eighteenth century debates on the trade to Africa, those of its northern shores steered a more conservative course. Considering Barnstaple and Bideford jostled each other for ascendancy after Exeter and Plymouth, and were deeply involved in the wool trade, their relaxed attitude to the question of Company monopoly is disconcerting. In fact, it can probably be attributed to their status as spinning rather than manufacturing districts. The latter areas (involved in weaving, fulling and dyeing cloth) lay in a broad semicircle around and to the north of Exeter. Barnstaple and Bideford's role, though not exclusive, was largely a result of their being the receiving ports for Irish wool which was spun into coarser English wool to produce a softer and more attractive product. During the fifteenth and sixteenth centuries Barnstaple had a considerable woollen industry and was the largest textile centre outside Exeter until 1600. However, as time passed the Taw estuary became blocked with sand and silt, severely hampering larger merchant shipping. No such problem presented itself at Bideford where the strong tidal currents of the Torridge made sure that its deep-water channels remained operative.[32] Thus it was to Bideford that most foreign trade, with its bigger vessels and deeper draughts, eventually passed in the late seventeenth and early eighteenth centuries.

England's colonial acquisitions in America helped sustain Bideford's growth. Until 1744 the town was the property of the Grenville family, who were deeply involved in the colonisation of Virginia and Carolina in the late 1500s. This led to sizeable American trade at Bideford which supplemented the port's woollen commerce with Holland and France and its considerable interests in the Newfoundland fishery trade. Predictably it was the tobacco trade with Maryland and Virginia which made the greatest financial impact in the period 1680–1730, and resulted in the town eclipsing its ancient rival, Barnstaple. With its ease of access to the Atlantic, strong trade connections with the American plantations, wealthy merchant families, and well established marine crafts of shipbuilding, servicing and repair, Bideford would seem to be an ideal candidate for mounting a venture to Africa. Yet despite its qualifications, no Guinea-trade venture – for slaves or otherwise – appears to have set sail from the port,[33] though at least one Bideford-registered ship was involved in the slave trade from Bristol. This was the *Castor* of 65 tons burden which left Bristol early in 1712 for Cork, where foodstuffs were loaded for Antigua. Captained by Richard Mullington (possibly brother or even the selfsame master of the earlier *Joseph Galley* of Bristol from Plymouth), the *Castor* cleared Antigua directly for the coast of Africa[34] with 9 hogsheads of rum, evidently designing for a 'double voyage'. None the less this was a Bristol venture, not a Bideford one.

The supply of labour to the new colonies of America and the West Indies entailed the shipping not only of black human cargoes, but white ones too, and here Bideford came into its own. Along with Scotland and Ireland, the west of England provided a significant proportion of indentured servants in the seventeenth and early eighteenth centuries.[35] Although their departures are not recorded in the Port Books of the time, as they were not a dutiable cargo, their arrivals were often recorded at their destinations. Unfortunately the picture cannot be entirely clear; Bideford vessels in the plantation trade often called at Cork or Dublin both for provisioning and for cargoes of foodstuffs on the outward leg of the voyage. A number of indentured servants arriving at the colonies aboard Bideford vessels may have been of Irish rather than West Country origin. Be that as it may, the volume was considerable. Two large groups arrived in Maryland in 1698 aboard the *Crown* and the *Integrity*, both of Bideford.[36] Between November 1699 and the following January, the colony of Virginia saw the arrival of no fewer than six vessels carrying goods and servants. These were the *Pearl* and the *Samuel* from Bideford, the *Mary and Elizabeth* from Bridgwater, the *George* from Plymouth, the *Unity* from Lyme Regis (owned by John and Robert Burridge) and the *George* from King's Lynn in Norfolk, the only vessel not from the West Country.[37] Bideford merchants, long connected with the founding of Virginia and Carolina, obviously realised the importance of regularly replenishing the colonies' pool of manpower. Since all transport costs were paid by the servants' new masters in the plantations, there was little financial risk in this traffic.

Though few, if any, of the vessels carrying indentured servants from Barnstaple and Bideford to the West Indies were also used in the slave trade, it may well have contributed to the Burridge family's eventual induction in that trade from Bristol, Lyme Regis and London; but not from Bideford or Barnstaple. The two ports, Bideford especially, remained tantalisingly close to entering the trade to Africa.[38] Certainly the basic cargoes lay close to hand. Woollen products were manufactured in the immediate area, vast quantities of tallow were daily imported from Ireland and many north Devon ships in the colonial trade carried consignments of iron, pewterware and even beads. However, until 1725 at least, these Bideford and Barnstaple vessels steered well clear of the African coast.

Despite the lack of vessels clearing Bideford for Africa it should not be assumed that the town's merchants were uninterested in the Guinea trade. It was much more that the proximity of Bristol tempted them to enter the trade there, rather than from their home port, and in this they were undoubtedly paralleled by their counterparts in the Somerset ports of Minehead and Bridgwater. As outport merchants habitually took their lead in the slave trade from others more firmly established at its centre, the Burridges of Lyme initially followed in the footsteps of Benjamin and Joseph Way of London and Bristol. At Exeter, Daniel Ivy and Henry Arthur relied greatly upon James Gould's London connections. Similarly in Bideford, where tobacco merchant John Parminter relied upon Bristol agent William Lisle to freight a Bristol ship – the *Elizabeth Galley* – to the Guinea Coast in January 1700.[39]

The similarity in date of departure of the *Elizabeth* and the *Daniel and Henry* is more than coincidental. John Parminter was Daniel Ivy's son-in-law, having married his daughter Elizabeth (after whom the vessel was named), in 1698.[40] The *Elizabeth*'s captain was William Levercombe, who had recently returned from a triangular voyage to Africa and the West Indies as commander of the *Beginning* of Bristol; much of this voyage had been carried out in tandem with the *Betty Galley* of Exeter and Levercombe probably came to Parminter on Daniel Ivy's recommendation.

It was not to be such a successful second bite of the cherry for Levercombe. Like Roger Mathew of the *Daniel and Henry*, he found competition on the Guinea Coast extremely tough, and was forced to complete his slave trading at Old Calabar (now in Nigeria). Notorious for the concealed bar across the mouth of the sheltered estuary, Old Calabar was to claim the *Elizabeth*, Levercombe allowing the vessel to run against the flukes of her heaviest sheet anchor as she lay awaiting the tide.[41] This was an unmitigated catastrophe for she was fully slaved. So fierce would have been the rush of incoming water that the crew would have taken to the ship's boat immediately, leaving those packed in the slave-hold to a watery grave. Levercombe, however, lived to slave another day.[42]

Following this disaster neither John Parminter nor his brother Richard ever speculated again in the slave trade. They continued to trade in a conventional way to the American and West Indian colonies for sugar and tobacco – the fruit of slave labour – but eschewed becoming directly involved in the quest for slaves.[43] Lured into the trade by the Act of 1698 they found – like many other Devon merchants before and after them – that the much-vaunted profits of the slave trade were to be found in the commodities resulting from it, rather than within the trade itself.

CHAPTER NINETEEN

Falmouth to Lancaster

CORNWALL, which points a delicate toe out into the Atlantic and gets a buffeting for its temerity, has two sides to its character. Its south coast is generously supplied with harbours and sheltered anchorages, and its indigenous tin-mining and smelting industry attracted a voluminous seaborne trade of a coasting and European nature in the eighteenth century. In comparison its north coast, which takes the brunt of the prevailing westerlies and is liberally studded with treacherous reefs and rocky headlands, offers little hospitality or safe refuge for the mariner.

Lacking passable roads for most of the year and with no major urban centre, Cornwall was practically a law unto itself in the early eighteenth century. In 1698 the south coast attracted the attention of the Navy Board, who hoped to establish a naval base overlooking the approaches to the Channel. Having scoured the coast for a suitable location the two principal candidate ports, Fowey and Falmouth, failed to find favour. The former was categorically eliminated from consideration as a naval base with a curt 'inadvisable to be chosen for any service for the Navy'. The latter fared only marginally better being 'clogged with very many inconvenient shoals and sudden soundings'.[1]

None the less, for those ready to run risks, Falmouth had its attractions. Smuggling was by far the largest and most profitable industry (as it was the length of the coast), and Falmouth's extreme westward position made it a natural choice as a base for the packet service to the American and Caribbean plantations. Primarily a mail service which began in 1688, it brought unprecedented prosperity, linking the port with the colonies and encouraging merchants to consider settling in Falmouth. The packet service was hardly typical of the merchant marine. Though the ships were of a considerable size

– between 150 and 200 tons burden – they relied on speed, not capacity, for their livelihood. Certainly cargo was carried, but it tended to be lightweight luxury items such as fine calicoes, silk, buckles, hats, lace and wine. As such it may be viewed as the 'air freight' of the early eighteenth century. The round trip to the colonies and back under an experienced captain took an average of a hundred days.[2] Often veterans with many years at sea, and occasionally past slave ship masters, these captains brought new horizons to Falmouth.

Apart from the packet boats, most long-distance overseas merchant shipping only touched at Falmouth for last-minute orders or used its harbour as a temporary refuge from storms. One ship which did so early in 1667 carried a ship's doctor, an Irishman from Connelstown, County Westmeath, though his family had originated from Huntwick in Yorkshire.[3] Few ships, apart from privateers or slave traders, carried seafaring doctors and the ship may have been on her final leg back from the West Indies when she was forced into Falmouth by foul weather. The doctor's name was Thomas Corker. He took to Falmouth and Falmouth, in the shape of Jane, daughter of merchant John Newman senior, took to him. They were married on 25 April of the same year.[4]

Nine months later – almost to the very day – a son, baptised Robert, was born to them. Another son, Thomas, was born two years later. Daughters Jane and Anne followed in 1672 and 1674.[5] The timing of these biennial occasions suggests that Doctor Corker continued to be regularly employed at sea on long-haul ventures. Not long after the birth of Anne Corker, however, her father died and her mother was left to bring up the family on her own. In this she was financially assisted by her brother, John Newman junior, then practising as an attorney. One of his clients was Bryan Rogers, the leading Falmouth merchant, and Newman prevailed upon him to take the eldest son, Robert Corker, off his hands as an 'apprentice gratis'. The lad proved to be 'of insinuating worldly parts': being commercially minded he progressed well under his master. Meanwhile his younger brother Thomas was packed off by his uncle John Newman to the Guinea Coast at the tender age of fourteen as an apprentice to the Royal African Company.[6]

Robert Corker learned his master's business well. So well that, as soon as he was out of his apprenticeship and in business on his own, he worked hard to bring his master down and set himself up in his stead. His success was such that, over the years between 1687 and 1693, Rogers found it increasingly difficult to remain solvent and

was forced to mortgage his house to his erstwhile apprentice. In 1693 he died and Robert Corker lost no time in making the house his own, 'turning with very little ceremony his late, very indulgent Mistress out of it'.[7]

Though Robert Corker now dominated the overseas export trade from Falmouth, Penrhyn and Truro,[8] his rise to prominence could not compare with that of his younger brother Thomas. Having entered the Company as a junior Writer, Thomas Corker quickly became Agent at the Company fort of York Island in the estuary of the river Sherbro. Securities for this responsible position (which Thomas Corker appears to have attained at the tender age of sixteen) amounted to £800 and were raised by Robert Corker and Alexander Cleeve,[9] one-time Company factor on the Guinea Coast, and later an active London separate trader. Though Robert Corker appears to have been pulling strings of his brother's career, probably envisaging himself as an eventual Guinea trade merchant, Thomas Corker had quite clear ideas of his own. Young, ambitious and more than ordinarily resilient – he had already outlived all his Company colleagues – this Corker could see an empire of his own taking shape.

By contemporary accounts – most notably that of Thomas Phillips, commander of the slave trade ship *Hannibal* in 1693 – Thomas Corker was a pleasant enough fellow. Corker was trading for ivory in his Company sloop the *Stanier* when Phillips arrived at Cape Mesurado. It was his first visit to West Africa and Corker made him most welcome, supplying him with an interpreter and provisioning his table with venison, courtesy of Corker's own band of *grommettoes*, or free hired Africans. Phillips had even more cause to feel gratitude when Corker, using his intimate knowledge of local customs, helped extricate him from a threatening encounter with a hostile chief which might otherwise have cost the newcomer his life. But Corker was not universally popular, and it is more than likely his treatment of Phillips was inspired not so much by charity as by hopes of future pecuniary gain. In fact Corker seems to have been heartily loathed by his subordinates. On his return from Cape Mesurado to the fort at Sherbro he was refused entry by his second-in-command. In the ensuing struggle firearms were discharged and several people were wounded before Corker regained possession.[10]

In the years immediately following Corker quickly consolidated his power base, first at Sherbro, and then at the Gambia. He took as his African wife a formidable lady known as Señora Doll, Duchess of Sherbro, a member of the Ya Kumba family, who ruled on the shore of Yawry Bay between the Sierra Leone peninsula and the Sherbro estuary.[11] Señora Doll became a resident wife; that is, she was taken to live within the factory compound and her maintenance charged to the Company, an arrangement which raised a few eyebrows in the counting house back in London. Corker also enrolled two of his young half-caste sons, Benjamin and Lawrence, on the Company books. When questioned about their place on the payroll he emphasised the dearth of reliable mulatto labour and the Company – for the time being – acquiesced.[12]

Corker's empire building proceeded apace. By the late 1690s he had developed the very profitable but fraudulent practice of keeping the best of the Company goods sent out for himself (by claiming they were damaged, and reporting them as such back to London), exchanging them for the highest-quality slaves and then requisitioning whatever ship came handy to freight them on his own account to the West Indies.[13]

Such was his organisation that he relied not only upon local shoreline caboceers for his slaves, but created 'feeder' lines of fresh slaves by employing his own small fleet of local boats to trade close inshore and upriver. The Company was not his only source of goods for barter. With Thomas now in a position of strength in Africa, and Robert's affairs progressing favourably in Falmouth it did not take undue imagination to envisage the possibilities of a profitable illegal private trade between the two.[14] Between October 1694 and January 1698, at least £550 worth of bills of exchange was remitted to Robert by Thomas to facilitate such trading.[15] This was only the tip of a huge iceberg of malpractice, involving shipping substantial numbers of slaves to the West Indies from the Gambia on Thomas Corker's own account (though the goods for barter had probably been sourced by Robert in Falmouth) which culminated in the ill-fated voyage of the *Dragon* from Topsham in 1699.[16] Throughout this time there was an absolute Company prohibition on private trading ventures by its employees.[17]

News of Thomas Corker's activities regularly reached London, so the Company appears simply to have turned a blind eye to his various misdemeanours. His approach to the Company was little less than cavalier. In 1696 the Company ship *Edward and William* had arrived in Jamaica with a consignment of slaves from Corker on the Gambia. So appalled were the Agents in Jamaica at their state – most were either diseased or afflicted with hernias and ruptures – that they complained bitterly: 'the ship had delivered the best at some other Island and carried only the Refuse thither'.[18] Corker survived, but the tide was beginning to turn against him.

The passing of the 1698 Act, severely reducing the Company monopoly, also helped concentrate the minds of senior Company officials in London. Faced with very real competition, they began to tighten up procedures, recognising that the freedom introduced by the opening of the trade to Africa would vastly increase opportunities for further malpractice. They warned Thomas Corker their patience was running out:

> Notwithstanding our extravagent misfortunes by your most egregrious delays in despatch of our ships, and not sending us any returns, and on the contrary encouraging Dutch interlopers & other Traders expressly against our orders, yet we continue still to make a further trial.[19]

Old habits die hard, and when news of the *Dragon* and other transgressions filtered back to Company headquarters in 1700, Corker was summarily dismissed, allegedly for 'living a very negligent and extravagent life'.[20] The dismissal took place while Corker was engaged in diplomatic activities of intricate importance, and smacked of using a sledgehammer to crack a nut.

Nothing could be easier than for the Company to point the finger at Corker and cry foul. But his years at Sierra Leone and the Gambia, while not free from peccadillo, were hardly unmitigated orgies of embezzlement. Though the Company conveniently chose to ignore the fact, its presence on the Gambia after the destruction of its fort at James Island by the French in the war of 1687–97 was largely due to Corker. Following the Treaty of Ryswick he had been instructed to 'resettle the Gambia and the Factory there . . . with conveniency and security and with no great expense'. Indeed, their own figures indicated that the cost of rebuilding James Fort would amount to £16–20,000. Naturally Corker was not made privy to these calculations. Neither did he have a clear field. The Gambia was now besieged by ten per cent ships and Dutch interlopers. But most serious of all was the arrival of emissaries from the French Senegal Company, eager to re-establish their former trade and political influence. For this purpose they sent out the redoubtable André Brue as Director-General in 1697. He quickly concluded a series of treaties with local chiefs and sent a chief factor and staff to re-establish the factories at Albreda and Geregia, as part of the effort to exclude English ten per centers from the river and coastal areas, which he did by seizing their vessels.[21]

Corker had rather a lot on his plate, yet he set about reasserting English influence with commendable zeal, settling factories close to the French, and on the River Gambia itself he insisted that any French boat wishing to trade above James Island could do so only with his consent. Those which failed to secure a pass from him were subjected to a barrage of cannon fire. Inevitably this led to diplomatic representations between France and England, and Corker was judged to have overstepped the mark. By this time Corker was aware that a *modus operandi* would need to be formulated between the French and English Companies and to this end he had already instigated a number of conferences with his French opposite number, André Brue. Horse trading was conducted amidst scenes of glorious ceremony which were marred only by Corker's insistence on wearing slippers to relieve what had been diagnosed as gout but was probably rheumatoid arthritis. The final conference was held aboard an English vessel. Brue put forward a series of proposals in which the English factories at Portudal and Joal would be closed down but freedom assured for English Company ships to trade there, provided his own French ships were allowed to proceed above James Island. Since these proposals incorporated several of Corker's own, he – according to Brue – felt personally prepared to accept them. It would be, in any case, a basis for a sound and workable agreement that would benefit both parties.

On 23 April 1700, while these discussions were still under way, news arrived via the vessel *Ann and Sarah* that Corker was being charged with embezzling Company property and indulging in private trade on his own account.[22] He was instructed to hand over immediately to his second-in-command, Paul Pindar, and return to England aboard the Company frigate *William*, expected at the Gambia within two or three days. Meanwhile, anxious lest he should slip though its fingers and set up in business for himself, the Company warned all their factors on the Coast:

> You are to take notice that Agent Corker is discharged our service and ordered home, but as already wrote, you must be upon your guard if he should desert and come to you he may not be entertained in any of our Forts or Factories, and the same of all that Gang of Rioters which he took with him to Gambia: we have already suffered too much by them.[23]

The premature truncation of Corker's career caused several of his money-making ventures which were in progress at the time to go sadly awry. Though he had amassed substantial capital in his stay on the African coast – Brue estimated 50,000 livres (£5000 sterling) – much of it was tied up in his own vessels and cargoes.[24] Naturally the Company believed he was worth much more, 'a great personal estate to the value of £20,000',[25] and was gunning for him as soon as the ship carrying him, the *William Frigate* under Captain Joseph Soames, anchored at Falmouth from the Gambia on 22 July 1700.[26] Corker even ran true to form on this occasion by importing a quantity of ivory and other Gambia produce under Soames' name without paying the 10 per cent tax due to the Company, though that did not come to light until 1713.

When Corker landed he was a sick man. Plagued by gout and weakened by malaria, he was unable to travel to London to face the inquiry the Company was eager to mount against him. He finally eluded their net altogether by dying in September 1700. At this final piece of impertinence the Company redoubled its efforts for compensation. In June 1704 their attorney, Martin Keigwin, travelled to Falmouth to prosecute the suit already brought by the Company against his mother, Jane, and brother, Robert Corker, for a share of his estate.[27]

Though Thomas Corker spent only sixteen years on the Guinea Coast, his influence – via his mulatto descendants – was to make itself felt well into the nineteenth century. But whereas a degree of sympathy can be felt for Corker's manoeuvrings and machinations, no such quarter can be allowed his mulatto offspring. They became the Borgias of the Upper Guinea Coast.[28] Through their mother, Señora Doll, they inherited the maternal claim to the chiefdom; through their late father they had learned fluent English. No other family group on the Coast was as well placed as the Corkers (or Caulkers as they later became) to profit by the slave trade. They reinforced their power with an intimidating standing army of *grommettoes* which became the basis of their military might in the numerous inter-tribal conflicts and territorial disputes that their activities caused.[29]

During times of peace these *grommettoes* were employed in the production of food and manufactures, often to provision European slave trade vessels, and assisted slave ships as pilots, canoemen and porters. From the vast area of land the Caulkers held in thrall (and indeed from their extensive slave labour plantations) slaves could be provided virtually on tap. Should their supply temporarily run dry, debtors to the Caulkers – and there were many – were often collected bodily and shipped off. In sum, the Caulkers, and their later cousins the Clevelands, directly facilitated through violence, oppression and corruption the sale of thousands of their fellow blacks to the West Indian and American plantations throughout the eighteenth and nineteenth centuries.[30] As elsewhere on the West African coast, but most clearly in Upper Guinea, the African ruling class – in the case of the Caulkers conveniently owing allegiance to neither African nor European codes of behaviour – joined hands with the Europeans in exploiting the African masses.[31]

The parish church of Falmouth contains a particularly fulsome (and misleading) commemorative tablet to the memory of Thomas Corker. As a piece of sanctimonious eulogy it is hard to see it as other than composed, possibly on Robert's orders, by one of his tame clergymen in later years, with tongue stuck firmly in cheek. Though perhaps a shade less resounding and pompous than the Latin original, this English translation captures the spirit of the occasion eloquently enough:

SACRED TO THE MEMORY
OF MR THOMAS CORKER
WHO DIED THE 10TH SEPTEMBER, AD 1700
IN THE 31ST YEAR OF HIS AGE.

The youth who lies here was renowned both in England and Africa. The former was his native land, the latter witnessed his warlike

deeds. After having driven the avenging Moor from the walls of
Gambia, he claimed sovereignty, not just for himself but for his
country. Returning home, he brought with him ivory, gold and
precious woods, laying down his life alas, not for himself, but for
his country. He died in the prime of life, snatched away by cruel
death, and England and Africa alike mourn his loss. Now marble
celebrates his virtues. He deserved a better memorial, and that he
himself might stand in this place for ever, cast in gold. Remember
that thou must die.[32]

Though this tablet is the outward and visible sign of Robert's
esteem for his brother, he commemorated him in a much more
pertinent manner by organising a voyage to Africa. For this he
engaged, late in 1700, the services of a sea captain called James
Brusser (who had recently returned to London from the Guinea
Coast with the *Happy Return* for John Lewis and Company) and a
vessel, which he christened the *Thomas* in honour of his late brother.
The venture was a considerable one and the variety of goods detailed
in the cargo manifest displays an intimate knowledge of those items
most favoured by the Guinea Coast caboceers. Before his untimely
death Thomas Corker undoubtedly had a hand in the selection of
goods: he may well have had a proportion of his capital invested in
the venture too. No one else was concerned in freighting the vessel
except for Samuel Eyre, a London merchant prominent in the slave
trade, whose cargo of beads, iron, cloth and metalware had been
shipped coastwise to Falmouth aboard the *Rebecca*, a London coastal
trader captained by Anthony Jenkins.[33]

Corker cleared the *Thomas* through Falmouth Customs on 8
January 1701. Her first port of call was Madeira, whither local
Falmouth merchant Robert Taylor had consigned four hogsheads of
salted pilchards, before Captain Brusser settled down in earnest to
trade on the Gambia. Doubtless the late Thomas Corker's erstwhile
family made Brusser feel extremely welcome for he took an uncon-
scionable time upon the Coast, eventually returning to London with
nearly 29 tons of redwood and 7 cwt. of ivory for Samuel Eyre
towards the end of February the following year.

There is no evidence that the *Thomas* was scheduled to carry out a
triangular voyage via the Caribbean or America, but it is virtually
inconceivable that Brusser traded neither for slaves nor gold. Equally
unlikely is the prospect of the *Thomas* returning directly to London
without calling at Falmouth. Unlike ivory and redwood – which
attracted Company import taxes of 10 per cent and 5 per cent

respectively – neither slaves nor gold were liable for duties on landing in England. Robert Corker would have had little use for redwood, which was used as a dye for cloth, since Cornwall had no industry that could process it. Gold was another matter entirely, and Robert Corker, already a man of substance, suddenly became richer still. He invested in four privateers, the *Betty Galley* of 1702, *Bachelor's Endeavour* of 1703, and the *Sea Nymph* and *Hooker Galley* of 1706.[34] (None paid dividends on its letters of marque with the exception of the *Sea Nymph*, which captured the Turkish vessel *Holy Cross* homeward bound from Malta via Cyprus in 1710.)[35]

If we cannot be sure that gold was landed at Falmouth from the *Thomas*, slaves certainly were. In fact Robert Corker presented his mother with one, a girl of sixteen called Chegoe whom she later took the unusual step of baptising in the parish church at Falmouth with the name Elizabeth.[36] The contemporary belief being that Africans, once baptised, could not be regarded as slaves and property, it is not surprising that of the handful of Africans it may be supposed the *Thomas* landed at Falmouth, she alone was accorded such a privilege.

Though he never indulged again in the trade to Africa, Robert Corker's career in Falmouth proceeded apace. True, there were setbacks. His brother Thomas, who had died at such an untoward time, had also done so without making a will. His mother expected to hold powers of administration, but these were delayed by the pleas of lawyer Martin Keigwin, representing the Royal African Company, who was about to launch into litigation in an attempt to recover some of the damage he alleged Thomas Corker had caused his clients on the Gambia. The case wound its tortuous way through Chancery without reaching any perceptible conclusion and Jane Corker was not granted letters of administration for her son's estate until April 1709.[37] However Robert Corker had more than enough to occupy his mind in his attempts – largely successful – to usurp the power of the local landowner, Sir Peter Killigrew. This he did by repeatedly holding the office of mayor and packing the corporation of the town with his own men, including merchants Edward Pearce and Stephen Jackson (Corker's brother-in-law). For more than three decades he ran the governing body of the town as his own and

> would not suffer any man to come into it who was not his own depending creature; and in his latter days set up a rule that none should be admitted into the body who were tenants to the estate [of Sir Peter Killigrew].[38]

As well as subverting various courses of justices (he had had plenty of practice on that score with the Company's entrammelled cases against his brother in Chancery) he introduced a number of novel ideas for raising revenue, the most outrageous of which was that newcomers into the corporation had to be licensed by that body before they could open a shop window; fees were payable to the mayor.

All of this was extremely parochial and Robert Corker sought a wider stage for his talents. In 1708 he was sufficiently well connected to be appointed Receiver of the Duchy of Cornwall and in that capacity was entrusted with large sums of money from tin mining.[39] About the same time, and perhaps not unconnected with the huge flow of capital passing through his hands, he began acquiring substantial properties around Bossiney. Possibly because of his Whig sympathies or because he was not considered trustworthy (both amounting to much the same thing in Lord Chancellor Harley's eyes), he was dismissed from the Receivership in 1712.[40] From tin he turned to copper, becoming heavily involved in Sir William Pendarves' smelting works in the following years.[41] Though firmly resident in Falmouth, Corker was not unaffected by the mania of speculation that unbalanced England, France and Holland in the years 1719–20 and that spawned such chimeras as the South Sea Bubble. Doubtless distance lent a certain enchantment to the eye, and these tempting 'bubbles' looked even more substantial when viewed from Falmouth. Though curiously loath to invest in the South Sea Company itself, Corker rushed to subscribe to Humphrey Morice's African Company (which was a solidly based and viable proposition),[42] and invested in a patent for a whale fishery off the Cornish coast (which was not). Fortunately he suffered no serious financial penalties as a result of his precipitate forays into speculation; even more providentially he was once again appointed to the Duchy, this time as Receiver-General to the Prince of Wales.

Morice's abortive Africa Company apart, Corker's dreams were now fixed in England. In 1722 he was returned as Member of Parliament for the Tintagel constituency of Bossiney, which he held to his death. His career as a parliamentarian was less than brilliant, and his tenure of the receiver-generalship less than honest. By 1729 he found himself in debt to the Duchy (on the receipts of the tin he had sold on their behalf) to the tune of £11,000. In a desperate bid to repair the damage he attempted to liquidate his holdings in land, but here he came a cropper for these were the very securities that guaranteed his position as Receiver: 'the bond of the Crown was such a terror to everybody that I could neither sell nor borrow any money on my estate . . .'

After all the years of wheeling and dealing Robert Corker had painted himself into a very tight corner. Inevitably the Duchy annexed all his property, a blow from which he could not recover. He died at the relatively early age of sixty-three, owing Frederick, Prince of Wales, as Duke of Cornwall, £23,000 in respect of arrears since June 1727.[43]

Any account of the mercantile life of Falmouth between 1690 and 1730 must needs concentrate on Robert Corker, for all other merchants of the time were little more than his auxiliaries. After his interest in the Guinea trade blossomed, bore fruit and withered in the short season of the *Dragon* and *Thomas* there remained in Falmouth little more than a marginal concern for trading with Africa. Fish merchant Edward Pearce had supplied the ten per cent ship *Mary Galley* of London with a few hogsheads of pickled herrings ('scadds') for her voyage out in 1701, and both he and Stephen Jackson consigned small cargoes aboard the *Expedition Galley* in November 1703.[44]

The *Expedition*, commanded by Samuel Parker, carried letters of marque and was bound for Madeira and the Guinea Coast on behalf of the London slave traders Houlditch and Brook. It was their occasional habit to use west of England ports (as they did Plymouth in 1708), shipping the goods coastwise from London or transporting them, as in this case, by land carriage. This would have added considerably to their overheads so either the merchants were attempting to improve the schedule of a particular vessel or, as here, war had recently broken out and the Channel was a dangerous place. In the larger outports crews were liable to be impressed, and the ships restricted to travelling in convoy.

Neither Jackson nor Pearce paid the 10 per cent tax on their cargoes so they may have been consigned to Madeira, not Africa. Though Houlditch and Brook had correctly deposited their 10 per cent payment (£63) with the Collector of Customs for Falmouth on the *Expedition* being loaded,[45] it took him an age to remit payment to the Company. This was by no means uncommon. As far as many Collectors in the outport were concerned, the 10 per cent tax was an interest-free capital loan until the Company heard from another source that an Africa-bound vessel had sailed. A sharp reminder letter would then be sent and the Collector would cough up. This did not happen at Falmouth until 1713. In reply to the Company's request for a complete breakdown of all ships and goods cleared in or out of Falmouth for and from Africa between 1698 and 1712, the Collector cited only the *Expedition*.[46]

What the town lacked in mercantile interest in Africa it made up in miners. If the Gold Coast was to live up to its name, miners would be needed to extract the gold. In comparison the lure of tin was pale indeed. As with all labouring men and women in the late seventeenth and early eighteenth centuries, the lot of the Cornish tin miner was a hard one. The intense hardship in the mining communities was aggravated by the fact that all sales of tin were channelled into 'coinages', which were held only twice a year. During the brief period of the Commonwealth the system fell into disuse and the restrictions placed upon sales were lifted. This deregulation sent the price of tin to new levels and wages rose accordingly. All this was lost with the Restoration. Coinage was reimposed and the bad old ways reigned again. During the period under examination, miners had to endure a long depression, and thousands came close to starvation.[47] To those given the chance, Africa beckoned like an El Dorado. In the opening years of the eighteenth century the Company organised a series of haphazardly planned expeditions in search of gold in the hinterlands behind the Cape Coast Castle, though the proportion of Cornishmen who embarked on these ill-conceived schemes is not known. The expeditions were ultimately inconclusive and there the matter rested, at least for the time being.

The year 1714 heralded a change. In this year the Earl of Yarmouth and a select band of wealthy subscribers formed the Company of Adventurers to the Gold Mines in Africa. Though more specific in tone, the venture differed little in substance from other aristocratic treasure hunts to Africa which had marked the latter half of the previous century. In 1715 two ships were dispatched from London: the *Melcombe Galley* under Captain John Wall, and the *Queen Anne* under the command of Drew Harris.[48] The manpower for the expedition came from Falmouth; a complement of miners embarked on each ship on her arrival at the port. Although tons of earth were returned to London, expert analysis revealed little trace of gold and the Earl of Yarmouth's Company slipped into abeyance.

In 1720 the Royal African Company, which had aided and abetted the Earl of Yarmouth's Company by giving their employees protection, board and lodging at their castles, took up the running itself. An experienced Cornish miner called Trengrove was commissioned to gather a band of men to proceed to Cape Coast Castle and search for gold. They boarded the Company ship *Onslow* at Falmouth in 1721 but were taken by the notorious pirate Bartholomew Roberts, whose two heavily manned and armed vessels, *Fortune* and *Ranger*, were wreaking havoc upon merchantmen on the Guinea Coast. The *Onslow* fell victim to the *Fortune* and was comprehensively robbed of her cargo, though the pirates seem – in general – to have respected life and limb. Except, that is, for William Mead. He was accused by Elizabeth Trengrove, wife of the captain of the miners, of behaving 'very rude, Swearing and cursing and forcing her hooped Peticoat off, and to prevent more of his Impudence which She was afraid off, went down into the Gun Room'.[49]

Miners were no use to pirates and they were released without ransom within a day or two, put ashore, and left to make the best of their way to the Cape Coast Castle.

When the Royal Navy, not long afterwards, ran down the two pirate ships and brought their crews to stand trial at the castle, William Mead was ordered to the Marshalsea prison for his offence. Henry Glaseby, master of the *Fortune*, was given a good reference by both Trengroves, turned King's evidence, and was acquitted. The band of miners was not quite so lucky. For them the Guinea Coast was a sentence of death and they all, with the exception of Trengrove and his wife, perished within a few months.

Following the dispatch of the *Onslow* the Company retained John Haughton of St Agnes, Cornwall to go to the Gambia as captain of another band of miners. Haughton agreed to supply the instruments for boring, collected a deputy, a smith, two swelterers and five labourers, and at Christmas 1721 embarked on the Company ship *Otter*, captained by Thomas Forster, at Falmouth. The difficulties of working in heavy tropical rains, their unfamiliarity with the terrain, the hostility of the local Africans and the constant threat of disease proved too much for this group for they all died shortly after their arrival at the Gambia. Nevertheless the Company persisted in its attempts to enlist Cornish miners – witness the ill-starred *Northampton* of April 1722 described in Chapter 17 – but only the dogged Trengrove developed any taste for Africa. His proposals were accepted by the Company, which sent yet another band of miners aboard the *Chandos* for the Cape Coast Castle in February 1723. This time the Company was far less sanguine about their prospects, remembering despondently in a letter to their factors at the castle that 'Trengrove has buried one set of miners already'.[50] The Company's gloomy forecast was only too justified, according to this contemporary report from one of their doctors on the Coast:

> at Cape Coast . . . I heard your Honours had sent from England a certain Number of Miners with two Gentlemen Overseers, who had made the Mineral Kingdom their particular Study and Practise. I found, at my Arrival, most of them dead, and those alive was now and then a digging of little Holes or Pitts in the Ground by the Sea-side, and searching that Earth for Gold; which appeared to me rather a Burlesque than any real Enquiry: But I was told afterwards that they durst not venture the Miners out of the reach of the Castle Guns lest the Negroes, who certainly took them for Conjurers, should make Incursions on them, to the Hazard of their lives.[51]

Presumably this remnant group of miners fared no better than their predecessors. Nothing further was recorded of them and with their decease Company interest in gold mining came to an end.

Though the county is surrounded on two of its three sides by sea, the men of Cornwall – unlike those of Devon – were reluctant seafarers. Like the great rocky cliffs and headlands of their native land they stoutly resisted the pull of the sea, beyond fishing or smuggling. Certainly Cornwall's geological structure and geographical outline was far from helpful. On its southern coast, only one port truly had the capacity to handle oceangoing merchantmen. On its northern shores there was not even that. In all this cliff-girt coast there are only two harbours, St Ives and Padstow, offering relief from the sea. Neither is ideal, the former being extremely dangerous in winds from north to east, the latter hazardous of entry at all times. Nor do they afford shelter for any craft larger than a coaster. Shipping from both ports in the early eighteenth century was largely limited to vast amounts of pickled and salted pilchards and herrings to Ireland, France, Leghorn and Venice. This required vessels of 10–40 tons burden, which would have severely cramped the ambitions of any local merchant who dreamed of making his fortune in the plantation trade.

So early eighteenth century trade between Cornwall and the colonies was slight. At a time when the ports of Devon were engaged in a roaring trade with both American and West Indian plantations, Cornwall lagged far behind. Setting aside the special service provided by the Falmouth packet boats, only five ships cleared from all the ports of Cornwall for the West Indies between 1697 and 1705, and two of those vessels came from London and Plymouth respectively.[52] Sparsely populated, industrialised only with regard to tin, boasting a local economy kept alive by smuggling rather than strong legitimate enterprise, and far from any vital route or financial centre, it is surprising that Cornwall had any connection at all with the slave trade.

Land's End provides both a geographical and a metaphorical turning point. Virtually all the ports we have looked at, from Berwick upon Tweed to Plymouth, have been characterised by extensive trade with Scandinavia, the Netherlands and France, according to their latitude. The ports of the western coastline of England (with the exception of Bristol and Liverpool, both major rather than minor outports), had much less scope for trade since their natural trading partner was Ireland. As shown in Chapter 18, special conditions there ensured that those two ports remained closely linked by historical precedents and a strong tobacco trade to the American plantations. Further up the Bristol Channel, the ports of Bridgwater Bay had no such advantages. Any Minehead or Bridgwater merchant contemplating a venture to the Guinea Coast would have sought to throw in his lot with a Bristol-based consortium, and take advantage of that port's expertise and availability of Guinea-trade goods.

No self-respecting merchant of either Minehead or Bridgwater would care to admit to that dependence. Instead they fostered the impression that the towns had a healthy trade with Africa and joined wholeheartedly in the pursuit of a free and open trade to that continent. Minehead merchant adventurers blandly observed 'That, since settling the Trade to the Coast of Africa, great Quantities of Woollen and other Manufactures of Great Britain have been exported to Africa' – a tactical statement which fell short of claiming direct involvement but reflected concern in the trade. Much bolder was the petition from Bridgwater, whose burgesses declared in 1710

> their Livelihood very much depends on Navigation to the Plantations, whose Products are raised by the Labour of Negroes, brought from the Africa Coast . . . the Petitioners fear [that the recovery of the monopoly by the Company] will very much lessen the Plantation Trade, for want of Negroes, and tend to the Decrease of Navigation, and confine most of the Plantation Trade to London only.[53]

The petition mentions neither woollen goods nor shipbuilding, so what was the trade which Bridgwater citizens feared would suffer a reduction if the number of slaves shipped to the plantations decreased? For an answer one must look at the commodities most in demand in the colonies, and though clothing and building materials came close to the top of the list, the perennial demand was for food. In that connection Minehead and Bridgwater warrant a special mention because of their herring fishery fleets. Though most active in trading to Cadiz, Leghorn and Venice (as with their Cornish cousins), they often went well beyond the limited aspirations of their Cornish counterparts. By the end of the seventeenth and beginning of the eighteenth centuries a flourishing trade with the West Indian plantations had been developed.[54] It was almost entirely limited to the supply of herrings, but such a supply was crucial to the West Indies: all their cultivated land had been given over to cash crops such as sugar, rather than subsistence farming for wheat or beef. Salted fish thus became the staple ingredient of a slave's diet, and still figures largely in Caribbean cooking. Though not playing an active role in the slave trade, the merchants of Minehead and Bridgwater benefited indirectly from its results.

Dominated by the prevailing westerlies and distant from large route and population centres, the remaining minor outports on England and Wales' west and north-west coastline show few dealings other than with Ireland. Gloucester's trade is limited to Dublin and Belfast. No records survive for Cardiff before 1714. Swansea is entirely given over to coal, most of which fed the insatiable proto-industrial centres of Bristol and Dublin. The survey is almost equally blank for Chester, Lancaster and Carlisle. However the *Friendship* of Chester, a small ship of 50 tons burden, did trade with Jamaica in 1700;[55] and the *Employment* of Lancaster made five voyages to the West Indies between 1698 and 1702, with massive quantities of manufactured goods.[56] Chester was not entirely indifferent to the prospect of the Company regaining its monopoly to Africa. Mindful of their past glory as a great medieval port and hopeful of a revival, Chester merchants wanted to keep their options open, petitioning Parliament in 1709 'that the said City was and is a Place of Considerable Trade, and situate commodiously for the Export of Welch Flannels and other Manufactures proper for the Trade to Africa.'[57]

The petition – like so many of its type – smacked of a heady and misguided optimism. Chester failed to exercise its options to Africa until well into the eighteenth century when the *St George* sailed from the port for Guinea and Barbados in 1753.[58] By that time Liverpool dominated the trade to Africa and the enormous expansion of manufactures in the vicinity resulted in trade goods for Guinea being much more easily acquired.

Chester took its time to enter the trade, and was never prominent in it, but Lancaster readily took up the challenge. First the town's shipbuilders constructed the *Penellopy* in 1720 for the Liverpool slave trade. Then, a decade later, the *William and Elizabeth* was both built and registered in Lancaster, though entering the slave trade from Liverpool. As the final step, from 1736 an occasional series of slave trade voyages actually issued forth from Lancaster. This turned into a flood in the mid-eighteenth century, with a total of eleven ships clearing Lancaster for Africa in 1755. Between then and 1776 Lancaster dispatched so many slavers that it became Britain's fourth-largest slave trade port. In its wake were dragged merchants and ships from other Lancashire ports including Preston and Poulton. Even Ulverston, on the other side of Morecambe Bay in what is now Cumbria, was tempted to follow suit.[59]

Given the interest taken by south and west of England merchants in the freeing of the trade to Africa and the consequent setting forth of ventures, it seems extraordinary that it took over half a century for their counterparts in the minor ports of England's north-west to mount their own response. But England in the early 1700s was vastly more provincial and insular than can be imagined today, being closer in spirit and character to medieval times than to our own world, which is dominated by time, media, transport and telecommunications. Nevertheless, in the early eighteenth century the minor ports of the north-west, England's 'forgotten corner', had one surprise up their sleeves. Cloaked by its overwhelming trade in coal to Ireland, hidden from the rest of the country by forbidding fells, this small town – truly a dark horse, despite its name – is the subject of the next chapter.

CHAPTER TWENTY

Whitehaven

THERE are few more desolate stretches of coast than that between Barrow-in-Furness and the Solway Firth. For much of the year it is pounded by the great grey rollers of the Irish Sea and lashed by rain-laden westerly gales. Dense tussocky grass crowns its headlands in defiance of blustering storms which, unappeased, threaten to uproot the gnarled and twisted trees that lean inland, their backs bent permanently double by force of wind and time. It seems the very beaches themselves have been scoured of sand, for bare rock predominates as one moves north. Here England, a green and pleasant land, seems turned to iron. In vain one searches for relief, a quiet corner of warm reflection; but instead is faced with the inhuman, the rearing head of Sellafield's nuclear excrescence which dwarfs all before it, nurturing deep within its heart the seeds of total destruction.

If Sellafield is the cuckoo, eternally demanding more land, labour and resources, then Whitehaven is the unfortunate nest. Situated a few miles to the north of Sellafield, the time will come when it will discover it hatched not a bird but a basilisk. Yet the future reflects the town's past, for it was built on the promise of power; the landscape, as desolate in the seventeenth century as today, held unseen riches in the shape of abundant coal seams. The local landowner, Sir John Lowther, established the town (then little more than a fishing village) as a coal port during the latter half of the seventeenth century. It thrived to such an extent that no seventeenth- or eighteenth-century Lowther could envisage a time in which coal would not be the backbone of the west Cumberland economy.[1]

Coal lay at the heart of Whitehaven, but arteries were needed to pump it to the growing industrial centres of Dublin and Belfast where a ready-made and expanding market existed. Ultimately this market was to provide the foundations upon which all other developments in west Cumberland were built. At the beginning of the last quarter of the seventeenth century, however, Whitehaven gave little indication of the meteoric rise in fortunes which would firmly establish it as one of the major ports of the kingdom, a rise for which Sir John Lowther was chiefly responsible.

Realising that his problem was twofold – lack of labour and only the most rudimentary of harbours, offering little protection against the prevailing westerlies – Sir John embarked on an ambitious plan of expansion. To attract labour a grid of streets was laid out to the north-east of the village, and some houses constructed.[2] Others shortly sprang up helped by Lowther's grants of 'estates of inheritance' and loan of capital at 5 per cent. An early and active member of the Royal Society, Sir John's enlightened paternalism and vision led him to plan wide streets and substantial plots. It may well be that his early friend and associate, Sir Christopher Wren, helped him to specify the general layout of the new town as well as advising on the kinds of houses he wished to have built there. For Sir John, though enlightened, was not negligent: a manorial court regulated both builders and owners in much the same way as a municipal council would today. Nor was Sir John's paternalism merely altruistic: it was coupled with a commercial drive to build his family fortunes that would do credit to any twentieth-century businessman.

Hand in hand with the development of the new town went that of

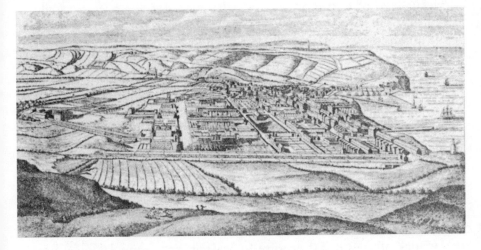

East prospect of the town and harbour of Whitehaven, 1738

the harbour. Despite being poorly endowed with what even the most optimistic could hardly claim was more than a sandy indentation on the coast, a major construction programme was instituted, financed by Lowther money, to enable the colliers to anchor safely. By 1690 the new harbour and breakwaters were in position. The cumulative effect of new town and harbour can be seen in population and trade figures over the ensuing quarter-century: the population rose from 2,222 in 1693 to 4000 in 1713.[3] Only a handful of vessels were registered at Whitehaven prior to 1690, yet more than 70 ships were based there by 1705. And tobacco imports, negligible before the building of the new port, totalled a colossal 1,639,193 lb. in 1712 – and still rising. Coal, fuelling the industrial growth of Dublin at the end of the seventeenth century, remained the core of this activity; and every chaldron exported benefited Sir John Lowther. By 1693 he was by far the biggest supplier of coals to Whitehaven's collier fleet: his customers were the collier owners, for Sir John did not own or operate any vessels of his own in the coal trade, though he did dabble on occasions in the plantation trade to Virginia. His method of supplying the collier fleet meant that the more voyages each collier made in a year the greater his revenue from coal. The efficiency and maintenance of the harbour was of crucial importance in guaranteeing stability and growth: the Lowther family refused to relinquish control over the harbour until 1709 and even then they dominated the board of trustees and retained a power of veto.[4]

Remarkably, the expansion of Whitehaven took place against a background of European wars which suppressed the overseas trade of many similar ports in the rest of the country. The reasons behind the expansion are not immediately obvious but fall into two categories, location and illusion. Whitehaven, far to the north of England, lay well outside the normal shipping lanes and so was relatively free from harassment by enemy privateers. Some merchants from outside the Cumberland area took advantage of Whitehaven's 'north channel' to the Atlantic and rerouted their cargoes in that direction. The security of the 'north channel' had particular relevance to the tobacco trade with the American colonies. As a result Whitehaven was to vie with both Bristol and Liverpool for domination of this traffic throughout the first half of the eighteenth century. But by far the most significant reason behind Whitehaven's stupendous rise in overseas tonnage clearances in the eighteenth century is a simple statistical illusion: coal exports to Ireland were counted as foreign trade even though liable only to coastal duties.[5] The distortion this created has resulted in Whitehaven standing second to London in tonnage clearances for much of the eighteenth century.

As the 1660s gave way to the 1700s, Whitehaven rode on the crest of the industrial wave which rolled steadily northwards in search of fuel. Though his heart lay with coal, Lowther was not blind to new industrial possibilities. There was, after all, no alternative fuel supply to his coal. Accordingly he took a keen interest in local developments,[6] and occasionally invested in industrial facilities which related to the processing of imports. Raw sugar was boiled in the town before being re-exported or sent by land carriage to Newcastle upon Tyne, or coastways to southern Scotland and Carlisle.[7] In 1699 a pipe-making factory was established to complement the industry in tobacco processing which was already in existence. But Lowther seemed loath to invest in new developments relating to exports, being content to supply fuel when and if the time came. The brunt of the financial burden for establishing new industries was borne by the area's lesser gentry, the overseas merchants.

Whitehaven's coming of age was never short of growing pains. In the 1690s Ireland prohibited the export of corn, and grain had to be shipped into Whitehaven from elsewhere in England, revealing the town's dependence upon outside sources for even the most basic foodstuffs. Following this setback a clause in the Irish woollen manufacturing Act of 1699 denied Whitehaven the right to import Irish wool for fear it would pass to Scotland.[8] The outbreak of war in 1702 brought embargoes on sailings from the port: the point of an embargo was to tie up vessels and create a pool of maritime labour in the town, which the Navy could then impress. Since an embargo was always taken as the harbinger of the press-gang, all the sailors left town and trade came to a standstill. Finally the union with Scotland in 1707 paved the way for unwelcome competition from the Scots in the English coal and tobacco trade: the direct intervention of Scottish merchants in the re-export of tobacco proved especially detrimental to Whitehaven interests.[9]

Of all these setbacks the most serious in relation to trade with the plantations was the Irish Wool Act. Vessels bound for the colonies needed an export cargo, and cloth was especially popular. Cumberland textiles were unsuitable for the colonial market, being too coarse in texture, but Lowther had great hopes of alleviating the rough northern fibres with softer Irish wool in much the same way as Exeter producers softened Devon cloth with Spanish wool. In 1699 he optimistically predicted that Cumberland broadcloth – with the addition of Irish wool – would soon stand comparison with any others.[10]

The 1699 Act dashed these hopes and brought his textile enterprise to a standstill. It also drove home Whitehaven's absolute reliance on secondary sources of supply if the port was to entertain any further hopes of trading with the plantations. So Whitehaven vessels joined the plantation trade at Dublin or Belfast by loading quantities of Irish beef and other provisions (including colossal numbers of candles made from Irish tallow) for the West Indian and American colonies. The colonies' agricultural state was so dominated by the cash crops of sugar, tobacco and cotton that – though in the midst of plenty – they were unable to feed themselves adequately. Sadly the only contribution that Whitehaven could make in terms of direct exports to the plantations was manpower: large numbers of indentured servants, many little more than children, were persuaded aboard Whitehaven merchantmen. To his credit Sir John Lowther became extremely concerned about this 'labour trade' – it was after all a drain of resources and taken from an area which could ill afford it – and took steps to proscribe it.[11]

The passing of the 1698 Act curtailing the monopoly of the Royal African Company and freeing the trade to Africa passed unremarked by Lowther or his stewards, despite Sir John's being one of the few country gentlemen (though he lived mainly in London) to hold stock in the Company.[12] Apparently oblivious to the debate that had raged about the bill's passing, Whitehaven merchants refused to be drawn into the trade at that stage.[13] Indeed Whitehaven was in a difficult position to export anything of consequence in the slave trade: shipping coals to Africa would have made carrying them to Newcastle look distinctly profitable. Nevertheless Whitehaven merchants, though geographically isolated, had been monitoring the possibilities of colonial trade through contacts and relatives. Late in 1697 John Gale,[14] Lowther's steward of collieries at that period, wrote to Sir John in London:

> My son George is expected here to navigate the ship *Cumberland*[15] bound for Virginia . . . my son Matthias sails from London to Jamaica as mate but is first to victual at Cork . . . that voyage is an undertaking of Mr Bennett's and Mr Isaac Milner's . . .[16]

The excerpt, though short, reveals links with the Royal Navy, the plantations, the slave trade and Ireland which would benefit Whitehaven merchants in the coming years. Both George[17] and Mathew[18]

Gale were naval officers turned merchant master mariners and George's appointment as master of the *Cumberland* must have been a matter of some gratification for him. She was a capacious, newly built vessel straight from the Whitehaven stocks and was designed specifically for the Virginia tobacco trade; most Whitehaven tobacco trade ships were colliers on off-peak summer voyages across the Atlantic.

Brother Mathew Gale's presence aboard 'an undertaking' of Isaac Milner's was not coincidence. A near contemporary from White-haven whose family was fiercely Nonconformist,[19] Milner had settled in London and was deeply involved in the wine trade from Madeira and Lisbon, where a distant branch of the Milner family had important trade connections. In these early days Isaac Milner's partner was Humphrey Morice, later to become (with assistance from Milner) London's pre-eminent slave trader, then director of the Bank of England, and finally that august institution's most notorious embezzler.

Though now permanently resident in London, Isaac Milner was to exercise a decisive influence upon Whitehaven merchants who were considering the option of trade to Africa. He showed them the way; after the 1698 Act he dispatched a prodigious number of slave trade ventures to the Guinea Coast from London and Bristol. Between September 1698 and June 1712 (shortly before the trade was finally thrown open) Milner was the prime mover behind twenty-four Guinea ventures with an aggregate cargo value in excess of £24,000.[20]

Vociferous in his demands that the 10 per cent tax be abolished and the trade thrown open, Milner displayed an unflagging energy in the cause of the separate traders and was the rallying-point for the anti-Company lobby.[21] During the first three decades of the eighteenth century he also fulfilled an important political and financial role for Whitehaven's colonial trade merchants. His presence in the capital and his access to policy-makers of the day made him an unparalleled channel of communication. Many Whitehaven bills of exchange were drawn on him during this time.

The appearance of such families as the Gales and Milners shows how successful Sir John Lowther had been in attracting mercantile and maritime expertise into Whitehaven in the last quarter of the seventeenth century. He had no hesitation in enlisting Dissenters – indeed wished to attract them by toleration and encouragement, granting them land on liberal terms for the erection of a chapel in February 1694[22] – but the Dissenting families of Gale, Lutwidge,

Milner and Gilpin among others later proved a handful for Sir James Lowther, his son.

By the turn of the century Whitehaven was fully able to take advantage of its Atlantic-facing position. It had the location, the capital, the merchants and the marine expertise.[23] Prominent amongst the merchants was Thomas Lutwidge, a witness to the 1694 grant of land for a Dissenting chapel and subsequently one of its trustees, and a powerful voice in the cause of Dissent. He was of Anglo-Irish stock and had started his career as an officer in the army of William III.[24] About the year 1690 he had set up in business in Whitehaven as a wine merchant, then branched out into tobacco. Since tobacco plantations were conveniently close to sugar plantations it was not long before Lutwidge, with the sweet smell of profit in his nostrils, made a bee-line for the Caribbean. Early in 1707 he freighted the *Hannah-Maria*, under the commmand of his nephew Walter, to Jamaica and Antigua. She returned in September of the same year, groaning under a cargo of West Indian produce. Even dour old John Spedding, Lowther's colliery agent, ever unwilling to admit money could be made out of anything but coal and even less willing to acknowledge the same to Sir James Lowther, was forced to concede that Thomas Lutwidge would 'be a Great Gainer by the Voyage'.[25] Both Thomas and Walter Lutwidge – and their respective descendants – were destined to spearhead much of Whitehaven's trade to Africa and the New World during the ensuing half-century.

For the present they were much concerned with the attempts of the Royal African Company to regain its monopoly of trade to Africa. Not that any Whitehaven merchant had ever traded to Africa, but they had of course a very direct participation in the tobacco trade. And tobacco was grown by slaves of whom the plantation owners, in the days of the Company monopoly prior to 1698, could never receive enough. So it was because tobacco, not Africa, was close to their hearts that Mathew and Lowther Gale, Samuel and William Bowman, Robert Biglands and Thomas Lutwidge (amongst others) penned the following rather exaggerated solicitation to Parliament:

> your petitioners depend wholly upon their Trade and Navigation, especially to the plantations of Virginia and Maryland where Tobacco is principally produced by Labour of Negroes, furnished hitherto Chiefly by the Separate Traders to and from Guinea . . .[26]

Perhaps the hand of Isaac Milner, then one of London's leading

separate traders, can be detected behind Whitehaven's two petitions,[27] but the responsibility was by no means entirely his. Merchants throughout the country repudiated anything which smacked
of monopoly, and doubtless Whitehaven – like anywhere else –
wished to see its options kept open. Africa, as had been heard from
Isaac Milner, was not a destination devoid of profit and might be
gainfully included in a voyage to Virginia or Maryland.

Trade with the West Indies had been desultory in comparison with
the constant but hardly spectacular trade with Virginia, but from
1710 a major expansion occurred in dealings with the plantations. A
new confidence imbued Whitehaven merchants, who now felt they
could stand on their own mercantile feet without financial aid from
Sir James Lowther. Local industries were gearing themselves up to
new trading possibilities. At nearby Furness the introduction of blast
furnaces in 1711 dramatically improved the area's production of iron;
in 1712 Sir James Lowther engaged a Mr Barwise to construct and
manage a sugar house in Whitehaven.[28] This was no altruistic move,
for Lowther-owned coal fuelled the sugar processing. Nor was it a
flash in the pan development: the sugar boiling house continued
under Mr Barwise's supervision until 1726 when it was taken over
by Lowther's erstwhile estate steward William Gilpin, and his
brother John. Perhaps most importantly of all, for the mainstream
plantation trade in sugar and tobacco demanded larger vessels than
the colliers that usually tripped to Ireland and back, control of the
harbour – though still under Lowther influence – was no longer
directly in his hands. In 1709 the trustees had the harbour deepened,[29]
and the sea defences reinforced with a counter mole: in 1712 the Old
Pier was extended.

A new order was rapidly overtaking the old, for these improve-
ments could not benefit the coal trade, but were crucial to the
development of the plantation interests. An irresistible mercantile
optimism swept through Whitehaven. Thomas Lutwidge, by now
the principal merchant, engaged three apprentices in 1711 in an
unprecedented expansion.[30] Shipbuilding yards were a hive of activity
with as many as six vessels on the stocks.[31] The mood in Whitehaven
reflected the spirit of the nation. An end could be seen to the war
and, perhaps most pertinent to Thomas Lutwidge's plans, the Royal
African Company had signally failed in its attempt to reimpose its
monopoly on the trade to Africa.

Long familiar with the eastern seaboard of the American colonies,
Whitehaven's ships' captains and their merchant backers had no

experience of maritime and trading conditions on the West African coast. Most merchants contemplating the Guinea trade would have ventured a few cargoes upon a ship bound from London or Bristol on an experimental basis, but not Thomas Lutwidge. In early 1710 he engaged a sea captain called Thomas Rumball, not a local mariner, to take his *Hannah-Maria* (an ex-privateer of some 90 tons burden) to Dublin for provisions and then on to Jamaica[32] with her cargo of foodstuffs. Having safely arrived at her destination, all transactions were doubtless carried out to Thomas Lutwidge's satisfaction for on Rumball's return Lutwidge assigned him the command of the brigantine *Swift* for Africa. As far as can be ascertained, Rumball had never ventured to Africa, and indeed there is no evidence he had actually been to sea before 1710.[33] Given the nepotistic character of mercantile life it is highly probably that he was the brother of Hannah Rumball, Thomas Lutwidge's first wife, who had died some years before.[34] The main branch of the Rumbold family in the seventeenth century had been staunch Royalists and had been rewarded for their pains come the Restoration. One of them, William, was made Surveyor-General of Customs in 1660 and his son Edward followed in his footsteps in the early eighteenth century.[35] This connection may have borne fruit later on, for Thomas Lutwidge's eldest son Charles (from his second marriage) made a spectacularly swift rise through the Customs and Excise to become Surveyor-General and Comptroller of the coasts of Westmorland and Cumberland.

Thomas Lutwidge was not alone in contemplating the riches to be gained by participating in the Guinea trade. The extensive and powerful Gale family could see the barometer of fortune pointing that way as well as any, but their mode of operation was less precipitate than Lutwidge's. Where he plunged in, they tried the temperature of the water. This was the reverse of what could have been expected. Slaves were hardly an unknown commodity to the Gales, for George Gale utilised them to work his plantation in Maryland and had previously brought at least one of them, a domestic slave called Jane, back to live in Whitehaven.[36]

The Gales' candidate for the slave trade was Lowther Gale, then in his late twenties. In the summer of 1710 he was commissioned master of the *Nancy Galley* of London,[37] bound for the Guinea Coast on behalf of Peter Hollander, leading slave trade merchant. The voyage was not a success: Company factors at the Cape Coast Castle reported that she had been taken by an enemy privateer early in March 1711 while under Captain Gale's command.[38] Some anomaly is evident here since in early January Lowther Gale had been named as captain of the letter of marque ship *Cumberland* owned by Nicholas Gale of Whitehaven.[39] Lowther Gale's sureties on this occasion were provided by the London merchants Henry Cairns and Peter Prompaind of College Hill; it is conceivable that the *Nancy* was captured late in 1710 and that the letters of marque were taken out in expectation of Lowther Gale's early return home. However, privateersmen generally ransomed ship, crew or cargo and occasionally all three, a procedure which took some considerable time; hopes of Lowther Gale's early release could not have been seen as other than impossibly optimistic.

No such irreconcilable mystery shrouds the career of Thomas Rumball and the *Swift*. She declared letters of marque on 4 November 1710 (on bonds again put up by courtesy of Henry Cairns and Peter Prompaind)[40] and cleared Whitehaven for River St Vincent on the Guinea Coast in the first few days of 1711, Thomas Lutwidge being her sole owner and setter-forth. The declared value of her cargo when clearing Whitehaven was a paltry £260; the suspicion must be that Lutwidge was severely underestimating the value to minimise payment of the 10 per cent tax due to the Company or that he intended to load a substantial addition to his cargo at Dublin, or both. Initially the sun seemed to shine on the *Swift*; Rumball traded easily around the Cape Coast Castle during April and May and cleared the Guinea Coast by late June.[41] Towards the end of the middle passage and probably within a few days' landfall of Jamaica, his good fortune ran out.

At precisely the time that Robert Lowther, Governor of Barbados, was reading

> the French privateers that infest this Coast are all Sloops, which sail very well, that in such smooth seas as we generally have here it is absolutely Impossible for any Man of War to come up with them. And that you seeing any in the Latitude they only stretch farther to the Windward and still Continue Cruising for our Merchant Vessels and do often take many of them.[42]

disaster struck the *Swift*. Despite her substantial armament and numerous crew (now debilitated after weeks at sea, and months spent standing off the African coast) the *Swift* was overhauled and captured by a French privateer, and relieved of her cargo of ninety-five Negroes. She arrived in Jamaica on 21 August 1711 with nothing to show for her trouble but ballast.[43]

Clearly Whitehaven's baptism into the slave trade was hardly auspicious. But whereas the Gales shunned all further consideration of it to concentrate on more traditional outlets for their mercantile talents, Thomas Lutwidge found it suited his interests and complemented other areas of trade in which he had a stake. He also sought redress for his losses occasioned by the taking of the *Swift*'s cargo, news of which had reached him from Jamaica: in January 1712, before Rumball's return to Whitehaven with tobacco from Carolina, he set forth his ship the *Friendship* under Isaac Langton on a privateering expedition.[44]

In the meantime, though Lutwidge's tobacco import–export business was undergoing an unparalleled period of growth, plans were being laid for his next slave trading venture. All that held it back was the lack of suitable locally produced goods, a factor that plagued all ventures to the Guinea Coast from Whitehaven at this time. For, despite the availability of northern cotton goods, Irish tallow and Irish iron, the area offered little else.

The problem of procurement is clearly seen in Thomas Lutwidge's next venture for the Guinea Coast. The 1698 Act expired in July 1712 and was not renewed: henceforward the trade to Africa was free and open to all on payment of the usual export duties, where these applied. Lutwidge correctly foresaw that a host of merchantmen would be gathering in the Atlantic and Channel ports to clear for the Guinea Coast. To give Thomas Rumball in the *Swift* a more competitive edge he brought together the most exotic cargo that had ever been seen in Whitehaven, including photaes, tirlannas and japanned scales, to the considerable discomfiture of the Customs officials who vainly attempted to record them accurately in the Whitehaven Port Books. The *Swift* sailed early in November 1712, ostensibly bound for Dublin and the Madeira islands, a cover story which suited Thomas Lutwidge well for Rumball repeated it on all subsequent voyages in his employ. Quite why is another matter; since no 10 per cent tax was now payable, the true destination would not attract any financial penalty. The *Swift* was certainly bound for Dublin, a regular port of call for Lutwidge's Guinea ventures. In all probability she also made landfall at Madeira, whose wines were acceptable both to Guinea Coast caboceers (who actually preferred French wines by this stage) and planters in the West Indies. This pattern of trade to Guinea via Dublin and Madeira was unusual but not unique: in 1720 the Company ship *Otter* sailed from the Thames to Dublin for salt beef and pork, thence to Madeira for wine and so to the Gambia for slaves.[45]

This time around, Rumball's presence on the Guinea Coast attracted neither comment nor notice from the Royal African Company. Competition for available slaves was intense and the *Swift* cleared from the Guinea Coast in the first week of May 1713 in company with the *Sacheverell Galley*, of Bristol. On 26 June the two vessels made landfall safely in Barbados. Next day the slaves were discharged in groups, the *Swift* delivering 122 in all. Unfortunately neither of the captains observed the rule that silence is golden: when the news spread that three Company ships and a multitude of independent traders were on the Guinea Coast, shortly bound for the West Indies, the bottom dropped clean out of the market in anticipation of a glut. Company Agents, always pleased to see independent traders in difficulties and still smarting from their reversal of fortunes the previous year, informed Africa House:

> the slaves imported per the *Sacheverell* and the brigantine were sold to some persons who send them to Martinico where they bear a good price. They bear very indifferent prices at Barbados by means of the sickness there is among them, the Dearness of Provisions and the Numbers they are advised they may shortly expect.[46]

Rumball, aware that a small flotilla of slave ships was heading for Barbados, and fearing a sharp rise in the price of sugar in the face of so much competition for a return cargo, quickly took 47 tons of muscovado sugar aboard and departed. His fears were not groundless, though calamity was on its way from a more capricious quarter than he imagined. The *Sacheverell*, which had not been so quick off the mark, was still in Barbados when the weather suddenly broke and a massive storm drove her and several other vessels ashore, causing them serious damage. By this time the *Swift*, true to her name, was within a few days' sail of Whitehaven, which she reached on 31 August. In considerable need of a refitting, the *Swift* was temporarily taken out of commission.

Meanwhile the signing of the Treaty of Utrecht in 1713 signalled the cessation of war. It also marked the end of Lutwidge's profitable sideline in privateering. His *Whitehaven Galley* (under the command of his nephew Walter Lutwidge), which had been remorselessly harrying French shipping off the Newfoundland banks, was ordered home and Thomas Lutwidge had her fitted out for a voyage to Guinea. He may have been prompted by hearing of the success of the *Whitehaven*'s old companion-in-arms, the *Provost Galley*. Under the command of veteran slave captain Nurse Hereford, the *Provost* had delivered 240 slaves to Jamaica in September 1713.[47] Just two months later Thomas Rumball cleared the *Whitehaven* for the Guinea Coast. There he traded profitably at Sestos, just north of Cape Palmas, where his activities caused dismay to Kendall Hudson, commander of the Company ship *Union*, who expected the Coast to be clear and instead

> found Capt. Rumball in the *Whitehaven Galley*: that going to pay his respects to the King he found a great Gun Mounted, which was sold him by Capt. Rumball ... made but little trade there being dogged by said Rumball.[48]

Having loaded some 300 slaves, Rumball cleared for Barbados in company with the *Fanteen Galley* of that island, under John Forster. Arriving in Barbados on 31 August 1714 with only 148 slaves still alive (the death rate on the *Fanteen* was even worse; only 140 survived of the 350 taken aboard) Rumball, mindful of his loose talk on his previous visit, complained bitterly about 'the price of Negroes on the Coast, men being at £31 per head'. Notwithstanding this ploy, Rumball's destination was actually Jamaica. Eight more slaves died on the passage there which, probably because of the contrary winds or poor navigation, took a further month to complete. Eventually, on 21 September, Rumball delivered '140 Negroes which sold at £15 per Head'.[49] Though this seems an extraordinarily low return and could scarcely have covered Lutwidge's costs, the Company ship *Worsley Galley*, arriving at the same time, could do no better, selling 290 slaves for £4,280 or £14 15s. each. Three weeks later the *Whitehaven* cleared for the Bay of Campeche in ballast, hoping to load logwood, which provided dye for the Cumberland cloth industry. Early in 1715 she doubled back to Jamaica and topped up with sugar for the return leg to Whitehaven, entering her home port on 20 March 1715 with muscovado and logwood.

Sugar was no longer an unusual cargo to be discharged at Whitehaven. The number of ships freighted directly to the Caribbean in 1710[50] had doubled by 1715 when the *Hopewell*, *William*, *Peace* and *Confirmation* cleared for Barbados and the *Stanhope* and *Susannah* for Antigua.[51] The last of these vessels – a French-built pink of 42 tons burden – was an ex-French privateer chased and caught by Walter Lutwidge in the *Whitehaven Galley* in 1711 for which Thomas Lutwidge had paid £100.[52] In 1715 her outgoing cargo consisted almost entirely of candles, and her return cargo of sugar, most of which was exported directly to Dublin and Belfast. As with tobacco, any profit on sugar derived primarily from export to larger population centres.

It is tempting to view this expansion of Whitehaven trade with the Caribbean as linked to the appointment of Robert Lowther, cousin to Sir James Lowther, as Governor of Barbados in 1710. Though Sir James instructed his agents to assure all Whitehaven merchants that 'if any ships will venture to Barbados they may expect all the favour that my cousin Robin Lowther, the new Governor can show them',[53] there is little to suggest any Whitehaven merchants took him at his word. For his part, Robert Lowther looked far more to London than the comparatively insignificant port of Whitehaven for his trade links. Though he owned a sizeable Barbados plantation from 1713 to about 1731 there is no indication he bought any slaves during this time direct from Whitehaven Guinea-trade ships: in the periods 1715–16, 1719–20 and 1725 Robert Lowther's plantation factor recorded the purchase of slaves solely from Barbados slave merchants Robert Harper, Thomas Withers, William Cogan and Thomas Ward. Nor was any sugar dispatched to Whitehaven from his estates: it was all consigned to Messrs Tilden and Mayne of London.[54] Whitehaven's ventures in the slave trade were simply a reflection of an increased expansion in colonial trade, perhaps more marked in Whitehaven's case, but common to all the ports of England. Sir James Lowther's remark about his cousin Robert is almost a *non sequitur* in the correspondence between Lowther and Spedding: the letter books of the time reveal a single-minded concentration on the vicissitudes of the coal trade and only occasionally admit details on the harbour, the new church, and the collection of outstanding debts – of which Lowther as the main source of capital was chief creditor – from such families as the Gales and Gilpins.

Of all the merchants the least indebted was Thomas Lutwidge. For him one trading venture fed directly into the next and by the time Thomas Rumball had returned from Jamaica in March 1715, Lutwidge's plans for a fourth triangular venture were well under way. Accordingly the *Whitehaven Galley* again cleared Whitehaven Customs in the following September for Dublin and 'Madeira'. Her cargo for Dublin consisted of coal and though an unlikely and hardly promising start for a Guinea-bound vessel, this short first leg across the Irish Sea was virtually the rule for Whitehaven ships in the plantation and Guinea trades. Sometimes tobacco was substituted for coal, sometimes both commodities were carried. The reason was an economic one: duties on coal, though Ireland counted as an overseas destination, were only charged at the cheaper coastways rate. And the original import duties on tobacco could be 'drawn back' or refunded when that tobacco was exported. The Irish leg was intensely profitable, for both commodities sold well there, and provisioning a ship for a long sea voyage could be achieved more cheaply in Belfast or Dublin than anywhere in England. Indeed the profit on coal or tobacco could pay for a ship's provisions; as John Spedding had remarked in 1706: 'Some ships before they proceed the Virginia Voyage take in a loading of Coals for Dublin and these victual their ship'.[55]

Thomas Lutwidge, ever mindful of the bottom line in all his ventures, always instructed them to call at Dublin first when they weren't actually clearing directly from Dublin for Virginia, an option favoured by many Whitehaven tobacco merchants.

Captain Rumball had learned his lessons well on his previous voyages to Guinea and this time his presence passed unremarked by the Company factors. No accurate information can be supplied on the number of slaves he embarked or discharged, nor where he delivered them, for the colonial shipping registers for 1716 are sadly deficient. Suffice it to say that the length of the voyage – Rumball did not sight Whitehaven again until January 1717 – and his substantial cargo of sugar, ivory, logwood and anatta dye is indicative of a successful voyage. Whitehaven Customs noted that the last port of call was Montserrat, but the commodities carried show that the *Whitehaven* had also traded at Jamaica and Honduras in much the same way as she had done on her previous voyage. This was to prove Rumball's last Guinea voyage for Thomas Lutwidge as he was shortly to go into business on his own account.

The sailing of the *Whitehaven Galley* in October 1715 had preceded the Jacobite Rebellion by just a few weeks. Whitehaven, close to the Scottish border and vulnerable to attack, was thrown into consternation by news of the uprising:

the Town was alarmed with a false report of a party of 200 Rebels coming this Way, & Mr Lutwidge with Several Masters of Ships & others then upon the Customhouse Key, were of the Opinion that the best way to keep off would be to plant Some Guns upon Brackonthwait Hill & beyond Tangier, Designing, if the main Body came this way & were found to be too strong, to plug up the Guns; if a party only, then they might be of service. And accordingly it was agreed by all them present to Carry up the Guns, and one of them was carry'd up to the head of King Street where the Mob rose immediately, to the Number of 3 or 400, Abused the Carrmen & threw down the Guns. Afterwards went to Mr Lutwidge's house & threatened to pull down his, & all the Presbyterian Houses in Town.[56]

Obviously not all was sweetness and light in Sir James Lowther's model town, and the rebellion polarised the population, catching the bourgeois merchants by surprise. The mob was probably composed largely of exiled Scots who had flocked to Whitehaven to make up the labour force, but John Spedding, in his weekly dispatches to Lowther in London, laid the blame at the feet of 'a Certain Family that have shown themselves too barefaced of late', but gave no further clues. Thomas Lutwidge, not a man to trifle with at the best of times, though he used his 'best endeavours to find out the bottom of this Matter' could do no better. Importantly the incident served to confirm Lutwidge as a Dissenter and his loyal but frustrated action did him no harm at all with the Dissenting Whig hierarchy.

As Lowther's steward of collieries, John Spedding had a vested interest in keeping his master's attention firmly fixed on coal. Thus, though the richness of the cargoes with which Captain Rumball returned from the triangular trade stirred the interest and envy of Whitehaven's merchant community, little of this reached Lowther's ears in London. All he heard from Spedding was a catalogue of disasters calculated to undermine any thoughts he might have entertained about diversifying his business interests and entering the tobacco trade. In any event, Whitehaven merchants played their cards very close to their chest when any representative of the Lowther faction came within range. It is doubtful whether Lowther could ever have received a true picture of the profitability of the Virginia trade by relying on Spedding's usual pessimistic offerings:

> there's little to be got by dealing in partnership with some Merchants in this Town, who are so very Dilatory, & drive things to such a Length before they are settled that they make nothing for any but themselves. Mr Anthony Benn has sold his sixteenth part of that ship [the *Hopewell*, frequently engaged in the Virginia trade] to Mr Feryes for £50, which is not half of what it cost, & thought he had made a good Bargain in quitting himself of it.[57]

Fired by the profits he had estimated Lutwidge was making on his imports from the Caribbean, leading tobacco merchant and Dissenter Robert Biglands (a fierce opponent of Lowther) was the next to be tempted into the slave trade.[58] He had, it is true, been a signatory to the 1710 Whitehaven petition against the reintroduction of the Company monopoly, so perhaps that should have been interpreted as an early marker for intended future involvement. Whatever the case, in the summer of 1716 he fitted out a sturdy collier, the *Thomas*, for the Guinea Coast, commissioning Nathaniel Walker to take her there. Her lading for 'Madeira' was an unimaginative assortment of cottons, heavy worsteds (it would be difficult to conceive of a more unsuitable cloth for Africa) and felt hats, so it must be assumed the *Thomas* completed her cargo with gunpowder, weapons, alcoholic spirits, beads and metalware in Dublin or Belfast. The mix of goods, wherever it was obtained, enabled Walker to trade without difficulty – though slowly – for it was not until late July the following year that he delivered ninety slaves to Barbados. On the *Thomas*'s return to Whitehaven in November 1717 the bulk of her cargo of muscovado sugar was exported directly to Dublin, suggesting that a substantial proportion of the capital behind the venture was of Irish origin and that Dublin was the source for her supplementary Guinea cargo. Neither Robert Biglands nor Nathaniel Walker, having satisfied themselves as to the profitability (or otherwise) of the slave trade, felt sufficiently keen to repeat the experience.

Thomas Rumball had no such qualms. His employment under Thomas Lutwidge had given him a host of contacts on the Guinea Coast and in the West Indies, as well as valuable experience in the trade. Eager to start trading on his own account he had been taking his time in selecting a vessel and, as luck would have it, struck a buyer's market. Amongst the collier-owners the realisation was beginning to dawn that the coal trade was oversupplied with tonnage. And as the depression of 1718–24 began to bite,[59] colliers were put on the market. Some of them – like the *Princess*, which Rumball eventually chose – were still on the stocks.

Colliers appear unlikely candidates as slave vessels, yet they had much to recommend them. Many were double-bottomed, a sheathing of timber covering the underwater section of the hull and a 'filling' of tar and oakum being packed between the two.[60] This, it was believed, offered some protection against the teredo worm prevalent in tropical waters. Though small, colliers were immensely strong. Unlike the deep-water anchorages of the south coast (Lyme excepted), the harbours of west Cumberland emptied at low water leaving the ships high and dry, so colliers were built to withstand the stresses imposed by a hefty cargo of coal both at sea and when 'taking the ground'. They were not the sweetest sailing ships in the Atlantic swell of the coast of Africa, but shallow-bottomed colliers were ideally suited to navigating the estuaries and rivers of the Gambia where Rumball had previously purchased the bulk of his slaves. (Sixty years later an obscure sea captain called James Cook was to make even better use of a similar vessel called the *Endeavour*. Unlike Rumball, Cook could choose whatever vessel he desired, but he still decided on a collier, for much the same reason as Rumball did now.) The purchase and freighting of the *Princess* was shared by John Gilpin,[61] Whitehaven merchant and Dissenter, who was to be in partnership with Thomas Rumball for many years. Eventually Gilpin's imports of sugar from the West Indies led him to purchase the sugar house which had been established in Whitehaven at Lowther's instigation in 1712.

Following sea trials, the *Princess* was set forth on her maiden voyage, Thomas Rumball commanding. Her ostensible destination was Barbados and her first port of call Dublin. Here her meagre cargo was supplemented with Guinea-trade goods of all descriptions, and the vessel provisioned. The contacts Rumball had established on his previous voyages to the West African coast stood him in good stead this time around; landfall was quickly made in Antigua at the end of June the following year, and 106 slaves were delivered. The *Princess* spent less than six weeks in Antiguan waters – an astonishingly short time for the sizeable cargo she loaded – before returning to Whitehaven in early October 1719 with ivory, sugar, cotton wool and anatta dye. This proved to be Rumball's last essay in the slave trade, a curiously sudden and inexplicable end to what looked like a promising career. Part of the profits from the voyage of the *Princess* were invested in the South Sea Company in which he held £1,000 worth of stock from the first money subscription of April 1720.[62] On the strength of that he borrowed £3,000 from the Company just before it crashed, and was in Stockholm loading timber aboard the *Princess* when the bubble finally burst.[63] Rumball appears to have ridden out the ensuing financial storm easily enough, settling into the colonial trade – Barbados in 1721,[64] Virginia in 1723[65] – before the coal trade overcame its depression. As soon as the coal trade picked up the *Princess* returned to her original calling as a collier, occasionally making traditional summer voyages to the plantations.

It was now some six years since Thomas Lutwidge had participated in the trade to Guinea. In the intervening period all his energies were being directed towards his burgeoning wine and tobacco businesses. The possibility remains that Lutwidge had not abandoned the slave trade between 1715 and 1720 but had entered it via Glasgow or Dublin, but it is not until 1722 that firm evidence establishes his vessel *Susannah* at Barbados from Africa.[66] Under the command of George Gibson, a prominent Whitehaven Dissenter who was well acquainted with Virginian and West Indian waters,[67] she delivered a total of fifty slaves to James Crowe of Barbados on 6 June. Though the number of slaves was not great it should not be inferred that Gibson was simply shipping slaves from one island to another: the *Susannah*, of 42 tons burden only, probably had a maximum capacity of little over a hundred slaves. Her small size facilitated a quick turnround time and enabled her to clear Barbados for Whitehaven by the end of June. Within the year she had sailed for Barbados again, returning directly with a cargo of rum, some of which she discharged at Dublin but the bulk of which was offloaded on the Isle of Man. The Whitehaven Customs were under no illusion about its eventual destination:

> the Isle of Man has long been a Common Warehouse for all high duty commodities, where they are put into proper and convenient package for the more easy running them into G. B. and Ireland.[68]

By this time Lutwidge was an even more formidable opponent, for in 1720 he had proposed marriage to Lucy, daughter of Sir Charles Hoghton.[69] Such a step, if successful, would propel him into the ranks of the Cumberland gentry but would not compromise his Dissenting sympathies. The Hoghtons of Lancashire were, despite their elevated rank and wealth, a prominent Nonconformist family who had borne arms for Parliament in the Civil War. Their immense family seat at Hoghton Tower, which stands to this day, was a bastion of Dissent and a beacon for democracy in the north-west of England. Dissenting ministers were maintained by the family under the guise of chaplains and tutors and religious services were regularly held in the banqueting room.[70] About 1715 the family could afford to feel more secure about their unconventional affiliations for they had mobilised volunteers under arms to oppose those factions in Preston sympathetic to the Jacobite uprising. By this action they had aligned themselves firmly behind George I and the new order of Whig ascendancy that his accession had initiated. The family was well rewarded for its pains. Lucy's brother Henry Hoghton,[71] who had inherited the title and estate and was renowned as a Whig, was immediately created a Commissioner for Forfeited Estates and later became Advocate-General of the Land Forces.

A new spirit of religious toleration was abroad following the suppression of the Rebellion. Both King and country at large recognised the invaluable support provided by Dissenting Whigs and Parliament sought to make amends for the outrages they had suffered. The Riot Act of 1715 outlawed the destruction of Dissenters' meeting houses, and Dissenters were able to claim up to £5,000 from the Treasury in compensation for past damage to their property. Four years later the Act for preventing occasional conformity and the Schism act were both repealed.[72]

Nevertheless, there can be little question of Sir Henry Hoghton entertaining proposals for his sister's hand from any but the Dissenting elect. Despite his age and questionable trading practices, Thomas Lutwidge was undoubtedly well received and there was little incongruity, for business was business and religion quite another thing altogether. Though 80 miles north of Preston, Whitehaven was a known centre of Dissent which had a permanent preacher, Thomas Dixon, and a congregation of some 350 hearers, including 20 gentlemen. Amongst them was 'one merchant worth above £20,000 and four merchants more worth each about £4000',[73] presumably Thomas Lutwidge himself, followed by the Gales, Gilpins, Feryes, and Bigland families.

News travelled easily from one Dissenting community to another, carried by peripatetic preachers and circulated by the merchant community. Doubtless Lutwidge's credentials had been immeasurably enhanced in Hoghton eyes by his forlorn but worthy attempt to defend Whitehaven against the imagined advance of the Jacobites in 1715, an action which faintly paralleled Sir Henry's raising of a volunteer force in Preston. Thomas Lutwidge's proposal was accepted and he married Lucy Hoghton in February 1721. Perhaps as a result of his rise in the social scale he became High Sheriff of Cumberland some five years later.

By this time Lutwidge was a father several times over, for he carried out his duties as a husband with the same unflagging energy and enthusiasm he had displayed as a merchant. Not that his mercantile career ceased, though his slave trading days were apparently over. During the third and fourth decades of the eighteenth century Lutwidge owned and freighted a number of vessels in the tobacco trade to Virginia including the *Carolina, Hoghton,*

Whitehaven[74] and *Wharton*.[75] Though some authorities have suggested he died penniless in a Dublin debtors' gaol in 1745,[76] this seems an unlikely fate for one whose business acumen was so renowned and who had amassed such a considerable fortune by his efforts.

Certainly the careers of his children – seven sons and two daughters were born to Lucy between 1724 and 1737 – bear no sign of having been blighted by reduced circumstances. His eldest son Charles, too delicate to go to sea himself or make his way successfully in the rough-and-tumble of merchant life, found himself a career in his father's erstwhile adversaries, the Customs and Excise. Rising swiftly through its ranks he achieved the post of Supervisor of Preventative Officers in Cumberland within his father's lifetime. History does not record whether this irony proved the final one for Thomas Lutwidge; he died about the same year, 1746. Charles went on to become Surveyor and Comptroller-General of the coasts of Westmorland and Cumberland and the first Receiver-General of the Isle of Man. On taking the latter office his first action was to draft plans for annexing Man to Cumberland, a scheme that caused widespread consternation and would have caused his father to turn in his grave.[77] Little is recorded of the second son, Henry, except that one of his great-grandsons achieved fame in a manner no other Lutwidge descendant could equal. He was an Oxford mathematician called Charles Lutwidge Dodgson, better known now as Lewis Carroll. Of Thomas Lutwidge's other sons, his namesake Thomas became a merchant (and caused endless confusion for historians).[78] The youngest son, Skeffington, commanded HMS *Carcass* on her epic voyage of discovery to the North Pole in 1773 and, as Admiral of the Red, was an early preceptor of Lord Nelson.[79]

Thomas Lutwidge senior played no further part in the slave trade after 1722, yet this was far from the end of Whitehaven's involvement. Lutwidge's nephew Walter, last seen as a successful privateersman, had quickly been building up his own business as a merchant. He was accorded the title 'captain' for the rest of his life, but his interests had largely turned landward. By 1721 Walter was actively campaigning against the Lowther faction and even managed to persuade his uncle to throw in his lot with the anti-Lowther lobby.[80] With the coal trade in recession and mercantile feeling united against him, Sir James Lowther crashed to defeat in the 1722 elections for the constituency of Cumberland. In comparison, Walter Lutwidge went from strength to strength, eventually surpassing his uncle as

Whitehaven's leading merchant. Though he had displayed little interest in the Guinea trade during the time it was held by his uncle, Walter made up for this by mounting three voyages to Angola for slaves between 1733 and 1737. More were planned only to be reluctantly abandoned owing to the dire financial straits in which Walter found himself at the end of that decade.[81]

These thwarted plans failed to discourage further Whitehaven participation in the slave trade. Merchants of the port, reluctant to commit themselves to a full-scale Guinea voyage, kept their hand in the business by way of the re-export trade. Joshua Dixon and Edward Tubman financed the voyages of the *Griffin* of Whitehaven to Barbados and then with slaves to Rappahannock, Virginia in 1741 and 1743. A decade later the *Expedition* of Whitehaven followed the same route.[82] By this time, led by James Spedding (whose grandfather John, Lowther's old steward of collieries, had railed against any diversification from coal), the merchants of Whitehaven had entered the trade in earnest. Their ships, the *Betty* and *Providence* of 1752,[83] the *Black Prince* of 1755, the *Willington* of 1756, the *Prince George* and *Neptune* of 1762,[84] and the *Elizabeth* of 1767, all sailed success-fully to Guinea for slaves.[85]

From the concentration of Africa-bound voyages in the middle years of the eighteenth century, it is clear that Whitehaven's involve-ment in the slave trade during that period was not a casual one. Yet compared to Liverpool – or, for a time, Lancaster – its participation remained in a minor key. Finally the slave trade ceased from Whitehaven for precisely the same reasons that the tobacco and sugar trades, its progenitors, moved elsewhere. First and foremost came the fraught question of the harbour and the deep division of interests between the plantation traders and the colliers. This characterised all harbour developments at Whitehaven throughout the eighteenth century. The division was never satisfactorily resolved – nor could it ever have been, due to a crucial lack of room to expand and the incompatible characteristics of the two trades. The colonial traders required deep-water access and secure berths in which they could anchor for long but infrequent periods both to discharge and to load their considerable cargoes. On the other hand the coal traders, happy to ply in shallow waters and content to let their vessels take the ground when the tide ebbed, encouraged any suggestion by Lowther that improved their turnround time and hence their profitability.[86] There was never room at Whitehaven to accommodate both parties amicably and the result was a foregone conclusion: the colonial traders left, one after the other, for the deep-water harbours of Liverpool and Glasgow. Harbours such as these lay close to large manufacturing centres with excellent road connections. As such they could not only process the inbound cargo from the colonies more easily and profitably, but they could provide the right quality and mix of goods for the all-important export cargo at short notice and without hefty carriage charges.

Gone were the days when the pioneer spirit of the American colonies had been content to clothe itself in the unassuming rough country cloth of Cumberland. Now the colonies called increasingly for the latest fashions and the most sophisticated stuffs, which proved beyond the capability of Whitehaven either to manufacture or to supply at reasonable cost. Over the fells and to the south, however, they were doing a roaring trade. Manchester, Sheffield, Bradford and Leeds were in full swing but the impassability of the Cumberland fells by wheeled traffic and their sheer inaccessibility for much of the year kept Whitehaven isolated from the mainstream of this booming cloth industry. The fells not only surrounded Whitehaven but confined the role it could play. Nor could industry come to Whitehaven: such a desolate landscape could never support the large population needed to man the factories and mills that might have propelled the town successfully into the following century. The fells were ultimately its downfall.

With the port of Whitehaven this survey has reached its northern borders. Though its limits are geographical as well as temporal, it should not be imagined that interest in the slave trade stopped dead at the border with Scotland, or failed to survive crossing the Irish Sea. Both Scotland and Ireland sought to share in the imagined riches generated by the trade and both countries pursued an energetic trade with the Guinea Coast throughout the eighteenth century. Before the Union with England, Scotland already boasted an African Company of its own, the Company of Scotland Trading to Africa and the Indies. This was in existence by 1695. After the Union – which came shortly before England's Royal African Company attempted to regain its monopoly – Scotland added its substantial voice to that of the separate traders in their bid to resist the monopoly and declare the trade open. All the merchants of the Royal Boroughs of Edinburgh, Dundee, Inverness, Aberdeen, Glasgow and Montrose felt, with some justification, that

a revival of the Royal African Company's monopoly would be

contrary to the Articles of the Union which state that all the Subjects of Great Britain shall have full Freedom and Intercourse of Trade.[87]

During a period of just over two years the Scottish lobby presented Parliament with eight such petitions. In reality Scotland was protecting its tobacco trade at Glasgow which had made huge strides during the last decade of the seventeenth century. Operating a Guinea-trade ship from a Scottish base did have a number of advantages, however. Western Scottish waters were less subject to privateers in times of war and the lower scale of duties payable on alcoholic spirits gave Scottish merchants an edge when bartering for slaves, gold or ivory in Africa. By at least the end of the second decade of the eighteenth century Glasgow was well established in the slave trade. Between August 1717 and December 1719 no fewer than three vessels from that port, the *George, Hanover* and *Loyalty*, were trading off Africa for a total of more than 400 slaves whose destination was Barbados.[88]

Across the Irish Channel the flourishing cities of Dublin and Belfast (and to a lesser extent Limerick and Kinsale), were ideally placed to enter the trade, either on their own account or on behalf of the English merchants who sought to evade the 10 per cent tax payable to the Company between 1698 and 1712. Irish ports were regularly used to provision ships owing to the cheapness and quality of Irish pickled beef and pork, and it was but a short step to freighting entire vessels from Irish resources. It is doubtful whether this clandestine trade was ever very substantial, but Ireland sent a sizeable contingent of her own ships to Africa during the first quarter of the eighteenth century. Amongst them were the *Sylva* of Dublin recorded slaving at the Gambia in May 1716 and bound for Jamaica,[89] accompanied by the *Sophia* of the same place, commanded by a Captain Spring. The latter vessel was attacked and taken by the very slaves it was attempting to transport: Captain Spring alone escaped the slaughter. A happier fate awaited the contemporary brigantine *Prosperity* of Limerick, though not its slaves: ninety-six of them were delivered to Barbados on 31 July 1718.[90]

CHAPTER TWENTY-ONE

The Re-export Trade in Slaves

GENERALLY blessed by light winds, (the hurricane season excepted), fair weather and placid seas, the Caribbean basin of the early eighteenth century was criss-crossed by a web of trading routes which encompassed its diaspora of islands and extended to the South, Central and North American mainlands which form its perimeter or rim. Much of the trade was coasting in nature, and a fair proportion was clandestine in both destination and goods carried. In theory it was illegal to export any produce grown in the British colonies to any destination outside Britain or its colonies. In reality a thriving trade in colonial produce brought rum, sugar and tobacco of British plantations to the Dutch West Indies and the Spanish-American mainland. Destinations were disguised and cargo manifests falsified as the first mate of this sloop stated in 1703:

> we went down again to Curacao laden with Sugar, Tobacco, Rum and bottle Liquours as beer and Cider. The Sloop was entered for Anguilla, and the Tobacco . . . for bottle beer, the Sugar for Flour, and the Rum for Tar.[1]

In this way trading across national boundaries within the Caribbean was much more common than the authorities would have liked to assume, or the Colonial Shipping Registers – where they still exist – would have us believe. Owing to the disappearance of many of the latter group of records due to the depredations of insects, careless officials, hurricanes, earthquakes or social upheavals, it is only with some difficulty that an account of conventional trade in the area can be pieced together. As for the slave trade, slaves being a non-dutiable commodity in most of Britain's colonial possessions during the early eighteenth century and thus not entered in the shipping registers, this account is more a marker indicating the existence of such inter-island trading than an exhaustive survey.

The main beneficiaries of the re-export trade in slaves were those Caribbean islands or North American colonies not directly served by the Royal African Company or separate traders. Usually they could neither absorb many slaves for their own use nor produce enough sugar or tobacco to assure slave trade captains of a profitable return leg to England. However variations on the re-export theme abounded. Sometimes slaves were shipped to the Spanish mainland, and occasionally from Spanish America to the English West Indies. In short, wherever trade flowed in the Caribbean, slaves were transported. Of course the two greatest route centres or distribution points in the early eighteenth century were Barbados and Jamaica.

Even when they had reached the plantation for which they had been purchased at the dockside, slaves were not fixed assets. Neighbouring plantation owners would hire slaves from other plantations when they were short-handed. Plantations which went bankrupt or suffered from overmanning sold their slaves either on to other plantations or to the island's slave merchants, and these were frequently consigned to other colonies. In addition, slaves could be directly regarded as a currency. The re-export trade to the Spanish mainland, though not at all evident from any official sources, is presumed to have resulted in much-needed silver and gold for plantation owners with liquidity problems.[2]

As with most conventional trade, re-export slave trading fell into certain set patterns. By far the most predominant was the flow of black labour which fanned out from the island of Barbados to St Kitts and Nevis, rarely visited by Guinea trade ships. This stream of black labour was usually carried by local sloops and brigantines which relied upon their speed and knowledge of local conditions to outrun and outmanoeuvre pirates and privateers. Sometimes English merchantmen in Caribbean waters were freighted with slaves by local traders or – less typically – attempted speculative short-haul ventures on their own account. As such ventures – perhaps to Carolina or Virginia from Jamaica, Antigua or Barbados, with rum and sugar to exchange for tobacco – were generally peripheral to the main aim of the voyage, space was usually at a premium and the number of slaves carried was rarely large. In addition slaves, even from one island to another, were a labour-intensive cargo, requiring feeding, cleaning, keeping healthy and guarding against any attempt to escape or revolt. It was never regarded as anything but legitimate trade: slaves, like tobacco, sugar, rum or cotton, were a commodity much in demand.

Occasionally the re-export stream flowed in a contrary direction. This had been especially true of St Kitts and Nevis in the last quarter of the seventeenth century when Guinea-trade captains were happier to deliver their slaves at smaller islands than risk the pirate-infested 2,000-mile round trip to Jamaica. Shrewd Jamaican plantation owners could plan ahead and instruct west-bound vessels to load slaves in Nevis at competitive rates. One such instance is revealed by William Helyar of East Coker, Somerset in a letter to John Read, master of the *Samuel*, bound for Jamaica in December 1684 and largely freighted by the Helyars for their Bybrook plantation:

> You are to dispose of the abovesaid Goods in Nevis for good Negroes and carry them down to Jamaica in your ship the *Samuel*; and there to send them to Thomas Hilyard the Steward of my plantation there, and oblige him to load on your Ship Sugars or other Commodity to the Value of what the Negroes shall cost you there.[3]

The re-export trade ebbed and flowed the length and breadth of the Caribbean. Jamaica in particular, starved of labour in its formative years, welcomed blacks from a variety of sources. Again in 1684, the *John's Adventure* under William Evert can be found arriving there from Curaçao with 60 sheep, 6 barrels of fish, 2 barrels of onions and seven Negroes, listed in that order by the Collector of Customs at Port Royal.[4] Typical of the vessels which traded in and around the Caribbean, the *John's Adventure* was no substantial oceangoing merchantman but a ketch of New England with an estimated capacity of little more than 14 tons.

Despite the French attack of 1694 and the consequent loss of hundreds of slaves, the labour situation in Jamaica improved considerably in the following decade. In 1707 London slave trader Benjamin Way informed the Commissioners for Trade and Plantations that the only reason there was not a surplus of black labour was 'the Spaniard being at hand to take off what can there be spared at a considerable Profit'.[5] One vessel which participated in this branch of the trade was the sloop *Union* of 1709. It is not recorded how many slaves she attempted to sell on the central American mainland but her captain John Toms notified the Jamaican authorities on his return (from the 'Spanish Coast') that he still carried seventeen Negroes 'returned for want of sale'.[6] Undeterred by his failure, Toms increased his complement of slaves to twenty-six, loaded cocoa, indigo and sugar, and cleared for Carolina. Based in Jamaica, trading the length and breadth of the Caribbean, and even found trading off the Guinea Coast exchanging rum for slaves, the *Union* typifies many vessels participating in re-export.

The reasons behind the re-export trade were predominantly economic. Hurricanes could suddenly destroy potentially valuable harvests and reduce the abilities of island planters to afford more slaves. Plantation owners preferred to take their slaves on credit, sometimes with years to pay, and slave ship captains and supercargoes, often balking at these arrangements, sailed onwards to find more suitable outlets. Occasionally a number of slave trade ships would unintentionally arrive in port within a few days of each other, creating a glut. Rather than accepting the lower prices this would entail, many a ship's captain preferred to seek out a better market on the Spanish Coast or Martinique. Should he have no option but to accept the fall in the market, local slave merchants would profit by shipping the slaves on.

Price was not the sole criterion behind the decision of plantation owners to sell their slaves on to other markets. Occasionally, as in the case of insolent, rebellious and intransigent slaves, the owner would dispatch them as the final disciplinary measure. In other cases, those of slaves damaged by beatings inflicted on the plantations, suffering from psychological trauma, chronic disease or simply exhaustion, onward shipping was carried out on the grounds of convenience. Finally there was a category of slaves bought purely for their re-export potential. These were the 'refuse' slaves, those men and women so close to death when they stumbled or were carried off a newly arrived Guineaman that no planter or merchant would be bothered to bid for them. Many were simply left to die on the dockside; others were bought for a pound or two by merchants – often Jewish – who specialised in 'feeding up' these distraught wrecks in the expectation of selling them on at a profit at some later stage. In general the further slaves were from the major 'reception centres' of Barbados and Jamaica the less likely they were to be of 'prime quality'.

Difficulties in assessing the re-export trade are made no easier by the haphazard survival of the Shipping Registers for the North American colonies to which it is probable much of the trade flowed. There are no records at all for this period for New England, New Hampshire, New Jersey or Pennsylvania and all others suffer from being severely intermittent. A small indication is supplied by a single Company memorandum entitled *Negroes Imported into the Plantations*, which records the separate traders importing 236 slaves into

Virginia by way of Barbados in addition to the 6,371 imported
directly from Africa for the period 24 June 1698 to 31 December
1707.[7] Though Virginia and Carolina with their tobacco and rice
plantations were profitable destinations for all slave trade merchants,
other areas of the American mainland were less attractive. Francis
Harrison, an early New York merchant, wrote to the Company in
1724 with proposals to set up an agency on their behalf and revealed
that

> from sometime before October 1717 no more than 138 negroes
> have been imported to New York from Africa; whereof 117 were
> from Madagascar which trade is now entirely defeated . . . such
> slaves as are sent from the West Indies being but very rarely, and
> seldom more than two or three at a time.[8]

Since the jurisdiction of the New York colony at that time
extended over East and West Jersey, Connecticut, Rhode Island,
Narragansett and southern New England, Harris' remarks cover a
good deal of ground. His historical perspective is extensive too – the
Company lost its monopoly of Madagascar to the East India Company in the last quarter of the seventeenth century – so the records
to which he had access reveal a very low level of slave imports into
the northernmost American colonies during the first quarter of the
eighteenth century. Unfortunately his data also reveals a low level of
accuracy. New York Customs records show 382 slaves entering the
colony from the West Indies, 556 from the coast of Africa, in the
years 1701–17.[9] None the less, compared to Virginia, the slave intake
was small. That is not to say New York merchants were not involved
in the trade, but simply that their investment was not seen by way of
slaves entering the port. Instead they probably operated very much
as their neighbours did to the West Indies, shipping out to the
Caribbean with timber for building, picking up a cargo of rum for
the Guinea Coast, returning with slaves which were sold for the
inflated prices they could be relied upon to fetch in Barbados,
Antigua or Jamaica, and completing the final return leg to New York
with muscovado sugar, logwood, tobacco or indigo. The *Fauconberg*,
a Company ship of 1699–1700, recorded 'a small ship bound for
Guinea, belonging to New York' sailing from Antigua:[10] other such
departures can be traced in the relevant West Indian documents
where extant.

In view of all the preceding caveats, the table in Appendix 7 must
be regarded as providing only the barest outline. As expected, vessels

from the southern and south-western ports of England dominate minor outport involvement. Amongst them are some familiar names: John and Robert Burridge of Lyme Regis were the owners and freighters of the *John* of 1702 which cleared for Barbados with cloth, pantiles, twine, lampblack and 100 cwt. of bread and then traded on to South Potomac with nine slaves from Barbados. Given the later predominance of the Burridges in the slave trade from the minor outports, this early instance can hardly have been unique. Nearly two decades later they repeated the process using the same ship, the *John* under Samuel Courtenay; this has been detailed in Chapter 16. Henry Pascall of the *Friend's Adventure* of Dover, which cleared for Nevis with a huge cargo of cloth and wrought-metal goods, bought two slaves there and sold them on in Barbados. On his return to England he put his knowledge of West Indian waters to good effect, being commissioned to take the London slave ship *Dolphin* to Guinea and Barbados where he delivered 160 slaves in 1715.[11]

The predominance of the West of England outports is reaffirmed by Richard Randall, owner and captain of the Topsham-based *Dolphin*. Though he cleared from Exeter with ostensibly American destinations, Randall seems to have made a habit of calling at Barbados for a supplementary cargo of Caribbean produce and slaves. Another West of England sea captain was Thomas Gollop, who made a name for himself as captain of the privateer *Crown*, a London ship of 200 tons, 18 guns and 50 men, between 1708 and 1711.[12] At that time a resident of Bermondsey, then a small Thames-side village close to London, he later moved back to Dorset. Since he was both owner and captain of the *Neptune* of Weymouth, which cleared for Antigua in 1717 with 16½ tons of strong beer, wrought stone, cotton and haberdashery and finally arrived in New York with four slaves in 1718, it is possible he had made his fortune by privateering. Finally there are the Barfoot brothers of Poole who mounted a conventional venture to Barbados and there shipped aboard 90 gallons of rum and 24 slaves for Charleston, Carolina in 1722. Two and a half years later William Barfoot was back in West Indian waters as master of the *Eagle* of Poole which had arrived via Madeira. Whether this was a full-scale Guinea voyage or not has been impossible to ascertain. What is certain however (and already documented in Chapter 15) is that William Barfoot re-entered the Guinea trade from Poole in mid-century.

Never more than a supplementary arm to the main body of the slave trade, the re-export trade may yet have fulfilled an important function for the trade as a whole. To begin with it demonstrated to merchant sea captains and their backers who had never been to the Guinea Coast that black human beings were a viable commodity. It also gave them the opportunity to engage in the trade on low-risk, short-haul voyages. And it allowed them potentially valuable contacts amongst colonial slave merchants most of whom, after all, dealt in conventional merchandise too.

Thus the re-export slave trade, like the trade in indentured white servants, may well have acted as a 'nursery' for slave trade captains. For all its tangential nature, its influence may have been far more central and much more widespread than has been recognised.

Epilogue

THOUGH this study has now reached its temporal and spatial borders, the process of the forced transportation and enslavement of over 12 million Africans knew no bounds. During the first quarter of the eighteenth century Britain's share of the slave trade was merely getting into its stride. Another half-century later is generally regarded as the 'golden age' of the trade, if such an epithet can be applied. At the same time as the trade reached its peak, and plantation profits reached undreamed-of heights, a new humanitarianism was painfully being born.[1]

The abolition of the slave trade was not achieved in a day. Though the activities of the abolitionists have rightly been accorded a wide measure of appreciation, this has undoubtedly contributed to the widespread modern delusion that Britain was primarily acting as a whiter-than-white knight, a St George on behalf of black Africa, who had never been greatly involved in the trade itself. In the first quarter of the eighteenth century – which can really only be regarded as the 'seeding' of the trade – that is nonsense. Abolition itself took time, for a whole trade structure had to be dismantled and vested interests of vast wealth and influence had to be placated. The much-vaunted Act of 1807 only prohibited the carriage of slaves in ships; slavery in the British colonies was not prohibited until 1834, and in some part of Europe – notably Portugal – it was not abolished until 1869, little more than a century ago.

Britain's stance as St George rescuing the slaves hides a complex train of events and perceptions, and the torment that afflicted West Africa was not over when the slave trade was abolished. Let us briefly consider other circumstances which ran contemporaneously with the new 'dawn of humanitarianism', and which may have played an equal part in the abolition of the trade, then of slavery as an institution.

First the increasing use of mechanisation on the plantations contributed to the decline in demand for black labour. Since virtually all the cultivable land was now under crops there no longer existed the need to expend black labour on the back-breaking task of clearing virgin territory, and the very real possibility of a surplus of black labour was beginning to worry plantation owners. Secondly, events in Europe at the beginning of the nineteenth century made trade links difficult to maintain. This was the responsibility of Napoleon Bonaparte, whose blockade of British ports cut the plantation trade to a minimum and forced the introduction of home-grown sugar beet in England as an alternative to imports based on sugar cane. Following this, the West Indian plantations never recovered their predominance in sugar.

If the abolition of the slave trade was irritating, but not unforeseen to the plantation owners, it was nothing less than catastrophic for the caboceers of the West African coast. In the years 1701–1810 they had largely been responsible for gathering and exchanging nearly 60 per cent of all slaves exported from Africa,[2] and the economy of the region, plus their own power base, was largely orientated towards the slave trade. With its abolition the power of local chiefs, some of whom led tribal nations, was severely compromised and a vacuum resulted. Given Britain's appetite for empire, nothing could be more natural than for the British to step into the breach. This they did with alacrity, concluding deals with African ruling families in which the latter surrendered their sovereign status and helped the British to achieve total economic and political subordination of their kingdoms.[3] From being virtually unknown traders living a precarious existence on the seashores in the latter quarter of the seventeenth century, the British, in the space of two centuries, became lords of all they surveyed in the Gambia, Sierra Leone, Ghana and Nigeria.

On the other side of the Atlantic the fears of the early white settlers in the Caribbean – that their islands would lose their 'whiteness' under the flood of forced black immigration – have long been realised. It is the descendants of slaves and not of slave-owners who now run the Caribbean and shape its destiny. Thankfully this is not history coming a full circle. European visitors to the many islands scattered through the Caribbean are merely enslaved by the beauty around them. Hopefully, on the subject of slavery, history will never repeat itself.

Vessels Clearing Deal, Portsmouth, Southampton, Cowes and Weymouth for Africa, 1698–1720

Date	Vessel	Captain	Merchant
10 March 1699[1] Portsmouth	*Ekins Frigate* of London, square sterned, 350 tons, 20 guns	Francis Stretell	Stretell & Co.

Cargo: 3 casks containing 520lb of new shoes.
(Freighted from London by the Royal African Company and designed for 600 slaves,[2] the *Ekins* delivered 359 to Jamaica, 26 Feb. 1700).[3]

13 Aug. 1700[4] Portsmouth	*Mary Anne* of Warsash	Israel Browne for Guinea in Africa and intended for Jamaica	William Pafford, Peter Hawkesworth & Co.

Cargo: 40 pieces of perpetuannas, weight 800lb; 7 doz and 4 felt hats; 16 doz ordinary pendants; 12 doz small looking glasses; 6 doz small toys; 30 doz glass necklaces; 4 doz small burning glasses; 6½ pounds of glass beads; a parcel of screw boxes, sets and nests of boxes; 20 doz gilt rings and 38 dozen ditto stone; 5 bundles of silver washed chains; 3 doz small horns for drams; 8 doz glassrings; 6 doz beads; 31 Hamboro cases and 31 doz bottles; a parcel of brass pans, weight 1cwt 2qr 22lb; 3 drums; 5 doz leather trunks; 2 hhds acquavitae; 30 doz pewter spoons, 3 doz basins, 3 doz tankards and 3 doz pots all of pewter, weight 1cwt 1qt 14lb; 60 gross tobacco pipes; 12 doz and 6 Monmouth[5] caps plain; 4 pieces dyed linen of English manufacture in remnants; 25 doz horn

Date	Vessel	Captain	Merchant

(*continued from p. 359*)

combs; 14lb haberdashery; 3 doz powder horns; 4000 flints; 4 barrels gunpowder weight 4cwt; 154 bars of copper, English produce, weight 1cwt 1qr; 54lb cowries; 56lb rangoes; 65lb tobacco; 1 ton and ½cwt of foreign iron (from Norway).

2 boxes of wooden toys; 1 box containing 20 gross of tobacco pipes; 4 barrels of pitch; 33 trading guns; 8 pairs of pistols; 114 doz knives; 20 hammers; 20 doz scissors; 21 doz razors; 106 doz steels; 2000 needles; 12 doz fish hooks; 100 large bream [hooks?]; 100 middle short points [hooks?]; 7½ doz chisels; 3 broad axes; 8 doz gimlets; 3½ doz hammers; 20 scimitars; 6 doz hatchets; 10 saws; 3 old swords & belts; [virtually all the hardware and ironmongery ware was described as second-hand but perfectly worn]. In addition: 18 doz Jews harps; 2 doz small bonnets; 1 chalder of sea coals.
Total value of cargo: £282 15s. 5d.
10 per cent tax paid: £28 5s. d.

Number of slaves delivered at Nevis unknown. Cast away at Cork, June 1701.

---

10 March 1704[6]	*Austria Galley*	John Cross	John Cross & Co.
Portsmouth	of London	for Guinea	
	(200 tons, 16		
	guns 24 men)		

Cargo: 13 cwt 13qr 8lbs wrought pewter; 100 birding pieces; 2 blunderbusses; 20 doz steeles; 600 flints; 709 galls English spirits; 22 demi-casters; 13cwt 3qr 12lb brass manufacture; 220½ lbs bugles; 20 lbs shoes and slippers; 12 lbs silk stockings; 40 yards flannel; 1 cwt knives.
Value of this cargo: £461 5s. 0d.
10 per cent tax paid: £46 2s. 6½d.

(By land carriage from London). 30 byrampants; 100 brawles; 30 chintz; 12 rumals; 6 lungees; 35 pieces foreign linen.[7] } Elwick & Co.
Value: £130
10 per cent tax: £13

2 tons of iron (by land carriage from London).[8]   Wm Browne & Sons

Date	Vessel	Captain	Merchant

21 Nov. 1706[9] Portsmouth — *Barbados Merchantman* of Plymouth — John Russell for Cape Coast — David Faulkner (probably for Joseph Bingham)

Cargo: 1 case containing: 5 pieces two-tenths calicoes: 5 pounds weight of tea; 3½ pounds of tea; 30 ells of Holland linen; 60 kittisoles; certain china and Lacquered ware; one malmul; two salempores; 2 felt hats; one piece of woolen stuff weight 12lb; 11 pounds weight of copper manufacture; 1 doz thread stockings.
(Balance of cargo transhipped from the *Resolution* and *Maurice and George* for the Royal African Company.)

23 Dec. 1706[10] Portsmouth — *Adventure* of London — Daniel Lewis for Africa and Virginia[11] — Anthony Tourney. Thomas Colthurst per Daniel Jamineau

Cargo: 40 cwt 1qr iron. 442 lbs great bugles; 10000 crystal beads; 4 cwt battery; 11 lbs coral beads; 3 lbs amber beads; 1cwt and 7qrs of copper Bars; 4000 rangoes; 1cwt cowries; 2 short cloths; 3 cwt wrought iron; 60 lbs of worsted fringe. (Arrived by land carriage from London).
Balance of the cargo previously loaded in London 5 Sept. 1706, valued at £894 13s. 3d., 10 per cent tax paid £89 9s. 4d.[12] Delivered 92 slaves to Maryland 11 Aug. 1707.

6 Aug. 1708[13] Portsmouth — *Prince of Mindelheim* of London — John Gordon for Africa — Houlditch & Brook (also owners)

Cargo: 10 chests containing 650 old sheets.
Balance of the cargo, amounting to a value of £1,247 10s. 9d. had been loaded in London, 16 Feb. 1708. The bulk of the cargo was for Houlditch and Co.; James Berdoe also had a share.[14]

7 Jan. 1710[15] Portsmouth — *Three Crowns* of London — Digby Keeble for Guinea — Joseph Martin

Cargo: 4 bales containing 100 perpetuannas, weight 1000 lbs.
Balance of the cargo previously loaded in London, 8 Nov. 1709, valued at £1,552 18s. 5d. Tax paid £155 5s. 10d.[16]
Delivered 200 slaves to Nevis.[17]

Date	Vessel	Captain	Merchant
July? 1713[18] Portsmouth	*Isle of Wight* galley of Portsmouth.[19]	John Mellish[20]	Not known

Cargo: Not known
Delivered 123 slaves to Barbados, 13 July 1714.[21]

Date	Vessel	Captain	Merchant
Jan? 1715 Deal	Not known. A snow of Deal.	Not known	Tobias Bowles

Cargo: Not known. Wrecked at the Gambia.[22]

Date	Vessel	Captain	Merchant
2 April 1717[23] Weymouth	*Flying Brigantine* of London, 50 tons	Stephen Patrick (part-owner) for Maderas	Thomas Randall

Cargo: 1 pack (60 pieces) sletia lawns; 6 reams writing paper; 1 cask with 126 lbs woollen manufacture and fringe; 1 piece of broadcloth (20lb); 30 qr of beans; 25 casks (7 hhds) of acquavita; 2 vats (50 small barrels) containing 10 cwt gunpowder; 3 cwt wrought iron; 8 tons of foreign iron.
Delivered 17 negroes to Charleston, So. Carolina, 9 Oct. 1717.[24]

Date	Vessel	Captain	Merchant
18–24 Dec. 1719 Deal[25]	*Samuel* sloop of London	Joshua Anley	Henry Alexander Primrose (supplied by Samuel Betteress and Christopher Astley of London)

Cargo: 12 cwt iron; 5 cwt pewter; 4 cwt lead shott;(?) hundred one-sixth ells Narrow Germany linen; 879 lbs great Bugle; 224lbs great Bugle; 5 cwt:1qr:25lb brown sugar; 400 Christall Beads; 9 pieces two-tenths calicoes; 2000z coral beads; 1:0:7lb cowries; 200 goads cottons; 45lb worsted fringe; a parcel of old wearing apparel; 2 doz felt hats; 1½ doz castors; 20 phottees; 50 chilloes; 10 romalls; 20 allabanees; 30 niconees; 15 tapseils; 10 Bajudipotts; 30 brawles; 10 long blue cloths; 1000 rangoes.

Contradictory figures of 95 and 98 slaves are reported as having been delivered to slave merchant William Allen of Barbados in June 1720.

Vessels Clearing London, Bristol and Lyme Regis for the Burridge Family of Lyme, 1704–25

Date	Vessel	Captain	Merchant
March 1704 Bristol[1]	*Union Galley* for Guinea	Not known	John Burridge junior

Cargo: Iron; Hemp; 6 chests of old sheets and other linens; 165½ bushels of beans; 500 single ranters.
Value: £511 16s. 11d.

15¾cwt Irish tallow; 585 old sheets; 30 tapseils; 70 niconees; 2 short cloths; 400 perpetts; 32 says; 5cwt iron.			Benjamin Way

---

Date	Vessel	Captain	Merchant
14 Jan. 1706 London[2]	*London Galley* of 190 tons 14 guns and 30 men	John Maxwell, subsequently Abraham Battell.	Benjamin Way and John Burridge junior

Cargo: 800 serges; 30 stuffs; 1430 old sheets; 29¾cwt tallow; 50 niconees; 50 tapseils; 50 calicoes; 160 bars of iron; 35cwt wrought iron; 30qrs of beans; 5cwt pewter; 50 cases of spirits; 280 lbs of tobacco; 100 brawles.
Value: £1,265 1s. 9d.
10 per cent tax: £126 10s. 2d.

105 perpetts.			John Maxwell

Value £57; 10 per cent tax £5 14s. 0d.

Arrived in Jamaica in late Nov. 1706 with slaves, ivory and gold. Departed at the end of February but was disabled and ran aground off the Cammanna (Cayman) Islands in the Caribbean.[3]

Date	Vessel	Captain	Merchant

20 Aug 1709
London⁴

Martha frigate

William
Courtenay for
Africa

John Burridge

Cargo: 20qr of beans; 600 perpetuannas; 10 says; 34cwt wrought iron; 6cwt pewter; 1 ton acquavitae; 16⅛cwt gunpowder; 10 whole and 20 half cases of spirits; 10 pieces of darnicks; 520 old sheets; 59¾cwt and 16lb foreign iron; 1⅙cwt broad German linen; 14¼cwt and 1lb Irish tallow; 60 pieces of brawls.
Value of cargo as given on oath by Walter Burridge: £798 3s. 0d.
Tax paid £79 16s. 4d.

2cwt wrought iron; 18 perpetuannas.   Walter Burridge
Value by oath: £19 2s.0d.
Tax paid: £1 18s.2d.

Landed 160 Negroes at Jamaica 25 March 1710.⁵

Entered Bristol 26 June 1710 with muscovado, indigo, fustick, cotton, lime juice and ivory.⁶

---

23 Feb. 1710⁷
London

John & Robert

Robert
Collins for
Africa

John Burridge

Cargo: 9½cwt wrought iron; 4cwt lead shot; 60lb wrought brass; 83lb wrought pewter; 250 gallons acquavitae; 30 cases spirits; 4cwt gunpowder; 48lb worsted fringe; 1 piece of cloth; 7 tons 11¾cwt and 7lb of iron; 4cwt battery; 10 reams paper; 100oz coral; 4000 rangoes; 388lb great bugles; 15000 crystal beads; 1⅙cwt narrow and one-third cwt broad German linen; 8 rumals; 1cwt copper; 10qr of beans.
Value sworn on oath by Walter Burridge: £421.
Tax paid £42 2s. 0d.
Designed to take 130 slaves.⁸

---

8 Aug.–4 Sept.⁹
1710
Bristol

Martha

Wm
Courtenay

John Burridge

Cargo: 18qr beans; 1 hhd acquavitae; 20 gross tobacco pipes. 520 old sheets; 40 photaes; 20 longees; 10 says; 700 perpetuannas; 9 boysadoes; 8 pennistones; 175 guns; 1057lb pewter; 150 cags of tallow; 250 iron

Date	Vessel	Captain	Merchant

(*Continued from p. 364*)

bars; 20 barrels gunpowder; 25½ gross knives; 30 half-cases of spirits; 144 gallons of molasses spirits.
Value of this cargo: £814 3s.5d.

80 perpetuannas.   Robert Poole
Value: £35. Combined value: £849 3s. 5d.
10 per tax paid: £84 18s. 4d.

2½ doz felt hats.   Samuel Packer

John Burridge also shipped: 2½ hhds of acquavitae; 23cwt wrought iron; 3cwt worsted stuffs.[11]

---

7 March 1712 London[12]	*Mary and Elizabeth*	John Willimott for Africa	John Burridge

Cargo: 18cwt wrought iron; 8cwt gunpowder; 4cwt shot; 1cwt wrought brass; cert. spirits; 3 doz felt hats; 140 goads of cotton; 4½ long cloths; 13qr beans; 1cwt pewter; 13 ton 4¾cwt and 17lb foreign iron; 613lb bugles; 11lb amber; 20,000 crystal beads; 5200 rangoes; 2cwt cowries; 200oz coral; 30 pieces sletia; 40 reams paper; 80 ells German linen; 7cwt battery.
Value £814 3s. 5d., no tax paid in lieu of cargo lost on the *Martha*.

10cwt wrought iron.   Anthony Tourney[13]
Value: £8   Tax paid: 16s.0d.   for John Burridge

2cwt wrought copper; 100lb worsted fringe.   John Burridge
Value: £31 6s. 0d.   Tax paid: £3 2s. 7d.

277oz coral; 5lb 2oz amber; 820 rangoes; ⎫
1500 crystal beads; 50 ells narrow   ⎬   James Wayte
German linen; ½ long cloth   ⎭
Value: £317
Tax paid: £31 14s. 0d.[14]

Delivered 113 slaves to Potomac, Virginia out of a total of about 200. Entered Lyme Regis 1 June 1713 from Guinea and Virginia. Declared 10cwt ivory, several arms and other small goods returned from Guinea for John Burridge Jnr; 1cwt 2qr 9lb ivory for John Burridge & Co.; 111,600 lb tobacco[15] for John & Robert Burridge & Nathaniel Gundry.

Date	Vessel	Captain	Merchant
19 Dec. 1714[16] Barbados	*John Frigate* of Lyme; 65 tons, 2 guns	Samuel Courtenay for Guinea	John Burridge senior and junior; Robert Burridge

Cargo: 5000 gallons of rum; £350 worth of dry goods.
Intended for 200 slaves. Re-entered Barbados 27 Sept. 1715 delivering 91 slaves.[17]
Arrived Lyme 6 Dec. 1716 with muscovado, ginger, cotton wool, fustick and indigo.[18]

Date	Vessel	Captain	Merchant
13 Feb. 1717[19] Lyme Regis	*John Frigate*	Samuel Courtenay for Cape de Verde and Maryland	John Burridge and John Pitts

Cargo: 7cwt wrought iron; 2cwt lead shot; 1cwt pewter; 1 hhd acquavita; 60lb crewel fringe; 4 single bays; 6 Barnstaple bays; 2 doz felt hats; 48lb serge; 3 reams ordinary paper; 2cwt 2qr 7lb battery; 1000 arrangoes; 3⁹⁄₁₀ pieces calicoes (damaged); 4000 crystal beads; 4½ masts (11¼lbs) of rough amber; 8¼lb coral beads; 107 Great bugle; ⁷⁄₁₂cwt narrow German linen; 3¼ ton of foreign iron; 1 barrel (100lb) cut tobacco; 1 cask (6cwt) muscovado sugar. (7lb. pewter and 18lb. shoes failed to sell on the Guinea Coast, returned to Lyme Regis and was re-exported on 9 March 1719 via the *Princess* for Virginia.)[20]

Date	Vessel	Captain	Merchant
April 1718 (from London?)	*John and Robert*	James Wyatt junior	Robert Burridge Jnr & Co., James Wyatt Jnr

Cargo: No reference to clearing Lyme Regis; entered from Guinea 18 Feb. 1719 with 32 elephants teeth and 15 ton of redwood. (19cwt of Swedish iron, 58lbs great battery and 1cwt of battery were returned from Guinea for want of sale.)[21]
Half the cargo of ivory was landed at Lyme, and all the redwood: Cobb duties on these amounted to 13s. 2d.[22]

Date	Vessel	Captain	Merchant
22 Aug. 1720[23] Lyme Regis	*Princess*	James Wyatt, Jnr for Guinea	Robert Burridge Jnr & Co.

Cargo: 7 hhds (513,316lbs) of tobacco (for Cork); 3cwt wrought iron; 8cwt brass manufacture; 5lbs silk manufacture; 3cwt 3qr wrought pewter; 50lb shoes; 1 hhd acquavita; 1cwt and 3qr of gunpowder; 2000

Date	Vessel	Captain	Merchant

(*Continued from p. 366*)

rangoes; 7lb coral beads; 57lb great bugles; 8cwt muscovado sugar; 2 reams copy paper; 36 suits of wearing apparel; 1 piece broadcloth, 12 pieces Welsh plains; 20lb worsted fringe; 1½ doz felt hats; 170 bars (2 tons) Swedish iron; 355lb great bugles; 4cwt battery; 203 quarters and 7 ells narrow Germany linen; 25²⁄₁₀ pieces of calicoes; 5000 crystal beads; 146⁶⁄₁₀ yards of printed calicoes; 555lb of tobacco.

Entered Lyme Regis 16 Oct. 1721[24] with:

17 tons 14cwt 2qr 21lb redwood; 63cwt and 11lb elephants teeth.	Robert Burridge Jnr
4cwt and 1qr elephants teeth.	Arthur Raymond

| 17 June 1722[25] Lyme Regis | *Princess* | James Wyatt for the Cape de Verde Islands and Guinea | Robert Burridge Junior & Co. |

Cargo: 34cwt 1qr16lb iron; 5cwt muscovado sugar; 2cwt 2qr battery; 2cwt 1qr prepared metal goods; 2cwt 1qr narrow German; 1cwt and 10⁄₁₂qr narrow Germany; 25 pieces calicoes; 448lb great bugles; 2000 crystal beads; 1cwt cowries; 1cwt marangoes; 1 barrel (250lb) rolled tobacco; 1 ream ordinary copy paper; 78 bars (12cwt 3qr 5lb) foreign iron; 18 stone pots; 85 arrangoes; 18lb bugle beads; 4lb coral beads; 6lb English manufactured silk; 1 doz thread stockings; 1 doz mens worsted stockings; 5cwt 1qr wrought pewter; 30lb worsted fringe; 3 doz felt hats; 1½ doz caster[26] hats; 5cwt lead shot; 4cwt wrought iron; 20 kegs (500lb) gunpowder; 11 pieces Taunton plains; 12 suits wearing apparel; 4 casks (141 gallons) English spirits.

10 kegs (200lb) gunpowder; 2cwt wrought iron; 1cwt wrought pewter; 1 doz felt hats; 14 pair thread stockings; 1 cask (19 galls) English spirits; 18lb shoes.	James Wyatt
118lbs tobacco	Arthur Raymond

Entered Lyme Regis on 2 Aug. 1723 from Guinea:

43cwt elephant teeth 18 tons redwood for dyers' use.	Robert Burridge Jr & Co.
8cwt 3qr 9lb elephants teeth.	Arthur Raymond
6cwt 2qr 21lb elephants teeth. 14cwt 1qr 16lb redwood.[27]	Robert Burridge

Date	Vessel	Captain	Merchant
? May 1724 Lyme Regis	*Princess*	Arthur Raymond for Guinea	Robert Burridge III & Co.

Cargo: Outward cargo not known. Returned to Lyme 1 June 1725 with 21 tons of redwood for dyers' use and 45cwt. of ivory.[28]

Date	Vessel	Captain	Merchant
22 Dec. 1725 Lyme Regis[29]	*Friendship*	Arthur Raymond for Guinea (via Madeira)	Robert Burridge III & Co.

Cargo: 46cwt of iron; 6cwt 1qr 4lbs of Battery; 4:0:7 of Mettle; 10:0:16 of brown sugar; 1:0:21 of Cheshire Cheese; 3:0:14 of pewter; 100 cast stone pots, uncovered; 433lbs of Great Bugles; 4000 Christall Beads; 3lbs coral beads; 2cwt of one-sixth ells of narrow Germany linen; 1cwt of cowries; 1 hhd (618lbs) of tobacco; 3000 arrangoes (from the last voyage of the *Princess*); 1 chest containing Byram-pants, 24 Guinea stuffs, 1 Negannepant, 3 Bejutapants, 2 Necanees, 12 Chintz, 4 Chelloes, 3 Romalls. And 12 chests, 3 boxes, 7 half hhds, 11 barrells, 4 bags, 3 Maunds, 2 baskets, 2 hhds containing 25cwt wrought iron; 18 Catouch boxes; 4000 gun flints; 2 Drums; 50 kegs containing 1000lb of gunpowder; 6cwt lead shot, 233½ gallons English spirits; 10 gallons of Geneva; 84 yards of ribbon; 2 dozen bottles of Staughton's Elixir; 3 dozen Painted Sticks, 20lbs of worsted fringe; 3 coiles containing 6:1:16 lbs of English Cordage; 5 & one-third gross small Bells; 40 copper bars weighing 1qr 7lbs; 3 brass trumpets; 1 scrutoe [escritoire] value 30s; 7 pieces of Taunton Plains; 20 yards of red broadcloth; 14 suits of wearing apparrel; 40lbs of shoes; 3½ doz Felt hats; 2½ doz Castor hats; 1 piece of Shalloon weight 6 lbs; 3 doz thread stockings, value £3:12:0, 1½ reams of ordinary coppy paper, value 16s; 20lbs Haberdashery ware; 4 pieces containing 155 yards of English sailcloth; 1 piece sail canvas containing 35 yards; 8 barrels of Pitch and Tar; 22 English Chequered Shirts; 14 Silk Caps; 10 gross small English tobacco pipes; 2 gross empty Glass bottles.

For Madeira only. 7000 Rind Butt Hoops.

The *Friendship* was hired on the Guinea Coast by John Carruthers of the *Resolution* of London (sunk off the Coast) to transport his cargo of 130 slaves to Barbados, arriving there 16 Aug. 1726. Raymond delivered 119 slaves to merchants Morris and Harper (presumably on Carruther's behalf) and 5 slaves to John Cogan (son of William Cogan).

Vessels Clearing Exeter, Topsham and Dartmouth for Africa, 1698–1725[1]

Date	Vessel	Captain	Merchant
Jan. 1698 Bristol[2]	*Betty Galley* of Exeter. Plantation-built, 80 tons & 4 guns	Charles Ellard for Cape de Verde	John Ellard

Cargo: 150lbs serge; 700lbs serge; 4cwt wrought iron; 1cwt haberdashery; 50 guinea cloths; 5cwt pewter; 16cwt brass & copper manufacture; 1250lb serge perpetuannas; 4cwt wrought iron; 8cwt gunpowder, 1 hhd acquavitae; 3 nests of trunks; 250(lbs) glass beads; 10 suits of wearing apparel; 32 pairs of old sheets for private use, not for sale.

140lb great bugles from Daniel Jamineau in London; 6 tons of foreign iron. }   Charles Ellard

448 lbs tobacco.   George Mason

Entered Barbados 15 Nov. 1698[4] from Guinea, landing 97 Negroes, 400 elephant teeth, and a parcel of dry goods from England. Cleared for Plymouth with 72 hhds of muscovado, 40 bags of ginger and molasses, on 31 Jan. 1699.

Entered Exeter 1 July 1699[5] from Barbados with:
24cwt of ginger & 8cwt of muscovado sugar.	Francis Lidstone
7000lb of tobacco.	Roger Prowse
7000lbs of tobacco.	Robert Lyall
20cwt of muscovado sugar.	Charles Ellard

Date	Vessel	Captain	Merchant
15 Feb. 1699[6] Exeter	*Dragon* of Topsham. Plantation-built, 60 tons, 6 guns	Christopher Butcher for Africa	Arthur Jeffry & Co.

Cargo: 2 cwt ironmonger wares; 1½cwt tapseils; 1 chest of glasses and glassware; 4 cwt wrought pewter; 56lbs shoes; 1 hhd acquavitae; 15cwt gunpowder; 3 doz felt hats with bands; 1 doz worsted stockings; 56 gross tobacco pipes; 159 bars of Swedish iron (3 tons); 23 doz corn necklaces with coral; stone pots; cut & rolled tobacco.
Arrived at the Gambia 25 Mar. 1699. Loaded ivory and 57 slaves, delivered 37 (of whom 4 died in port) to Joseph Hole in Barbados in June 1699.

Date	Vessel	Captain	Merchant
24 Feb. 1700 Dartmouth	*Daniel and Henry* of Exeter	Roger Mathew for Guinea	Daniel Ivy, Henry Arthur & James Gould

Cargo: As per account.
Loaded 452 slaves on the Guinea Coast.
Delivered 252 slaves to Jamaica 17 Nov. 1700. Seized by Customs in Jamaica. Released June 1701. Returned to Dartmouth 23 July 1701 with 104 cwt of muscovado sugar for James Gould.

Date	Vessel	Captain	Merchant
3 Sept. 1709[7] Dartmouth	*Dartmouth Galley* of Dartmouth	John Blake for the Coast of Africa	John Harris & Co

Cargo: 267 barrels (40cwt 10lb) of Irish tallow; 5 tons of iron; 15 chests containing 975 old sheets; 200 lbs of tobacco; 1 cask of battery (2cwt); 50 packs each of 25½ pieces of English ranters; 5 casks and 3 chests of ironmonger wares (9cwt); 30 small casks (6cwt) of gunpowder; 5 casks (7cwt) wrought pewter; 1 cask (20 gross) tobacco pipes; 1 pack (50 pieces) broad Germany linen; 10 packs of calicoes; 1 box containing 50 paper brawles and 20 rumalls; 1 pack (40) carpets English woollen manufacture; 14 packs (350) English ranters; 1 barrel (1 cwt) of wrought pewter; 22 small casks (5cwt) of gunpowder.
Cargo valued at: £1,151 14s. 7d.
10 per cent tax paid: £115 3s. 5½d.[8]
Taken by French privateers on the Guinea Coast in Jan. 1710.

Date	Vessel	Captain	Merchant

29 Nov. 1713[9]   *Anna*   Thomas Wills   John York, Roger
Topsham   for Oporto   Prowse, John Pyne,
                                                 Abraham Goswell

Cargo: 5 packs containing 120 pieces of perpetuannas; 6 ordinary wigs. 6 ends (18 pieces) of cotton. 225 qrs of barley. 2 bales (40 pieces each) of serge.
Arrived at the Gambia 2 Jan. 1714[10] bound for Brazil.

---

16 Feb. 1714   *Surprise*   Captain Tibby   Roger Prowse for
Exeter[11]   *Galley* of   for Guinea   John Burridge &
                Exeter. 80   Co.
                tons, 6 guns[12]

Cargo: 5 hhds containing 713 brass pans weighing 8cwt 1qr 11lb; 1 hhd (74lb) of fringe; 1 piece (3½yds) red cloth; 6½ reams of paper; 5 chests (7800) cristals; 1cwt 4qr of maungie; 1cwt and 9lb red Pocado; 1cwt 23qr of Olivetto Reds; 580 rangoes; 6cwt of mock coral in 58 strings; 2×½ pieces of Holland; 1 box of laced hats; 1 barrel (1935lb) cowries; 1 case with 57 copper bars; 3 buckaneering guns; 799 bars and 18 pieces of iron; 1 box containing a parcel of weights and scales.

---

15 Sept. 1714[13]   *Sylvia Galley*   John Vennard   George Barons
Dartmouth   40 tons, 4   junior for
                guns[14]   Terceras

Cargo: 2cwt wrought pewter.
Bulk of cargo loaded at Rotterdam, arrived at the Gambia in late Oct. 1714.[15]
The *Sylvia* re-entered Dartmouth from South Carolina 8 Aug. 1715. Her cargo for George Barons amounted to: 764cwt 5qr 14lb of rice; 64 beaver skins; 4cwt 2qr of logwood; 3cwt 1qr 21lb of elephants' teeth. Most of this cargo was exported to Rotterdam on the *Sylvia* within the month by George Barons[16] on the following voyage.

---

19 Aug. 1715   *Sylvia Galley*   John Vennard   George Barons
Dartmouth[17]   junior for
                                  Rotterdam

Cargo: African cargo loaded in Rotterdam, cleared there for the Gambia about Jan. 1716. Delivered 9 slaves to Barbados in July 1716.[18]
Entered Dartmouth with 14cwt 9qr 7lbs of ivory and 40 tons 13cwt 2qr 21lb of fustic for George Barons,[19] re-exported to Rotterdam.

Vessels Clearing Plymouth for Africa, 1698–1719 Including the *Elizabeth Galley* of Bristol Freighted by Bideford Merchants to Africa in 1700[1]

Date	Vessel	Captain	Merchant
16 Jan. 1701[2]	*Rochester* of London	John Dennis for Guinea	Edw. Nicholson

Cargo: 2770 lbs of tobacco.

Date	Vessel	Captain	Merchant
6 Oct. 1704[3]	*Michael Galley* of London	John Prior for Guinea	Mordecai Living & Co.

Cargo: 6cwt 18lb wrought pewter; 6cwt lead; 25cwt wrought iron; 20lb shoes; 1½ tons English spirits: 6 calico quilts; 2 long cloths containing 46 yards; 30 felt hats; 429 yards red Plains; 2doz mens worsted stockings; 6¼cwt battery; 20cwt wrought iron; 196lb great bugles; 29⅝ ells Holland Linen; 20 pieces of ³⁄₁₀ calicoes; 8 slesia lawns; 60 ells broad Germany; 10 Goanhoncherulas; 20 pieces Chocarees; 40 Guinea stuffs; 20 Rumalls; 20lb Great Bugles; 9m chrystal beads out of time; 17cwt 1qr 14lb brass kettles; 28 pieces of chintz; 4lb brown thread; 6 gross white thread buttons; 6 pieces of allejas, 314½ gallons spirits; 20 whole and 20 ½ cases of spirits; several Sheffield wares; 10 muskets; 40 Jamaica guns.[4]
Value: £551 2s. 8d.
Tax paid: £55 2s. 3d.

Date	Vessel	Captain	Merchant
13 July 1705[5] Plymouth	*William* brigantine of London	John Collingwood for Guinea	Joseph Martyn

Cargo: 10 chests containing 650 old sheets valued at 246[d] per p . . . came hither per land caridge; 20 little barrels weighing 20cwt Irish tallow; 85 bars of Swedish iron weighing 20cwt; 22 packs of serges (540 pieces) weighing 4320lb; 2 packs of says (20 pieces) weighing 160lb; 2 packs of Cape cloth (7 rolls) weighing 400lb; 4 bundles of 140 negro waistcoats; 10 quarters of beans customs free; 1 barrel of wrought pewter; 10 barrels of English gunpowder (9 quarters 10lb weight); 60 rundletts & 75 cases of acquavitae (3 hogsheads); 6 chests & 1 barrel of ironmonger wares (14cwt); 1 barrel of wrought pewter (¾cwt).
Value of cargo: £688 5s. 8d.
10 per cent tax paid: £68 16s. 6d.[6]
Delivered 120 slaves to York River Virginia in April 1706.

Date	Vessel	Captain	Merchant
6 Jan. 1707[7] Plymouth	*Pindar Galley* of London	John Taylor for Jamaica	Royal African Company

Cargo: 1 chest of apothecaries' wares, weighing ¾cwt, for delivery to Sir Dalby Thomas at the Cape Coast Castle.

Date	Vessel	Captain	Merchant
10 Nov. 1708[8]	*Joseph Galley* of Bristol	Robert Mullington	Houlditch & Brook

Cargo: 18 cases, 6 bales, 12 casks, 6 chests viz; 300 demy blue long cloths; 18 pieces blue cloth; 240 paper Brawley Dukes (came by land carriage); 80 nicanees; 100 brawles; 15 Photaes; 3cwt 7lb battery; 16cwt 3qr 6lb battery; 21 pieces of $^9/_{10}$ calicoes and 12 pieces of $^8/_{10}$ calicoes; 8 salempores at 23s.8d.; 6 pieces long cloths at 51s.6d. (all of which came by land carriage from London); 2400 pieces of English fustians; 1 piece scarlet long cloth; 1 piece double bays; 26cwt wrought iron; 5cwt wrought pewter.
Value of cargo: £960
10 per cent tax paid: £96[9]
Delivered 280 slaves to Jamaica, 5 Nov. 1709.[10]

Date	Vessel	Captain	Merchant

8 Nov. 1710[11]   *Sylvia Galley*   John Vennard   Phil: Pentyre for
                   of Plymouth   for Guinea   Geo Barons

Cargo: 3 tons 10cwt 3qt 7lb of Swedish iron (300 bars); 5 chests
containing 14cwt 3qt copper bars; 1 cask earthenware; 139 gross Great
glass beads; 1018lb bugle great beads; 4lb bugle small beads; 3doz pair
glass earrings; 2doz vizards; 2doz looking glasses (halfpenny ware); 50
earthen pots covered; 3 casks containing 10cwt 3qr 12lb of pewter.
Value of cargo: £234 10s. 0d.
10 per cent tax paid: £23 9s. 0d.[12]

---

11 Apr. 1711[13]   *John & Robert*   Robert   Phil: Pentyre for
                    of London   Collins for   Robert Burridge
                                       Gambia   junior & Co.

Cargo: 5 chests, 4 cases, 3 boxes & 2 casks containing 280lb of great
bugles; 4cwt battery; 5200 rangoes; 8lb 6oz coral beads; 200lb bugle
beads; 1cwt cowries; 12 reams paper; 56 ounces coral; 17500 cristal
beads; 54lb of scarlet and yellow worsted fringe; ½cwt wrought iron;
50 fowling pieces weighing 2cwt; 60lb wrought brass; 100 copper bars
containing 3qr 14lb in weight; 750 bars Swedish iron (8½ tons); 20
pieces of paper Silesia; 2 packets (100 ells) of holland linen; 3 barrels of
gunpowder (2cwt 2qr 20lb); 2cwt lead shot; 5 pieces blue cottons for
the negroes; 2 doz felt hats; 35 small casks and 20 half casks of English
spirits (300 gallons).
Value of cargo: £408 8s. 9d.
10 per cent tax paid: £40 16s. 10d.[14]

---

9 Feb. 1700   *Elizabeth*   William   John Parminter and
Bristol[15]   *Galley*   Levercombe   Co., Bideford.
                                  for Guinea   Agent: William
                                  and Calabar   Lisle of Bristol.

Cargo: 28 pieces of checks; 80 niconees; 20 broad tapseils; 3000
rangoes; 6 pieces of checks; 55 dozen hats; 3000 rods of copper; 4
groce knives; 4194lbs of pewter; 10 ton: 16 cwt: 0 qr: 17 lbs of iron; 10
ton: 18 cwt: 1 qr: 14 lbs bars of iron; 2:0:17 copper bars; 3:1:14
pewter; 9 dozen hats; 25 dozen hat bands; 1 piece of worsted stuff; 1
piece of striped linen; a parcel of belts.
Value: £1,050 5s. 1¼d.
10 per cent tax: £105 0s. 5d.
Ran upon her anchor at Old Calabar in July 1700 and was lost.

Vessels Clearing Falmouth for Africa, 1698–1719[1]

Date	Vessel	Captain	Merchant
15 Feb. 1697[2] Falmouth	*Restore* of 380 tons, 46 men, 24 guns	Hesketh Hobbiman	Royal African Company

Cargo: 2 hhds of tobacco
(delivered 470 slaves to Barbados, 13 Nov. 1697)[3]

8 Jan. 1701[4]	*Thomas*	James Brussers for Guinea	Robert Corker

Cargo: 13cwt 2qr 14lb ironbound brass kettles; 6cwt wrought pewter; 2cwt knives; 24 fuzees and bullet guns, locks, moulds &c; 2000 flint stones for guns; 2 pairs of stilliards; saws, files &c. weight 28lb; 6 doz hawks bells; 2cwt haberdashery; 1cwt 7lb brass kettles; 3cwt 3qr 17lb brass pans; 6 brass trumpets; 2cwt copper bars; 2qr 21lb brass pans and kettles; 1qr 17lb pewter; 10 doz knives; 24 guns and locks; 100 flints; 1qr haberdashery; 5cwt cloth; 2 chests of tapseils, sletias, chintz; 1cwt and 10lb brass pans; chests of bugles; 6 tons 1cwt iron bars. (All details entered at London and duties paid there.)[5] 2 barrels gunpowder; 1cwt lead bullets; 1 seine net; 6 casks English spirits; 1 surgeon's chest; 11 casks of wine & beer in bottles; 2 cases of salvoes for ships stores; 20 winchesters of French salt.

6 tons iron value £96:16:0; 1120lb bugles;
3500 crystal beads; 2cwt 2qr 26lb cowries;
2000 rangoes; 11lbs amber; (value £235:12:11). } Samuel Eyre
21 ⁶/₁₀ calicoes; 12 tapseils; 1 cwt battery;
¾cwt Germany linen: (Value £39:10:0).[6]

(for Madeira only) 4 hhds pilchards. Robert Taylor

Date	Vessel	Captain	Merchant

(*Continued from p. 375*)

The *Thomas* anchored in the River Thames on 24 Feb. 1702 and discharged 25 tons of redwood value £1,250, a further 70cwt 1qr 14lbs of redwood and 7cwt 7qr 16lb of ivory with a combined value of £231 3s. 9d., all consigned to Samuel Eyre.[7]

12 Aug. 1701[8] Falmouth	*Mary Galley* of London	John Haslewood for Guinea	Edward Pearce

Cargo: 6 hhds of scadds.

19 Nov. 1703[9] Falmouth	*Expedition Galley* of London 150 tons, 16 guns, 30 men[10]	Samuel Parker for Guinea	Houlditch & Brook of London

Cargo: 1566 Calicoes; 50lb stuffs; 60 doz looking glasses; ½cwt haberdashery; ½cwt wrought iron; 15lb small bugles; 1 bundle of blood stones; 1 bundle of Venice pearl; 1lb of amber necklaces; 4 $\frac{3}{10}$ pieces of calicoe; 1 piece muslin. All entered at London, duties paid there – but not the 10 per cent tax – & transported to Falmouth by land carriage. Total value of this cargo, £630; 10 per cent paid, £63.[11]

2cwt 2qr of molasses; 1cwt 2qr 6lb of ironwares; 20 gross of small pipes; 226lb tobacco.	Stephen Jackson (of Falmouth)

12½ hhd pickled scadds; 2qr of wrought pewter.	Edward Pearce (of Falmouth)

The *Expedition* was also carrying 38¼ hhd of preserved pilchards for the Madeira islands. Not long after leaving Falmouth, the *Expedition* was lost at sea,[12] Houlditch and Brook being given leave to ship another cargo to the same value in 1704.

Vessels Clearing Whitehaven[1] for Africa, 1698–1725

Date	Vessel	Captain	Merchant
3 Jan. 1711[2] Whitehaven	*Swift* brigantine. Plantation-built, 70 tons, 4 guns	Thomas Rumball for the River of St Vincent, Guinea	Thos Lutwidge

Cargo: 13cwt & 2qr Irish tallow; 100 bars Irish iron weight 36cwt 2qr 6lbs; 1cwt 3qr 25lb wrought pewter; ¼cwt and 11lbs wrought brass; 3cwt wrought iron; 723lbs British woollen manufactures; 154 goads[3] of cotton; 40 casks of tobacco; 72 pieces of plains; 3 pieces of sempiternas; 17 serges; 10 striped linseys.
Total value of cargo: £260
10 per cent tax paid: £26

Date	Vessel	Captain	Merchant
23 Oct. 1712[4]	*Swift* brigantine	Thos Rumball for Dublin and Madeiras	Thos Lutwidge

Cargo: 24 chalders of coal; ½ton of Nicaragua wood[5] (both items for Dublin); 260 old sheets; 20 pair of salempores; 50 pieces of calicoes; 1694 ffoho [photaes]; 2 pieces of garlits [?]; 30 tirlannas; 30 lots of battery; 10 Japanned scales; 10 boxes of cut and 38 roles of tobacco; 522 Jasper watter;[6] 15cwt 3qr of wrought iron; 114lb wrought pewter; 10cwt 2qr gunpowder; 2322 goads of Northern cotton; 922lbs perpetuannas; 7 doz felt hats; 200yds British made check cottons.

10 remnants containing 2 pieces English linen; 2 doz checkered handkerchiefs; 4cwt worsted stuffs.	Consigned by William Hicks to Barbados

Date	Vessel	Captain	Merchant

(Continued from p. 377)

Delivered 122 slaves in Barbados 27 June 1713.[7]
Entered Whitehaven 31 Aug. 1713 with 3cwt. 4lb. elephants' teeth and 940cwt muscovado sugar.[8]

---

27 Nov. 1713[9] Whitehaven	*Whitehaven Galley*	Thos Rumball for Dublin and Madeira	Thos Lutwidge

Cargo: Tobacco, train oil and 38 calders of coal (all for Dublin); 1300 old sheets (from Newcastle); 5 bolts of canvas; 1 [?] & one-sixth ells of Holland Duck; 2 casks of rolled tobacco; 4 boxes containing 22 doz & 9lbs weight of tallow candles; 5 pieces of British linen cloth under 40 ells each; 100 remnants (of the same); 72qr of wrought iron; 10cwt gunpowder; ¼cwt and 15lb wrought brass; 1440 goads of northern cottons; 13 doz felt hats (for Maryland); 90lbs of British woollens dyed.
Delivered 140 slaves to Jamaica.[10]
Returned from Jamaica with muscovado sugar and 34 tons of logwood.[11]

---

20 Sept. 1715[12] Whitehaven	*Whitehaven Galley*	Thos Rumball for Dublin and Madeira	Thos Lutwidge

CARGO   66 chalders of coal (for Dublin); 5 pieces of British linen cloth; 1cwt wrought iron; 1qr wrought brass; 2 [chests] of old sheets; a parcel of necklaces; 560lbs woollen manufactures, dyed; 28lbs worsted stuffs; 456 goads of Northern cotton; 9 made garments.
Returned from Montserrat on 2 Jan. 1717[13] with 68 elephant teeth, 310 cwt brown sugar, 1680lbs indigo, 3590lbs coconuts, 37cwt fustick, 4000lbs cotton, 620lbs anatta.

---

15 Aug. 1716[14] Whitehaven	*Thomas*	Nathaniel Walker for Madeira	Robert Biglands

Cargo: 20 plains containing [?] & 112lbs weight of British woollens and worsted manufactures, dyed; 1½ doz felt hats.
Although ostensibly for the Madeiras, Walker landed 90 slaves in Barbados on 22 July 1717[16] and entered Whitehaven with a cargo of muscovado sugar on 16 Nov. 1717.[17] 105cwt of this was then freighted direct to Dublin.

Date	Vessel	Captain	Merchant
14 Oct. 1718[18] Whitehaven	*Princess* 80 tons, 4 guns[19]	Thos Rumball for Barbados	Thos Rumball

Cargo: 15 chalders of coal (for Dublin); 406lbs British woollen manufactures dyed; 2 doz hats; parcel of small glass beads returned from Monserrat for want of sale;[20] 192 goads of Northern cotton; a parcel of gunflints; 54lbs British copper bars.
Entered Antigua 30 June 1719[21] from Guinea, delivering 106 slaves.
Cleared for Whitehaven 31 July, entering Whitehaven 3 Oct. 1719[22] with 62cwt muscovado sugar; 53 elephant teeth, 2cwt annatto.

121cwt muscovado sugar 5cwt elephant teeth 5040lb cotton wool			John Gilpin & Co.[23]
15cwt muscovado			James Jopson

Date	Vessel	Captain	Merchant
?Oct 1721[24] Whitehaven?	*Susannah*	George Gibson	Thos Lutwidge

Cargo: Not known. Delivered 50 slaves to James Crowe of Barbados on 6 June 1722.[25]
Cleared Barbados for Whitehaven with 10,000 lb sugar, late June 1722.[26]

Minor Outport Involvement in the Re-export Trade in Slaves, 1698–1722

Date and port of origin	Vessel	Captain	Acknowledged destination	Final destination
April 1698 Exeter	*Hopewell* of Guernsey[1]	Benj. Garrett	Barbados & Boston, New England	Rappahannock, Virginia: arrived 6 Nov. 1699[2]

Final cargo: Rum, sugar, molasses, saltfish and 2 Negroes.
Returned to Dartmouth with tobacco.

17 April 1702 Lyme Regis	*John*	Robert Read	Barbados	South Potomac: arrived 12 Jan. 1703[3]

Final cargo: Plantation goods and 9 Negroes

26 Dec. 1712 Dover[4]	*Friend's Adventure*	Henry Pascall	Nevis	Barbados: arrived June 1714[5]

Final cargo: Mixed cargo and 2 Negroes

4 Nov. 1713 Plymouth[6]	*Industry*	Joseph Howell	Barbados	Upper James, Virginia[7] (arrived May 1714?)

Final cargo: included 2 Negroes

11 Feb. 1716 Plymouth[8]	*Duke of Cornwall*	William Butcher	Virginia	Upper James via Barbados (arrived July 1716?)

Final cargo: included 9 Negroes

Date and port of origin	Vessel	Captain	Acknowledged destination	Final destination
30 May 1716 Lyme Regis[9]	*Martha*	John Wallis	Barbados	Potomac (arrived Feb. 1717?)

Final cargo: included 15 Negroes

| Not traced Whitehaven | *Swift* | Albert Kirkpatrick | not traced | Potomac *via* Barbados (arrived 1714–18) |

Final cargo: included 1 Negro

| 20 Aug. 1716 Exeter[10] | *Dolphin* of Topsham. 60 tons registered in Bermuda | Richard Randall (part-owner) | South Carolina | Charleston: arrived 30 Dec. 1717 via Barbados[11] |

Final cargo: European goods (freighted by Heathfield and Parsons of Exeter); sugar; rum, 14 Negroes. Cleared for Topsham, 5 Feb. 1718.[12]

| 16 Nov. 1717 Weymouth[13] | *Neptune* 80 tons, 8 guns, 10 men | Thomas Gollop | Antigua | New York: arrived 3 March 1718[14] |

Final cargo: 3 Negroes and European goods

| 22 Aug. 1718 Exeter[15] | *Dolphin* of Topsham | Richard Randall | Philadelphia | Charleston: arrived 2 Feb. 1719 via Barbados[16] |

Final cargo: Cocoa; European goods; 4 Negroes

| Dec. 1718 Ramsgate[17] | *Elizabeth* of Ramsgate 100 tons | George Long | (Jamaica ?) | Charleston: arrived 2 Sept. 1719[18] |

Final cargo: 48 Negroes and ballast from Jamaica

Date and port of origin	Vessel	Captain	Acknowledged destination	Final destination
April 1719 Lyme Regis	*John*	Sam Courtenay	Barbados and Virginia	Rappahannock (Dec. 1719 ?)

Final cargo: 48 slaves and rum, molasses, sugar & lime juice[19]

Date and port of origin	Vessel	Captain	Acknowledged destination	Final destination
Nov. 1720 Lyme Regis	*John*	Sam Courtenay	Cork, Barbados and Virginia	Rappahannock (Aug. 1721 ?)

Final cargo: 10 slaves with rum and sugar

Date and port of origin	Vessel	Captain	Acknowledged destination	Final destination
19 Sept. 1721 Poole[20]	*Two Brothers* 60 tons	William Barfoot (part-owner with Stephen Barfoot)	Barbados[21]	Charleston: arrived 7 Feb. 1722[22]

Final cargo: Rum, sugar, 24 Negroes

Vessels Clearing Plymouth for the West Indies, 1697–1704

Date	Vessel	Destination	Cargo
1697 Jan.	*Land of Promise* of Topsham	Barbados	Gunpowder, cloth, mixed cargo including 18 English paintings
Feb.	*Dolphin*	Barbados	Mixed cargo, cloth
June	*Harding* of London	Barbados	Pewter, gunpowder, cloth
July	*Speedwell* of London	Nevis	Cloth, gunpowder
	Tiger of London	Barbados	Cloth
Sept.	*Margaret & Anne*	Of & for Barbados	Candles
	Cock	Barbados	Mixed cargo
Nov.	*Charles & Richard*	Of & for Jamaica	Cloth
Dec.	*Thomas & Francis*	Barbados	Mixed cargo
1698 Feb.	*Employment* of London	Barbados	Cloth
	Catherine	Antigua	Cloth
	Daniel	Barbados	Cloth
	Faithful Galley	Antigua	Mixed cargo
	James & Thomas	Barbados	Cloth
	Britannia of London	Barbados	Gunpowder & cheese
March	HMS *Speedwell*	Barbados	Haberdashery (1cwt)
	Tryon of London	Barbados	Ironmongery & herrings
	Barbara	Barbados	Cloth

Date	Vessel	Destination	Cargo
May	*Land of Promise* of Topsham	Barbados	Cloth & mixed cargo
June	*Josiah & Betty*	Barbados	Cloth
July	*Hope* of London	Barbados	Canvas
Aug.	*Daniel* of London	Barbados	Cloth
Oct.	*Palm Tree*	Barbados	Cloth
Nov.	*Orange Tree*	Barbados	Cloth & herrings
1699 Jan.	*Susanna*	Barbados	Herrings, soap, biscuits, cloth
	Friendship of Lyme	Barbados	Herrings
	Daniel	Barbados	Herrings & mixed cargo
Feb.	*Faithful Galley*	Antigua	Herrings & Cloth
	Adventure	Barbados	Mixed cargo
March	*Sarah & Mary*	Barbados	Mixed cargo & herrings
April	*Katherine*	Barbados	Mixed cargo
Oct.	*Palm Tree*	Virginia & Barbados	Mixed cargo
Dec.	*Sarah & Mary*	Barbados	Mixed cargo
	Adventure	Barbados	Mixed cargo
1700 Jan.	*Neptune* of London	Antigua	Serge
	Sarah & Mary	Barbados	Cider & herrings
	Faithful Galley	Antigua	Cloth
	Thomas & Edward	Barbados	Cloth
Feb.	*Providence*	Antigua	Cloth
	Daniel & Elizabeth	Barbados	Cloth & herrings
May	*Barbara*	Barbados	Cloth
	Daniel	Barbados	Salt
Sept.	*George*	Barbados	Mixed cargo & herrings
	Clarinda of Topsham	Barbados	Cloth [& hakefish from Mount's Bay]
Oct.	*Adventure*	Barbados	Bricks (14,000), cloth, arsenic (12cwt)
Dec.	*Catherine*	Barbados	Cloth
	Land of Promise of Topsham	Barbados	Foodstuffs, 1 tombstone

Date	Vessel	Destination	Cargo
1701 Jan.	*Daniel & Elizabeth*	Barbados	Cloth
	Blossom	Barbados	Beer
Feb.	*James & Thomas*	Barbados	Cloth & herrings
July	*Daniel & Elizabeth*	Barbados	Herrings & soap
	Mary	Barbados	Cloth & mixed cargo
	Lyme of Lyme	Barbados	Cloth, soap, gunpowder
	Content	Jamaica	Serge & dry foodstuffs
Dec.	*Land of Promise* of Topsham	Barbados	Bacon & cider

1702 has no extant records

Date	Vessel	Destination	Cargo
1703 Jan.	*George*	Barbados	Lime
Feb.	*Adventure* of London	Nevis	Soap
	Happy Return of Margate	Antigua	Soap out of the *Goodluck*, a prize
March	*Land of Promise* of Topsham	Barbados	Cloth & herrings
March	*William* of London	Barbados	Herrings & mixed cargo
April	*Daniel & Elizabeth*	Barbados	Beef, pork, peas, gunpowder
May	*Lewis* brigantine of London	Jamaica	Cloth
June	*Golden Frigate* of London	Jamaica	Cereals and candles
	Orange Branch of Topsham	Antigua	Building materials, stoneware, mixed cargo, 3 children's coaches
Dec.	*Orange Tree*	Barbados	Mixed cargo
1704 Feb.	*Somerset* frigate of London	Barbados	Beer & biscuits
March	*Virginia Merchant*	Barbados	Cloth
	Land of Promise of Topsham	Barbados	Cloth & mixed cargo
April	*Friendship* of Lyme	Barbados	Cloth

Date	Vessel	Destination	Cargo
May	*New Frisby* of London	Antigua	Copper cooler & copper teach*
July	*Maryland*	Barbados	Rugs & clothing
Oct./Nov.	*Prince* [packet boat]	Barbados	100 dozen hats
Dec.	*Thomas & Edward*	Barbados	Cloth
	Ely	St Christophers	Pewter

* Teach, usually spelled 'tache', a flat pan used to evaporate sugar cane juice.

Vessels Clearing Minehead and Bridgwater for the West Indies, 1697–1703

MINEHEAD

Date	Vessel	Destination	Main cargo
1697 March	*Friendship*	Barbados	Soap, sacking, herrings, serge
Oct.	*Willing Mind*	Barbados	Soap, serge, herrings
1698 Oct.	*Patience*	Barbados	Herrings
Nov.	*Willing Mind*	Barbados	Herrings
1699 Jan.	*Trial* of Boston, NE	Barbados	Herrings: 491 barrels[1]
March	*Friendship*	Barbados	Herrings: 894 barrels
Nov.	*Taunton Merchant*	Barbados	Herrings: 539 barrels
Dec.	*Trial* of Boston, NE	Barbados	Herrings: 465 barrels
	Endeavour of Cork	Antigua	Herrings: 354 barrels and cloth
	Joan of Topsham	Barbados	Herrings: 160 gross and 55 gross of mohair buttons
1700 Jan.	*Elizabeth & Francis*	Barbados	Herrings: 279 barrels, cloth
Nov.	*Taunton Merchant*	Barbados	Herrings: 481 barrels, cloth
Dec.	*Elizabeth & Francis*	Barbados	Herrings: 302 casks
1701 Oct.	*Taunton Merchant*	Barbados	Herrings: 341 barrels
Dec.	*Elizabeth & Joan*	Barbados	Herrings: 219 barrels
	Somerset	Barbados	Herrings: 600 barrels
1702 March	*Trial*	Barbados	Herrings: 478 barrels

BRIDGWATER

Date	Vessel	Destination	Main cargo
1698 April	*Hannah*	Barbados	Herrings
Nov.	*Willing Mind*	Barbados	Herrings
Dec.	*Friendship*	Barbados	Herrings: 292 barrels
1699 Jan.	*Betty* of Watchet	Barbados	Herrings: 357 barrels
March	*Hope*	Jamaica	Nails, wrought iron, serges, silk, fustians, sletias, herrings
Nov.	*Michael*	Barbados	Herrings: 329 barrels
1700 Jan.	*Unity*	Barbados	Herrings: 479 barrels
Dec.	*Unity*	Barbados	Herrings: 659 barrels
1702 Jan.	*Emily*	Barbados	Herrings: 566 barrels
1703 July	*Emily*	Barbados	Herrings: 470 barrels plus foodstuffs

Glossary of Trade Terms

Note: spelling was far from standardised in the early eighteenth century and the terms below can be found in a multitude of variants.

Ackey: gold-based Guinea currency equivalent to one-sixteenth ounce of gold, value 4s.9d.; sometimes spelt 'acchae', occasionally termed 'angels' or angles, and often abbreviated to 'A'.

Allejas: cloth – type not traced, but of Eastern origin.

Amber: yellow translucent fossil resin used for ornament.

Anker: measure of brandy (8½ gallons), hence cask holding that amount.

Annabasses: cloth often referred to as fustian.

Anatta: orange-red dye.

Aqua vitae: alcoholic spirit such as brandy or whisky.

Arangoes: red carnelian beads from Bombay, usually abbreviated 'rangoes'.

Asiento: the contract to supply the Spanish colonies in the New World with slaves.

Baffts: coarse and cheap cotton cloth of oriental origin.

Barracoon: enclosure where slaves were held awaiting shipment.

Battery: metal goods (usually of brass or copper) that have been beaten into shape.

Bays: ('baize') a fine woollen fabric originally from Holland; Colchester was the prime centre of eighteenth-century English production.

Bejutapant: East Indies cloth.

Benda: measure of gold (2 oz); hence a currency with that value (£7 12s.).

Birding pieces: a fowling piece or gun specifically designed to shoot birds.

Bloodstones: semiprecious stone streaked with red.

Boysadoes: a variant of baysadoes or baize.

Brawles: blue and white striped Indian cotton cloth.

Brawley Dukes: cloth – type not traced, but possibly a variant of brawles.

Buckanearing guns: long muskets originally used to hunt wild oxen.

Bugles: small cylindrical beads, usually black, often sewn on to clothing as ornamentation.

Bunter: corruption of 'buntine', a thin woollen worsted from which flags were made.

Burning glass: magnifying lens.

Byrampants: cloth – type not traced, but of Indian origin.

Caboceer: headman of Guinea Coast village. Eventually loosely applied to any African with whom trade for slaves was effected.

Calico: cotton cloth from Calicut (now Kozhikode) in India.

Cape cloth: cloth manufactured specifically for the Guinea trade (i.e., for the Cape Coast Castle) and probably identical to 'Guinea stuffs'.

Carbine: firearm of an intermediate size, half-way between a pistol and a musket.

Carpet: a thick fabric, normally of wool.

Cartouch: rolls of paper containing powder and shot (cartridges).

Casters: popular fur hats, usually of beaver but increasingly made of rabbit in the eighteenth century; also known as demi-casters.

Chalder: measure of coal, varying between 32 and 40 bushels.

Chelloe: East Indies cloth.

Chintz: a painted or stained calico from India.

Chocarees: cloth – type not traced but of Eastern origin.

Clout: measure of cloth, usually silk or other precious fabric.

Corn: Indian wheat, known now as maize.

Cowrie: small shells from the Maldives, used as currency by the Sudanese and West Africans.

Crewel fringe: ornamental bordering of tassels or twists made from crewel, a thin worsted yarn.

Cristals: clear glass beads, but often used to describe small hand mirrors.

Crocus: heavy sailcloth used for packing and protection.

Currell: coral (as a semiprecious stone).

Darnicks: corruption of the Flemish town of 'Tournai' and applied to the characteristic fabric produced there and its imitations.

Dashee: customary present distributed at the start of trading on the Guinea Coast to the chief (African) negotiators.

Double voyage: a voyage for slaves from the colonies to Guinea and back.

Duck: strong linen or cotton cloth from Holland.

Elephant teeth: ivory, chiefly made into combs, toys (trifles) and false teeth.

Ell: a type of cloth and also a common measure (45 inches).

Ends: a half-length or half-piece of cloth, usually many yards long (despite its name).

Factor: chief executive or Agent of a Royal African Company establishment on the Guinea Coast or at slave trade destinations such as Jamaica or Barbados.

Factory: warehouses of the Company; often loosely applied to the whole trading post itself.

Ferrenoe: not traced, probably a corruption of *farinha*, the Portuguese for flour.

Filletted: tied in a bundle, usually cloth.

Firkin: a small cask.

Fowling piece: gun for shooting birds.

Fustian: coarse cloth made of cotton and flax.

Fustick: wood yielding a yellow dye, from Central America and the Caribbean.

Fuzee: light musket.

Garlits: light brown cloth from Silesia, probably coarser than slessia.

Geneva: gin.

Goad: measure of cotton cloth (4½ feet): sempiternas and linseys also used this measure.

Goanhoncherulas: cloth – type not traced, but of Indian origin.

Gold Coast: stretch of the Guinea Coast from Cape Three Points to the River Volta, now known as Ghana.

Grommettoes: free black Africans employed at the Company forts who occasionally manned Company ships.

Gross: twelve dozen (144).

Guinea Coast: the West African coast from Cape Verde to Nigeria.

Guineaman: vessel bound to or from the Guinea Coast: usually synonymous with slave ship.

Guinea stuff: coarse woollen fabric specifically manufactured for trade on the West African coast.

Hamboro' Case: a packing or travelling case; its exact description has not been traced.

Hangers: loop or strap from which the sword or scabbard was hung from the belt; eventually applied to the sword itself.

Hogshead: large cask; occasionally – as in the case of brandy – it refers to a specific quantity (60 gallons).

Horn: drinking vessel made from horn, often used to dispense drams of whisky.

Hostage: see 'pawn'.

Hounscott seas: says were cheap worsted cloth predominantly of Devon manufacture. Hounscott is possibly from the village of the same name in the parish of Ashwater, or Huntscott near Dunster in Somerset.

Indigo: blue powder from Central American and Caribbean plants of the genus *Indigofera*, used as a dye.

Jew's harp: a simple lyre-shaped musical instrument held between the teeth and played with the finger, the cavity of the mouth giving it tone and resonance.

Kittisole: parasol (from the Spanish *quitar* + sol).

Latin: brass.
Lawn: kind of fine fabric, usually linen.
Lignum vitae: Caribbean hardwood from which the resin was extracted for medicinal purposes.
Linsey: coarse material, probably wool mixed with flax.
Lockram: a coarse French cloth used for clothing and hangings.
Logwood: wood from Central America, especially Honduras, used for dyeing.
Lungees: plain Indian cotton cloth, used in India as loin-cloths (*lunghis*).

Mallaguetta: pepper, used aboard ship as a spice and traded on the Guinea Coast.
Malmul: an expensive sheer muslin with the consistency of silk, imported from the Far East.
Manioc: cassava meal.
Marangoes: apparently a misinterpretation of arangoes, red carnelian beads.
Mark: gold-based currency equivalent to £30 8s.
Mast: measure of weight (2½ lb.) applied only to amber, gold or silver thread.
Matt: bag or sack made of matting; generally also indicates a heavy, coarse fabric (like tarpaulin) used to protect goods.
Maund: a wicker or woven basket with handles.
Maungie: a type of oriental bead.
Middle passage: the Atlantic crossing from Africa to America on which slaves were carried.
Molasses: black treacle, the uncrystallised residue drained from raw sugar during refining.
Monmouth cap: a flat, round cap traditionally worn by soldiers and sailors.
Muscovado: unrefined brown sugar. It attracted a lower rate of duty than white when imported into England.
Muslin: delicately woven fine cotton fabric.

Negannepant: East Indies cloth.

Nehallaware: cotton fabric from India, possibly a corruption of Nel-lore-ware.

Neptunes: large thin brass pans. Cut into elaborate shapes they provided ornament for neck, arms and ankles.

Niconees: cotton fabric of Indian origin.

Old sheets: second-hand cotton bed sheets, often imported from Rotterdam and exported to Guinea as a staple item of barter.

Olivetto: a kind of mock pearl made for the Guinea trade.

Ounce: weight of gold equivalent to £3 16s.

Pawn: quantity of gold held as a guarantee of delivery of slaves after terms of barter had been agreed; occasionally human pawns were taken.

Penistone: coarse woollen fabric from the West Riding (Yorkshire) town.

Pentado: printed chintz or calico from the East Indies.

Perch: measure of length equivalent to a rod (5½ yards).

Perpetuanna: hard-wearing woollen cloth of predominantly West Country origin.

Photaes: Indian cotton fabric.

Pipe: cask for wine, usually containing 105 gallons.

Plains: kind of flannel material produced largely in the West Country and Wales.

Pocado: a type of oriental bead, often red in colour.

Qua-qua cloth: woven cloth of Sudanese manufacture, popular with the West Africans.

Rangoes: red carnelian beads, imported from Bombay.

Ranters: English woollen cloth favoured by the Guinea trade.

Rod: measure of length (5½ yards).

Rumal: silk or cotton square used as a handkerchief or neckerchief.

Rundlett: cask of varying capacity and dimension, frequently used for gunpowder.

Salempore: cotton cloth from Nellore in India, the usual 'slave cloth'.

Say: cheap worsted woollen cloth from Devon and Norfolk.

Scadd: herring.

Seam: a horse-load.

Seas: corrupt plural of 'say'.

Seine net: fishing net which hangs vertically in the water, the ends of which are drawn together to trap the fish.

Sempiternas: long-lasting woollen fabric, probably identical with perpetuannas.

Serge: staple woollen cloth, usually of Devon origin.

Shag: worsted cloth with a velvet texture on one side.

Shalloon: closely woven linen, often used for linings.

Slessia: fine linen or cotton fabric from Silesia, occasionally spelt 'Sletia'. Occasionally described as paper'd, presumably referring to the protective tissue in which this fine cloth was wrapped.

Steels: applied to a wide variety of goods from needles to sharpeners for knives. Here it probably refers to the piece of steel shaped for the purpose of striking fire with a flint, usually in a pistol or firelock.

Stilliard: balance or scale.

Supercargo: agent appointed by merchant to supervise and account for loading and disposal of ship's cargo.

Tackey: African gold-based currency equivalent to 4¾d. Usually abbreviated 'T' and occasionally spelled 'taccae'.

Tallow: solidified animal fat used for making candles and smearing on ships' hulls to prevent teredo worm and marine growth.

Tapseils: Indian cotton cloth, frequently re-exported to Africa.

Ticking: cheap striped cotton fabric.

Tirlannas: not traced: 'lana' (the Spanish for wool) suggests a fabric of that type.

Train oil: fish oil, usually from cod or whale.

Trunk: slave pen or stockade.

Venice pearl: solid artificial pearl.

Vizards: beads, but of an unknown type, possibly from Persia.

White sugar: refined sugar that attracted a higher rate of duty when imported into England in this state.

Winchester: a dry and liquid measure often used for salt.

List of Abbreviations

For locations of collections of papers or other records, see Primary
Sources, p.448.

ADM.8	List of Ships on Station, 1699–1703
ADM.36	Ships' Musters Series 1
ADM.50–53	Admirals', Captains', Masters' and Ships' Log-books
B7	Lyme Regis Borough Archives
B.57–63	South Sea papers
BL	British Library
BMHS Journal	*Barbados Museum and Historical Society Journal*
C.33	Chancery Decrees
CJ	*Journal of the House of Commons*
CO.5	Colonial Shipping Returns – Virginia, South Carolina etc.
CO.33	Colonial Shipping Returns – Barbados
CO.142	Colonial Shipping Returns – Jamaica
CO.157	Colonial Shipping Returns – Leeward Islands
CO.388	Board of Trade Original Correspondence
COU	Humphrey Morice papers
CSP	*Calendar of State Papers*
CTB	*Calendar of Treasury Books*
CTP	*Calendar of Treasury Papers*
CUST.50–101	HM Customs and Excise, Outport Records
CUST.102	HM Customs and Excise, Port of London, books of minutes and orders
D/LONS/W	Lonsdale papers
DNB	*Dictionary of National Biography*
DX	Letter books of Walter Lutwidge
E.190	The Port Books for England and Wales
HCA	Records of the High Court of the Admiralty

HHC	*Histories of the House of Commons* (the portion central to this study – 1690–1715 – has not yet been published)
HLRO	House of Lords Record Office
IGI	International Genealogical Index
IJAHS	*International Journal of African Historical Studies* [Boston, USA]
IND.1	Index to Shipping Captured by Letter of Marque Vessels
JAH	*Journal of African History*
JRIC	*Journal of the Royal Institution of Cornwall*
LJ	*Journal of the House of Lords*
PRO	Public Record Office
PROB	Wills and Administrations of the Prerogative Court of Canterbury
RO	Record Office
SLB	Spedding Letter Books, in the Lonsdale papers
T.64	Treasury Papers
T.70	Papers of the Royal African Company
VCH	*Victoria County Histories*

Notes

PREFACE

1. Charles Davenant, *Reflections on the Constitution and Management of the Trade to Africa* (1709), from Whitworth's edition of Davenant's *Collected Works* (1771) Vol. V, p. 79.
2. By John A. C. Vincent, copy made for Charles G. Prideaux-Brune of Padstow, Cornwall. Vincent was a professional antiquary and genealogist.
3. The *Journal* contains copious notes from the *Lex Mercatoria*, especially Chapter 22 'Of the Master of a Ship, his Power & Dutie of the Mast^r to the Mech^{ts}', and Chapter 23 'Of the Duties and Privillidges of Marriners'. In addition, Prideaux lists the commodities of Great Britain, Ireland, France, Spain and so on. Since all this material derives directly from the *Lex Mercatoria* and reflects nothing of Prideaux himself, being merely an *aide-mémoire*, it has not been transcribed into the present *Journal*.

CHAPTER I   An Introduction to the Slave Trade

1. *The Voyages and Travels of Captain Nathaniel Uring*, (1726, repr. 1928), p. 107.
2. A small percentage of her slaves derived from contraband dealing with islands in the Caribbean held by the English, French, Dutch or Danes.
3. *Some Memoirs of the First Settlement of the Island of Barbados* (1741), Appendix.
4. CO.388/12 part 2: 13 November 1709, letter from the Committee of Separate Traders signed by Peter Paggen, Humphrey Morice, John Burridge junior and others.
5. CO.388/7. fol.285.
6. Ibid., fol.337.
7. T.70/1199, 19 February 1702. In the *Hopewell*, Captain Roberts for Venice, freighted by John Munday, 1531lb. of great bugles.
    Not all Italians were oblivious to the profits of the slave trade. A

group of Genoese merchants in Seville played an important part in the seventeenth-century Spanish slave trade. When Spain resumed the Asiento system in 1662 it was the expatriate Genoese community who again benefited. Overall however, Italy, lacking colonial possessions, could muster only the most marginal presence on the slave trading stage. See James A. Rawley, *The Transatlantic Slave Trade* (1981) for an extensive overview of the trade in general, an account to which the opening chapters of this book are greatly indebted.

CHAPTER 2   Merchants versus Monopoly

1. James A. Rawley, *The Transatlantic Slave Trade* (1981), p. 150.
2. Richard Jobson, *The Golden Trade* (1623) p. 89, quoted by James A. Rawley, *The Transatlantic Slave Trade* (1981), p. 151. I am indebted to Professor Rawley's scholarship for much of the background to the slave trade of this period.
3. R. Porter, 'The Crispe Family and the African Trade', *JAH* ix (1968).
4. Later writers have represented this as a black slave conspiracy. For a detailed account of the incident and the role of poor whites in the West Indies see Jill Sheppard, 'The Slave Conspiracy that Never Was' *BHMS Journal* xxxiv, no. 4 (1974), and *The Redlegs of Barbados* (1977), also Hilary Beckles, *Black Rebellion in Barbados* (1984), pp. 111–2.
5. *CSP* Colonial, (1693–6), para. 1738.
6. R. N. Bean, *The British Transatlantic Slave Trade 1650–1775* (1975), p. 109.
7. See Henry A. Gemery and Jan S. Hogendorn, 'The Atlantic Slave Trade: a Tentative Economic Model' *JAH* xv (1974): 223–47.
8. Ibid. See also Hilary Beckles, *White Servitude and Black Slavery* (1989), p. 124.
9. Bean, p. 260, from *CSP* Colonial (1661–8), p. 266.
10. Charter reprinted by Elizabeth Donnan in *Documents Illustrative of the Slave Trade to America* (1930–5) Vol. I, pp. 177–92. The first two volumes of Donnan's magisterial four-volume discourse on the slave trade to the Americas are particularly relevant to the late seventeenth and early eighteenth centuries, though scant attention has been paid to the involvement of minor English outports. The standard history of the Company is K. G. Davies' *The Royal African Company* (1957).
11. Support for the Company in the provinces was largely restricted to Kidderminster and Shrewsbury cloth-workers and weavers: *CJ* xi (1696).
12. *CJ*, X (1695).
13. *CJ*, X (1690).
14. Especially the petitions of Bristol and Dartmouth, *CJ*, XVI, 15–19 March 1711.
15. T.70/57.
16. Ibid.
17. T.70/52. Letter to Cape Coast factors, 11 December 1712. The question

of free trade to Africa remained a vexed one. After much further debate, on 13 April 1713 the House of Commons resolved that the trade should be open, subject to charges for the maintenance of forts, and a bill was brought in to give effect to this resolution. After passing the Commons, it was rejected by the Lords: the respective rights of the Company and separate trader remained undetermined. The latter group took advantage of the vacuum by resolutely pressing ahead with what amounted in effect to free, open and unfettered trade. And so, despite Company fury, it remained. See W. R. Scott, *The Constitution and Finance of English, Scottish and Irish Joint Stock Companies to 1720* (1910), Vol. II, pp. 20–5.

18. T.70/45.
19. T.70/132.
20. T.70/5.
21. T.70/61.
22. T.70/43. For William Coward (1648–1738) see *DNB*.
23. Ibid.
24. See T.70/44 for an instance of this: the *Michael* of Glasgow arrived in Bristol with two black sailors, servants of the Company (probably *grommettoes*) aboard. They were ordered to London on 6 June 1710.
25. T.70/51.
26. T.70/132, Sir Jonathan Andrews.
27. T.70/43. The *Boughton* also brought back a 'tiger'. No import duty was payable on slaves, gold or silver.
28. Ibid.
29. T.70/135.
30. T.70/43.
31. Peter Fryer, *Staying Power* (1984) pp. 113–14.
32. T.70/52.

CHAPTER 3 Background to the Voyage

1. Described in CO.5/749 as a hack-boat, Samuel Stafford commanding. As we shall see later the term hack-boat is misleading.
2. E.190/973/3.
3. E.190/841 (12 August 1699).
4. E.190/960/7. Cleared for New England under Samuel Stafford: since trade with the Guinea Coast was controlled by the monopoly of the Royal African Company, this apparent destination was little more than a simple ruse to avoid detection. Stafford handed over to Mathew somewhere in the Atlantic, probably at the Azores.
5. T.70/12. The name of the vessel has not been entered, again to avoid detection.
6. E.190/962/1. The Royal African Company appears not to have questioned the import of Guinea redwood by an independent trader.

7. Devon RO. 3372A add/PZ3.
8. The blank against the number of crew in the Port Book entry for the *Daniel and Henry* reveals that when clearing the Customs at Dartmouth the ship was far from fully manned.
9. James Pope-Hennessey, *The Sins of the Fathers* (1967), p. 108.
10. *CSP* Colonial (1696–7), para. 287.
11. As has been noted in Chapter 5, tonnage is liable to arbitrary judgements. Thus the *Prince of Orange* is described in the Barbados Shipping Registers as 456 tons in 1700 and 300 tons in 1701: she had suffered no truncating rebuild in the intervening period.
12. K. G. Davies, *The Royal African Company* (1957), p. 193.
13. BL Add.MS39946.
14. T.70/350, which is also evidence of the 10 per cent tax being paid.
15. Charles Davenant, *Reflections on the Constitution and Management of the Trade to Africa* p. 296. (1709)
16. *CTB* (1690–1), pp. 975–6.
17. *CSP* Domestic (1700–1), p. 251.
18. J. L. Vivian, *The Visitation of the County of Devon* (1895), p. 248.
19. Ezra Cleaveland, *A Genealogical History of the Courtenays* (1735). Francis Courtenay (father of Frances), b.1633, d.1672.
20. Apprenticed to John Mayne, merchant of Exeter, early in his career.
21. For James Gould (c.1625–1707) see B. D. Henning (ed.) *The House of Commons 1660–1690* (1983), pp. 422–3. George Gould (1634–1720) is mentioned in Hutchins' *History of Dorset* (1861) Vol. II, p. 842.
22. As an indication of their importance as tobacco merchants, Ivy and Arthur had imported 687,954 lb. of tobacco in 1694–5 and re-exported 543,583 lb. of it (*CTB*, 1699, p. 181).
23. Engledue Prideaux, *Pedigree of the Family of Prideaux of Luson in Ermington* (1889). Exactly a century later, much more material relating to the Prideaux family is available in Roy Prideaux's *Prideaux. A West Country Clan* (1989), and shows that Nicholas Prideaux, Company Agent in Barbados in 1700, was a very remote cousin.
24. HCA. 26/2.
25. Dottin of Barbados references can be found in an anonymous work, *Some Memoirs of the First Settlement of the Island of Barbados* (1741); J. C. Hotten (ed.), *Original Lists of Persons of Quality* (1874); Vere Oliver, *Caribbeana* (1910–19) Vol. II; Sir R. H. Schomburgk, *History of Barbados* (1848). The slave ship *Dottin Galley* is recorded at CO33/13, and in E. Donnan, *Documents Illustrative of the Slave Trade to America* (1930–5), Vol. II. p. 32.
26. Dartmouth Port Books (E.190 series) and MSS detail in the *Journal*. Part of the 1717 voyage (on behalf of Benjamin Ivy) has been reprinted in the *Mariner's Mirror* vi (1920).
27. Royal Commission on Historical MSS, NRA 9926, p. 35.
28. David Brion Davis, *The Problem of Slavery in Western Culture* (1966), pp. 291–332.

29. Charles Davenant, *Reflections on the Constitution and Management of the Trade to Africa* (1709), from Whitworth's edition (1771) Vol. V, p. 104.

CHAPTER 4 Slave Ship Cargoes

1. Barbot, *A Description of the Coasts of North and South-Guinea* (1732), p. 172
2. K. G. Davies *The Royal African Company* (1957), p. 115.
3. T.70/2; T.70/58.
4. Barbot, p. 274.
5. T.70/350.
6. E.190/974/11.
7. T.70/350, p. 12.
8. Ibid.
9. CUST.65/39: Board to Collector at Dartmouth, 30 December 1699. A marginal note – £203:14:5¾ – probably refers to the value of the casks.
10. T.70/58: seizure of the *Daniel and Henry* recorded in Jamaica.
11. There is an obvious discrepancy between £2,036 and £2,252 (total declared to the Company in London): perhaps not all figures were adjusted upwards by exactly 50 per cent.
12. Charles Davenant, *Reflections on the Constitution and Management of the Trade to Africa* (1709), from Whitworth's *Collected Works of Sir Charles Davenant* (1771), Vol. V, pp. 321–4. T.70/135 records the petition of the inhabitants of Kidderminster of 1708 in which they, as manufacturers of carpets and boysadoes, saw greater opportunities for themselves if the Company monopoly was not reinstated.
13. Davies, pp. 177–8.
14. *Improvement of the African Trade* (1708).
15. T.70/1223.
16. Davies, p. 177.
17. Daniel Ivy and Company's fuzees (light muskets) are described as fine and probably not strictly comparable with Company fuzees. The last thing the Company intended to do was arm its local African traders with fine, accurate weaponry.
18. The figure in brackets includes the cost of the hogshead.
19. The figure in brackets includes the cost of the chest.
20. I.e. 1700. All cargo details were required to be with the Customs House at least fifteen days before the ship cleared the home port. This explains the discrepancy between Port Book entry date and log-book record of actual departure.
21. Thus the real cost of the cargo was £2,036. In fact official documents put it at £2,252 (T.70/350).

CHAPTER 5   A Description of the *Daniel and Henry*

I am grateful to Captain A. J. B. Naish CBE, RN, retd. – descendant of the *Daniel and Henry*'s supercargo, Walter Prideaux – for his generous help in compiling this chapter.

1. Though not addressing the subject of the slave trade, Dr Nancy Eaglesham's unpublished thesis '*The Growth and Influence of the West Cumberland Shipping Industry*', University of Lancaster, 1977, highlights much of the financial minutiae of shipping in this period.
2. ADM. 52/36.
3. See log for Tuesday, 26 March 1700 when the *Daniel and Henry* encounters a tornado (p. 66).
4. See log for Tuesday 27 February 1700 (p. 58).
5. See log for Saturday 14 September 1700 (p. 159).
6. Notes apparently present in the original *Journal*.

CHAPTER 6   The Voyage Out

1. Details from the IGI registers compiled by the Church of Jesus Christ of Latter-day Saints
2. HCA. 26/2. Nicholas Lidstone, Exeter and Dartmouth merchant, was the *Franke*'s commander in 1692.
3. CUST. 65/173.
4. HCA. 26/18 and HCA. 26/14.
5. *The Mariner's Mirror* vi (1920). Curiously, a Thomas Rogers is recorded on the muster roll for HMS *Scarborough* as having been impressed on 20 March 1701 – before the war ship left Portsmouth – but as having deserted in Jamaica on the following 23 June (ADM. 36/3381).
6. David Waters, *The Art of Navigation in England in Elizabethan and Early Stuart Times* (1978), p. 581.
7. T.70/134 contains the 'outline' log-book of the *Fauconberg*.
8. Will of Robert Mather of the *Sarah* dated 2 January 1699, proved 15 February 1700; PROB. 11/454. An account of the finances behind the *Sarah*'s Guinea venture are detailed in the account book of John Burwell, Devon RO.3372A add./PZ3. This document also reveals Roger Mathew was part-owner of the Newfoundland fisheries ship *Blessing* of Dartmouth, and that he acted on behalf of his son during the latter's command of the *Elizabeth* (1697) and *Prudence* (1698) of Dartmouth.
9. That is, with both the fore topsail and main topsail reduced in size by reefing.
10. E.190/974/4. The *America Merchant* of between 120 and 160 tons burden, 12 guns, 22 men, was frequently employed between the Caribbean and Exeter/Topsham in the years 1698–1710.
11. T.70/1199, December 1706.
12. 'Starboard tacks on board' is equivalent to the modern 'on the starboard

tack'. Steering was mostly carried out by adjusting the sails as a ship's rudder was very small to avoid damage by waves and had only a limited capacity to control the direction in which the ship sailed.

13. Variation is the difference between true and magnetic north. In England in 1700 it was about 10° west, i.e. the magnetic compass pointed 10° west of true north. Variation fluctuated widely in different parts of the world. As all courses steered, and all bearings taken had to be corrected for variation, it was important to ascertain this with some accuracy. Variation could be checked because, given the sun's declination and the approximate latitude, it was possible to calculate the true direction in which the sun rose or set. The word 'amplitude' means the angle between a rising or setting celestial body and true east or west. The difference between this true direction and the direction shown by the magnetic compass, after allowing for the known compass error (deviation) gives the variation.

Walter Prideaux may well have had tables (or calendars such as the first mate, John Chapman, had) similar to those found in modern nautical almanacks, showing the true bearing of the rising or setting sun against declination and latitude. The sun was officially rising when it was bisected by the horizon, but to allow for refraction – the bending of light near the horizon – the sun was taken as rising when it appeared to be a distance of half its diameter above the horizon.

Weather was crucial to the success of determining variation. The sky had to be clear down to the sea's horizon so that the sun could be seen actually setting. Secondly, the sea itself had to be calm so that the magnetic card would not swing about too much. Walter Prideaux describes the weather as fair and the water as very smooth, which also made it easier to take an accurate bearing with the compass. In addition, he was able to take a latitude observation, so the sky at noon was reasonably clear.

At sunset the variation was measured and found to be 5° east.

14. The vagaries of the current were rendering it impossible to reconcile the ship's position by log with that ascertained by observation. Strong currents the length of the West African coast made this a common problem.

15. Elizabeth Donnan, *Documents Illustrative of the Slave Trade to America* (1930–5), Vol. I, p. 445.

16. Presumably 'hummocks'.

17. James Barbot, 'An abstract of a Voyage to the Congo River ... and to Cabinda in the year 1700', in Awnsham and John Churchill, *Collection of Voyages and Travels* (1732), Vol. V, p. 540.

CHAPTER 7 Africa and the Africans

1. N. Uring, *The Voyages and Travels of Capt. Nathaniel Uring* (1726), p. 112.

2. T. F. Garrard, _Akan Weights and the Gold Trade_ (1980) is an invaluable study of African trading history and much of this chapter derives from that source.
3. J. L. Vogt, 'Notes on the Portuguese Cloth Trade in West Africa 1480–1540', _IJAHS_ viii (1975).
4. Garrard pp. 44–5, quoting C. Loyer, _Relation du Voyage du Royaume d'Issyny_ (1714).
5. Quoted by Garrard, p. 93.
6. Roland Oliver, _The African Experience_ (1993), pp. 125, 128.
7. J. E. Inikori (ed.) _Forced Migration_ (1982), pp. 51–4.
8. Alexander Falconbridge, _An Account of the Slave Trade on the Coast of Africa_ (1788).
9. Uring, p. 108.
10. _Certain Considerations Relating to the Royal African Company of England_ (1680), BL MS Harley 7310 (pamphlet).
11. Quoted by J. A. Rawley, _The Transatlantic Slave Trade_ (1981), p. 272.
12. Phillips, p. 214.
13. Orlando Patterson, _The Sociology of Slavery_ (1967), pp. 119–38.
14. Phillips, p. 198.
15. Ibid., p. 206.
16. Ibid., p. 218.
17. T. 70/1185.
18. Ibid.
19. Phillips. p. 218.
20. T. 70/1185 extract by permission Controller HMSO.

CHAPTER 8   Forts, Factors and Fraud

1. Albert van Dantzig, _Forts and Castles of Ghana_ (1980). The standard work on the subject is still A. W. Lawrence, _Trade Castles and Forts of West Africa_ (1963).
2. T.70/43.
3. Ibid.
4. T.70/1435, a loosely inserted leaf entitled 'Salaries Allowed the Company's Servants in Guinea'.
5. Thomas Phillips, _A Voyage Made in the 'Hannibal' of London, 1693–4_, in Awnsham and Churchill, _Collection of Voyages and Travels_ (1732) Vol. VI, p. 204 reveals these were maintenance men only employed at the larger Company establishments. Their duties at the Cape Coast Castle involved maintaining the water supply to its cistern.
6. K. G. Davies, _The Royal African Company_ (1957), p. 372.
7. Ibid., pp. 109–10.
8. Peter Kemp, _The British Sailor: A Social History of the Lower Deck_ (1970), pp. 31–2. Although concentrating on the mid-eighteenth cen-

tury, N. A. M. Rodger's *The Wooden World* (1986), pp. 128–30, shows the situation in the Royal Navy to have been much more equitable.

9. T.70/1225.

10. T.70/1443 and 1444 for some particularly flagrant examples.

11. T.70/376.

12. Davies, p. 256.

13. T.70/50.

14. Phillips, pp. 210–11; also provides the source for the preceding quotes in this passage.

15. Ibid., p. 201. Coincidentally, Thomas Buckeridge was factor at Winnebah in 1699. Company records indicate that little love was lost between the two brothers.

16. Ibid., p. 223.

17. Ibid., pp. 209–10.

18. T.70/1428 and T.70/50: Buckeridge, his father Edmund (a Commissioner of Prizes), Sokeford Cage of Sokeford Hall, Essex and Mr Deane of the Inner Temple each provided £400.

19. T.70/11.

20. T.70/376.

21. Quoted by A. van Dantzig, *The Dutch and the Guinea Coast 1674–1742* (1978), p. 72. A benda = 2oz. of gold.

22. Later the author of *A New and Accurate Description of the Coast of Guinea* (1705).

23. T. F. Garrard, *Akan Weights and the Gold Trade* (1980), pp. 142–3. A half-hearted attempt was made by the English to mine gold not far from Winnebah, but the geologist appointed by the Royal African Company – Joseph Baggs – quickly succumbed to disease. Mindful of the salutary experience of the Dutch at Commenda, the attempt was finally shelved; Garrard, p. 143.

24. Garrard, p. 157. Quoting letter from van Sevenhuysen to the Assembly of X, 1 March 1699. The Amsterdam chamber of the West-Indische Compagnie was governed by ten directors, hence the Assembly of X.

25. Garrard, pp. 91–2.

26. T.70/51. 'The Private Book of the Cape Coast Castle' (T.70/1463) also records Buckeridge's predilection for murdering local African dignitaries for political and financial ends. Buckeridge's replacement as Agent, the geologist Joseph Baggs, did not live long enough to effect a change, (T.70/1209A), and it was not until the arrival of Dalby Thomas in 1703 that the Company could put its house in order.

27. T.70/51.

28. See Dalby Thomas' *An Historical Account of the Rise and Growth of the West India Collonies* (1690). This work is dedicated to Sir Robert Davers.

29. T.70/2. Daniel Thomas, his third brother, captained several Company slave trade ships before being appointed Company surveyor of ships.

30. T.70/14.

31. T.70/1199.
32. T.70/1184.
33. T.70/14 (1704).
34. T.70/52. John Pery, Secretary to the Company, to Sir Dalby Thomas.

CHAPTER 9   Along the Guinea Coast

1. Nicholas Gellibrand to the Lords of the Council of Trade, January 1700 (CO.5/715).
2. T. Phillips, *A Voyage Made in the 'Hannibal' of London, 1693–4* (1732), pp. 194–5. When compared to Phillips' concise and accurate account, Prideaux's looks decidedly garbled, indicating he was rarely certain exactly which small town or river the *Daniel and Henry* was actually standing off. For this he probably had to thank his inaccurate charts.
3. T.70/350. The *Amity*'s cargo was valued at £841. Described as of 50 tons, 10 guns, she arrived Barbados on 2 September 1700 but left the same day 'with all her slaves for Jamaica' (CO.33/15), where she delivered 170 (T.70/175). Richard Smallwood later commanded the slave ship *Ann and Judith* in November 1704 (T.70/1199).
4. John Barbot, *A Description of the Coasts of North and South-Guinea* (1688) in Awnsham and John Churchill, *Collection of Voyages and Travels* (1732), Vol. V, p. 130.
5. That is, the *Daniel and Henry* sailed towards the shore (on), and then away for a short distance (off), and repeated the process. By this means she remained in roughly the same place, without having to anchor, and was ready to collect her long-boat as soon as it returned.
6. Good sandy ground suitable for anchoring. Foul ground normally indicated a rocky bottom where an anchor might become jammed in the rocks and lost.
7. Phillips, p. 196.
8. Cape Palmas divided the Grain Coast from the Ivory Coast and Windward or Upper Guinea from Leeward or Lower Guinea.
9. One-tenth of a nautical mile; so about a cable (or 200 yards) off the Cape the water became shallow. This feature extended about a league off shore. Even at a distance of 3 leagues offshore the depth was still only 20 fathoms.
10. Usually a corruption of Rio St Andero, but this still lay three days' sail to the east.
11. Barbot, p. 137.
12. Ibid., p. 139.
13. Phillips, p. 197; see also Barbot, p. 139 as corroboration.
14. Possibly slaves bought as part of a private venture since the *Daniel and Henry* did not load her first 'official' slave until 11 April at Dixcove, a date also corroborated by the Burwell Account Book (Devon RO 3327A add./PZ3).
15. N. A. M. Rodger, *The Wooden World* (1986), pp. 100–4.

16. Barbot, p. 432, who describes Visser as 'wanting even common sense'.
17. Burwell Account Book (Devon RO. 3327A add./PZ3).
18. Garrisoned by 16 white men and 14 *grommettoes* (free blacks employed as servants and soldiers). The local natives were 'so intractable, fraudulent, villanous and obstinate, that the English cannot deal with them'; Barbot, p. 433.
19. Dalby Thomas was not appointed until 1702. Details of Colborn from T.70/1184, T.70/51, T.70/14 and T.70/52.
20. A. W. Lawrence, *Trade Castles and Forts of West Africa* (1963) p. 292, which also confirms the suitability of the *Daniel and Henry*'s anchorage.
21. T.70/1184. Africans were habitually lampooned with intensely disparaging names. In the event of their visiting England, which a few powerful chiefs did as guests of the Company, ridiculously inflated titles were invariably bestowed on them.
22. Phillips, p. 203.
23. Barbot, p. 153.
24. ADM. 8/7 and ADM. 51/4261.
25. Peck had only arrived on the Coast in 1699. On 30 June 1701 he wrote to the Company: 'As to slaves, the ten per cent men are my only interruption in acquiring any, they giving 6 or 8 angles more than your honours allow . . .'. Sir Dalby Thomas reported to London that Peck was guilty of breach of trust, alleging that cloth was dispatched to him on all ten per cent ships under the guise of Company goods. With this he no doubt traded for slaves on his own account – though probably feeding and housing them at Company expense – before selling them to the separate traders (T.70/14). A poor salary was not the reason for his freelancing; on 17 September 1702 his wage is recorded as 6 marks and 2 ackeys per annum, an unusually high amount (T.70/661).
26. Van Sevenhuysen, 15 April 1700. Quoted by A. van Dantzig in *The Dutch and the Guinea Coast, 1674–1742* (Accra 1978), pp. 70–1. Since England's calendar was eleven days behind Holland's, the date of the letter corresponds to 4 April 1700.
27. T.70/1183 and 51.
28. The career of the *Prince of Orange* and her commander, Josiah Daniel, can be traced through *Acts of the Privy Council*, Col. Series 11, 274(7); HCA. 26/1, HCA. 25/11; *Acts of the Privy Council*, Col. Series 11, 365(16) and 477; ADM. 52/80; ADM. 51/4298; *CSP* America and West Indies (1697); CO. 33/13; T.70/376 and 1223, 350, 61, 1433, 1209b. Josiah Daniel's will is recorded by J. M. Sanders in *Barbados Records 1701–1725, Wills* (1981) p. 85. His brother, Peter Daniel, was the commander of the celebrated 'wreck ship', the *Terra Nova* of 1689 described by Charles May in 'The Voyage of the *Terra Nova*', in Awnsham and John Churchill's *Voyages* (1732), Vol. VI pp. 343–54.
29. Governor Markham of Pennsylvania to William Penn in a letter of February 1697, *CSP* America and West Indies (1697).

30. T.70/61.
31. Detail concerning Ralph Sadler and the *Encouragement* (which was owned by the Sadler family) occurs at *CSP* Colonial, America and West Indies (1701), para. 790; CO. 142/13; Jill Sheppard 'The Sojourn in Barbados of 2000 Disbanded Soldiers', *BMHS Journal*, xxxv (2) (Mar. 1976), pp. 138–43. Jill Sheppard, *The Redlegs of Barbados* (1977); T.70/ 1223 and 376; Elizabeth Donnan, *Documents Illustrative of the Slave Trade to America*, 4 vols (1930–5), Vol. II, p. 25; T.70/58.
32. Peter Duffield's various misdemeanours at T.70/1433 and 1463, 1183; his cargo for Guinea at T.70/350.
33. Benjamin Curtis was later transferred to Dixcove and was discharged from the Company in 1702.
34. T.70/376. Consigned to Philip Broom, who shipped them on to Antigua. See also T.70/61 and 51, 58 and 1184.
35. *New Adventure* of 150 tons and 10 guns. Dunn spent at least ten years in the slave trade, invariably shipping rum to Guinea and slaves back (CO.33/13). *Happy Return* of 55 tons and 4 guns. One of her rare deviations from slave trading occurred in 1698 when her captain landed 120 disbanded soldiers in Barbados as indentured servants (CO.33/13). For slave delivery figures see Donnan, Vol. II, pp. 29–30.
36. Barbot, p. 177.
37. Thomas Mathews had only arrived in Africa in February (T.70/376).
38. T. F. Garrard, *Akan Weights and the Gold Trade* (1980), p. 59. Phillips, p. 224, characterises the Akannis as being the best traders and having the purest gold.
39. Donnan, Vol. II, pp. 29–32.
40. Barbot, p. 266.
41. The Gold Coast was 'perilous and toilsome to land either men, goods or provisions: the waves of the ocean rising in great surges and breaking so violently on the strand, for better than a musket shot in breadth one after another; which requires a great deal of activity and dexterity to carry canoes through without being sunk, overset, or split to pieces, and often occasions the death of many men, and considerable losses of the goods' (Barbot, p. 157).
42. Anchors came in four sizes: sheet, the largest and strongest; bowers, large and small, lowered over the bows; stream; and kedge. Losing any of these was a major problem for ships far from their sources of supply, and a common occurrence on the Guinea Coast.
43. Gerrard Gore had previously been factor (with Benjamin Curtis) at Anamabo, but had quickly been transferred to Accra. As befitted a descendant of Jerrard Gore, recorded by Hakluyt as being a London merchant and member of a syndicate granted a 12-year monopoly of trade on the Barbary Coast in 1585 (Richard Hakluyt, *The Principal Navigations . . . of the English Nation*, 1927, Vol. VI, p. 419), Gore was a career Company man and member of an influential and extensive London family who were primarily financiers. (See John Carswell's

The South Sea Bubble, 1960, for details of their involvement in that catastrophe.) In 1713 he became Chief Agent at the Cape Coast Castle with a salary of £300 p. a. He died in 1717. Accra was an important posting, being the southern terminus of a busy African trade route.

44. Christiansborg, sometimes termed St Francis Xaverius from the time it was held by the Portuguese (1679–83), was the Danish castle.

45. Barbot, p. 457 (both quotations).

46. Barbot, *A Description* p. 185 (John Barbot, uncle to James). Phillips in the *Hannibal* ascribed his problem with anchors – with which he had his fair share of disasters – to the soft clay sea-bed into which they settled too deeply (Phillips, p. 213).

47. The *Wormley Berry*'s cargo was valued at £1,405 (T.70/350). Her Jamaican destination is revealed at CO.142/13.

48. It is unlikely that the marking iron was for slaves since John Fort was not a senior officer and had no dispensation to freight a slave as a personal venture; it was probably intended for ivory or for stamping casks of sugar on the voyage home.

49. John Barbot, pp. 404–5.

50. Donnan, Vol. II, p. xvi, n.

51. Probably a Dutch East India vessel, bound for Holland's colonial possessions and settlements at Ceylon, Bengal, Sumatra and Java.

52. Probably *farinha*, the Portuguese for flour.

53. Barbot, p. 406; he advocated only the very best, clean water for slaves on the middle passage: 'it is so essential . . . that it often contributes very much to save or destroy whole cargoes of them, according as it is good or bad'.

54. Donnan, Vol. II, p. 25.

55. The dollar was a confusing unit of currency, commonly worth 3 shillings; the specie dollar, however, was worth 5 shillings. Here Prideaux is probably using the term for a piece of eight, or peso, worth approximately 4 shillings. An anker was a cask.
    Judging by Phillips in the *Hannibal*, August 1694, the prices quoted here are for quantities of 100 of each commodity. Firewood, used in the ship's galley, was estimated by the boatload. The 'corn' seems to have been Guinea corn or sorghum.

56. Barbot, p. 547.

57. BL Add.MS 39946, pp. 9–11, also recording the use of dead slaves as shark bait.

58. Barbot, p. 465–6: see p. 406 for details of taxes on food and goods unloaded.

59. ADM.51/4261; HMS *Milford* January 1701. Despite the supposed 'infestation' of pirates along the Guinea Coast, Moses never caught sight of a single one.

60. The 'full and change' refers to the times of full and new moon; i.e. the times of spring as opposed to neap tides.

CHAPTER 10   The Financial Reckoning

1. From the local Akan language, 'Tackey' derives from *taku*, a seed or pea used to weigh minute quantities of gold. See T. F. Garrard, *Akan Weights and the Gold Trade* (1980), pp. 252–6, 232–3.
2. *An Account of the Disposal of Capt. Rog. Mathew's Cargo in the 'Daniel and Henry' on the Gold Coast for Slaves 1700*: Account Book of John Burwell, Devon RO.3327A add./PZ3.
3. Men aged 16–40,; women 15–35; boys 10–15; girls 10–14. Elizabeth Donnan, *Documents Illustrative of the Slave Trade to America*, 4 vols (1930–5), Vol. II, p. 244.
4. Four chests of corn were also purchased in this transaction.
5. Spirits were heavily used to ease the commercial relationship between slave buyer and slave seller, as commission, bribe, customary payment and gift. No doubt their use also had a similar significance for factors of the various forts on the Guinea Coast, who had a reputation for hard drinking and whose clients, both African and European, shared their predilection.
6. Ankers were storage casks for spirits and may well have formed part of the cargo of '310 ironbound casks of several sizes' which caused the Customs so much trouble at Dartmouth in December 1699.
7. 'Coffee' probably signifies Kofi, a common Gold Coast name.
8. For further detail on trading practices see Marion Johnson, 'The Atlantic Slave Trade and the Economy of West Africa', in *Liverpool, the African Slave Trade and Abolition*, edited by Roger Anstey and P. E. H. Hair (1976).
9. *The Mariner's Mirror* vi (1920):3
10. Per thousand.
11. Virtually all iron and copper bars were of Baltic origin. Though a popular item of trade on the Gambia, they were much less saleable on the Gold Coast: a check of the inventory of the *Daniel and Henry* compared with the account of goods put off for slaves reveals iron bars were seldom accepted in exchange for slaves.
12. Tied.
13. In 1683 the Royal African Company specified that perpetuannas should be 20–1 yards in length and 9 lb. in weight. In 1700 they were usually 18 feet long by 2 feet wide, singles weighing 5½ lb., doubles about 11 lb.: hence piece and ½ piece.

CHAPTER 11   The Middle Passage

1. T.70/2 and T.70/58.
2. T.70/8. See also Appendices 8 and 9.
3. Orlando Patterson, *Slavery and Social Death* (1982), p. 78.
4. Ibid. p. 96.
5. *Narrative of a Voyage to Guinea* (1714) BL.Add.MS 39946.

6. John Barbot, *A Description of the Coasts of North and South-Guinea* (1688) p. 272; James Barbot, 'An abstract of a Voyage to the Congo River . . . in the year 1700', ibid., p. 547.

7. Henry Greenhill, Henry Spurway and Daniel Bridge to the Royal African Company, 6 April 1681. Quoted by E. Donnan *Documents Illustrative of the Slave Trade to America*, 4 vols (1930–5), Vol I, p. 272. The term 'extraordinary' refers to the incentive payment or bonus for slaves delivered alive to the plantations.

8. J. A. Rawley, *The Transatlantic Slave Trade* (1981), pp. 301–4 examines the practice of 'tight-packing'.

9. For an extensive and masterly analysis of racial prejudice and slaves, see Winthrop D. Jordan, *White over Black* (1968).

10. P. Curtin, *The Atlantic Slave Trade. A Census* (1969) pp. 282–3.

11. Kenneth F. Kiple and Brian T. Higgins, 'Mortality caused by Dehydration during the Middle Passage', *Social Science History* 13 (1989), pp. 421–437.

12. Richard B. Sheridan, *Doctors and Slaves* (1985) p. 115.

13. Barbot, p. 545.

14. For many years the impression has been put about that this was a disease peculiar to the Negro race. It is true that it probably originated in Africa but it was (and is) a highly contagious disease that could infect Europeans and Africans alike. However, since it is transmitted directly by skin contact – usually venereal – reports of it were comparatively uncommon in the white communities of the plantations, for obvious reasons. Sheridan, pp. 83–9.

15. Curtin, p. 277.

16. Richard Ligon, *A Time and Exact History of the Island of Barbados* (1657).

17. T. Aubrey, *The Sea-Surgeon or the Guinea Man's Vade Mecum* (1729).

18. Rawley, p. 297.

19. Aubrey, p. 107.

20. Rawley, p. 297.

21. Aubrey, p. 133.

22. Ibid. pp. 126–30.

23. Barbot, p. 548.

24. *LJ*, Vol. XVIII (1708) p. 467 registers the complaint of slave trade associate William Coward of Walthamstow in Essex (1648–1738), brother of Henry Coward of Petworth and Jamaica, that 'Year after Year, from the Beginning of the War, not one of his Ships had escaped having Men pressed out of them, both at Jamaica and upon their return . . . all the Captains he had employed to the West Indies have declared to him that they who impressed his Men at Jamaica never showed any Authority or Consent from the Governor for so doing.'

25. John Coad, *A Memorandum of the Wonderful Providences of God* (repr. 1849), pp. 23–6. Also quoted by Jill Sheppard, *The Redlegs of*

Barbados, (1977), p. 29. Similar accounts can also be found in *A Relation of the Great Sufferings and Strange Adventures of Henry Pitman* (1689). Pitman was consigned in Barbados to Charles Thomas, brother of Sir Dalby Thomas (later Chief Agent at the Cape Coast Castle).

26. Aubrey, p. 121.
27. Ibid., p. 132.
28. Phillips, p. 237.
29. Barbot, p. 270.

CHAPTER 12   Jamaica Bound

1. James Barbot, 'An abstract of a Voyage to the Congo River . . . and to Cabinda in the year 1700', in Awnsham and Churchill, *Collection of Voyages and Travels* (1732), Vol. V. p. 542.
2. This course is the result of geometrically combining the three courses actually sailed which are recorded in the left-hand margin in miles.
3. The *Society* had been continuously employed in the slave trade since at least 1696 when she entered Anapolis, Maryland with 175 slaves. Darold Wax, 'Black Immigrants: the Slave Trade in Colonial Maryland', *Maryland Historical Magazine* lxxiii (1978): 32.
4. CO.33/13.
5. T.70/1435, 1184 and 1209.
6. The allowance of 27° 23' for leeway sounds, at first sight, rather a precise figure for something which had to be 'estimated'. In fact, of course, 27° 23' is only the 2½ compass points, turned into degrees (one point equals 11¼ degrees) which Walter Prideaux allowed for leeway, based on experience, when going to windward in a strong wind.

On this day it is recorded that the captain took an observation and made the ship's latitude 2° 54' south. Although this agrees well with Prideaux's calculated latitude (2° 50'), he does not record it as an observation. He also appears to ignore his own observations on 24–25 September, possibly because observations taken when the sun was very close to the Equator were of doubtful accuracy. From 28 September (modern date 9 October) when the sun's declination had increased to about 6° south, his observed latitudes began to agree very well with his calculated latitudes.

It gives a good impression of sailing to windward in a small, fully rigged ship of 1700 to think that they were steering west or slightly south of west for 24 hours, with a fresh breeze, and finished up 75 miles further to the west but also 31½ miles further north. Their actual average speed during this time, sailing against the wind, was just over 3 knots – a fast walking pace. (With thanks to Capt. John Naish R. N., ret'd.)

7. Nine degrees 27 min difference of longitude: sailing away from England the difference of longitude was measured from the Lizard as this had been their point of departure. For this voyage their departure was made

from São Tomé. At the Equator 1° of longitude equals 60 nautical miles or 20 leagues. For the whole of the voyage recorded here they are so close to the Equator that 1° of meridian distance is always taken as 20 leagues. At noon today they calculate they are 189 leagues west of São Tomé which equals 9° 27' of longitude from that island.

8. Studding sails were auxiliary sails set beyond the leeches (the perpendicular or sloping sides of a sail) of the principal sails during a fair wind.

9. St Pauls is a rocky outcrop in mid-Atlantic, reckoned today at 0° 23'N, 29° 23'W. Acroll has not been traced.

10. A puzzle. The difference in longitude from São Tomé has now reached 29° 45', then without explanation Walter Prideaux initiates a second way of recording longitude by taking a second point of departure 26° west of São Tomé and calling this point 360°. He then reckons longitude by substracting the distance travelled west from this new 360° point. The only interpretation possible is that Walter Prideaux had run off the edge of the old chart and started a new one, calling the right-hand edge of the new chart 360° and making it 26° west of São Tomé. In the following days longitude is recorded both in difference of longitude from São Tomé *and* in this new system. Thus the next day (11 October) they are 626 leagues or 31° 18' meridian distance from São Tomé, and in longitude (by the new system) 354° 42' meridian distance from the same place. The latter figure is arrived at thus: 360° minus 31° 18' plus 26° equals 354° 42'. (With thanks to Capt. John Naish R. N., ret'd, for this explanation.)

11 A pissing-clout was a child's nappy (*Oxford English Dictionary*: usage in 1672), but whatever the literal meaning of Foxworthy's remark, its pejorative tenor is unmistakable. 'Clout' was in common usage, as in Barbot (p. 131) describing the men of Sestos on the Guinea Coast 'wearing only a single clout about their waist'.

12. With grateful acknowledgement to Canon Ronald Brownrigg for this reference.

13. *CSP* America and West Indies (1700) para. 500: 'all the news of America is the swarming of Pirates, not only on the Coast but all the West Indies over . . .'.

14. Originally called the *Jersey* and renamed in 1698, HMS *Margate* was of 262 tons and carried 22 guns.

15. *CSP* Colonial, (1700) paras 17, 274(i), and 454. See also *CSP* Colonial (1701), para. 814.

16. David Waters, *The Art of Navigation in England in Elizabethan and Early Stuart Times* (1978), p. 579.

17. BL Sloane MS 2496, previously unidentified. The same source is also used to provide meteorological data for the log-book entries 13 November to 17 November.

18. ADM.52/56.

19. Quoted in *The Mariner's Mirror* (1920), vi, no.5.

20. ADM. 52/36. And ADM.7 L/F/197 (National Maritime Museum

Library, Greenwich, London).
21. T.70/51.
22. ADM.8/7. Other Navy ships on the West India station at the time included HMS *Ludlow* off Barbados and HMS *Deal Castle* off the Leeward Islands. Captain Peter Pickard's career is partly detailed in Wm Laird Clowes, *The Royal Navy* (1898) Vol. II, pp. 358, 362, 465, 473, 535.
23. The Controller of Customs at Jamaica reported 250 slaves delivered (T.70/135). The discrepancy is probably due to the presence of 'privilege' slaves carried privately by the officers of the *Daniel and Henry* and thus not part of Ivy, Arthur and Gould's venture.
24. Quoted by J. A. Rawley, *The Transatlantic Slave Trade* (1981), p. 305.
25. T.70/1183, p. 55 and T.70/58.
26. 'Much Vermin in the Ship, as Rats, Cockroaches, Ants and other bugs as destroys both Provisions and Sails likewise and other things' (T.70/ 134, from the log of the *Fauconberg* of 1699).
27. BL, Sloane MS 2496, 3 June 1701.
28. Ibid., 5 June 1701, recording four merchant ships sailing for London. Although none is mentioned by name it is highly likely that the *Daniel and Henry* was amongst their number.
29. E.190/975/3.
30. Will at PROB.11/460, fol.88.
31. HCA.24/128 fol.128.
32. CUST.65/40 and 173.

CHAPTER 13   Counting the Cost

1. J. A. Rawley, *The Transatlantic Slave Trade* (1981), p. 264. For the years 1701–20 the estimated profit per slave was £8 9s.2d. quoting Engerman: 'The Slave Trade and British Capital Formation in the Eighteenth Century: A Comment on the Williams Thesis', *Business History Review* xlvi (1972), pp. 430–43.
2. Rawley, p. 265, cites the Liverpool merchant William Davenport, based on seventy ventures from 1757–1784, who reckoned his annual profits at 8 per cent: quoting P. D. Richardson, 'Profits in the Liverpool Slave Trade: the Accounts of William Davenport 1757–84', in Roger Anstey and P. E. H. Hair (eds) *Liverpool. The African Slave Trade and Abolition* (1976), pp. 60–90.
3. James and John Barbot, pp. 384, 423, 457, 465 in Vol. V of Awnsham and John Churchill, *Collection of Voyages and Travels* (1732).
4. CO.33/13.
5. Philip Curtin, *The Atlantic Slave Trade. A Census* (1969), p. xv.
6. K. G. Davies, *The Royal African Company* (1957), p. 364.
7. M. Craton and J. Walvin, *A Jamaica Plantation* (1970), p. 54.
8. David Galenson 'The Slave Trade to the English West Indies', *Economic History Review* (1979).

9. *CSP* Colonial, America and West Indies, 1700, para.15.
10. T.70/175 'List of Vessels into Jamaica': 246 is Walter Prideaux's figure. The *Mayflower*'s ownership is established in T.70/350.
11. E. Donnan *Documents Illustrative of the Slave Trade to America*, 4 vols (1930–5), Vol. II, p. 362.
12. Rawley, pp. 247–81, deals with this in great detail.
13. T.70/1183, p. 31.
14. Barbot, p. 142. The custom probably predated the European arrival on the West African coast; T. F. Garrard, *Akan Weights and the Gold Trade* (1980), p. 81.
15. O. Patterson, *The Sociology of Slavery* (1967), p. 9
16. T.70/350.
17. Ibid., entered 23 January 1700.
18. E.190/975/3 and 13.
19. E. H. Phelps-Brown and Sheila V. Hopkins, 'Seven Centuries of Building Wages', *Economica* xxii, no. 84 (1955), pp. 195–206.
20. T.70/135.
21. CUST. 65/39 and 173.
22. Based on charge to the *Davers Galley* of 1704 (T.70/1183).
23. Crew costed on a monthly basis. Salary structure: captain £5, chief mate £2 18s.; boatswain £2 10s.; 2nd mate £2 10s.; gunner, cooper, carpenter and other skilled tradesmen £2 1s.6d.; skilled assistants £1 14s.; skilled seamen £1 12s.; ordinary seamen £1 5s. (figures based on Kemp, Course and Company records); doctor £4 3s.2d.; supercargo £2 10s.; captain's son £2. Had the entire ship's company completed the voyage the wages bill would have been approximately £1,268.
24. The incentives to Mathew are based on £4 for every £104 of the net proceeds from the sale of the slaves; those of the ship's doctor, one shilling per head for every slave sold.

CHAPTER 14   A Lawful Calling?

1. J. A. Rawley, *The Transatlantic Slave Trade* (1981), p. 3 quoting Hakluyt.
2. Elizabeth Donnan, *Documents Illustrative of the Slave Trade to America*, 4 vols (1930–5), Vol. I. p. 63.
3. T. Knox, *A Brief Account of the Woollen Manufacturing of England* (1708): CO.388/11.
4. Rawley, pp. 183–90, examines the socioeconomic background, especially of Bristol slave traders.
5. R. H. Tawney, *Religion and the Rise of Capitalism* (1926; repr. 1965) pp. 197–251.
6. Maurice Ashley, *England in the Seventeenth Century* (1952; repr. 1963) p. 112.
7. Tawney, pp. 236–7.
8. Ibid., p. 269.

9. Ibid. p. viii. Professor Tawney's classic work contains many penetrating insights into Dissenting philosophy especially as related to trade and commerce. Of particular value and relevance are pp. 197–270, the chapter entitled 'The Puritan Movement'.

10. Jeanette Tawney (ed.) *Chapters from a Christian Directory by Richard Baxter* (1925) p. 26.

11. Samuel Wright, *The Great Concern of Human Life* (1729) p. 120 quoting from Eccl. 9:10. Wright was the favourite author (and casuist) of the Lyme Regis merchant family of Burridge whose involvement in the slave trade is chronicled on pp. 248–70.

12. Anthony Benezet, *Observations on the Inslaving, importing and purchasing of Negroes with some Advice thereon extracted from the Epistle of the Yearly Meeting of the People called Quakers held at London in the Year 1748.* (2nd edn 1760), p. 4.

CHAPTER 15   Berwick to Weymouth

1. E.190/206/11, 207/6 and 207/13.

2. E.190/334/19 and 336/6.

3. E.190/514/12.

4. Much information on Deal and the Goodwins appears in Stephen Pritchard, *The History of Deal* (1864), John Laker, *History of Deal* (1917), Richard Larn, *Goodwin Sands Shipwrecks* (1977) and Edward Hasted, *History of the County of Kent* (1799), Vol. IV.

5. The tackle for hoisting and lowering the lower yards.

6. T.70/354 and 13. Details of the Bowles family occur in *HHC*, Laker pp. 233, 241, 257–8. See also W. H. Bowles, *Record of the Bowles Family* (1918). Tobias Bowles' will, which clarifies his relationship with Henry Alexander Primrose and in which the fate of his niece Thomazine is mentioned is at PROB.11/616, quire 156. Tobias' son James, Agent for the Royal African Company at the Patuxent river, Maryland between 1709 and 1729, is frequently mentioned in connection with the Company's importing slaves, especially in T.70/4. For Valentine Bowles' naval career, understandably ignored by the family history and glossed over in John Charnock's *Biographia Navalis* (1795), see ADM.1/5260 and Wm Laird Clowes, *The Royal Navy* (1898) Vol. II, p. 495. Valentine was provisioning ships at Deal by 1700; see E. Donnan, *Documents Illustrative of the Slave Trade to America*, 4 vols (1930–5) Vol. IV, p. 69, where James Westmore, master of the *Africa* of London for Guinea notifies Thomas Starke, merchant of London, that he has received £14 worth of supplies for the ship from Valentine Bowles.

7. T.70/6.

8. E.190/695/15. There are no Port Books for Deal prior to 1719. The Barbados records contained at CO.33/15 are later abstracts: they list the *Samuel* as arriving in 1719, but are in error.

9. E.190/698/8 and 701/12.
10. E.190/701/12. A full account, edited by William Boys junior, the historian of Sandwich, is entitled *An Account of the Loss of the Luxborough Galley by Fire* (2nd edn, 1787), but he is not altogether reliable as to dates.

William Boys senior was neither the first nor the last of the Boys family (who were concentrated in the county of Kent) to take part in the slave trade. A Thomas Boys was master of the brigantine *Adventure* at Jamaica in 1709 with 120 slaves from Guinea (CO.142/14). Later in the eighteenth century John Boys, having gained experience of the trade as commander of the Company sloop *Fame* in 1731, and as master of the *Fortune* in 1734 (delivered 85 slaves from the Gambia to Lower James, Virginia), formed his own company. Between 1735 and 1736 he made two voyages to Virginia via the Gambia and Barbados in his ship *Pretty Betzie*, delivering a total of 358 slaves (Donnan, Vol. II, pp. 401, 431; Vol. IV, pp. 193, 195, 197). Neither Thomas nor John Boys have been conclusively linked to William of the *Luxborough*.

11. Boys, p. v. *DNB* awards the killing of Blackbeard (Edward Teach) to Captain Maynard of the Royal Navy, who shot him. The name assigned to Hammose suggests he first reached England at Hamoaze in Plymouth Sound; 'Merry Pintle' is an interesting compression of two phrases – 'merry pin' meaning good-humoured, and 'pin-tailed', small in stature and narrow-hipped.
12. Boys, pp. 10–11.
13. William Page (ed.) *Victoria History of Hampshire &c* (1908), p. 175.
14. E.190/841/8. Port Book records for Cowes (Portsmouth, Southampton and the Isle of Wight) in the first quarter of the eighteenth century cover only 1699–1713.
15. HCA.1/16,29,31 and HCA.15/31 for the *Mary Anne*. Briscoe went on to deliver 64 slaves to Maryland (Donnan, Vol. IV, p. 17). The Briscoe family were involved in the slave trade as sea captains from before 1698 until at least 1798; see Donnan, Vols I and II. Pafford is mentioned in N. W. Surry and J. H. Thomas (eds), *Portsmouth Record Series: Books of Original Entries 1731–1751* (1976), p. 91. For Brown's reappearance at Barbados in 1719 see CO.33/15.
16. T.70/349–52; CO.142/15; and Donnan, Vol. IV, p. 208. The *Molly* delivered 206 slaves to Upper James, Virginia; the *Broomfield* 195 to Jamaica.
17. T.70/43.
18. K. G. Davies, *The Royal African Company* (1957), pp. 194–6.
19. 24 February 1706 (T.70/14).
20. T.70/1209 and T.70/44. Legal proceedings concerning the *Resolution* are at HCA.15/32. Galloway still sailed for the Caribbean however, taking a prize into Baltimore in 1706–7; W. R. Meyer 'English Privateering in the War of the Spanish Succession', *The Mariner's Mirror* lxix (1983):440.

21. T.70/44.
22. 15 August 1706 (T.70/44).
23. HCA.25 and 26.
24. T.70/43.
25. T.70/2, 44 and 52.
26. Donnan, Vol. II, p. 1.
27. HCA.26/21.
28. T.70/1198 and 1184; CO.388/12; T.70/5.
29. Also known as Degory Herle (T.70/1199). As master of the *Wiltshire* he delivered 247 slaves to Buenos Aires in Sept.–Oct. 1715 as contraband, returning to London with thousands of hides. E. F. Scheuss de Studer *La Trata de Negros en el Rio de la Plata durante el siglo xviii* (Buenos Aires, 1958), table v. See also Donnan, Vol. IV, p. 18, where as master of the *Delight* of London, he brought 114 slaves to Maryland in May 1708.
30. Donnan, Vol. II, p. 116.
31. CO.33/15. The *Betty* which delivered 134 slaves to Jamaica from Calabar in 1718 is detailed at CO.142/14. Mellish returned to the *Isle of Wight* for a voyage from Portsmouth to Antigua via Madeira in 1719. See CO.157/1, where the vessel is described as a galley of Portsmouth.
32. T.70/1225.
33. Peter Fryer, *Staying Power* (1984), p. 51.
34. T.70/354.
35. E.190/841/1, (the beer being for the consumption of the crew.) Southampton records are extremely patchy; there are no Port Books for 1714, or from 1717 to 1747.
36. E.190/906/17 and 907/16.
37. CO.5/509.
38. *DNB* XIV, though comprehensively reviewing Oswald's life, coyly omits any mention of his slave trading empire (as it fails to do also with London slave merchant Humphrey Morice). Oswald's career as a slave merchant is noted however by Donnan, Vol. II, pp. 111n. and 565n.; Vol IV, pp. 191, 245, 347; and J. A. Rawley *The Transatlantic Slave Trade* (1981) pp. 243, 270. Bence Island was named after John Bence, appointed to the Royal African Company's Court of Assistants in 1692.
39. The ventures of Jolliffe and Barfoot to Guinea can be traced in the Port Books for Poole (E.190 series) between 1752 and 1759, and the Register of Shipping for Carolina, CO.5/509 and 510. These sources are supplemented by Donnan, Vol. IV, p. 310. The number of slaves delivered during this time by Poole shipping exceeded 1,500.

    Occasional references to Poole occur in *The Papers of Henry Laurens*, ed. Hamer and Rogers (1968), especially Vols. I–III. William Jollife, member of the Court of Assistants to the Royal African Company 1699–1706, was not a close connection of the Poole Jolliffes.
40. Donnan, Vol. II, pp. 30–2; as commander of the *Content* he delivered 96 slaves to Barbados in 1709.

41. Lest it be thought that the *Flying Brigantine* had also joined in the re-export trade, CO.5/508 specifically states she arrived at Charleston from London and Guinea. The Randalls – especially Thomas – were the subject of many Customs examinations, especially during 1720–5, when Thomas, amongst others of his family, suffered prosecution on charges of smuggling 2,000lb. of tea, 88 gallons of rum etc. (T.64/143).

CHAPTER 16 Lyme Regis

* Much information has been derived from Mr John Fowles, whose contribution to this chapter cannot be overestimated and whose generous help has gone far beyond that which the occasional note may suggest. For a wider view of the town's history his *Short History of Lyme Regis* (1985) provides an admirable introduction to the subject.

1. Cyril Wanklyn, *Lyme Regis, a Retrospect* (1927), p. 24.
2. *CSP* Domestic (1683–4), p. 179 quoted in *HHC* pp. 216–18.
3. W. Macdonald Wigfield, *The Monmouth Rebels 1685* (1985) quoted by John Fowles in *Lyme Regis Museum* (Curator's Report, 1986), p. 19.
4. Typical of these was Richard Russell's *Dissertation on the Use of Sea-water in the Diseases of the Glands* (3rd ed, 1755).
5. John Hutchins, *History of Dorset* (1861), Vol. II, p. 68; and *Somerset & Devon Notes & Queries* xv (1917): 206–8.
6. George Roberts, *History of Lyme Regis* (1823), p. 31.
7. Roger North, *The Life of the Rt. Hon. Francis North* (1742) pp. 118–19. Francis North was the presiding judge on the western circuit from about 1674 to 1680 and – oddly – had a soft spot for Lyme.
8. T.64/139.
9. *HHC*, p. 752.
10. Information kindly received from Mr Gordon Reed of Ruislip, Middlesex, who has made an exhaustive study of the Tucker family of Dorset. Walter Tucker died in 1682, John in 1667, Samuel in 1678 and William in 1668.
11. E.190/881/2 (1672) and E.190/882/11 (1678).
12. *HHC*, p. 217.
13. Married at Chardstock (IGI register), where the Burridge family may well have originated, there being a hamlet and farm called Bowditch or Burridge about a mile to the north of the village. Much confusion has resulted from Walter Tucker's will, which erroneously names John instead of Robert Burridge II as his son-in-law. Examination of the Burridge papers at the Dorset Record Office and Burridge wills at the PRO, Chancery Lane, London, confirms that Mary Tucker was Robert Burridge II's wife.
14. E.190/886/2.
15. *CSP* Domestic (1683), p. 179. Granville, a West Country MP for Liskeard 1667, Plymouth 1685 and Saltash 1679, 1681, 1689, specialised

in anti-Dissent. In 1668 he was appointed to a parliamentary commission specifically set up to receive information about the insolencies of Nonconformists (*HHC*, pp. 432–3).

16. *CSP* Domestic (1685), p. 243; 4 July 1685. The revelation regarding Messrs Andrew and Tucker derives from the careful research of Gordon Reed and is reported in Fowles, *Lyme Regis Museum*, p. 14.

17. *CTB*, (1685–9) Vol. VIII; 27 July 1685.

18. Maurice Ashley, *England in the Seventeenth Century* (1952; repr. 1963), pp. 171–2.

19. Dorset RO. B7/A3/2a.

20. *HHC*, pp. 217, 752.

21. E.190/888/1.

22. CUST.102/68. By 1718 this practice had exceeded all reasonable proportions and smaller scoops were specified.

23. *HHC*, pp. 217, 218, 752.

24. E.190/890/5.

25. HCA.26/1, 27 August 1691.

26. Dorset RO.B7/N2 (entry dated 1720).

27. Ibid., recording 'a silver watch which my uncle Burridge gave me when I was his apprentice'.

28. Herbert W. L. Way, *A History of the Way Family* (1914), pp. 6–26.

29. E.190/879/11.

30. A. G. Mathews, *Calamy Revised* (1934), p. 515. See also J. E. Acland, 'The Founding of Dorchester, Massachusetts and the Rev. John White', *Proceedings of the Dorset Nat. Hist. & Antiq. Field Club* xlii (1922): 87–95.

31. PROB.11/368.

32. Died in 1738 leaving £100 to the Congregational fund but, more importantly, established the Coward Trust which still provides grants for ministers to train for the Congregational Church. I am grateful to Dr John Thompson for his help in clarifying Coward's career.

33. See pp. 18, 411 note 24. Coward chartered his ships for slave-trading ventures but apparently – at least from 1699 – mounted no such ventures of his own.

34. Abbot E. Smith, *Colonists in Bondage* (1947), pp. 12, 35–9, 58, 140.

35. Dorset RO.B7/M9.

36. CO.5/1441. The *Lyme* of Lyme delivered more the following year.

37. Dorset RO. B7/G7/7 records payment of £9 to Robert Burridge for interest of the £150 principal in 1704.

38. Document lodged in Lyme Regis (Philpot) Museum: information courtesy of John Fowles.

39. Dorset RO.B7/F2.

40. Dorset RO.B7/G7/7.

41. R. H. Tawney, *Religion and the Rise of Capitalism* (1926; repr. 1975), pp. 262–4.

42. Dorset RO.B7/G7/7.

43. Tawney, p. 273.

44. Dorset RO.B7/A4/4 (reverse).
45. For more information on the Halletts of Stedcombe see Mark Girouard, 'Stedcombe House, Devon', in *Country Life* 26 December 1973, and G. P. R. Pulman, *The Book of the Axe* (repr. 1969), p. 873. I am grateful to Mr John Fowles for bringing these to my notice. See also Bridget Cherry, 'A Perfect Restoration', *Country Life* 4 July 1991, pp. 90–94.
46. Dorset RO. B7/B2/12.
47. Dorset RO.B7/A4/4 and 5; B7/H2.
48. PROB.11/449; *Somerset & Dorset Notes & Queries* xiv (1914):150.
49. Dorset RO.B7/N2. Francis Read returned with the *Africa* bringing tobacco and West Indian produce (T.70/14), and almost immediately shipped out as captain of the *Siam* of London to the Guinea Coast for slaves in 1704–5 (T.70/354). The *Siam* was neither owned nor freighted by the Burridges.
50. J. G. Alford, *Alford Family Notes* (1908), p. 95. It is not entirely certain that Joseph and Daniel Alford of London were closely connected to the Winsham family but circumstantial evidence points that way. See T.70/349–52 for details of their Guinea ventures. A Benjamin Alford was Agent for the Company in 1702 at Boston, New England and in 1703 at New York but appears to have had little or no connection with the Dorset branch of the family (T.70/353).
51. T.70/350. One of Joseph Way's slavers was the *Dorset Brigantine*; she went to Guinea from Bristol at least twice, 1707 and 1709 (T.70/355).
52. William Cogan, baptised October 1677 at Lyme (B7./B6/10), owned a house and garden in Lyme at the time of his death in 1719 (J. M. Sanders, *Barbados Records: Wills and Administrations 1681–1700*, 1981, Vol III, p. 73). The house was willed to his son John, who apparently never took up residence in Lyme, and the property was still managed by Robert Burridge III as late as 1736 (Dorset RO.B7/N3). William Cogan's slave trade ventures as a separate trader are detailed at T.70/353–5.
53. T.70/353.
54. T.70/354.
55. T.70/1199. The cargo detailed in this document and the one in John Burridge junior's memorandum may partly overlap.
56. Dorset RO. B7/B2/12. Joseph Paice and his sons Joseph and Nathaniel were to handle much of the Burridges' finances over the ensuing decades. Based in London they were the financial and commercial agents for Lyme's corporation in the first decades of the eighteenth century. The same source claims that the senior Joseph Paice was born at Exeter but educated by the Burridges of Lyme, one of them being his uncle. A strong Dissenter, he maintained close connections with William Coward – note 32 *supra* – see G. F. Nuttall, *Correspondence of Philip Doddridge* (1979), letter 418.
57. E.190/884/3 and CO.5/1441. Freighted the *Mary and Anne* (1700) and the *Virginia Merchant* (1702), both of Weymouth, to Virginia for tobacco.

58. Dorset RO. B7/N2.

59. No Bristol Port Books for overseas trade exist for 1703 and 1704. The Company record of clearance, compiled in part from this source, is equally silent on the *Union Galley*, as are the Colonial Shipping Registers. Her likeliest destination was Virginia, but there are no records for that colony in 1704. The voyage is not recorded by Donnan.

60. Dorset RO.B7/N2.

61. *CTB* Vol. XX (9 July 1706).

62. E.190/896/7.

63. *London Galley* of 170 tons, 14 guns and 30 men, victualled for twelve months. None of her crew appears to have been of Lyme origin. Her captain was initially John Maxwell, later Abraham Battell (HCA.26/21; *LJ* Vol XVIII, pp. 390–1).

64. T.70/354.

65. I.e. the stress caused by the wind in the extra sail resulted in the foremast shearing off at deck level. The stays for the two upper sections of the mainmast were secured to this foremast and so the two sections – main topmast and main topgallant mast – also came tumbling down.

66. Somerset RO, DD/WHL/1089/5; 2 April 1706, Benjamin Way to John and William Helyar. English and Jamaican currencies, though notionally the same, did not exchange at par, hence the allowance for difference in monies.

67. *HHC*, p. 550.

68. CO.388/10; CO.388/11, fol.95.

69. T.70/175; *An Account of Exports made by Private Traders from September 1702 to Michaelmas 1707.*

70. Reprinted in full by Elizabeth Donnan, *Documents Illustrative of the Slave Trade to America*, 4 vols (1930–5), Vol. II, pp. 75–9.

71. PROB.6/85; administration granted to Joseph Way, brother and Elizabeth Way, widow. Joseph Way continued in the slave trade until 1720, engaging in seventeen voyages to Africa for slaves between 1702 and 1720. (David Richardson, *The Bristol Slave Traders: a Collective Portrait*, 1985). Benjamin Way's eldest son Lewis, born 1698, became a barrister and director of the reconstituted South Sea Company in the late 1720s (Way, p. 26).

72. John Burridge junior's marriage to Martha Ledgingham, who was probably somewhat older than him, at Dorset RO.B7/N1. For Warwick Ledgingham see C. D. and E. Whetham (eds), *A Manor Book of Ottery St Mary* (1913), pp. 64–6.

73. COU/B.119 and 293, D.442 etc. in the Humphrey Morice papers.

74. HCA.25/16. The Jamineaus are frequently cited in the T.70 records.

75. The career of the *Severn Galley* can be gleaned from IND.1/9017 and Damer Powell, *Bristol Privateers and Ships of War* (1931), p. 101. Abraham Elton (1654–1728) was born of humble origin, the son of a poor market gardener. He rose to be sheriff of Bristol, mayor and MP. He was also the Master of the Society of Merchant Venturers and was

created a baronet in 1717. His namesake son, like John Burridge junior, lost a small fortune speculating in South Sea stock. He himself eschewed such speculation and died worth over £100,000. See *HHC* for his political career and W. E. Minchinton *et al*'s *Virginia Slave Trade Statistics 1688–1775* (1984), p. 8.

76. The previous year a Walter Burridge had signed the petition of the Weavers, Tuckers and Dyers of Exeter (T.70/175 and Donnan, Vol. II, p. 97). From all five petitions from Exeter relating to the African trade this was the odd one out as it supported the return of Company monopoly, so the likelihood is this was not the same Burridge.

77. T.70/8 and Donnan, Vol. II, p. 94. The Jamaican shipping registers record the date of arrival as 27 March 1710 with 158 slaves. This voyage must not be confused with that of the *Martha Brigantine* of Bristol under Captain John Sorrell, which also traded to Guinea and Jamaica at the same time.

78. T.70/1199.

79. Donnan, Vol. II, p. 116.

80. T.70/1198; 26 January and 25 August 1711.

81. Somerset RO.DD/WHh/1089/2 and 6; his commission was 2½ per cent of the sale price.

82. T.70/175; presented to the Commons 15 March 1711; *CJ*, Vol. XVI.

83. T.70/356, where the *Martha*'s cargo is listed as Joseph Way's venture. The Bristol Port Book for 1710 (overseas: E.190/1166/3) clearly shows John Burridge (junior) as the principal merchant. According to Roberts, p. 297, Richard Henvile had married a granddaughter of Williams Ellesdon of Charmouth. In 1728 Henvile was named as sole executor of the will of Arthur Raymond of Lyme (documents at the Lyme Regis (Philpot) Museum communicated by Mr John Fowles). During the years 1709–44 Henvile managed a total of thirty slave trading voyages from Bristol (Richardson, 1985).

84. T.70/5.

85. Wiltshire RO., Trowbridge; documents from the Prebendal Court of Lyme Regis, Wills and Administrations.

86. Minchinton *et al.*, p. 35; Donnan, Vol. IV, p. 182.

87. Dorset RO., photocopy ref.483, revealing a loose affiliation rather than any organised partnership between the 'middle' Burridge brothers and the Gundrys during the early eighteenth century; Daniel Gundry was part-owner of the *Africa* during this period.

88. Will of John Burridge senior at PROB.11/661. A note at Dorset RO. B7/B6/10 suggests that Lyme suffered a large conflagration in 1713, with many houses destroyed. The roofs of course were thatched, making fire-fighting extremely difficult. Chimneys and mantels were often in poor condition, which created extra hazards. In August 1722, perhaps during a long hot summer but certainly mindful of his uncle's experience, Robert Burridge III ordered a fire engine on behalf of the town corporation from John Bastard of Blandford at a cost of £7 18s.

The advertising puff which accompanied it claimed it was 'easily carried by two men . . . will throw water over any house in the town' (Dorset RO.B7/N24/3). It is now in the Philpot Museum in Lyme.

89. CO.33/15; also attributes ownership of the *John Frigate* to John uncle and nephew.

90. E.190/903/2; CO.33/15; Dorset RO.B7/N2; T.70/8. Letter to the Royal African Company from Major William Cogan, Writer to the Company at Barbados, 19 December 1714. The document reveals that the owners (of the *John*) 'ordered Cogan to take out no licence', presumably a reference to the fact that the trade to Africa was now an unlicensed one and not dependent upon payment of the 10 per cent tax.

91. Dorset RO.B7/N2. Barbados shipping registers record 91 delivered so the balance were either private ventures, disposed of independently, or died in the intervening period.

92. Dorset RO.B7/A4/7. A comprehensive list of suppliers and their services in the Lyme Regis area (1710–20) would include Mary Cookney (oakum), Richard Cookney (water pumps), John Staple (blocks and timber), William Churchill (cordage), William Cooper and John Bowdidge (casks), Thomas Clarke (bread and brooms), John Morris (cooper) John Bushrod (weights, scales and balances), Benjamin Beeve (twine for making and mending sails), Robert Clothyer (ship's kettle and pewter ware), Henry Cox (graver) (Dorset RO.B7/N2).

93. Roger Prowse was a prominent Exeter merchant. He also acted for the Burridges' Guinea venture aboard the *Surprise* from Exeter in March 1714.

94. A drawback was the duty repaid to merchants when dutiable goods they had imported – such as tobacco – were re-exported.

95. Collector of Customs at Lyme.

96. A mast – the term is applied solely to amber and gold or silver thread – had a weight equal to 2½lb. The sale of the amber is recorded in Dorset RO.B7/N2.

97. Minchinton *et al.*, p. 35.

98. CO.5/1441.

99. Dorset RO.B7/N2.

100. One conventional African trade ship of this time which plainly colluded in the slave trade was the *Anglesea* of London, John Bickford commander, which cleared Gravesend for the Guinea Coast on 19 October 1712. Forced to haul ashore at Sierra Leone for repairs, it fell in with the *Douglas* of Bristol. In the following months it cruised between the rivers Punge and Nunez, purchasing 60 cwt. of ivory and a total of 32 slaves. This collaboration ended equitably with the *Anglesea* exchanging her complement of slaves for the *Douglas'* cargo of ivory: whilst the latter set sail for the West Indies the *Anglesea* headed north for home. She was in dire need of further repairs, and

was again forced to refit at Sierra Leone. Once again she fell in with another English Guinea-trade ship, commanded by a Captain Gordon (almost certainly the *Pearl* John Gordon commander, owned by Humphrey Morice). This second collaborative venture netted her a further 6 cwt. of ivory and six slaves. Bickford sold the slaves to Gordon, who was bound for the West Indies, and sailed northwards a second time, arriving at Dartmouth on 18 July 1713 (T.70/1184).

101 The charter-party agreement is at HCA.25/135 fol. 244. A petition for wages from the *Resolution*'s crew is at fol.239. I am grateful to Glanville J. Davies' article, 'A Dorset Ship in the Slave Trade', *Somerset & Dorset Notes & Queries* xxx (1974–9):241–2, for bringing this voyage to my attention.

102. John Burridge junior's wine debts are the subject of *CTB*, Vol. XXXI (1717), p. 686; *CTB* Vol. XXXII (1718) pp. 32, 299; *CTP*, Vol. CCXIII (1718), para.42; and mentioned in *HHC* p. 509. His *Account of such Real Estate or securities for money which at the time of my failing in Credit in the World I was or am now interested in or intituled unto* is lodged at Dorset RO.B7/N1, and makes clear the dealings with Receiver-General John Bowdidge of Taunton. Bowdidge's case appears at *CTB* Vol. XXIX (1715) pp. 292, 623; *CTB* Vol. XXX (1716), p. 168; *CTB* Vol. XXXI (1717), pp. 14, 378, 631; *CTB* Vol. XXXII (1718), pp. 158, 654.

103. *CJ* Vol. XIX, p. 590.

104. *HHC*, p. 509.

105. MS detail in George Roberts' own copy of his *History of Lyme Regis*, kindly communicated by Mr John Fowles.

106. *CTP*, Vol. CCXLI, pp. 205, 233.

107. Cholmondeley (Houghton) MSS, quoted *HHC* p. 509.

108. PROB.11/661

109. PROB.11/799.

110. *HHC*, pp. 234–5.

111. BL. Dept of MSS. Add.MS 32707, fol. 405.

112. John Burridge junior is not mentioned in the will of his brother Robert Burridge III (made 1744, proved 1752) who predeceased him.

113. PROB.11/799 (1752). Dorset RO.B7/N1 contains an inventory of Robert Burridge III's library, in all 378 volumes in folio, quarto and octavo, fairly equally divided between history and divinity. The latter numbered a substantial proportion of books by or about Dissenters and Dissent, including titles by Richard Baxter, Ames Short and, significantly, Calamy's *Defence of Moderate Non-Conformity* (1703).

114. Samuel Wright *The Great Concern of Human Life* (1729), pp. 109, 128. The great concern was 'to fear God and keep his commandments'.

115. Dorset RO.B7/M16.

116. With thanks to Betty Mitchell's 'Lyme Regis Charities' in the Lyme Regis Society *Newsletter* March 1993.

CHAPTER 17 Exeter, Topsham and Dartmouth

1. An excellent account of this last voyage, and much background information on the Hawkins, can be found in Rayner Unwin's *The Defeat of John Hawkins* (1960).
2. Cecil T. Carr (ed.), *Select Charters of Trading Companies 1530–1707* (1913). See also K. R. Andrews, *Elizabethan Privateering* (1964), p. 103 for details on the trading and privateering activities of this company.
3. W. G. Hoskins, *Devon* (1978), p. 207.
4. Christopher Morris (ed.), *The Journeys of Celia Fiennes* (1947). pp. 245–6, quoted in Frances Wood, 'Merchants and Class' (1977), unpublished Monash University MA thesis.
5. Hoskins, p. 128.
6. BL Harley MS7310: *Certain Considerations Relating to the Roy. Afr. Co. of England*.
7. Ibid.; MS untitled p. 196: no date (c.1692).
8. K. G. Davies, *The Royal African Company* (1957), p. 130.
9. BL Add.MS12430. The Jamaican Assembly quoted the final loss at 2,006 slaves and awarded £8 per head compensation to those planters affected by loss – many being both planters and members of the Assembly.
10. E.190/960/12 with CO.33/14. The *Speedwell* was of 100 tons burden.
11. The Port Book entry is not clear. The name could be Ivyie or Joyce. Christopher Coke shipped a quantity of serge aboard her; John Hodge sent tobacco to Cape Verde, where it would probably have been exchanged for slave trade goods (E.190/960/12).
12. Madagascar later came under the jurisdiction of the East India Company's monopoly and was out of bounds to Royal African Company and ten per cent ships alike. During 1670–90, however, it was a popular region for slave ships.
13. *Speedwell* recorded paying £112 to the Company at Barbados (T.70/1199, loose papers) on account of her status as an interloper. Varloe captained another slave ship in 1687, delivering 200 slaves to Barbados from Madagascar (T.70/12).
14. Davies, p. 177.
15. E.190/1157/1. Described in the PRO Shipping Lists as Xmas 1698–Xmas 1699, the cover of this Port Book appears to have been subsequently transposed with 1156/1 and should read Xmas 1697–Xmas 1698. Her arrival at Barbados is recorded in CO.33/13.
16. E.190/1059/4 and T.70/350.
17. E.190/973/1.
18. HCA.25/16, owned by John Sikes of Dartmouth. In April 1704 a further *Betty Galley*, perhaps the same one, but owned by Lord Willoughby and Dean Swift, was granted letters of marque in Exeter.
19. Hoskins, p. 498.
20. E.190/973/2.
21. T.70/1434.

22. T.70/1434 mistakenly states that Agent Corker shipped sixty slaves. Details of the *Dragon* at HCA.13/135, 15/29 and 24/128.
23. CUST.64/60.
24. 1718, HCA.25/21 and HCA.26/16.
25. T.70/354; Elizabeth Donnan, *Documents Illustrative of the Slave Trade to America*, 4 vols (1930–5), Vol. II, p. 94: E.190/982/3.
26. T.70/5: 12 February 1710.
27. HCA.26/15.
28. *Holdsworth* of 200 tons. Owners and setters-forth were Arthur Holdsworth, captain, Nicholas Wood of Exeter, and Nicholas Hutchins of London (both merchants) (HCA.26/15).
29. T.70/44.
30. See T.70/24 for the full correspondence and accounts. Veale had earlier (1716) been the Receiver-General for part of Devon, including Exeter (*CTB*, Vol. XXX).
31. *CJ*, Vols XV, XVI, XVII.
32. E.190/987/17.
33. T.70/5. Brazil was not a new destination for English slave traders. In 1696–7 the *Eagle* of London, though ostensibly for Jamaica, had eventually delivered her slaves to Brazil. See HCA.15/19 for her logbook, and HCA.23/23 for the legal proceedings.
34. HCA.1/99.
35. Joseph Tibby of Southampton recorded as being part-owner of the *Manley* at Rappahannock, Virginia, in 1699 (CO.5/1441).
36. John Cabess, most important of all the early eighteenth-century African traders with the Cape Coast Castle, had a particular predilection for such fashions (T.70/14). A useful account of parasols as symbols of majesty can be found in S. Baring-Gould, *Strange Survivals* (1892).
37. This follows the general pattern of Burridge ventures of the period, detailed under Lyme Regis (Chapter 16). Neither the Jamaican nor the Virginia records cover this specific time, but the *Surprise* was not lost at sea or taken by pirates. In September 1715, described as a brigantine of London of 80 tons and 6 guns, the *Surprise* delivered provisions and dry goods to Antigua from Galway and London. Once again her master was Joseph Tibby; she carried a crew of ten and returned with sugar, cotton and ginger (CO.157/1).
38. Devon RO.Z1/10/483. See also HCA.24/127 fol.180 and HCA.24/132 fol.173 where the *Neptune* is taken by the pirate Charles Vane off Providence Island in 1718.
39. CO.157/1 (Antigua: April 1719).
40. CO.33/13.
41. E.190/987/4.
42. T.70/6. 'There are three interlopers from England . . . say they brought their cargoes from Holland, cleared from England. Two of their names are Wennard in a small ship, & Deverell in a sloop. ' Company factors to Africa House, 20 October 1714.

43. E.190/988/4.
44. T.70/6: factors at the Gambia to Africa House, 21 December 1716: 'in June the *Selby Galley*, Captain Vennard, had a rising among the slaves . . . Mr Francis (factor) assisted him &c . . .'.
45. CO.33/15.
46. E.190/989/12.
47. E.190/989/6. Yet another John Vennard captained small sloops and brigantines between New England and the West Indies between 1712 and 1715 (CO.157/1).
48. Donnan, Vol. IV, pp. 258–62, 285.
49. Full details of these ventures can be found in the account book of John Burwell, Devon RO 3372A add./PZ3. The *Fly* commanded by Robert Roberts, was bound for Old Calabar, with a cargo valued at £649 17s. 7½d., which she exchanged for 69 men, 57 women, 11 boys and 8 girls. Most of the linen (Indian cottons) knives, bells and cowries in her cargo remained unsold. The *Wydah* (170 tons), captain John Warren, was bound for Calabar or Bandy for 450 slaves. Her cargo was valued at £1,230 4s.7d., and Burwell's 2½ per cent commission on this came to £34 16s.4d. No serges or perpetuannas were loaded, all the cloth for barter being either Kendal cottons or blue Indian fabrics. Burwell's main interest in this voyage seems to have been gold. The *Sarah*, named after Robert Mathew's wife, of 90 tons burden was bound for Calabar. Burwell's ³⁄₃₂ share of her cargo cost £54, of the ship itself £56, and in extra private arrangements a further £21. The second voyage of the *Wydah* with a cargo valued at £1,685 netted him in commission on the supply of goods and services, a total of £40 16s. The *Two Brothers*, master Roger Gray, sailed in the late summer of 1700 for Guinea with a cargo that included gooseberry beads, three Spanish tables, cane chairs, beaver fur-lined hats, and a sceptre and crown made of laquered tin, valued at £1,000 3s.6d. Burwell's commission on this and other services came to £29 1s.1d., his ¹⁄₁₆ share of the venture to £70 10s. It was the last Guinea venture in which he had a hand.
50. E. A. G. Clarke, *The Estuarine Ports of the Exe and Teign* (1957), pp. 815–16.
51. T.70/46.
52. T.70/1185.
53. T.70/1225.
54. T.70/46, Letters from Francis Lynn, Secretary of the Company, to Sharrow.
55. T.70/7.

CHAPTER 18   Plymouth, Barnstaple and Bideford

1. W. G. Hoskins, *Devon* (1972), pp. 453–61.
2. Thomas Moore, *The County of Devon* (1831), p. 396: 'Plymouth has never been a town of manufacturing notoriety'.

3. A list of ships clearing for the Caribbean (1697–1704) and their cargoes is the subject of Appendix 8.

4. E.190/1061/13. No record has been found of the *Love's Increase* commanded by John Pertescue, freighted by London merchants John Silke and Brough and Arnold from Plymouth. A cargo valued at £800 was shipped coastwise from London to meet her at Plymouth in August 1700 (T.70/350).

5. E.190/1063/35.

6. In the *Peace* of 1699 as Mordecai Lenin (Elizabeth Donnan *Documents Illustrative of the Slave Trade to America*, 4 vols (1930–5), Vol. II, p. 31. In T.70/165 and 353 his name is spelled 'Living', though present-day orthography would probably be 'Levine'.

7. E.190/1064/8. Joseph Martin's career is detailed in John Carswell, *The South Sea Bubble* (1960), p. 282.

8. T.70/1184, p. 121.

9. T.70/5 and T.70/1199. The *William* usually designed to take 180 Negroes (CO.388/11), and here delivered 120 to York, Virginia on 19 April 1706 (W. E. Minchinton *et al.*, *Virginia Slave Trade Statistics 1688–1775* (1984), pp. 16–17.)

10. T.70/1199.

11. E.190/1066/37.

12. T.70/1184, p. 18.

13. T.70/44.

14. T.70/132.

15. Probably Hypericum or St John's Wort.

16. A variety of sources has been used to determine the functions of these herbs. The two most useful are Sir John Pringle, *Observations on the Diseases of the Army* (1775) and 'The London Dispensary', in Vol. II of Culpeper's *Works* (1802).

17. T.70/44.

18. 6 January 1708; she also carried 150 marks of gold and 15 cwt. ivory (T.70/1290B).

19. E.190/1067/21.

20. T.70/1199.

21. Damer Powell, *Bristol Privateers and Ships of War* (1931), p. 97.

22. HCA.26/3.

23. CO.142/14. Donnan, Vol. II, pp. 92–4, quoting from CO.388/13 and presumably following their error, transposes the *Joseph*'s cargo with that of another *Joseph Galley*. The origin of the misunderstanding is due to the unlikely coincidence of two vessels of the same name arriving in and departing from Jamaica within a few days of each other. The *Joseph Galley* under Mullington arrived 5 November 1709 and departed 14 January 1710. The *Joseph Galley*, under Thomas Rogers on behalf of the Royal African Company, arrived on 14 November with 200 slaves and departed on 15 January 1710 for London (CO.142/14).

24. George Barons has already been a subject of discussion in the section

on Exeter and Dartmouth (see pp. 291–4). He may well have been involved in previous trade with Africa from Rotterdam, but there is no evidence for that.

25. E.190/1069/17.
26. Devon RO. Z12/31/22.
27. E.190/1070/12. The link with George Barons is clearly shown in Dorset RO. document ref. B7/N2.
28. See Chapter 16.
29. No Port Books survive for London, either imports or exports.
30. The *Royal Africa*, a Company hired ship of 130 tons and 10 guns, made two voyages to Guinea apparently from Plymouth under Samuel Foot. The first was in 1713 when she delivered 250 blacks to Nevis, the second in 1714 (T.70/1183). A third voyage, under Henry Cornwall, took her to Cabenda and straight back to London in 1721 with gold, ivory, mallaguetta and redwood (T.70/1225). This ship did not take her cargoes aboard at Plymouth, so the assumption must be that she was owned by a Plymouth businessman, and her terms of charter started from there.
31. *CJ*, Vol. XVI, 19 April 1711. The burgesses' petition, along the same lines, had been presented on 11 January 1710.
32. Hoskins, pp. 327–37.
33. Bideford Port Books appear for this period under Barnstaple, the head port.
34. 27 July 1712 (CO.157/1).
35. Gordon Ireland (ed.), 'Servants to Foreign Plantations from Bristol to Barbados', *BMHS Journal* (1946–50) XIV–XIX.
36. CO.5/749.
37. CO.5/1441.
38. Witness the *Concord Galley* of 1705 (E.190/970/7), which left for Cork with tobacco, then on to Madeira and Carolina with old draperies, serges, bays, pewter, iron and 140lb. of great bugle beads supplied by Daniel Jamineau of London (much of whose trade was with Guinea merchants). However the quantities of beer and herrings aboard the *Concord* – presumably for Carolina – suggest she was bound on a conventional voyage. Beads were, of course, popular trading items with the North American Indian.
39. T.70/350 and E.190/1158/1.
40. Daniel Ivy's will is at PROB.11/460, quire 88. The date of the marriage (IGI) was 6 July 1698 in Upton Pyne, a tiny village a few miles to the north of Exeter. The Parminters were predominantly a north Devon family with their main branches at Bideford, Barnstaple and Ilfracombe.
41. Recorded in Walter Prideaux's *Journal*, 27 August 1700 (p. 120).
42. Witness his presence at Virginia with 67 slaves in December 1701 commanding the *Expectation* of Bristol owned by Quaker slave trade merchant Charles Harford, and again in August 1707 aboard an unnamed galley with 158 slaves (Minchinton *et al*, pp. 3–14).

43. CO.157/1: for example, freighting the *Betty Galley* of Barnstaple at Nevis for sugar, cleared for Bristol, 21 November 1705.

CHAPTER 19   Falmouth to Lancaster

1. William Page (ed.), *The Victoria History of the County of Cornwall* 4 vols (1906), I, p. 504.
2. Nathaniel Uring *Voyages and Travels* (1726) gives a first-hand account of the service.
3. *JRIC* ix (1886–9):182–216. Though drawing on contemporary documents which reflect an adherence on the part of the writer to the interest of Sir Peter Killigrew and his descendants, the article is valuable for shedding some light on the origins of the Corker family. It does not, alas, clarify the relationships between other Corkers present in Falmouth at the same time, such as Chambre Corker Esq.
4. *The Registers of Baptisms, Marriages and Burials in the Parish of Falmouth* (1914), transcribed and edited by Susan E. Gay and Mrs Howard Fox, p. 2. Corker is spelt variously, Calker and Caulker. In the latter form it has survived to this day in the Gambia and Sierra Leone.
5. Gay and Fox, p. 126 but various mistakes in the transcriptions, or perhaps in the original records.
6. T.79/51 records his indenture for seven years. Walter Rodney's *History of the Upper Guinea Coast 1545–1800* (1970) includes a brief profile of Corker in his chapter 'The Rise of the Mulatto Traders', pp. 216–20.
7. *JRIC* ix (1886–9).
8. E.190/1062 and 1063.
9. C.33/308.
10. Thomas Phillips, *A Voyage Made in the 'Hannibal' of London, 1693–4*, in Awnsham and Churchill, *Collection of Voyages and Travels* (1732), Vol. VI pp. 192–3, 203.
11. Christopher Fyfe, *A History of Sierra Leone* (1962).
12. Walter Rodney 'African Slavery . . . on the Upper Guinea Coast', in J. E. Inikori (ed.) *Forced Migration* (1982), p. 216.
13. T.70/1434.
14. Some shipments to Thomas Corker were legal. For example the *St Quintin* cleared London for the Gambia in September 1699 with a small cargo of clothing and other items valued at £54 (T.70/349).
15. C.33/308, p. 276.
16. T.70/1434.
17. K. G. Davies, *The Royal African Company* (1957), p. 110.
18. T.70/50.
19. T.70/51.
20. C.33/308.
21. J. M. Gray, *A History of the Gambia* (1940), pp. 122–34.
22. T.70/1434.

23. T.70/51.
24. T.70/43 and 51. An anonymous compilation *A New General Collection of Voyages and Travels* (1745) Vol II, pp. 77–84, relates much detail concerning the negotiations between Brue and Corker. According to this account, Brue reckoned Corker's fortune – the post being 'very lucrative' – as £13,500. Brue held Corker in high esteem.
25. C.33/308.
26. T.70/2.
27. T.70/43.
28. See Christopher Fyfe *A History of Sierra Leone* (1962), and 'The Caulker Manuscript', *Sierra Leone Studies* iv (1922).
29. Walter Rodney, 'African Slavery' p. 268.
30. See Cyril P. Foray, *Historical Dictionary of Sierra Leone* (1977) for an account of some latter-day Caulkers, happily famous rather than infamous.
31. Rodney, 'African Slavery'.
32. Susan E. Gay, *The Parish Church of Falmouth* (1897), pp. 18–19.
33. T.70/350.
34. HCA.26/14, 25/15 and 26/21.
35. IND.1./9021.
36. Gay and Fox, p. 177: Elizabeth Chegoe 'a Negro servant of Mrs Corker brought over from Guinea', was baptised on 8 July 1705 at the age of nineteen. The surname Chegoe bears a curious similarity to 'Chigoe' a tropical water-borne flea which burrows into the skin, usually of the feet, causing acute discomfort. It may well have been a nickname.
37. PROB.6/77.
38. *JRIC* ix (1886–9).
39. BL Add.MS5755, fol. 260 and 'Collectanea Cornubiensia' in Polsue's *Lake's Parochial History of the County of Cornwall* (1867–73; repr. 1974), p. 161.
40. *The History of the House of Commons 1715–1754* ed. Romney Sedgwick (1970), pp. 578–9.
41. *VCH Cornwall*, p. 568.
42. COU., Humphrey Morice papers, document 532.
43. *HHC*, pp. 578–9.
44. E.190/1061/16 and 1062/25; the *Expedition* carried letters of marque (HCA.25/15).
45. T.70/353.
46. T.70/2.
47. *VCH Cornwall*, pp. 558–9.
48. T.70/46.
49. HCA.1/99/3. Much criticism of Captain Gee of the *Onslow* in T.70/4.
50. T.70/53.
51. James Houston, *Some New and Accurate Observations . . . of the Coast of Guinea* (1725), p. 23.
52. E.190/1057/31. Penzance, November 1697; the *Phoenix* of London for

Barbados with candles, tobacco pipes and handpikes. E.190/1059/14, Fowey, October 1699; the *Great John* for Barbados and Virginia, with a large mixed cargo, predominantly woollen goods and clothing. E.190/1061/6, Padstow, January 1701; the *Katherine* of Plymouth for Barbados with herrings. E.190/1062/25, Falmouth, April and September 1703; the *Vine* and the *Vigilance* for Barbados with hats, haberdashery and cloth.

53. *CJ*, Vol. XVI, 17 April 1711 and 12 January 1710.
54. See Appendix 9, 'Ships Clearing Minehead and Bridgwater for the West Indies, 1697–1703'.
55. CO.142/13. Loaded 41 hogsheads of sugar, 18 April 1700.
56. E.190/1359/16 to 1364/4.
57. *CJ*, Vol. XVI, 19 February 1709.
58. CO.33/16. See also James A. Rawley, *The Transatlantic Slave Trade* (1981), pp. 241–6 for a useful summary of minor port involvement in the slave trade.
59. Peter Fryer, *Staying Power* (1984), p. 50 for the *Penellopy*. The *William and Elizabeth* recorded at CO.33/16 delivering 98 slaves in May 1731. The role of Lancaster is examined in M. M. Schofield, 'The Slave Trade from Lancashire and Cheshire Ports outside Liverpool', *Transactions of the Historic Society of Lancashire and Cheshire for the Year 1976* (1977):30–72.

CHAPTER 20 Whitehaven

1. J. V. Beckett, *Coal and Tobacco* (1981), p. 177.
2. D. R. Hainsworth (ed.), *The Correspondence of Sir John Lowther of Whitehaven (1693–1698)* (1983), pp. xx, xxi ff.
3. Edward Hughes, *North Country Life in the Eighteenth Century*, Vol. II (1965).
4. Beckett, p. 161.
5. Ibid., p. 48.
6. Hainsworth, p. 661.
7. Beckett, p. 145.
8. Hainsworth, p. 661.
9. Beckett, p. 105.
10. Hainsworth, p. 661.
11. Ibid., p. 666.
12. K. G. Davies, *The Royal African Company* (1957), p. 66. Company stock was probably just one element in a typical mixed portfolio of assets of the time (1675).
13. Since no Whitehaven Port Books are extant for the period before 1707 this assertion is based on a close study of T.70 material and Colonial Shipping Registers. A John Lowther is recorded as captain of the slave trade vessel *Lyttleton Galley* of London in 1704 and 1705 (T.70/1199), but there is no evidence of any but the most tenuous family connection.

14. John Gale (c.1645–1716), Lowther's steward of collieries. His brother Ebenezer was a fierce opponent of Lowther. John Gale had six sons; John, George, Matthias or Matthew, William, Lowther and Philip; and three daughters, Mary, Suzanne and Elizabeth. Other Whitehaven Gales include Elisha, master of the *Restoration* at Jamaica in 1715 (CO.142/14); Thomas, Surveyor of Customs in 1718 (CUST.82/1) and in partnership with Thomas Lutwidge from 1719; another Thomas, master of the *Swan* of 50 tons burden registered at Barbados in 1718 (CO.33/15) and owned by brothers John and Matthew Gale and John Anderton; and Nicholas, owner and setter-forth of the *Cumberland* in 1711.

15. *Cumberland* of 150 tons, built in Whitehaven in 1697.

16. Letter quoted by Hainsworth, p. 452.

17. George Gale, 1671–1712.

18. Matthew Gale, 1677–1751.

19. Isaac, born about 1672, the younger son of Isaac Milner senior who is recorded as signing the letter of Whitehaven Dissenters in 1694. Jacob, elder brother of Isaac II, was tenant of land at 38 King Street, Whitehaven, in 1696, though by 1698 was in Dublin as a merchant. Another Isaac, possibly Jacob's son, was master of the *Restoration* of 35 tons (later commanded by Elisha Gale) recorded at Jamaica in 1712 from Whitehaven and Dublin with provisions; and also master of the *Hopewell Betty*, an Irish-built brigantine of Whitehaven, 35 tons, which cleared Barbados for Newfoundland with sugar in 1715 (CO.142/14 and CO.33/15 respectively). A further Milner – Joseph – whose biblical nomenclature probably entitles him to membership of the same family, was riding officer at Workington from at least 1718 (CUST.82/1) until 1731 (CUST.82/46); though 'always an active, careful officer', he was also proprietor of the warehouse at Workington, which suggests a profitable sideline in confiscated goods that was perhaps not wholly above board. See Hainsworth, p. 285 for details of conflict between William Gilpin (Lowther's estate steward) and the Milners.

20. T.70/349–56. At least four of Milner's ventures were lost (T.70/1199).

21. CO.388/11.

22. William Jackson, *Papers and Pedigrees mainly relating to Cumberland and Westmorland* (1892), Vol. I, p. 234. The chapel was in James Street. The foundation deeds state it is for Protestants dissenting from the Church of England, whether Presbyterian or Congregational. The original grant was made to Elisha Gale, one of the three sons of John Gale senior who, like other settlers in Whitehaven of the time, came from Newcastle upon Tyne.

23. Though rope-making had been established in the area early in the seventeenth century (Beckett, p. 147) shipbuilding was of comparatively recent date and many Whitehaven vessels continued to be built in Wexford or Wicklow (CO.5/749). The first recorded Whitehaven-built vessel, the *Dove*, was completed in 1686 (Anon. *Shipbuilding in Whitehaven*, 1984).

24. *Notes and Queries* x (1896):335. Jackson, pp. 243–4.
25. D/LONS/W: SLB, 12 September 1707.
26. T.70/175.
27. January 1710 and March 1711 (*CJ* Vol. XVI).
28. Beckett, pp. 6 and 146.
29. Ibid., pp. 161–2. Trustees numbered 21 in total, 14 elected triennially from amongst the masters of vessels, the owners of not less than 1/16th shares in a vessel belonging to the port, and inhabitants dealing in dutiable goods. Sir James Lowther nominated the rest and had the power of veto.
30. William Walker of Co. Westmeath, Ireland; John Relfe of Stoneycroft, Cumberland and Francis Graham of Athwerid, Cumberland (Guildhall Library, London, *Apprenticeship Books 1710–1811* pp. 6074, 4862 and 2744).
31. Beckett, p. 149.
32. CO.142/14.
33. A George Rumball had commanded the London slave ship *Rebecca and Margaret* to Guinea and Barbados for Peregrine Browne (T.70/350 and 1198). Elsewhere the vessel is recorded as the *Robert and Margaret* (CO.33/13). There is, however, no trace of Thomas Rumball in these sources.
34. Died 1704. A young son, Palmer, was buried in the same year (Burke's *Landed Gentry*, 1894, p. 1259).
35. Sir Horace Rumbold, 'Notes on the History of the Family of Rumbold in the 17th Century', *Transactions of The Royal Historical Society*, NS vi (1892): 145–65.
36. *The Registers of St Bees' Cumberland*, transcribed H. B. Stout (Parish Register Section of the Cumberland and Westmorland Antiquarian and Archaeological Society, 1968). There is a possibility that Jane had been the maid of Mildred Warner Washington and had embarked with her on the *Cumberland* of 1699 following Mildred's marriage to George Gale. Jane was baptised in January 1700 and died the following month.
37. T.70/356. Cargo valued at £1,615 10s.
38. T.70/5.
39. HCA.25/24; 27 January 1711. *Cumberland* of 250 tons, 10 guns, 60 men.
40. HCA.25/24 *Swift* of 130 tons, 16 guns, 50 men (recorded elsewhere as 70 tons and 4 guns). Carried 50 small arms, 50 cutlasses, 12 barrels of powder, 70 rounds of great shot, 4 cwt. small shot, victualled 18 months, 2 suits of sails, 4 anchors, 4 cables, 2 cwt. spare cordage. Crew: Robert Hawkes, lieutenant; Sisson Roberts, boatswain; James Astree, gunner; Henry Tennison, carpenter; Robert Berry, cook.
41. T.70/5.
42. D/LONS/W; Barbados Council Minute Book, Captain Charles Constable of HMS *Panther* to Robert Lowther, 13 July 1711.

43. CO.142/14.
44. The *Swift* returned 13 April 1712, D/LONS/W; SLB of that date. The *Friendship* was of 200 tons, 14 guns, 40 men. Carried 40 small arms, 30 cutlasses, 10 barrels of powder, 40 rounds of great shot, 2 cwt. small shot. Crew: John Cartmell, lieutenant; Jeremiah Lucas, boatswain (HCA.26/16).
45. T.70/1225.
46. T.70/8; 30 June–13 July 1713.
47. CO.142/14.
48. T.70/5, 5 June 1714.
49. T.70/8; 8 September–6 October 1714.
50. E.190/1450/4 records the *Mary* for Antigua, *Globe* for Barbados, *Eleanor Galley* for Jamaica.
51. The year 1714 had also seen six ships clearing: the *Holly*, *Eleanor Galley*, *Betty*, *Parton* and *Restoration* for Barbados with cargoes of candles, and the *Bridget and Hudleston* for Jamaica (E.190/1451/13).
52. E.190/1450/21. For an account of the capture of the *Susannah* see D/LONS/W: SLB 16 July 1710.
53. See the invaluable and encyclopaedic work by Dr Nancy Eaglesham, 'The Growth and Influence of the West Cumberland Shipping Industry', unpublished Ph.D. Thesis, Cumbrian RO, Carlisle, p. 89.
54. D/LONS/L: Barbados Plantation Journal, 1713–31.
55. D/LONS/W: SLB, 2 March 1706.
56. Ibid., 16 November 1715.
57. Ibid., 13 March 1707.
58. Robert Biglands, now part-owner of the *Cumberland* (according to CO.5/1441), second-generation Whitehaven merchant of the same name. Hostile to the Lowther cause, he traded extensively with the plantations and often colluded with Scots interlopers in the colonial – predominantly tobacco – trade (Hainsworth, pp. xxii, 245 and 672).
59. Beckett, p. 86.
60. Nancy Eaglesham, *Whitehaven and the Tobacco Trade* (1979), p. 2.
61. CO.33/15, also revealing the date of construction as 1718.
62. HLRO, South Sea Papers, Box 157.
63. CUST.82/1 detailing an allegation regarding one of the crew, a Benjamin Rumball, for smuggling tea.
64. CO.33/15.
65. D/LONS/W: Lists of Ships Belonging to Whitehaven. These record yet another Rumball – Joshua – as master of the coasting trader *Mary Anne*. Whitehaven Museum records reveal Thomas Rumball was still at sea in 1731 when he captained the *Rachel and Betty* to Virginia for tobacco. Unfortunately it has proven impossible to link him with his later namesake, Thomas Rumbold, who headed a company of Liverpool merchants in the middle years of the eighteenth century. Between 1758 and 1763 they set forth four slaving voyages in the vessels *Hare* and *Rainbow* of Liverpool and the *Rumbold* of Lancaster (Elizabeth

Donnan, *Documents Illustrative of the Slave Trade to America*, 4 vols (1930–5), Vol. IV, pp. 228, 370.)

66. CO.33/15.

67. Gibson captained the *Thomas* of Whitehaven at Virginia in 1700 (Eaglesham, 'Growth and Influence', p. 257).

68. CUST.82/1, Letter to Commissioners, 25 October 1723.

69. Burke's *Landed Gentry* (1894), p. 1259. Sir Charles (1644-1710) MP for Lancashire 1679, 1681 and 1689, married Mary Skeffington (1656–1732). See also George Edward Cokayne, *Complete Baronetage*, Vol. I, p. 11.

70. William Farrer and J. Brownbill, *The Victoria History of the County of Lancashire* (1906–14), Vol. VI, pp. 41–7.

71. MP for Preston 1710, 1715 and 1727–41. MP for East Looe, 1724; *HHC*, p. 556.

72. Michael R. Watts, *The Dissenters* (1978), p. 267.

73. *The Evans List* (1715–29), held at Dr Williams Library, Gordon Square, London, WC1.

74. Information kindly supplied by Mr Harry Fancy and Ms Jane Protheroe-Beynon of the Whitehaven Museum.

75. The *Wharton*, wrecked in 1725, was on hire to three Glasgow merchants and was the subject of a lawsuit in the House of Lords in 1734 (BL Add.MS36152, fol.27).

76. Although Thomas Lutwidge is generally assumed to have died in 1745 his wife Lucy did not prove his will until 12 December 1747 (PRO. of Ireland, BET/1/42), which suggests his death was actually in that year. C. Roy Hudleston and R. S. Boumphrey *Cumberland Families and Heraldry* (1978), pp. 214–15, clarify some of the Lutwidge history. Jackson, pp. 213 and 228, states that Thomas Lutwidge was a Governor of St Bees Grammar School from 1730.

77. Ronald T. Gibbon, *To the King's Deceit. A Study of Smuggling in the Solway* (1983), pp. 23, 29. Charles Lutwidge DL, JP (1722–84).

78. Eaglesham, 'Growth and Influence', p. 285.

79. Hudleston and Boumphrey, p. 215n.

80. D/LONS/W: SLB, frequent references in 1720 onwards.

81. DX/524/1–2, Lutwidge Letter Books. Quoted by Eaglesham, p. 78 ff. Walter Lutwidge eventually managed to stage a recovery and became High Sheriff of the county in 1748 (Jackson, p. 245).

82. Donnan, Vol. IV, pp. 207, 212, 223.

83. Elizabeth Lawrence-Dow and Daniel Hay, *Whitehaven to Washington* (1974), p. 15. The *Betty* under Henry Harrison delivered 116 slaves to Rappahannock, Virginia. The *Providence* delivered 111 slaves to Jamaica (CO.142/15).

84. Eaglesham, 'Growth and Influence', p. 90. The *Black Prince* delivered 200 slaves, the *Willington* 149, and the *Prince George* 220. The last ship may be the same as the *King George* of Whitehaven, a slave trader of the 1760s, chiefly famous for her third mate, John Paul Jones: see

Daniel Hay, *Whitehaven* (1979), p. 33, who asserts it is 'one of the few references that can be traced to the port's connection with the [slave] trade'. The *Neptune* under John Eilbeck delivered 383 slaves to James River (Lawrence-Dow and Hay, p. 15).

85. Peter Fryer, *Staying Power* (1984), p. 51, claims an average of four ships a year left Whitehaven 1758–69.
86. Eaglesham, 'Growth and Influence', p. 232 ff.
87. *CJ*, Vol. XVI, 29 January–4 March 1709, reiterated 11 February 1710 and again on 19 March 1711.
88. The *George*, commander David Buckland was bound for Barbados and Virginia (T.70/6). The *Hanover* delivered 90 slaves on 10 May 1718, and the *Loyalty* 51 slaves on 4 December 1719 (CO.33/15).
89. T.70/6.
90. CO.33/15.

CHAPTER 21   The Re-export Trade in Slaves

1. CO.388/12.
2. Leslie Imrie Rudnyanszky, 'The Caribbean Slave Trade: Jamaica and Barbados, 1680–1770, Ph.D thesis, University of Notre Dame, 1973.
3. Somerset RO, DD/WHh/1089.
4. CO.142/13.
5. CO.388/11.
6. CO.142/14.
7. T.70/1205.
8. Bodleian Library: MS Gough Somerset 7; *Observations . . . on the Royal African Company Settling an Agency at New York* (23 November 1724).
9. Elizabeth Donnan, *Documents Illustrative of the Slave Trade to America*, 4 vols, (1930–5) Vol. III, p. 444.
10. T.70/134 contains the log of the *Fauconberg*.
11. CO.33/15.
12. HCA.25/20.

CHAPTER 22   Epilogue

1. David Brion Davis, *The Problem of Slavery in Western Culture* (1966), contains an invaluable chapter entitled 'The Enlightenment as a Source of Anti-slavery Thought: the Ambivalence of Rationalism', p. 391. For numbers of slaves see Paul Lovejoy, 'The Impact of the Atlantic Slave Trade', *JAH* 30 (1989), p. 368.
2. James A. Rawley, *The Transatlantic Slave Trade* (1981), p. 430.
3. It has been persuasively argued that 'abolition was a mere pretext for seeking economic and political domination' of West Africa: see *Economic History Review* xxv (1972) for J. F. A. Ajayi and R. A. Austen's article, 'Hopkins on Economic Imperialism in West Africa'.

APPENDIX 1   Vessels Clearing Deal, Portsmouth, Southampton, Cowes and Weymouth for Africa, 1698–1720

1. E.190/841/8; named after Thomas Ekins, a prominent London merchant.
2. T.70/51.
3. T/70/1183, p. 43. The *Ekins* initially called at Barbados; she cleared Jamaica on her homeward run on 15 June 1700 bound for London with sugar, indigo, ginger, cotton, 4 tons of fustick, and 161 tons of logwood (CO.142/13 and CO.33/13).
4. E.190/842/8 and T.70/351. No shipping registers survive for Nevis, the *Mary Anne*'s destination, 1700–3.
5. Flat round caps, traditionally worn by soldiers and sailors.
6. E.190/846/6.
7. T.70/353.
8. T.70/1199.
9. E.190/848/2.
10. Ibid.
11. T.70/1209.
12. T.70/1199. Entered London from Maryland 9 December 1708 with 79 lb. of ivory (T.70/355). For delivery of slaves see Elizabeth Donnan, *Documents Illustrative of the Slave Trade to America*, 4 vols (1930–5), Vol. IV, p. 17.
13. E.190/850/1.
14. T.70/1199. Donnan, Vol. II, p. 73 mistakenly calls this vessel the *Prince of Mindchim*.
15. E.190/852/8.
16. T.70/1199; T.70/356.
17. Donnan, Vol. II, p. 116.
18. Estimated date. No reference has been found to her departure.
19. CO.157/1.
20. Later captained the slave ship *Betty* (CO.142/14).
21. CO.33/15.
22. T.70/6.
23. E.190/695/15.
24. E.190/913/1.
25. CO.5/508.

APPENDIX 2   Vessels Clearing London, Bristol and Lyme Regis for the Burridge Family of Lyme, 1704–25

1. Dorset RO.B7/N2. Benjamin Way's cargo sent 'by land carriage to Bristol & so to Africa' on 28 July 1703 (T.70/1199).
2. T.70/354 mentioning only Benjamin Way. Two *London Galleys* plied in the slave trade during 1704–5; one for Houlditch and Brooke of London under John Beckford, the other for Richard Tudway and John

Bryant of Bristol (T.70/1199 and 354).

3. *LJ*, Vol. XVIII, pp. 390-1.
4. T.70/1199. Details also at T.70/354 with slight variations.
5. T.70/8.
6. E.190/1166/3.
7. T.70/1199.
8. Elizabeth Donnan, *Documents Illustrative of the Slave Trade to America*, 4 vols (1930-5), Vol. II, p. 116.
9. E.190/1166/3.
10. T.70/356.
11. E.190/1166/3. Further slight discrepancies between cargo detailed to the Royal African Company and that actually recorded as shipped from the port of departure. Robert Poole and Samuel Packer were both Bristol merchants.
12. T.70/1199 and 356.
13. Humphrey Morice (COU/B.119 and 293) describes Tourney as an ironmonger, though the scope of his operation went far beyond the modern-day interpretation of that title. The central part that iron bars and metalwares played in slave trade cargoes led Tourney to become directly involved in the trade and he financed many London ventures to Guinea during the early 1700s.
14. T.70/356 states a value of £37. James Wayte was a leading London slave trade merchant, particularly active 1700-15.
15. E.190/903/9.
16. T.70/8.
17. CO.33/15.
18. E.190/906/12.
19. E.190/907/1.
20. E.190/908/1.
21. Ibid.
22. Dorset RO.B7/F2.
23. E.190/910/2.
24. E.190/911/12.
25. E.190/911/6.
26. Originally beaver but by the eighteenth century, rabbit.
27. E.190/912/7.
28. E.190/914/4. There are no Port Books for Lyme for 1724 and 1727-33 inclusive.
29. Ibid. For the involvement with Carruthers and the *Resolution* see HCA.24/135, fols 239 and 244. The *Friendship*'s arrival in Barbados at CO.33/15.

APPENDIX 3 Vessels Clearing Exeter, Topsham and Dartmouth for Africa, 1698-1725

1. Port Books for Exeter cease in 1723.

2. E.190/1157/1. Whereas this item is described as Xmas 1698–Xmas 1699 the cover appears to have been transposed with 1156/1, Xmas 1697–Xmas 1698.
3. CO.33/13.
4. Ibid.
5. E.190/973/1, E.190/1059/4 and T.70/350 reveal that the *Betty* had delivered the bulk of her cargo to Plymouth merchants on 15 June 1699.
6. E.190/973/2.
7. E.190/982/3.
8. T.70/359; Elizabeth Donnan, *Documents Illustrative of the Slave Trade to America*, 4 vols (1930–5), Vol. II, p. 94 mentions the *Dartmouth* had 1,650 pieces of woollen goods aboard.
9. E.190/987/17.
10. T.70/5.
11. E.190/987/11.
12. As described on a later voyage, CO.157/1.
13. E.190/987/4.
14. From a later entry in Antigua Shipping Registers, CO.157/1.
15. T.70/6.
16. E.190/988/4.
17. Ibid.
18. CO.33/15.
19. E.190/989/12: a cargo of 2,600lb. of tobacco and 550lb. of indigo was also entered for Roger Prowse.

APPENDIX 4 Vessels Clearing Plymouth for Africa, 1698–1725, Including the *Elizabeth Galley* of Bristol Freighted by Bideford Merchants to Africa in 1700

1. There are no Plymouth Port Books for the period 1720–54.
2. E.190/1061/13.
3. E.190/1063/35.
4. Extra detail added from T.70/353.
5. E.190/1064/8.
6. T.70/353. See Elizabeth Donnan, *Documents Illustrative of the Slave Trade to America*, 4 vols (1930–5), Vol. IV, p. 173 for *Williams'* arrival in Virginia.
7. E.190/1066/37.
8. E.190/1067/21.
9. T.70/355.
10. CO.142/14.
11. E.190/1069/17.
12. T.70/356.
13. E.190/1070/12.
14. T.70/355.

15. T.70/350; cargo detailed between 24 January and 9 February 1700.

APPENDIX 5   Vessels Clearing Falmouth for Africa, 1698–1719

1. Port Books for Falmouth are in existence only until 1719.
2. E.190/1057/37.
3. CO.33/13.
4. E.190/1061/16.
5. T.70/51 (some details may be duplicated).
6. Ibid. and T.70/350. Eyre's cargo arrived on the *Rebecca*, commanded by Anthony Jenkins from London. Samuel Eyre was a prominent London slave trade merchant.
7. T.70/1198. There is no record of the *Thomas* discharging cargo at Falmouth or any other Cornish or Devon port. Brusser claimed her last port of call was the Guinea Coast, but the length of the voyage and Robert Corker's track record reinforce the very real possibility that Corker's share of the return cargo may have been smuggled ashore at Falmouth.
8. E.190/1061/16.
9. E.190/1062/25.
10. HCA.25/15: 17 September 1703.
11. T.70/353.
12. T.70/1198.

APPENDIX 6 Vessels Clearing Whitehaven for Africa, 1698–1725

1. The Port Books for Whitehaven (E.190 series) exist only for 1707–20: they generally fail to mention the African leg of the journey. Elizabeth Donnan, *Documents Illustrative of the Slave Trade to America*, 4 vols (1930–5), Vol. II, p. 118 quoting CO.388/13, records a vessel clearing for Guinea from Whitehaven in the summer of 1710, but no evidence that this voyage actually took place has been found. In all probability this refers to the *Swift* of 1711.
2. E.190/1450/10 and T.70/356.
3. Traditional measure of cotton cloth equal to 4½ feet. 'Sempiternas' and linseys also used this measure.
4. E.190/1450/17 and 21.
5. Logwood (fustick) for dyeing. Lutwidge had previously imported supplies from Jamaica via the *Galley Prize* and *Kent* of Whitehaven.
6. This expensive cloth – recorded by the Customs at 26s. a piece – is presumably a watered silk which has been jaspered or speckled. However, a note of caution: the spelling is difficult to decipher owing to the Searcher being unsure of the names and categories of these stuffs which had presumably been imported via London. 'Jasper Watters' may simply be a rather extravagant misunderstanding, since Jasper Water &

Co. were London merchants of the time who carried on a considerable trade with the American plantations.

7. CO.33/15. William Hicks had been Sir John Lowther's London clerk before being apprenticed to Thomas Lutwidge in the wine trade. Like Lutwidge, he became prominent in the tobacco trade, dying in 1758 worth about £20,000. Dr Nancy Eaglesham, 'The Growth and Influence of the West Cumberland Shipping Industry', unpublished Ph.D. thesis, Cumbrian RO, Carlisle, p. 87, J. V. Beckett, *Coal and Tobacco* (1981), p. 113.

8. E.190/1451. The *Swift* was redeployed to Virginia via Dublin with beef and provisions for her next voyage (CO.142/14).

9. E.190/1451/6 and 2.

10. CO.142/14.

11. E.190/1452/7: 20 March 1715.

12. E.190/1452/8.

13. E.190/1453/7.

14. E.190/1452/9.

15. CO.5/1441.

16. CO.33/15.

17. E.190/1454/8.

18. Ibid.

19. CO.157/1.

20. Via the *Whitehaven Galley* – see entry for 20 September 1715 (p. 380).

21. CO.157/1.

22. E.190/1455/2.

23. Brother of William Gilpin.

24. Approximate date: no Port Books for Whitehaven have survived for the period 1721–38 inclusive. The *Susannah* was owned by Thomas Lutwidge.

25. CO.33/15.

26. T.70/1664.

APPENDIX 7 Minor Outport Involvement in the Re-export Trade in Slaves, 1698–1722

1. Despite her name, a Dartmouth vessel usually engaged in Channel Island trade.

2. CO.5/1441.

3. Ibid. Robert Burridge II and husband and wife tobacco merchants Robert and Elizabeth Fowler were the merchants behind this voyage.

4. E.190/689/16.

5. CO.33/15.

6. E.190/1072/8.

7. This entry and the following three all derive from W. E. Minchinton *et al.*, *Virginia Slave Trade Statistics 1698–1775* (1984), pp. 23–37, though loosely described there as arriving in Virginia between 10 December

1710 and 10 December 1718. By use of the Port Books (E.190 series) a more exact timetable has been established, with the exception of the *Swift* of Whitehaven, which was under Thomas Rumball's command until 1713 so must have arrived in Virginia subsequently.

8. E.190/1075/7.
9. E.190/906/10.
10. E.190/989/12.
11. CO.5/508.
12. Return cargo consisted of rice, pitch, tar and sassifrax roots.
13. E.190/907/11.
14. CO.5/1222, also Elizabeth Donnan *Documents Illustrative of the Slave Trade to America*, 4 vols (1930–5), Vol. III, p. 465.
15. E.190/991/10.
16. CO.5/508.
17. Despite the presence of such a substantial re-export cargo, the *Elizabeth* appears not to have been a fully fledged Guinea-trade ship. Usually the Charleston port authorities were careful to note whether ships carrying slaves had called at the African coast. Neither London's nor Ramsgate's Port Books survive for this period.
18. CO.5/508.
19. Dorset RO.B7.N/2: approximate date of arrival in Virginia (as with *John* of 1720).
20. E.190/910/4.
21. T.70/1664: cleared Barbados in January 1722 with 90 gallons of rum for Carolina.
22. CO.5/509.

APPENDIX 9   Vessels Clearing Minehead and Bridgwater for the West Indies, 1697–1703

1. A barrel of herrings weighed 228 lb. and contained approximately 900 herrings (Richard B. Sheridan, *Doctors and Slaves*, 1985, p. 162).

Select Bibliography

Primary Sources:

Public Record Office, Chancery Lane, London
E.190   The Port Books for England and Wales
HCA.   Records of the High Court of Admiralty
IND.1   Index to Shipping captured by Letter of Marque vessels
PROB.6 & 11 Wills and Administrations of the Prerogative Court of
             Canterbury
C.33   Chancery Decrees

Public Record Office, Kew, Surrey
T.64   Treasury Papers
T.70   Papers of the Royal African Company
CO.33   Colonial Shipping Returns – Barbados
CO.157   Colonial Shipping Returns – Leeward Islands
CO.142   Colonial Shipping Returns – Jamaica
CO.5   Colonial Shipping Returns – Virginia, South Carolina etc.
CO.388   Board of Trade Original Correspondence
CUST.50–101 HM Customs & Excise, Outport Records
ADM.8   List of Ships on Station 1699–1703
ADM.50–3   Admirals', captains', masters' and ships' log-books

Bank of England
COU. Humphrey Morice papers

Somerset Record Office, Taunton
DD/WHh. Walker Heneage/Helyar papers

Dorset Record Office, Dorchester
B7. Lyme Regis Borough Archives

Devon Record Office, Exeter
3327A add/PZ.3. Account Book of John Burwell

Cumbria Record Office, Carlisle
D/LONS/W. Lonsdale of Whitehaven papers

House of Lords Record Office, Westminster
B.57–63; Box 157–8 South Sea papers

British Library
Sloane MS 2496   Log of HMS *Margate* by Lt William Carr, 1700–1
Add. MS 39946   *Narrative of a Voyage to Guinea*, 1714
Add. MS 12430   Journal of Col. William Beeston

Official Published Sources
Calendar of State Papers, Colonial: America and the West Indies
Calendar of State Papers, Domestic
Calendar of Treasury Books
Calendar of Treasury Papers
Journal of the House of Commons
Journal of the House of Lords

Secondary sources:

Anon., *Some Memoirs of the First Settlement of the Island of Barbados* Barbados: William Beeby, 1741.

Ashley, Maurice, *England in the Seventeenth Century* 1952; repr. Harmondsworth: Penguin Books, 1963.

Atkins, John, *A Voyage to Guinea &c.* London: Ward & Chandler, 1735.

Aubrey, Thomas, *The Sea-Surgeon or the Guinea Man's Vade Mecum* London: John Clarke, 1729.

Barbot, John, 'A Description of the Coasts of North and South-Guinea' (1688) in Awnsham and John Churchill, *Collection of Voyages and Travels* London: Churchill, 1732, Vol.V, pp. 1–455; James Barbot, 'Abstract of a Voyage to New Calabar River . . . in the year 1699', ibid., pp. 455–66, 'An abstract of a Voyage to the Congo River . . . and to Cabinda in the year 1700', ibid., pp. 497–522, and 'An Account of the Rise and Progress of our Trade to Africa', ibid., pp. 665–8.

Bean, R. N., *The British Transatlantic Slave Trade 1650–1775* New York: Arno Press, 1975.

Beckett, J. V., *Coal and Tobacco* Cambridge University Press, 1981.

[Bonner-Smith, D., et al.] *The Commissioned Sea Officers of the Royal Navy, 1660–1815* Greenwich: National Maritime Museum, 1954.

Bosman, William, *A New and Accurate Description of the Coast of Guinea* London: D. Midwinter, 1705.

Carr, Cecil T., *Select Charters of Trading Companies 1530–1707* London: Selden Society, 1913.

Carswell, John, *The South Sea Bubble* London: The Cresset Press, 1960.

Cary, John, *An Essay on the State of England* Bristol, 1695.

Clowes, William Laird, *The Royal Navy* 1898; repr. New York: AMS Press Inc., 1966.

Coad, John, *A Memorandum of the Wonderful Providences of God* repr. London: Longman, 1849.

Course, A. G., *A Seventeenth Century Mariner* London: Frederick Muller, 1965.

Craton, Michael, *Searching for the Invisible Man* Harvard University Press, 1978.

Craton, Michael and Walvin, James, *A Jamaican Plantation* London: W. H. Allen, 1970.

Cundall, F., *The Governors of Jamaica in the XVIIth Century* London: West India Committee, 1936.

Curtin, Philip, *The Atlantic Slave Trade. A Census* Madison: University of Wisconsin Press, 1969.

van Dantzig, A., *The Dutch and the Guinea Coast 1674–1742* Accra: GAAS, 1978.

—— *Forts and Castles of Ghana* Accra: Sedco, 1980.

Davenant, Charles, *Reflections on the Constitution and Management of the Trade to Africa* (1709) in *The Political and Commercial Works of Charles Davenant*, ed. Sir Charles Whitworth 5 vols., London: R. Horsfield, 1771, Vol. V.

Davies, K. G., *The Royal African Company* London: Longmans, Green, 1957.

Davis, David Brion, *The Problems of Slavery in Western Culture* New York: Cornell University Press, 1966.

Deerr, N. F., *The History of Sugar* 2 vols., London: Chapman & Hall, 1949–50.

Donnan, Elizabeth, *Documents Illustrative of the Slave Trade to America*, 4 vols., Washington: Carnegie Institution, 1930–5.

Dow, G. F., *Slave Ships and Slaving* Salem, Mass.: Marine Research Society, 1927.

Dunn, R. S., *Sugar and Slaves. The Rise of the Planter Class in the English West Indies 1624–1713* Chapel Hill: University of North Carolina Press, 1972.

Falconbridge, Alexander, *An Account of the Slave Trade on the Coast of Africa* London: J. Phillips, 1788.

Faust, Drew Gilpin (ed.), *The ideology of Slavery* Baton Rouge: Louisiana State University Press, 1981.

Foray, Cyril P., *Historical Dictionary of Sierra Leone* London: Methuen, 1977.

Fowles, John, *A Short History of Lyme Regis* Wimborne, Dorset: Dovecote Press, 1985.

Fry, E. A., *Calendar of Wills . . . Relating to Dorset* London: British Record Society, 1900.

—— *Calendar of Wills . . . Relating to Devon and Cornwall* London: British Record Society, 1908.

Fry, G. S., *Calendar of Dorset Wills* London: British Record Society, 1911.

Fryer, Peter, *Staying Power* London: Plato, 1984.

Fyfe, Christopher, *A History of Sierra Leone* Oxford University Press, 1962.

Galenson, David W., *Traders, Planters and Slaves* Cambridge University Press, 1986.

Garrard, T. F., *Akan Weights and the Gold Trade* London: Longman, 1980.

Gay, Susan E. and Fox, Mrs Howard (eds.), *The Registers of Baptisms, Marriages and Burials in the Parish of Falmouth* Exeter: Devon & Cornwall Record Society, 1914.

Gibbon, Ronald T., *To the King's Deceit, A Study of Smuggling in the Solway* Carlisle: Whitehaven Museum, 1983.

Gray, Sir J. M., *A History of the Gambia* Cambridge University Press, 1940.

Hainsworth, D. R. (ed.), *The Correspondence of Sir John Lowther of Whitehaven 1693–1698* Oxford University Press, 1983.

Hakluyt, Richard, *The Principal Navigations, Voyages, Traffiques and Discoveries of the English Nation* 1589; 12 vols., repr. Glasgow: James Maclehose & Sons, 1903–5.

Harlow, V. T., *A History of Barbados* Oxford: Clarendon, 1926.

Hay, Daniel, *Whitehaven* Beckermet: Michael Moon, 1979.

Henning, Basil Duke, (ed.) *The History of Parliament. The House of Commons 1660–1693* 3 vols., London: Secker & Warburg, 1983.

Hoskins, W. G., *Industry, Trade and People in Exeter 1688–1800* Manchester University Press, 1935.

—— *Devon* Newton Abbot: David & Charles, 1978.

Hotten, J. C. (ed.), *The Original Lists of Persons of Quality &c.* London: Chatto & Windus, 1874.

Houstoun, James, *Some New and Accurate Observations . . . of the Coast of Guinea* London: J. Peele, 1725.

Hudleston, C. Roy and Boumphrey, R. S., *Cumberland Families and Heraldry* Ambleside: Cumberland & Westmorland Antiquarian and Archaeological Society, 1978.

Hughes, Edward, *North Country Life in the Eighteenth Century* 2 vols Oxford University Press, 1952–65.

Hutchins, John, *History of Dorset* 4 vols., London: J. B. Nichols, 1861–73.

Ingram, K. E. *Sources of Jamaican History 1655–1838* London: Zug, 1976.

Inikori, J. E. (ed.), *Forced Migration* London: Hutchinson University Library, 1982.

Kemp, Peter, *The British Sailor: a Social History of the Lower Deck* London: Dent, 1970.

Klein, H. S., *The Middle Passage. Comparative Studies in the Atlantic Slave Trade* Princeton University Press, 1978.

Lawrence, A. W., *Trade Castles and Forts of West Africa* London: Jonathan Cape, 1963.

Ligon, Richard, *A True and Exact History of the Island of Barbados* London: Humphrey Moseley, 1657.

Mannix, D. P. and Cowley, M., *Black Cargoes* London: Longmans, 1963.

Mathews, A. G., *Calamy Revised* Oxford: Clarendon Press, 1934.

Moore, Thomas, *The County of Devon* London: R. Jennings, 1831.

Patterson, Orlando, *The Sociology of Slavery* London: MacGibbon & Kee, 1967.

—— *Slavery and Social Death* Harvard University Press, 1982.

Phillips, Thomas, *A Journal of a Voyage Made in the 'Hannibal' of London, Ann. 1693, 1694* First published in Awnsham and John Churchill, *A Collection of Voyages and Travels* (1732) Vol. VI, pp. 173–239

Pitman, Henry, *A Relation of the Great Sufferings and strange adventures of H. Pitman, Chyrurgion to the Late Duke of Monmouth* London: Sowle 1689.

Polsue, J., *Lake's Parochial History of the County of Cornwall* 4 vols., 1867–73, repr. Wakefield: E. P. Publishing, 1974.

Powell, Damer, *Bristol Privateers and Ships of War* Bristol: Arrowsmith, 1931.

Prideaux, R. M., *Prideaux. A West Country Clan* Chichester: Phillimore, 1989.

Rawley, James A., *The Transatlantic Slave Trade* New York: Norton, 1981.

Roberts, George, *History of Lyme Regis* Sherborne, 1823.

—— *History and Antiquities of the Borough of Lyme Regis* London: Bagster, 1834.

Rodger, N. A. M., *The Wooden World* London: Collins, 1986

Rodney, Walter, *A History of the Upper Guinea Coast 1545–1800* Oxford: Clarendon Press, 1970.

Sanders, J. M., *Barbados Records, Wills and Administrations 1681–1700* Houston: Sanders Historical Publications, 1981.

Schomburgk, Sir R. H., *History of Barbados* London: Longman, Brown, Green & Longmans, 1848.

Scott, W. R., *The Constitution and Finance of English, Scottish and Irish Joint Stock Companies to 1720* 3 vols., Cambridge University Press, 1910–12.

Sedgwick, Romney (ed.), *The House of Commons 1715–1754* 5 vols., London: HMSO, 1970.

Sheppard, Jill, *The Redlegs of Barbados* Millwood: KTO Press, 1977.

Sheridan, Richard B., *Doctors and Slaves* Cambridge University Press, 1985.

Tawney, R. H., *Religion and the Rise of Capitalism* 1926; Harmondsworth: Penguin, repr. 1975.

Thomas, Dalby, *An Historical Account of the Rise and Growth of the West India Collonies* London: Jo. Hindmarsh, 1690.

Uring, N., *The Voyages and Travels of Capt. Nathaniel Uring* 1726; repr. London: Cassell, 1926.

Wanklyn Cyril, *Lyme Regis, a Retrospect* London: Hatchards, 1927.

Waters, David, *The Art of Navigation in England in Elizabethan and Early Stuart Times* Greenwich: National Maritime Museum, 1978.

Watts, Michael R., *The Dissenters* Oxford: Clarendon Press, 1978.

Williams, Eric, *Capitalism and Slavery* Chapel Hill: University of North Carolina Press, 1945.

Index

Appendices and footnotes have not been included in this index.

abolition of the slave trade, 357–8
Accra, 112, 114, 115
Accra, 223
Act of Toleration, 239
Acts of Trade and Navigation, 10
Addis, John, 301
Adventure, 221–2
Africa, 69–80; British supremacy in, 358; sub-Saharan: effects of slavery, 72, *see also* Gold Coast; Guinea Coast; individual countries
Africa (1699), 16
Africa (of London and Lyme Regis), 247, 258
Akan tribe, 70, 71, 89, 124
Albion, 113, 121, 158, 185
Alford, Daniel, 247
Alford, Gregory, 231
Alford, Joseph, 247
Allen, William, 209
Amber, Captain, 283
America or *America Merchant*, 58–9
American colonies, 34, 348
American War of Independence, 223
Amity, 93, 94, 109
Amsterdam, 6, 292
Anamabo, *see* Annamabo
Ando (black manservant), 246, 247
Andrew, Solomon, 235
Angola, 5, 170, 347
Anley, Joshua, 209
Ann and Sarah, 314
Anna, 290–1
Annamabo, 20, 89, 104, 108, 109, 222
Annapolis, 218
Anne (of Bristol), 257
Anne (of Exeter), 292
Anne and Priscilla, 300
Anning, John, 233

Antelope, 54
Anthony, Joseph, 282
Antigua, 26–7, 30, 73, 108, 281, 305, 343
Arbuthnot, David, 249
Arcadians, tribe, 21
Arcaney Merchant, 110
Arcania Galley, 110
Arthur, Henry, 22, 23, 27, 28, 29, 32, 36, 40, 48, 55, 100, 182–3, 188, 292, 306
Ashburton, 281, 289
Asseney, 70
Atkins, Robert, 223
Atkinson, James, 164
Aubrey, Thomas, 149–50, 152–3
Austria Galley, 218
Azores, the, 19, 23

Baale, Christopher, 56
Baker, John, 285
Baker, Thomas, 209
Bale, Christopher, 29
Ball, Dorothy, 32
Barbados, 7, 12, 16, 22, 30, 31, 34, 35, 52, 56, 107, 108, 109, 110, 119, 141, 281; and the re-export of slaves, 351, 353, 354; Lyme Regis trade with, 233, 234, 237, 246, 268, 269, 270; Portsmouth trade with, 233; Whitehaven trade with, 343, 344
Barbados Council, 31
Barbados Merchantman, 218, 219–21
Barbot, James, 113, 121, 147, 158, 224
Barbot, John, 34, 35, 94, 109, 154, 185, 187, 223–4
Barfoot, William, 225, 355
Barnstaple, 232, 277, 279, 304, 305, 306
Barons, George, 291–2, 293, 303
Barons, Samuel, 292, 293–4
Barra, King of, 208
Barrett, Mathew, 288–9

Basnio, Richard, 54, 56
Batchelor's Endeavour, 317
Battell, Abraham, 251
Beeston, Sir William, 186
Beginning, 120, 282, 306
Belfast, 324, 349
Bellerby, Isaac, 250
Bembridge, William, 56
Bence Island, 225
Benezet, Anthony, 201
Benn, Anthony, 341
Berwick upon Tweed, 202
Betty (of London), 223
Betty (of Whitehaven 1752), 347
Betty Galley (of Exeter), 120, 282, 306
Betty Galley (of London), 215
Betty Galley (privateer of 1702), 317
Bideford, 277, 279, 304–6
Bigbury Bay, 54
Biglands, Robert, 332, 342
Billingsly, Rupert, 174
Bingham, Joseph, 218, 219, 220–1
Birkett, Henry, 347
Birmingham, 20, 274
Biscay, Bay of, 57
Bissagos (Bijuagos) Isles (Guinea-Bissau), 170, 267
Black Prince, 347
Blake, John, 287
Blake, Robert, 228
Bojador, Cape, 53, 61, 62
Bosman, Wilhelm, 89, 90
Boughton, 19
Boughton, Consul at Venice, 8
Bourdeaux Merchant, 202
Bourne, Patrick, 17
Bowdidge, John, 265
Bowles, George, 205, 208
Bowles, James, 205, 207
Bowles, Thomas, 207
Bowles, Thomazine, 207–8
Bowles, Tobias, 205, 207–8, 209
Bowles, Valentine, 205–7
Bowles, William, 207, 209
Bowles family, 204–8
Bowman, Samuel, 332
Bowman, William, 332
Boys, William, 209, 210–11
Bradford, 348
Bradley, Stephen, 210
Bragge family, 245–6
Branscomb, Bartholomew, 55, 57, 148
Brazil, 5, 6, 118, 170
Bridgewater, 160
Bridgewater, 15, 306, 323–4
Briscoe, Edward, 215–16
Bristol, 15, 22, 148, 191, 195, 196, 197, 202–3, 230, 245, 250, 274, 279, 294, 295, 306, 323, 324, 328

Bristol Merchant Venturers, 280
Broderick, Martha (Brodridge), 58–9, 282
Broomfield, 218
Brotherhood of St Thomas Beckett, 230, 245
Brown, Israel, 213, 214, 215, 216, 217–18
Brue, André, 313
Brusser, James, 316
Buckeridge, Nicholas, 85, 86–7, 88–90, 104, 105, 123
Buckeridge, Thomas, 87
Bunston, Henry, 265
Burridge, John, 225, 233, 234, 235–6, 237, 238, 243, 244, 246, 248, 253, 256, 258, 259, 268, 269, 270, 273, 275
Burridge, John junior, 238, 239, 242, 248–9, 250, 251, 252–9, 272–3, 274, 291
Burridge, Mary (later Gibbs), 233, 238
Burridge, Robert I, 232–3, 234–5, 240, 246, 273
Burridge, Robert II, 235, 236–8, 239, 243, 256, 258, 259, 269, 270, 271, 273
Burridge, Robert III, 270, 273, 275–6
Burridge, Walter, 255, 256
Burridge family, 232–3, 234–9, 244–5, 247, 248, 250, 251, 303, 306, 355
Burwell, Henry, 24, 124, 294
Burwell, John, 124
Butcher, Christopher, 283
Butcher, John, 250, 261

Cabestera people, 21
Cairns, Henry, 335
Campeche, Bay of, 338
canoes, 110–11
Caotre (Ivory Coast), 98
Cape Coast, 223
Cape Coast Castle, 17, 19, 77, 78, 79, 81–2, 85, 86, 87, 88, 90, 91, 103, 105, 106, 108, 123, 215, 320, 321–2, 334, 335
Cape Mount, 218
Cape Verde Islands, 52, 60, 224, 267, 281
Carcass, HMS, 346
Caribbean, 9, 11–13, 358; re-export of slaves to, 350–4; Whitehaven trade with, 338–9, *see also* individual islands, e.g. Barbados
Carless, Mr (surgeon), 301
Carlisle, 324
Carolina, 52, 225, 226, 354
Carolina, 345
Carruthers, John, 271–2
Castor, 305
Catchpole, Samuel, 179–80, 182, 187, 188
Catherine, 59
Caulker family, *see* Corker
Cecilia, 248
Chandos, 321
Chaplin, Charles, 16
Chapman, John, 55, 56, 160, 161, 163–5, 190; inventory of, 164–5

Charity, 233
Charles, 183
Charles I, King, 198
Charles II, King, 198
Chauncy, Ichabod, 241
Cherubim, 230
Chester, 15, 324–5
Christian, Robert, 224
Christiansborg (Dutch fort), 81
Clapp, John, 57, 148
Clarendon, Earl of, 170
Clarinda, 293
Clarke, Mrs Anne, 19
Cleeve, Alexander, 310
Clement, Henry, 102
Coad, John, 152
Codrington, Christopher, 73
Cogan, Elizabeth, 232–3
Cogan, John, 235, 248
Cogan, William, 248, 260, 267, 269, 339
Colborn, William, 100, 101
Colchester, 202
Collingwood, John, 300
Collins, Robert, 256, 303
Colthurst, Thomas, 222
Columbus, Christopher, 3, 4–5
Colyton, 279
Commenda, 102–3, 108
Commenda Wars, 89
Company of Adventurers to the Gold Mines in Africa, 320
Company of Cacheu, 170
Company of Merchants Trading into Africa, 11, 205
Company of Royal Adventurers into Africa, 13–14, 279
Company of Scotland Trading to Africa and the Indies, 349
Concord, 202, 233
Confirmation, 338
Congo, 223
Congregationalism, 198
Cook, James, 52, 343
Cooke, John, 36
Corker, Benjamin, 311
Corker, Jane, 309, 314, 317
Corker, Lawrence, 311
Corker, Robert, 283, 286, 309, 311–12, 314, 315, 316, 317–19
Corker, Thomas, 86, 283, 309–16, 317
Cornwall, 308–23
Coromantine slaves, 73–4
Costin, Thomas, 257
Courtenay, Frances, 29
Courtenay, Samuel, 244, 255, 259, 260, 261, 267, 268, 269, 270, 355
Courtenay, William, 255, 257, 259
Coward, Elizabeth, 241–2
Coward, Henry, 241

Coward, William, 18, 241
Crawford, Thomas, 8
Crispe, Nicholas, 11, 204–5
Cromwell, Oliver, 10, 12, 30
Cross, John, 218
Crossman, Richard, 100, 101
Crowe, James, 344
Crown (of Bideford), 305
Crown (privateer of London), 355
Culliford, William, 231
Cumberland, 330, 331
Cumberpatch, Zachariah, 80

Daniel, Josiah, *see* Daniell
Daniel and Henry, 286, 294, 306; accounts, 124–38, 187, 188–91; in Africa, 93–117; anchors, 113; armament, 50; at Cape Mesurado, 92, 93; cargo, 27–8, 36–45; construction, 46–8; crew, 24–7, 53–7, 111, 146, 148, 151, 154; fitting out costs, 48–9, 53; navigation, 50–2; officers, 55, 151; repairs and maintenance, 48, 180–1; rigging, 49–50; in São Tomé, 117–21; slaves on board, 73–4, 100, 117, 120–1, 141–54, 156, 165–6, 168, 172–3, 177–9; voyage to Jamaica, 142, 155–83; watch bill, 56–7
Daniell (Daniel), Josiah, 104, 106, 107, 112, 113
Danish West African Company, 114
Dartmouth, 23, 24, 25, 27, 28, 29, 52, 53, 54, 182, 289, 290, 292, 294
Dartmouth or *Dartmouth Galley*, 39, 287–8
Davenant, Charles, xiv, 32–3, 39, 183
Davers, Sir Robert, 90
Davers Galley, 187
Davis, John, 108, 109
Davis, Nathaniel, 258
Davis, Robert, 8
Deal, 203–4, 205, 207, 208–9
Dean, Anne, 265
Delagoa Bay, 295, 296
de la Palma, William, 71
Denmark, 81
Dennis, Captain John, 299
Devis, William, 57
Devon, 23, 195, 277–307, 322
Dissenters, 198–201, 232–3, 235, 239, 241, 244, 252, 275, 331–2, 341, 342, 343, 344–5
Dixcove (Dickey's Cove), 87, 100–1, 106, 114, 124, 214, 215
Dixon, Joshua, 347
Dixon, Thomas, 345
Dodgson, Charles Lutwidge (Lewis Carroll), 346
Doliffe, James, 287
Dolphin (of London), 222
Dolphin (of Topsham), 355
Donegal, 218

Dorchester, 22
Dorset Brigantine, 251
Dottin, George, 30, 58, 188
Dottin, William, 31
Dottin family, 30–1
Dottin Galley, 31
Dover, 211
Dowrish, William, 110
Dragon, 39, 59, 282–6, 312, 319
Drake, Andrew, 265
Drake, Sir Francis, 278, 298
Drax, Sir James, 7
Drewin (Ivory Coast), 97, 222
Dring, Simon, 216
Dublin, 324, 336, 339, 343, 349
Duffield, Peter, 107, 108, 109
Dunkervell, 224
Dunn, John, 108, 109
Dupont, Stephen, 185
Dutch forts, 81, 89, 90, 101–2
Dutch West India Company, 7, 11, 103, 282

Eagle, 356
East India Company, 15, 83, 204, 290, 295, 354
Edward and William, 312
Ekins Frigate, 212–13
Elizabeth (1767), 347
Elizabeth and Katherine, 236
Elizabeth Galley, 120, 183, 306, 307
Elizabeth I, Queen, 230
Ellard, Charles, 282
Ellard, John, 282
Elmina (Dutch fort), 81, 89, 90
Elton, Abraham, 255
Elton, Jacob, 302
Emilia Galley, 254
Employment, 324
Encouragement, 26, 40, 103, 107–8
Endeavour (of Jamaica), 214, 215
Endeavour (of Ramsgate), 233
England, 9–11; legal status of slaves in, 19–20
English Civil War, 30, 227–8, 274
Evans, James, 287
Evans, Silvanus, 286–7
Evert, William, 352
Exeter, 15, 22, 23, 25, 29, 195, 196, 245, 279–82, 289, 290, 291–2, 292, 294–5, 304
Exeter, 23
Expedition (of Whitehaven), 347
Expedition Brigantine, 257
Expedition Galley (of London), 319–20
Eyre, Samuel, 316

Falconbridge, Alexander, 72
Falmouth, 295, 296, 308–10, 314, 315–20, 321, 322
Fane family, 274

Fanteen Galley, 338
Fauconberg, 56, 220, 354
Faulkener, David, 220–1
Fenner, Edward, 55, 57, 76, 147, 190
Ferdinand, King of Spain, 3, 5
Feryes family, 345
Fiennes, Celia, 279, 295
Florida, 26–7
Fly, 294
Flying Brigantine, 225–6
Formosa, Cape, 95
Forster, John, 338
Forster, Thomas, 321
Fort, John, 54, 57, 83, 124, 146, 148; inventory of, 115–16
Fort Nicholas, 56, 115, 148
Fortune, 291, 321
Fowey, 308
Fowey, HMS, 174, 175, 177
Fowler family, 244, 247
Foxworthy, Phillip, 53–4, 57, 148, 169, 170, 178
France, 7, 9–10, 298
Franke, 53
Franklin, William, 248, 250
Freeman, Howsley, 90, 104, 105
French Senegal Company, 313
Friend's Adventure, 355
Friendship (of Lyme), 237, 244, 250
Friendship (of Lyme, built 1706), 261, 271–2
Friendship (of Whitehaven), 336

Gale, George, 330–1, 334
Gale, John, 330
Gale, Lowther, 332, 334, 335
Gale, Matthew, 330–1, 332
Gale, Nicholas, 335
Gale family, 334–5, 336, 339, 345
Galloway, Patrick, 218–19
Gambia, River, 313
Gambia, the, 11, 14, 48, 160, 208, 230, 311, 312–14, 321, 343
Gambia, 223
Gambia Castle, 85, 223
Gambia Galley, 17
Gardiner, John, 90
Geare, John, 274
George (of Glasgow), 349
George (of Plymouth), 305
George (of Topsham), 292
George of Denmark, Prince, 252
Germany, Brandenburg Company of, 99
Germoon, HMS, 176
Gibbs, Henry, 233, 238
Gibbs, Thomas, 108
Gibson, George, 344
Gilpin, John, 333, 343
Gilpin, William, 333
Gilpin family, 339, 345
Glaseby, Henry, 321

Glasgow, 348, 349
Gloucester, 324
Godferry, John, 54, 57, 148
Gold Coast, 35, 62, 67, 71, 83, 95, 99, 111, 114, 320–1; scheme for colony on, 92
Gold (or *Gould*) *Frigate*, 18, 241
Golden Cross, 8
Gollop, Thomas, 356
Goodwin Sands, 203, 204
Gordon, John, 222
Gore, Gerrard, 112
Goree Island, 14
Gotley, Joseph, 302
Gould, George, 29
Gould, Henry, 57
Gould, James, 27, 28, 29, 36, 40, 48, 55, 100, 183, 188, 240, 249, 306
Gould, John, 250
Grain Coast, 68, 96
Granville, Bernard, 234
Grenville family, 304
Greyhound, 223
Griffin, 347
grommettoes, 82, 91, 311, 315
Groot, Arendt de, 11
Grove, John, 119
Growa (Ivory Coast), 97
Guadeloupe, 9–10
Guilford, 212
Guinea Coast, 7, 15, 16, 17, 19, 23, 35, 38, 55, 56, 59, 76–7, 78, 84, 86, 87, 88, 105, 107, 110, 113, 114, 205, 245–6; accounts, 123–5, 138, 139–40; Lyme Regis trade with, 248, 249, 250, 251, 255, 267, 268; scheme for colony, 91–2; Scottish and Irish trade with, 349; Whitehaven trade with, 335, 336, 337, 342
Guinea Company, 11, 205
Guinea Frigate, 220
Guinea Hen, 248
Guinea Packet, 209
Gundry, Daniel, 237, 258
Gundry, John, 258
Gundry, Nathaniel, 236, 258, 265, 269

Hale, George, 56, 182
Hallett, John, 247
Hallett, Meliora, 246
Hallett, Richard, 246
Hallett, Richard II, 246, 247
Hallett family, 246–7
Handcock, Humphrey, 56, 148, 160, 161, 163
Hannah-Maria, 332, 334
Hannibal, 71, 74, 75, 77, 87, 95, 98, 153, 220, 310
Hanover, 349
Happy Return (of Barbados), 109
Happy Return (of London), 316

Happy Return (of Stockton), 202
Harper, Robert, 339
Harris, Drew, 320
Harris, John, 286–7, 288
Harris, Richard, 253
Harris, William, 214, 215, 216, 217
Harrison, Francis, 354
Harrison, John, 52
Hastings, HMS, 176
Haughton, John, 321
Hawkesworth, Peter, 213, 216, 217
Hawkins, Sir John, 11, 22, 195, 278–9, 298
Hawkins, William, 278
Helderenburgh, 235
Helyar, John, 252
Helyar, William, 252, 353
Henvile, Richard, 257
Hereford, Nurse, 338
Herle, Degory, *see* Keeble, Digby
Heysham, Giles, 16
Heysham, Robert, 16, 17
Heysham, William, 17
Hicks, William, 287
Hodge, Thomas, 54
Hodge, William, 56, 117, 155
Hoghton, Lucy, 344, 345, 346
Hoghton, Sir Henry, 344–5
Hoghton, 345
Holdsworth, Arthur, 288
Holdsworth, Robert, 288
Holdsworth, 288
Hole, Benjamin, 293
Hole, Joseph, 284–5
Holland, 5, 6–7
Hollander, Peter, 334
Hollwell, William, 182–3
Holt, Lord Chief Justice, 20
Holwey, Jeremy, 241
Holy Cross, 317
Hooker Galley, 317
Hopewell (of Plymouth), 23
Hopewell (of Whitehaven), 338, 341
Houlditch, Abraham, 222, 253, 302
Houston, John, 268
Hudson, Kendall, 338
Hull, 202
Hunt, William, 55, 57, 76, 138, 147
Hutchings, Richard, 54, 56

India, 39
Indigo Merchant, 302
Integrity, 305
Ipswich, 202
Ireland, 305, 323, 324, 325; and Whitehaven, 328–9, 333, 339–40, 348–9
Isle of Wight, 223
Italy, 7–8
Ivory Coast, 68, 70, 97–9
Ivy, Benjamin, 29

Ivy, Daniel, 22, 23, 27, 28–9, 32, 36, 40, 48, 55, 100, 120, 182, 188, 197, 292, 306
Ivy, William, 281

Jackson, Stephen, 317, 319
Jacobite Rebellion, 340–1, 344
Jago, Thomas, 30, 38, 189
Jago, Walter, 30
Jamaica, 7, 13, 22, 25, 34, 35, 54, 141, 186; Lyme Regis trade with, 248, 249, 250, 251, 255, 267, 268; and the re-export of slaves, 351, 352–3, 354; voyage of *Daniel and Henry* to, 142, 155–83; Whitehaven trade with, 338
James (African prince), 296
James II, King, 169, 170, 198, 228, 235, 236
James, 212, 256
James Island, 313
James Island, 223
Jamineau, Claude, 222, 224, 254
Jamineau, Daniel, 222, 224, 254
Jeffreys, Judge, 152, 170, 228, 235
Jeffry, Arthur, 58–9, 282, 283, 284, 285–6
Jenkins, Anthony, 316
Jenkins, Sir Leoline, 232
Jennings, Sir John, 251
Jesus of Lubeck, 278
Jobson, Richard, 11, 13
John (African prince), 296
John (of Topsham), 23
John or *John Frigate* (of Lyme Regis), 48, 49, 259–70, 355
John and Robert, 255–6, 303
John and Thomas, 177, 179, 186
John's Adventure, 353
Johnson, Peter, 57, 111, 112, 148
Johnson, Richard, 56, 115, 148
Jolliffe, Peter, 225
Jolliffe, William, 225
Jolliffe's Adventure, 225
Jones, Joseph, 224
Joseph or *Joseph Galley*, 302, 305
Joseph and Thomas, 287

Kearley, George, 265
Keeble, Digby, 223
Keigwin, Martin, 314, 317
Kellaway, William, 209, 211
Kerridge, Elizabeth, 240, 242
Kerridge, John (mariner), 265
Kerridge, John II, 239, 240, 242
Kidderminster, 9
Killigrew, Sir Peter, 317
King, John, 237, 265
King, Samuel, 257
King Solomon, 223
Kingsbridge, 280

Lancaster, 324, 325, 347
Langton, Isaac, 336

Lascelles, 212
Laurel, 108
Law, William, 175
Ledgingham, Martha, 253, 254
Ledgingham, Warwick, 253–4
Lee, Thomas, 240
Leeds, 348
Levercombe, William, 120, 282, 306–7
Lewen, Sir William, 224
Lewis, Daniel, 222
Lewis, John, 316
Lewis, Raphael, 121
Lidstone, Francis, 282
Ligon, Richard, 148–9
Lind, James, 99
Lisbon, 170, 331
Lisle, William, 306
Liverpool, 15, 148, 191, 195, 197, 274, 294, 323, 324–5, 328, 347, 348
Living, Mordecai, 299
Locke, Thomas, 54, 57
London, 15, 20, 27, 35, 148, 191, 195, 196, 197, 202, 205, 279, 294, 295, 306, 323, 329
London, 212,
London Galley, 251–2
Lone, Arthur, 293
Lorenz, John, 118
Lowther, George, 85
Lowther, Robert, 335, 339
Lowther, Sir James, 332, 333, 339, 341, 346, 348
Lowther, Sir John, 326, 327, 328, 329–30, 331
Loyalty, 349
Loyer, Father, 70
Ludlow Galley, 293
Lutwidge, Charles, 334, 346
Lutwidge, Henry, 346
Lutwidge, Skeffington, 346
Lutwidge, Thomas, 332, 333–4, 336, 337, 340–1, 342, 343–6
Lutwidge, Thomas II, 346, 347
Lutwidge, Walter, 332, 337, 338, 346–7
Luxborough Galley, 209–10
Lyme Bay, 277
Lyme Regis, 29, 48, 170, 227–76, 306
Lyne, Joseph, 175

MackEvoy, Evander (McIvor), 210
Macpherson, Michael, 114
Madagascar, 281, 355
Madeira, 17, 57, 60, 206, 207, 225, 271, 316, 319, 331, 336, 339
Malynes, Gerard, xiv
Manchester, 9, 348
Mande traders, 70
Mann, Daniel, 209
March, Nicholas, 54, 57, 148
Margaret, 223
Margate, HMS, 174–5, 177

Marsh, Stephen, 108
Martha (Company ship), 223
Martha (frigate of London), 254–5, 256, 257, 259
Martha (of Lyme), 269
Martin, Hales, 56
Martin, Joseph, 253, 300
Martinique, 9–10
Martyn, Joseph, 223
Mary I, Queen (Mary Tudor), 228
Mary, 257
Mary and Anne, 52
Mary and Elizabeth (of Bridgwater), 305
Mary and Elizabeth (of London), 257, 258
Mary Anne, 213–17, 224
Mary Galley, 319
Maryland, 23, 28, 48, 106, 243, 270, 304–5
Mason, George, 257
Matham, Ralph, 57
Mathew, Robert, 24, 56, 247, 294
Mathew, Roger, 23–5, 31, 37, 41, 54, 55, 56, 57, 95, 103, 148, 183, 190, 306; in Jamaica, 175, 176, 177–9, 182, 187–8; on slave deaths, 153; slave trading by, 73–4, 108–9, 113–14, 115, 125
Mathew, William, 37, 55, 57, 148
Maurice and George, 219, 221
May, Isle of, 52, 224
May, John, 214, 215, 216
Mayflower, 177, 179, 186
Meacome, John, 56
Mead, William, 321
Melcombe Galley, 320
Mellish, John, 223
Merchant Adventurers of Bristol, 196
Mesurado or Monserado, Cape, 67, 68, 80, 92, 93, 96, 102, 114, 214
Mexico, 5
Michael Galley, 299
Milford, HMS, 102, 121
Milner, Isaac, 223, 253, 331, 332–3
Minehead, 15, 306, 323, 324
Modbury, 280
Molly, 218
Monk, Edward, 119–20, 159–60, 161, 162
Monmouth rebellion, 170, 228, 235
Monney, Stephen, 56
More, James, 56, 119
Morice, Humphrey, 186, 253, 254, 257, 318, 331
Morice, Sir William, 30
Moses, William, 121
Mount, Cape, 66
Mozambique, 5
Mullington, Richard, 305
Mullington, Robert, 302

Nancy Galley, 334, 335
Napoleon Bonaparte, 358

Neptune (of France), 94
Neptune (of London), 292
Neptune (of Weymouth), 355
Neptune (of Whitehaven), 347
Nevis, 216, 351, 352, 355
New Adventure, 108, 109
Newcastle upon Tyne, 9, 202
Newman, John junior, 309
Newman, John senior, 309, 310
Newport, 212
Nicholas, 30
Nicholson, Edward, 299
Nicholson, 19
Nonconformists, *see* Dissenters
Northampton, 295–7, 321
Northumberland, HMS, 251
Norwood, Richard, 164
Nowell, Jacob, 94

Onslow, 321
Orange Branch, 292
Oswald, Richard, 225
Otter, 336
Oxford, HMS, 175–6

Padstow, 322
Pafford, William, 213, 216, 217
Paggen, Catherine, 254
Paggen, Peter, 243, 252–3, 254
Paice, Joseph, 248–9, 254, 270, 421
Paice, Nathaniel, 294
Palmas, Cape, 68, 96, 338
Palmer, William, 268
Parker, Samuel, 319
Parminter, John, 120, 183, 306, 307
Parminter, Richard, 307
Pascall, Henry, 355
Patrick, Stephen, 225, 226
Peace, 338
Pearce, Edward, 317, 319
Pearce, Nathaniel, 268
Pearl, 305
Pearson, Josiah, 20–1
Peck, John, 114
Peck, Thomas, 91, 102, 103, 108, 114
Pendarves, Sir William, 318
Penellopy, 325
Penn, William, 32
Pentyre, Philip, 303
Pernambuco, 6, 170
Perry, Micajah, 243
Peru, 5
Pery, John, 18, 19
Peterborough, 149
Phillips, Thomas, 71, 74, 75, 87, 88, 95, 98, 102, 153, 154, 310–11
Phippard, Caleb, 8
Phoenix, 285
Pickard, Peter, 176

Picsson, Nicholas, 56
Pike, George, 265
Pindar, Paul, 314
Pindar Galley, 300–2
Pippenose, Charles, 57
Pitts, John, 266, 268
Pitts, Thomas, 235
Plymouth, 29, 234, 277, 278–9, 284, 289, 290, 298–304, 304, 323
Plymouth Company, 196
Pole, John, 234
Poole, 224–5, 237, 255, 355
Portsmouth, 23, 212, 213, 218, 219, 223, 299
Portugal, 5–6, 81, 118, 170, 267, 357
Postilion, 19
Poulton, 325
Pounick, William (Penneck), 282, 285, 286
Presbyterianism, 198
press-gangs, 26
Preston, 325
Price, Peter, 56
Prideaux, Arthur (Walter's brother), 32
Prideaux, Arthur (Walter's grandfather), 30
Prideaux, Walter, xiv, 27, 30–2, 37, 38, 49, 52, 55, 58, 59, 60, 61, 62, 63, 64, 67, 68, 94, 95, 98, 102, 108, 110, 112, 113, 120, 148, 176, 197; accounts, 133–40; attitude to slaves, 154, 156; on deaths of slaves, 146, 172–3; in Jamaica, 176–7, 179–80, 182; on São Tomé, 118–19, 121–2; slave trading by, 74, 108–9, 113–14, 115, 125; on the voyage to Jamaica, 158, 164, 170–1, 172–4, 183
Primrose, Henry Alexander, 209
Prince George, 347
Prince of Mindelheim, 222–3
Prince of Orange, 26, 40, 104, 106–7, 112
Prince of Orange (Company ship, 1689), 220
Princess, 342, 343
Principe island, 121
Prior, John, 299
Prompaind, Peter, 335
Prosperity, 349
Providence (1752), 347
Provost Galley, 337–8
Prowse, Robert, 249
Prowse, Roger, 183, 282, 291
Pyne, Malachy, 292

Quakers (Society of Friends), 32, 148–9, 183, 198
Quamboers (tribe), 87
Queen Anne, 320

Randall, Richard, 225, 356
Randall, Thomas, 225
Randall family, 225–6
Ranger, 291, 321
Raymond, Arthur, 270, 271, 272

Read, Francis, 247
Read, John, 352
Read, Robert, 261, 269
Rebecca, 316
Recovery, 218
religion, *see* Dissenters
Reserve, 202
Resolution (1706), 218–19, 221
Resolution (1726), 271–2
Richard, 291
Richardson, Alexander, 214, 215
Riot Act (1715), 345
Roberts, Bartholomew, 291, 321
Roberts, Isaac, 257
Rochester, 299
Rogers, Bryan, 309
Rogers, Thomas, 54, 57, 178
Rose, 53
Rotterdam, 22, 23, 30, 229, 230, 269, 281, 282, 292, 294
Rouse, Nathaniel, 93
Royal Africa, 18, 220
Royal African, 223
Royal African Company, xiv, 7, 8, 14–21, 26, 28, 29, 35, 39–40, 40, 63, 68, 69, 75–7, 78–80, 81–92, 103, 106, 195–6, 204, 205; accounts, 123, 184–5, 186; and Cornwall, 320–2; and Devon, 288–90, 294, 295, 296–7, 300; factors, 81–92; forts, 81–2; and Lyme Regis, 256; and Portsmouth, 223; salaries, 82–3; and Scotland, 249; and Whitehaven, 330, 332, 333, 337
Royal Navy, 26, 35, 53, 83, 84, 151, 175–6, 212, 226, 321
Rudd, John, 53, 56, 115, 148, 182
Rumball, Hannah, 334
Rumball, Thomas, 334–43
Rumbold, Edward, 334
Rumbold, William, 334
Russell, Charles, 85
Russell, Governor of Barbados, 12
Russell, John, 220, 221
Rye House Plot, 241
Ryswick, Treaty of, 7, 107, 174, 182, 243, 245, 313

Sacheverell Galley, 337
Sadler, James, 268
Sadler, Mary, 107
Sadler, Ralph, 103, 106, 107, 108
Sadler, Thomas, 107
St George, 324
St Ives, 322
St Kitts and Nevis, 351, 352, 355
Salkeld, Samuel, 111
Sally Rose, 220
Salter, Robert, 265
Samuel (1684), 352

Samuel (of Bideford), 305
Samuel (of London), 209
Santo Domingo, 7
São Tomé, 5, 11, 54, 117–22, 155, 157, 158, 160
Sarah, 24, 56, 247, 294
Sarah (Company ship), 223
Satisfaction, 212
Savage, Robert, 57
Scarborough, HMS, 174
Scotland, 202, 249, 305, 329; attitude to Company monopoly, 348–9
Scott, John, 257
Scrope, Adrian, 241
Scrope, John, 241, 273–4, 275
Scrope, Thomas, 241, 273
Sea Nymph, 317
Seaflower, 8
Searle, Edward, 91, 223
Sedgemoor, battle of, 170, 228, 235
Sellafield, 326
Seller, John, 164
Sestos, 93, 338
Sevenhuysen, van (Director-General at Elmina), 89–90
Severn, 255
Seymour, Colonel, 205
Sharrow, John, 295–6
Sheerness, HMS, 205–7
Sheffield, 9, 274, 348
Sherborne, 22
Sherbro, Señora Doll, Duchess of, 311
Short, Ames, 243
Shovell, Sir Cloudesly, 106
Shutter, John, 54, 57, 148, 180
Sierra Leone, 86, 92, 225, 271, 272, 285
Smallwood, John, 93
Smallwood, Richard, 93, 94, 109
Smith, Thomas, 302
Snelling, Francis, 53, 56, 83, 148
Soames, Joseph, 314
Society, 32, 114, 119–20, 159–60
Society of Friends, *see* Quakers
Soldados Prize, HMS, 176
Somers, Sir George, 229, 230, 242
Somerset, 306, 323–4
Somerset Frigate, 241
Sophia, 349
Sorlings, 287
South Sea bubble, 318
South Sea Company, 204, 207, 258, 272, 343
Southampton, 223–4
Spain, 5, 6, 7, 10, 298
Spedding, James, 347
Spedding, John, 332, 339, 340, 341, 347
Speedwell, 281
Spring, Captain, 349
Stafford, Samuel, 23, 24
Stanhope, 338

Stanier, 310
Steele, Richard, 201
Steydervil, Stephen, 224
Strangways, Thomas, 234
Stretell, Francis, 212–13
Surprise or *Surprise Galley*, 39, 258, 261, 291
Susannah, 338–9, 344
Swain, Elizabeth, 246
Swansea, 324
Swetland, Joseph, 265
Swift, 334, 335, 336, 337
Sylva, 349
Sylvia or *Sylvia Galley*, 292–3, 303

Taguarim (Sierra Leone), 65
Tancomquerry, 110
Tanner, James, 16
Taunton, 15, 22, 227, 228, 230, 232, 243
Taylor, Henry, 283, 284, 285, 286
Taylor, John, 301
Taylor, Robert, 316
Teach, Edward, 210
Templeman, Thomas, 246–7
Thomas, Daniel, 19
Thomas, Charles, 90–1
Thomas, James, 56
Thomas, Sir Dalby, 16, 17, 19, 83, 90–2, 101, 106, 221, 287, 301
Thomas, 316–17, 319, 342
Thorne, Thomas, 57
Three Crowns, 223
Three Points, Cape, 99–100
Tibby, Joseph, 291
Toms, John, 353
Topsham, 25, 29, 274, 277, 282, 290, 295–7
Totnes, 15, 245, 289
Tourney, Anthony (Tournai), 221, 257
Tremlett, John, 57, 148, 182
Trengrove (Captain of gold miners), 321
Trial, 293
Tubman, Edward, 347
Tucker, Andrew, 235
Tucker, Elizabeth, 255
Tucker, James, 235
Tucker, John, 233
Tucker, Mary (later Burridge), 234, 255
Tucker, Samuel, 233
Tucker, Walter, 233, 234
Tucker, William, 233
Two Brothers, 294

Ulverston, 325
Union, 19, 338
Union (sloop of 1709), 352–3
Union Frigate, 54
Union Galley, 248, 249
Unity, 237, 305
Uring, Nathaniel, 5–6, 70, 77
Utrecht, Treaty of, 212, 258

Varloe, Philip, 281
Veale, Joseph, 289
Venice, 8
Vennard, James, 292
Vennard, John junior, 292, 293
Vennard, John senior, 292, 293, 303
Verde, Cape, 282
Virginia, 23, 27, 28, 106, 230, 243, 244, 247, 258, 269–70, 304, 305, 328, 340, 354; Lyme Regis trade with, 233, 234, 237, 251, 268; Whitehaven trade with, 340, 341, 343, 345, 347
Virginia Company, 242
Visser, Jan, 99–100

Waghenaer, Lucas Jancz, 164
Walker, John, 214
Walker, Nathaniel, 342
Wall, John, 320
Wallis, John, 269
Wallis, Samuel, 90, 104, 105
Walpole, Robert, 273, 274
Walthamstowe Galley, 241
War of the Spanish Succession, 107, 224, 244, 250, 258, 282, 299
Ward, Thomas, 339
Way, Benjamin (preacher), 240–1, 256, 273
Way, Benjamin (slave trader), 240, 241–2, 247–8, 250, 251, 252, 253, 256, 306, 352
Way, John, 240–1
Way, Joseph, 240, 241, 248, 251, 255, 256, 306
Way, Richard, 240–1
Way, Thomas, 240
Way family, 240–2
Way Galley, 248, 257
Wayte, James, 222, 253, 257–8
West Indies, 3, 12–13, 17, 19, 26, 34, 35, 153

Westbury (Wiltshire), 15
Weymouth, 29, 224, 225–6, 237
Wharton, 346
White, John (of Dorchester), 240
White, Martha, 240
Whitehaven, 326–50
Whitehaven or *Whitehaven Galley*, 337, 338, 339, 340, 346
Whydah, 87–8, 106–7
Whydah, 209
Wilkison, John, 206
William III, King (William of Orange), 236, 332
William (of 1705), 299–300
William (of 1716), 224
William (of Whitehaven), 338
William Frigate (Company ship, 1700), 314
William and Elizabeth, 325
William and John, 224
Williams, John, 58
Willington, 347
Wills, Thomas, 290–1
Winnebah, queen of, 87
Wisehard, Robert, 54, 57
Withers, Thomas, 339
Wollacott, Benjamin, 58
Wood, Samuel, 57
Wormley Berry, 114, 179
Worsley Galley, 338
Worth, John, 56
Wren, Sir Christopher, 327
Wright, Samuel, 275
Wright Galley, 217
Wyatt, James junior, 270, 271
Wydah (Company ship), 223
Wydah (of London), 294

Yorke, George, 54, 56, 178